All the officers watched as various ships' numbers were hauled aloft to break out at the *Victory*'s masthead. Orders were sent to *Excellent, Blenheim, Orion* and *Prince George*. That was followed by the message instructing them to support HMS *Captain*. Nelson felt a release of tension, of which he had been unaware in the excitement and trepidation of his actions. The responsibility was no longer his: Admiral Jervis had approved.

Nelson allowed himself one more look around at the ships holding their course to follow Troubridge and those moving directly to his support. He felt his heart swell with the certainty that the fleet would be victorious. That he might not survive didn't matter. If he expired in the moment of triumph he would have achieved the single most important aim of his life, making it worthwhile.

'Lay me alongside the enemy, Captain Millar,' he cried, in a voice that travelled the whole length of the ship.

David Donachie has had more jobs than birthdays. He now writes full time and lives in Deal with his wife and two children. He maintains a website at *www.firsteditionshighway.com/daviddonachie*

By David Donachie

THE DEVIL'S OWN LUCK
THE DYING TRADE
A HANGING MATTER
AN ELEMENT OF CHANCE
THE SCENT OF BETRAYAL
A GAME OF BONES
ON A MAKING TIDE

Writing as Tom Connery:

A SHRED OF HONOUR
HONOUR REDEEMED
HONOUR BE DAMNED

DAVID DONACHIE
ON A MAKING TIDE
The epic novel of Nelson and Emma

Volume 1

ORION

An Orion paperback

First published in Great Britain in 2000
by Orion
This paperback edition published in 2001
by Orion Books Ltd,
Orion House, 5 Upper St Martin's Lane,
London WC2H 9EA

Maps and diagrams by John Gilkes.

A CIP catalogue record for this book is
available from the British Library.

ISBN 0 75284 425 3

Typeset by Deltatype Ltd, Birkenhead, Merseyside

Printed and bound in Great Britain by
Clays Ltd, St Ives plc

To my son Thomas.
A delight!

GLOSSARY

Aft The rear of the ship.

Afterguard Sailors who worked on the quarterdeck and poop.

Bilge Foul-smelling water collecting in the bottom of the ship.

Binnacle Glass cabinet holding ship's compass visible from the wheel.

Bowsprit Heavy spar at the front of the ship.

Broadside The firing of all the ship's cannon in one salvo.

Bulkhead Moveable wooden partitions, i.e. walls of captain's cabin.

Capstan Central lifting tackle for all heavy tasks on the ship.

Cathead Heavy joist that keeps anchor clear of ship's side.

Chase Enemy ship being pursued.

Crank A vessel that won't answer properly to the helm.

Fish To secure the raised anchor to the ship.

Forecastle Short raised deck at ship's bows. (Fo'c's'le)

Frigate Small fast warship; the 'eyes of the fleet'.

Larboard Old term for 'port': left looking towards the bows.

Leeward The direction in which the wind is blowing.

Letter of Marque Private-armed ship licensed to attack enemy. (Privateer)

Log Ship's diary, detailing course, speed, punishments etc.

Logline Knotted rope affixed to heavy wood to show ship's speed.

Mast Solid vertical poles holding yards (see below).

Mizzen Rear mast.

Muster List of ship's personnel.

Ordinary Ship laid up in reserve.

Orlop Lowest deck on the ship, often below waterline.

Quarterdeck Above maindeck, from which command was exercised.

Rate Class of ship 1–6 depending on number of guns.

Rating Seaman's level of skill.

Reef To reduce the area of a sail by bundling and tying.

Scuppers Openings in ship's side to allow escape of excess water.

Scurvy Disease caused by lack of vitamins, especially C.

Sheet Ropes used to control sails.

Sheet-home To tie off said ropes.

Ship of the Line A capital ship large enough to withstand in-line combat.

Sloop Small warship not rated. A lieutenant's command.

Spar Length of timber used to spread sails.

Starboard Right side of ship facing bows.

Tack To turn the head of the ship into the wind.

Topman Sailor who worked high in the rigging.

Wardroom Home to ship's officers, commissioned and warrant.

Watch A division of the ship's crew × 2. A portion of the day.

Wear To turn the head of the ship away from the wind.

Windward The side of the ship facing the wind.

Yard Horizontal pole holding sail. Loosely attached to mast.

Yardarm Outer end of yard.

LIST OF SHIPS

Raisonable
Victory
Triumph
Dreadnought
Swanborough
Seahorse
Racehorse
Carcass

Ramilles
Vixen
Euraylus
Dolphin
Worcester
Lowestoffe
Torbay Lass
Ardent
Hinchingbrooke
Badger
Victor

Albemarle
Daedalus
Harmony
Iris
Barfleur
Boreas
Bristol
Agamemnon

Battle of St Vincent
Captain
Santissima Trinidad
Culloden
Orion
Excellent
Diadem
Blenheim
Prince George
San Salvador
San Nicholas

San Josef
Theseus
Fox
Vanguard
Alexander
Goliath
Mutine

Battle of the Nile
Swiftsure
Zealous
Minotaur
L'Orient
Le Guerrier
Audacious
Le Spartiate
Guillaume Tell
Généraux
Bellerophon
Le Peuple Souverain

Southern England and the
Major Channel Route

NORTH
SEA

ENGLAND

The Burnhams

Burnham
Thorpe

London

The Nore

Bath

Spithead

HMS Lowestoffe

Plymouth

The Needles

ENGLISH CHANNEL

FRANCE

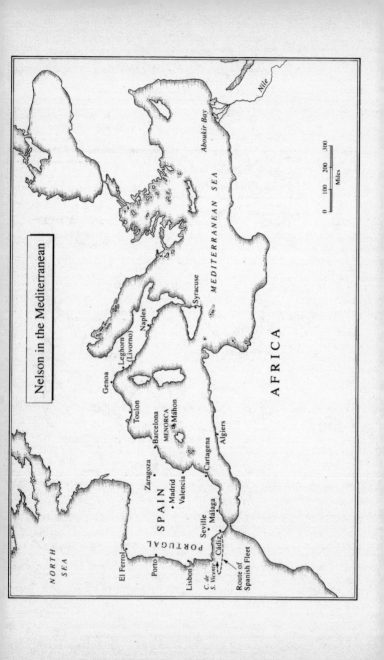

Nelson in the Mediterranean

Nile

Aboukir Bay

MEDITERRANEAN SEA

Syracuse

Naples

Leghorn
(Livorno)

Genoa

Toulon

Barcelona

MENORCA

Máhon

Zaragoza

SPAIN

Madrid

Valencia

Cartagena

Algiers

AFRICA

Seville

Málaga

Cádiz

C. de
S. Vicente

Lisbon

Route of
Spanish Fleet

Porto

El Ferrol

PORTUGAL

NORTH
SEA

Miles

0   100   200   300

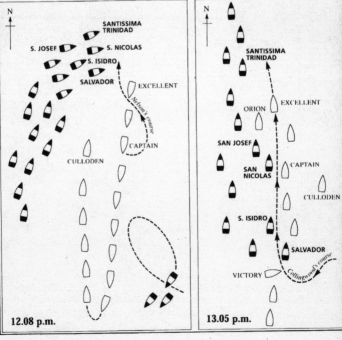

The Battle of Cape St. Vincent
14th February 1797

N

Wind →

Spanish fleet commanded by de Córdoba

English fleet commanded by Admiral Jervis

CULLODEN

11.31 a.m.

N

SANTISSIMA TRINIDAD

S. JOSEF   **S. NICOLAS**

S. ISIDRO

SALVADOR

EXCELLENT

Nelson's course

CAPTAIN

CULLODEN

12.08 p.m.

N

SANTISSIMA TRINIDAD

ORION   EXCELLENT

SAN JOSEF

SAN NICOLAS   CAPTAIN

CULLODEN

S. ISIDRO

SALVADOR

VICTORY   Collingwood's course

13.05 p.m.

PROLOGUE

1771

His boots were wet and the dew that clung to the Norfolk marsh grass had soaked both his stockings and the bottoms of his white breeches. As he was small, Horatio Nelson had to push hard to open the door and its creaking hinges added to the eerieness of his errand.

The pews of the chapel at Burnham Thorpe were empty, while the bare stone walls of the interior, open to the elements at the south nave, ensured that on this March morning it was even colder inside the chapel than out.

He shivered as he approached the black marble slab that lay to the left of the nave and stepped round the bronze outline of the knight buried centuries before. He felt somehow that this was a fateful moment. He knelt between the two graves and put his hands together in prayer, his lips moving silently as he asked a blessing on his future

His mind was full of images of himself and his mother. He could see her now, on the day they had gone to King's Lynn to visit the *tableau vivant*, based on the painting by Benjamin West, detailing the death of General James Wolfe, his life sacrificed in far off Canada in the battle to capture Québec City. Muffled music, heavy with the deep beat of the funeral drum, had played in the background. Wolfe lay in the arms of his officers and the regimental flags held over his head were limp and tattered, ripped asunder by shot and shell, stained with mud. But the Union Flag of Great Britain showed red, white and blue above them all, extended so that the entire world should know that here, on the Plains of Abraham, Albion had triumphed over Gaul.

The mortally wounded general stared at the stiff flag, the sky behind it black, streaked with dark grey. Doleful soldiers gathered round him, while the figure of a Red Indian chief lent an exotic element to the heart-wrenching scene. To the right stood a pale, blue-coated figure, the ghost of Wolfe's opponent, the noble Marquis de Montcalm, holding out his sword in abject surrender, a crumpled *fleur de lis* wrapped around the hilt, proof that this dead Frenchman was handing over the power of his nation, as well as the province of Canada, to Britannia.

His mother had explained each nuance to her golden-haired, wide-eyed son: how, in 1759, that Year of Victories, Wolfe had delivered the final telling blow to the enemy, sacrificing his life for the well-being of his country, and earning himself a memorial in Westminster Abbey. The crowd pressed hard behind them, impatient that this woman should linger so long before a drama they, too, wished to observe. Catherine Nelson ignored them. Turning, she took her child by the shoulders and looked into his bright blue eyes. 'That, my son, is nobility indeed. God, who must hate a Frenchman as much as I do, favoured the arms of the most righteous nation on this earth. General Wolfe must surely now sit by His right hand, ready to direct His attention to those places where He must yet intervene, so that the plague we call France may be confounded at every turn.'

Now Horatio traced the letters on the black slab, brightly lit by the huge arched north-facing window. First the Latin inscription that told visitors Catherine Nelson had died four years previously, in 1767. Her husband Edmund, heartbroken at the loss, had added another inscription in English: 'Let these alone: Let no man move these bones.'

The boy's stammered words echoed off the bare stone walls: 'I hope and pray, Mama, that God will look kindly on me, and that I may make you as proud of me as you were of all Albion's heroes. And that if I give my life for my country, let it be in circumstances that would meet with your approval. I ask your blessing and that you will, from your celestial abode, guide me and keep me true.'

The solid image of his father replaced the idealised one of his dead mother. Tall, beetle-browed and unsmiling, even when absent from his parish, as he was now, the Reverend Edmund Nelson was a potent force in his son's life. Stern and unbending, trusting in his Maker, the Rector of Burnham Thorpe had a fixed notion of his place in society. When he was not castigating sin and sloth, or railing against ecclesiastical neglect of his churches, he would talk of the family lineage, so that his children's antecedents, of whom they should and could be proud, were indelibly imprinted in their minds. Horatio knew he had to live up to them too.

On his mother's side the Sheltons, granted the right to arms in the seventh century after the siege of Adrianople; Bullens who had resided at Hever Castle and the Manor of Blickling, playing host to Henry VIII and his Boleyn bride; Woodhouses, Jermyns, Townsends graced the family tree. Sir John Suckling, his coat-of-arms a scallop shell and a sprig of honeysuckle, who had ridden north to greet the successor to Good Queen Bess, his reward the office of Secretary of State to the newly crowned King James I.

The Walpoles claimed pride of place, first Captain Gadifrus, who had lost an arm in battle at Vado Bay and had ended his days Treasurer of the Greenwich Hospital; and then his puissant brother Sir Robert Walpole, First Earl of Orford, who had dominated the nation for three decades. Uncle Maurice, a still living and breathing naval hero, would now become his captain and mentor. The burden of all that history seemed to bear down on the boy, an almost physical presence, pushing his knees into the hard flagstone floor.

'Horace!'

The shout, echoing off the church walls, startled him and he leapt to his feet. Susanna, his sister, emerged from behind a thick round pillar, her pretty oval face under a linen mob cap half worried, half angry. When she saw where he stood her expression softened, and the words of admonishment she had been about to deliver were spoken kindly. 'Dawdle and you'll miss the King's Lynn coach.'

'I came to say farewell to Mama,' he replied, with just a hint of defiance.

Susanna came up the aisle and stood beside him. She put her

3

arm round his shoulders, and gave him a gentle shake. 'To her bones. Her spirit is with us always, wherever we go.' Her fingers tugged first at his stock, then she brushed back his fair hair, at which he recoiled. 'I cannot quite believe that you're going away, Horace. My little brother, just thirteen, yet a sailor in the King's Navy. And I daresay all set to be a hero.'

'I will miss you, sister.'

She shook him again affectionately. He couldn't help acting like a man any more than Susanna, three years older, could help seeing him as a boy. She took his arm, and allowed him to lead her out into the grey morning, chattering as they descended the slope through the still bare trees. Arms linked they crossed the field that was a short-cut between the yellow brick L-shaped Parsonage, which looked so drab in the winter light, and the equally uninspiring stone of the square-towered rectangular church. Around them the north Norfolk landscape, gentle slopes criss-crossed with dense hedgerows, was silent, but for the odd mournful cry of a distant rook.

The whole family was gathered to say their farewells, sallow-faced, brown-eyed and silent: William, one year older, his three younger brothers, Edmund, Suckling and George, Anne, just old enough to know what was happening, and Catherine, confused at four years old, clutching the hands of two older siblings. Collectively they made him feel like a changeling, with his blond hair and blue eyes. He took his looks from his mother. The father whose colouring the others had inherited was at King's Lynn waiting to accompany him to London.

'We will all miss you,' Susanna said. There were tears at the rims of those warm brown eyes, a flush on the round rosy cheeks, a tremble on the point of the chin and a catch in her voice. 'But everyone knows that you will make us so very proud.' The response was a smile so warm and engaging that it wrenched her heart. 'Come back to us often, Horace, as your duty permits.'

The dray, his chest already loaded, was waiting by the gate. The driver, in a thick shawl, drew contentedly on his clay pipe, the smoke drifting up into the chill air. Susanna wrapped Horace in his heavy boat-cloak. Then she kissed him on both cheeks before placing his hat squarely on his head. The whole family came down to the gate and his brothers raised a ragged cheer, while the girls, with deft use of their handkerchiefs, showed him how much they had feared this parting.

As soon as he was aboard the driver flicked his whip and the skinny horse moved off. One wave of his hand was all Horatio allowed himself as the metal-rimmed wheels rattled across the short wooden bridge that spanned the river Burn. It was a scene he had imagined often, his leaving home to take up his duties. What had made him think that the sun would shine, that flowers would be thrown, and that everyone would be happy? How different the reality! He felt a cloying dread that he might never see those faces or this place again; worse, that he might disgrace his house. The pain that thought induced in his chest was sharp and it seemed doubly hard to keep his eyes set firmly forward.

Emma's eyes, large and green, seemed to fill half of her face. Now they were entranced. Her fingers traced each detail of the dark, carved oak, the outlines of semi-clad figures and flowers on the giant newel post. The flames from the hall fire combined with the light from the window to throw the delicate woodwork into sharp relief, while dust motes danced in the shafts of bright sunlight. The Glynne family portraits, murky and forbidding, looked down on Emma with what the child imagined was scant approval.

'Stand up straight, now, Emma.'

Her mother's sharp tone was accompanied by a hefty shove. Footsteps echoing off bare wood above her head filled the cavernous hallway, changing in tempo as the owner of the house descended the top flight of stairs. On the landing, framed by the light behind him, Sir John Glynne had the air of an avenging angel as he examined the duo who stood below. When he spoke his deep, sonorous voice echoed down on them.

'So, Mrs Lyon, this is she?'

'It is, Sir John.'

'How old?'

'Coming up nine.'

'Just nine?' There was surprise in his voice. Emma was tall

for her age, nearly the same height as her mother, and to a practised eye like that of Sir John Glynne already showing the first signs of bloom. Her hair, long and shining, caught the firelight in a way that matched the suddenly illuminated edges of the banister. 'And behaving, Mrs Lyon. I see no sign of that independent spirit you complain of.'

'Emma could scarce be other than awed in the presence of so puissant a man.'

The child turned to look at her mother, in her best dress and bonnet. The lips, pale pink in a slightly olive face, were open as though amused, the brown button eyes dancing. Her words struck a false, insolent note that matched her expression. Sir John started to descend, and Emma could see him properly for the first time. Florid-faced, broad-shouldered and confident, he was grinning at her mother. He kissed the proffered hand in an overtly gallant way before turning his attention, sternly, to her.

'Is she worth the endeavour?'

'Who's to say, Sir John? She's bright enough, even if she is more'n a touch wild. But if Emma is denied books and learning, her future is like to be bleak.'

Sir John took Emma gently by the chin, forcing her to raise her head and look at him. A finger moved, feeling the alabaster texture of her milk-white complexion. 'A fair skin. If she stays unmarked by the pox, madam, she may get by on her beauty.'

'That is scarce enough in this world.'

'Your beauty serves you well!' The reply was swift, the tone sharp.

That made Emma look at her mother again. She had never heard her called a beauty before, and now she examined her closely. The dim winter light didn't favour a complexion that benefited from sunlight. Was the face too square, the chin too straight for beauty? And her frown detracted from whatever it was Sir John admired. Then she spoke and her voice was far from friendly. 'It allows me to serve the interests of others, sir, rather than freeing me to my own inclinations.'

His voice dropped to an urgent whisper. 'I've never known you disinclined, madam.'

Emma's mother responded just as quietly, but there was force in her tone. 'I'm not one to plead, Sir John, you knows that. I derive as much pleasure from our association as do you. But a promise was made, sir, that if I accompanied you to London, you would make some provision for my Emma. If I leave her with my mother she'll be fit for nowt but selling coal on the Chester road.'

He tweaked Emma's chin. 'That would, indeed, be a great loss. She's made for warmth, I wager, but not from vending coal.'

'So you will hold to your word, sir?' Mary Lyon paused, before adding, with a hint of longing. 'It was freely sworn.'

'I plead the location.'

Mary Lyon's voice lost any hint of supplication, bringing a dark look to Sir John's face, and a painful pinch to Emma's chin. 'I was not aware, sir, that a gentleman required his breeches buttoned to sustain an obligation. I made one and I require that you do likewise.'

Sir John let go of Emma's chin and swung away. 'I'm not one to be "required" of, madam. And it ill becomes you to adopt such a tone. You go too far!'

'I shall not set foot outside the confines of your demesne, sir, if that obligation isn't met.'

She tugged at Emma's hand to pull her away, but the child's feet seemed rooted to the bare oak boards. Emma didn't want to leave. To some this hallway would be forbidding, but to her it spoke of a warmth and comfort she scarcely knew. A log dropped in the wide fireplace, sending shafts of red light to sparkle on the polished wood. Sir John had raised a hand, as if he intended to strike her mother, but he hesitated to make contact.

'Hold, madam. I shall keep to my word. But you must not address me so. Beauty and a lively intelligence permit you many things, but not that.'

'Proper schooling in letters and numbers, paid for in coin.'

There was an air of resignation in his response. 'Yes.'

'So, Sir John, when I see you instruct the curate, I'll hold to my end of our bargain.'

Then an odd light came into Sir John's eyes. He walked to a door in the panelling and pushed it open. 'I am a poor host, madam, to carry on our business in the hallway. Will you not come to a place that will afford us more comfort?'

Emma didn't see her mother nod sharply in her direction. She was too busy trying to imagine a life that could encompass so much space. Her family home would fit into this hallway twice over. And here was Sir John inviting them into a huge parlour, full of brocaded couches and other beautiful furniture.

'The child may wander the house if she promises not to be light of finger.'

'My Emma is honest, sir.'

Sir John's voice had taken on a husky quality. 'Good! Then let it be madam. But I require you to join me in private.'

Her mother's hand forced Emma round. 'You're not to go up them stairs, Emma, do you hear? You are to look round on this floor, or make your way to the kitchens. The cook will give you a bite. I'm going to talk with Sir John and settle all points regarding your learning.'

'How long will you be, Ma?' she asked.

The grunt from Sir John made her mother grin. 'Not long, I reckon.'

She lifted the hem of her skirt and cloak, then swept through the doorway. Sir John followed swiftly, and Emma heard the latch rammed down. She walked across to the door, put her ear to the wood, and soon heard the half-strangled grunts. Emma grinned, spun round and skipped up the stairs. She had been told that rich folk slept on soft feather down, not horsehair, and though there was much to inspire her curiosity in this great house, that was paramount: she longed for nothing more than to experience the luxury – her grandmother had said it was the closest thing to heaven.

What her mother was doing in this house concerned her not at all. She had been a distant parent, coming to Grandma Kidd's house, the Steps, once or twice a year, bearing gifts certainly, but hard words too about the way Emma was being raised and the freedom she was given.

The open door at the end of the landing revealed a huge bed with four carved posts and a ruched silk roof. The heavy red curtains, with gold-tasselled edges, were closed. Emma tiptoed into the room, parted the curtains and her hand sank down into the snowy white coverlet until feathers enveloped it.

'Why, my old gran has the right of it an' no error.'

'What are you about, child?'

Emma spun round to face the sharp voice, bobbing a curtsy as she registered the formidable shape, feathered quill in hand, sitting at the table in the window. 'Who gave you permission to enter my house?'

The old woman's round face was shaking with indignation, and her eyes promised dire punishment.

'Sir John did.'

'Did he, indeed?' she snapped. Then she extended the hand that held the quill over the parchment on which she was writing and beckoned. 'Come here, child.'

Emma moved with caution, her heart still pounding with fear, until a sharp gesture indicated that she should hurry. Finally she stood before the old woman, who examined her minutely, noting that her dress was well-made and clean, the plump, childish face healthy with rosy cheeks. However, all Emma saw was the deep frown, which she took for anger not interest.

'I know you, don't I? I've seen you by the roadside selling coal.'

'I does that for my grandma, Mrs Kidd.'

'So your mother is the widow Lyon?'

Emma nodded. The woman's face relaxed and Emma realised that the lines had been wrought by pain not age. This was underlined by a wheezing cough that lasted several seconds.

'You didn't arrive here unaccompanied then?' the lady gasped.

'No,' Emma replied, with an enthusiasm so natural she forgot her fear. 'Sir John is with my mother now. He's set to pay to see me put to learning.'

At the stern look engendered by that remark Emma gabbled. 'She says she will not accompany him to London lest he keeps his sworn word to do so . . .' Her hand flew to her mouth. She had said too much to this stranger. But the face softened with a look that made Emma think of her grandmother, and the quill stroked the back of her hand.

'Hush, child. I am Lady Glynne and you tell me nothing of my husband that I do not already know. He may go to hell or London, for all I care. Just as long as I am spared his attentions and his conversation. As for your mother, I feel pity that any member of my sex should be so put upon.'

'I wanted to see a feather bed,' Emma said, hoping to change the subject, which was ten times more delicate now that this lady had identified herself.

'See?'

'Well, my grandma says I'd feel like an angel on a cloud if'n I was to rest on one.'

Lady Glynne smiled then, her heart melted by the look of wonder in the child's wide green eyes. How could the oaf to whom she was married have any connection to such a fetching creature? 'You may lie upon that bed, child,' she said, 'for it is entirely mattressed in feathers.' She watched, amused, as Emma skipped across the room, opened the red curtains and again pushed her hand into the feathers. It brought back a memory of her own mother's room and how pleasant a haven it had been.

'You must test your grandmother's contention and lie upon it. An angel on a cloud, she claimed, did she not? It may be that she has the right of it. Had I a harp available, it would make for a pretty tableau.'

At Lady Glynne's encouraging nod, Emma jumped on to the bed. She lay back and closed her eyes, arms and legs spread. If the lady noticed that her feet were bare, she didn't say so, but Emma had walked down the muddy lane from the cottage and knew their condition. That had her back on her feet in a trice, lest she mark the linen.

'Well, is it as your grandmother said it would be?'

Emma bobbed another curtsy. 'It is, your ladyship. I pray that one day I shall own such a thing.'

'Perhaps you shall, child. Now you'd best run along. I know my husband, and I'll wager your mother is already looking out for you.'

BOOK ONE

BOOK ONE

CHAPTER 1

An almost intolerable excitement had replaced Horatio Nelson's melancholy at parting from his family. From King's Lynn to London, it had chafed for two whole days in his gut, but he had suppressed it to avoid his father's disapproval. Edmund Nelson, dark of countenance and pessimistic by nature, could not abide agitation, and constantly bemoaned the duty that had forced him to leave Bath and the curative waters he claimed made his life tolerable to see his son safely through the perils of the metropolis. It gave him scant pleasure to deliver him into the Navy, which he knew to be full of sin and temptation. Yet he could see no other way to advance Horatio in life. Even with the income of three clerical livings he had too many children to support.

The boy's excitement survived a night in Kentish Town, a modest dinner and ample advice heaped upon him by his uncle William Suckling, an official in the Customs Service who claimed to 'know a thing or two about the Navy'. He was now alone atop a coach on the London–Chatham road. And, by the time the coachman yelled that they'd arrived in the courtyard of the Angel, the itch that could not be scratched had turned to pangs of hunger.

The wind whipped through the narrow streets to swirl round the cobbled courtyard, but for a time the activity served to ward off the cold. However, as the coachman unloaded the luggage and the crowd thinned, Nelson realised that not one of the people left in the courtyard was naval, and that, of those who were still present, no one had the slightest interest in him. That was worrying: his father had assured him that he would be greeted warmly and whisked aboard his ship, that he would not need much money – which he would only waste, given half a chance.

'You never can leave that there!' barked the man in the streaked leather cap and apron, as Horatio stepped down and headed for the door of the inn.

Turning, the boy looked into the battered purple face. 'It will only be for a moment. I must go inside.'

That earned him a hiss of censure from a mouth that seemed to contain only one yellowing tooth. 'As you say, young sir. Why, that's time enough for me to take a tumble and break my neck. Can't have any cove that fancies leaving his boxes about. Many's the time Ah've found myself flat on my back, with only the good God to thank for bein' whole.' The porter's face was only a few inches from Horatio's and the smell of stale beer on the man's breath almost made him retch. 'But I don't s'pose a young gent would give two hoots for that!'

'I would, sir, I would,' Horatio protested, stepping back two decent paces, suddenly aware that being free of a parental overseer had pitfalls as well as advantages. 'But I believe that I am to be met. I must look for the person who's been sent for me.'

Two fingers squeezed the cratered nose, and a loud blast of air served to clear it, sending a flurry of yellow mucus on to the cobbles. 'An' two seconds is what it takes to lose it, boy, what with the villains we have round here.'

'If I may be allowed just a moment, sir, to enquire?'

'Not half a second, that is lest you want me to guard it fer you?'

Horatio was just about to say yes when he saw the gleam in the man's rheumy eyes. 'Twopence will see it safe.'

'That's more than I can spare.'

'Then you'd best take it along with you.'

Horatio's pleading glance did nothing to soften the porter's stance. He bent down and took hold of the new rope straps fitted to the battered old sea chest. Perhaps it was the cold, but it seemed so much heavier now than when he had tried to lift it at home.

'If I take an' end it will only run you to a ha'penny.'

Horatio shook his head and heaved, the brass edge moving

14

an inch, scraping across the cobbles. By the time he had dragged the chest to the back door of the Angel the thick dark clouds, which had layered the sky since first light, began to pour forth the rain they had been promising all morning. Looking back, Horatio saw the porter standing as the water cascaded off his leather cap, silently cursing.

'Look at Alfred Mace a-chunterin' out there,' said a light, pleasant voice behind him. 'That rain five minutes afore would have been worth a shilling of ale.'

'Then thank Christ it held off,' snapped a stocky girl. She had come close to Horatio to peer through the thick panes of glass. 'Too much ale frisks him. My arse is black and blue from his drunken nippings.'

'Excuse me, miss?' The girl looked down at Horatio, her round face red from the heat of the taproom. 'Would it be possible for me to leave my chest here while I look for someone?'

'No need to look so fessed, lad,' she replied. 'As long as it's out of the way.'

'I can't afford to pay.'

'Why, what are you bletherin' about? There's no need for to pay, young sir. How much did that sod Mace try to dun you for?'

'Twopence.'

'Miserable old bugger, he is,' she retorted, which made Horatio blush. 'I'd damn 'im to hell if I didn't think that Old Nick would send him right back twice as nasty.'

The lobby was full of people and smoke, some blowing out from the logs on the fire, even more from long clay pipes. The taproom was heaving, abuzz with loud talk, and the fug was so dense it was hard to see. Several men in naval uniform sat there, though not one spared Horatio a sideways look. It would be rude, he thought, to interrupt their earnest conversations and enquire if they had come to meet a Mr Nelson.

He went outside again, through the front entrance into the street, which only increased his confusion. The road was teeming with people, carts, horses, running dogs and a dozen coaches fighting to make their way through the throng. Horatio was sure he'd never seen such a crush, nor heard such a babble of sound. His questions as to the whereabouts of HMS *Raisonable* were met with stony incomprehension.

'Must be a ship,' barked one man, the fifth he had asked.

'She is, sir. A sixty-four gun line-of-battle ship.'

'Then it be a waste seeking for that in the middle of the King's highway. You'd best make your way to Anchor Wharf.'

The directions that followed, accompanied by much pointing, were complex. The youngster knew he had gained little more than a general direction but he offered his thanks. He set off, crossing the main thoroughfares, and more enquiries sent him downhill, through narrow, stinking lanes of tall, wood-framed houses, with workshops on the ground and homes above, concentrating on keeping his feet out of the stream of sewage that overflowed the central gutter, while keeping a sharp eye out to avoid the contents of a chamber pot that might suddenly be emptied above his head.

Eventually he could see the River Medway. Broad and tidal, it was full of boats of all shapes and sizes, but none from what he could tell looked anything like a King's ship. The prints of warships he had studied had been specific enough. None of the vessels in the basin, floating or tipped over on the mud banks, had any trace of the array of flags, rigging and guns he remembered.

The gates of the great naval dockyard, surmounted by the royal arms carved in stone, produced no more help than the streets of Chatham. It was late afternoon now, even colder. There had been several heavy showers so it was a wet, bedraggled young man who spoke to the marine sentries, only to be told in no uncertain terms that they were not employed as guides for lost sailors.

Disconsolate, Horatio turned to walk back towards the Angel, wondering if he had enough funds to pay for a night's lodging in the hayloft. His shoulders were hunched and the bottom of his cloak soaked and stained with every trace of Chatham filth. His spirits were so low he was close to sobbing.

'Did I hear you enquire for *Raisonable*, young fellow?'

Horatio looked up, hope welling in his breast. The man before him, tall and erect, was most certainly a naval officer.

The shape of his hat said so, as well as the gold braid on the blue coat that showed through his open cloak. More than that, he was smiling in a way that exuded genuine concern.

'I am, sir,' Horatio stuttered, trying to control his trembling, frozen limbs. 'I'm assigned to join that vessel, which is commanded by my uncle Maurice.'

'You are nephew to Captain Suckling?

'Yes, sir.'

'*Raisonable* lies beside my own ship, out at Saltpan Reach.' Horatio's incomprehension was evident. 'You do not know where that is?'

'No, sir,' Horatio replied, shuddering once more.

The man put a hand on his shoulder. 'I daresay you would like me to show you where she's moored?'

'Yes, please, sir.'

'I will, if you wish, take you out to her. My ship is tied up no more than a cable's length from her mooring. But I think such a journey would be ill advised before we've dried you out and fed you.'

'I must retrieve my sea chest.'

'Which is where?'

'I left it at the Angel, the inn where the coach stopped.'

Looking down, Frears could see that those bright blue eyes were close to despair, brought on by weariness and cold. But this young fellow was biting his lip in a vain attempt to restrain any notion that he might be a charity case. It would have been a bravura performance if he hadn't been shaking so much.

'Then that, young fellow, is where we will go. They have as good a fire as you will find in Kent, and the food is passing edible, certainly better than anything you will get aboard ship.'

'As long as it is within my reach, sir, I'd be obliged. But if it is not, I would be happy to wait upon your pleasure.'

Frears was thinking, you would too, boy. You'd wait out in the cold and rain rather than admit to need. And, no doubt, you'd haul your chest through the streets even if you risked collapse. He wasn't sure if that was admirable or foolish.

'I, young sir,' he said, finally, 'will stand you dinner.'

'B–but . . .' Horatio stammered.

'And quell your anxieties. I was in your shoes myself not

many years back. I remember it well, mostly for the hollow feeling I always seemed to carry in my gut. It will give me pleasure to treat you to a meal, and engage someone to porter your chest. And who knows? One day, when you're a lieutenant like me, you may be able to return the compliment. Now, what's your name?'

'Horatio Nelson, sir, but my family call me Horace.'

'Nelson of the *Raisonable*. It has a pleasing ring to it. I am Lieutenant Frears.'

'Of which ship, sir?'

'*Victory*.'

The rain stopped before they reached the Angel where a table was quickly procured in the warm, smoke-filled room that had seemed so unfriendly just a few hours before. Without his hat the lieutenant seemed less imposing than hitherto. He had jug handles for ears, a soft, fleshy face and a permanent worried frown for which, perhaps, there was good cause: Horatio learnt that Frears had just enough interest with influential acquaintances to keep himself in employment, if the ship to which he was assigned wasn't ready for sea. *Victory*, built ten years earlier, had never been commissioned, which suited him fine.

'Better to be laid up, young feller, with no yards crossed and an empty sail locker, than stuck on the beach! Any berth has the legs on half-pay.' He was also the father of three boys, whom he hoped one day would follow him into the Navy.

Frears had listened with understanding to the youngster's tale of himself and his family, of his father, a widower who showed little inclination to remarry despite his brood, and the need for a man on a clerical stipend to place his children where they might prosper, taking advantage of a family relationship to get his third son a naval berth.

The sky had cleared to reveal twinkling stars by the time they hired a wherry from the naval dockyard. Out in the main channel, close to the point where the Medway joined the River Thames, a whole fleet lay moored. Horatio Nelson had never seen a ship-of-the-line close to, so the size of the great warships was astounding. The boat swept him past the *Victory* as Frears reeled off details about her size, complement when commissioned, and armament. A hundred guns, displacing two and a half thousand tons fully rigged and supplied, she was enormous, towering above the little boat he had hired to bring them out. 'There's your vessel, young Nelson,' Frears said, finger pointing past the oarswomen, square-faced brutes with bad skin and arms like tree trunks. He was indicating a ship just visible in the gathering gloom as they ran under the gilded décor of the *Victory*'s stern.

Raisonable lacked the third deck that made Frears's ship so impressive, yet up close she seemed even bigger. Horatio understood a fraction of what he was being told about her crossed yards and the standing rigging. That was partly through ignorance, but more because the knot of anxiety in his stomach made it difficult to concentrate. The rowers, pipes clamped firmly in their mouths, took their wherry deftly in a long arc, and swung it in expertly to touch against the platform at the bottom of the long, sloping gangway.

'You will visit me, I hope, young man,' said Frears, as a rope appeared and was lashed to Horatio's chest, which disappeared into the night air. 'And pray be so good as to mention me to your uncle, Captain Suckling.'

Horatio nodded to the older man and, with some assistance from the hard-faced Medway women, stepped over the counter from the bobbing boat on to the empty, floating platform. Climbing the gangway brought him to the entry port, which led on to a long, dark, deserted main deck spliced by two sets of open stairways that led aloft. From the bottom of the nearest he could see starlight, and ascending that he rejoined his chest where it had been dropped. The men who had hauled it aboard were nowhere to be seen.

The upper deck was empty and *Raisonable* rocked gently, creaking and groaning. Occasionally someone would appear from a companionway and walk to another part of the ship, but they didn't acknowledge him, and he was left to pace back and forth, once more shivering and a victim of the penetrating cold.

Horatio wondered if he was forever to be a deserted soul in an unfamiliar landscape. Did the jolly tars he had been led to expect, the decorated fellows singing and dancing that were the

19

stuff of naval legend, really exist? Was that image a myth? Could this be the reality? A cold, harsh, indifferent world that made him long for the comfort of home?

A man emerged from a door aft. Looking at an hourglass he stepped towards the carved belfry that enclosed the ship's bell, which he rang with little enthusiasm. Then he murmured, 'All's well.'

'Excuse me, sir. I'm looking for Captain Suckling.'

'He's not 'ere,' the man replied, as he turned to go back whence he had come. 'Ain't been aboard the last fortnight, an' not like to be back this comin' week.'

He disappeared, and Horatio felt more bereft than ever. His father had told him the sea was a hard occupation, but nothing had prepared him for this. He sat on a pile of neatly coiled ropes and leant against the hard metal of a still-warm chimney, close to tears, until eventually his eyes fluttered and closed.

The fitful dreaming that followed, continually interrupted by the bell, as well as the need to move around and keep warm, meant that when the drummer came on deck to herald the dawn, Horatio was fast asleep. The new midshipman lay crumpled in his cloak on the deck planking with his head on his hat. He slept through the long, soft drum roll that saw the sky turn from black to grey, jerked but remained still when the Port Admiral's gun fired from distant Sheerness. The eight bells of the middle watch that summoned the crew failed to disturb him; the noise of the master at arms, rousing men from their hammocks, demanding that they 'show a leg', was muted by the wood of the deck. But the hard kick on the sole of his shoe woke him immediately.

'Who the devil are you?'

Horatio tried to stand up quickly, to respond to the officer, but his limbs were stiff. When he gained his feet, having stooped quickly to grab his falling hat, he was momentarily unsteady.

'Are you drunk, sir?'

The man who asked this was no older than Horatio's brother, Maurice, but his tone and the way he held himself had an authority that belied a five-year difference.

'No, sir,' he protested weakly.

One pair of bare feet made little noise on wooden planking, but there was no missing the growing sound of a hundred pairs, or of men being harried on to the deck by the harsh yells of the petty officers.

'You will oblige me by getting out of the way,' the officer barked. 'You're in danger of interfering with the running of the ship.' He added, 'And smartly!' but this was unnecessary, for Horatio was faced with a wall of sailors rushing towards him. Being small, he could slip between a pair, as they made to ram the long round bundles of their rolled hammocks into the nets that lined the ship's side. Not many noticed him, and those who did were only prepared to glare, especially at his sea chest, which was in the way. A convenient gap existed between a mast and those nettings. He dragged both the chest and himself clear, and from that vantage-point watched in the grey dawn light as the ship came to life.

Buckets were thrown over the side, to be filled with seawater, which was cast before men with large mops. They worked behind the sweeper, who in turn followed a line of sailors on their knees, with blocks of wood in their hands, grinding them over a thin line of sand. The ensemble was brought up at the rear by a line of men flogging the deck dry with cloths.

'And who, sir, for the second time, are you?' demanded the officer.

'I'm Nelson, sir. Horatio Nelson.'

All around him sailors were carrying out tasks, some mysterious, others obvious, like the hauling aboard of fresh greens or casks that had been fetched from the shore. Their laughing, joking and cursing made it hard to concentrate on his interrogator. He was hungry and fearful, but curious too.

'That means nothing to me,' the officer barked. 'Nor did I ask for your name. I am more determined to root out your purpose.'

A cask that had been lifted high inboard suddenly dropped towards the deck, seeming certain to smash to pieces. Horatio held his breath, then let it escape as the cask halted on its rope, the planking no more than a hair's breath away.

'Well?'

Horatio dragged his eyes back to the puce-faced officer. 'I have come aboard to serve, sir, which my uncle, the Captain, will confirm.'

The eyes widened, and the face reddened even more. 'Captain Suckling is your uncle?'

'He is.'

He had expected the man's tone to mellow at this but quite the opposite happened. 'You are telling me you're related to the Captain when you don't have the faintest idea of how to present yourself aboard his ship?'

Horatio gave something between a nod and a shake of the head, which did nothing to improve the impression he had created. 'You report to the premier, that is the first lieutenant, Mr Fonthill. He, and he alone, will decide whether to let you stay aboard, or tell you to sling your hook.'

'Can you tell me where I'll find him, sir?' Horatio enquired, looking first at the poop, then at the bows.

'Officers reside abaft the mainmast. And I don't suppose you know which is aft and which is forrard?'

Two of the men labouring close by laughed, which earned them a glare.

'You will proceed down on to the main deck. Then make your way aft to the wardroom, and stop once you encounter the marine sentry – hard to miss since he is coated in bright red. There you will ask for the premier. You will say to him that the officer of the watch sent you. You will then introduce yourself, and throw yourself upon his tender mercy.'

That produced another laugh, and a reprise of the previous glare. 'Belay that damned noise.'

A lack of certainty ensured slow progress, and every time he stopped it appeared he stood in someone's way. He was jostled on his way down the companionway and an object of curiosity on the main deck, which he followed aft to where the promised marine stood, his back to a door set into a wall of panelling.

What to ask for, premier or first lieutenant? He reckoned them the same, two appellations for the one rank, but in a mood of some confusion certainty was at a premium. In the end he asked for Mr Fonthill.

'It's customary to come aboard with letters of introduction!'

Fonthill was a tall, gangling man, every feature on his bony frame, from nose to throat, clearly defined by the lantern that cast a faint glow around his crowded cabin.

'My father led me to believe my uncle Suckling would be here, sir.'

'Then your father was mistaken. And, since you have no letters, how do I know that you are who you say? The purser won't thank me for another mouth to feed, especially one that's not on the books.'

Only the fear of being slung off the ship gave him the courage to reply. 'But I am, sir. My uncle wrote to inform my father that I was entered as captain's servant on January the first.'

'Were you, by damn?' Lieutenant Fonthill replied, though the expletive was muted. He reached for the muster book, a thick, leatherbound volume in a deep shelf behind his head, opened it and flicked through. His lips moved along with his finger as he ran it down the list of names, until finally he said, 'Nelson, Horatio. That's a damned awkward appendage.'

The boy squared his shoulders and gave a reply that would have pleased his father, who never feared to advise a stranger of the family bloodline. 'It comes to me through my Walpole relations, sir, ennobled as the earls of Orford.'

It didn't please Fonthill. He gave Horatio a hard look, which made his thin eyebrows quite threatening. 'It don't do to go boasting of your connections, young man.'

'I didn't—'

He got no further, and was treated to such a fine piece of sophistry that he wondered if he was back at school. 'Silence. Do not speak unless spoken to.'

'Sir.'

'Proceed to the gunner's quarters, and there introduce yourself to his wife.'

'I'll need some help with my chest.'

Fonthill leant forward, his face screwed up in distaste, every feature sharper still as he was right below the lantern. 'You're a poor specimen, Nelson, runtish in fact, with a tendency to flaunt your relations in the hope of impressing. But you are, for your sins, a young gentleman. As such, you do not carry your own dunnage. You may tell the officer of the watch to have your chest taken below. He will detail some hands to oblige.'

'And the gunner's quarters, sir?'

'Damn you, boy!' Fonthill barked. 'Do you expect me to sketch you a map of the ship?'

He was out of the premier's cabin before Fonthill had finished the sentence.

CHAPTER 2

Emma Lyon looked forward to Thursdays, to the weekly journey to Chester market. It was the one day, barring Sunday, that she was free of the burden of learning. Attending classes at the curate's house, she had soon discovered, was a misery; a dozen children at the mercy of a grubby creature who was free with his cane and never sounded as though he had much of interest to say. For all that, being quick, in three months she had got to grips with writing and counting, though with the former she had run up against the twin obstacles of spelling and grammar.

Home was little better. The Steps was a thatched cottage, old and draughty, with whitewashed walls and leaded windows streaked with the effect of wind and weather. It stood on rising ground on the edge of the muddy road that led out of Hawarden village. To get away from both, in the company of Grandma Kidd, was a treat to savour, even if a seat on the box of an unsprung cart was an uncomfortable way to travel.

She left behind her not just schooling but the constant laments of her elders. They never varied, nor were they ever resolved, just set aside to be raised at the next encounter. Grandpa moaned daily about his lot, stuck out in his shallow pit, rusting musket in hand, there to stop the local dogs from attacking the sheep he was employed to watch; this while Uncle Willy lay about all day, setting off disputes every time he claimed that he hadn't been born to work. The two unmarried aunts, who knew as well as anyone that there was little to spare in coin, wailed about the difficulty of snaring a husband with nothing to offer but passable looks. And Grandma Kidd herself, chief breadwinner and undoubted ruler of the roost, silenced them all by reminding them of every fault they possessed.

'Stop fidgeting, girl!' Grandma Kidd was sucking hard on her clay pipe, which, in a toothless mouth, robbed the admonishment of any force. Not that she was often fierce: the indulgence shown to Emma was another ongoing source of family strife. She hauled on the tarpaulin that had been laid on the box seat to keep the girl clean. 'That there dress'll be streaked with coal dust if you don't set still.'

The road from Hawarden ran across the flat landscape of Saltney Marsh, the ramparts of the medieval castle plain now, jutting up into the bright blue sky. Emma loved Chester; the arched gates that had once been shut against invaders; the bustle in the narrow streets that promised both danger and safety. Best of all was the market, quiet now in the early morning, soon to be teeming with trade. Her grandma knew the value of a pretty little girl, tidily dressed, for attracting custom. Not that Emma was tied down: having taken the horse to the livery stable, she would run around to talk with other children and extract favours from the vendors – sweetmeats perhaps, or an occasional bit of ribbon or lace.

'How's the dipping, Fred Stavely?' she squealed.

'Ssh!' Fred responded, putting a grubby finger to his lips. 'You'll get me hung by the thumbs.'

Five years older than Emma, he was smaller, a stunted orphan who worked the square on market day. Many was the time she had seen Fred filch a handkerchief or sometimes even a purse from some unsuspecting mark. Small, bright-eyed, like a bird of prey, Fred would steal anything, even fish or poultry, but only after it had been bought and paid for. He couldn't keep it, of course: he had to hand it over to the two villains who controlled the crime.

Brand and Potts, they were called, low-looking coves who bribed the market steward to leave them in peace. Everybody knew them, and some of the bigger stallholders paid them a regular stipend to protect their steady customers from the likes of Fred Stavely. They had approached Grandma Kidd with their demands, only to be sent away with a flea in their ear. Although Fred might work under their control, he wasn't like them. He was the type to share his good fortune with someone he thought of as a friend.

'I got my eye on that fat goat over yonder, the one with the flat round hat. He's wearing a watch and chain, an' keeps hooking his thumbs in his waistcoat pockets so that all can observe his prosperity.'

The market was getting crowded and Emma had to look hard to see who Fred had his eye on. Every stall had an awning, as well as a cart covered in produce of every colour imaginable. Orange carrots vied with dark brown potatoes, which sat next to deep green cabbages. On the cloth stalls the rainbow was represented in all its hues, which contrasted with burnished brass, dank pewter and bright iron. The noise was distracting too, the babble of vendors set against the arguments that went with every notion that a purchase might be made.

'There,' Fred said, breaking a dip's rule and pointing at his mark.

Emma looked along his finger to the fellow he had targeted. Even through the crowd, with all that noise, he oozed pomposity. The object Fred had spotted was his watch, on open display. 'He's asking to have it lifted,' she said, trying to sound adult.

Fred grinned, his puckish face creased in delight and puzzlement. 'You sounded just like Brand then. He would see me strung up on the Chester gibbet just to get his hands on a piece like that.'

'I don't want you strung up, Fred.'

'I know you don't,' he replied, giving her a gentle push as his mark turned towards them, the sunlight glinting on the chain across his belly. 'And nor are you like to see such a thing. Now you just go and stand over by Hargreaves' wet fish stall an' watch me work.'

Emma had heard her grandmother rail about pickpockets often enough, with many a warning of what to look out for or avoid. Working alone, as Fred Stavely did, was unusual. Dips normally worked in teams of three or four, using their numbers and quick transfers to avoid being nabbed. The knowledge that what Fred was about to attempt was dangerous thrilled Emma rather than alarmed her. As he had asked, she sidled over to the fish stall, her nose wrinkling at the familiar smell.

Fred's mark was bargaining loudly for some French lace,

tugging at his own jabot, insisting that it was of a far superior quality to what was on offer and demanding that the vendor should drop his price. Florid of face, his belly was prominent under his watch chain, and his clothes, though of good quality, were well worn, the velvet on both coat-collar and elbows showing thread. He looked like a tenant farmer, who had his hunting horse, enough coin to finance his alehouse boastings, and sufficient pride to wear his watch on market day so that folks could see his worth.

Fred was running now, darting through the shoppers, matching his pace and course to the state of the continuing bargaining, trying to time his arrival at the point when the loud transaction would have gathered the curious, without creating a throng that would impede him. Being so small in a crowd where only the costermongers knew him, Fred was taken for a child at play, afforded the odd impatient look yet never challenged. Just as the mark, with an imperious, dismissive wave, turned away from his bargaining, Fred barged into him with enough force to bring forth a shocked 'Damnation!'

Fred, as if hurt, fell at his feet, then hauled himself up by his mark's legs. The man swung his hand but his thick coat handicapped the force of the blow. However, it was enough to send Fred flying. He glared after the child, too triumphant to notice that his watch and chain had gone. That didn't last. Once again he poked his thumbs into his waistcoat pockets.

Fred was three feet from Emma when the roar went up. She could see the shock on his face, knew that he could sense what she could observe, as the bull-like victim began to push his way in pursuit, elbowing people aside as he yelled, 'Stop thief!' The shock of the cold metal in her hand, as Fred brushed past, was total, and the chain started to slip through her fingers. She caught the watch just before it hit the ground and, for lack of anywhere else to hide it, pushed it up under her skirt and jammed it between her thighs.

Fred ran behind the fish stall, emerged from the other side and went straight for his mark, aiming to pass him by, just like the innocent he now was. The large, rough hand took him by the collar and lifted him bodily, bringing forth a strangled cry from the boy's throat. Emma, feeling the metal against her inner thighs, acted instinctively to cover her own presence. She turned to the fishmonger and asked for half a dozen dabs, then made a show of searching for the means to pay. 'I've gone an' left the money and the sack with my Nan, Mr Hargreaves,' she piped, her face contorted with worry.

'Don't you worry about that, Emma girl,' the fishmonger replied, his red, beery face beaming kindly as he pulled a precious piece of paper from under the counter. 'You just take them over to Mrs Kidd and tell her to send you back with a sixpence and this here brown paper.' They were wrapped and handed to Emma before the nearby commotion really registered with her. It took the owner of the watch little time to search the two pockets on Fred's threadbare jacket, but since he knew the ways of dips, he was soon looking round for an accomplice. His eyes traced the route Fred had taken, to alight on the little girl in the long dress, brown paper parcel in her hands.

With a dozen huge strides he was towering over her and pointing, shaking Fred with the other hand. The curious came with him, surrounding the stall in such numbers that Hargreaves threw a piece of canvas over his wares lest they be pilfered in the mêlée.

'What's in that parcel?' the man demanded of Emma.

'Fish, sir,' she replied, meekly, head bent.

'Liar!'

'Hold your wheest, there,' barked the fishmonger. 'I sold her them dabs not a minute past, and she's telling truth.'

Fred's victim shook him again, producing numerous squeals and requests to be spared. So fearful did Fred look, eyes rolling and a dribble of spit running down his chin that Emma nearly laughed, but the seriousness of the situation put paid to that notion. Fred had dropped her right in it, and the consequences were almost too terrible to contemplate. She could recall the names of half a dozen girls her age who'd been condemned to the stocks, gaol or even transportation for what she would stand accused of. Offering up the watch and chain was no solution; that would see her taken up for certain.

The gruff voice of the mark, as he spat back at Hargreaves,

made her look up. 'You, sir, will mind your own, and this creature will unravel that paper and show me the contents.'

The metal of both watch and chain was warm now, digging into her tender flesh as she pressed her legs together to stop her knees trembling. Timidly, she offered up the parcel, which he grabbed. Half of the dabs fell to the ground as it was opened and, slowly Emma bent to pick them up.

'You know this villain?' the man demanded, throwing the rest of the dabs, still in their paper, at her feet.

She looked up, the big green eyes luminous with assent. 'Everybody knows Fred Stavely, your honour, what with him bein' a mite witless, an' all.'

'Witless?'

Emma tapped the side of her head with one finger, while Fred, responding like a natural, rolled his eyes and muttered gibberish. The man pushed him away, as if the taint of madness might be transferred by touch.

'Fred Stavely, you say?'

'That's him,' Emma replied, nodding to the creature now rolling on the ground. The mark looked at the fishmonger for confirmation, which came with a sharp nod. 'Check it with the Charlies of the watch, if you like, sir. They knows about him well enough.'

'I'll do that!' he barked, then turned away. The crowd who had followed him watched as he elbowed his way through, to return to the lace stall and investigate further. Emma slipped the paper to the edge of her dress, fell on to her knees so that it was covered, opened her thighs and let the watch and chain fall silently on to the remaining dabs. The rest, grimy from the cobbles, were quickly laid on top.

'You can give over writhing, Fred Stavely,' said Hargreaves, sharply, as he uncovered his fish. 'An' don't think if that fat sod asks me again I'll lie for you. If he hadn't been so bloody stuck up I wouldn't have done it once.'

'You're a right gent, Mr Hargreaves,' Fred replied, his grin given carefully, lest anyone should see his sudden recovery.

Hargreaves leant forward, without taking his eyes off Fred, and spat on the cobbles.

*

'You fuckin' near did for me, Fred Stavely!' Emma hissed. They had taken refuge in a narrow doorway and the echo doubled the pleasure she took in using forbidden language.

'Right sorry I am, girl, but it was that or the Tollbooth. Those bastards Brand and Potts wouldn't pay so much as a brass farthing to get me free.'

But Fred's troubles were of little concern to Emma: she had enough of her own to worry about. 'I've got sixpennyworth of dabs here that need settling. What am I goin' to tell if'n my Nan finds out what I did?'

Fred unwrapped the parcel. Watch and chain nestled amongst the grubby fish. He took it by one end and lifted it out. Not much light penetrated the deep doorway, but what did flashed on the polished metal. 'I wish you hadn't used my name, Emma. If that fat bugger goes to the watchman I'm done for, even if I have got rid this. And if he's asked, Hargreaves might tell him more truths than he did afore.'

'Sixpence!' Emma demanded, holding out her hand.

It was as if Fred hadn't heard her. 'Brand and Potts will give me precious little for this, even if'n it is worth a decent bit o' coin.'

'They'll give you enough to pay me back.'

Even in the gloom she could see that he wasn't listening. Those bright bird-like eyes were looking past her, as if she didn't exist, and his voice, when he spoke, was wistful. 'I've been reckonin' to make a move afore this. Things is gettin' hot round here, and they grant me less an' less for what I do lift.'

'Fred!'

He looked at her at last and smiled. 'I ain't got sixpence, Emma, and if I had I would need to hold it hard to see me on my way.'

'Way to where?'

'I'll head south, I reckon. Who knows? I might end up in London town, dipping the pockets of German George hisself.' Seeing the look in Emma's eye, he spoke more quickly. 'Tell your Nan that you fancied the dabs for supper. She's so soft on you she'll pay out even if she does bark. Maybe Hargreaves'll take one of her rabbits instead of coin.'

He lifted a hand to chuck her under the chin. 'I'll recall you kindly, Emma. We was friends even afore what happened today.'

'You're not goin' right off.'

'What's to stay for?' he replied, holding up the watch and chain once more. 'I ain't got no one to say farewell to, 'ceptin' you. Brand and Potts will have heard about this bein' lifted soon enough, and if my name's mentioned they'll be looking for me to take it.'

Fred turned once, then spun back, his eyes hard in a way that she had never seen before. 'They two sods have been at your Nan for money, right?'

'She told 'em to bugger off.'

'They won't. It's not their way. If you was to ask around you'd hear that when Brand and Potts get refused, they're like to wait on a lonely road, takin' by force what folks won't part with willin'. An' I heard them discussin' your Nan not a day past, and sayin' as how she needed to be taught her place.' Emma put her hand to her mouth. 'Best tell Mrs Kidd that, and say it comes from me. Now, wish me good fortune, lass. And remember, should you ever come to London, look into every coach and four, 'cause, like as not, you'll find Fred Stavely, Esquire, alolling on velvet cushions like the cock of the walk.'

There was a rattle as Fred gathered the watch and chain into his hand. Then, with a final smile, he turned round and strode off.

He might have thought that Grandma Kidd was soft enough on Emma to forgive her, and maybe she would have done so if the fish had been clean. But the grubby offering, 'with half the muck of the market on it', was not accepted. Emma spent the rest of the day under her baleful looks with sharp reminders about the state of the Kidd finances, though in honour, before they packed up to go home, she sent to Hargreaves the money he was owed.

As always, it took an age to get out of the town, carts clogging up to leave through the narrow gateways. So it was under a darkening sky, full of low, troubled clouds, on Saltney Marsh, that Emma first spied the men loitering by the side of the road. She knew her Nan had seen them too, just by the way she stiffened up. That was the moment she chose to tell her what Fred had hinted at.

'Your eyes is better 'an mine, child. Is that Brand and Potts up ahead?'

'I think it is. The tall one is so like Brand.'

They had chosen a good spot in the middle of the marsh with only this one road. And the fading light was security against anyone seeing what they were about from a distance.

'Get in the back, girl,' said Mrs Kidd, sharply.

'But—'

'Do as you're bade for once this day.'

Emma climbed over on to the flat bed of the cart, her heel going over on the coal that her grandmother had failed to sell. 'What will you do, Nan?'

'I'll not part with a penny, that's for certain.'

'Fred told it like they were prepared to offer violence.'

'Happen,' Mrs Kidd replied enigmatically.

They were close now, the features distinct of the pair of villains. Both stepped out at once, barring the narrow road, with the taller one, Brand, holding up his hand. Grandma Kidd flicked her whip to get the nag moving faster. One of the cartwheels dropped into a pothole, which made Emma stagger and fall to her knees. Putting out both of her hands to save herself, she grasped two sizeable pieces of coal. Potts stepped forward, hands outstretched to take hold of the horse's head-collar. As soon as he got close, Grandma Kidd was on her feet, the whip flashing out in front of the horse's nose, to drive Potts backwards.

'You get away from there, Ismail Potts,' she shouted, 'or for certain I'll mark you.'

'You had best hold up,' shouted Brand, lifting a heavy stick.

'I'll do no such thing,' the old lady replied, applying the whip to the horse's hindquarters.

'We've come only for what's due,' yelled Potts, reaching out to catch the traces again.

The whip took him right across the face, making him duck as he yelled in pain. Emma was on her feet, the two lumps of coal sent forth, not with any real force, but enough to make Brand move back instead of forwards. The whip drove him back another step. Now they were abreast of the wagon, Emma rained lumps of coal at them, ignoring her grandmother's command to get back on the box and take the reins. One lump caught Brand on the temple and he spun away to join Potts, who was holding his cheek and swearing in pain and anger. But he was standing still, making no attempt to pursue the bucking cart.

Chest heaving, Emma's face was full of triumph. She and her Nan, two females with forty years between them, had seen off two of the biggest rogues around, proving that they were nowt but stuffed bullies of no true account. She had seen a picture once, at the curate's lessons, of a man in a chariot after winning some ancient biblical fight. That was what she felt like now.

'Get back on the box, girl, this instant!'

Brought back to reality with a bump, Emma obliged, glancing at her dress, which was covered in streaks of coal dust. Grandma Kidd, transferring the whip, sat down herself. Her free hand took Emma round the shoulders.

'I'm sorry for the state I'm in, Nan.'

'You'll do for me, lass, clean or dirty,' the old lady said, as she hauled her granddaughter hard to her so that she could give her a kiss. 'An' even stinkin' of fish.'

CHAPTER 3

Mrs Killannan, wife to HMS *Raisonable*'s gunner, was a substantial woman. Rosy-cheeked, broad in the hip and with huge breasts, she terrified not only her husband but most of the officers as well. She would bend in knee and spirit to the premier, and to the second lieutenant at a pinch. But no one inferior to that dared challenge her, especially when it came to the behaviour of her charges in the midshipmen's berth. She had two precepts that were paramount: cleanliness in both body and mind, so that as long as the boys stayed spruce, and were attentive to their prayers, she left them to their own devices. She believed, quite wrongly, that even with a touch of wildness, her 'boys' were too in awe of her to countenance disobedience.

'This 'ere is Mr Nelson,' she said, to the assembled mids who occupied a space no bigger than eight feet by twelve. 'Now, he is nephew to the captain, but that don't signify 'cause you know that he's a man who would shudder to see special treatment afforded.'

In the dim lantern light, here below the waterline, it was possible to make out with certainty only the faces of the half dozen closest to him. Yet each person had some feature that marked him out as an individual, even if in one case it was a face so bland as to be remarkable for that alone. A square chin here, a prominent nose there: the looks of indifference that were real contrasted with those more contrived. One, with the dark stubble of a heavy growth, seemed older than the lieutenant who had discovered him asleep on deck. Another's face was so round and cherubic that he had the appearance of an overgrown baby. The only thing it seemed that they all had in common was a determination to ignore him, as though the arrival of a new member of the mess was an everyday occurrence.

Although unaware of it, Horatio Nelson was likewise the object of surreptitious examination. Those he had joined saw a slight youth, thin, handsome but pale, with very fair hair and grey-blue eyes that were slightly hooded and shielded whatever thoughts he harboured. His skin was clear, his lips slightly feminine in their fullness, with no trace of the flickering tongue that denoted nerves.

He had been in this situation before, suddenly required to face a potentially hostile group, with which he would have to co-exist. But he had attended school in the company of his elder brother, and although that had provided little in the way of physical defence, at least he had had someone to associate with until he found his own friends. This, he knew, as the gunner's wife began the introductions, was different.

'Now this here is Mr Dobree,' she said, patting the fellow with the dark chin, 'and he is senior in this mess. So you will bide with what he says. He answers to me, an' answers well.'

'What peril would I risk if I failed to respond to you, dear lady?' Dobree asked, his voice soft and supplicating, an odd look in his watery, chestnut eyes as he leant forward into the light.

That was nothing to the warmth of the response from Mrs Killannan. The apple cheeks reddened a touch more and the hard countenance melted fleetingly, like that of a mother looking upon a favourite son. Yet Nelson could see the insincerity in Dobree's expression and picked up a hint, from the nods and winks that rippled through the other members of the berth, that this was a game they enjoyed.

'You will find, Nelson,' Dobree added, his voice silky, 'that your own dear mother would struggle to match the grace and comfort afforded us by Mrs Killannan.'

'My mother is dead,' the newcomer replied quickly, only realising after the words were out of his mouth that, in some way, he had failed his new shipmates, several of whom frowned at him for dampening a situation that clearly amused them. The next words were blurted out and, judging by the stony faces, did nothing for his standing. 'I am sure you are right.'

36

Dobree's expression hadn't changed, and his moist eyes were locked on those of the gross-faced gunner's wife. He put out a hand to brush her thick forearm. 'You may look here for comfort, sir. That is, if you feel the need.'

The face that pushed past that of Mrs Killannan was as gaunt as hers was fat, a comedic combination, framed by the curtain, which produced suppressed sniggers. 'Where's this chest to be let down?'

'I'll leave you to square that away, Mr Dobree,' the lady said, spinning round, her sheer bulk enough to force the man who had fetched the chest to jump back. His eyes still fixed on the other members of the mess, Nelson heard her curse the carrier, bidding him shift out of her way in a voice full of venom.

'Leave it outside for the present,' Dobree said, as the thin face appeared again, his voice much harder now. He stood up, too tall to complete the motion, even bent his head brushing the deck beams above. He towered over the newcomer, who tensed. There was a pregnant pause, before Dobree spoke in the same silky tone he had used with Mrs Killannan.

'Well, Mr Nelson, do you have a brain in that limited top hamper of yours?'

The softness of the voice did nothing to help the youngster relax. Instead he bunched his fists, which didn't go unnoticed. Every member of the berth seemed to edge forward slightly in anticipation.

'Why we have a gamecock in our midst,' the senior midshipman crowed.

'Get on with it, Dobree,' said another voice, almost as deep, from just outside the range of the lantern. As he spoke, its owner leant forward to show a square, broken-veined face, with thick, widespread eyes, and a button for a nose. His mere presence caused all the others to withdraw to the edge of the lanternlight, like tortoises seeking the shelter of their shell.

Horatio Nelson didn't relax. If anything this new voice added to his anxieties. He knew that his every action, every expression on his face, would be judged by those present against patterns of which he knew nothing. All he could do was maintain his stance until things became clearer. Dobree didn't turn to face the voice, but an expression bordering on distaste crossed his face.

'That's Rivers, Nelson. You must mind out for him, since his morals are as thin as his patience. But that is as nothing to the needs of his belly, though I regret to say he's not singular in his hunger. Now, you must, in all conscience, have some food in that chest of yours?'

He did, and his willingness to share gained him a place at the table, which was a board suspended from two hooks in the deck beams above and removed at night so they could use the space to sleep. That first night was strange: his futile attempts, a cause of much hilarity, as he tried and failed to get into his unfamiliar hammock. Rivers and Dobree eventually hoisted him in so that they could get some sleep, the former making much play of goosing him in the process before killing the lanterns and plunging the berth into Stygian blackness.

There was an element of terror in the dark, which was full of strange sounds and what seemed like surreptitious movements, the creaking of the ship as it moved on the tide removing any similarity to his old school dormitory or to his bedroom at home. He lay, eyes open, thinking of his family, the two brothers and four sisters who had always seemed like a shield against any hostility in the world. The image of his mother floated in and out of his mind, sometimes smiling, at other times scowling, warning him never to do anything to shame her.

The word 'shame' conjured up the face of his father: dark, stern and pessimistic. It was a word he was much given to using, as though it represented a fate he struggled against in vain, the knowledge that it was only a matter of time before one of his motherless brood let him down. He presided over a cold house, due to parental frugality in the matter of wood, where meals were a purgatory of short commons and sharp-eyed fatherly observation. No laxity was allowed either in posture or table manners: a Nelson back touching a chair was held sinful, and meals were consumed with a posture that would not have shamed a Prussian grenadier.

Greed was a sin too, so the natural hunger of a boy who had

been out in the fresh air all day had to be kept in check so that only his share of the family repast made it to his plate, and that was never enough. All the while his father dominated the table from his position at the head. The Reverend Edmund Nelson was no storyteller, which rendered his sermons as dull as his conversation. For all that, Horatio missed his family, father, sisters and brothers, as well as the Parsonage, and had to fight now to stop himself sobbing with homesickness.

He couldn't recall what he had been thinking about when sleep took him, but he did know, when he woke up, that he had had the most vivid of dreams, all centred on home and family. What had been the name of that cowherd? It was ten years ago and Horatio had been only four . . .

'That looks a likely tree, young Mr Nelson. You can see the lapwings a flying in and out, and ahovering o'er the edge building it up. Now that means there's eggs in that there nest, an' all it will take is a leg up from old Dan . . .'

'Dan,' he hissed to himself. 'That was his name, Dan.'

He had met him in a field close to his grandmother's house and, with the innocence of childhood, had just started talking. Old Dan must have taken to him, because they were soon off into the woods nesting, with Dan saying that it was never too early to start a collection of eggs. That a gentleman, which he most certainly must grow up to be, should collect them, and butterflies, and press flowers in a book so that he would always have a memory of his countryside childhood to hand.

He recalled how Dan had lifted him up on to that lower branch. 'Now, watch how you go, young sir, allus make sure ye has a handhold, 'cause that will save you from a fall. And don't go right near that nest when the birds are about, 'cause their flapping will see you tumbling.'

Coached inch by inch he had made his way up several branches till he could put a hand into the nest. His size had driven the lapwings away, regardless of old Dan's warning. It was easy to get the eggs out.

'There's four and they're warm,' he squeaked.

'Don't take 'em all, lad. Leave a pair for them to raise. That way there's a nest for someone else to look into in the future.'

Getting down took twice as long as getting up and old Dan,

as he said, 'had to go about his occasions'. Taking the boy, who now cradled his treasures in his shirt, to the edge of the wood, he pointed across a deep grass meadow. 'See that oak tree yonder, standing solitary like it were there to hang a poacher? That be your way home. There's a stream t'other side, which you can wade. You'll see your grandma's house from there.'

'Can I come again, Dan?'

'If you can find me, lad. I don't stay in one field for long.'

Now he could smell his way across the meadow, the sharp scent that tickled his nostrils as he crushed grass and meadow flowers on his passage. They came up to his chest, and as he looked back he could just see how his route marked a deep trail, made dark and obvious by the dropping sun. He was picking flowers too, a posy for his grandmother, because he knew she would be pleased. A happy grandmother meant a mincemeat tart.

It was the stream that had flummoxed him. Old Dan might say to wade it, but to his four-year-old eyes it had looked deep and menacing, clear water that showed a bottom made up of grasses that bent in the current and, as he looked hard, the occasional darting fish. Unsure of how to cross he sat down, not unhappy since the sun was still warm, content to arrange his posy and wait for the stream to go away.

That was how they found him, sitting there in the dark, the posy sagging sorrowfully, his father angry, and not mollified by his childish explanation that he had gone nesting with old Dan, or even the evidence of the eggs.

'Do you not fear to wander off with strangers?' his father demanded.

'I don't know fear, Papa. What does it look like?'

No wonder his brother William had called him a pious little turd. But that had been over the theft of the pears from Classic Jones's garden. Every boy in the school had eyed them as ripe for plunder, but Jones the headmaster was so free with the birch sapling that no one was brave enough to act. Each, though, seemed stalwart enough to accuse every other boy in the room of being a scaredycat, an accusation that the younger Nelson could not countenance.

'I'll go.'

'Shut up, Horace,' said William.

'I will not, brother. I make a genuine offer. If you and the others will aid me in the manufacture of a rope I will pinch Jones's pears.'

'You don't like pears,' William muttered.

But he was too late. Others, less fearful that the younger Nelson might get a good flogging, had already set to with their bed sheets, twisting and knotting them to make the rope necessary to lower him from the first-floor window. Within five minutes he was out, hands clasped hard over one of the knots, being eased down to the ground.

A windowful of heads and whispered jabbering watched him climb the pear tree. Hands shot out to direct him to the most fecund branches. His pillowcase was full when he descended, and was sent aloft before the thief, who arrived in the room to see that a goodly half of his haul had tooth marks in them already.

'Here, Nelson. Have some.'

He waved away the pears pressed on him. 'I cannot abide pears.'

'So why did you steal them?' demanded a frustrated William.

'The others were afraid to, brother. I was not.'

In his own head now those words sounded as though they had emanated from a pious little turd. Was he that? How would he fare here in this berth? What would he become in the Navy? Would future nephews sit at table while he, like his heroic uncle, moved cruets and cutlery to describe a historic battle? Would he make his late mother and dour father proud of him? The terror of failure was very real, and it was with deep gratitude that he heard the gunner's wife come to rouse them so that they could wash, say their prayers and partake of breakfast.

No cleaner or any more pious than other boys their age, they spent much of their time circumventing the strictures of the gunner's wife. Midshipman Nelson, almost as his first lesson, learnt that she was a slave to flattery. Praise for her natural maternity, judiciously mingled with hints that there was a desirable woman in that huge, squat body, could usually melt the frown that appeared when she espied anything amiss.

He also realised quickly that, for all his height and need to shave, Dobree was weak in the article of discipline, more interested in peace, food and a good pipe than any exercise of authority. Two of the others, Rivers and a fifteen-year-old called Makepeace, exerted whatever terror was going in the berth. This mostly extended to stealing victuals from the plates of those too young, small or cowardly to challenge them. Like all societies of youngsters, they revelled in vulgarity, never using a proper expression where slang, preferably larded with filth, would do. And for all the books he had brought, none referred to nautical vernacular so that initially a lot of the conversation went over his head.

And then there were the ceremonies by which boys initiate others into their group. It was in these that Rivers and Makepeace showed that their attitude wasn't entirely harmless. In an undermanned ship at anchor, some of the usual jokes could not be played. But fertile minds found plenty with which to tease. Dobree sent the new arrival to the Bosun, to ask for a long weight; to the yeoman of the sheets to demand a skyhook. Midshipman Buckle, only a year older than him, gave him a kid and sent him to the wardroom to demand that it be filled with the midshipman's daily ration of claret. On the first day that the breeze blew with any strength, Midshipman Foley, the same age as Nelson but with two years' experience, challenged him to a pissing competition, with a sixpence for the winner, which was when Midshipman Nelson discovered the inadvisability of urinating to windward. They were embarrassing but harmless pranks. Slightly less comfortable was the ritual stripping of the new boy, initiated by Makepeace and enthusiastically carried out by the entire mess. Horatio Nelson was a scrapper by nature, but faced with ten pairs of hands his efforts were useless. He was therefore forced to undergo in silence the humiliation of having his breeches pulled off and his parts, hairless and undeveloped, examined and disparaged. He squirmed the most when Rivers fondled them, aware and ashamed of the instant erection as the older midshipman's face leered over his.

42

'We've got a Jemmy Jessamy here, by the feel of things,' Rivers crowed. 'What's stirs ain't much, but it do stir.'

The curses he emitted, and the names he called his attackers before a hand stopped his screaming, earned his groin and belly a double dose of boot-black. Restored to his feet he tried as hard as he could to make light of his humiliation, rubbing hard at his blackened genitals with a piece of tow, half laughing in an attempt to hide his upset. He could not weep before this group: to do so was to invite another drubbing. And there was no good to be had from a display of anger.

Such rituals were commonplace and, though not so violent or thorough, he had received and administered them himself at his old school. He knew that a few amiable curses and insults allied to a display of acceptance would do more to endear him to this mess than protest. Likewise no complaints could be passed to a higher authority.

In the next few days he experienced the first stirring of acceptance: the jokes dried up, there being only so many to be played on a fellow now deeply suspicious of anything. His name was changed to Nellie, which he knew from his past was a good sign. Inclusion in conversation became automatic instead of forced, and he began to comprehend some of the vernacular jokes of this particular berth. He knew he had arrived when he was included in the 'cocks on the table'. Not that he was up for a prize, but he put out what he had for display and his examination of the opposition was furtive but fascinating.

His problems started when Rivers got him into the lower holds to hunt for rats. It was an entertaining game, played in the faint light from a single lantern, since the older midshipman knew well how to stir them from their hiding places. That gave the tyro, strategically placed, a chance to club them as they emerged. They changed roles, Rivers and he so close as they poked the crevices that Nelson could smell the musk of the older boy's sweat. Inevitably, as the number increased, it ended with the pair of them racing around as best they could bent near double, squeaking rodents running in all directions from their swinging cudgels.

Breathing heavily they collapsed, their gasps for air mixed with mirth and comments on each other's hunting prowess,

Rivers's arm over Nelson's shoulder in a firm grip. It was a strange sensation, that hand on the back of his neck pulling him forward suddenly to be kissed, to feel a strange tongue forcing itself into his mouth and a hand running slowly up the inside of his thigh. Horatio Nelson didn't react for several seconds, not sure of what he should do, aware that there was excitement in this as well as danger, that there was a delicious sensation in his groin. Rivers was at his breeches buttons, opening them just enough to slip his hand inside.

He pushed away the older boy as soon as Rivers reached his goal. 'It's a good game, Nelson,' he whispered. 'Better than Rat and Trap.'

In the half-empty holds, with no one else present, the older boy felt free to unbutton his own breeches without being observed, his voice hoarse as he invited the other boy to do likewise. 'One hand clapping is all very well, Nelson, but this is better, as you will find when you grow a bit.'

He took the younger boy's hand and pulled it on to his prick. Nelson, not looking, was aware of dry soft flesh and wisps of thin hair but most of all he was conscious of the size, so much greater than his own.

'No.'

'Come on,' Rivers insisted, pulling hard to restore contact.

Nelson stood up and tried to edge past him, only to be grabbed and pushed until his back was against the end of a barrel, with Rivers, now upright, trapping him.

'It's nowt but a bit of play.'

Nelson pushed him hard, to little effect. 'Go play with yourself, damn you.'

Rivers laughed, a throaty sound. His square face and button nose were so close that the saliva on his lips gleamed. The fist that took him on the ear didn't inflict much pain, but it surprised him, and he took a half-step back.

The follow-up blow caught him on the lip, which split and began to bleed. Rivers had his hand to it, which muffled the string of curses aimed at the back of his escaping victim.

Breeches fully undone he couldn't follow.

CHAPTER 4

The rest of the day had an endless, surreal quality, full of confused imaginings, not least about what might have happened if he hadn't fled. Part of him had wanted to stay, he knew that; to experiment with what had only ever been the subject of hushed discussions or inaccurate jokes. He couldn't rid himself of the feeling that part of Rivers was still there, in his hand, which induced mixed emotions.

Nelson felt even worse in company than he felt alone. He was convinced that every member of the berth had an inkling of what had occurred, which made him examine every remark to try and glean if it was innocent or barbed, which made him appear moody and suspicious. Rivers, subdued at first, soon latched on and proceeded to heap on his head a stream of insults.

Nelson had yet to learn that the berth was split: a few liked Rivers and actively encouraged him; the rest laughed at his sallies for fear of seeming weak. Dobree remained aloof: he just smiled at the references to pretty blond catamites being perfect for the Captain's servants, to jokes about being stretched across a gun for a thick whip, or the best way to trim the wick on the Captain's candles.

Faced with a silent, stone-faced victim, Rivers grew bolder. Allusions to 'bum boys', and the pleasure they gave their superiors, came thick and fast. The others watched the victim closely, supposing through his occasional shudders that he was taking it badly, unaware that in reality he was wondering if Rivers's slurs were true. There had been pleasure mixed with terror in the depths of the ship, and he wasn't sure where one had begun and the other ended. He tried to block the images from his mind, glad that the table hid the effect of memory, but he couldn't block out the abiding question: had he run from fear of Rivers or for fear of his own inclinations?

Examining the faces of the others produced a confused answer to that question. His shipmates refused to meet his eye. Was that from disgust? He couldn't know that they were waiting for the inevitable outcome: a sobbing plea to be left in peace.

That didn't happen. When Nelson's self-control shattered, he dived across the table to attack his tormentor. For the second time Rivers was taken by surprise and absorbed half a dozen blows before he could retaliate. But, given their respective height and weight that mattered little. Nelson was soon knocked to the floor, with his opponent stepping in to boot him. 'You snivelling little shite,' Rivers spat, as his foot swung.

Trapped by the bulkhead, Nelson tried to rise, only to be knocked back by another blow, more of a heavy slap than a punch. Following through, Rivers called for the others to join in. His friends, especially Makepeace, had already moved forward. Nelson grabbed Rivers's foot and pulled hard, sending the older boy flying. That gave him enough room to begin to rise until Makepeace landed a punch that felled him again, forcing him to curl up into a ball, with his hands around his head. He began to feel the impact of the kicks now raining in on his body.

It was odd listening to the sounds of anger and excitement, feeling the strength of the blows without much pain. His senses, except his hearing, seemed numb, as though the assault was being inflicted on another. Each voice was clear: Rivers spluttering as he cursed and swore; Dobree calling feebly to them to let Nelson be. He guessed that Makepeace, a silent attacker, was inflicting the greatest hurt, his boot beating a tattoo on his unprotected back. Everyone, it seemed, had joined in, Rivers's deep growl set against a background of high-pitched squeals. But many seemed token in their efforts, careful as they added their contribution, using the confined space and ample noise to amplify the apparent extent of their labours.

It took the senior midshipman a good minute to begin a vain attempt to stop the fight. Given the ballyhoo, this allowed time for Mrs Killannan to arrive, her shout bringing immediate relief

46

to Nelson. Nearest the door, and between the gunner's wife and the fray, Dobree took a thudding clout, which threw him out of the way. Her hands and forearms were not all fat and she had little difficulty in dragging or punching everyone back from the boy still huddled on the floor. 'You miserable swabs,' she cursed, dragging Nelson upright and hauling his face into the apron that covered her ample bosom. 'Don't you surmise no better'n to batter the Captain's nephew?'

The bloodied face was pushed back for examination, the note in Mrs Killannan's voice carrying more than a trace of desperation. 'And who's to excuse this away when the Pig comes aboard?'

She caught her breath, as if to try to cover her inadvertent use of the Captain's nickname. But the boy wasn't listening. He was wriggling to get free. Nelson knew he was hurt, but could still feel no pain. The salty taste of blood in his mouth seemed quite pleasant. That didn't last the distance between the mid's berth and the gunner's quarters. Agony came as the force that had animated him subsided and his hurts were not aided by the less than gentle ministrations of Mrs Killannan and her neat rum.

Her husband sat through this, chewing on his tobacco, a glint in his eyes, which twinkled every time he moved the quid to one side so that he could repeat, 'You're fer the 'igh jump now, me girl. It'll be roast Sow, stuffed and trussed, when the Pig comes up that there gangway.'

Which he did the following morning, the ceremony of piping the Captain aboard attended by everyone. To avoid any further trouble his battered nephew had spent the night in the gunner's quarters. Captain Suckling spotted him right away and his all too obvious wounds. But the needs of his office took precedence and the formalities were punctiliously observed. Only when they were complete was his nephew summoned, first to account for his presence but much more for his condition.

Stepping into the great cabin of HMS *Raisonable* for the first time terrified him, almost as much as the stern look in his uncle's eye. Pacing back and forth, Captain Maurice Suckling was silhouetted against the casement windows that ran across the rear of the ship. Thus, the angry look he wore was apparent each time he turned to retrace his steps. Yet there was something else, a similarity to the memory of Nelson's mother. This meant that the boy's eyes, which would have been better cast down in shame, were occupied in close scrutiny of his relative's features. That made his uncle stop and growl. As Nelson didn't know him well, it was impossible for him to deduce if the wrath was genuine or contrived, but the voice was certainly peppery when he spoke.

'I come aboard only to find you already here when you're not supposed to be.'

'My father was eager to return to take the waters at Bath, sir.'

'You mustn't interrupt me,' his uncle insisted, though in a tone less abrupt. He was slim, like his nephew, and shared in some measure the Suckling gentleness of feature, which made it hard for him to sustain outrage. 'Being blood makes no odds.'

'I'm sorry, sir.'

'And try to remember the correct form of response to a superior. You're supposed to say, "Aye, aye, sir".' Nelson complied immediately, just as his uncle was about to continue, which earned him a searching stare. The older man was clearly wondering if the boy was baiting him. 'How am I going to explain to your father the condition I find you in?'

It was lucky that his uncle Maurice couldn't see the bruises that covered his body and legs. They were well hidden by his breeches and blue uniform jacket. But the marks on his face bore ample testimony to the beating he had taken. Every time the youngster moved his tongue he could feel the extra thickness of his lips and rock the tooth that had come loose on one side. He had a black eye that was turning yellow at the fringe, plus a prominent lump on his forehead, the result of Rivers's most telling punch.

Captain Suckling was no fool. He had been a midshipman himself once, so knew what a bear pit the berth could be, even if he was careful of the quality of the youngsters who occupied his. He wondered if that word 'youngsters' was accurate. Those aboard *Raisonable* ranged from a pair of children of even more tender years than his nephew, to Dobree and Rivers who were so long serving that they had grown to be men of eighteen.

'Am I to be granted an explanation, sir?' Suckling demanded.

Nelson hesitated, partly because he had no idea of what to say but more because he was so struck by his uncle's looks. Take away the wig and replace it with a cap, add a touch more flesh, though less colour, to the cheeks, and he might have been facing the wrath of his late mother.

'Well, boy?'

'I f-fell down a companionway, sir. It was an accident.'

There was no doubting the nature of the family likeness as Suckling digested that, and Nelson saw the rage coming long before his uncle delivered his response. 'Fell? Do you take me for an idiot, nephew?'

'No, sir,' he replied.

'Then you will explain to me who is responsible for this. And I will point out to you that I command here and that every member of the berth you occupy is here because I have taken them on.' His fingers clicked loudly. 'I can have any one of you off this ship in an instant.'

Horatio Nelson didn't know much about the Navy as yet, but he knew that that was stretching the truth. Maurice Suckling had filled his mid's berth with the relatives of people to whom he either owed a favour or from whom he sought one. Even if one or two were no-hopers, who might sit the lieutenant's examination till Doomsday without passing, he was obliged to keep them on his books, so that their relatives or patrons would look favourably on any request the captain of *Raisonable* put forward. In his own case, he prayed that the family connection would exert too much pressure on his uncle for him to take any precipitate action.

'It is, sir, the truth.'

Suckling responded slowly, his voice a good octave deeper than it had been previously. 'How long have you been aboard my ship, nephew?'

'This is my third day, sir.'

'And has anyone had the presence of mind to point out to you the masthead?'

'Yes, sir.'

'Then you will oblige me, Mr Nelson, by making your way to that station, and you will stay there until I call you down. I would advise you to contemplate the folly of your response, and reflect that with a father who is a clergyman, and myself as your relative, I have the right to expect from you the complete truth.'

'Aye, aye, sir.'

Suckling observed the stiff way his nephew turned and left the cabin. He knew little of the boy. Given the size of the Rector's brood occasional visits to Burnham Thorpe had tended to cause all the nephews and nieces to take on a single personality. According to his father, Horatio was the terrier of the bunch, as well as the runt, never content to let an older sibling hold sway. He had questioned in his letters the Rector's notion of sending him to sea, which by its very nature was a hard, dangerous life. His brother-in-law had informed him that if anyone was inured to a world of rough and tumble, it was his third boy. The long-suffering cleric had tried and failed to calm the beast of transgression that lay within the child's breast.

The Captain smiled as he recalled the last lines of his final letter. It had been a warning, in some sense, to the Rector of the worst he might expect: 'Let him come, and the first time we go into action, a cannonball may knock off his head and do for him at once.' The smile evaporated as the recent memory of his nephew's swollen face swam back into his mind. Given the state of him, it looked as though he might not survive long enough to face a day's sailing, never mind a proper sea fight.

'Mr Fonthill!' he yelled. 'If you please.'

The first lieutenant, seated in the wardroom below the Captain's feet, heard the faint sound of his name through the deck beams. But he was the senior officer on the ship – barring the Captain – and with a proper sense of his place in the scale of things, he didn't move until the officer of the watch sent a messenger to fetch him. He entered Captain Suckling's day cabin with a degree of confidence, since the man behind the desk was not only his own patron but had a deep appreciation of his subordinate's efficiency in running the ship. 'Sir,' he said, removing his hat in the required fashion.

Fonthill was not received with the civility he had come to expect. He was subjected to a baleful look, and there was a rasping note in his superior's voice. 'What in the name of God has been going on in the mid's berth, Fonthill? My nephew looks like he's come off second best in a cockfight.'

The Captain's nephew looked aloft to the tiny platform called the top foremast cap, over a hundred feet in the air. The drawings he had studied had done nothing to show the dimensions of these great lengths of fir. Had *Raisonable* been at sea, he would have seen, several times a day, men make their way up to that place with an ease born of long habit. No sail could be set without it. So it was effortless, in a rational way, to look at the task as one that presaged no danger, a mode of thought an idle mind might contemplate when not required to do likewise. But rationality be damned: he was scared stiff.

He knew he was being watched by the very people he had failed to name in the great cabin. Not all of them were ill disposed. But even those who sympathised with his plight would do nothing to aid him, fearing, as much as he did himself, the ridicule that must ensue from being thought soft. He was on his own, faced with a direct order he dare not disobey, required to go aloft by a route that was something of a mystery to him.

Grabbing one of the taut lanyard ropes that held the shrouds, he jumped up on to the bulwark, his first thought to look down at the grey tidal waters of the Medway estuary. It was an unpleasant sight. Flotsam, the filth of the thousands of ships that used the Thames, had been brought up by the tide, and was drifting beside the warship. In a flash he saw his body floating among that nautical debris, a corpse that would, for years to come, be washed in and out by the continuous ebb and flow.

'Take your time, Nelson. Never look down. Don't try going up by the futtock shrouds, use the lubber's hole. And always keep one hand clapped on.' He turned at the soft voice, partly in response but more in mystification, only to elicit, for his pains, a harsh whisper: 'Don't look at me, in the name of Holy Christ.'

Foley, sharp nose set dead ahead, went walking by, for all the world as though he hadn't a care. Not much bigger than the boy to whom he had spoken, he'd been one of those in the mid's berth who had not seen the need to take this new arrival down a peg or two: the escapade with the pissing competition had been prompted by humour rather than dislike. This had caused Nelson to wonder if he, too, had been an unwilling victim of Rivers's attentions. Laughter – young and high-pitched mixed with the gruff older sounds – floated from the quarterdeck to his ears as Foley joined his peers, leaving Nelson to wonder what he'd said to them to make them laugh.

Tentatively, Nelson put his foot on the first rung, feeling it dip beneath his weight as he looked up at the long, rising stretch of square knotted ropes; the shrouds, which ran like a hempen ladder from the ship's side, all the way up to the wide platform he thought was named the foremast top.

'Clap on with one hand,' he repeated to himself, as, taking a deep breath, he began to ascend.

Though the ropes moved, seeming to have a life of their own, he was pleasantly surprised at the ease of ascent, the strands of hemp being easy to grip. On a relatively windless day, they sloped in at an angle, so when he paused gravity laid him safely on the rope surface. The admonishment not to look down was one he knew from climbing trees, so he kept his eyes fixed upwards on his destination. This was the point at which the narrowing ropes passed the mainforemast yard, and touched the wood of the top, right by the lubber's hole that would take him on to the wide fighting platform.

He was followed by hoots of derision that were quickly silenced by whatever authority was on deck. The top, over fifteen feet across, felt secure in these inland waters, where the roll of the ship was slight, and that was made even easier as *Raisonable* snubbed gently at her cables. The edge had no barrier except the next set of shrouds. Stepping out on to the exterior of those reprised all his fears and imaginings. This was a much narrower avenue, the roll more exaggerated as the height increased. The smaller upper foremast cap felt less secure, three connecting beams barely big enough for two men to stand on together. But he reached it, hooked his arm through a taut, convenient stay, then looked down gratefully and began to consider his position.

The way down was simple, the requirement being that he tell

his uncle the truth. This was something he could not do, regardless of the consequences. After only two full days in the berth, he had formed an opinion about all his fellows; socially, morally and sexually. But what he had learnt was as secret as the fumblings in the holds. Recalling that, and the smell of rot that pervaded the bottom of the hull, bilge water that no amount of vinegar and burning sulphur could make sweet, nearly made him gag.

To distract himself he spent the rest of the morning looking at the flat marshes that surrounded the anchorage, at the warships still anchored, with fishing smacks, bum boats and yachts either still in the water or racing for some unspecified destination. From this height he could see over the low marshes and the Kentish coast to the great watercourse of the river Thames. Upriver he imagined he saw the haze that covered London, smoke from a hundred thousand fires that filled the atmosphere of that great city, a noxious brew that had amazed a country boy from deepest Norfolk.

'Mr Nelson.' He looked down, to see the premier standing on forepeak. 'You may return to the deck.'

'Aye, aye, sir,' he replied, putting a foot over the edge to search for the first ratline rung of the shrouds.

'What kind of lubber are you, sir?' Fonthill yelled, in a voice that the boy imagined could be heard on land. 'Do you not know to use the windward side?'

'Sorry, sir,' Nelson yelled back.

He crossed the platform to come down on to the weather side wondering as he descended whom he could ask to explain to him the reason for what he had just been told. But the slight wind on his back, pressing him in, provided its own explanation. He felt the ropes moving long before Rivers came into view. His tormentor shot past him before he could respond to the delivered insult. Arms moving like a monkey, Rivers swung out on to the upper cap, then grabbed hold of a backstay that ran from above his head to the deck, threw himself into seeming thin air, and shot down towards the deck, feet round the rope, hand over hand, whooping to demonstrate his superiority to the dumbstruck newcomer.

Nelson knew he had just been challenged, and wearily

restarted his climb. He hauled himself without enthusiasm, back on to the narrow platform. The rope that Rivers had used to descend could not be reached by merely holding out a hand – he would have to jump for it. Looking down to the deck, a hundred feet below, he felt sick, as much by the faint straight lines of the caulking as by the sea of faces looking up and watching him. The dare was too stupid to accept, too blatant to be refused, and no order came from a superior to desist.

In those fleeting seconds he thought about his father and his family, all the pets lodged at Parsonage Farm and the friends he had had at school. But when he jumped, the image in his mind was of his mother, smiling benignly as he arced through thin air to catch the thick, rough stay with one hand. The leg that he got round it didn't support him, and he dropped sickeningly, forced to use his other hand to prevent his arm being wrenched from its socket.

The attempt to clamp his free foot round the line was only partially successful, as the pace of his descent increased alarmingly. Only his burning palms stood between him and disaster. At last he got some purchase with his legs, was able to slow down a fraction, in which moment he saw his proximity to the bulwark and the deck. It gave him the chance to judge the right moment to let go and he landed in an untidy heap, rolling over several times until he found himself close to stockinged legs, looking up into the frowning face of Lieutenant Fonthill.

'Creditably done, Mr Nelson, for a first effort. But I will point out to you that what is necessary in an emergency will not answer at anchor. Skylarking in the rigging while berthed is forbidden. Since you are new you would not have been aware of that. Should you transgress again, however, I'll stretch you across a gun, with your breeches down, and give you two dozen of my very best.'

'Aye, aye, sir,' the boy replied, struggling to his feet, to stand trembling before the premier. A cough behind him made him turn round, to find a pigtailed seaman holding out his hat.

'Your coat is a disgrace,' Fonthill continued. 'Go and change it at once, then report back to the Captain.'

Rivers stood to the rear of Fonthill, surrounded, barring

Dobree, by the rest of the mids. Keenly, Nelson examined their faces, gratified to see that if he excluded his tormentor and Makepeace, there was something close to respect in their stares. He clapped on his hat, raised it in salute, then headed for the companionway, the rest trailing in his wake.

'Mr Rivers, you will report to me just after defaulters in the morning.'

The older midshipman raised his own hat to acknowledge the order. As a result he didn't see Nelson lift a belaying pin from the rack. Nor, as he came down the companionway, out of strong light from the deck, were his eyes adjusted enough to pick out his adversary. So when Nelson clipped him round the ear with the long, round piece of wood, using enough force to stun him through his hat without breaking the skin, it came as a complete surprise.

CHAPTER 5

Emma was right about Lady Glynne being ill. She died in high summer, and within a month the funds for Emma's education had dried up. Sir John had not returned to Hawarden to see his wife buried, and the curate's pleas that outstanding fees be remitted had been ignored. Word eventually came through Emma's mother, and though carefully couched it was clear that the connection with Sir John, who was now free to pursue a second wife, had been broken.

Money did come, enough to pay for Emma's keep, but not her schooling and no information either as to how Mary Lyon had earned it. Grandma Kidd was quick to kill off any speculation, as though Emma couldn't help but notice how the whole family, who had boasted often of her mother's good fortune, fell silent now, given to mumbling responses rather than clear answers when their neighbours made enquiries.

The news that her mother was coming home 'to sort matters out for Emma's future' induced mixed feelings. Emma's sense of attachment to both Hawarden and her nan, the pleasure she took in the tasks she now performed, made her unsure if she wanted anything to be different. Yet the other half of her reasoning engaged with her innate sense of adventure: the little voice that insisted that change was best. What worried her was the kind of transformation her mother had in mind.

'If she's not to be put to learnin',' insisted Mary Lyon, 'then she'll have to be put to something other.'

'Leave the child be,' hissed Grandma Kidd. 'She ain't of an age for toil.'

'I don't recall you saying that when I was just gone nine.'

'Times alter,' the old lady barked.

Anything but school, was Emma's single thought. Her ear was pressed to the door, not that it needed to be. Like everything in the Steps, windows and roof included, it was a poor fit, a source of fierce draughts in winter. It was no aid to slumber when the men of the house, her father and uncle Willy, decided to stay up late over a jug of grain spirit, waste a candle and their breath, noisily putting to rights the county of Cheshire, as well as King George's domains. Nor did the door disguise the grunts of copulation between her grandparents, a rare occurrence but never a silent one, which taxed her powers of belief. Now, neither woman was making any effort to keep quiet and Emma's mother continued in the same hard tone in which she'd made her opening remark.

'It's a burden to me that is hard to bear, Ma, though I'll stand it to see her lettered and able to count. But I can't be paying out good coin just so she can loaf around here.'

'She don't loaf around. She helps.'

'Do what? Ply coal by the road for a few pennies a day so folk can cook their vittles? Is that to be the lot of my girl, a-squatting there waiting for some bright jay with half-torn breeches to come along and catch her fancy?'

'She's too sharp for that.'

'How come you're so damn sure, Ma? You fell for my pa in like manner.'

'Am I to be recalled for every sin in my life? That was in times past, an' we ain't done so bad neither. The Kidd house owes nowt to nobody.'

'Then how come I'm required to send so much?'

'It be 'cause I'm raising your bairn.'

'All the more reason why it's got to stop. I saw her when she came in, filthy she were, her hair all matted with the black dust. I could scarce bear to kiss her cheek.'

'If she be that covered in filth,' Grandma Kidd growled, 'you've no fear for her being taken up by any passing fancy man.'

'Ain't I? Well, let me tell you I knows more about that than you. As for times, they don't change when it comes to falling for the wrong blade, and I stand as testimony to that.'

Ordered to wash and brush her hair, Emma left the door and

went to the rickety washstand, the voices fainter but still audible as they continued the argument. It was odd to the girl, who recalled that her mother and her gran had been right friendly at the time she had gone off with Sir John. But there had been more coin around then, enough for ribbons and a new dress. She decided, as she watched the water in the basin turn from clear to dark grey, that she would wear that same dress now, even if it was a mite small for her. The sight of it might cheer her ma, who looked very fine and fancy in what she was wearing, even to the quality of the buckles on her shoes.

The water was near black by the time she finished, so dirty that she chucked the contents out into the lane at the back of the house and refilled the bowl with what was left. Even that was discoloured when she had finished, testimony to how much of the coal stuck to her on a windy, August day. Yet for all the filth it was a job she enjoyed. There were her regular customers, who used the purchase as much to pass the time of day as to buy fuel for their fire. Naturally, given her age and the way she was growing there were boys around, gawky, spotty fellows in the main, who would guy her as a group and blush to the roots if faced with her on their own.

Work wasn't all plain sailing, of course. Some of the women were shrews, and it wasn't confined to the old crones either. And there were the goats: men who couldn't look at young girls without thinking themselves beauty enough to be considered swains. Age was little barrier to their fooling themselves. There were those who were old, at least thirty years, all the way up to men who could give years to her grandpa. What they had in common was a sweet tongue and a look in the eye that she now knew too well.

At first, Emma had taken as friendship their dallying by her handcart. The first untoward hand on her backside had soon disabused her of that notion, and she had to thank her stars for her grandma's pitch being on such a busy spot, so that even a muted squeal was usually enough to deter the lecher. Failing that a cry of 'There's my grandma' drove them far enough away to restore her safety.

Sometimes it was true. Grandma Kidd, on the box of her cart

with the old nag puffing along, would come in from the coastal marshes with a fresh supply of sea coal heaped in the back. Beach scouring always produced something, and when the wind was right, strong and north-westerly, an abundance of washed up coal.

By the time she got to brushing her hair, a dampened cloth placed around her shoulders so that the dust dislodged didn't spread, the heat had gone out of her elder's argument. She counted the strokes in her head and fell into daydreams of herself on the arm of a handsome fellow, well dressed and about to enter his carriage and four. By a hundred strokes she was in a grand house, with a dark panelled entrance and a stairwell lit by a huge window. And there was always a bed at the end of a long corridor, soft, full of feathers, and because she was so young, it was a bed she occupied alone.

'Two hundred,' she said aloud, and stood to slip off the dirty dress she was still wearing. Even filthy it was neatly folded, as it was required for the morrow. No point in wearing something clean that would get just as dirty. With no smalls or petticoats on underneath, she stood naked for a second, looking down at the spreading nipples and hint of breasts she had sprouted these last weeks, and below them the first signs of silky hair between her legs. None of the other girls her age were, as yet, anything more than children, still squealing like infants when they played. Emma knew she had left them behind, and the thought was pleasing.

The scraping noise alerted her to two things: that she should have pulled the shutters before disrobing and that she wasn't the only one looking at her body. Fighting back the temptation to glance round at the window, she went to the chest by the far wall that contained her dress and bent to open it. Part of her mind told her she should be outraged, that she should scream blue murder and have these peepers taken up. Yet another part of her took a delicious thrill in being watched.

Emma reckoned she knew who it was. Tom Meehan and Bart Higgins: two of the most tenacious of her workplace admirers, neither much more than two years older than herself. They thought she had no idea they followed her home, but Emma knew all right, and that gave her pleasure too.

The smell of mothballs filled her nostrils as she shook out the blue dress and slipped it carefully over her head. Only then did she spin round sharply, quick enough to catch a glimpse of a pair of disappearing, becapped heads. Then, in a loud voice, as she tied her ribbons and finished her hair, she sang a song she had heard in the market, standing outside the Red Bull Inn, that she knew would increase the discomfort of her peeping Toms.

They took old Cain to 'Merica, cause his crimes were manifest,
There weren't not one of his neighbours, who'd swear he weren't a pest,
Some were wont to hang him, and from a gibbet swing,
Yet others swore a gibbet's too fine, a sill is just the thing,
For Cain he was peeper, who spied on spouse and maid
So they packed him off to foreign parts, a trussed and bonded slave . . .

There were several more verses, which saw the peeper tarred and feathered, whipped, pilloried and finally blinded, but the scrabbling sound that came through the ill-fitting window made the continuation of the ditty unnecessary. That made Emma glow even more and, with a final look in her little glass, she went through to the parlour to greet her mother properly.

The pair sat on either side of the fire, her mother smiling and straight-backed in a low-cut dress of fine green silk, her brown eyes alight. Nan was frowning and shaking her head, muttering to herself in a way that alarmed Emma. It seemed that while she had been brushing her hair, decisions had been taken.

'Well, Emma,' Mary Lyon said, her voice confident. 'What do you say to a chance to enter household service? We shall find you a good family and a nice establishment, and maybe you can get back to your books.'

Her mother carried on, talking about rising in the household or maybe becoming a governess, if she could apply herself to learning, none of which did anything to cheer her grandmother. Emma wasn't sure if she should be pleased or upset, the only idea in her mind that wherever she ended up might be more comfortable than the Steps.

'What kind of bed does a girl get in service?' she asked, breaking into her mother's flow of assurances.

Mary Lyon's eyebrows, pencilled to twice their normal size, went up in surprise. 'Whatever do you mean, girl?'

'Might they be allowed a feather mattress?'

'I've no desire to accord my nephew favours, Mr Fonthill. But neither do I wish to see him expire before he ever gets sight of salt water.'

'I've done what I can, sir, short of undermining Dobree or Mrs Killannan.'

Maurice Suckling knew that there were things he wasn't being told. Fonthill couldn't be in ignorance of the true nature of events, even if he chose not to intervene. His nephew was engaged in a feud, the root cause of which he refused to divulge. Childless himself, Suckling was unaware that he was facing a perfectly normal parental dilemma. While demanding honest answers, he had to admire the way these were refused. Whatever punishment Nelson was being subjected to had to be suffered without recourse to either outside authority or family connection.

'Things can't go on like this,' said Suckling, with a hint of a groan. 'My arm aches from wielding that damned birch sapling. I've belaboured more haunches this past week than I have in the whole of my last commission.'

Fonthill didn't reply, there being little he could say. There was nothing wrong with the Captain fetching a relative aboard, plenty of officers favoured their own, and though those sons and nephews often faced a torrid time in the mid's berth, it usually died down when they learnt their place. Certainly there was bullying, and quite probably thievery in the article of food. Drinking was commonplace, and after life in a conventional home the shock of joining such a place was terrifying. But service life was harsh, a lesson that a midshipman best grasp as soon as possible.

'Will there be anything else, sir? asked Fonthill, after a short pause.

Suckling glared at him. 'Send my nephew to me.'

Nelson wasn't winning his private battle, but neither was he losing. His reasons for fighting were simple: to prove to a group that must already have guessed the background to the conflict that he was more of a man than any of them. The berth had been split asunder for weeks now. The pups, led by him, now openly challenged the oldsters, with Dobree and Mrs Killannan trying and failing to hold the ring. Nelson was proud of his party, each willing to take what retribution was meted out to them rather than succumb to what he termed 'arbitrary power'. He was fond of reminding them that they were trueborn Englishmen, using words recalled from his mother's litany to raise them when spirits flagged.

Most of the day was spent in the carpenter's walk. In a vessel at anchor inspections of the hull were infrequent. This was the quietest part of the ship, with a number of entrances and exits should danger threaten. They would go nowhere alone, lest the older boys waylay them – but that applied equally to their tormentors. Makepeace had certainly received a drubbing for ignoring that constraint, his howls of pain deeply satisfying as the smallest mids belaboured him with ropes' ends while the remainder held him down. But the chief target was Rivers, who now bore a bandage on his head so that he couldn't wear a hat. A typical bully, he never went anywhere unattended.

Foley, the bravest of Nelson's companions who had been left as lookout, popped his head through the narrow hatchway that led to the orlop deck, his eyes bright, his long thin nose twitching as if he smelt danger.

'Premier's looking for you, Nelson. He's sent a marine.'

Nelson shot out of the hatch, looked left and right to make sure it was safe, and scooted for the companionway, yelling in response to the marine calling his name. Fonthill was on the quarterdeck, pacing back and forth with a black look, the full force of which was turned on the Captain's nephew as he appeared. He hated the lack of discipline. With the crew it would have been easy – a few men fetched up at the grating was enough to quell whatever ardent spirits had got out of control.

But with the so-called 'young gentlemen' it was different: the traces of interest were deep, and Captain Maurice Suckling would not share them with him. That made the imposition of discipline more complex, since in chastising them, he had only a limited idea of how they stood in terms of his own commander's career.

'It is not my habit to be kept waiting, Mr Nelson,' Fonthill snapped, 'and I am sweetness and light compared with the Captain.'

'Sir!' Nelson replied, as he slipped past the premier, to his uncle's cabin, trying to adjust his hat and coat to make himself look presentable. His attire was one thing, his face quite another.

The original bruises had long since faded. As he stood before his uncle, the boy was unaware that there was a look in his eye that had been absent the first time they had met. It wasn't defiance, though it had a trace of that, more an expression hinting at the kind of confidence that bordered on insolence. It was obvious enough to rile his uncle.

'There is a smugness about you, young man, which is unbecoming,' he snapped. 'You seem to have some trouble understanding your station, and not just in my cabin.'

The expression disappeared, to be replaced by one of concern, as the Captain continued. 'I am going to breach the grounds of strict convention and speak to you as a father would. I have no idea what caused such mayhem below decks, all I know is that it is so. It also seems as though no amount of chastisement with a crop will clap a stopper on it. This I subscribe entirely to your presence and behaviour.'

'Sir, I—'

'Silence! I asked you the first day I came aboard to tell me why you were in such a bruised condition. You chose not to answer. I have an abiding hope that you feel your honour would be impugned if you did so, since it would grieve me even to suspect a hint of arrogance.'

Suckling paused, and his nephew stiffened at the increased scrutiny. He knew his uncle was trying to discern, from his reaction, whether what he had just said was true. If he had found the answer he gave no indication of it. 'On my last visit to Norfolk, your father informed me that the word honour means something to you. Yet I must warn you against too strict an affection for it. It leads to trouble and, what's more, it makes the proper maintenance of discipline impossible. Half the courts martial in the service are caused by wounded pride.' A sudden change of subject caught Nelson off guard. 'What do you know of the laws of the Navy?'

'Not as much as I should, sir.'

That was the only reply to such a general question, though the thought of what it might presage was unmistakable.

'Quite. Do you, for instance, know that I am forbidden by statute to take you to sea before you have reached the age of fourteen?' Nelson tried to keep his face a mask, but he knew he was failing, and could almost feel his shoulders drop in anticipation of what would come next. 'There is also a general feeling that the armament that has led to my command of this vessel may come to nothing.'

'The Spaniards have backed down?' Nelson asked, his voice cracked.

'They are inclining that way.' Suckling picked up a piece of folded parchment. Even broken, the thick seal that had held it was imposing. '*Raisonable* is to be paid off and laid up in ordinary, and I have here an order transferring me to another ship, a seventy-four.'

'Congratulations, Uncle,' the boy responded, weakly.

'I am to take over *Triumph* forthwith. Naturally I am allowed to take my own people with me, and that includes midshipmen and my servants.'

The youngster's eyes had locked on his uncle's, and his mind was working furiously. What, if anything, was he being offered?

'That doesn't alter the fact that we are likely to remain at anchor. *Triumph* is a guardship. There will be no action, nor are you likely to enjoy any sea-going experience. And the plain fact is, young man, that such a situation will never do.'

Suckling sat down abruptly, and signalled his nephew to do likewise. As he continued Nelson noticed that his tone was noticeably softer.

'I took you aboard for several reasons. Certainly I wished to please your father, but there was the memory of my sister, your dear mother.'

That made the boy drop his head. In his heart he knew what his uncle was working towards: that he should return to his

Norfolk schooling and give up all thoughts of a naval career. To plead was alien to him, but necessary. His uncle having paused, he took the opportunity to do so. 'If I have disappointed you, sir, I am truly sorry.'

'Nephew,' Suckling sighed, 'I have no idea if you have disappointed me or not. All I do know is that since you came aboard my ship, matters have been at a stand.'

'If I could be indulged with another chance, sir, I would not let you down.'

'No more fights in the mid's berth? No more running battles on the orlop deck?'

He was tight-lipped as he replied, 'No, sir.'

'I find that hard to believe.'

'Yet it is true, sir.'

'It won't do, Horace,' Suckling said. 'What would your mother want for you, boy?'

That was like rubbing salt into his wound. He kept his eyes down as he said, 'That I should do well, sir, both for myself and the honour of my family.'

'A feeling that I share,' Suckling replied, reaching for another of the letters on his desk. 'I have here a note from a Mr John Rathbone. You will not know that he was a master's mate aboard *Dreadnought*, and took part with me in the action off Cape Francis Viego. I would have most heartily recommended him for a commission if the war had continued.'

Interest fought with despair as Nelson looked up, suddenly less sure of the direction in which this conversation was heading.

'Rathbone now captains a merchantman, having been unable to find employment in the service. A damn fine seaman but beached in any terms, for want of interest. He wrote to me, with his compliments, to tell me he was about to set sail for the West Indies. I then dropped him a note asking, as a favour to me, if he would take you along with him. I have here his affirmative reply.'

'Sir, I—' the boy said, but no more words came quickly enough to interrupt his uncle's brisk flow.

'You're no good to me as a lubber with no sea time. The service is awash with officers, including admirals, that haven't been at sea for decades, and it is my view that a captain who cannot sail his own ship is a sad case. So you will go to the West Indies and, on that voyage, free from the bonds of naval discipline, will put yourself to learning your trade. While you are at sea you will remain on the books of HMS *Triumph*. And on your return, should you so wish it, you may resume your place.'

His uncle Maurice glared at him now, as if determined to ensure that his nephew understood what was required. 'I hope and pray that when you do so, it will be in a calmer state of mind than you have exhibited to date. For I warn you, any repeat of what has happened aboard *Raisonable*, and I will send you straight back to your father. Do I make myself clear?'

He could have promised the fires of damnation, and they would have had no effect of the elation that suffused his nephew's mind and body. The prospect laid out before him was nothing short of glorious, with the added advantage that it would bring his running feud to a close without loss of face. There was a twinge of conscience when he thought of the others, those he would leave behind, to face the wrath of Rivers without his leadership.

They must look to their own resources, he thought, as he stood up, and looking at a point just above his uncle's head he said in a clear crisp voice, 'Aye, aye, sir.'

CHAPTER 6

The journey back to London was different from that which had brought him to Chatham five months previously. Horatio Nelson sat on top of a coach in warm August sunlight instead of a March chill, with adventure on his horizon instead of worry. Dropped off at the north end of London Bridge, he hired a drayman to take his chest to the dock where his new ship lay.

The *Swanborough*, some five hundred tons, was nothing like a navy vessel, not in size or in the way it was run. The crew was small, a mere dozen souls, and even if the Captain was ex-Navy, there was a limit to the order he could impose on a merchant ship. The deck lacked the pristine whiteness of a man-o'-war. Hen-coops and a pig-sty amidships, and numerous articles like barrels and boxes left lying around, only served to heighten the difference. But the main point of departure compared to a King's ship was the behaviour of the men.

Orders to warp the ship out from the wharves and moor her near the main channel were issued crisply, but were subject to a moment's scrutiny before compliance, as if each man aboard wanted it known that he was obeying because the command was correct. John Rathbone had sailed as a merchant captain for a year so, as he explained to his new recruit, his initial surprise and frustration at such an attitude had worn off. A tall, raw-faced man, with a fleshy nose, he had penetrating blue eyes and a warm deep voice.

'It's not the Navy, young fellow,' he said, glancing over the side at the boat, which was paying out the mooring rope, 'and maybe that's just as well. There will be no showing away aboard this ship, with younkers having their brains smashed out on deck for want of a little knowledge about sail drill. You will dine with me tonight, then you will berth forward with the rest of the hands. I would not wish them to think you over indulged.'

'Aye, aye, sir.'

Rathbone smiled down at him, his eyes making the journey from blond head to polished toe, taking in the blue coat and the snow-white breeches. 'Mr Rathbone will do nicely, Mr Nelson, or Capt'n if you prefer it.'

'Aye, aye, sir.'

Nelson registered his own stupidity and Rathbone laughed and patted him softly on the shoulder.

The first mate, called Verner, was also Navy, a tattooed ex-topman who still wore his pigtail sewn with coloured threads. As a mark of office he wore a short blue mate's jacket. He also sported a round black hat of tarred straw as stiff as brick. This he used in moments of unbearable frustration to belabour the backs of men he held to be 'lubberly slow sods, no better than cows stuffed of milk'.

Nelson dreaded dinner with the captain, in the way that all youth abhors the idea of adult company. But after a stiff opening, in which each response was dragged out of him, Rathbone began to talk of the time he had spent serving with Maurice Suckling. This including a retelling of the action that had made Nelson's uncle's name, the battle off the north coast of Hispaniola in the Caribbean. Cape Francis Viego had seen three British ships engaging and defeating a superior French force. Nelson had watched the battle fought on the dinner table, with knives and forks, on every subsequent anniversary. But he was still eager to hear more, from a new, non-family source.

As Rathbone spoke, Nelson conjured up the scene in the cabin of the flagship. Outnumbered by a squadron of French ships the British admiral had asked his subordinates for their opinion. All three captains had stated, without reservation, that they should attack the enemy. This they did, driving them from the scene of battle, badly damaged, their pride chastened. In his imagination Horatio Nelson was one of those captains, the first to insist, with a rousing speech, that they force the French to do battle.

Rathbone then began a rambling account of his uncle Maurice's connections and the nexus of contacts an officer needed to prosper in the Navy. Horatio learned, between stifled yawns, that Captain Suckling was assiduous in the way he cultivated those with the power to advance his career, politicos as well as senior naval officers. Even without a ship he had been able to place relatives of both in the vessels of his employed friends. Rathbone named him as that rare creature, a man with few enemies. 'For that, young fellow, is death to advancement. I've known many captains who ran crack ships stay on the beach for offending the wrong admiral. Your uncle never made that error. As he once said to me, since prominence in the service had nothing to do with ability, you never knew who was going to end up on the Board of Admiralty, deciding who was appointed and who remained on half pay. Best not to antagonise any of them if it could be avoided. His connections will stand you in good stead. As long as Captain Suckling is there to guide and protect you, you'll never want for influence.'

Did Rathbone sense that his visitor was bored? He stood up or, rather, half-crouched under the low deck beams, which robbed the stern nature of his parting words of their force.

'And now, young sir, you cease your previous self and become no more than a ship's boy on the fair vessel *Swanborough*. I will ask you to remove your naval uniform, which I will keep here in my own cabin, and change into a set of ordinary seaman's ducks. Then Mr Verner will issue you with a hammock and take you to your place on the maindeck, there to sling it. We shall not dine together again – at least not until you are ready to quit the ship at the end of the voyage. If the wind stays true, we sail on the ebb at first light.'

There was a sense of ritual in the shedding of that blue midshipman's coat, the feeling that he was surrendering something of value. But that could not compete with the excitement engendered by the thought that he was, at last, going to sea. There was a twinge of fear as well as the almost physical ache of stimulation, the sure knowledge that not every ship that set sail from the upper reaches of the Thames made a happy return. But no young mind could for long dwell on the idea of risk, when faced with the prospect of adventure.

'Domestic service' sounded grand Emma thought when 'drudgery' was a better word to describe the toil of blacking a stove and all the implements in the fireplace. Her knees hurt from kneeling on the flagstones and more of the blacking seemed to be on her than on the articles she had been set to clean.

'Dirtier now than they ever were selling coal,' she growled to herself, furiously. 'I'd like to see my ma on her bloody knees doing this work, with rock-hard horsehair to bed down on of a night.'

All those fine words her mother had mouthed seemed sour now, for all the praise she heaped on Emma's employers. First impressions let Emma see the Thomases as fine, upstanding folk. First of all they lived in Chester, which was much more exciting than Hawarden. Mr Honorius Leigh Thomas was a noted surgeon, a member of a profession that had moved from the barbershop of old to become steadily more dignified. His wife, daughter of a local worthy and from a higher social class, was determined that in appearance the family should be elevated further. The proper number of servants was a must to attest to the place to which the family aspired to in society.

Nothing would make Emma admit that it was her fault that she now had to perform these disagreeable tasks. Originally engaged as a nursemaid, she had enjoyed the prospect of taking care of Benjamin, the smallest of the Thomases' seven-strong brood, a late child, and much cosseted. The family appeared friendly, Mrs Thomas a distant but formidable figure, who always managed to be close by when Emma made a mistake or used words of which she disapproved. The eldest daughter, Honoria, treated her in a friendly manner. Struck by Emma's looks and her long auburn hair, Miss Thomas, an accomplished artist, had even asked her to sit for a drawing while the child was asleep.

Boredom soon set in, though. The wet nurse, Mrs Carey, was so attached to her own child as well as the Thomas infant, that any surrender of duty, even those that didn't fall to her, was unwelcome, and Emma found herself pushed to one side. The only thing that that did not extend to was fresh air, especially if the weather was in the least inclement. Mrs Carey's definition of bad weather included too much sun, a hint of wind, lowering clouds as well as rain, which made going out impossible. The new nursery maid had little to do except take Benjamin for long walks in his small-wheeled carriage. Mrs Carey's child was held to share her mother's disposition, and stayed at home.

On Thursdays the Chester market was like a magnet to Emma. It was a place of fond memories and familiar faces, from traders to urchins, folk with whom it was unnecessary to guard against offending by some misplaced word or expression. And she could act the customer, with means to buy certain things, and could recommend wares to her employers, which made her doubly welcome. All her old friends, even her own grandma, would bill and coo at little Benjamin. They liked to touch him, either stroking his cheek or offering a finger to his baby grip, which was held to bring an adult luck.

'State of 'im,' was the usual response when she got back, sometimes late for his feed. 'How come you let all and sundry poke at him?'

'They don't poke at him,' Emma replied, in a voice that was well above what was required of her station. Nursemaids did not argue with anyone. They took what was said to them and remained silent. 'There's nowt but affection in the way folk go on when they see him laying there smiling.'

'That and dirt.' The child was washed now, and feeding greedily from Mrs Carey's breast. Her own baby daughter, two days older than Benjamin, had already been fed. 'You wants to stay away from that there market. God knows what the child will pick up from the foul air round some of them stalls.'

'Didn't do me no harm. I used to fetch up there every market day with my nan.'

'Happen you're not genteel enough, then,' snapped Mrs Carey. 'But this bairn is.'

'And your mite will be as well, I suppose.'

Mrs Carey screwed up her face at a response that should never have come. 'Not bred like this 'un, I grant you, but a cut above anyone carryin' the name of Lyon.'

Emma opened her mouth to deliver the requisite reply, but Mrs Carey snapped, 'Mind your station, Emma Lyon. One more word out of you and I'll be telling Mrs Thomas that we has a vacancy in this here nursery.'

Intent on switching Benjamin from one breast to the other, Mrs Carey didn't see Emma's protruding tongue.

The following week Tom Meehan joined her in her slow walk through the market. He had sprouted a few inches since her coal-selling days and most of the spots that had ravaged his cheeks had disappeared. He had a lively face, under dark curly hair, with cat-green eyes that testified to his Irish parentage. He had his hand in the baby carriage, and little Benjamin was tugging on it happily, gurgling away.

'Honest to Christ, Tom, she's a harridan.'

'I should get back to working for your gran, Emma.'

'Can't Tom. My ma has said no to that by indenturing me. Nursery maid wouldn't be bad if there was owt to do.'

'Not for me. I get little chance to see you now when I used to get to have a word every day.'

Given her sense of mischief, Emma couldn't stop herself. 'Not just a word, Tom Meehan.' That made him blush to the roots of his hair. 'Your knees must be worn bare the times you've crawled through the back hedgerow at the Steps.'

'I don't know what you're saying.'

'Yes, you do, Tom Meehan! You and Bart used to follow me back every day, thinking I never knew, creeping up to look through my window.'

'Never.'

'I ain't told no one.'

'Nothing to tell,' he insisted. 'If anybody was like to look through your window it weren't me.'

'It were, and I reckoned you liked what you saw.'

The reddened face changed from embarrassment to lechery. 'What would I have saw?'

Emma laughed, in a way that entertained the baby. 'Me without so much as a stitch. Like a new-born babe.'

'Not like that,' protested Tom.

'See? You're owning up now.'

'I ain't,' he replied, covering his renewed embarrassment by tickling Benjamin.

'I caught you out. Just as I caught sight of you and Bart at my window the day my ma came home.' He opened his mouth to renew his protest, but Emma cut him off. 'And a dozen times following on from that. Now, you either own up or happen I'll just inform someone that matters that you're inclined to be a peeper.'

The hand came out of the carriage so swiftly that young Benjamin's face crumpled in surprise. 'Christ, don't do that Emma.'

'Case you end up like Cain?' *They took old Cain to 'Merica . . . ,* she sang, her lilting voice settling the child. 'Just own up, Tom, and you can die old in Hawarden.'

'All right. Weren't no harm in it, and if you knew and didn't say you should have pulled the shutters to.'

There was no doubting the truth of that. Her behaviour, passed on to the wrong ears, would be branded scandalous. Yet the memory did not induce shame, more a feeling of mastery.

'Happen I didn't want to, Tom,' Emma replied coquettishly.

'Fer certain I didn't want you to. Not a night goes by I don't close my eyes and see you afore I go to sleep.'

'That be a long time to remember.'

'Not for me, Emma,' Tom replied, his face flushed again, but not with embarrassment. 'I can see it as clear as if it were an hour past.'

'So you wouldn't care for another look?' Tom was too shocked to nod for a whole half minute, during which Emma Lyon laughed. 'And here's me thinking you'd grown, Tom.'

'I've grown, Emma,' he said emphatically, 'and that's something I could show you.'

'Never,' Emma pealed. 'Benjamin there's got more to show than you, I reckon.'

'Come here,' rasped Tom, taking her hand and dragging her into a narrow alleyway. Emma had to let go of the carriage, it being too wide to fit. What happened next was so swift she had no chance to fight against or even protest, as Tom took that same hand and pressed it into his groin. 'Now tell me that's no better than Ben there.'

'Ten minutes?' Emma snarled, as she dipped the brush into the blacking pot once more, transferring the mixture of tallow and soot to the metal of the stove. 'No more than ten seconds was I in that alley with Tom, and never doing what Miss Thomas said I was.'

*

'I had Mr Fort read it fer me,' said Grandma Kidd. 'Yer ma has found you a place in London.'

The old lady wasn't happy about that either. It was in her voice, that tone of mixed anger and sadness that her green-eyed girl would be going away, just like her own daughter, leaving her in the Steps under the burden of her family without benefit of relief. Her manner forced Emma to moderate the excitement she felt. Like everyone, she had heard tales of the Great Wen, of a city so large it was unimaginable, the whole place so teeming with noise and people it was like another world.

More than anything, it was what she wanted. It wasn't just that the Thomas family had taken against her, moving her from nursery maid to skivvy. She might have been the family governess and she would still have wanted to go south, to where everyone knew opportunity abounded. It hadn't taken her long to discover there were few princes to catch in Cheshire, but the streets of the capital city, every girl knew, were crammed with them.

'There's a lot more, Emma,' said her grandma. 'You and your goings on have cost your mother a pretty penny, and I daresay she be set to scold you when she sees you.'

Money had been paid to Mr Honorius Leigh Thomas to release Emma from her bond to the family. More, no doubt, would have been expended on the household to which she was to go to, that of a London doctor called Budd, who owned an establishment run by one of her mother's oldest friends. That wasn't a good thing. When they heard the lies that had caused the rift in her last employment, there would be scant chance of freedom.

In the days that followed, before she took a seat on the roof of the coach, Emma suppressed all thoughts of work and constraints. Instead, she filled her every waking hour, and a goodly portion of the sleeping ones, with dreams of luxury. There would be no fumbling in alleyways when she got to London. It was easy to see in her mind's eye the shocked face of her mother when Emma presented her to the man she would marry, a man very much above their own station. There would be no more scolding after such a day!

If anything, rocking about on that coach roof, with a

tarpaulin round her shoulders to keep out the rain, reinforced her flights of fancy. She watched the manners of speech and movement of those wealthy enough to pay for an interior seat, and practised them in the few moments she had alone on the week-long journey. And she lied to her fellow passengers with an ease that thrilled her. To them, she was no housemaid but a girl from a good family, fallen on times so hard she could no longer travel as she used to. In her enthusiasm to guy them it never occurred to her that no one believed a single word.

Then came that day of dreams, the thrill of her first sight of London. The coach always set off in the pre-dawn, to make maximum use of daylight, and that didn't alter for proximity to the capital. From the top of Highgate Hill, the whole city was spread out beneath her in the orange glow of the morning light, a pall of smoke from the numerous fires drifting in the air above the mass of buildings.

The masts of hundreds of ships filled the river basin to the east, seemingly attached to a string of vessels with sails aloft, working their way towards the wider reaches of the river Thames and the open sea. Another fantasy filled Emma's thoughts, of herself sailing away with some foreign beau, to a land of high turreted castles, where white horses pulled gilded carriages. Everyone on the coach roof, even those who had seen it before, was affected by the sight on such a clear morning. But Emma knew in her heart that none was as touched as she. This was like coming home.

CHAPTER 7

The Thames pilot came aboard *Swanborough* at midnight, in good time to take advantage of the combination of dawn light and the ebb that accompanied it. With a whole day, barring a wind that was strong and foul, they would clear the Thames estuary at the North Foreland before dusk, which would allow him to bring another ship in on the morrow. He stood now by the binnacle, a swarthy face peering out from the high collar of his cloak, unsmiling, saying few words, and generally confirming the opinion that most sailors had of pilots; that they were miserable, stuck-up sods.

All hands were roused at four to man the capstan and haul close to the mooring buoy, with a fiddler on the top playing an encouraging tune. Nelson, who had hardly slept in an inferno of adult snoring, found himself on the end of a twelve-foot bar, cheek by jowl with the men who would be his messmates all the way to the West Indies.

Most had been in their hammocks by the time he made it to his berth, greeting him with no more than a curt nod. He had to sling his own in the confined space, aware that eyes were on his back, with their owners probably wondering what level of trust they should place in a lad who was invited to dine aft. The realisation of that made him curse Rathbone, as well as the clothes in which he had come aboard. Would he need to fight once more for acceptance?

These thoughts were still with him as he dug his bare feet into the planking. They heaved on command to shorten the cable, warping the ship closer to the buoy to which she was moored. Nelson strained as hard as anyone to get the inert mass of the ship moving, aware of round smooth wood in his hands, the naked backs in front of him, the shoulders either side of men who had not smiled, all this mingled with the overpowering smell of human sweat. A curse calling for more effort, right in his ear, made him close his eyes as he sought to increase his exertions. His previous excitement had evaporated, leaving him with just doubts. Was he right to be here? Would he find friends on a voyage that might last as long as a year?

Matters eased as the ship began to move, until he was walking round the capstan easily. Men slapped each other's backs in shared achievement. Someone, he didn't see who, patted him and that one act lifted the gloom that had assailed him. Once she was in the desired position, with a boat standing by to unhitch, all hands went on deck, some going aloft to free the sails, others manning the falls, the ropes that controlled the positions in which they were set. Nelson obeyed every instruction he was given, aware that those issuing them were as careful to avoid eye contact as he was.

The early morning sun had risen in the east, an orange ball in a clear sky that tinted the sails and silhouetted the masts of the hundreds of ships that filled the greatest seaport in the known world. Eased out into the main channel under topsails, they joined a convoy of others using the same tide to make their way out to sea, each with a river pilot to take them round the treacherous shallows and sandbanks that dotted the river Thames. Ebbing quickly, with the sails used more to hold the course than provide steerageway, the river carried them downstream past the buildings of Greenwich Hospital, all trim lawns and Portland stone, on past the dockyards, wharves and boat builders' docks of Blackwall Reach and Woolwich.

Horatio Nelson had never seen such a sight, and it made his heart swell with patriotic pride: so many ships, so much maritime activity that, for all the width of the great water-course, the *Swanborough* was never more than a biscuit toss away from another merchant deck. The wind was steady in the north, the sky clear and bright because of it, the yards hauled round to take it. Even so, the pilot was obliged to call for slight adjustments as they encountered occasional gusts from a local breeze. New buildings, warehouses, homes and wharves were being built all the way down both banks of the river. Nelson could imagine a time when there would be no gap between the great city they had just left, and the naval anchorage they were approaching at the Nore.

'Come on, young 'un,' said a voice behind him. He turned to see a wiry individual he had heard called Judd smiling at him. He was not tall, with a thin crooked face, deep-tanned from years of sea and wind. 'Old Rattlebones will indulge you in yer dreaming, but Mr Verner has eyed your back and lifted off his black hat more'n once.'

There was something in Judd's face that engendered trust, so Nelson spoke openly. 'I was looking to see if I could spy my old ship.'

'You'll not see owt from here. Best go aloft.'

'Can I?

'You must ask Mr Verner, lad, that's the proper way. And I must advise a bit of busy before you do that.' Seeing the look of confusion on Nelson's face, he grinned again. 'Them falls by the weather shrouds is sheeted home well enough but they is all ahoo. Why don't you and I tidy 'em, man-o'-war fashion, which'll please him. Then you can ask yer favour.'

'Thank you, Judd,' he replied, looking the man right in the eye and smiling, in a manner so open and natural that the older man seemed thrown.

'Name's John, but most aboard calls me Little Bitt,' the sailor said, looking away. He pointed to another of the hands, a great, barrel-chested fellow who was hauling a huge roll of canvas up through one of the hatches. 'You'll have spotted Eamon McGrath, who's termed Big Bitt. We was named thus since we came down the gangplank together, an' it's stuck. You can call me by my true moniker, if you'd rather.'

'My name's Nelson.' That was answered with a grunt. 'My given name is Horatio but my family call me Horace.'

'Ain't much better to my mind, either one. But never fear, we've got no end of wits on the barky who'll baptise you different in no time.'

Judd had taken hold of one of the ropes that fell from the end of the yards to the bulwarks, there to be lashed off taut in a figure of eight to a belaying pin. To pull the pin was to release the rope. Naturally there was an excess of untidy hemp and he had to haul it out so it was straight.

'See, young 'un? You gets the kinks out first off, then you puts your foot to hold one end, and coils it thus.'

Nelson watched for a few seconds, as one coil was laid, with the second just inside before he took hold of a rope.

'Now since you're Navy, you'll have seen how the falls end up on a man-o'-war deck. That's how Mr Verner likes 'em, so we might as well give the bugger one happy day on a long cruise.'

As they worked Judd talked away about the ship and the voyage. Every time he used a nautical term, he raised his eyes to see if it registered, careful not to take too much notice of the slight flash of annoyance each time something had to be spelt out. He explained that a square rigger was the best ship afloat, seeing as how it had yards that were separate from the masts, and could be swung round to take the wind for near three quarters of the compass. 'Deep keeled, see, so if the wind is coming in right on the beam, that be over the side of the barky, you can swing the yards round to take it.'

'The ship won't go sideways?'

'No, lad. Keel's too deep. It'll trend away a bit, what with leeway an' all. That's the run of the sea. But stands to reason, though, if it won't go sideways it's got to go somewhere, and that somewhere is forwards if the wind ain't dead foul. Ship might heel a bit, an' look as though it's set to tumble, but it ain't. It just be goin' on its way.'

Nelson was confused, and it must have shown.

'It'll come in time, lad,' he said, aware that his young charge knew he was ignorant, and was angry with himself because of it. 'How would you know what was in a kitchen grate if'n no one never told you? Imagine a black savage, just hauled out of the Bight of Benin, faced with a set of andirons. He wouldn't no more ken their name or what they was for'n you do on a ship.'

Judd's manner had sucked Nelson in, and it was with pleasure that he realised that many of his anxieties had evaporated. That is, until he saw the first mate move from his position by the binnacle.

'Are you after something, Little Bitt?' said Verner, making his way across the deck towards them. 'I ain't never seen you a-tidyin' afore without being telt to attend to it.'

'Young 'un's idea, Mr Verner,' Judd replied, looking up and grinning. 'Said that's the way of the Navy, and with you bein' a fellow who'd taken the King's shilling, that's how you'd like it.'

'Bollocks,' Verner replied, without rancour.

'Lad wants to go aloft as we pass the Nore Banks see if'in he can spy his old ship.'

Verner looked towards the wheel to where the pilot stood next to Captain Rathbone, his eyes darting left and right as he checked his landmarks on the Kent and Essex shores. 'Shouldn't make no odds for a bit, since we'll hold to the Yantlet Channel. If you ask the Captain nice enough he might lend you a glass.'

Rathbone obliged and the boy ran for the mainmast shrouds, dashing aloft with the telescope tucked into his belt. The *Swanborough* couldn't match the majesty of *Raisonable*'s top hamper, and even on a clear morning he stood little chance of seeing a hull behind the low-lying Isle of Grain. But the masts were visible, especially those with senior officer's pennants. Once he'd recognised the flagship, and placed *Raisonable* in relation to it, he found himself subject to a series of conflicting emotions. He should have been glad to be able to look at her topmasts, safe in the knowledge that not only was he at sea but also away from the trials that he had endured below those decks. Yet there was an inexplicable sadness too, a feeling of something lost.

Clearing the Thames past Margate and Ramsgate, they dropped round the North Foreland, then used the Brake Channel as a passage through the northern end of the treacherous Goodwin Sands. John Judd informed him that they were to anchor in the Downs, to complete their wood and water as well as take on twenty more hands, including another boy of Nelson's age. There followed a riotous night ashore in the taverns of Deal, from which Rathbone was brought back in a local bum-boat, alternately cursing and singing, another boat to his rear carrying the extra hands.

For the first time Horatio Nelson was introduced to the pleasures of a proper seaport. Deal might lack a harbour, but with the Goodwin Sands acting like a great breakwater to stem the fury of the North Sea, and three castles bristling with cannon to protect it, the anchorage between sands and shore was one of the safest in England. It was home to hundreds of merchant ships, either returning from a voyage or setting out on one.

The town existed to provide for that, every second house a tavern of some sort, full of hard looking individuals in need of a berth. They had, as Judd informed him, spent every penny they possessed from their previous voyage, in the way of all sailors, on one continuous stream of pleasure-seeking: drink, dancing, singing and the comfort of one of the dozens of whores who lined the narrow streets. Nelson saw too much in one night to register anything but the sense of near riot that attended the revels. Yet what he saw excited him greatly, even if it brought to mind his father's warnings, which never failed to equate all matters nautical to sin.

At mid-morning the Deal pilot saw them out through the southern exit to the Goodwins and, with the jutting white cliffs of Dover on their starboard quarter, they raised more sail, heading for the English Channel and the open sea.

The new boy, Amos Cavell, was just as much a novice to the sea as Nelson. He was small, thin and pale, with thick dark hair that stood up straight from his head and dark eyes that were never still. After circling each other on the first day, mutual necessity turned them into companions. The crew were something less than pleasant during the first days of the voyage. Most were out of sorts, either beached so long that they had mislaid their skills, or still drunk from the last parting. A few were seasick, though they were sent aloft regardless.

When these sufferers had been exposed to a verbal drubbing or the back of Verner's tarred hat, ship's boys were easy targets. So, being nimble was the first requirement for Nelson and Amos Cavell. Proximity to an adult meant that one eye was always on them and when the thought of home, hearth and comfort became too much for the men to bear, their swipes at the nearest head whistled through thin air. Four eyes being better than two, the boys soon learnt to look out for each other's welfare.

The hands brought aboard at Deal had to sort out their

respective stations with the men who had brought the ship down from London. Mostly this was satisfied with mutual growling, issued but unfulfilled threats, and the occasional heavy nudge. But in the case of one it had to come to blows, at a point below decks where others, watching the hatchway, could make sure that neither Rathbone nor his mate knew anything about it.

Eamon McGrath saw himself as top dog below decks. An ugly hardcase called Streeter, who had come aboard at Deal, decided to challenge for that title. The pair stood toe to toe, rules agreed in advance, to trade telling punches, the prize no more than the right to be occasionally deferred to in the matter of a seat at the mess table or a place in the queue for some captain's treat. Streeter was the better boxer, but McGrath, beetle-browed and seemingly insensitive to pain, wore down the newcomer with brute force instead of science. The fascination for a boy whose parson father had never let him near a boxing booth was tremendous, though when the bout was over and McGrath victorious, Amos Cavell pronounced it a poor affair, nothing like as exciting as he had seen on Walmer Green for a penny.

John Judd was a special friend of McGrath, which meant that he was afforded a respect out of all proportion to his own ability with his fists. And, either from his own inclination or under direct instruction, he had adopted the youngsters, taking it upon himself as though it was his sworn duty to ensure that the boys shouldn't suffer too much in the way of casual punishment, nor be left in ignorance of the knowledge needed to perform their duties.

'There's two things that you need to hold paramount to pass through this life,' he said, supervising them as they prepared to collect their meal from the galley, his face serious in the light from the stove. 'Whatever, think what you're about afore you does it, 'cause more men die at sea from not minding to their task proper than ever went to disease or a gun.'

The boys had two wooden kids each, full to the brim with good East Kent beef, mixed with potatoes and broken ship's biscuit. Earlier in the day they had been happy to accept John Judd's help but now they were impatient for their food. Amos

Cavell cracked first, seeking to hurry Judd in his explanations. 'So what's the second, Little Bitt?'

'Why, that's easy, lad. You find the 'ardest bastard on the ship, the finest man in a fight, and make sure you're his very best friend.'

Routine is everything aboard a ship, and a compact vessel like *Swanborough* was no exception. It didn't take either boy long to become familiar with his new home. High prowed, with deep holds and a prominent poop, she was 120 feet long, two-masted and broad in the beam. Fully laden there was little room for the crew. The forepeak, where they messed, was smaller than any mid's berth. But the main gripe was the lack of rest: it took every available man to sail her, and with a crew of over thirty, in the chops of the Channel, time was spent either on deck or aloft trimming sails, with Nelson often shouted at for his ignorant fumblings.

But even under such trying conditions the steady nature of the days took hold, ironing out the differences between crew contingents, as well as providing a cure for ailments caused by past carnality or just plain hankering for the shore. The crewmen became names, not just faces, while Rathbone, keen to remain in contact with his well-connected supernumerary, was eager to explain his motives for various actions.

'It don't do to apply the harsh word early on a cruise, Mr Nelson. A wind takes days to clear the heads of the worst of the drinkers, pining for loved ones notwithstanding. There will be one or two cases of pox aboard for certain, and that's as debilitating an affliction as is known to man. Thank God, the cook can work his coppers and provide us with our meals, but is also handy with the mercurials.'

Each change of sail was alluded to, and the reason for the course explained on the chart. But Nelson came to dread being singled out: he hated to be seen as in any way different, and that applied especially with Amos Cavell. He took to dodging the Captain, especially at mealtimes, happier to help the other youngster fetch the grub. Then he would sit down to listen with equal devotion to the tales of the older men with whom he now messed.

Half the crew had been in the Navy, and one or two had even observed a gun fired in anger. Officers under whom they had served were named and compared for their seamanship and their standards of discipline, many cursed and few praised. He listened avidly to yarns of men pressed on land as well as at sea; of a life locked away from society as long as the country was at war; of anger caused by official abuses perpetrated by an uncaring government.

All agreed there was a right way to go about things and a wrong way; that rations issued were sacred in both weight and measure; that pursers were rogues who would steal your eyes and come back for the holes. There were good captains and right sods, who would trim the skin off your back for pleasure. The most often quoted word was 'rights', applied to everything from pay to punishment. Every member of the crew, from landsmen to topman, had rights, and it was a foolish captain who gainsaid them.

Every one of them, King's Navy or merchant, had gone foreign. An exchange of opinion on numerous exotic-sounding ports tended towards an examination of the relative merits of taverns and bawdy houses, and Nelson's innocent enquiries regarding physical particulars of the landfalls, tides, currents and hazards were met with incomprehension. Naturally, disagreements were loud and continuous, with accusations of 'gilding it' commonplace. Every one of the men claimed to have lived through the biggest storm the world had ever known, with waves high enough to engulf the tallest house, to have seen the most gigantic whale, the prettiest mermaid with the finest jewelled mirror, as well as icebergs the size of England.

But most of all each and every one had rogered the most expensive, beautiful and accomplished whore, and left her sated, gasping with pleasure, having performed throughout the entire night like the veritable prize bull in the quality of their couplings. That was the point at which he and Amos Cavell's views parted company, with the Deal boy sneering at the claimed prowess as nothing more than fancy.

'And how the devil do you know that, smart arse?'

Amos Cavell looked at Nelson, his dark eyes narrowed and

his thin face insufferably superior. 'It be 'cause I've done it, and I know it ain't like they say.'

That caught Nelson out. He and his siblings had been raised on a thirty-acre smallholding, with chickens and livestock, so acts of procreation, in the general sense, held no mystery. But human carnality did. So care with his words would be necessary, as essential as the look of scorn he gave Amos.

'Takes no more'n a minute at most,' said Amos, with so little emphasis that it rang true, 'though I will say it's pleasurable enough. All that about being at it all through the night is bollocks.'

Maintaining his air of disbelief was hard, but Nelson tried, though he was aware that the look of doubt on his face had slipped halfway to curiosity. 'Don't you josh me, Amos Cavell.'

'I ain't joshing, mate. It's no hardship to get your end seen to in Deal. I reckon we has more whores than any other town in the land, and some of 'em are younger than me. If that don't provide, a walk in the country around will see you attended to quicker than you can pick an ear of corn.'

Amos, who had been more interested in his own words than the attitude of the enquirer, suddenly looked hard at his companion, and a grin spread across his face that depressed the other boy. 'You ain't never been there, Nelson.'

He wanted to lie, to boast in the same tone he had heard at the mess table, but his tongue was stuck to the top of his rapidly drying mouth.

'Makes no odds to me, mate,' Amos continued, his expression giving the lie to that statement: there might be no discernible difference between them, but he had seen the way Rathbone treated Nelson. This intelligence served to redress the imbalance in their respective stations. 'It ain't all it's cracked up to be. And now we're on water there ain't nobody doing nothing but talk on. Mind, I should think there's no end of puddin'-pullin' goin' on. Have you had your first purl yet?'

Nelson blushed and shook his head, the long fair lashes covering the shame in his eyes. He was reminded of the mid's berth in *Raisonable*, of the below belly conversations in which he had taken part, conscious of the lies needed to maintain face; and of that moment in the hold with Rivers, and his own reaction to the older boy's attentions.

'Then you'd best haul away every chance you get,' Amos added gleefully, landing an over-emphatic punch on Nelson's shoulder. 'Milk don't come from an ignored teat. Nothing like pulling your own to bring matters on.'

If sexual prowess was the stuff of dinnertime, both boys soon discovered that allusions to it were constant both on deck and aloft. Every item of equipment seemed to have a name that invited some jocose innuendo. Some, like the cunt splice or the arse on a block, were without subtlety. Others were hardly less obvious, like the hand organ, a huge block of sandstone used for cleaning the deck. Amos Cavell could never be brought to say futtock shrouds without giggling, nor call 'bear a hand' without a wave of his right wrist, an action that became wearing to Nelson and John Judd alike.

But as they laughed, and sometimes groaned, the two boys also learnt. There was none of the cracking on that Rathbone had told Nelson he would find in the Navy. It was steady as you go in the merchant service. But sails had to be set each morning, and properly to get the best out of the ship. And the wind, which never seemed to be in the same place two days running, meant that every time they went aloft at first light to re-rig the top hamper, they were working to a different sail plan.

Grey skies and westerlies accompanied *Swanborough* down the Channel all the way to Portland Bill, but then they cleared to a bright blue, and the wind shifted into the north, which allowed Captain Rathbone to port his helm and set a southerly course to open the Bay of Biscay. For once, Horatio Nelson broke his self-denying ordinance and got close enough to hear the master and his mate discuss the alternatives.

'Arse lickin', are we, Nellie?' whispered Cavell, who had sidled up unseen. More infuriating was the way he skipped clear of the sweeping blow Nelson aimed at him in response.

It was still summer, with long sunlit days, in which the ship, under a mass of white canvas, made good progress. With little to do, there was time to make, mend and entertain. At the Parsonage there had always been sisters to sew for a male

Nelson, and when spare canvas was issued to make fair weather ducks, this became obvious. His efforts with the needle produced much blood from the pinpricks that covered his hands. Judd came to the rescue once more, by showing him the proper use of a thimble, as well as how to sew, then watching over the less than perfect results. However, the pricks he suffered paled into insignificance as he watched those in venereal pain take their cure, a service delivered by the cook.

After dinner was the best time. There wasn't a man aboard who couldn't, at the very least, recite a patriotic ode. With the clement weather and clear night skies, these could be delivered on deck. Rathbone had a fine, if unsteady tenor voice, while Verner prided himself, as most topmen did, on his ability to hornpipe. Once he had been persuaded that there was no shame in his attempts to entertain, young Mr Nelson, with his voice unbroken, added a touch of the counter-tenor. The fiddler, a toothless stick of a man called Catgut, would saw away all night if need be so that every man would get his chance.

John Judd was no mean shantyman, and he taught Nelson to dance as well as to hand and reef. The boy absorbed quickly what he was taught, especially aloft. Knots, which had been like cat's cradles, became simple till he could do a clove or half hitch eyes shut. It was he who got the running bowline first but he was beaten to the sheepshank by a determined Amos Cavell, who, when bested, always talked about first purls to even matters out.

No day was brighter, no knot more satisfying, as the morning that particular jibe could be laid to rest. His cracking voice accompanied by angry spots had signalled the change and an inspection of his hammock was called for before he could scrub it clean. The result of his nocturnal emissions was pronounced a true picture, though the ribbing he had to endure over the following weeks every time he went forward to the heads or sought a peaceful place to say his prayers brought no end of rouge to his cheeks.

John Judd continued with his self-imposed task, often taking the boys aloft to demonstrate some of the finer points of seamanship. The nautical words became second nature as the voyage progressed. By the time they reached latitude 20 degrees north, there was no mystery in parrels and cheeks, chain slings, trusses or a Flemish horse. Judd didn't seem to mind when the other hands passed on tasks to the trio, like greasing blocks or re-reeving ropes. As they worked he talked, stating his opinions on everything in a quiet but emphatic way.

So they learnt their trade, from the lowest lanyard to the highest topgallant stay, where the shrouds were so narrow that they would scarce contain one foot, and a hand on the royal stay was essential to avoid falling. Heights held no terror now: jumping for the backstay hawsers that held the masts in place, and racing to the deck, were a ten-times-a-day occurrence, despite the number of rebukes they earned for skylarking from Rathbone and Verner. Down and down they dropped, with the temperature rising inexorably, until on latitude 14 degrees north they picked up the trade winds and Rathbone set his course for Antigua.

Water that had been fresh in the English Channel had suffered from heat and time – it was now turning green and brackish – the biscuits were full of bargemen, and the rats in the holds had multiplied until they were a menace. The routine of the nautical day, with its three square meals, began to chafe as the unchanging nature of the food replaced gratitude for being fed at all. The dolphins that accompanied the ship for several days only lifted the spirits for a while, though both the youngsters had a great deal of fun lowering themselves from the pitching bowsprit, to stand on the outer martingale stay in an attempt to reach down and touch them.

'Belay that, you stupid little buggers,' yelled Verner, his face made pink by his passion and his adherence, in stifling heat, to his blue coat of office. 'Where's that sod Judd?'

'Here, Mr Verner,' said Judd, rising from the heads and pulling up his ducks.

'Can't you keep an eye on them, man? If they come off that there stay the bows will crack them wide open.'

'I keeps an eye on them as much as I can, Mr Verner,' Judd replied, crossly. 'And never do I complain that others leave me to it. But even I must be allowed my occasions.'

'Well, tell them, if they're going to take so much interest in dolphins, to get a line overboard and haul one in for the Captain's supper.'

'Is that a shark, John Judd?' called Amos Cavell, pointing to a fin cutting through the water. Nelson was still lowering a hand to try to touch the dolphins as they flew up and apart, diving in all directions.

'It is, young feller,' Judd replied, 'and you best get yourself back inboard.'

'Why?'

' 'Cause them sharks has teeth as long as your arm. And they can climb the planking.' Both boys had their soles back on the foot-ropes in a flash, as the fin cut under the bows, missing them by inches as the great fish swung in an elegant arc. Judd spat loudly as he sat on the thick line of wound ropes that gammoned the bowsprit and attached it to the ship. 'Partial to a boy, they are, an' all.'

'Can they really climb?' asked Amos Cavell, squinting in disbelief.

His good friend Nelson tried to contain a grin as Judd replied, his face serious. 'You wait till Antigua, Amos. The locals there train 'em to scale up and fetch down the coconuts. Then they places them in those great jaws, jumps on the shark's head, and cracks the buggers open.'

'You're havin' me on.'

'Am I?' replied Judd, spitting on his hand. 'A whole commission pay I'll place on that.'

CHAPTER 8

The mood of the ship changed even more as they crossed the wide ocean. Boredom set in, a longing to be on the land that lay somewhere over the bowsprit. That produced an increase in fractiousness, a series of petty disputes that destroyed any harmony. McGrath seemed particularly affected, though the mood was general. Horatio Nelson noticed it and confirmed his impression with Amos Cavell, then broached the matter with John Judd.

'It was ever thus. A cruise starts off with a levelling, then settles down to peace an' quiet. Most of the lads we fetched on board can't run to one meal a day ashore, let alone three. So once they're settled in they's happy for a full belly. But that don't last, an' all the vice that's stayed pent up starts to break out.'

'Vice?' demanded Nelson, intrigued.

John Judd's eyes were on him, for once without the light of humour. 'When I tell you, at certain times, to stay clear of the hold, there's a purpose. Some of the crew have attachments and need peace.' Nelson fought to keep his face still, determined to pretend he had no idea what Judd was on about. 'And I tell you no lie when I say that those near a young 'un who might be troubled keeping their hands to themselves have been warned off. It ain't always so for a ship's boy, I can tell you.'

Even here on an open deck, the smell of *Raisonable*'s bilge water was in Nelson's nostrils, the breath of Rivers, his spittle, his voice. 'Warned off by you?'

'Not me, but I'm friend to McGrath, ain't I?'

'He's the most miserable sod afloat this minute,' said Amos, who was clearly bored by this. 'I ain't seen him smile for near a week.'

'Happen he has reason.'

'Like what, Little Bitt?' Nelson asked, his breaking voice half-growl, half-squeak.

Judd was really frowning now, as though what he had to say was more unwelcome than either pederasty or bestiality. 'We don't get saints serving. There are some right good men, don't get me wrong. But it stands to reason that if'n you take a body of tars from all and sundry places, one or two are bound to be less than right honest. It makes no odds what ship you serve in, Navy or trade, the one thing that drives a fid though peace and quiet is the thought that one of your mates is thieving.'

Neither boy responded, so after giving them a meaningful look, he continued, 'It's the bane of ship life, with men bein' all mewed up close. You can't hide or make safe all you value, and half the time there's no money worth to what goes astray.'

'McGrath has had something stolen?'

Judd looked keenly at him.

'Which is why he's got a monk on,' Amos added.

'You'd be in a hermit mood too, if you'd been robbed. I'm just guessin' mind, since he ain't said owt. But all the old signs are there.'

The angry looks that McGrath had been casting around were easy to recall but whatever they had made plain to John Judd had escaped Horatio Nelson. 'Does he know who's done it?'

'Would he be a-broodin' if he did?' Judd replied, slowly. 'Seems to me he ain't got a clue, which is bad, 'cause it means he's uneasy about every party in the mess.'

'Including you?' piped Amos, amazed.

'Never in life. But what about you, boy? There's no law says a thief has to have hair on his chest.'

'Should he not tell Rathbone?'

'None of the Captain's business, Nellie. This is the lower deck.' Judd sucked his cheeks in, clearly troubled. 'Never take your troubles to the master, 'cause he has to apply the proper law. Below decks we have our own ways, though with a hard bargain like McGrath you never know what could occur. He's a brooder any road, an' he could explode in the next minute.'

'And what happens then?'

'He'll hit someone for certain. But, worse than that he'll start accusing, which means that every man jack in the mess will get shirty. Then they'll start looking at one another for a clue to the miscreant. Next thing, another few accusations will fly about, which'll lead to a fight. If it ain't sorted it could last us all the way to the Windies.'

'There must be something that can be done.' This particular statement was made before the perpetrator realised how pompous he sounded, indeed how like his own father.

Judd looked at him and gave a wry smile. 'Oh, yes, young Nellie, there is. An' happen John Judd is the man best placed to do it.'

Over the next two days McGrath's face grew darker, his beetle-brow shrinking even more as he examined everyone with deep suspicion. Even Streeter, who had given him a fair fight and not disgraced himself, was walking around the Irishman as if broken glass lay under his feet. It was a situation that the two boys couldn't resist. Seeing a man about to explode, they were determined to witness the event at the point of combustion, unconcerned that watching only added fuel to an already flaming temper. To extend their observation to a point where they even had their quarry at his place of easement was carrying things too far. Luckily for Horatio Nelson, Amos was closest to McGrath when he cracked.

'You stinking little toe rag,' the Irishman yelled, leaping to his feet, one huge hand hauling up his trousers while the other shot out to catch the boy by his collar. The garment was worn loose to ward off the sun and it seemed as if the youngster was going to slip bodily out of it as McGrath lifted his arm. But Amos, squealing with terror, stayed inside, the white linen stretched above his head.

'I've a good mind to wipe my arse with you. Then we'll see how much you want to stay dogging my every step.'

'Please, McGrath,' Amos screamed, as he was swung out over the bows, well clear of the nettings.

As they were right at the peak of the prow, few people could see what McGrath was doing. And if they could hear the squealing, they could also hear the Irishman's angry voice, and were not about to come forward to investigate. Let down as far as possible Amos's calves were soaked by the forward motion of the ship. As soon as the sea dropped back he was hauled in again, close to the angry sailor's face.

'You'll be after telling me what you've done wi' my Pigtail or, Jesus bear witness, next time I duck you I'll leave go.'

'What Pigtail?' Amos shouted, turning his head away from McGrath's eyes. Nelson was shouting too as his bantam-sized fists pummelled the Irishman to little effect.

'My fuckin' baccy. A whole wad of prime Pigtail. I want to know who you sold it to.'

Amos tried to say he knew nothing about McGrath's tobacco, but the man's grip had tightened and the shirt was now knotted over his throat. Then one of Nelson's punches swung wide, taking the huge man in the groin just below the hand that was still holding his trousers. McGrath roared in pain, and swung a fist at his assailant's head. Not only did he miss the nimble lad, but the ducks ended up round his ankles, and tripped him up.

This was mostly bad news for Amos who, if he was saved from drowning was nevertheless roughly hauled over the bowrail. McGrath let him go and he crumpled on to the wet planking, still unsure as to which way was up by the time the Irishman got his ducks up round his waist. Nelson was standing just out of reach trying to tempt McGrath to follow him by cursing him roundly as 'a no good swab, a grass-combing bugger not fit to be boiled for tallow'.

John Judd arrived just as the huge sailor, roaring like a bull, was about to launch himself on the boy. Judd pushed Nelson behind him, his hands held up to his friend in fearful supplication. 'Now, stow it, McGrath.'

It was only in that place of relative safety that Nelson realised what had just happened. Without thinking he had landed several blows on the hardest man in the ship. The burst of fear was mingled with pride at his own audacity.

'Step aside, Judd.'

'What?' Judd replied with disbelief. 'So you can beat up a nipper?'

'Did you cock an' ear to what he said?'

'I did, and it was cheek for certain. But I reckon he's just spoke to save young Amos.'

Clearly McGrath had forgotten about Amos, who was now crouched on his hands and knees watching the Irishman's back. As the sailor turned, he shot for the bowsprit.

'Where's my damned baccy you little sods?' he growled, his head jerking back and forth. ''Twas in my chest and some skulkin' low life bastard has gone an' lifted it.'

'Weren't locked,' said Judd, almost to himself, since a man like McGrath felt, quite rightly, that he had little need to protect his possessions. While both men were pondering this, and at a cocked thumb from Amos, Nelson took the opportunity to slip away.

'Thanks mate,' gasped Amos, and Nelson's chest swelled with pride.

'You'll be after tellin' me I'm to blame,' growled McGrath.

'I can see how such as that would work on you,' said Judd, moving forward, his finger tapping his head, well within the range of those bunched fists. 'That's why you've been a-brooding.'

'There's not a man on this barky would cross me, mate, an' well you know it.' The use of the word 'mate' was reassuring, hinting that some of McGrath's anger had dissipated. But he could still be heard on the forecastle as he continued, 'But them tykes might pinch my Pigtail to sell on.'

'Never in life,' said Judd. 'They might be imps, but they ain't light-fingered.'

McGrath looked unconvinced, but Judd pressed home his advantage being the hard man's friend. 'What if I was to say to you, McGrath, that John Judd could find out for certain who snaffled your Pigtail?'

'An' how, in the name of Brian Boru, are you going to do that?'

'You wait and see.'

'I've been mullin' on it since well before he blew,' said Judd, clearly pleased at the looks of certainty on the two boys' faces. At least they didn't doubt him. The rest of the crew did, and were placing bets that it would be Judd himself who would feel the weight of McGrath's displeasure, which was to be welcomed since it was like to save them. 'Now, you just run along and attend to your duties while I get my little surprise ready.'

Amos, Nelson and the rest of the crew watched Judd like hawks. As Rathbone made his noon observation, he was spotted standing by the lee rail, muttering incantations and throwing various objects into the sea. This included the innards of a chicken, whose neck had been wrung to provide the cabin dinner. Some of the bird's blood followed, which, added to the dirge-like tones of Judd's prayers, caused much unease among a deeply superstitious crew.

Dinner was eaten in silence, with the Irishman's eyes never still as he sought guilt in every move or gesture. Only Judd was relaxed. Taking advantage of the tension, he helped himself to twice the normal allowance of food. Being Saturday, there was grog to consume, but no one really seemed to want it until they were sure what was afoot.

Observing this, Judd reached behind him, and pulled from a ditty bag a set of thin sticks. In the lantern-light, every eye was drawn to the dark blood that tipped the end of each one. 'Do all concur that there be such a thing as sea justice?' he asked, to nodding heads and grunts of assent. 'An' that McGrath here has been cruelly robbed of his rightful chattels?' His eyes ranged round the table. 'We're all tars at this mess table, an' we know that there are laws and retributions that have nowt to do with judges and courts. Have we not all seen the won't-take-no-for-an-answer sodomite fall from the yards, his vile blood to stain the deck, the slack-arsed swine who crows on his mate lost o'erboard on a dark and windy night, with no man's hand anywhere near him?'

Judd's voice had dropped low, seeming to draw in the deck beams above their heads. 'Now, there are those that cry mishap an' refuse to see the power of old Neptune at work. But there are others, men like us, who knows that venerable laws govern the lives of sailors, doctrines that go back to a time hidden by the mist.'

Horatio Nelson felt his skin crawl, such was the effect of John Judd's litany. All his father's admonishments regarding sorcery and devilry, which tried to well up and force him to leave, could not stand against the power of a present speaker. Judd's eyes seemed to have grown larger, as if he was no longer the same gentle fellow who took such care of his boys. He looked at Amos, seeing that he, too, was deeply affected. They both started, as Judd's words cracked like a whip.

'There be a thief among us,' Judd cried, 'an' that, as you know, is enough to summon the old spirits. I have said words to the waves, summoned Neptune's aid in cantos that are death to the hound that lies. I have spoken with the spirits, as a few of us can, and they say that McGrath shall have his Pigtail returned, and his vengeance on the villain who lifted it.'

The bundle of thin sticks was shoved into the middle of the table, the base in his fist, the bloody tips held upright. 'In here there is one piece for each man. They must be returned to my hand by suppertime, and he that stole McGrath's Pigtail baccy will have the longest one of us all, for with his guilt and my spells, the wood will grow in his possession and nail him as sure as my name is John Judd. Let no man see it as you choose, for the evil eye rests in the miscreant, and he may do to yours, with no more'n a look, what should be done to his own.'

Tentatively, each man took his choice, some quickly, others hovering over the tips. The last two were offered to the ship's boys for, as Judd observed, the spirits required them all to hold a piece of the true wood. Slowly the sailors moved away, to carry out the duties that had been assigned to them for the late afternoon. As the work progressed they would stop suddenly, pull their sticks from their pockets and turn to examine them. No genius was required to see the relief on the faces when they observed that theirs was the same length as when they had drawn it.

Time dragged until supper, began to seem near standstill as the men ate, so by the time Judd called for the sticks to be returned, the atmosphere was as taut as a bow string. One by one they laid them, even in length, on the table. As the line increased, so did the fear, for the number of potential culprits diminished. Catgut the fiddler was near the last to oblige. Heads turned in wonder when they saw that his stick was a good inch shorter than the rest.

'You are undone, Catgut,' said Judd softly. The scrawny

fiddler tried to laugh, but one look into John Judd's eyes killed the sound in his throat. 'All the sticks were the same, each and every one. To be shorter, a man would have to break a bit off. Why would he trouble to do that, lest he thought himself guilty and wanted to be sure his stick hadn't grown? Now, delay no more an' tell me where you've hidden McGrath's Pigtail.'

Catgut waved his skinny arms in feeble protest as he looked into rows of accusing eyes. Lower than the others, Horatio Nelson could see tears appear in the fiddler's eyes. His jaw was set in denial, but his rapidly dampening cheeks told the truth.

'Holy Mary Mother of God,' cried McGrath, moving forward. Horatio Nelson closed his eyes, not wishing to witness what was about to happen, but relieved that the thief had been exposed.

'Stand!' snapped John Judd, and such was the authority he had acquired that even the ship's hard man obeyed him. 'The thief must confess to stave off damnation.'

Nelson, eyes wide open now, watched as Catgut's shoulders slumped, and he loosed the first of several sobs. The words followed slowly, in spurts. 'In the manger ... by the straw where the hens alay.'

'You mean, paltry swab.' Judd whispered. 'Go down on your knees this second, and beg for the forgiveness of Neptune, as well as the man from who you stole.'

The fiddler's bony knees thudded on to the planking. He was babbling away, to God, Neptune and Eamon McGrath, pleading for absolution, promising every drop of his grog for the whole voyage if he could be spared the drubbing he was owed.

'I'll not forgo it,' said McGrath, emphatically, his fists clenched.

Judd put his hand on McGrath's arm and spoke softly. 'Take it easy on the sod, shipmate. He's a miserable wretch, and what's more the only fiddler we have aboard. Wound him too deep and you'll find yourself dancing the capstan in his place.'

It was a bruised and bloodied specimen that crawled from his hammock the following day, but McGrath had heeded Judd's wishes. The fiddler could still play, if only a scratch and a scrape, but enough to pace all hands as they swung round the capstan, pushing to get a new topsail yardarm aloft. The boys went up the shrouds after John Judd, and followed him out on the footropes, nagging him to answer their most pressing question. Finally, acting like a man driven to distraction, he obliged. 'Why shipmates, it was all stuff and nonsense. But there is nowt as daft as a superstitious tar. You'll never go astray preyin' on that particular habit. Take that blood now, which got everyone so. They thought it was from that chicken, but I tipped the whole of that o'er the side in plain view.'

'So where did it come from?' asked Amos eagerly.

'No more'n a lucky mishap.' Hooking his arm around a sling, he showed them his thumb, the thin gash where the knife had caught him now no more than a thin white line in the callused flesh. 'Bled like a stuck pig I did. But seeing as I had it to hand, and was set to prey on the fancies of my messmates, I thought it added a touch of the devil to the business.'

'Land ho!' came the cry from above their heads. 'Fine on the larboard bow.'

Every eye on the ship strained for their first sight of solid earth for two months. Captain Rathbone's voice boomed out, cursing the crew and telling them to get on with their tasks. They obliged, but as they worked their eyes strayed, until all had seen the white clouds that hovered over what must be land.

'Now my boys,' said John Judd, 'you think you's seen excitement since we weighed from the Downs. But just you wait. You ain't seen nothin' as yet. Over yonder there's rum, women and make merry, and old Rathbone has coin in his sailing chest that makes sure we'll get the chance to partake of it.'

The brilliance of St John's was astounding, everything Nelson had been told to expect and more, a combination of bright sunlight, deep blue skies and sea set against the green and brown of the island of Antigua, which was dotted with buildings of startling whiteness. Beyond lay the land of fabled fortunes made from sugar cane, of great sea battles, sieges, of islands changing hands in bewildering rotation between the warring French, Spanish and British.

In the seas between here and the Spanish Main the pirates and buccaneers had plied their bloody trade, creating legends that he and his friends had re-enacted on the beaches and chill waters of the north Norfolk shore – Drake, Henry Morgan, Blackbeard. This was the arena in which his uncle had risen to martial fame. And here he was about to land on one of the islands.

What would they be doing at the Parsonage now, his brothers and sisters? The mornings, hot here, would perhaps be frosty in Norfolk. If Father were at home the strict regime he insisted on would be in place: proper dress, cleanliness, prayers three times a day and not enough food to go round. Nelson had been homesick on this voyage from time to time, either in his daily prayers or lying in his hammock longing for the familiarity and security of Burnham Thorpe. He wasn't now, though, and he knew that every one of his siblings, perhaps even his pessimistic father, would envy him what he was about to experience.

To land and see the very ordinary faces of those who occupied the place was a great disappointment. There were no scarred scallywags and villains, flagon of rum in hand, or black-browed rogues thirsting to fight over a wayward look. There were only tradesfolk of the most mundane hue. The wharves that followed the horseshoe shaped bay were crammed with warehouses, full to the brim with everything from ambergris to wine. The place reeked of prosperity, not danger.

'Now, I have knowledge of this port of St John's,' said McGrath, pointing to an area where narrow lanes led off the quay, 'and it is not, thank the Lord, a place where a Christian would wish to spend too much time. So we leave Jesus and St Patrick in the boat, John Judd, and get our feet under a tavern table.'

The two boys followed in their footsteps, curious onlookers to the sights, sounds and smells of the place. His first sight of so many black faces had had no effect on Nelson, but outside a drawing smuggled into his schoolboy dormitory, he had never before seen bare-breasted females, who were seemingly unashamed by the exposure. Though it was warm, the air was clear and dry, and the women, as they passed close to them, gave off a musky smell that tantalised the boys as much as it did McGrath and Judd.

The tavern the Irishman chose was so dark and full of smoke that, at first, they could hardly see. But with elbows put to good service McGrath found them a place to sit. Then slapping some silver coins on the bare wood of the table, he loudly demanded attention. Looking around Nelson could see girls in bright patterned shawls, who sat at the tables and encouraged the customers to divest themselves of their money.

Within seconds rum had arrived, strong, undiluted liquor that nearly made him choke until it was cut with water and lime juice. He felt the warmth of the drink spread through his limbs. Pipes arrived too, and soon Judd, McGrath and Amos were puffing away, adding to the dense clouds that hung thick under the low rafters. McGrath had downed his first rum in one, then called for and consumed another before he rose to his feet and grinned at Judd. 'That's set me up fine and dandy, John boy, but you know, as I do, that too much of one good thing does no favour to another. You just keep an eye on these nippers while I test the mettle of what lays at the top of them stairs.'

Six eyes followed him. They had adjusted now to the gloom and they could see the open wooden staircase that ran up to a landing that lined the whole of one wall. Most of the doors were closed, but the two that remained open had handsome young negresses standing in them, demure in their looks despite the flesh they showed. McGrath had stopped at the base of the staircase and was haggling with the man who sat at the table. Finally a bargain was struck, money changed hands, and the Irishman had his foot on the first step.

Distracted by the arrival of more rum, when they looked back he'd disappeared. Amos Cavell grinned and nudged Nelson, indicating that one of the open doors was now closed. Suddenly John Judd was fidgeting like an infant, swaying back and forth as though trying to find the seat of a particularly galling itch. Setting down his tankard, he pronounced himself unwilling 'to hold such for an instant longer', and was at the foot of the stairs in an instant. His business at the table was as quickly concluded and the boys saw him run up, slap something into the last girl's hand, before both disappeared behind the closed door.

'Give me rum any day, mate,' said Amos to Nelson, leaning back in a superior way. 'There's more pleasure in a good jug of rum than in any black-skinned trollop.'

'You're right at that,' was the reply, though doubt was evident in Nelson's voice. The pair sat there as Judd and McGrath satisfied their corporeal needs, trying hard to look like men rather than boys. This took the form of an exaggerated loucheness, which with more rum soon turned raucous. Puffing on his pipe, Amos was showing away, as if a tavern was his natural habitat, shouting lewd comments that earned him many a baleful look. It also attracted to the table two of the whores working the room.

'You're a noisy one,' said the older of the pair, as she sat on the bench beside Amos.

The younger girl perched next to Nelson. He squirmed along his bench to avoid her. Close to, her skin didn't look quite so smooth, and her shawl was garish rather than colourful. 'This one is quiet and deep, I can tell.' Her voice was low and rasping, her face round and pockmarked, but her touch was light as she laid a warm hand on his.

'The question is,' said the other, 'what are they doing here? This be a place for men, not boys.'

'I ain't no mere boy,' said Amos, loudly, reaching under the table to his own crotch. 'There be the making of a smile down here.'

'Thin and fleeting, I'll wager.' The older woman laughed, showing a couple of broken teeth, then patted his waistcoat pocket. 'Never mind what's in that pouch below the board. Is there the wherewithal in here?'

'Depends,' Amos replied, sucking hard at his pipe and trying to look manly. 'I ain't no Simple Simon waitin' to be dunned.'

The older woman's eyes had narrowed just a fraction, while the one close to Nelson had put her hand in his lap. As he watched Amos lean close to negotiate, he wanted to run, but that would make Amos sneer.

'What have you got hidden away in your breeches?' asked the

girl next to him. Her voice was husky and insincere. 'I promise that whatever trade they agree will do for me.'

He couldn't speak, much as he wanted to, and neither could he move when, on hearing Amos agree a fee of two shillings, the girl's hand moved from his lap to his arm, and with a hearty tug she hauled him to his feet. Amos was already at the foot of the stairs, and the whole place seemed to have sunk away from him, the babble of the tavern somehow distant. And all the time, the smiling negress propelled him forward, with whispered promises of the delights to come. When it came to payment he felt as though he was outside his own body and the sweating face of the man who took his coins was too ill-defined to register.

Then they were on the stairs. At one point he managed to stop and look into her grinning face, which earned him an admonition not to be afraid, that every boy had to come to manhood one day. It was that, allied to the feeling that every eye in the smoke-filled room was on him, that turned him back up the stairs. If this whore knew he lacked experience then so did everyone else. To balk would be to invite ridicule from the entire assembly, so he allowed himself to be pushed along the landing, then through a door.

The hands that spun him round as soon as the door shut were not gentle, neither was there a smile on the girl's face. The fingers that scrabbled at his breeches buttons were eager enough, but the words she breathed now betokened impatience rather than lust. His erection sprang out into her avid, jerking hand, and the ache he had felt in his groin at the table concentrated so much that he had to close his eyes. When he opened them a second later he saw that he had shot semen all over the hem of her brightly patterned shawl.

'My, you're a quick one,' she said, in a voice that had no hint of the earlier sensuality. Her hand was in the folds of the shawl, to be wiped clean. But she was looking at his breeches. 'Best do likewise, young sir. Half the contents of your sack are running down your ducks.'

CHAPTER 9

As they worked to reload *Swanborough* with the cargo of molasses, Nelson wanted to kill Amos Cavell. It wasn't the notion of what he had got him into that chafed, or what had happened in that upstairs room. That, as he knew from mess table conversation, was an old bawd's trick, which earned them their money without any effort. Besides he had kept it secret. What annoyed him was the way the other boy reprised every second of his own experience. Since he had been gone a lot longer than Nelson, there was little doubt that he had been successful. In his boasting, Amos sounded like the older hands, and his tale always ended with the words, 'Best two shillings' worth she's ever had, I'll wager. Wasn't fit for the knacker's yard after a bout with Amos Cavell.'

This went on until well after they had weighed, which made Nelson grateful that a shortage of coin and the work of disgorging the cargo and reloading had confined his friend to that one carnal outing. Then, one morning, after Amos had made several trips to the heads, the boasting stopped. No explanation was given, but Amos took to watching Nelson closely. They were basically inseparable anyway, because of their duties and the other boy's curiosity deepened. His constant allusions to Nelson's health made no sense until the day when Amos had to admit that, like McGrath and Judd, he had been forced to consult the cook.

'How come?' he moaned, stroking his groin, 'that out of a pair I get the one that's poxed, an' you get away scot-free? McGrath and Judd are in the same state. You must have had the only clean whore in the whole fuckin' place.'

'Pot luck, I reckon.'

The dark eyes narrowed and Amos looked hard at his blond friend. 'You did do the service, didn't you, Nellie?'

'By the pint, Amos,' Nelson responded gaily. 'By the pint. The prize bull himself couldn't have done better.'

The way to England was the third arm of the triangular passage, north from the sugar islands, the coast of the American colonies to leeward, searching for the trade winds that would take them east and home. So far it had been a good voyage, with few accidents and no deaths. But the risk of that was a constant, and never more so than once the ship had touched land and the crew had been exposed to ailments alien to the sea.

They lost one man to a fever of unknown origin that had them sousing the whole ship with vinegar; that was followed by a week when everyone watched everyone else carefully for any sign of a malaise that might threaten them all. Tales of a whole ship's crew perishing, leaving the vessel to drift, were the stuff of nightmares. Amos stopped boasting and took to regaling them with tales of his fortitude when faced with the cook's mercury-tipped metal implements.

John Judd kept silent about what he had endured in the same line, but he still watched over them, ensuring that they did what they had been taught. He told Nelson that now he was a full member of the crew, like to be trusted, being seen in close conversation with the captain would not be taken amiss. As soon as the boy showed interest in the more difficult nautical skills, Rathbone practically fawned on him. Learning the rudiments of spherical trigonometry was harder than tying knots, but Nelson fetched his seamanship books from the chest in which they had lain undisturbed, and set himself to learn as much as he could.

Yet he still messed forward, with the same men, who now hankered after home instead of foreign adventure. It took him time to realise what it was that made him feel so at ease. It gradually dawned on him that the men shared a sense of tolerance he had experienced nowhere else. They were at ease with their differences and forgiving of transgressions, once a point had been made or a score settled. No one shunned

Catgut, or hid their possessions from him. He was now, almost with affection, named a fiddler on two counts. He had suffered McGrath's retribution and that was enough.

At home, at school, even in his limited time in a midshipman's berth, Nelson had seen how every mark counted against a person's character: it was knowledge to be husbanded for future use. No sin was forgotten, no misdemeanour forgiven in a world where people jockeyed for advantage, in which standards must be maintained, where change was treated with suspicion. Here, 'tween decks, a man's ability was what marked him out; and live and let live was the order of every work-filled day. That, and a keen anticipation of whatever it was that lay over the horizon.

'You'll never satisfy a blue water sailor, young Nellie,' said John Judd, as they worked on some old ropes, picking out the shakings so that they could be reused. 'They ain't like fisher folk and men who work the coast. For those that go deep grass is always greener, don't matter where they are.'

The youngster wanted to disagree, since he was himself a blue water sailor now, and he was as happy as he had ever been in his life, unsure that the future could hold better than the world he now inhabited. But he needed to keep that to himself. Better a joke than maudlin emotion. 'Excepting Fiddler's Green,' he replied, grinning.

'The land of milk and honey,' Judd intoned, 'where the money never runs out, and the women are as obligin' as the rum is pure. God grant you get there one day, Mr Nelson, cause it's as sure as hell is hot that I never will.'

'Fiddler's Green don't exist, John Judd, and you know it.'

'It's there for some, lad, though I daresay your pa the parson would term it heaven.'

'Not with obliging women he wouldn't.'

As if on cue Amos Cavell came back from his latest visit to the cook, his face as grey as the sea under the keel. 'How many more times has he got to stick that probe down my prick? The pleasure the man gets ain't natural.'

'Just be thankful you're alive, Amos,' said Judd. ''Cause that is what matters most.'

Once they had found the prevailing westerlies, well north on latitude 40 degrees north, the sun was rarely out. Behind them, in the Caribbean, the hurricane season was in full swing, and the tail of that weather pursued them across the grey Atlantic, sending black clouds scurrying eastward and whipping up storms that, even when they abated, left them in the midst of a heaving, troubled sea. Going aloft in sheeting, wind driven rain was misery. And, as John Judd never tired of reminding them, it was dangerous. He was at his charges constantly to keep both arms over the yard, both feet well spread on the foot ropes slung below, religiously supervising their work even as he carried out his own.

'Hands aloft!' yelled Verner, head down the hatchway for the tenth time since dawn.

Groaning and moaning Nelson, exhausted from little sleep and too much toil, dragged himself on to the deck, as the mate ordered another reef in the topsail to take account of an increase in the wind. He was still wet from his last outing, when a black squall had swept across the ship, rain so heavy that he could barely breathe, so he felt he must be drowning. The ship was rolling and pitching on a heaving grey sea, under glowering, cloud-filled skies that, even in the gathering twilight, promised a deluge in the near future. He was cold already but the wind chilled him even more as it took what little heat his body had generated. Rathbone was by the wheel, where he had been since the day before, red eyes caked with salt, water cascading off his oilskins. Verner was beside him now, speaking trumpet in hand.

'Clap on there, Nellie,' Judd barked, pushing him slightly as the ship pitched into a deep, broken trough. Nelson had forgotten to lash himself on, but there was no time to reach for the line he wore round his waist for the purpose. He grabbed at the man-rope that stretched from the top of the companionway to the bulwarks, his feet slipping on the wet deck as it canted, leaving him stretched out practically face down. Above his head he heard the cry, and Amos Cavell screaming. John Judd slipped past him, hands scrabbling for a hold that didn't exist, on a deck that the running sea had swept clear.

Judd made his feet just before his body hit the bulwark, with the ship rising on a wave to help him upright. He stood like a man on a tightrope, grasping at the air for balance, his eyes on the lifeline that was just beyond his reach. Nelson was on his feet too, lashing himself to the man-rope while the deck was horizontal. The ship should have continued to lift, threatening to throw Judd all the way across the deck as it canted to larboard. Instead she pitched again as a sudden gust of wind, allied to a freak in the run of the sea, threw her over until she was nearly on her beam-ends. John Judd, wide-eyed and with nothing to hold on to, was lifted bodily and, as his back hit the bulwark, he tumbled over the side.

'Man overboard,' yelled Nelson, a cry that was taken up all around him as he battled his way along the man-rope to the side of the ship. Using the shrouds to secure himself he leapt on to the rail and arched his body out over the hull. John Judd was in the water, arms waving, bobbing away towards the stern, the opening gap testimony to the speed *Swanborough* was making. Someone astern threw a rope, but it missed him by several feet, which in this sea was as good as a mile.

'Get aloft, Nelson,' screamed Verner, his mouth close to the youngster's ear. Words wouldn't come as Nelson pointed at Judd's fast disappearing form. The mate's salt streaked face held little sympathy for his distress, and the voice was a harsh growl. 'How in Christ's name are we to come about and save the poor sod without we have men to work the fuckin' sails?'

Nelson was already climbing when he heard Rathbone give the orders for a figure of eight. He wondered as he ascended what that meant then put it to the back of his mind as he made his way out on to the topsail yard – the need to survive the journey out to the end of the narrowing pole had to take precedence over everything. The ropes beneath his bare feet were soaked, but rough enough to give grip and, true to Judd's teaching, he had half his body across the yard, a hand holding anything that would aid his purchase.

Once in place he managed a look over the stern. Judd was clear in the wake, bobbing in the troughs and rising on the tops, going under occasionally but resurfacing, his arm raised in supplication. Then the orders came, sails loosed as Rathbone bore up into the wind in a long arc. The yards, worked by those still on deck, spun until they were nearly fore and aft, with the wind pushing the ship to leeward at an increasing rate. Rathbone called for them to be sheeted home then let the bows fall off across another heavy gust. Nelson felt himself pulled through the air as, with the wind now pushing on the starboard bow, the trim of the yards was reversed. Rathbone had his speaking trumpet raised to call out the orders to take the ship back across its own course.

'Sheet home, lively,' Verner screamed. 'Aloft there, let fall the topsail.'

The sail already reefed, Nelson scrabbled at the ties that had halved the area of available sail, the men inboard of him doing likewise. Habit overbore anxiety, and the task was carried out as if the sea were calm, and the toiling topmen were not rising, falling, pitching and rolling through an arc of fifty feet. Nelson knew that the Captain was taking a risk, showing so much canvas to a gusting wind. He would be safe if he could come up into it again and make some headway before another gust hit the ship. That would take him beyond John Judd in the water; he could then come round to complete the figure of eight with the gale on his quarter, shortening sail to shield Judd. Then they could try to get a line on him to haul him inboard, a manoeuvre that would have to be performed with way on the ship. Any attempt to heave to in this swell would see them founder.

With a darkening sky, time was short, but a glance told him Judd was still alive. He knew Rathbone was trying to rescue him, so he had stopped waving and put all his effort into staying afloat. The Captain made his figure of eight, and brought *Swanborough* to a point to leeward of Judd before he wore to come back on to his original course. Now the swell was the problem. That and the fear that by getting too close to Judd, a sudden gust would ship them sideways and drive him under.

The task aloft was finished, and Nelson chivvied those ahead to clamber down the shrouds. Sensibly they wouldn't be hurried, insisting that they lash themselves off to avoid sharing Judd's fate. Descending at a pace set by others, Nelson saw the lines fly out again and again, as the best men on the ship tried to cast a rope close enough for Judd to reach. He was calling encouragement to them now, his voice carrying over the wind. Before Nelson touched the deck, he knew the gap was too great. The tide was carrying Judd at a rate close to that of the ship so the gap never closed. To put her before the wind and narrow it meant setting a course across the swell, bringing the risk that she might roll out her masts.

'Let me try and swim to him,' he said, tugging at Rathbone's sleeve with one hand while the other was occupied releasing his safety line.

The captain turned to look at him, clapped a hand over the still tied knot and shook his head. 'I'll not risk losing two, Mr Nelson.'

There was a look in the red-rimmed eyes that seemed to hint that if another had asked he might have said yes. The notion that he was being favoured made Nelson both angry and intemperate. 'I'll go without permission,' he shouted, trying to prise off Rathbone's hand.

'You will not, Mr Nelson. But if you can find a grown man to accept the task I will sanction an attempt.'

McGrath was beside them, and heard Rathbone's words. He tugged at Nelson's sleeve so hard that the boy slipped on the wet deck. When he spoke, his voice was an angry growl. 'Get up, you grass combing bugger and lash me up.'

'Can you swim?'

The beetle-browed hard man swung round and shouted to Amos Cavell. 'Fetch me a cask from below. If it ain't empty make it so.'

Judd's voice came again, asking why they'd given up casting a line to him.

'How long till full night, Captain?'

Rathbone looked up at the scudding black clouds, full of rain and the indistinct lightness to the west. 'Half an hour, no more. Get a line ready for McGrath, and one to put round the barrel in case the bugger lets go. Mr Verner, when our man is ready, I want to put the ship before the wind for no more than a minute.'

There was no need to go aloft. This was all deck work, easing the yards a fraction while Rathbone worked the rudder, then hauling them tight again. But the risk they ran was soon evident, as the ship, lifted sideways on to a huge wave, nearly broached to, saved only by the strength of the wind at the top of the rise, which took her head round. They had closed the gap with Judd but not by much.

'We'll not be risking that again, I hope, Capt'n,' called Verner, as he struggled to hold the wheel. Rathbone silently shook his head.

McGrath was helped on to the bulwark, four men holding him as he lay backwards, feet on the ship's side, walking backwards on the planking into the water. A sudden flash of lightning illuminated the seascape, followed by a crack of close-by thunder. That flash of light underlined to everyone on deck just how little time they had.

'Topmen aloft, Mr Verner,' said Rathbone. 'We'll need to re-reeve those sails.'

'Aye.'

'I'll delay as long as I can, boy,' Rathbone growled, 'but that lightning is running ahead of a heavier storm, and that means an increase in the wind.'

Going aloft had two advantages. It kept him occupied and afforded a better spot from which to view McGrath's endeavours. He had struck out from the side of the ship, slowed by the barrel but clearly with the strength to cope. Judd had started calling to him, his voice noticeably more feeble. On the yards, every man was in his place, ready to haul up the sails and tie them off. What little light remained faded and John Judd was swallowed up by the darkness, then the struggling McGrath. Just as it seemed full night was on them, another flash of lightning lit the sky, showing both men in the water still too far apart. The thunder was instantaneous, and mingled with yet more streaks of lightning. Rathbone could wait no longer.

'Aloft, reef the topsails. On deck, haul round on those falls. Mr Verner, resume the course.'

'Move yourself, Nellie,' shouted the man inside him, forcing Nelson to go to work. But each flash of lightning made his heart sink, and he saw McGrath being hauled back to the ship, while John Judd, still gesturing, drifted away. Tears streamed down his face, as the man who had taught him so much crested on a wave. Was it in his imagination that he heard one last faint cry, before John Judd was carried into the next trough and oblivion?

The sight of England, as they spotted the Lizard three weeks later, brought a lump to Nelson's throat, which seemed to grow the closer they came to making their landfall. He felt very different from the youth who had set sail six months previously, more of a man than a boy, aware that for all the skill he had absorbed the most important lesson had little to do with seamanship, and much with companionship.

The talk now was of where the men would meet again, and those whose friendships were deep swore to find a new berth together. For almost the first time since coming aboard *Swanborough*, Nelson felt separate from the crew. He was going back to his uncle, back to the King's Navy and that midshipman's berth. And if he failed to fit in a second time, it would be back to his father and his Norwich school.

He wasn't afraid, but he was sad. The loss of John Judd still weighed heavily. He and Amos endured long silences, as they tried to come to terms with his absence. When Nelson contrasted the present with the unwelcoming nature of a mid's berth, set against the sense of easy fellowship he had had these last months, he felt a terrible temptation to damn the Navy to hell and stay in the merchant service. Rathbone saw the gloom, guessed the cause and, in a surprisingly gentle way, dissuaded the youngster from any such madcap idea.

'Why, your uncle will see you advanced, lad. I told you that when you came aboard, and it holds as true now as it did then. You're destined for a quarterdeck, not a slung hammock. And if you can find employment for such as John Rathbone, old as I'll be, then I will be obliged to you for it.'

The point at which the anchor hit the water off Deal was the full stop to the trip, with most of the crew going ashore there. The Nelson to whom Amos Cavell said goodbye was a different creature from the fresh-faced, nervous youth he had encountered on coming aboard. And, in the nature of things, Amos had no real idea of how he himself had changed.

That which they had both been taught had been absorbed

into a body of knowledge acquired as much by observation as learning by rote. The legacy of John Judd would stay with them for life. The daily toil of shipwork and his attention to their ways, with rope, canvas and wood, meant that they were sailors now; no longer ship's boys to be kicked aside, but close to full-grown men in the level of their skill.

'Take care, Nellie,' Amos said, 'and if there's a war, God pray they don't press me into any ship in which you're a servin'. I've got you marked down, in a blue coat, as a hard-horsed, floggin' bugger.'

The grin took the sting out of the words, as Nelson responded in the same vein of humour. 'You won't escape me, Amos. I'll insist on having you in my crew, with a special grating rigged just so the bosun's mate can stripe your back at my whim.'

They stopped off at Deal only long enough to get seamen ashore and paid off. Rathbone, sober, was back aboard *Swanborough* within two hours, eager to weigh and get home. They picked up a Thames pilot off Margate, and a small extra payment took the ship south of the Isle of Sheppey so that they could close the Great Nore anchorage.

Horatio Nelson, dressed once more in his dark blue coat, was boated to Chatham. The Captain, very obligingly, came with him, and his last act as the boy stepped on to dry land was to hand him a packet of letters for his uncle, and various other officers believed to be on the station.

'Good luck, Mr Nelson,' said Rathbone. 'If you're ever stuck for a berth in a peace, look me up. If I have ship, you shall have a place in her.'

McGrath had helped row the boat ashore. He didn't say anything, but his smile and wink spoke volumes. Nelson couldn't reply in kind, since he knew to do so would give away how close he was to tears. Rathbone was back in the thwarts, and as the cutter spun away from the steps, he called after them.

'God be with you all.'

No novice now, he called at the Port Admiral's office to check if his uncle was still serving. The lieutenant he spoke to confirmed that Captain Suckling was aboard the guardship *Triumph.* He produced a chart to show her position, and was kind enough to take from him the letters that Rathbone had addressed to other serving officers. This time, as Nelson approached the side he was spotted by the officer of the watch. He placed himself carefully to ensure that all proper forms were observed, then came up the gangplank and made his way up on to the pristine quarterdeck. Once there he raised his hat to Mr Fonthill. 'Permission to come aboard, sir.'

'Granted,' the officer replied.

He looked up and down at the youth before him, noting the deep tan on the previously pallid face. He had grown a bit and the shoulders had broadened. But the greatest gain was in the sense of presence, most tellingly in the steady look in those deep grey-blue eyes. He shouted to a group of sailors working by the hammock nettings. 'You there. Look lively and fetch Mr Nelson's gear aboard.' Then he turned back. 'I sent to tell your uncle that you were returned. He desires you to proceed to his cabin at once.'

'Aye, aye, sir,' Nelson responded briskly.

'Well, well,' said Suckling, standing to receive his nephew, 'you've put in some sea time.'

'Captain Rathbone desired that I deliver these, sir,' Nelson replied, handing over the letters.

There was a pause of a few seconds while each relative examined the other. Nelson saw the faint smile on his uncle's lips, which hinted at pride in his nephew. The knowledge that he had pleased his uncle filled him with happiness. Whatever doubts he had harboured, he knew for certain that life for him in the King's Navy now would be different from his first experience.

'Steward, a glass of wine,' Suckling called, as he opened the packet, and indicated that his nephew should sit down. The wine was poured as Suckling read. Finally he laid the letter aside, picked up his glass, and looked at Nelson. 'So, nephew, you have gone from one ship, sailed to the West Indies, acquitted yourself well judging by Rathbone's opinion, and returned to my new command. Raise your glass to a scheme well complete.'

Nelson did so, noticing the twinkle in his uncle's eye. The full, slightly feminine lips parted in a grin, just before he spoke. 'Ha, ha, boy. You could be said to have had a *Raisonable* voyage, and returned to a *Triumph*.'

CHAPTER 10

1773

Emma grew impatient with the sudden doubts of Jane Powell, her fellow housemaid, and had to take her arm to get her out through the basement door of Dr Budd's house. Jane, the elder of the pair, should be taking the lead, not her. Dinner had been served, Mrs Lane the housekeeper had nodded off in the pantry and Gill Tooley, the head footman, with his two under-footmen, was on hand to provide anything their master and mistress required. Everyone would take it for granted that after a long hard day which had started with the laying of fires before dawn, the two girls had retired to their attic beds.

Her own blood was racing, part from fear and part from excitement, since to leave the house without permission was forbidden. Employers of serving wenches, one just coming up thirteen, the other a mere fifteen, wanted their girls to be sober, cheerful, chaste and asleep after dark, not gallivanting on Autumn nights around the fleshpots of London.

The streets around Blackfriars were still busy, the wharves that lined the Thames hives of activity with cargoes being loaded into the barges that would take them up and downriver. They picked their way delicately through the throng of carts, carriages and people, hems held clear of the filth, horse and human, that coated the walkways. Though Jane was still nervous, Emma was filled with a sense of freedom, gabbling away nineteen to the dozen as they stopped to finger the goods at every covered stall that sold trinkets, lace or ribbons.

However, neither had the means to buy, and frustration grew as they made their way on to London Bridge, which was lined with tiny shops. There, behind glass, were gold jewellery, fans decorated with elaborate eastern patterns, dress materials of the finest satin, wool and silk and gay shawls. Downriver of the bridge, silhouetted in the fading light, stood the masts of thousands of ships, the very vessels that had fetched in this abundance. Beneath their feet, the river transport surged through the narrow arches; barges, small boats and the rivermen's tiny wherries.

'Do you not long to go to sea, Jane,' Emma asked breathlessly, 'to see the world's wonders?'

'I could think of nothing worse. My uncle Gabriel was a sailor, and he said that all that blather about the world's wonders was stuff. It were backbreaking toil and barely a farthing to roister on ashore. That was before the pox he got from his voyaging took away from him the power to speak.'

'If I were a man, that is what I should do, go to sea.'

Emma caught Jane looking at her full breasts, a source of deep envy, she knew, to her less well endowed companion, but of some pride to herself. Although she was younger than Jane, Emma was taller by a good two inches, with a fuller figure that made her look several years older than her years. Yet Jane Powell had beauty as well: an olive complexion and near black eyes to contrast with Emma's green, though her short chestnut hair, however well brushed and shining, could not compete with Emma's three feet of auburn.

'You'll never pass for a man, Emma Lyon,' Jane said, trying to sound more grown up than her companion. 'If it's salt water you're after, find yourself a sailor. And while he's traipsing round the globe, making the money to keep your affections, enjoy yourself with any of his mates who happen to be ashore, 'cause that's what he'll be about in every port he calls at.'

'That's a sure way to please my ma,' said Emma, with a trace of anger.

She had visited today, an unbidden call that had nearly killed off the plan for this nocturnal adventure. A friend of the housekeeper, Emma's mother could come and go as she pleased to a house where Cath Lane ruled the roost. She had the key to the tea caddy, and a sharp eye for the lecherous eye of Gill Tooley, who was a touch free with his hands.

Emma knew that her mother thought her too boisterous for

her station, but Cath Lane seemed to enjoy her lively nature, encouraging both her and Jane to sing as they wished. The sound was pleasing to the mistress of the house, Dr Budd's invalid wife, though not to her husband, who demanded peace and quiet when he was about.

'She fears to see you out on your ear again, that's all,' said Jane.

'I'm not sure I do,' Emma replied, immediately realising that she had said the wrong thing. Jane Powell's dark eyes showed real alarm as the consequences of what they were doing crossed her mind. 'You don't reckon on service all your days, do you?'

That was the way to steady Jane: to remind her of how often in the eighteen months they had been together they both spoke of a better life than that below stairs, at Dr Budd's or anywhere else. They had fantasised about other avenues to advancement – to becoming actresses or singers, owning a shop or marrying a rich man captivated by their uncomplicated charm.

Emma wondered if her mother knew how she added to that sense of disquiet. How could she insist that this was a proper life for her daughter when she wore well-made clothes of silk and velvet, a fashionable hat on her head and trailed a waft of expensive scent that hinted at a life far better than Emma's? How she achieved such was never discussed, but it was scarce a secret that she worked for a lady called Mrs Kelly, who owned a fine house in Arlington Street; that everything she owned was provided either by her or by male admirers. Cath Lane had worked there too, which was why they were friends, until her beauty had faded. Now Cath Lane was near as broad as she was high, with a round face in which her nose had near disappeared between bright red cheeks, and she had forearms like a drayman.

'And how are we to know what's to be had,' Emma added, taking Jane's arm to propel her along, 'if'n we don't go abroad to see it?'

Jane was smiling again as they traversed the other half of the bridge. Over the sound of vendors shouting of the beauty and value of their wares, they could hear fiddles, fifes and drums, the sound of the camp that occupied the Southwark bank opposite the city. Once military, it was now a permanent fairground, as well as home to any number of travellers. Crowded and bustling, the rule was that if you could find a space and a way to attract attention, you were free to perform. There were jugglers by the dozen, while others swallowed swords or fire. Moth-eaten bears were made to dance, and the cockfights in the central arena took turnabout with contests between battling dogs.

The girls were invited to Rat and Trap, play skittles, shy balls for prizes, and try their hand at short archery. Using dazzling smiles to slip into the boxing booth without payment they watched as the two pugilists hammered each other, the blood from their bare-knuckled blows spattering the crowd, who were yelling for the man on which they had placed their bets. They observed people who thought themselves wiseacres relieved of their coins on the hunt the thimble board, made dizzy by the way the three cups were switched.

Hardest to bear was the smell of food so powerful it overbore the human stink: pork on a spit, roasted potatoes and chestnuts, fresh sweetmeats that made their nostrils twitch. The hot spices from mulled wine rose to tempt them, overtaken suddenly by the fragrance of cool lemonade. Emma thought of Fred Stavely, and tried to reckon how much a quick, darting fellow like him could pick up in a crowded arena like this. Looking around the soldiers, sailors and ordinary citizens, an ache grew in her belly that demanded to be filled. She regretted that she had never asked him to teach her the skills of a successful dip.

'If I don't get something to eat I'll faint,' said Jane.

They had stopped in one of the lanes that criss-crossed the camp, with no real idea of where they were. It was pitch dark now, the only light coming from flaming torches that flared above each booth or stall. People milled around them, and some of the passing males, mistaking their purpose, made suggestions that brought a blush to their cheeks. One party of sailors, pigtails stretched down their backs, made so bold as to approach them, the smell of drink obvious on their breath.

'Hey ho, my beauties,' said the leader, who was dressed in his best shore-going rig, a short, brass-buttoned blue coat, wide trews and stripped stockings to match his waistcoat set off by buckled shoes. With his tarred hat in his hand, he executed a deep bow. 'My shipmates here, having observed as I 'ave that you're a pair of true sprites, was wondering if we might engage you for matters of a sporting nature.'

'Only in conversation,' said Jane Powell, archly.

'As long as it's criminal conversation,' said one of the others, to loud laughter.

Their leader waved his hat impatiently. 'As you will observe, some of my mates here are drunk to the point of bein' blind. They can't see your innocence as I can.'

'You get much closer and that innocence'll be forfeit.'

'Belay, you damned oaf,' their interlocutor said. 'The trouble with you is you only knows how to address whores. These be more gentle creatures.'

'Stuff your gentle creatures,' spat the man who had responded first. 'Get the price, an' let's either get them on their backs or seek elsewhere.'

The naïveté that had kept them in conversation was broken. Jane screamed and Emma turned and grabbed her as they ran away, pursued by a long string of lubricious catcalls. Yet for all her fear, there was a delicious thrill in Emma's breast. That sailor had marked their beauty, and the look in his eye, as he spoke to them, had hinted at something else.

'They took us for whores,' Jane wailed, as they rounded the corner to find themselves standing in a small open space, under huge lanterns, at the back of the boxing booth. 'Who could do that?'

'Not the one that came close,' Emma replied, putting her arm around Jane to comfort her. 'He was more of a gent than the others. The rest were just pie-eyed with rum.'

'And there was you prattling about goin' to sea.'

'What's to be afraid of in this mob? Except having no money. We'd have more of a time if we had some coin.'

'You're not suggesting we take up on them jack tars!'

'Don't be daft,' Emma snapped. 'I just said we had to get hold of some coin.'

'Well, there's the moon, Emma Lyon.' Jane pointed to the sky. 'You may whistle for it if you like.'

'What about singin' to it?'

'Sing?'

'Like we do in the house, when we're working.' Emma took off her cloak and laid it on the ground in front of them. Her hat followed that, and the long auburn tresses of which she was so proud tumbled down to frame her face. 'See, we can stand here and chant – perhaps that Granger air we both know – an' those going by may tip a coin into my cloak as payment. When we've got enough, we can get ourselves something to eat and drink.'

'It'll never work!'

'If jugglers can drop their beanbags and still get paid, so can we, even if we drop a note or two. You've got a better voice than me, so you take the lead part and I'll do the reprises.'

What came out of Jane Powell's mouth when she started singing was so far from the real item that Emma burst out laughing. Out of key, weak and tuneless, it would have driven people away if she had been loud enough. Emma began to sing herself, loudly, and with a *faux* assurance that covered the feeling of butterflies churning in her stomach. Slowly, as Jane gained confidence, her voice grew in strength until she was singing with enough gusto to allow Emma to drop to a softer tone.

They had plenty to compete with – the roars from the boxing booth at their back, the shouts of a crowd at pleasure, as well as the odd drunken yell 'to put a boot up the cat's arse' – but one or two people stopped to listen. Those accompanied by wives or sweethearts were swiftly dragged away, for the trilling girls were not very good – so it was more their youth and looks that attracted. The rougher element, on hearing a song of soft love and sweet muses, didn't linger either, though one or two, more from habit than generosity, threw a few coins into Emma's cloak.

They were left, as an audience, with young, unattached men, none of whom seemed to have the courage to approach too closely, nor the means to reward them for their efforts. But one duo did, though they waited till the end of the song to applaud and throw a sixpence. The one who tossed the coin was tall and thin, with sharp, unbecoming features, thick lips under a nose that seemed too big, and an eager look that rendered him unattractive. He was well dressed in a buff coat of good quality, white breeches and stockings that looked to be silk.

The other, in a plain black coat, was of medium height, round of face and fair skinned. He had a sullen air, though this might have been attributable in some measure to the tricorn hat pulled down low over his forehead. They listened to another song, made payment of a second sixpence, applauded again, then approached the performers, the tall thin fellow well to the fore. 'Bravely done, girls,' he cried.

'Bravely?' Emma demanded, stretching to her full height.

He smiled. 'If you listen carefully, and put aside the noise of the crowd, you will realise that the nightingales have fled the contest. You have, my beauties, triumphed over nature.'

He had a good voice, even and deep, so the insincerity in his eyes did little to diminish the compliment. Jane had stepped back slightly, so that her friend's greater substance shielded her.

'Allow me to introduce myself. I am James Perry, and this is my very good friend Owen Dunn.' The smaller man gave a grunt, as his friend continued, 'We are both of the opinion that we enjoyed your concert immensely.'

'The word "bravely" sits ill with that, Mr Perry,' Emma replied, thrilled at her own boldness.

'There are those who might flatter you, Miss . . . ?'

'Lyon,' Emma exclaimed, confidently. 'And this is Miss Jane Powell.'

That produced another bow, and Jane took a tight grip on Emma's arm. Perry looked down at the few coins in the cloak. 'I fear you'll never make your fortune as a fairground *chanteuse*, Miss Lyon, though you'd be amazed at what you might achieve with a trifling amount of tuition, especially at your tender age.' He gazed into the huge green eyes. 'Indeed, you have the necessary presence to overcome any flaw in performance.'

Emma bobbed a curtsy, then cursed herself for doing something so childish. 'I thank you kindly, Mr Perry. But you mistake our purpose. We are naught but a pair of housemaids.'

He interrupted her, and again the expression in his eyes was at odds with what he said. 'Why, you amaze me. Such beauty in a mere domestic servant is rare.'

'Jane and I were only singing to acquire the means to buy some food, and perhaps a drink.'

'Then I'd be very obliged if you and Miss Powell would allow Mr Dunn and me the honour of providing for you.'

Emma ignored the hearty tug from Jane, which Perry noticed. 'Why we'd be delighted, sir,' she said.

'If you were to state a preference, Miss Lyon, I'm sure I could take you to the very spot that sells whatever you fancy. There's a stall I spied selling hot rum mixed with cinnamon.'

'Lemonade will suffice, sir.' Emma looked down, in a way that obliged Perry to scoop up the coins swiftly, along with her hat and cloak, all of which he handed over.

'What are you about?' Jane demanded, in a whisper. All the time Perry had been talking, Dunn hadn't taken his eyes off her, as though they had decided before they had approached who would take whom. 'What do we want with a couple of old goats like 'em?'

'They're never more than twenty years,' Emma hissed. 'Why spend what we've earned, Jane, when we can get a pair of willing gents to lay it out for us?'

Perry helped her put her cloak back round her shoulders, but made a sudden gesture when she made to replace her hat. 'Please, Miss Lyon, do not deprive me of the sight of those engaging tresses.'

That was when Dunn spoke, requesting archly that Jane, too, remove her hat so that he could gaze upon her locks. When Jane refused, Emma reached out and did it for her.

'Will you take my arm, Miss Lyon?'

'I think not, Mr Perry,' Emma replied. 'That would not be proper. If you and Mr Dunn walk ahead, we will be following a few steps behind you.'

'I would prefer that we reverse the arrangement,' Perry replied.

'As you wish, sir,' Emma responded, moving off with Jane in tow. As soon as they were moving she called out over her shoulder. 'You don't seem the type for such a place, sir.'

'That one so young should be so discerning is singular, but good entertainment is not easy to find.'

'And this place obliges?'

'Why, I doubt my parents would approve, but we cannot always obey our elders and seek pleasure at the same time.'

'D'ye hear that, Emma?' said Jane, softly. ' "My parents". He's not for the likes of us. He's probably got housemaids of his own.'

Emma whispered. 'I daresay. And so will the other one. They're just a couple of rakes out seeking a good time.'

'Well, they can good time it elsewhere,' Jane retorted.

'If you turn left at the next corner, ladies,' said Dunn, 'you will come to a lemonade stall.'

Again it was Emma who responded. 'I see it, Mr Dunn.'

The quartet drew close, joining those queuing to be served. That was the moment when Perry and Dunn chose to move forward, trying gently to separate the girls. Emma knew what they were about, as did Jane, but was less alarmed by their attentions. Servants like her were expected to be grateful for being taken up by men of quality.

She could see in Perry's eyes that he was enjoying the thrill of the chase. She, in turn, liked the pursuit; a notion that was clearly alien to her companion, considering the way that Jane elbowed Dunn so that she could stay attached to Emma. There was satisfaction in knowing what the men were thinking. Perry and Dunn saw two young serving girls, wenches bent on adventure, who had had the good fortune to run into two lads who could provide it. Both would be certain their luck was in, assume that Emma and Jane were easy game. Perry was more forthright than Dunn, but in some way his quiet expectation of compliance was more revealing. At least he felt he had to try to seduce them, employing wit, flattery and refreshment. Dunn had made up his mind that if they were that sort, in this place, warbling badly to get a few pence, then the results for the night were a foregone conclusion. Emma was struck by another thought: she hadn't the faintest idea how she knew all this, but she did.

'I confess I'm faint with hunger,' she said, trying as hard as she could to sound ladylike.

'Then let us proceed to the roasting pit, where they are turning fresh pork,' said Perry, a leering note in his voice. 'Nothing like a bit of pork to set you up for the night.'

'Why that's the truth, Mr Perry,' Emma said, her huge eyes full of innocence. 'I'm truly fond of hot pork.'

'James, if you please,' he responded, with something akin to a whoop.

The girls went ahead again, Jane whispering in something close to panic, her arm looped round Emma's.

'Never fear, Jane,' Emma murmured. 'These two Jimkins think they've landed sweet. Next thing, after we eat, will be an invite of some sort that will get us away from the crowds.'

'Then what are we to do?'

Emma laughed, one of those pealing chuckles that had filled the Budd house earlier that day. She heard the two men behind her join in with their own ribald mirth, could almost see them nudging each other in mutual anticipation. 'Leave that to me. Let's just get them to feed us first.'

The heat from the pit brought an added glow to their cheeks. Perry's handkerchief was needed to stem the juices from the pork slices that ran down Emma's chin. It was a fine cambric square, of a quality that she had only ever felt on an ironing board.

'Please keep it, Miss Lyon,' Perry said. 'It is a trifle compared to your beauty, and the promise of your company.'

Looking up at him, in the stronger light from the lanterns that hung under the spit-roaster's awning, she tried to make out his age. Twenty had been her guess, though the puffiness she had taken earlier for a sign of youthfulness looked more likely due to over-indulgence.

'How often do you come here?' she asked.

'Why, this is but my second visit,' he replied as though suddenly afraid that the image he was presenting would fall apart with the truth. The truth that he and his friend came here often, hunting, no doubt, for fresh conquests. Emma knew he was lying. The raised voice had been to alert Dunn.

'What a memory you have, James Perry,' she said, with deliberate coquetry, 'to know Southwark Fields so well after only two visits. I swear I could never find a lemonade stall as quick as you, nor a roasting pit.'

The grin stayed fixed, but the jaw clenched, as though he was struggling to contain such a sally from someone so much his inferior. Out of the corner of her eye she could see Dunn leaning close to Jane. From the stiff way she was holding herself, he was making improper suggestions.

'In truth, I don't really care for this place,' Perry said. Emma pouted, enjoying the swift way he responded. 'Saving for your presence, of course. I much prefer the town, St James's and Covent Garden.'

'I ain't never been to such.'

'Have you not?' he cried, as though such ignorance was fatal. 'Then I see it as my duty to take you there.'

'Would you?'

He bent over, took her hand and lifted it to his lips. 'It would be my pleasure. And since I have a small set of rooms there, I can provide you with something a touch more refined than the provender you've consumed in this place.'

'What about my friend?' Emma asked, with a note of alarm.

'She may come too. I'm sure my good friend Dunn will pay her all the attention she requires.'

'Is it not a long way off?'

'Not in a hack, which I can easily call upon once we're on the north bank of London Bridge.'

Emma's voice became positively childish. 'I don't know, sir. We would be much troubled to get home.'

'It is to visit a place you've never seen. Did you not come here for that very purpose?' She smiled, bowed her head and nodded. 'Look upon it as an addition to the night's pleasure. And as to getting you home, what fellow with any claim to be a gentleman would not oblige you in that?'

'If we're late . . .'

'You will not be late,' he said, in a voice much more firm.

'How I long for adventure, Mr Perry.' She pouted. 'Life can be so dull below stairs.'

'The man who keeps you to that station must be blind.'

That husky compliment produced a full flutter of the eyelashes. 'You flatter too outrageously, sir.'

'I assure you I do not.'

Perry held her gaze for a second, then called to his friend, who was still having trouble with Jane. 'Dunn, I have engaged to take Miss Lyon to Covent Garden.'

The look that earned Perry was singular, half envious, half triumphant. Perry continued, his voice now sounding hard. 'Of course, you and Miss Powell must accompany us, if only for the sake of propriety.'

Jane shook her head violently, which made Dunn frown. Emma whispered reassuringly to Perry. 'Let me talk to her. She is a nervous creature, and no doubt feels unsafe.'

'What nonsense,' Perry scoffed.

'Truly,' Emma said, again looking up into his eyes, her own wide and trusting, 'what could we possibly have to fear from two kind gents like you?'

'Not a thing.'

'But I fear to try and persuade her with both of you close by. Your friend Mr Dunn, while I'm sure he's a gent too, has not your way of easing people.'

'Miss Powell will find him as kind and generous as you will find me.'

'That is what I intend to tell her, sir.' She spun away before he could respond, going towards Jane and Owen Dunn. 'If you were to wait on the bridge, Mr Dunn, with Mr Perry, I will undertake to fetch Jane to you.'

'On the bridge?' Dunn demanded, as Perry came to join them.

'In the very middle.'

'How long?' asked Perry, in a firm confident voice.

Emma touched the back of his hand, happy to see the way his eyes reacted. 'Minutes, no more.'

Dunn was unconvinced, but Perry gave him a look that bespoke certainty. He bent over, took Emma's hand, raised it to his lips once more and, very elegantly, kissed it. Emma watched them as they strode away.

Perry tried not to look too cocksure, but his gait gave him away. Jane, on the other hand, was glaring at her. 'I don't care what you do, Emma Lyon, but I ain't going no place with that worm.'

'And neither am I with the other,' Emma replied, her eyes still fixed on their retreating backs.

'Then how in hell's name are we to get back to the house, with them in the middle of the bridge?'

Emma held out the hand that Perry hadn't kissed, showing the money they had gained from their singing. 'Bridges go over water, an' water goes under them.'

They started to sing their song as soon as the wherry came into the arc of the great lanterns that lined London Bridge. Expertly, the boatman took them right through the middle channel, where there were no shops to impede the view. And, since the river was high, they were no more than thirty feet from the two swains awaiting them. The singing made both look over to where Jane and Emma sat in the thwarts, waving gaily and blowing kisses. They shot under the arch, and as they came out on the other side, it was gratifying to see Perry and Dunn had crossed over too. That was when Perry, clearly laughing, blew them a kiss of his own.

'Perhaps,' Emma said, 'he wasn't so bad after all.'

'Stuff,' snapped Jane Powell, as she made a rude gesture with her fingers, aimed at Dunn.

The boatman dropped them off at the Blackfriars steps, moaning that sixpence was stretching it for such a journey, and prattling on about the mouths he had to feed. Both girls were in high spirits, and laughed in his face. The streets were quieter now, which had them trying fruitlessly to guess the time. They were very late, in danger of being locked out if Tooley or one of his boys had set the latch.

With much mutual shushing, they crept down the steps to the basement door, Emma silently lifting the latch and pulling a gap as the hinges creaked slightly. They were inside, the warmth of the kitchen a great relief. Both let out a deep sigh, which turned to a frightened start when Tooley said, 'Had a good night out have we?'

Tooley might have kept quiet, but the price of that silence would be too high for both girls. He never stated what it was, but the look in his eye and the increase in his familiarity left neither Emma nor Jane in any doubt that he would soon be creeping about their attic bedroom. It was Cath Lane who rescued them, once she had made them admit the nature of the hold Tooley exercised over them.

'Well, it will never do just to walk out, an' even worse if that sod lets on to Dr Budd about your shenanigans.'

'Tooley's getting right bold,' said Emma.

'You leave him to me. If'n he don't behave he'll be singing like a cathedral boy with his stones in a jar on my mantle.'

It was the housekeeper's idea that they leave one at a time, replaced by new housemaids so that the master wouldn't pay too much heed. What she said to Tooley they never found out, but it worked since he began to avoid rather than annoy them. Jane departed first, electing to go off with a touring band of players rather than stay in service. The truth never dawned on her or Emma that Cath Lane hadn't acted towards them out of pure kindness: she had her own interests at heart. What would it profit the housekeeper if the master or mistress found out that the girls she had chosen were a flighty pair inclined to night-time excursions?

'I fancy goin' to be an actress,' said Emma dreamily, 'like Jane has.'

'Actress!' Cath Lane spat. 'I don't call it that, fetchin' an carryin' for all and sundry for nowt but half the food you need to sustain you. If she ever gets on the boards it will be to sweep them. Travelling players? Vagabonds and thieves, I say. You can put the notion out of your head. I had word from your ma, and where you are goin' is already decided. Let me tell you it's better than what Jane Powell has managed.'

'Where?' Emma asked, in a dispirited voice.

'You're going to the family that owns Drury Lane, the housekeeper bein' a friend of old to both me and your ma. But you mind and remember you're going there to occupy the same station that you 'ad 'ere, so don't go getting any fancy ideas.'

'No, Cath,' Emma lied. 'Wouldn't want to upset my ma, now would I?'

But she mouthed 'Drury Lane', and though she had never seen the place she conjured up the image of a brilliantly lit palace, of crowded stalls and gilded boxes full of rich suitors. And, naturally, when the lights shone they shone on her.

CHAPTER 11

1774

Captain George Farmer, commanding officer of HMS *Seahorse*, was not a man lacking in influence. He had a ship in peacetime, unlike the majority of his peers. His 28-gun frigate had been attached to the squadron being assembled by Commodore Sir Edward Hughes for duty in the Indian Ocean, a commission that would certainly last three to four years. But when a senior captain like Maurice Suckling, with connections that heavily outweighed his, asked for a berth for his nephew, a positive response was in order.

The letter that had arrived with the boy a week before alluded to the experience he gained on his West Indian trip. It also told him that Midshipman Nelson had spent a year in the guardship *Triumph*; that he had newly returned from a voyage of scientific exploration to the polar ice cap, an attempt to find a passage through the northern ice that would take vessels from the Atlantic into the Pacific. Subsequent enquiries addressed to the officer who had commanded that expedition placed certain question marks over Nelson's suitability, which left George Farmer wondering, as he sat perusing the replies, whether he had been right to take him on board.

'Message from Mr Durrand, your honour,' said his steward, softly, holding out his hat. 'Hands are mustered to witness punishment.'

'Very well.'

His Majesty's frigate *Seahorse* was crewed by peacetime volunteers, but once they had signed up for service they belonged to the Navy. This was something the frigate's commanding officer was determined they should not be allowed to forget. There was no shore leave on a ship preparing for sea, which was frustrating when Portsmouth harbour was visible from their mooring, as was St Helen's on the Isle of Wight. But with so many parties bringing in stores a certain amount of absenteeism was inevitable, and so was the punishment if the offender was caught.

'Seize him up, Mr Caldwell,' said George Farmer, the minute he came on deck.

Nelson stood by the mainmast between two other midshipmen, Bertie and Troubridge, not sure in his heart if he wanted to witness what was about to happen. Bertie, small, plump, with a bland countenance, was the same age as Nelson, a Londoner with all the cockiness of that breed. This was his first ship, but few would know it from his attitude, though the prospect of watching a flogging silenced him somewhat. The oldest of the trio, Troubridge, dark complexioned with a hooked nose and hooded eyes, was muttering indistinct imprecations under his breath, leaving Nelson unsure if he was cursing those who would administer the punishment or the man who would receive it.

Called aft to witness punishment, the crew were lined up behind them along the gangways and behind the hammock cranes that cut off the waist. Even those in the boats had been called on deck so that they would not miss this example. The bosun, Caldwell, and two of his mates had grabbed the offender, a tough-looking individual called Mallory, and hauled him forward to lash him to the upright grating, placed above a square of canvas laid to protect the deck from dripping blood. Above him, the marines lined the poop, their red coats and white belts a bright slash even under the grey March sky. The second lieutenant, Stemp, who headed Mallory's division, was invited forward to speak on his behalf, so that punishment might be mitigated.

Nelson had heard that Mallory was a hard bargain, a bit of a brawler who had little time for officers and scant inclination to hide his attitude from them. It seemed obvious that Stemp didn't like him. His voice lacked conviction as he put forth the defence that Mallory had been tempted by drink, that if he had not been fetched back by the Portsmouth watchmen, he would have returned in due course of his own volition.

Captain Farmer was an avuncular looking creature with a benign face and pastel blue eyes, rather slight and stooped even in his full dress uniform. He responded in a voice as mild as his appearance. 'We really cannot have men running around Pompey, Mr Stemp, drinking and whoring when they should be attending to their duty. The Commodore berates us daily for our want of readiness. We must, in some measure, pass that on to the hands.'

As Stemp replied, 'Aye, aye, sir,' Nelson wondered whether a rousing speech and a call to responsibility might not achieve more than the use of the cat.

'Carry out the sentence, Bosun.'

The petty officer nodded to one of his mates, who opened the red baize bag. The other bosun's mate forced a leather strap into the prisoner's mouth to stop him biting off his own tongue. Every eye, Horatio Nelson's included, was on the cat as it came out and was flicked sharply to open it out. The nine slim tails, each with several knots along its length, hissed even at such a slow pace, making him shudder. He suppressed a gasp as the second bosun's mate stepped forward again and, adding a further indignity, ripped Mallory's shirt from his back, exposing flesh that bore the serrated scars of previous floggings.

'Another shilling for the bloody purser,' said one of Mallory's mates, as the garment came apart.

'Silence there!' shouted Durrand, the first lieutenant, pock-marked and bellicose, turning round to glare. 'Any more talking and the culprit will join Mallory at the grating.'

There had been plenty muttering when the sentence had been announced. Nelson had heard his mates say that Mallory would certainly have come back aboard – he was a man with no place else to go sobered up, ''ceptin his own hammock'. But there were others who opined that he should have known he was dealing with the Ploughman. In the few days he had been aboard, Nelson had learnt that Farmer, for all the bland look and relaxed manner, was a taut captain, a mite free with the cat, in which he was ably supported by his premier, Lieutenant Durrand.

The buzz of dissent had been silenced, but the gist of it, to the boy's ears, had been the same as the original complaints. 'Forty lashes might be due for running in wartime, and that for doing so foreign, but for a Pompey volunteer who liked a jug, it was comin' it too damned high.'

'Carry on,' said Captain Farmer.

Nelson closed his eyes after the first blow, which covered Mallory's back in thin red weals, but he couldn't shut his ears to the sound of the second. He forced himself to think of John Judd, to recall the way that seaman had discussed flogging, his opinion being that it was the way of the world and that there was nothing to be done to gainsay it. As each blow was completed he could hear the whispered responses from the men behind him.

Crack! 'Right on the same spot as three.'

Crack! 'Skin's gone.'

Crack! 'I bet that blood he's spillin' reeks of gin.'

Crack! 'There's a rib, I swear.'

'Concentrate on John Judd,' he said to himself, trying to block out the sounds with his old mentor's imagined voice.

Crack! 'Knees goin', though he held for a dozen.'

Crack! 'But never a sound out his lips.'

'You got to reckon,' Judd had insisted, 'what would be the result without the cat being let out of the bag. In a Navy ship there be ten times the crew of a merchant ship, an' that means twenty times the trouble. Thievin', men beaten half to death below for a sideways look, hard-case sodomites buggering the boys at will, and when you get into a sea fight no man prepared to stand by his gun. You got to have rigour, lad, or else you get Paddy's Market.'

Crack!

Nelson couldn't help himself. He opened his eyes and shut them again as he observed the minced condition of Mallory's back. But it wasn't that image which stayed with him: it was the calm look on the faces of the officers, allied to the naked, near greedy interest of the majority of the crew. He had seen the same expression on Troubridge's face. Try as he might, he could not shift that image from his mind, or the words and sounds he was hearing from his ears.

Crack! 'Wondered when that bastard Caldwell would begin to tire.'

Crack! 'He's been layin' to, an' that's for certain.'

Crack! 'Feart to lose his rating if he fakes it.'

Crack! 'Bollocks. He's showing away to the Ploughman.'

Crack! 'A word in his shell-like might be handy later. If he lays into me like that, I'll chuck the bugger overboard.'

Crack! 'Look out!'

Crack! 'Mr Foster, take that man's name who was talking.'

Even with his eyes shut Nelson recognised Durrand's voice, but which of the three to his rear who had been talking was a mystery. One eye cast behind revealed only a row of blank faces, with eyes set to the middle, innocent distance.

Crack! 'Aye, aye, sir.'

Crack! 'Poor bastard's passed out.'

Farmer could stop it, he had the right, but Nelson knew that would never happen.

Crack! 'An' he's still got more'n a dozen to take yet.'

Sailors to their fingertips, men who had probably endured an even worse existence before joining the Navy, they were the same stamp of men as John Judd, if not bred to the sea so accustomed to it that no other life would suit them. Once more he thought how much he admired them and wondered at the justice of the world he lived in. There was supposed to be honour in naval rank, but in the face of such butchery he wondered if natural distinction lay before the mast.

Nelson jerked fifteen more times before he heard the bosun say, 'Punishment complete, sir.'

'A damn fine flogging that!' stated Troubridge, emphatically.

'By God, yes,' added Bertie, speaking with little conviction. 'Almost up to a Tyburn jig.'

Horatio Nelson's stomach churned and he said nothing.

'Cut him down and take him below to be attended to,' said Durrand.

Nelson forced his eyes open, made himself look at the ripped skin and white bones, as well as the blood that ran down Mallory's legs. The bucket of seawater they used on him made it flow on to the canvas beneath his bare feet, which was already dark red. Caldwell, chest heaving, stood with the cat in his hands, oblivious to the shards of skin that hung off it, and to the blood that ran round his own feet. Mallory was dragged towards the companionway, the strap dropping from his mouth. Even at this distance the boy could see how deep were the bitemarks in the hard leather.

'Mr Nelson,' called Durrand, 'a party, at the double, to get this deck cleaned up.'

Farmer had already departed so Nelson didn't see how he had reacted to the sight of Mallory's back. But he knew, even after only a week aboard, that what had taken place would not have affected the Captain at all.

'Everyone else, return to your duties.'

Nelson called together a party of seamen and set them to sluicing the mess off the deck. As he watched the water-thinned blood run into the scuppers the excitement he had felt at joining a ship due to go on active service abated. It seemed now to be something to regret rather than celebrate.

Durrand's voice cut into his thoughts, and he turned to face him. 'Captain Farmer wishes to see you in his cabin in ten minutes.'

'Nelson,' Farmer said, then he paused, mouth slightly open. 'Yes.' He rubbed his hand over his chin as though he had lost any idea of why he had called the boy into his cabin.

He picked up a creased piece of paper from his desk. 'I had this letter from Captain Skeffington. You served with him on his polar voyage?'

'Yes, sir.'

The blue eyes held his, seeming to see into his soul, causing Nelson, for reasons he couldn't understand, to blush.

'Remind me,' he said, dropping the letter. 'What were you rated as?'

'Captain's servant, sir, aboard HMS *Carcass*.'

The stare from those pastel blue eyes was disconcerting, giving no clue to what the Captain was thinking. Farmer had heard about the trip to the northern ice cap a month before the two ketches had set out, and the stipulation had been quite plain. No boys! Yet this youngster before him had got himself aboard, no doubt through the intervention of his uncle. Now

Suckling had exercised that same influence to get his nephew another prized posting.

They would be the only King's ships in the Indian Ocean, a small fleet of four 74-gunners and half a dozen frigates. It was bound to be a long commission, in an area where the peace that held between Britain and France in Europe was tenuous. Sir Edward was an active officer, who, six thousand miles and several months away from direct instructions, would respond with vigour to any transgression he perceived against Britain's interests in the Far East, be it from the French in southern India, or from the Dutch in the Spice Islands. There might even be a chance of some action, which would do this youngster's prospects no harm at all.

'I require you to tell me about it.'

Farmer, for all his benign and absent-minded air, proved a keen interrogator, his enquiries so searching that Nelson felt the ground shift on several occasions, as he dug deep in his mind for the answer to questions he had never even considered. He soon discovered that this was unproductive, a simple admission of ignorance serving better than bluff. He answered questions regarding the crews and their behaviour, the changing colour of the sea related to the tidal flows. Which wind blew and at what strength to free *Carcass* from the encroaching ice? Did the penetrating cold have any effect on the ship's instruments of navigation?

Nelson described the journey north, the day they woke, sure by the change in the smell of the air that they were close to ice. Soon they were upon it, great sheets that glinted in the sunlight and turned green through the long Arctic night, itself punctuated with several sights of the *aurora borealis*, fiery and awe inspiring. Shifting winds and dropping temperatures that turned salt water solid so quickly it seemed like magic to the naked eye. Farmer was a good listener, only interrupting Nelson's tale when the boy waxed too lyrical.

'A decent war would put an end to all that stuff and nonsense. I'm all for a spirit of enquiry, Mr Nelson, if the purpose is sound, but a route to India past the glaciers is mere fancy. Any vessel that enters those waters is bound to become stuck fast in an ice sheet, which is precisely what happened to you. You were lucky to get out. Many before you, including experienced Greenland traders, have had to take to their boats.'

'We very nearly did so, sir. Captain Skeffington was set to abandon both vessels, and led an advance party out in the boats to map out a route. Those left behind were sleeping in full rig, ready to depart, when the wind shifted. I cannot tell you what a difference it created as the warmer air cracked the ice. Those who had been in battle said it was louder than a First Rate broadside.'

Farmer looked from under disapproving lids at that simile, his impression that the boy's tale was peppered with too much poetic licence never more obvious.

Nelson carried on hurriedly. 'Captain Skeffington had just returned from seeking passage when the ice began to break up. We set to with axes, and got the ships afloat. Then, when the fissures opened up enough, and under a steady north-north-east, we got underway. We caught up with Captain Skeffington's boats in two hours, to find them bobbing in clear, ice-free water, though it was a hard passage for us.'

'How much damage did the ships suffer?'

'The bows of *Carcass* were bereft of a lick of paint, and holed in two places so badly they had to be frapped with tarred canvas. I believe *Racehorse* was similarly affected.'

'Well, it was a fine thing to have gone there and got back again. Useless, but fine, and you've told your tale well.'

'Thank you, sir,' Nelson replied, looking at him with an air of confidence that had grown as he had related the story.

That was dented when Farmer picked up the letter again and frowned. 'On balance, Skeffington was pleased with you, said you were attentive to your duties, though he did allude to some tomfoolery with a bear.'

'Sir,' Nelson replied, blushing furiously now.

The hardening of the voice was almost imperceptible. 'Is that all you have to say, Nelson? I had hoped for an explanation.'

Nelson looked over Captain Farmer's powdered wig, his mind drifting back to that freezing morning and that ice-bound landscape. To him and his shipmate, Tom Floyd, the idea of shooting a bear had seemed reasonable. The lack of permission to leave the ship mattered little to boys their age. The certainty of success would vindicate them.

Captain Farmer continued, 'Why did you choose to leave the ship, when you'd been expressly ordered not to do so?'

A raft of excuses presented themselves to someone who had sought hard to find good grounds for what had been plain stupidity. At the same time, Nelson suddenly realised what this interview was about, and that knowledge brought a knot of cold fear to his stomach. Skeffington's letter would have told Farmer a great deal about the polar expedition. Even more was available in the account of the journey printed in the *Naval Chronicle*. The Captain didn't need him to relate the tale unless he wished to test his honesty. There was no other reason for that unless he was considering turfing him off the ship. The truth, foolish as it sounded even to him, was all he could rely on.

'I wanted a trophy for my father, sir.'

'A bear?'

'Just the skin and the head, sir, which would look very fine on the Parsonage wall. We'd seen the creature the day before, near our detritus, which was piled well away from the ship, so we knew it was about.'

'So you went out with a musket to kill it?'

'Yes, sir.'

'Tell me, Nelson, what do you think of this exploit now?'

He had felt shame in the night when he recalled it, and he felt that now as he replied, 'It was foolish in the extreme, sir. Seeing the animal at a distance, we had no idea of its true size.'

They had soon learnt when it rose up from the ice, over eight feet tall on hind legs, with massive jaws that looked big enough to bite either of the boys in half. It was too big to be felled by one musket ball, unless they managed to wound some vital spot.

'I read that you tried to down it with the butt of the weapon.'

'That was after I fired, sir.'

'And missed?'

He hadn't been trying to hit it with the butt, just to stop the beast from leaping across a crevasse in the glacier. They couldn't run without either he or Tom Floyd being caught.

Keeping that gap between themselves and the bear, which it would have had no trouble in crossing, afforded them all the protection they had from the beast. If Skeffington hadn't fired the signal gun to recall them, thus frightening it off, he doubted he would be here now giving this weak explanation.

'I dislike disobedience, Nelson,' said Farmer, looking down and tapping the desk with his fingers. 'I hope you know that by now.'

What had happened on deck not an hour previously left no doubt about that. 'I do, sir.'

'And escapades of this nature will not be tolerated. Being a nephew to Captain Suckling affords you many advantages, but if you are to satisfy his desires and become a commissioned officer, you must show more self-discipline. You do yourself desire this, I take it?' Farmer looked hard at him, as if this needed to be confirmed.

'It is my earnest wish, sir,' Nelson replied, not sure that he was telling the truth. What he was sure of was his fear of being sent packing, then having to face his uncle and his father.

The silence lasted several seconds, as George Farmer considered his options: to take this young man to sea with him and risk whatever trouble that might cause, or to send him back to a well-connected uncle who might take that as a personal insult. Though not tall or broad of shoulder the youngster looked fit, healthy and eager. And there was an air of guileless sincerity about him.

'Very well,' Farmer said finally. 'Return to your duties. But be warned, Mr Nelson, I have my eye on you.'

'Thank you, sir,' he replied.

'Come and have a look, Nelson,' said Troubridge, hauling on Nelson's arm to drag him towards the sickbay. The sailor who had just pushed past the pair had carried a mess kid, and the smell of the scouse, like that of beef dripping, had wafted up into his nostrils to linger with the stench of the bilge. 'They're dressing Mallory's back.'

The attempt at resistance was brief, a momentary tug of war between fear and pride that lasted no more than a split second. Nelson allowed himself to be led towards the murmuring that was coming from the tiny cubicle. The canvas screen had been left open, and Mallory lay face down on a cot, a lantern beside him to illuminate his condition. Nelson felt the hot, acid bile rise in his throat as he looked at the mashed flesh. The loblolly boy was applying the scouse to the defaulter's back. The raw flesh glowed as if it had a life of its own; a separate hellish entity that shone and flickered as Mallory took deep, painful breaths.

Suddenly he arched his back, showing the faintest trace of the exposed white bones. His jaw was as taut as a bowstring, teeth biting hard into the leather strap that had been replaced in his mouth. But Mallory was aware of his surroundings, and as his head turned in agony he spotted the two youngsters filling the doorway. Nelson was fighting to avoid retching, but he registered Troubridge's deep interest. The most compelling image, however, was Mallory's grin, which seemed to change from a rictus of suffering to a terrible satanic smile.

Conscience made Nelson visit the sickbay the day after the flogging, glad that Mallory's back was now covered with a sheet. The sailor remained face down, and was still in some pain, though he had dispensed with the leather strap. His eyes, alert and suspicious, fixed on Nelson as soon as he appeared in the doorway, and watched him while he sought permission from the surgeon's mate to enter, then moved the few feet to the table.

'I brought you this,' he said, holding out a straw-covered flask, aware that his voice sounded nervous.

Mallory looked first at it, then at him, with little in the way of gratitude. Nelson felt the tremor in his voice even more as he continued. 'It is brandy, which I hope will help to ease the pain.'

The pause seemed long, though it was only a few seconds. Then Mallory pushed himself on to his elbows. Balancing on one, he took the bottle with his free hand and inspected it, his eyes conveying a clear lack of faith. 'If this be some mid's berth joshing I'll have your hide.'

'What do you mean?' Nelson was stunned by his ingratitude.

'It ain't beyond you lot to piss in a bottle like this and pass it on to an unsuspecting soul.'

Nelson was so shocked he spoke without thinking. 'Would I do that after I put you in my prayers last night?'

'Your prayers, boy? An' just what was it you was praying for?'

Nelson blushed, well aware of what the sailor was alluding to. 'Your full recovery to health was what I asked from God, and a remission of your sins.'

Mallory grinned and the youngster anticipated a jeer. But the sailor's voice, though harsh, was uncritical. 'Then you must be close to the Maker, lad, 'cause he would have told you that this is what Mallory would see as like a pardon.' Mallory passed back the flask.

'You don't want it?'

'Course I do,' Mallory replied, moving painfully. 'But I be in dire straits when it comes to haulin' out that fuckin' cork, savin' your presence.'

The surgeon's mate, who had been watching this exchange in silence, spoke. 'Best leave that to me, young 'un, otherwise this no-good sod will down the lot and rate himself another dose of the cat.'

Mallory's response contained real venom. 'You can stuff yourself, mate. If'n you get your hand on that, I'll scarce see a drop of what's inside.'

'How long before you're on your feet?' asked Nelson, hurriedly, as he broke the wax seal.

'Another day, an' then it'll be light duties for a week.'

'We might be at sea by then.'

Mallory took the bottle, tipped his head sideways, and drank a quarter of the contents. He handed the bottle back to his benefactor. His initial anger and suspicion had evaporated in the face of plain goodwill. It was not something he had experienced much in his twenty-five years but he could recognise it when he saw it. This youngster, with his innocent expression and honest blue eyes, genuinely cared, which brought a lump to the sailor's throat. A racking cough covered it as he spoke. 'You care for this. It's like to make me sleep, and as soon as I close my eyes the rest'll vanish down the first throat that nabs it.'

Nelson wanted to say that would not be the case, yet he knew from what Judd had told him about Navy ships that it would. A small merchant crew was one thing but three hundred Navy tars in a hull this size quite another. 'Would you like me to fetch it back to you tomorrow?'

'No, lad,' Mallory replied, his voice friendly now. 'I'll be in luck to get through this commission without another kiss of the gratin'. Save it for then, eh?'

'I do so hope that isn't true.'

'Get away with you boy,' Mallory growled, forced to turn away his head lest young Nelson see the tear in his eye.

Nelson's relationships on the ship were generally good. Many who shared the cramped accommodation of the midshipmen's berth had been serving longer than him, one a hopeless case who would never rise above his present station. But few had put in his sea time, which gave him an authority that was impossible to overcome. Troubridge, although cursed with a choleric nature, had become his friend; he might swear more than was strictly necessary, and use harsh words where soft ones would have served, but he was kindly underneath, and had endeared himself to his new messmate by the way he had stood up for the smaller boys in the berth.

So there were no more than the normal run of disputes. He had settled in easily, finding his niche in the hierarchy without difficulty, while making it plain that he was now too much of an oldster to be practised upon by the common midshipman's pranks.

Not that there was time for any such thing. They were kept busy, with the Commodore firing off endless requests for statements of readiness to get to sea. Not that the officers, masters and pursers were laggardly; being in port cost everyone money, so a desire to get to sea and make some instead of spending it was built into the system, while the dockyards, as well the Ordinance and Victualling Boards, who wished to husband what they held, had a keen interest in delay. They were therefore eager to query, several times, any request for spars, sails, spare canvas, powder and shot, beef, pork and peas in casks, fresh provisions and water, along with all the thousand other items it took to provision a ship of war for a voyage of several month's duration.

The new midshipman had his duties aloft, supervising the rigging of the ship's top hamper. He had to ensure that the clewlines and bunts were in place, that the lanyards were free to run; preventer stays tight to the jeer blocks that ran round the mast, getting to know those men for whom he would be responsible at sea. They were a cheerful bunch who sought to guy him, quick to notice that he took such in good heart and would often laugh as heartily as the men who had played the joke.

He was Nellie from the first day, and liked for his willingness, not least to learn from men who knew more than he did about how to go about rigging the mass of ropes, blocks and pulleys. They were all nimble, these topmen, young pigtailed individuals who took pride in their ability to do their task with a laugh.

He had the added responsibility of Thomas Bertie who, apart from being 'damned cocky', was as green as it was possible to be, though so willing he was a danger to himself. Working aloft was a gradual process, where risk had to be balanced against experience. Bertie wanted to go from knowing nothing to doing everything, so was constantly in receipt of instructions to 'Belay that damned nonsense, lest you're minded to kiss the deck at speed.' Greasy and black from head to foot, both youngsters were happy. Busy all day, they were kept apart, so when they met hunger was the common glue of their existence. Nelson had his likes and dislikes but on balance he rated his mess a happy one.

So it never occurred to him to wonder if his act of charity had been observed. Even less did he imagine that it might be misinterpreted. Needless to say it was Midshipman Bertie, too cocky to guard his tongue, who made the first unfortunate crack.

'Like 'em rough, do you, Nellie?'

Still lost in his own thoughts from talking to Mallory, Nelson missed the point of the allusion. But the knowing look and the rocking of the hips that accompanied Bertie's next remark, added to the grins on the faces of the others present in the mid's berth, didn't leave much room for doubt.

'Nothing like a bit of pain to get your pecker rampant, eh?

Daresay your next meeting with Mallory will be someplace quiet.'

The blow, a full tight fist, caught Midshipman Bertie right on the nose. Nelson had a vision of startled eyes before the blood began to flow in copious, satisfying quantities.

CHAPTER 12

Prevarication could last only so long, and even the various boards had to succumb to the pressure of the Admiralty. They wanted Sir Edward Hughes and his squadron at sea, on his way to relieve the ships that had now been on station in eastern waters for two and a half years. Nelson was on deck, ready to go aloft on the great day, impressed by the band playing on the hard, as well as the presence of several senior officers come aboard to see them off.

He was first to the shrouds when the order came to weigh, and from aloft he looked down on the quarterdeck to see Captain Farmer stagger till he clasped the binnacle. Having been entertaining or indulged by others for a full twelve hours, he was in no fit state to command a ship's longboat. Not that he tried. He stood on the quarterdeck trying to make his swaying look as if it was caused by the ship's motion rather than half a dozen bottles of claret.

Red-faced admirals were heading back to the Portsmouth sally port. As they landed the signal gun spoke from the Round Tower, a plume of white smoke preceding the boom. This was only a second ahead of that on the flagship HMS *Ramilles*. Signals broke out instantly at the masthead and on each deck the first lieutenants raised their hats to their commanding officers and set in train the actions that would not only get every vessel to sea but also allow their captains to return to their cabins and sit down.

Nelson, still waiting for his orders, watched the crowds that lined the ramparts, waving their scarves and handkerchiefs in time to the music of the band. Below decks the men began to move to that same rhythm, the off duty watch and the marines at the capstan, straining to haul HMS *Seahorse* over her anchor, a thousand tons of inert timber, guns, stores and a three-hundred-man crew, heaving till the call came that she was 'thick and dry'.

Durrand, head held back and speaking trumpet to his lips, called aloft to let fall the maintopsail, which followed as the bunts were released by the singular sound of falling canvas, like the slow wing-beat of a gigantic bird. The canvas beneath Nelson's feet changed quickly from a creased shapeless mass to a thing of white beauty, as the wind took the sail, billowing it out until it was as taut as a drum. A turn of the head saw the frigate fetch her anchor, sailing slowly over it so that it could be plucked from the bed of the sea.

'Anchors aweigh, sir,' came the cry.

'See it catted and fished,' called the first lieutenant, as the free anchor was hauled up on the cathead, well clear of the side of the ship, prior to being securely lashed. On the deck below, men were struggling with a wet, slimy hawser while on slippery planking, boys threw fast loops to attach it to the messenger cable so that it could be brought inboard and laid, head to tail, in front of the stout wooden bitts that held fast to the end. Every other ship in the squadron had carried out the same manoeuvre, creating, to a young, impressionable eye, a wondrous vision of a fleet going to sea. Sure it was a small one, but it was impressive nevertheless.

'Mr Nelson,' called Lieutenant Durrand, his voice a loud growl, 'I will thank you to attend to the fore topgallant sail, and to cease your damned daydreaming.'

He did as he was ordered, but it was hard. He had never seen so many ships put to sea at once: majestic two-deckers, several frigates, down to a couple of scampering sloops, all encouraged by the music of a band. That and a thousand relations, a great many of them wives who would be weeping with the fear that they might never see their loved ones again. He thought of his own family, his sisters and brothers, even his father, which brought a tear to his own eye and a rasping comment from his neighbour on the yard. 'Belay them tears, Nellie lad, for if they hit the premier's fresh-swabbed deck, he'll have your guts.'

Seahorse heeled over as the wind took enough of her sails to bring a tilt to her deck. Looking down, he saw the water running down the lee side of the ship, deep, green and cold . . .

Blue and warm and startlingly phosphorescent, the water was now even deeper, as the frigate ploughed through the great swell of the Indian Ocean. The crew of the *Seahorse* were now so practised in their sail drill that they could bend on a sail, take it in or reef it in their sleep. Durrand, his pockmarked face bereft of the ability to smile, might be a bad-tempered martinet but the ship ran well enough to be termed a crack frigate by the Admiral, one that could be detached for special duty when the need arose.

They had crossed the line so long ago that it seemed like a distant memory, all the numerous candidates for the ceremony daubed and ridiculed as they made their first foray into the southern hemisphere. The Cape of Good Hope, where they had taken on wood and water, had come and gone, as had Mauritius and La Reunion. Ceylon was behind them and the flagship had set her bowsprit well to the east so that the squadron would master the currents and winds that would carry them on to the Bay of Bengal and the mouth of the Hoogly. He learnt this from the man responsible for teaching him seamanship, the master of the *Seahorse*, Emmanuel Surridge.

'For failure to do so, Nelson,' Surridge said, as they carried out their fifth consecutive night of lunar observations, 'would see us hauled up westerly and foul of the Maldives.'

'Yes, Mr Surridge.'

'Tell me what that would mean, young man.'

There was no attempt to trap him in the question, just a desire to ensure that his pupil had absorbed all that he had been taught. Nelson had come to admire his teacher for the depth of his knowledge, the extent of his curiosity and to esteem him for his kindness and patience.

'Coral reefs and sandbars, sir, many of them uncharted and deadly danger to a ship's hull on a night without a moon, especially with any kind of wind blowing.'

'Now, sir, lay me a course to avoid that by taking a fix on Venus and the Orion's belt.'

John Judd had taught him to hand and reef aboard the *Swanborough*. Emmanuel Surridge had added spherical trigonometry, lunar and astrological observation, mathematical considerations about the consumption of stores related to the state of the frigate's trim, plus a thousand other points of learning required by a sailor. The process of assimilation was almost unnoticeable, and only the thickness of the boy's journals betrayed how much knowledge he had acquired.

Captain Farmer entertained them in rotation, an occasion for the ever-hungry midshipmen to fill themselves at a more well endowed table, and to drink more than was good for their young heads. Nelson was no exception, happy to let the conversation pass him by as long as he could keep his mouth full. On this occasion he had been invited along to hear in which position he was now going to serve, it having been decided that he had spent enough time aloft to be fully competent.

If he had thought the Captain didn't notice his greed then he was wrong, since Farmer posed a question just as he stuffed three slices of tough roast beef into his mouth. His attempt to reply was inaudible, and sent flying several pieces of meat.

'We must do something about your manners before we raise Calcutta, Nelson. And not just yours!'

'Slur,' Nelson replied, a wad of beef stuck in his gullet.

'Every midshipman I have aboard is the same,' he said to Durrand.

The premier, Durrand, responded with his habitual scowl, which looked even worse than it had previously on his peeling face. Nelson knew that the sun had not been kind to him on the voyage: it had left his visage, pock-marked under the shards of skin, looking like a piece of upholstery scratched by a cat.

Farmer had turned his attention back to his still chewing young guest. 'Once we anchor, Nelson, there will be a great deal of social activity, some of which might be of benefit to you – not that I want to deny you the common whorehouse, if that is your wish. I'm told the Bengal bawds are a cut above their English counterparts, perfumed, gentle creatures unlike the brutes you'd find in a home seaport.'

Surridge, also a guest, coughed slightly, to remind his

commander, whose voice had grown wistful, that he had strayed off his point.

'Quite!' said Farmer, recovering himself. 'I daresay it would be futile to hope that any of my midshipmen's manners should improve, since none of the young men I have aboard seem to possess an ounce of that commodity, have they, Surridge?'

Surridge replied with a heavy nod. 'I've often had occasion myself to bemoan the lack of polish in the mid's berth.'

'Shockin', Surridge! God help the Calcutta whores when they get that lot between their thighs, eh! I doubt the perfume will suffice to kill off the smell. And as for gentility they'll not last two grains of sand. And what am I to do with them in polite society, I don't know. Weren't like that in my day. We were born to be gentlemen and knew how to behave like one.'

He gave Nelson a hard look, just as the youngster managed to shift the last lump of his meat to one side of his mouth. 'That's what I'd like to see from you.'

'I'll do my best, sir.'

Farmer had leant forward and was peering at Nelson's bulging cheek. 'For God's sake, boy, get rid of that lump.'

The knock was so slight it was almost inaudible, and the door opened swiftly to reveal the round red face of Thomas Troubridge. 'Flag signalling, sir. Squadron to make more sail, dipped three times.'

Surridge had already made to leave, since that meant the Admiral apprehended danger, and Farmer had lost his vagueness. The eyes that had seemed sleepy were lively now. 'Anything from the masthead?'

'Nothing, sir,' Troubridge replied.

'If the best eyes are not aloft already, get them there.'

'Sir!'

'And my compliments to Mr Stemp, he is to comply with the signal.' The eyes were on Nelson next. 'What are you still doing here? Get about your duties!'

In the background Nelson could hear the cry of 'All hands'. Before that would have meant him going aloft, but he'd been removed from that station. 'With respect, sir, I'm not sure what my duties are.'

'You may act today as my aide. Mr Durrand, I would like things put in hand to clear for action.'

By the time Farmer appeared on deck they had heard the dull boom of distant gunfire. Every eye was straining to see the source of that sound, with the officers occasionally glancing aloft at the two men who occupied the masthead. Surridge was yelling orders through his speaking trumpet to the men aloft, while on deck canvas was coming up from below, sails to be laid out ready for bending on to the yards.

Seahorse was racing along, her deck canting to the angle of a steep-pitched roof, her bowsprit digging into the heavy swell of the Indian Ocean, throwing up a great mass of water. *Ramilles* and the other 74s were striving likewise, but their bulk slowed them down compared to the frigate, and Farmer had to shorten sail to remain on station.

Nelson felt as if his entire skin was itching, so quickly was the blood racing through his veins. All the ships in the squadron had a full suit aloft now. The sloop *Vixen* – on point duty – which had raised the alarm, had gained on everyone, increasing the gap between herself and the fleet, seemingly determined to get to the centre of the action first.

'Flagship signalling, sir,' said Durrand.

'What does he say?' Farmer asked Troubridge, who was now the signalling midshipman.

'Difficult to make out, sir. The wind is angling the flags away from us.'

'*Vixen* shortening sail, sir,' added Durrand, a telescope fixed to his eye.

'Flagship's orders being repeated by *Euraylus*, sir,' said Troubridge pointing to another frigate, then consulting his book to make sense of the message. He nearly screamed the order as Sir Edward's signal became clear. 'Flag is making our number, sir. The message reads, "Make all sail".' Everyone on board the vessel was watching as that set of coloured pennants disappeared and a fresh lot was sent aloft. 'General chase due east.'

'Mr Surridge,' said Farmer, calmly, 'I want the very best you can give us.'

'Aye, aye, sir.'

The next hour was a whirlwind of activity, as yards and sails were set up in an endless stream. Nelson was sent dashing in all directions with messages to the various divisional officers, all the time aware of what the master was about, trying to second guess each alteration to the sail plan before it was made, happy that he managed to anticipate about half of what occurred.

Studdingsail booms were lashed on, to be pushed out from the main yards, the canvas they carried spreading well beyond the side of the ship. Royals and Kites were hauled up to take what wind there was at the very top of the masts. *Vixen*, too lightly armed to go on alone, spilled the wind from her sails then joined company as the two ships opened up the gap between themselves and the rest of the squadron. The log was cast continuously, as Surridge trimmed sails, added to one side and subtracted from another, until, on the even Indian Ocean breeze, and taking account of the leeway, he had achieved the maximum speed.

'By damn, twelve knots, sir,' he called, as the log was heaved again.

'Thank you, Mr Surridge,' Farmer replied.

Nelson now stood beside Farmer on the quarterdeck, balancing himself against the motion of the ship, left leg extended to hold his position on the canted deck, right dipping to absorb the motion of the swell. Spray washed his face continuously, blown over the bows to hang in the air as *Seahorse* ploughed on through it. Cool as it was, it did nothing to dampen the excitement he felt, or the feeling that this was where he belonged.

It was what he had dreamed of in that cold coach that first took him to Chatham, the image of himself in command of a warship going into battle. It was the stuff of endless speculation among the youngsters he messed with; would they one day rise to a captain's rank? On this deck now it was easy to forget the presence of Farmer and imagine himself in the role of which he dreamed, to transpose their respective stations and conjure up the notion that he was issuing the orders. He would, God willing, rise to command, and when he did, he would be a better captain than the man he was standing by, at this moment, to serve.

Farmer's eyes were fixed on the scene ahead, an East India merchant vessel that had fought off a pirate assault long enough for the attacker to realise that warships were coming to the rescue. Still partly obscured by smoke the attackers had been close to success. The Indiaman's bulwarks showed several jagged areas where they were stove in, and what sails she had aloft were shot full of holes. Obviously the enemy had lain off her stern, out of the arc of her guns, firing through the casements of the main cabin, which were so shattered as to be non-existent.

The enemy must have been close to the point of boarding through that very cabin, but had disengaged as soon as they spotted *Vixen*'s skysails, running before the wind to make an escape. The East Indiaman cheered first *Vixen* then *Seahorse* as they went by, with all the officers raising their hats to each other in salute. But Nelson observed that blood was running out through the scuppers, and through the shattered sides he could see bodies strewn on the deck, proving that it had been a close-run thing.

'Signal the flag, Mr Durrand,' said Farmer. 'Enemy in sight, am engaging.'

Those last words proved to be at best premature. The ships they were pursuing turned out to be a couple of *Chasse Marées*, small, compact vessels with narrow lines and a low freeboard designed for speed. They were fore and aft rigged, so on their present course the square rigger lost a great deal of the advantage of being able to put aloft more sail. A wind dead aft meant that the maincourse took pressure off the forecourse, which in turn deprived the inner and outer jib, while to come off the wind slightly so that they could draw meant that *Seahorse* had to tack and wear in pursuit. Farmer decided to split with the sloop, himself taking a more southerly course, while *Vixen* trended north. That would create a triangle with the British ships at the base and the chase at the apex.

'Mr Surridge, we require subterfuge. I want plenty aloft, but I would wish them not to draw too efficiently. They have seen us struggle in their wake, let them see us wallow a trifle on a more favourable course.'

'If I could be appraised of your intentions, Captain?'

'We could stay on this course for days, if the wind stays true, and we'll lose them for sure. Their home port has to be north towards the Kerala peninsula. I want them to turn that way assuming that only *Vixen* stands between them and safety. Let them also believe that even with the most favourable wind we could never catch them.'

'Would they not have seen our true ability as we bore down on the action?'

There was a touch of impatience in Farmer's reply. Nelson surmised that the master had asked one question too many, exceeding his duty in that respect and annoying a man who disliked having to explain himself.

'That I cannot tell, Surridge. I'm hoping they were too busy to note it. Now you will oblige me by complying with my request so that I may discover if I have the right of things.'

Surridge took the rebuke well, having achieved his purpose, this being that all the men on the ship should know what was required. And Captain Farmer could not have had a better ship's crew for such a task. Nelson watched carefully as Surridge, employing skills honed over many years, did as he was asked. Now the idea of one sail interfering with the efficiency of another was deliberate, the canvas behind spilling just enough of the breeze to keep the one ahead taut, so that it looked as though it was drawing well, when in fact it was working at only three quarters of its capacity.

'Who do you think they are, sir?' asked Durrand.

'French dogs, for certain,' Farmer snapped, 'with local Indian crews, either out of Madras or Pondicherry.'

'Since we are at peace, they have engaged in piracy.' Durrand's peeling face showed real pleasure as he added, 'We can hang them.'

'There's no peace out here, Durrand, regardless of what happens in Europe. The best you can hope for is an armed truce, and those ahead of us have just broken it.'

Farmer threw back his head and shouted to the men in the

crosstrees. 'Keep an eye on the enemy decks. As soon as you see them prepare to alter course, I want to know.'

Nelson, who had considered George Farmer as bit of a duffer, was now looking at him with open admiration. The Captain's eyes were alight, and his whole frame seemed infused with a new spirit of animation. Horatio Nelson would be a kinder captain than Farmer, less inclined to employ the cat, but he would settle for the same competence as a sailor.

'Mr Surridge, I will require an increase in speed on this course, since I intend to deny them the opportunity, if they make an error, to correct it.'

'The chase is manning the braces, Captain,' the lookout called.

Nelson strained to see, but from his position on the deck, with a running sea creating waves fifteen feet high, he only glimpsed the two enemy ships when all three vessels crested at the same time. But he could imagine the men on the ropes, half an eye on the pursuing frigate, the other on their own captain, waiting for the orders that would change their course.

'Mr Surridge,' said Farmer.

'Aye, aye, sir,' the master replied. Having discussed what would happen next more words were superfluous. The main course was goose-winged into a triangle, the raised corner allowing the wind full play forward. Braces were tightened and yards trimmed so that every one drew, with the driver boom, holding the fore and aft gaff sail, hauled to leeward to take full advantage of the wind.

'Enemy going about, sir,' said Durrand. There was then a moment while he waited for them to sheet home again on their new course. 'Heading north-north-east.'

'Mr Troubridge, a signal to *Vixen*, if you please, to read, "Disengage, course north-north-east". Mr Surridge, stand by to go about. Mr Nelson, a message to the gunner. I intend a mixture of bar and case shot to be ready and loaded as soon as we clear. Tell him I require double charges to make them fly.'

'Sir,' Nelson replied crisply, running for the companionway. Desperate not to miss anything on deck he raced to the lower depths, hauling back the wetted screen on the hanging magazine to relay Farmer's order.

'Belay there, you daft swab,' the gunner growled. He was bent over, sorting charges by the glimmer of candlelight that filtered through the glass window. 'Don't you know better, boy, than to rush in here when there's powder laying about?'

'Sorry,' Nelson replied, before delivering the Captain's message. He got back to the deck just in time to hear Farmer order the new course. The chase was now off the starboard beam, with *Seahorse* at the end of a near straight line drawn from *Vixen*, through the two *Chasse Marées*.

The months at sea paid off now as the *Seahorse* came about almost in her own length. The deck was a mass of men hauling and running, first easing the ropes that held the yards in place, then, as the rudder bit and the ship began to turn, pulling even harder to tighten them at an angle to the wind, which was now coming in right over the frigate's quarter. Surridge was yelling and waving his arms, calling for a mass of adjustments, some tiny, others major, so that he could get the best out of the top hamper.

Farmer, immobile through all this, waited until *Seahorse* was settled on the new course, until the master himself, taking the wheel, nodded to say he was satisfied, before turning to Durrand. 'I think we may now clear for action.'

They pursued the *Chasse Marées* for hour after hour, the distance closing imperceptibly, while ahead of the enemy *Vixen* barred their escape. Having overheard the discussion, Nelson knew that Captain Farmer had no intention of exposing *Vixen* to a fight with two of the enemy. In such a small fleet and far from home the number of ships had to be maintained. Capture of these two pirate vessels would avail little if the sloop was rendered useless in the process.

Both the enemy helmsmen were good, as were the crews, quick to see an extra puff of wind or a path through the run of the seas that would keep them clear. The hands were fast workers when it came to slight alterations to the set of a sail, the combined skills keeping them out of danger for longer than Captain Farmer had thought possible.

As the sun began to sink, they saw the enemy trying to lighten their ships, throwing overboard anything deemed unnecessary to survival; water, food and personal possessions that bobbed on the water until the frigate ploughed through them. Having eased away from the Captain, Nelson had questioned Surridge as to what was likely to happen.

'He won't request *Vixen* to haul her wind unless the pirates throw overboard their guns. She will stay ahead of them, avoiding battle until we can overhaul.'

'But it will be night soon.'

'Aye, lad, and if you look at the sky you'll see nary a cloud. There's a moon due, and that will be bright enough for us to work by.'

'Why don't they change course?'

'Because, no matter which way they turn, the wind and leeway favour one of our ships. And that wind can hold steady for a week in these parts. They should have held to the west and run for two days, if need be, to get clear, waited for a dark night to go about and get home safe.'

'How long, sir?'

'See that one that's a touch laggardly?' he answered, pointing to the rearward enemy ship. 'We'll have him within long gunshot by dawn.'

'Mr Nelson,' called Farmer, 'gun crews to worm every second cannon. Please go round the officers and tell them to split their men into watches. Two hours' sleep each.'

'What about food, sir?' asked Durrand. 'They have not been fed.'

That remark surprised Nelson, who had always thought Durrand a hard-case premier who would see the men suffer rather than appear soft.

'Neither have we!' Farmer snapped, proving where the indifference lay, also killing any hope that the cook might be able to re-light his coppers. 'Give them cold water and biscuit.'

Night turned slowly to day, the sky full of moon and stars fading to a cold grey before the orange ball of the sun lit the western horizon. The first bow chaser fired, at extreme range, just after four bells in the morning watch, by which time any enthusiasm for what was to come had evaporated among the crew. They were hungry, and so was Nelson. And he was tired, not having been allowed to leave the deck all night. The ball skipped across the waves, dropping short on the second vessel's stern. Immediately the two ships changed course, heading in opposite directions.

Surridge was yelling again, bringing them round in the lead ship's wake, while a signal went out to *Vixen* to engage the other. The frigate was closing fast on her quarry. And since they knew their fate the pirates were determined to fight, lining the side in the low, brilliant sunlight and casting off their guns.

'Six pounders, Durrand,' said Farmer. 'I doubt we have much to fear from those.'

'Shall I reload the wormed cannon, sir?'

'No. Put the men into a boarding party, to gather on the forepeak. You, Mr Durrand, may lead it.'

The premier's cratered face positively glowed. If the ship was taken by his boarding, the honour would belong as much to him as to Captain Farmer. And if the Admiral at Calcutta bought it into the service, he might even get it as his first command.

'Message to Mr Foster, Nelson,' Farmer said. 'I want his maindeck cannon aimed well forward. He's to clear those swine away from their guns so that when we touch Mr Durrand can board.'

Going forward to relay this allowed Nelson to look over the hammock nettings. He could see several Europeans clustered around the enemy wheel, in breeches and shirts, but the rest of the crew were dark skinned, wearing nothing but white cloths around their loins.

By the time he was back on the quarterdeck, the range had shortened and Durrand had his party ready. Slowmatch smoke drifted up from below, the smell of saltpetre lingering on the nostrils. But that disappeared as Farmer gave the order to fire.

Nelson felt the vibrations through his feet, as the whole ship shuddered, the result of half a dozen guns going off at two-second intervals, sending a frisson of fear through him, not helped as, simultaneously, the balls from the *Chasse Marée* thudded into the frigate's side planking. The boom was deafening, the great cloud of greasy black smoke rising to obscure the target. Surridge, on the command, put the helm hard down, so that *Seahorse* ran alongside the chase. A second salvo was exchanged, the pirates aiming high at the elevated bulwarks of the frigate. Durrand, standing on the hammock right by the forward shrouds yelling to his men, took a ball that went right through him. Even over the din of battle, Nelson could hear him scream in agony, before he dropped back on to the deck, twitching like a freshly stuck pig.

Farmer's voice seemed devoid of emotion, even though he had just seen his first lieutenant killed. 'Ask Mr Stemp to take over the boarding party, Nelson. You take his place on the guns, which are only to fire if the chase looks like getting clear.'

Going below to the maindeck was to enter a different world, darker, full of smoke and sweating men, the only radiance coming in through the open gunports, streaks of sunlight on the red-painted deck. The crews were kneeling by their pieces and only the gun captains stood, crouched, peering through at the target, which was now a few feet away.

'What do I do, sir?' he asked Stemp, as the lieutenant hurried away.

'Fire them one at a time, and let the gun captains do the aiming.'

'What else, sir?' he shouted to the retreating back.

'Stay clear of the recoil, or you'll forfeit a leg.'

Every time the frigate's bows rose he could see the enemy's side, splintered and broken where the guns had struck home. Above his head, he heard the yells of the men getting ready to jump for the side. He was in command, with only the sketchiest idea what to do. True he had orders, but they were so vague as to be useless. Suddenly there was a voice in his ear. 'It's all over bar the shouting, young Nellie.'

He turned to look into Mallory's smiling face. Clearly he was the gun captain on the number one piece.

'Durrand's gone, cut in two by a ball.'

'That's no loss,' Mallory spat on the deck.

'Belay that, Mallory,' he shouted, offended. 'I'm in charge of this division now.'

'Nellie,' Mallory replied, unfazed, his face splitting into a grin, 'you've gone and joined the enemy.'

Nelson looked set to protest, but Mallory slapped him on the back. 'Had to come 'cause of the coat you wear. Never mind, when you'se high and mighty, lad, don't you forget your old shipmates.'

The ships, crunching into each other, killed any chance of a reply. Mallory ordered his gun pulled inboard, grabbed the wormer and poked himself half out of the gunport, jabbing at something unseen, the muscles in his scarred back flexing with each stroke. He blocked any view that his newest young gentleman had had of what was going on. All Nelson could hear were the muffled sounds, metal on metal particularly, accompanied by banshee-like screaming. Suddenly it went quiet for a split second, then a great cheer rent the air, some of it coming through the ports but the majority from the upper deck.

'Come on, Nellie,' called Mallory, tugging at his coat sleeve and heading for the companionway.

'Have we won?'

'How could we fail? It weren't no more'n a smack. Mind, old Farmer will carry on as if it were a ship of the line when he dines with the Admiral.'

Everyone was pouring up on to the deck. Hesitating for only a second, Nelson followed, to be greeted by the sight of a British Ensign being raised on the *Chasse Marée*'s mainmast. The boom of distant gunfire reminded them of *Vixen* and the task she had to perform, which was more difficult given her size.

'Belay that damned cheering,' yelled Farmer, before shouting across to the enemy deck. 'Mr Stemp, you will take possession of the prize. Mr Surridge, shape me a course to join *Vixen*.'

'Three huzzahs for Captain Farmer.'

Nelson didn't recognise the voice, but the cry was instantly taken up. He was standing close to Mallory's back, so close that each stroke of the cat seemed like a separate etching or ridge in the re-formed skin. But the tough gunner was cheering like everyone else, and for the man who had bestowed his scars, which made Nelson wonder where sense started and excitement ended. Mallory should surely hate the Captain more than any man alive. When he turned, the sailor provided the answer to why he was cheering. 'There's money, Nellie,' he whooped.

'Good coin to make our Calcutta visit one to recall in old age. I'll pay you back for that brandy you fetched me.'

'Nelson,' shouted Farmer, 'what the devil are you doing away from your station?'

'Sir,' he cried, before turning to Mallory, his face flushed: 'Get the men back on the guns.'

The two fingers that went to the cloth wrapped round Mallory's ears were a salute of sorts. 'Aye, aye, Mr Nelson.'

They buried Durrand on the way back to join the squadron. No plain shroud for him, rather the wooden cot he had slept in. It had been made to fit his body and was slung from the deck beams in his cabin. All it required was a lid and some roundshot to weight it. Had he ever pondered as he lay in it at night, that his bed might also be his coffin? Somehow, Nelson doubted it; Durrand had been a man who seemed bereft of imagination.

But there was still emotion in this funeral, with the captured French officers in attendance and Captain Farmer reading the words of the service in a sonorous tone. On the voyage he had lost the usual number of men to sickness and accident, but this was the first time Nelson had witnessed a burial caused by action, and it was different.

He hadn't liked Durrand, but his death had made him think differently of the man and see beyond the scabby face and bellicose manner, perhaps to glimpse the fellow who wanted the men fed. The work of a first lieutenant was thankless: they got no praise when things went well – that was expected – but were roundly damned when anything went wrong. Perhaps his manner had been the result of his office and not his true personality. Nelson would never know the truth now that the man was dead.

As Farmer spoke the final words, and the burial party tipped the body over the side, Nelson prayed for the soul of a departed shipmate with all the vigour of his faith. At the same time he shuddered at the thought of where Durrand's remains were going.

CHAPTER 13

As she had delivered her daughter to the Linley house, Emma's irate mother had informed her that this would be her last chance; that an endless supply of below-stairs places could not be taken up through parental good offices. An honest reply from her daughter would have been, 'Then thank Christ for that', for continued domestic service did not accord with the dreams she had harboured when she came to London, even less with those she had now. Yet the alternative, going back to Hawarden, was even less enticing.

But she had to admit her new situation was better than she had feared. Compared to dull Dr Budd's, the Linley household was afire with continual activity, always full of visitors, actors and actresses, writers, scene painters, seamstresses and tradesmen seeking business or payment, the latter always a cause for noisy dispute. Lively herself, she fitted in easily. Supine, bobbing housemaids were not required by a family who lived off the profits of the Drury Lane Theatre. As well as performing their domestic tasks Linley servants were required to run errands connected with the business.

Household chores completed, Emma was often despatched to the theatre, to deliver a costume or a message. The smell of the backstage area enchanted her, especially when the cast was rehearsing; dust, often hot from the footlights, a hint of dope from the scenery paint, the smell of humanity and greasepaint, a whiff of scented powder. To go from bright sunlight into the dark cavern of Drury Lane was to enter an enchanted world where reality vanished. Beyond the wings lay the stage and a world of fantasy.

No one troubled her if she hung around to watch, sitting in the darkness of the reveals outside the circle of stage lighting, listening to the performers declaiming long speeches, or short sharp exchanges interspersed with cursing when the line they required wouldn't come. There would often be a writer standing around looking anxious, or dashing about explaining to the cast the true notion he had formed of how the lines should be spoken.

There were fights, dances, horses and carriages, and bewildering changes of scenery carried out in what seemed like the blink of an eye. A forest would disappear, pulled on ropes into the great void above the stage, another cloth thirty foot wide dropping in simultaneously to create the background of a drawing room already half furnished. Within seconds the doors and windows would be attached and heavy weights laid on the wooden bar at the foot of the backdrop, turning the flapping cloth into what looked like a solid wall. Inside a minute actors in loose clothes who had been picnicking in a forest glade would enter a drawing room dressed for a masked ball.

Eventually Emma would remember her duties and rush back to the Linley house, to be scolded for her absence. But such was the chaos of the establishment that such strictures were lost in another tantrum or crisis. The place was exciting, alive and disordered, and connected to the theatre, which suited Emma perfectly. Then young Samuel Linley came home and life for the under-housemaid was transformed.

Emma's heart stopped the minute she clapped eyes on Samuel Linley. Sixteen years old, of medium height and slim, Samuel had fine blond hair that flopped over his brow, pale, delicate skin, and a wistful expression. That first day he was still wearing his midshipman's uniform coat, dark blue with snow white facing to match his breeches. But it was his eyes that riveted her, pale blue under heavy fair lashes, they seemed to be full of dreams. Until they locked on hers.

The attraction was instant and mutual. When they stole a moment of peace, Samuel loved nothing more than to gaze dreamily into her eyes and remark on their green beauty, while running his finger through the traces of auburn hair that had escaped from under her cap. Every time they held hands she felt a charge of excitement run up her arm and she knew he felt it too. Meetings in such a bustling house were of necessity brief and hasty, and his two weeks' leave was on its last day before he plucked up the courage to kiss her.

The infatuated pair saw themselves as star-crossed lovers in the mode of Romeo and Juliet, constantly kept apart by duty or circumstance, Samuel because he was an infrequent visitor who had to return to his naval duties, Emma because her station in the household should debar her from such an association. But intermingled with her sighs was the sure knowledge that in time she would be worthy of his attentions. She would be, perhaps, an actress employed by his father, a suitable companion to the son of the owner of the most famous theatre in the land.

Every time she served the family and guests she had eyes only for Samuel, so missed the looks of deep disapproval coming from a mother who had also observed the secret smile with which her only son reacted. She said nothing until the end of her Samuel's second visit, having allowed matters to rest so that she could see if the attraction would withstand the test of a month-long parting. That left her with a mooning housemaid whose spirits were only revived by the arrival of a *billet doux*. On Samuel's next leave, when the pair took up where they had left off, she knew it was time to act. Having contained her impatience until her son's leave was over, she called Emma into her workroom, which was strewn with cloth.

'It is not unnatural for the son of the house to find himself attracted to one of the female servants, Emma, and since you are a pretty creature I absolve Samuel of any blame in the association.'

Emma was wondering how she knew. They had been so careful.

'Indeed, if I were the only one to notice I might have let matters take their natural course. My boy is turning into a man, and they, poor creatures, have needs that must be met somehow. But neither of you has been discreet. Samuel cannot sustain a conversation while you are in the room and you cannot properly attend to your duties for staring at him.'

Emma was shocked, and dropped her eyes in the face of her mistress's stiff stare.

'The servants are aware of it, my guests are aware of it, even my family is aware of it. Except Mr Linley of course. He is as purblind as most fathers.'

'Ma'am.'

'It must stop.'

'But—'

'No buts, my girl.'

Then her voice lost its hard edge and became more comforting. Her face softened, showing the source from which Samuel had inherited his beauty.

'Do not think I do not understand the attraction. You are young, so is he, and puppy love . . .' She threw up her hands. 'Well! But understanding does not bring approval. My son has his way to make in the world and I know him well enough to admit the possibility that he might, out of kindness, act foolishly. But it is not to be, and I, as his mother, have a duty to ensure that is so. Do you understand that failure to abide by my wishes will see you dismissed? It will be a month at least before Samuel returns to the house. Think on what I have said, make sure you attend to what is yours and let what is not to be die a natural death.'

Those words came to haunt both of them. Samuel was home within a fortnight, suffering from a fever, confined to his bed, attended by doctors who could never emerge from his bedchamber with a cheerful expression. Emma, barred from that room, was dependent on bulletins from the male servants about her love's condition, every spare moment spent on her knees praying that God might spare him.

'Emma.'

Still on her knees, Emma turned to look at Mrs Linley. Strength that had previously been evident in the face of the woman who had chastised her was gone now.

'Samuel has asked for you. My own maid, as you know, has been in charge of the nursing but that brings on frustration in him, which the physicians says scarce does him good. They maintain that the vital spark necessary to pull him through this crisis is missing. Perhaps you can rekindle it. You have my permission to go to his room and take over such duties.'

Emma was gone so quickly that she didn't hear Mrs Linley's

sobs. She burst into Samuel's room and rushed to his bedside to take his hand, shocked to see that his skin was now translucent and that the bones now stood out starkly from his skull. His hair was lank, not floppy and boyish, and the eyes she adored had a faraway look that only flickered when they crossed her face. She was hardly aware of the others in the room, the shadowy figure of the physician and the outline of Mrs Linley's maid, hands clasped, mouthing indistinct prayers.

'Emma,' he croaked. She kissed the back of his limp hand in response, to convey her love, but also to hide her shock at his condition. 'My mother relented.'

'She did,' Emma whispered, her lips brushing his skin, her eyes stinging with the tears she sought to control.

'I fear I was harsh with her.'

'I can't believe that, Samuel. You don't know how to be harsh.'

That produced a wan smile. 'A naval officer must be a veritable tyrant, Emma, and, you do not see me at my duties. I had hoped that one day you would.'

'That day will come, my love,' she whispered.

Samuel's brow furrowed, and a look of deep sadness crossed his sweating face. When he spoke his voice was dry and rasping. 'I cannot think I truly have the qualities for the Navy.'

Emma picked up the glass that sat on the bedside table and gave him a drink. The water eased his voice, but there was no power in his speech and Emma had to lean forward to hear him.

'I command men so much older and wiser than I,' Samuel whispered. 'Even those my age are my betters as seamen. They laugh so readily that I often wonder if I am the object of their mirth.'

'I think it more like that you're the object of their admiration.'

'I saw myself in command, Emma, at sea, in my own ship, with a happy crew and you just as much at home in my cabin as I was myself.'

Even if that didn't accord with her own dreams, Emma's reply was sincere. 'I would be at home just by your side, Samuel, wherever that should be.'

There was sudden strength in his hand, which gripped hers tightly. 'Will it be?'

'Samuel, you are low now to be sure,' Emma answered, 'but you will recover – you must recover, because I have enough strength for that. It will flow from me to you, Samuel, and sustain you through the worst of this fever, sustain you till your own strength is restored enough to bring you back to full health.'

'When I am well again, I will take you away from here.'

'This is your home, where you belong.'

'Is it, Emma?'

She wanted to say, 'Of course,' but refrained.

They had never had time for much more than an exchange of endearments, never been together long enough to explore their thoughts. Emma loved to see him in his naval uniform, yet could not understand why he had been attached to a service that was full of ruffians. She was only vaguely aware that Samuel's parents had aspirations for their son that did not include theatre management, and would not have believed Mrs Linley had she told Emma that Samuel's professional future was merely an aid to raise his social position.

'Our future,' Emma said, kissing his damp forehead as Samuel closed his eyes and drifted off into a deep sleep.

Time lost its meaning then, and the long day turned to night as she sat beside him bathing his face, talking softly of how he would be restored to health while she would pursue his parents to let her progress from housemaid to actress. Their future would be glorious, him the theatre manager, she his leading lady both at home and on the stage. Her words conjured up carriages and houses, glittering balls and famous names, the greatest in the land bowing to Samuel Linley and his consort. And there were children; lots of them, all clever and obedient, beautiful and virtuous.

Emma was hardly aware of the people who drifted in and out of the sick room, the stream of anxious tear-stained faces. Only the physician could break her train of visions, his sombre face lit by the circle of candlelight that surrounded the sick bed allowing a desperate reality to intrude.

Samuel drifted from sleep to fragile wakefulness then back

again to sleep. Each time his eyes opened to meet hers he gave her another wan smile and she felt a slight increase in the pressure on her hand. Her heart nearly broke when that ceased, when those beautiful blue eyes showed no sign of recognition, just a blank, fearful stare, as if the terror of approaching death was stalking him. There was no affection in his speech now, just ramblings of past fears. The physician took over then, his long bony fingers pressing the pale soft flesh to prepare it for the hot glass ampoules that were applied to blister the skin.

The pain of that made Samuel arch, and produced in her a corresponding sensation that racked her body as much as it did his. Her agonies lasted longer though, for eventually the thin wasted body ceased to react to the applications. Her eyes met those of the doctor once more, and she saw in them the news that she dreaded.

'Best fetch Mrs Linley,' he intoned. 'Tell her to gather to the bedside those members of the family who wish to attend the final extremities.'

They filed in one by one, mother, father, sisters and cousins. It was hard to explain the anger and the depth of her despair as they moved her away. Mrs Linley was kind enough not to ask that she leave the room, merely requesting that she stay by the door while the family prayed. She prayed too, but not even the love of everyone assembled could save him, and as dawn approached Samuel Linley closed his eyes for the last time.

'I thought you understood that you were never to come here, Emma.'

The kitchen servants had been very close to turning her away. Any number of grubby creatures would beg a crust at their basement door of a day, so the sight of one more was not likely to dent their indifference. And asking for her mother had helped little: it was a well-worn and false device to elicit sympathy, there being no such creature as Mary Lyon resident at 5 Arlington Street. If the cook hadn't recalled that the woman who called herself Mary Cadogan had once gone by that name, Emma wouldn't have been in this room now.

'Where else am I to go, Ma?'

'Back to your employ, girl, at Mr Linley's.'

Emma responded with a violent shake of the head, which had the effect of holding back her tears as well as denying that proposition. She could never go back to that place because everything she saw and touched would remind her of her loss. The weeks since Samuel's death had eased her grief enough to let her know that drifting was unwise. To her cost she had learnt just how cold the city was, how few were the people who would like or employ her for her own sake. Selling flowers or vegetables from a market stall was worse than service, a corner of a room in a filthy rookery a hundred times less comfortable than a warm attic.

'Where have you been?' her mother asked.

'Here and there,' Emma replied, not wishing to list the odd jobs she had found, nor the desperate places where she had paid to lay her head, even less the doorways she had sometimes been forced to sleep in. Cold, hungry and full of self-pity she had felt herself part of the world that lived with nothing. What had seemed an age had been less than a month, but in such an existence time loses any meaning.

There was little companionship. Girls her own age, selling themselves, spat at her lest she interfered with their trade. Beggars defended their patch because their lives depended on it. There had been men who'd approached her, most rude in their demands for a price, others with kindness in their voices that did not extend to their eyes. Cocooned by family or service, Emma had been shielded until then from the narrow margin between security and death. But in the last month she had seen it close to, and was sure of only one thing: she wanted no part of it.

Now she didn't want to look her mother in the eye, so she glanced around the small anteroom instead. It was simply but tastefully decorated, the quality of the hangings and furniture as good as anything she had seen in domestic service. The floorboards shone with polish, their smell mingled with that of the fresh cut flowers in a vase on the table. Her appreciation of her surroundings was heightened by the fact that she was sitting on a comfortable chair, not dealing with the needs of others. How nice to feel like a guest instead of a servant!

'Happen we can find another household,' said her mother.

'This one would serve.'

'It would not!'

'Why?'

There was a long pause while they looked at each other, the mother wondering how much her daughter understood, the child willing the woman to open up and tell her the whole truth. Questions posed in the past had led to vague replies concerning the kindness of gentlemen, and being involved in entertaining no less than the ladies of the stage.

'I make my way, child, using what gifts God gave me to do so.'

That was the only answer Emma had ever received to her few direct questions. Yet she knew very well that there was more to it than that. The story of her mother's abandonment by Sir John Glynne had been bandied about so often in her grandmother's household when they forgot the girl was present. The residue of previous family arguments had led to the use of expressions that made more sense in this room than they had in Hawarden. And hints from the likes of Cath Lane had filled in most of what was still missing.

'Why are you known here as Mary Cadogan?'

Her mother turned to look out of the high sash window, to the quiet street outside and the gates of a rich man's redbrick townhouse across the way. That allowed Emma to examine the dress she was wearing, of heavy warm pink silk, embroidered at collar, cuffs and hem. She didn't need a mirror to see her own drab garment, the same grey dress with which she had departed the Linley house, not improved by a month on the streets. To rub the coarse cloth between her fingers served only to highlight the contrast in material.

'I liked the sound of it,' her mother replied eventually, 'and changing my name shut behind me some doors that left open only reminded me of sorrow, the loss of your father being but one. There's no Mr Cadogan wandering about if that's what you're thinking.'

'Is this a bawdy house?'

Emma's mother laughed then, full-bloodedly, spinning round with her head thrown back, seeming to shed the years and cares that had come to line her face. She was once more the beautiful mother Emma remembered; the woman with the trim figure and lively face who could never walk down a Hawarden street without attracting the open admiration that had made her daughter proud. Yet the change of expression underlined to Emma how much older her mother was now, and how she had come to rely on elegance to support her fading beauty.

Flesh had turned the fine-boned face square, and pouches had appeared beneath the brown eyes, fighting a losing battle against the powder used to disguise them. Her mother's smile had always been one of her best features, that and a pert nose. They, at least, were as she remembered them.

'A bawdy house, Emma? Don't let Kathleen Kelly hear you say that.'

'Who is Kathleen Kelly?'

'The lady that owns this fine, respectable establishment.'

Emma was irritated by the obvious condescension of that reply, the way it was delivered and her mother's arch expression.

'I'm not a child, Mother.'

When she replied the humour was still on her mother's face, but it had gone from her eyes. 'No, Emma, you're not. Yet neither are you a full-grown woman.'

'I'm old enough to be told what you do here.'

That brought forth a sigh, then a smile. How to say that Mrs Kelly, termed the Abbess, was a procuress? To tell her daughter that, no, 5 Arlington Street was not a bawdy house, but a place where men came to find companionship, even if consummation of any desire they might feel took place elsewhere? That the job of Mrs Kelly's ladies, nicknamed nuns, was to encourage the customers to spend money on highly priced suppers and wines by stroking male vanity.

'Mrs Kelly's house is a place of entertainment. Food is eaten, cards are played, songs are sung and often, late at night, there will be dancing. The good lady provides company of a charming nature. We can be taken out for picnics and the like during the day by her clients, that being at our own choosing. Other times – say after supper – we might consent to be escorted to Ranelagh and the Vauxhall.'

Her smile had faded. It was a long time since she had visited either. Nor had there been many picnics. The clients no longer seemed quite so keen to take her anywhere but their bed. To flatter and entertain her was no longer deemed necessary. She had slipped from the front rank of Mrs Kelly's nuns, but was not yet reduced to serving at table. Kathleen Kelly would hesitate to chuck her on to the streets, but the hints had multiplied that it might be time for her to consider moving on.

'God in heaven, now. Sure, what are you doing sitting here?'

Neither of them had heard the door open and domestic habit made Emma shoot to her feet. The newcomer was a red-headed woman, with a lined, over-powdered face. The mouth was large, the accent Irish, the voice loud and vulgar.

'And who would this be?'

'I'm Mrs Cadogan's daughter,' said Emma, before her mother had a chance to reply. There was extra pleasure in using the unfamiliar name, as if it created a distance between herself and her mother that had never existed before.

The woman was between them now, very close to Emma, exuding perfume. 'You never told me you had a daughter, Mary.'

'Emma, this is Mrs Kelly,' Mary replied, her voice flat with despair.

'I came looking for a place, Mrs Kelly,' Emma blurted out, wondering why her mother's eyes closed tightly as she said it.

Kathleen Kelly looked her up and down, inducing a blush as Emma recalled what she must look like: hair unclean, face likewise, her dress marked by where she had worked and slept these last four weeks. Then the older woman took Emma's chin between finger and thumb and squeezed gently. Suddenly Emma was back in that dark Hawarden hallway, looking into the florid face of Sir John Glynne.

'Would you look at those eyes, Mary Cadogan? Would they not just make your heart melt, now? And such hair, clean and dressed proper.'

'Kathleen?' said Emma's mother, a note of desperation in her voice.

Emma experienced a surge of pressure in her breast, a mixture of defiance and desire: the need to break free of control and a determination never again to serve others. There was a mass of other emotions as well: the feeling of being cast adrift by the loss of Samuel Linley, the worthlessness she had felt since his death, the certainty that the life she had been living was not for her.

'Will you take me in, Mrs Kelly?' asked Emma.

'Sure, I don't think we'd struggle to find you a place, girl.'

'Please!'

Mary Cadogan didn't get any further with her protest, as Mrs Kelly glared at her. 'Being so young, she will need grooming. Who better to look after a girl like you than her own dear mother?'

Emma missed the implications of that, not in the least aware that her mother had been threatened. She sat down again, taking a deep breath of the luxurious scent of the room, her hands running sensually along the silk coverings on the arms of her chair. The temptation to pick up the bell that lay on the side table and ring to order tea was almost overwhelming.

CHAPTER 14

The crew of HMS *Seahorse* caught the smell of the city of Calcutta before they ever clapped eyes on the place, another odour to add to those that had already assailed their nostrils. Dry, burnt earth contrasted with rotting swamp was at the base, but as they sailed slowly up the Hoogly there were sharp overtones of fruits, spices and humanity, all of which emanated from the boats traversing the river, many full of dark-skinned women, the rest with fresh victuals. All was for sale. Behind them the rest of the squadron followed under topsails, the Commodore's pennant of Sir Edward Hughes atop the mainmast of *Ramilles*.

The youngsters, Nelson, Troubridge and Bertie, could scarce be kept out of the chains, and were to be found, as their duty permitted, just behind Mallory, who was employed casting the lead. They searched the shore eagerly for some of the fabled creatures they had been assured populated the sub-continent, beasts with twelve legs hunted by giants with two heads being the least remarkable. It had been the sport of the ship since they had weighed from Portsmouth to work on the gullibility of the youngsters and landsmen, who fully expected on arrival to see the ship revictualled by trained birds of enough size and strength to carry a twelve-pounder cannon.

'Ah!' said Mallory, sniffing loudly as he picked up a particularly pungent, musky odour that had a hint of the unswabbed roundhouse about it. 'That smell's like the droppings of the weegee-weegee bird.' He turned away, cast the line in the muddy water, hauling it in with a cry of 'No bottom on this line.'

'The what?' the trio chorused.

Mock-horror filled Mallory's scarred face. 'Are you meaning

to tell me that you ain't never heard of the great weegee-weegee, that special bird that many an admiral has begged to see put on his own coat-of-arms, only to have the King deny him?' Incomprehension had to wait for another cast forward of the lead, then the sailor continued. 'It be special, royal like, and only for the anointed King, seeing how it flies in so particular a manner.'

'How does it fly?' demanded Bertie.

'Well, it starts off in a great sweep of a circle, more'n a mile wide, crying "Weegee-weegee" all the while. Then it shortens at each turn, the circles getting smaller like the inside of a right tidy set of falls, tighter and tighter till the circle is so small it finally jams its beak up its own arse.'

Credulity fought with scepticism, until the latter won out. But their doubt was tempered, just in case he was telling the truth.

'Four fathom ground on this line,' Mallory called, after his next cast. Extracting the rope from the water he examined the sand that had stuck to the tallow on the bottom of the lead. 'We're near there, lads, and there's ladies ashore by the ton weight, as well as in them there boats. Why, my gonads are aching already.'

'Like they was before we raised Trincomalee?' demanded Thomas Bertie.

His question earned him a dig in the ribs from Troubridge, who was relieved that Mallory, busy on his line again, had pretended not to hear. The cocky Londoner had trouble holding his tongue, and could never be brought to understand that truths discussed in the mid's berth were not always to be voiced in adult company. Bertie and his loose tongue had nearly landed the gunner's mate in a yardarm noose when he mentioned too near the premier that he and two other midshipmen had watched the man roger the ship's goat.

Every youngster knew there were parts of the ship to avoid at certain times, groups of sailors to stay clear of. The committed sodomites, as opposed to those who indulged occasionally, were few and secretive, keeping themselves to themselves, even if their shipmates knew their orientation. Some were identifiable by the over elaborate dressing of their pigtails, others brutes so ugly that many wondered how any creature, male or female, could consider sexual congress with such a beast. In the main, they stayed separate, never interfering where such attentions were unwelcome. If the ship's boys chose to indulge them that was their affair and no one else's business, provided it didn't challenge the proper running of the ship.

There wasn't an officer on board, from the Captain downwards, who wasn't aware of what went on in ships at sea, from the smallest merchant vessel to the biggest ship of the line. Sodomy, bestiality, gambling and theft were commonplace. An active commander could make a point of weeding out the first two by careful choosing of his crew, but would struggle to contain the others, even though according to the Articles of War they were all capital crimes. Most made good use of the blind eye to avoid a life spent in constant attendance at courts martial, floggings around the fleet, or hangings.

The sinners aboard a ship, from sodomites to rum robbers, were no different in their duties from the others. The good ones could hand, reef and steer as well as the next man, go aloft with ease in a howling gale, ply a gun with just as much venom, and when it came to boarding were just as keen to kill and maim as the most ardent psalm singing celibate. Good hands were prized and there was no point in an officer being too zealous about the law. Better the blind eye and a trim ship than the sight of men hauled up to swing from a yardarm.

And it wasn't confined to activities before the mast. Rumours abounded of captains who chose their servants with care, of premiers who had to fight temptation tooth and nail so that they could properly carry out their duties, and of others who failed in that and ruined their careers. Some ships, it was said, had wardrooms and mid's berths where such heathen carnality was the norm rather than the exception. Asking to name such officers or vessels didn't produce much in the way of evidence, but it was held to be true nonetheless. And when they were discussed, in the darkness of the night, the breathless quality of the conversation made Nelson wonder if he was the only youngster who could never decide if he was excited or appalled by the notion.

There were temptations: he worked with flashy topmen not

much past his age who seemed to have lived a hundred years given the depth of their knowledge. Occasionally, because he liked them as people and admired them for their skill, that, added to his own naivety, sometimes led to an invitation. Mostly hints, sometimes actually tactile, couched in gentle terms to persuade him that what hadn't been tried should not be gainsaid. He always declined, without anger, then wondered, as he tried to get to sleep, if he had done the right thing.

As to the scratching off Trincomalee, that had been an allusion to the activities of Grimface Adams. Ugly as sin, near toothless and textured, he could fold his face into half its true size, which, with a lantern below his chin, made him look like a true ghoul. His other sport was to take money off his mates in the cable tier, giving them the gammeroush to ease the tensions that could find no other relief aboard a near female-free vessel.

He did a brisk trade, at times when officers were thin on the decks, visited in near total darkness by dozens of his shipmates, not one of whom would admit to having been a customer. That common secrecy had been severely strained by the itching that had seized the ship south of Ceylon. Half the crew were at it, all ages and sizes, including the oldest midshipman, scratching away with their backs turned, or earnestly finding a quiet spot for a personal examination to see if they had somehow become poxed.

Grimface Adams might be the likely culprit but no one could openly accuse him of anything. However, the general suspicion soon surfaced, given that he was known to be less than fussy, that he had had himself a monkey at the Cape. Whatever disease he had picked up there he had passed on wholesale. When the truth emerged, only those who never went near him could laugh at it. Grimface, with no more than five teeth in his whole head, had, chomping on a ship's biscuit, chipped a splinter off the remaining front one. In carrying out his service in the dark cable tier, he had scratched half the cocks on the ship.

Thinking back to *Raisonable* Nelson was aware of just how much he had missed. Rivers's fumblings had been nothing, and it was probable that a goodly portion of those who had sided with him had done so to protect themselves from the same abuse. But that was nothing to what had been kept from him by John Judd. This long commission had opened his eyes, but it had also shown him that there were times to keep them closed. He had observed as much as the next midshipman what went on aboard. He heard the clacking of dice, had seen shadowy shapes creeping around on his night-time watches. His duty as an aspiring officer was to interfere, to clap a stopper on all illegality. But the other thing he learnt was this: that on a dark night, anyone, even the most brutal bully, might go over the side without so much as a cry for help. Captain George Farmer set the tone; Midshipman Nelson abided by it.

A shout from the masthead told those below that the lookout had spied the first of the ship's masts that would fill the Calcutta roadstead. That brought the new premier Mr Stemp, on deck, speaking trumpet at the ready, his task to beautify the already perfect, to make his captain proud of the ship as it sailed past the Port Admiral's residence and fired off the customary salute.

All the facilities of the Calcutta dockyard were thrown open to them, and an abundance of spars, sails and cordage to replace that which had been worn through or lost since the Cape. War, for the King's Navy, was always on the horizon. If it came there was an enemy at sea in the eastern waters: the French Admiral Suffren, well equipped with a strong squadron to threaten the China fleet and the East India convoys. So there was no shore leave. Instead they worked as hard as the Lascars the Port Admiral employed to get the squadron ready for sea. Once that was achieved, they could look to relax.

The captured *Chasse Marées* were bought into the service, so there was a small pay-out of prize money on the day that leave was finally allowed. For the officers, commissioned and warrant, that meant going ashore. For the hands, confined to the ship for fear they would desert, it meant that the boats full of women and trinket traders that had lain around the anchored ships might now disgorge their occupants on to the lower decks. These soon became so full it was impossible to walk from one end to the other without tripping over recumbent bodies. There was music, a strange amalgam of East and West, much dancing and, on that first day of relaxation, an excess of debauchery as each trader or whore worked to relieve every hand of his share of the recent captures.

Spared a daylight watch, the trio of midshipmen went sightseeing. To be untroubled by the exotic was de rigueur amongst those who had never been outside England. But Nelson, more experienced than his companions, had seen the West Indies and the polar ice, so could withstand any jibes directed at his enthusiasm. He was openly agog at what he saw in the teeming streets and bazaars of the Indian city.

Every spice was on sale, at a cost that would yield a handsome profit if taken home. Gold wrought into fantastic shapes filled shops that stood next to others overflowing with gaudy silks. The food markets were bedlams of excess, none more so than the fish quays, lined with stalls, produce piled high, and the traders yelling that they could not be beaten on taste, freshness or price. Anything bought was immediately cleaned and prepared by the boys who hung around the market, eager to earn a few annas for their labours.

The temples, even though the sailors had been told about them in advance, were a revelation, with their amazing sculptures of unknown and powerful heathen gods, the sight of which had Nelson crossing himself. Stone and wooden carvings of men and women in every carnal position, quite a few incomprehensible to those who gazed on them, even after what they had so recently witnessed on their own maindeck. They were boys, who, beneath the braggadocio and jokes, still blushed. Each saw fit to suggest a visit to a brothel; each was equally unwilling to press the matter when his companions suggested delay. And, in truth, there was too much to see, as well as their social duties to perform.

There were a few European women in the busy ballroom, but they were in the minority. Some were the wives of the guests, others disreputable creatures who had travelled to India to escape their reputation at home, and perhaps to snare a husband. In such a small, incestuous society, everyone in Calcutta passed on scurrilous details of everyone else. Those prowling for matrimony didn't suffer in this, since the wives were carved from the same block.

Most of the women present were Indian, concubines of East India Company officials colourfully dressed in delightfully revealing saris, possessed of flawless, pale olive complexions, with jewels in their noses. They also wore a great deal of gold, either in bangles around their wrists, or in elaborate buckles and pendants. Close to, they sent out the odour of strong, seductive perfumes, and their laughter was loud enough to echo off the high ceiling. Given the choice, Horatio Nelson would have sought their company, but to an aspiring gentleman that option was not available. He had to move among his own kind, drinking claret in a quantity that seemed excessive to him but perfectly normal to his hosts.

Everyone Nelson spoke to was keen that he should know the depth of his or her connections. He was assailed by the information that their presence in India was a mere sojourn, a pause for breath before they returned home to re-enter the busy social whirl that was theirs by right of birth. Good manners demanded that they enquire of him, just as they obliged him to respond.

The name Burnham Thorpe required that he locate it on the northern shore of the county, his father's occupation earning a sniff of indifference only eased by the added information that the Reverend Nelson held three livings rather than one. He was too young for the pastime of social gaming that was the bedrock of these conversations, too eager to describe his rural pursuits and the qualities of quiet charm and good humour of his siblings. But the disdain with which such snippets were received dawned on him eventually. As each conversation progressed Nelson realised that he was being condescended to, that those with whom he talked were inclined to look down on him socially. They saw before them a young fellow, the son of a mere parson, with few prospects and little in the way of interest to advance him in life. And the knowledge of how he was perceived hurt him deeply.

Just as painful was the sense of his own inadequacy. He lacked experience of adult company, excepting that of his naval superiors whose conversation tended towards the nautical.

Horatio Nelson felt himself exceptional, from a family that while not grand was to be admired. It galled him that these people were unable to see that he was not just some Norfolk ragamuffin.

'I know Norfolk well, sir,' a pregnant lady said. 'My cousin Lord Lychett has estates there.' The pause was timed to perfection, before she added, 'Substantial estates.'

'Quite,' added the red-coated officer, her husband and an East India Company major, who stood to her side. He had a bright red face to go with his coat and wispy carrot coloured hair to set it off.

'Lord Lychett positively plagues me with requests to call,' his wife added, with a gesture designed to demonstrate how shocking her reluctance was. 'I fear my endless refusals must vex him.'

'Very vexing indeed,' the Major added, puffing himself up slightly. 'We should really make the effort, my dear.'

'I accept when my diary permits, of course,' his wife added hastily, lest the impression of grandeur she was determined to create led to overstatement. Then she gently touched her swollen belly. 'Perhaps when the child is born. Lord Lychett will positively demand godparentage.'

The climate had not been kind to this lady, the third with whom Nelson had conversed in the space of ten minutes. Her skin was lined as though the heat, or her forthcoming child, had sucked out every ounce of its moisture, making her look older than her years. The other pair had been so over powdered it had been impossible to tell their age.

'I know the Lychett name, madam,' he said suddenly. 'I believe their estate abuts the property of my cousin the Earl of Orford.'

Those words produced confusion in the female face, but deep interest from her husband. 'You are an Orford relation, sir?'

Suddenly Nelson was granted a vision of his father, forever harping about his late wife's relations in monologues that had bored his son rigid. Perhaps they had a value, after all. 'The present Earl is my second cousin, sir, the consanguinity coming to me through my mother's family. We share a great-grandparent.'

'I have never had the honour of his acquaintance,' the Major said, clearly impressed.

The question loomed, even if it hadn't been asked. Nelson lied with surprising ease, pleased that it had the desired effect. He had made one visit to the Orford estates, memorable, as young as he had been, only for the chilliness of the reception. A blood tie to the family of an impecunious parson was not something the noble Earl had sought to encourage.

'He calls often upon my father, sir, when they are both in Bath, which is frequent.' The Major's eyes lit up, and Nelson plunged further into deceit. 'At other times he has travelled to my family home at Burnham Thorpe.'

'The Earl calls upon you?'

'He is very attached to my father, sir, as he was to my dear mother before she died. He makes the case that it is easier for him to come alone to us than that my overburdened parent should drag his large brood all the way across the county.' One of the Major's eyebrows moved enough to make Nelson add hastily, 'We do visit, of course, as often as we wish.'

The leather-skinned wife had been listening to this exchange with increasing wonder. Finally she found her tongue. 'A mother lost and a father needing the Bath waters. Why, the boy's practically an orphan, Major Higgins, in need of maternal care.'

'So it seems, Mrs Higgins, so it seems.'

'You must, young sir, treat our home as your own while you are here in Calcutta.'

'That is most kind, Mrs Higgins,' he replied, suppressing the alarm the invitation had induced in him.

'I think you might find it tolerably comfortable after the rigours of a ship.'

'Quite, my dear! Anything will seem palatial after a ship,' said Higgins, reaching out to take Nelson's arm in a fatherly way. 'Would you care to make the acquaintance of some of my fellow officers, Mr Nelson?'

'That would be most gracious of you, sir.'

'If you will excuse us, Mrs Higgins?'

'Most certainly, Major Higgins,' she replied, looking far from pleased. 'Do remember, Mr Nelson, our house is yours. I would be distraught if you did not call upon us.'

'Rest assured, madam,' he responded, with a bow deep enough to hide his expression, which might reveal his amusement at the way their opinion of him had altered, 'I will undertake to do that as an act of pleasure, not of duty.'

Once away from his wife Major Higgins began a series of noisy introductions, all to red-coated officers, many of whom seemed to be Scotsmen, and each one treated to an allusion to Nelson's high-born relations. It was gratifying to see languid boredom switch to interest.

'Do you play, sir?' asked Higgins, as they reached a table of men at the back of the room. They were playing whist, and clearly, given the degree of concentration, the game was a serious one.

'I have taken a hand in the wardroom, sir, at the premier's bequest, but I am no real player.'

The rubber finished as he replied, and two of the players rose from the table.

'Come, sir,' the Major exclaimed, moving towards an empty chair and inviting Nelson to follow. 'I'm sure that a fellow of your parts is only indulging in modesty. I am a judge of character, young man, and I think I can perceive a sharp mind as well as anyone. It is a skill upon which I immodestly pride myself.'

'If you will permit me to decline, Major Higgins.'

'Never in life, sir. Partake of a seat at the table of good fortune.'

'My present resources are limited.'

'Never fear,' Higgins replied, loudly and encouragingly. 'These fellows will not decline to take a note of hand from the blood relation of a belted earl.'

Horatio Nelson quietly cursed his big mouth.

CHAPTER 15

In a game of skill and chance, there was space for beginner's luck and it operated now. Nelson wasn't a complete novice, but the noisy card school of the mid's berth was very different. Garrulous Major Higgins was quiet now, all his concentration going into the cards, and after the introductions the other two men, another East India company officer and a civilian contractor called Colbourne, behaved likewise. Nelson struggled to recall what little knowledge of the game he possessed, but the state of his head was of no help, the claret he had consumed earlier addling his judgement.

The gasps that greeted some of his leads, as well as the cards he produced to follow, came as proof positive that his game displayed a want of finesse. But he made up in brio what he lacked in the finer points, which led to a steady accumulation of golden guineas, as well as promissory notes by his right hand. Higgins lost steadily but unspectacularly, the other officer held his own. But the civilian endured a cascade of failure, mainly because he thought himself an expert, whereas he was in truth some way behind the main winner. It was some indication of his wealth that when he finally called a halt, he accepted his losses with equanimity, enquired for an address and promised to send a servant to redeem his notes first thing in the morning.

'He'll make that up in a day,' Higgins explained, 'if not in half a morning, from his trading enterprise.'

There was anger in the Major's tone. His own losses clearly rankled. 'Nothing but a damned tradesman, with manners to match. I'd not be surprised to learn he's made more than his losses while sitting at the table.'

'There are notes here in excess of three hundred pounds, as

well as a pile of guineas.' Nelson blushed. Most of the cash had been the Major's.

'A trifle to a man like Colbourne.'

'Your own losses, sir?'

'Of no consequence, young sir,' the Major boomed, as if determined to tell not only Nelson but every other card player in the room. He dropped his voice though when he continued, bringing his bright red face closer to Nelson's, the grin he employed displaying his very yellow teeth. 'Though I won't say I'd be ashamed to take supper off such a handsome set of winnings. A proper supper fit to set up the belly of a fellow fighting man.'

Nelson wanted to go back to the ship. He had drunk too much, his tongue felt like sun-bleached sailcloth and his head was aching. A bottle had stood available throughout the game, yet he had not touched it. But, having won money from this man, could he in all conscience refuse?

'I am at your disposal, sir,' Nelson pointed to his money, 'and so, sir, are those.'

'Splendid!' cried Higgins, picking up the claret and charging both of their glasses. 'And handsomely said, sir, the kind of sentiments I want to hear from my own son, should the good Lord be so disposed to favour my wife and me with a boy.' He pushed a glass into Nelson's hand. 'That is something we most earnestly desire. A toast, sir, to the good Lord looking kindly on the provision of an heir to the name of Higgins.'

'The name of Higgins,' Nelson replied reluctantly. The Major had emptied his glass, and participation in the toast demanded that he do likewise. Yet as he drank, the wine revived him.

'Another bumper, sir, at our host's expense, before I take you out and show you what the fabulous East has to offer.'

It wasn't one but three bumpers that Higgins took, all of which seemed to increase his jollity. Nelson, however, was beyond the state he had been in earlier, so when the Major took his arm to sneak him out through a side entrance he made little protest. But before they left the premises, Higgins requested a servant to inform his wife that he had been called away on urgent business. 'Company business. Mind you tell her that. Company business.' Then he turned to include his young companion in the subterfuge. 'Best not to let on about the cards, eh?'

'The fabulous East,' said Higgins, for the tenth time, raising a glass of European claret. They were sitting, coats and waistcoats off, stocks loosened, on a long low couch, almost lounging like Romans as they ate.

Nelson was drinking too, though not as swiftly, wondering why the liquid did not quench the thirst intensified by the heavily spiced food that filled the bowls in front of him. The air too, seemed full of spice, the aroma of cooking mingling with that of the perfumed candles. He was aware that there were other parties in the room, some Indian, others European, mingling easily with no hint of any group being superior to another.

Lithe young girls attended each table, wearing flimsy wrap-a-round garments that did little to disguise their figures. Occasionally a member of a supper party would depart with one. An allusion to that opened him up to a lecture from Higgins.

'Were you to take up residence here, Nelson, you'd find soon enough that what our home country offers cannot stand comparison to the pleasures available in India. I have been to Bombay and Madras on my service and I can tell you that what stands for Calcutta stands for the whole of the sub-continent. They have no hypocrisy here in matters of the flesh. A man who claims to be of parts is lessened if he has no external attachments. For the Mussulman several wives are necessary to maintain status, without precluding other pleasures. Some have a predilection for male flesh that I do not share but, I must say, exposure to their ways has tempered what was initial hostility. You, in the King's Navy, would not in that matter have been hampered by my reserve, sodomites being so common in your service.'

The temptation to defend his profession was strong, to refute the constant allegation that the King's Navy was the home of rum, sodomy and the lash. But it failed from hesitation, and besides the Major, drunk and insistent, was speaking again.

'Being in the East teaches you to be at ease with carnality, teaches you to shed the guilt our parsons berate us with in England. They do it here, too, of course.' He emitted a loud laugh and inadvertently spat rice over the dress of the smiling young girl who had returned to serve them. 'You'll hear no end of sermons in Bengal about the sins of the flesh – from cassocked individuals who have concubines tucked away in the Vicarage, the filthy clerical dogs.'

Higgins took the girl's wrist and pulled her forward. Her look remained complaisant, with not even a momentary flicker of anger. The Major rolled closer to Nelson, bringing the young girl with him, making him aware of both her youth and her beauty, and the lemony scent of her dark skin.

'Temptation, Nelson, that's what undoes them, from pompous trader to High-Church divine. They can't get this close to willing flesh and resist the need to touch it.' The chuckle that followed was low and sensuous. 'And damn me, young fellow, if you ain't just as struck.'

She was smiling at him, her dark brown eyes sending forth an invitation. And Higgins was still talking, in that low, lewd tone.

'I'll wager, boy, whatever meat you've had will not compare to this. For these Eastern beauties have the one gift a man craves more than any other. They are patient enough to seek out that which pleases you, and submissive enough to provide it. Not, I think, that you will have any but the most everyday tastes.'

The move away from the table was seamless and natural, as though preordained to happen. The hand that led him was warm even to one whose blood was racing, the faint coarseness of the fingertips enough to register through his own callused hands. The cubicle they entered was barely large enough to accommodate the cot and two people, the faint light from another perfumed candle flickering off the hangings that stood for walls. Nelson was rooted to the spot, the back of his legs against the edge of the cot, as she slid his stock from round his neck.

It was folded neatly and laid on the small table that bore the candle and the jug of water. His shirt followed, and he gave an involuntary shudder as her hands touched his belly, one sliding into the back of his breeches, the other working on the first of the buttons. He was shaking, small tremors that racked his body as she eased them over his haunches and down his thighs, her forearms brushing his prick.

She spoke for the first time, her voice sweet and high pitched: an injunction for him to sit so that she could remove his pumps, breeches and stockings. He obeyed without protest, his eyes on the ceiling in a vain attempt to cool his passion. Having rendered him naked she stood up and undid her own cloth, a single movement followed by three more just as swift to fold and put it away.

A large part of Nelson's mind was saying that he should not be here, that to consort with a common whore was a sin. But his conscience could not compete with the image that greeted his eyes, especially as she moved forward a fraction to lay her hands on his shoulders, forcing him to bring his gaze down to her. Small, perfectly rounded breasts with deep burgundy nipples, very erect; a flat belly above a bush of dark silky pubic hair, with just a trace of a wispy line running up to her umbilicus.

The hands were behind his head now, pulling it forward till his face was in contact with her breast. Not to open his mouth and suckle the nipple was impossible. He was shaking even more now, a permanent trembling that racked his whole body. Had he looked up he would have seen her smiling, a girl younger than him, who knew so much more than he about the sexual act. His need was great, his resistance low. She knew she must relieve that before she could go on to provide the services for which she was employed.

She pushed him on to his back, one leg swiftly straddling both of his. The speed with which she grabbed his erection and inserted it inside her was only matched by the speed at which he ejaculated as soon as she began to move. The pleasure was unbearable, almost painful, as a dozen spasms rocked his groin. His eyes were closed, his lower teeth biting his upper lip, as the first seeds of guilt replaced that sensation of pleasure.

The girl was still rocking back and forth delicately, waiting for his eyes to open. When they did, she slid free and stood up, picking up the jug of water and a cool cloth with which to bathe him. She started with the sweat on his brow, dabbing gently before descending to his cheeks and upper lip. The water was so cool and pleasant that the sensation almost matched what had gone before. His neck was on fire until she ran the cool cloth over it. Then she lifted each arm to wash there, the strokes including his own breast. His belly was next and finally the coolness was between his legs, a gentle rubbing that cleansed him of the fluids of both their bodies, and put paid to those feelings of remorse.

Her hand, cooled by the water, replaced the cloth, and she fondled him gently. Nelson lay there for ten minutes, lost in the sensuality of her touch, his eyes closed. Within a few minutes those small gentle movements had to lengthen as he became erect again. Expertly the girl stroked, with one wetted finger, the point at which the membrane connected his foreskin to his penis, making him groan out loud again. Then he felt her lie down next to him.

He turned on his side, gazed into her huge brown eyes. With his body pressed to hers, her breasts against his chest as obvious as his erection on her belly, he kissed her, tasting the spice that lingered on her dark red lips.

He awoke alone, eyes parting only a fraction, his body bearing a languor that comes only to the truly sated. He felt as though every muscle had been removed, leaving only the skin and bones, so that he would never move from here, just remain a willing victim of endless debauchery.

'I didn't ask her name,' he said to himself.

His eyes snapped wide open and he sat up still naked, searching the tiny cubicle for his clothes. The cry that was supposed to alert everyone to his predicament came out as a croak, but that was clearly sufficient, since the curtain was pulled back to allow a bent retainer to enter with a tray, which he laid on the bed. Nelson could see that it contained tea, strips of unleavened bread and a bowl of saffron rice with small pieces of meat. It also contained his purse, which, judging by its flatness, was emptier than it had been the night before.

'The Sahib Higgins left a message for you, Excellency,' said the old man, who pulled a note from under the bowl and handed it to him. Nelson opened it, leaning towards the candle so that he could read it.

My dear Nelson,

I trust you enjoyed your night as much as I did mine. Duty obliges me to leave you here in the tender arms of the girl whose services you engaged. My losses at the table force me to bear upon you for the cost of our evening's entertainment. All your promissory notes are there, along with a new one from me, which I would beg you to delay before presentation, since my affairs are at something of a stand. The invitation my wife extended to you is still open, though I know that I can trust you not to let slip how much pleasure I derived from the duty that dragged me away from her side.

The fact that it was unsigned showed that Major Higgins, for all his bluff exterior and seeming simplicity, was cunning enough not to leave himself open to exposure.

'My clothes?' asked Nelson.

The old man bowed. 'They are being prepared, Sahib. When you have eaten and been bathed they will await you.'

He checked the notes, with Colbourne's florid signature, as he ate the repast, and recalled the events of the previous day: the drinking, the cards, but most of all the time spent in this cubicle. The tea was thick and sweet, the meat just as spicy as the food he had consumed the night before. Waves of guilt began to assail him, slowly at first, then in increasing fervour.

How far had he fallen from the standards he set himself? He blushed to think that his mother might look down on her son and see a gambler and a rake who had consorted with a common prostitute. Drink had lowered his resolve, and Higgins with his blandishments, had removed the protection of his faith. The lies he had told regarding his Orford relations swam round in his head.

When the old man returned with his uniform, he found Nelson kneeling by the cot, volubly begging his God, his father and his late mother for forgiveness.

But silently he was trying and failing to press down his glee. A question that had troubled him since his first days in the Navy was now resolved. He could take carnal pleasure from the company of a woman.

On Nelson's return to the ship Colbourne's Indian servant was waiting for him, at the foot of the gangplank, protected by two tall retainers, carrying a casket of coins, as well as a receipt that he required to be signed. Refusing to come aboard, the servant ensured that the payment of the gambling debt was made in public, the money counted out to the young man before the eyes of his shipmates.

Instead of feeling elated though, Nelson felt somewhat indisposed. He had a sore head and his mouth tasted of metal. His friends failed to lift his spirits with their jokes about where he had been, and the new nickname, the Nabob, that referred to his good fortune at the table. He wasn't sure that it had been good fortune, since he had felt increasingly unwell since he had exchanged Colbourne's promissory notes for golden guineas. He was sweating excessively, even given the heat, and lassitude made every physical act a chore.

Everyone aboard seemed to know precisely where he had been. Worse, most of the mids wanted a blow-by-blow account of his adventures. As a senior in the mess he could, and did, demand privacy, his growls chasing away the prepubescent, whose curiosity far outweighed that of his contemporaries. Gratefully, even in the fetid heat of the mid's berth, he lay on his cot, his mind filled with whirring images of God, devils, sea battles and naked dark-skinned whores disguised as mermaids. He fell into the first serious bout of the fever, thinking he was sinking into a refreshing sleep.

'Malaria, no doubt about it.'

The disembodied voices seemed like part of the troubled dream. Yet through half-open eyes Nelson could make out the vague shape of the master. Surridge was holding a lantern above his head and another shape was looking into his face, lamenting, 'Your young men will gad about the place as if it were part of England. I have said time and again that a warning should be issued. I'll wager that not one of those who went on a picnic bothered to ascertain if their chosen site was in any proximity to a swamp.'

'Surely the damaging vapours are confined?' asked Surridge.

'They are clearly not, sir,' the other voice responded angrily, 'as this young man in his cot testifies. The malodorous airs are on the winds, infecting all those in their path, even healthy young fellows eating cold collations on a sandy riverside beach. It is my belief that they take on an extra strength as the sun dips, the cool of the approaching evening giving them vigour. Have you not noted it, sir? The wind abates in the heat of the day, only to rise and stir as evening approaches.'

'I am a ship's master, Mr Underwood,' said Surridge, coldly. 'It is my trade to know such things.'

The name registered. Underwood was the chief surgeon of HMS *Ramilles*, a man noted for the forthrightness of his views, medical or not, a fractious, argumentative fellow who was a sore trial at the dinner table. This was true even to the Commodore, which Nelson had noted on his one visit to the flagship's dining cabin.

It was as though Underwood hadn't heard Surridge speak. 'The shore hospital is full of them, men who swore that alive to the risk, they had never exposed themselves. And I daresay my sickbay will follow on this commission, just as it did when I was surgeon to the *Dreadnought* on the Windward Islands station.'

'What can we expect?'

'A crisis in the fever, which this fellow—'

'Mr Nelson,' Surridge interjected.

'I know his name and it will not save him, Mr Surridge. He will either expire and go to meet his Maker, this within two days, or he will recover for a while. After that, it will be as God wills.'

'There is no release.'

It wasn't a question, and it wasn't treated as such. 'It will be with him for life, and if another affliction does not carry him off, I daresay it will do for the young man in the end.'

'Is there aught we can do?'

'First we must wait to see how he fares, and that, I fear, will depend on his own vital spark.'

'He's a robust young man.'

'That is of little account. I've seen physical giants go down in a twelve-hour bout and others who would not qualify to be called a yard and a half of piss survive to see old bones. It is the inner being that matters in these affairs – dare I call it the soul. But if he's still with us at the end of the week we must do

190

something to get him away from this deadly climate. A second malady is not impossible, and that will surely kill him. Get him to sea. Not even the strongest breeze can carry the disease out to the oceans. No man in any ship I have served on has fallen foul of the malarial disease unless close to an evil shore.'

Nelson closed his eyes as the cool wet cloth touched his forehead, which brought back memories of that narrow cubicle and the girl with whom he had shared it. An hour later, when they moved him, he was delirious, the sweat running off his body in rivulets, hardly able to drink the water that Mallory insisted he take, despite protests from the loblolly boy, who ran this sickbay, that it hadn't been prescribed by the surgeon.

'There's water pouring out of him,' Mallory insisted. 'Stands to reason that if he leaks like dried-out planking, the only thing to tighten up his seams is more of the same. Too much loss and he'll peg out for certain.'

'You gone soft, Mallory?' asked one of his shipmates, a pigtailed young topman, hovering to observe his ministrations.

'Just returning a favour, mate.'

'Or seeking to grasp hold of an easy duty,' added another. That earned the speaker a hard look, which was returned in full measure. 'You was overheard, mate, asking for the care of the lad.'

'That's my duty,' piped the loblolly boy, an emaciated individual with a high, squeaky voice. He had no medical training and had only been given the job because he was utterly useless anywhere else. One of the visiting sailors poked him in the ribs.

'Mallory here reckons Nellie's got more chance with the Grim Reaper than he has with you.'

'Then I've got to keep him mortal to prove it, ain't I?' Mallory snarled. 'Now, fuck off out of here, the lot of you, and give the poor bugger some air.'

The next forty-eight hours were harder to watch than to live, since the patient had no idea of his condition. Mallory tended him constantly, relieved from his other duties for the purpose, stuck in stifling heat that seemed increased to furnace level 'tween decks, which frayed his temper.

So did the attention of the officers, midshipmen and the

master, who vexed the able seaman with their questions as to the youngster's condition. The surgeon Mr Underwood was welcomed, though irritated himself as Mallory pressed forward, asking questions, suggesting remedies and interfering in the examination. No one else was well received, though Captain George Farmer and the premier, Mr Stemp, had to be indulged. They rated a rise to the feet and a touch of the forelock; other officers along with Mr Surridge, justified elevation to a half-crouch and a nod, with enough gruff in the voice to denote displeasure. All the mids got was a stream of blasphemy, especially if they woke Mallory from one of his frequent catnaps. The loblolly boy was confined to fetching buckets of cool water.

It was three days before Nelson opened an eye. Mallory had strict instructions to inform his superiors at the first sight of improvement, but he hesitated, bathing the face till both eyes opened, the drooped lids showing just a hint of the blue-grey eyes.

'There you are now, Nellie, back with us after a visit to the other side.'

'Where am I?' Nelson croaked.

'Below decks, still berthed on Calcutta shore.' Gently Mallory raised his head and allowed him to sip some water. 'You've been right ill, you have, scaring the whole ship.'

'Ill?'

'A fever that's laid you low these three days past, with half your berth wondering if your card winnings were to be shared if you pegged out or taken home to your family.'

The pale damp head, hair plastered to the scalp, shook slowly, the eyes flickering as Mallory told him about the card game and his winnings, as well as the place where he had spent the night. That started a babble of remorse, with more pleas for forgiveness to his Maker and his parents, and an insistence that his condition resulted directly from his sin.

'Hell's teeth,' Mallory said, easing him back and bathing his head again. 'Don't you go fretting o'er that. What you did were nowt but natural. God wouldn't have much to concern hisself with if men and women didn't get together, now, would he? And it strikes me, the way one man dies and another lives, with no rhyme or reason to it, he might be a dab hand with the old dice in that lair of his.'

The response was a stream of mingled prayers and psalms, snatches of one well-known verse mixed with another, none making any sense. Mallory shouted till one of his shipmates arrived and pulled back the cloth.

'Double up to tell the Captain Mr Nelson's a-showing signs of coming round.'

'Double up? Who the fuck do you think you are, Mallory? Double up, you order me, and you not even warranted let alone commissioned.'

Mallory raised his knobbled fist. 'This be better than either, if you don't shift your arse.'

'It has been represented to me by the surgeons that for you to remain on this station carries a grave risk.'

Seated in his dining cabin, Captain Farmer appeared a lot less imposing than he did on the quarterdeck, both in voice and manner more like a slightly forgetful uncle than a Tartar of a commander. He would have described the youngster before him as wasted, with his skin so pallid and his bones so prominent. Only the eyes still had power, which could be laid at the door of his recurring fever.

'Nevertheless, sir, I would wish it so.'

'You have been under the burden of this for near a month, Mr Nelson. Every slight improvement brings a fresh bout of debilitation in its wake.'

'With God's help, I will fully recover.'

'I cannot indulge you, Mr Nelson. Your pleas have swayed me once already, and I feel I have been foolish to comply. It is my natural instinct to support a brave face but in this I have been mistaken.'

Hardened as he was by his years of command, even George Farmer was touched by the look of loss that swept across the young man's face. But he knew he must hold firm. He had relented to that look once already, and that in the face of Surgeon Underwood's contrary advice, only to regret it.

'You must not see it as a stain, young fellow. The log of the ship will show that you made every effort to remain at your duties. No want of character can be attached to your name.'

Nelson heard the words, but not the sentiments. He was being discharged as unfit for duty, and that before he had even acquired a lieutenant's commission. Tears pricked his eyes as his thoughts turned to the sins he had committed, and the punishment and retribution that seemed so harsh. Had his transgressions really deserved this?

'HMS *Dolphin* has orders to sail for England,' Farmer continued. 'Captain Pigot has agreed to take you aboard and give you passage home. It is my earnest wish that you are fully recovered when you make that happy return. The service needs men of your stamp, Mr Nelson. God knows they are few enough in number.'

As Farmer spoke, the young man before him seemed to shrink into a uniform coat that was already too big. It was as though the glue that had held him upright was melting. His look of despair was obvious and Farmer had to look away.

Horatio Nelson was thinking of death, which at this moment he would have preferred to discharge. Somehow the small panes of the cabin's casement windows dissolved into the faces of his family, his sisters Susanna, Anne and Catherine smiling sweetly, as they would over a childish misdeed. His brothers' faces held a look of triumph, as if happy to see their bumptious brother brought low. He shut his eyes rather than gaze on the images of his parents.

'Mallory!' Farmer called. The able seaman stepped through the door, touching his forehead. 'Help Mr Nelson back to his sick bed. You will then undertake the packing of his sea chest, Mr Troubridge to assist. Take care that his books and journals are secure in there. He will need them to pass for lieutenant.'

That one word returned enough strength to Nelson for him to sit upright. He had held out for a month when even the most confident of his shipmates had despaired. He would hold out longer, and show them all that he was the better man, including all those upstarts who would condescend to his parentage and upbringing, wherever they might be. With a peremptory gesture he waved Mallory back, which caused him immediate regret.

'You can do it, Mr Nelson, I know you can,' the sailor said.

The smile they exchanged heartened him more than any words or terrors he could conjure up. 'You never gave up on me, did you, Mallory?'

'Wouldn't be right, your honour, seeing as how you never did for me.'

Farmer coughed then, since the exchange of affection between the two men threatened to get out of hand. Nelson got to his feet and grasped Mallory's hand and gave it a vigorous shake. 'I would take it as an honour, Mallory, if you would count me as your friend, and that you would call upon me when you are next in England.'

He bowed to a shocked Captain Farmer, and walked stiff-legged out of the cabin. Mallory sniffed loudly, then followed him.

'Not that you'll get as far as England,' Farmer said softly, to himself. 'I wager you won't even raise the Cape.'

James Pigot was a fine sailor, as well as a deeply religious man respected by his crew, a group honed over years of service and careful transfers to reflect their captain's piety. Men addicted to gambling, drinking and pursuits of the flesh had been sent into less scrupulous vessels. Not all those who remained, after three years in the East, had white skin, but the men who replaced those who had died on the commission had their own binding faiths, which Pigot was careful to honour. Thus the *Dolphin* carried everything from Catholics, through High- and Low-Church Anglicans, to free-thinking Anabaptists and Hindus.

Having served with and been a friend to Maurice Suckling as a youngster, he would not suffer to see the nephew confined to a sick bed below decks. Nelson was accommodated in his own coach, off to the side of his great cabin, the care for his health physical and spiritual the personal responsibility of the Captain. Natural daylight came through the casements as well as fresh air. Though his steward administered food for the body, the care of the young man's spirit was a duty that fell to Pigot. Given the wavering nature of the boy's illness, in and out of deep fevers that continued to waste an already skeletal body, he veered between sermons on hope and tracts to prepare a troubled soul for the rigours of eternity.

In lucid moments Pigot and Nelson read psalms together. If he was well enough he was taken out on deck to attend the Sunday service. That was an obligatory gathering for the whole ship's company, a requirement that could not be laid aside for anything other than danger from battle or the elements. An inspection of the ship, by the Captain, followed before the various elements of the crew were permitted to worship in their own manner. When sick, in a half-comatose state, smitten by another bout of fever, Nelson would lie in his cabin listening to Pigot read his service, his grip on reality often tenuous.

'He has a faith that I fear shames mine.'

A voice close by was inclined to bring Nelson out of his troubled sleep, and Pigot's voice was the cause of that now. He knew, even with his eyes closed, that he had again been very ill, so much so that he had lost all track of time. He was too exhausted even to open his eyes, as he heard the purser of HMS *Dolphin* reply: 'Either that or a will that bespeaks pride.'

'Never. Remember, I have sat with him. I know he loves his God as much as we do ourselves. Odd that though I never clapped eyes on the boy till he came aboard sick, I have come to esteem him almost as much as if he were my own son.'

'That is a dangerous fancy, Captain Pigot. And if it is true that you feel so you must steel yourself to the prospect of loss.'

'That I have done already, though I have prayed for a better conclusion.'

'In truth, he should have expired already. The final spasms cannot be long in coming.'

So I am going to die!

That notion was not new to Nelson, nor was it wholly unwelcome. Death was a constant, as his father was fond of saying, quoting from Corinthians, 'As in Adam, all die', though he would never fail to follow with a message of uplift, like, 'The last enemy that shall be destroyed is death.'

Nelson was subject to the contradictions of the very sick; death, and the release from pain, suffering and shame, held a deep attraction; against that, life held out a vision of fame and fortune, of a lieutenant's commission, of being gazetted as a post captain, then an admiral's command, manoeuvring great fleets and confounding England's enemies. There was a beautiful wife, too, and a hoard of smiling children, broad acres to shame his Orford cousins and a great palace, a gift from a grateful nation to rival the Marlborough edifice at Blenheim.

The *tableau vivant* of Wolfe, the hero of Québec, the nobility of his death, the fluttering of the flags recurred in his troubled dreams, a great many of which were attended by his mother, albeit a younger vision of her than the one he remembered. Her message varied little in substance, even if he conjured up new wordings. Duty and diligence were the foundations of her refrain.

She came again now, as he slipped once more into semiconsciousness, wavering between benign concern for a sick child and a hard remonstrance to be about his duty. Anyone still watching him would have seen his lips move, though they would have struggled to hear the whispered words as the boy spoke what he was sure were his mother's utterances.

'Step back from the gates of the abyss,' he hissed, unaware that the ship in which he lay turned on to another tack that brought sunlight streaming through the window above his head. He felt the heat on his face as the hand of benign Providence, and through thin eyelids the world was suddenly the colour of bright gold. 'Let death be stayed so that you can commit yourself to your nation, free to sacrifice your life, if need be, to raise her standard high.'

He ran the gamut of positive images again: lieutenant, captain, admiral, hero.

Pigot was on deck now, supervising the weekly running in and out of the guns, which rumbled mightily through the deck timbers and carried the tremor of their passing into the fevered brain sweating in the swaying cot. Visions of a stately mansion dissolved into the flame of battle as, using a private supply of powder, James Pigot set one watch against the other in firing the *Dolphin*'s great guns.

The intensity of the golden light increased behind the invalid's eyelids, concentrating into an ever-narrowing beam, his mother's face to one side and that of General James Wolfe to the other. His lips moved again in translation of her pleas, which followed immediately on the boom of the second cannon.

'Death will spare you only to a purpose, Nelson.'

'I must be a hero!' he said out loud, in a cracked voice of enough power to alert Pigot's steward, who had been preparing a light repast in the pantry and now rushed to the patient's side.

The whole ship shuddered at the third shot, which heralded an emphatic 'Yes!' from his mother, again evident only on her son's lips, and not witnessed. But the words that followed were audible and, to a deeply religious man, which Pigot's steward was, they sounded like portents.

'I see before me a golden orb,' Nelson said, 'a light so strong as to burn the soul.' The steward crossed himself, then leant forward to try to hear the whispered words that followed.

'That is the light of the Lord's grace, Nelson, which shines upon you calling you forth to greatness.' The voice deepened. 'That shall be my destiny.'

Pigot's steward didn't know whether to run or stay, didn't know if these utterances were the words of the devil or the incantations of angels.

'You will be spared if you accept your fate.'

The image melted as two of the great guns fired simultaneously. The worried steward placed a cooling cloth across the sweating brow. Beneath it the face carried a smile, beatific to the impressionable observer, the look of a man at peace with his Maker. Fearing he was about to pass over, the steward ran out towards the deck to alert the captain.

BOOK TWO

CHAPTER 16

Emma Lyon, now resident in the attics at Arlington Street, learnt many things in a short time, mingled with much teasing from the other residents. Among those was the deep dislike Mrs Kelly had for the word 'whore'. Any man loose tongued enough to use it faced immediate ejection from her establishment. All those employed at the house were ladies, even if the euphemism 'nuns' was quietly applied. There was no prudery, but discretion was everything.

London enjoyed many layers of licentiousness, from street-walking strumpets through rookery moll houses to the more salubrious bagnios of Covent Garden. Arlington Street in St James's was in a different league, close to coffee houses like White's and Brooks's. It was a house that few men were ashamed to be seen entering or leaving, styling itself a place of entertainment. The nun's morality was loose certainly, but the attachments formed were expected to last longer than the few minutes allotted to a heated lecherous coupling with a moll.

In her first few months Emma wasn't allowed a hint of that. Her employment was simple: to keep the house clean by day and stay out of the way after dark. Time and her own insistent desire changed that. Cleaning remained her true chore, but within six months she was permitted to attend tables and guests, chastely dressed in a maidenly costume, serving wines and sweetmeats, smiling prettily and ensuring that her flawless complexion and fetching green eyes were noticed.

In this she was coached by her mother, who taught her to bob while placing a dish, to serve from the left, allowing the faintest brush of bare flesh to connect with the flapping male hands that came her way. Avoiding anything more telling came naturally to a girl who had been the object of male desire since her earliest years. She knew as she worked that she was under triple scrutiny, the first maternal, the second male and sensual, the third and most exacting, Mrs Kelly's.

The proprietor watched her whenever chance permitted, coolly appraising her ability to deal with men, and judging the worth that could be placed on the unsullied virtue of such a lively and beautiful young creature. If she made a mistake, it was to mention the subject in the presence of Emma's mother.

'Jesus,' Mrs Kelly protested, when Emma's mother had finished spitting blood, 'you make it sound as if I have no notion of how to proceed in such matters.'

'How can that be, when I've seen you carry it through a dozen times?'

'With proper discretion, for sure. And I know how to take my time. Mother of God, the way you're talking anyone would think I'd peddle her off to the first guinea-laden rake with the wit to enquire.'

That had the ring of truth: the Abbess knew her stuff, knew that virtue could be milked, but that once surrendered the loss was permanent. Conversing with her customers she would promise much and deliver little. But eventually she would surrender Emma, charging a price for the privilege. Emma's mother was in a bind, and that had much to do with her own standing as well as the rating Kathleen Kelly put on Emma's virginity. She could only watch as the Abbess prepared Emma for the inevitable, using kind words and flattery to persuade the girl that what must be surrendered one day was best done in comfort, an arranged affair in which the older woman's experience could be employed on Emma's behalf.

'The right fellow can open the gate to a life of pleasure. I'm sure, young as you are, girl, I don't have to tell you what the alternative is.' Kathleen Kelly was enough of an actress to make her next word strike terror into an inexperienced mind. '*Pain!*'

Virgins were highly prized, especially by the older men, and a clean, guaranteed one, as opposed to the numerous scruffy urchins on the streets, created a demand that made temptation impossible to resist. Kathleen Kelly had her clients' trust. They knew she would never sell them short, vend the same girl twice, or lie about the hymen, employing tricks like sheep-blood sacks inserted to expend false virginal blood. And the deflowering would be a pleasant affair, with the girl well prepared, fed with good wine and advice, willing instead of tense and anxious. Hardly surprising that bids for Emma had already been placed.

From her own experience, Emma's mother knew where that would lead. And there was another consideration: the longer Emma spent in the comfort of Arlington Street, the harder it would be to persuade her to return to a less glamorous existence. She would not see that the prospect that faced her mother now would face her in fifteen years' time. But to complain too emphatically might see them both on the street without a farthing to sustain them. Getting Emma out of this place was a project that needed time for both mother and daughter to garner a little money.

Emma was no help, revelling in the freedom that came her way. As soon as Mrs Kelly saw that she had a way with her, the personality to make her customers laugh – which in turn encouraged them to spend money – her morning duties evaporated steadily. There was a wardrobe full of clothes to wear and, properly chaperoned, she was allowed to go out with the other nuns, to walk in Kensington Gardens, even on picnics at which some of Mrs Kelly's clients were present to pick up the bills.

It was an alluring life to a girl of Emma's age: free from expense, full of laughter and the finer things in life, wine, sweetmeats and attentive companions willing to insist that she was the comeliest thing. Looking older than her years added to her allure and offers from men to attend to her well-being were frequent. Quite a few were genuine, in the sense that a man might take her for a mistress, provide her with rooms, food and comfort so that he could enjoy the exclusive right to her favours. She might have succumbed without competition, but her companions on every occasion were not about to allow this newcomer a clear run at advantage, and scotched any overture that was broached.

Her mother was even more active, scouring the parts of London she knew well, talking to those she could trust to be discreet, hinting to those in whom she had less confidence. She knew that during her service at the Linley house Emma had been attracted to the world of theatre, and although acting was not, for a woman, perceived to be much different from whoredom, Mary Cadogan knew it to be a far more respectable occupation.

'I have managed to secure a position for both of us, Emma,' said her mother, having got her daughter alone.

'We have that here.'

'You might, I don't.'

Mary Cadogan fought to remain calm in the light of Emma's pout; there was no doubt that her daughter relished the life, loved the clothes and male attention, and would put up not one jot of resistance to Kathleen Kelly when the time came for her to fulfil her side of their bargain. She also knew there was a wilful quality in that heaving breast.

'Emma, do you believe me when I say I care deeply for you?'

That took Emma by surprise, making her answer sound weak. 'As a mother should.'

'More than most I know. Do you remember Hawarden?'

She nodded, her first recollection being of that huge feather bed, the kind she occupied by right now. It was soon replaced by the memory of the dark, heavy countenance of Sir John Glynne.

'I gave myself to a man for whom I had little affection on the promise that he would see you educated.'

Emma's reply had all the defensiveness of someone who had not appreciated the gift. 'He didn't, though.'

The smile on her mother's face showed a real awareness of her own past foolishness. 'No. I won't say he lied to me – the attachment and the way it were governed was plain enough. But he evaded his word at the first chance presented, leaving me to fend for myself in a way that I did not relish.'

'Here?' Emma demanded, looking her mother straight in the eye.

'It's better in Arlington Street than it could have been. I don't know that I'd have fallen so far as the street – I would have gone home rather than that – but have you ever stopped to ask yourself that with all the time I have been in this house, I have never scraped together much in the way of money?'

Emma couldn't hold that eye contact. She knew that her negative answer would wound before she uttered the word 'No.' She heard the sigh though, not deep but a measure of the hurt.

'You've seen the other nuns with the gifts they've been given stuck on finger or dress? Look, Emma.' Mary held up her ringless hands, and rubbed the top of her dress, which was free of jewellery. 'Look back to the Steps, to your uncle Willy sat by the fire, shirking for a living. My da, stuck out on that damned marsh to keep marauding dogs from the sheep, was never much to bring food to the table. And your gran, for all her wiles, can't fight increasing years. Then there was you!'

There was pain in those eyes, a glistening of tears that spoke of years during which her mother's desires had played second fiddle to the needs of the family, and an unspoken hint that it had scarce been worth it.

'I know you sent money home.'

'As often as I could, even selling that which I was gifted.' The maternal voice was firm again, as Emma's mother suppressed her memories and focused on her purpose. 'Now, if you want to stay under this roof, I don't know as I can stop you. But I hope and pray that you believe I have your best welfare at heart, and that if I was to advise you, you'd abide by what I say.'

Emma's surrender was so meek and swift that it took her mother, geared up to continue the argument and unaware of how much guilt she had loosed, by complete surprise. It was a bonus that Emma was still young enough to see the need for conspiracy as a game. They had to get out of the house without Mrs Kelly finding out, and have rooms waiting for them to move into. London was no place to be on the streets. A few days without a roof and the deterioration in appearance became manifest. That meant accommodation was even harder to find.

James Graham was the provider. A Scotsman by birth, a doctor by training, he was also an innovator who sought cures outside the tenets of his profession, with its addiction to bleeding, blistering and laudanum. He was not a handsome man, rather stooped in his posture. His wig was rarely properly powdered and his narrow face with large bags under the deep-set brown eyes was far from attractive. But he was blessed with a silver tongue between his thick red lips and a persuasive personality, based on the assumption that if he believed something it must be true.

Graham, determined, forthright and sure of his own brilliance, had thrust himself into the world of fashion, claiming that he held the secrets of cures to innumerable ills that refused to answer to traditional methods, particularly in the article of procreation. Such nostrums, especially delivered with assurance, fell on eager ears. The rich and fashionable felt they had a God-given right to good health and were always willing to pay exorbitant sums to achieve it. But Graham's great coup was to interest Georgiana, Duchess of Devonshire, the most fashionable hostess in London, in his electrical cures. With her endorsement, every door in the capital was open to him. If electrical therapy was good enough for her, causing her to shower fees on the Scotsman's shoulders, it was good enough for the whole *ton*. Society clamoured for his attention in such numbers that he couldn't cope.

His answer was a fanum, medicine with a touch of the theatricals, to be called the Temple of Aesculapius, which he was in the process of setting up at the Adelphi on the Royal Terrace in Bond Street. A mock Grecian edifice, it would be dedicated to health, with particular emphasis on all matters related to long life and the begetting of children. There he could treat people in numbers denied to him in a mere drawing room.

It also allowed Graham to extend his experiments. That it also added lustre to his name, by spreading it to a sector of society he had yet to reach was an added bonus. Dr James Graham became what he had always wanted to be: the talk of the town. In this round neo-classical hall, he had the perfect conditions he believed, to advance his ideas and take them to an audience that included the merchants, traders and business-men of London, as well as the landed gentry.

It was no great distance from Arlington Street to Bond Street and Mary Cadogan had come to him through a friend, just at the moment when both were in need. The good doctor was sure that the physical presence of beauty would enhance his lectures, just as the purity of a sweet voice would help to set the tone and calm the nervous. With her connections to the world of the *demi-monde*, Mary was able to provide him with half a dozen handsome women who could be trusted not to disgrace his efforts, while she secured for herself the position of managing them. Emma, with her sweet, high voice, gained the place of *chanteuse*.

Not that either was right away thrust into work. Flush with money from the indulgent Duchess of Devonshire, Graham seemed indifferent to the fact that he was employing a pair for his spectacle without them, at that point, having much to do. He was an odd creature, evangelical in the way he propounded his beliefs, yet unable to shake off the impression that a charlatan lurked in his hollow chest. Tall, thin and stooped, with arms and legs that never seemed quite to co-ordinate with his body, he nevertheless had facial features that became compelling when combined with a deep, reassuring voice that in full rhetorical flow was quite spellbinding.

A man who had treated the Duchess and her friends to a dose of electricity was hard to argue with when he insisted on treating Mary and Emma. All his employees must see the benefits too. Emma was thrilled by the idea, unlike her mother, to whom the tingling that coursed through her limbs was the cause of alarm not pleasure.

The Adelphi was transformed: the windows were painted with portraits of the relevant Greek goddesses, those who spoke of good health, wisdom and fecundity. Doric columns stood at either side of alcoves where at night those recruited and costumed by Mary Cadogan would disport themselves, revealing just enough flesh and outline of figure to titillate the audience. Emma was given song sheets, which she was obliged to learn, her role to sing and so soothe those who came to visit, especially the night-time clients. They paid heavily, a crown a head to enter for the privilege of listening to the good doctor speak, to see him treat a patient or two while enjoying the suggestive portraits and the possibilities latent in the still life, semi-nude figures in the alcoves.

Any medicines or treatments they purchased occasioned

great expense, swelling Graham's profits. But to prove his philanthropic credentials, Dr Graham opened his temple during daylight hours to anyone who was sick or infirm at no charge for either treatment of curatives, leading to a queue made up of London's unhealthy. This displeased everyone in the neighbourhood, except the quondam benefactor busy dispensing his free supply of pills and mild shocks. When they entered both groups, rich and poor, had to pass two enormous footmen, dressed as the heirs of Hercules, followed by a pile of walking sticks and crutches, physical evidence that the remedies proposed and administered were truly efficacious. The clients limped in and walked out.

Graham's lectures were concerned with long life and procreativity, with much reference to the causes of sterility, and were full of expressions like 'the staff of creation' and the 'valley of man's entry to the light of life'. He would thunder at the point where he insisted that a dutiful act was no bar to that same manifestation occasioning pleasure. Fluids unmentionable by name took on different properties from their natural state when, using the properties of electricity, he had a hand in preparation for the 'act of conception'.

At the centre of the room, roped off to the audience but preached over by Graham, stood his celestial bed, a gorgeous construct covered in silk and decorated with gilded lilies. This was available to childless couples for the princely sum of fifty pounds per night, the Latin inscription above reminding these educated patrons that it was a sad thing for a rich man to have no heir to his property. That was the last act of the night, when all others had gone home. Graham would admit whichever couple had booked his facility, treat them to the prescribed regimen, then leave the pair to cavort on his bed, assuring them that their union, previously unblessed, could not now be anything but fruitful.

For a man who spent so much time talking in a roundabout way about sexual congress, Graham was strangely indifferent to the possibilities he had created for himself in the fanum. The ladies who occupied his alcoves, indeed Mary Cadogan herself, were not prudes, and as a wealthy man – as well as their employer – he was in prime position to take advantage. Mary watched him closely, with particular regard to his dealings with Emma. But she had no cause to worry: he was benign in his dealings with all his female employees, vague and paternalistic rather than libidinous.

With the stipend from Dr Graham, Emma and her mother were free to depart Arlington Street, leaving at an early hour when only the skivvies were at large to see them go. They repaired to the Liberties of the Savoy, just south of the Strand. The streets might be narrow and the smell of the Thames too close for comfort, but it was a safe place, beyond the reach of bailiffs and the like. As Emma's mother explained, 'It's where I came to when that scrub Glynne left me high, with debts that he failed to pay. That's the first thing you must do if ever debt threatens, get into the Liberties where those who nab for Newgate are barred from operating. Change your name, as I did, so that everyone knows you by it. You're safe in the Liberties but it's no spot to make the means to eat. You has to go out for that, and a new name is just the thing to keep you out of debtors' prison. So, as soon as I ran for here, I ceased to use the Lyon name.'

'Can you not go back to it?' Emma asked.

Emma's mother had no desire to tell the truth, that she had no intention of ever reverting to the Lyon name, which held for her, in association, nothing but disappointment and hurt.

'I've no desire to. The name Cadogan has a ring to it, which I'm fond of.'

'I still wonder who they are addressing when people say Mary Cadogan.'

'You'll get used to it, Emma. I just hope that you've no cause one day to change your own.'

The shared room was small and cramped yet comfortable and Emma's mother seemed content, although her daughter was not. She liked singing well enough, but when performing she was hidden from view. She longed to appear before the audience, ached to don one of her mother's simple Greek costumes. And, though it was never mentioned, she missed the gaiety of Arlington Street, the gossip and the laughter shared with the other nuns, the picnics and the open carriages that made those people forced to walk regard her with envy. The comfort was another thing, as well as the pleasure to be had from acting the temptress while serving the tables.

Often she lay awake at night, listening to the sound of her mother's gentle snoring, reflecting on the way that her life had been ordered by parental instruction. From the attempt at schooling to every domestic post she had occupied her mother's hand had been present. Liberty from that held fear as well as anticipation and she would sometimes fall asleep wondering if she would ever be allowed to lead a life of her own.

CHAPTER 17

1776

'Remarkable, sir,' exclaimed Captain James Pigot, 'close to a miracle given the depth of your last bout. You begin the New Year a new man.'

Nelson was sitting up for the first time in a week, able to feed himself. The faint tinges of pink in his cheeks were a long way from being termed colour, but it was a distinct improvement on the translucence that had been his lot since leaving Calcutta. The yellow tinge was fading too, though the weakness in his legs prevented him walking on a heaving deck.

'I have a question to ask you, sir.'

The voice was still far from strong, but Pigot noted that uncertainty made it soft, not want of good health. Nelson seemed nervous. 'Ask away.'

There was a pause of several seconds before the question was posed, during which Nelson rehashed all the pros and cons of enquiry that had filled his mind since the fateful day when his fever had reached crisis.

'Do you believe in visions?'

'Visions?'

'They are related often in scripture, sir,' he said, aware that he was speaking too quickly, 'as being afforded to saints and the like.'

Pigot's face darkened at the mention of saints. 'There is a danger here, Mr Nelson that you may border on blasphemy.'

'I do not mean to claim any such elevation for myself, sir,' Nelson protested. 'I only wish to enquire if mere mortals, a sinner even, is also open to such divine favour.'

'I detect a notion here. You feel you have experienced such?'

He had to force out the reply. Divine retribution for blasphemy was not something to be trifled with. 'I do, sir.'

'The nature of this is?'

'I feel I have been close to death, yet spared, called forth by God to a heroic future, called to serve my country.' Seeing the other man's doubt he continued hurriedly. 'I need no longer fear death, having been so spared.'

'Death is not to be feared, Mr Nelson. Dying in sin is.'

'I would not claim purity, sir, only purpose.'

He went on, stammering, to describe the experience, the images of a dead yet saintly mother, the golden halo that had attended the vision, until it had turned into a blinding orb attended by thunder that beckoned him to some distant but weighty destiny. As he spoke Pigot picked up the Bible that lay on the table by Nelson's cot, as if by doing so he could protect himself from the risk of transgression.

'I cannot believe,' Pigot said, as the youngster's voice trailed off, 'that heavenly visions are confined only to candidates for sainthood. Many times myself I have felt close to God, in that time between waking and sleeping, and, I confess, on my own deck. But I've never mustered the arrogance to claim a vision.'

Nelson replied with genuine humility, 'It is the thought of such arrogance that checks me.'

Pigot laid a hand on his shoulder, which was skin and bone with little flesh. 'You have been ill, Nelson, very ill indeed. At one time I was rehearsing the words I would give to your uncle to describe your demise. Yet here you are, sitting up unaided, able to take victuals by your own hand. I do not doubt that you were close to death, and in that state you may have been blessed with insights denied to those who go through their days in robust health.'

The young man's eyes flashed at that moment. 'Then I should act upon it.'

'If you believe it, yes. Damnation awaits you if it is fancy, just as it awaits you if, having been so sanctified, you ignore the divine injunction.'

'My desire is to serve my country, sir. Whatever God has seen fit for me to achieve I would wish to place at the nation's feet.'

Pigot was taken with the expression on the youngster's face. The bright blue eyes, now in hollowed sockets, seemed to blaze. Colour filled the pallid cheeks and the cast of the head, as though fixed on a distant destiny, inspired rather than troubled him. Clutching his Bible harder he said with deep conviction, 'We are all servants of God, and we are humbled before His majesty, just as we are all ordered by His grace.'

'Thank you, sir.'

'I think that what thanks might be offered are due to God,' replied Pigot, sinking from his chair to his knees, Bible in hand. 'Let us pray.'

Nelson was a walking invalid, albeit a weak one, when they raised the Cape of Good Hope, and able to stand as a member of a watch before they crossed the Equator going north. The cooling air seemed to invigorate him. Though not on the muster roll of HMS *Dolphin* he soon became a valuable member of the crew, taking on the full set of duties that went with the role of an aspiring officer. That included continuing his nautical education, which he pursued with a singular zeal that impressed his less driven colleagues and his uncle's good friend, James Pigot.

Dolphin sent a pinnace into Portsmouth with despatches, then touched at the Downs to receive orders and return mail. It was there that Nelson heard the news that his uncle had been appointed to the office of Comptroller of the Navy Board, one of the most powerful positions to which a commissioned sailor could aspire. Ordered ashore at Deal, he was to join Captain Robinson with all despatch as acting fourth lieutenant aboard HMS *Worcester* at Portsmouth.

Setting foot ashore in England once more, on the steep shingle of Deal beach, Horatio Nelson was no longer what he had once been in the Indian Ocean, a shadow of his former self. But the disease had marked him in another way: there was an air about him, a look in the eye of a man who was sure of his course in life.

To be cosseted as an invalid had a certain natural ring to it. But to receive equal attention when in good health was a surprise.

One-legged Captain Mark Robinson of HMS *Worcester* greeted Nelson like a visiting dignitary rather than a midshipman yet to pass his lieutenant's exams. The letters Nelson brought were taken kindly and read without delay. Enthusiasm shone out of the Captain's knobbly face, which was set off by long whiskers and a pair of eyebrows bushy enough to hide half his forehead. He had hardly had time to stow his dunnage before Robinson yelled for his coxswain and whisked him off in his own barge to meet his patron, Admiral Sir James Douglas.

A sense of normality came with the next dawn, as Nelson set about his duties, victualling the ship for convoy duty to Gibraltar, craning livestock aboard – no easy task in the case of cows and bullocks, which might be dangerous if allowed to get loose. The water hoy was alongside pumping full barrel after barrel in the holds while other hands were set to hump all manner of provender up the long sloping gangplank.

Later, he was summoned once more to the great cabin to be told that he was to be taken to dinner with the Mayor of Portsmouth. The reason for the invitation was obvious, now that he was the Comptroller's nephew. By the nature of his office his uncle Maurice would assume the parliamentary seat of the town when it became vacant. Ignoring the relative of such a powerful individual was poor policy.

It was a long time since Nelson had been treated as a child, but he had never been afforded full adult status. He found the dinner trying because of that one fact. He was not left, as most men of his rank would have been, to eat his food and respond politely to the odd remark designed to keep him in the conversation. Both the mayor and Captain Robinson consulted him for an opinion on all manner of topics. The state of the Navy was high on the agenda, a discussion of ships building and those close to being broken up, and especially the nature of Spithead as the main naval base for the future.

The mayor insisted that France was the enemy and a prevailing westerly wind would force the southernmost naval base into pre-eminence, that to sink more money into the Medway ports, Woolwich, Rochester, Sheerness or Chatham, to face the Dutch, was foolish. This was a message he wished passed on to Nelson's uncle, the man who ran all of the Navy's dockyards, with a plea that any available funds should come to his town.

Matters took a less favourable turn when they alighted on the actions of the American colonists in refusing to agree to be taxed, the mayor insisting that they were 'Damned rebels, sir, half of them of criminal stock.'

'I believe the problem hangs on representation, sir,' said Nelson.

The mayor choked and would have added a crushing rebuttal if he hadn't known the connections of the youngster who had made the remark. But he was not to be overborne and the next few minutes were taken up by the natural dissenting sentiments of a Norfolk Whig set against the certainty of the mayor that such rebellion should be punished.

Robinson intervened and moved the pair to safer ground: the cost of poor relief falling on Portsmouth when sailor's wives took up residence in the town. The dinner concluded in a sober but friendly mood, with the mayor pressing on his young dining companion an invitation to come ashore the next day and partake of his hospitality before the ship sailed.

When the *Worcester* raised Gibraltar, Nelson had another example of the status granted him by his relationship to his uncle. Captain Robinson sent him ashore with the letters and despatches. Naturally these included one that alluded to Nelson's connections so he found himself once more in receipt of invitations that bore little relation to his station. By the time he returned from his first voyage, he was laden with messages, both written and verbal, for his uncle Suckling.

But the news he received on his return was better: dates had been set early in the following spring for his examination for a commission, to be chaired by his uncle and served by a committee of officers Captain Suckling knew and trusted. Over the forthcoming winter the Gibraltar voyages would complete his sea time, and he was abjured to set his mind to his manuals in the intervening period so that he could answer the questions the panel of captains would pose.

When the day came, it was a nervous and fragile looking Midshipman Nelson who presented himself at the offices of the Navy Board. The high-ceilinged room was forbidding in the way that it echoed the voices of those asking the questions, four unsmiling captains who had already reduced a drove of aspirants to weak-kneed jelly. His uncle, occupying the central seat of honour, showed no sign of recognition. He examined the logs as if the man before him was a stranger, books from *Carcass*, *Raisonable*, *Triumph*, *Seahorse* and *Worcester* that proved the candidate had the requisite six years' sea time.

No one questioned the figure inscribed in the muster roll on which he had first been entered that put him a good two years above his real age. But they did test his competence as a seaman, firing questions at him like a rolling barrage. As he answered his nervousness eased, but he was still unsure if the examiners saw before them an officer whose competence could never be in dispute, a man who had a right to a lieutenant's rank. The grim faces never relaxed as they conferred in hushed tones, even when Maurice Suckling rose to his feet.

Nelson wasn't privy to what was coming, and the dull sensation in the pit of his stomach, the fear that he was going to fail, was not assuaged by the avuncular smile. Suddenly the room took on a frightening air, the echoes of voices from the plastered walls and bare floorboards threatening. To founder here would see his career stalled. Perhaps he would become like those midshipmen he had encountered too frequently, men past their prime, going nowhere and bitter because of it.

The reaction when his uncle introduced him as a relative was very strange, the way the examining officers expressed surprise seemed insincere. The view that Captain Suckling had not wished to see a relative unduly favoured was greeted with pronounced nodding that did nothing to convince the candidate that these gentlemen were not playacting.

But when called to attest to his obvious abilities the voices were honest enough, and slowly it dawned on Nelson that he was going to be passed for lieutenant. Fear turned to an almost uncontainable joy, and while he had to stop himself from leaping to his feet and shaking every hand in the room the whole examination was brought to a cheerful conclusion. Nelson walked out knowing his commission was a certainty, smiling into the worried faces of those who were slated to follow him.

The following morning he received orders to join a new ship, HMS *Lowestoffe*, captained by one William Locker.

Every King's ship was a self-contained world, which applied just as much to *Lowestoffe* as it did to any other frigate. Joining a new vessel was a rite of passage endured by every commissioned officer and all the members of the wardroom had similar experience. On first acquaintance members of the wardroom were generally guarded, careful of what they said as much to protect themselves, as to avoid offending newcomers. But a shared profession, with ports, journeys and sometimes acquaintances in common, usually helped to break down the reserve.

Lieutenant Waddle, the premier, didn't like Nelson from the moment he clapped eyes on him and he made no secret of the fact. There was no apparent reason for this other than a natural antipathy, which was troubling, especially since his relations with his new commanding officer began well. Captain William Locker tried to be a friend to all his officers. Open, cheerful and more inclined to advise than criticise, he was a stocky red-faced man of thirty-six years. He walked with a permanent limp, from a wound which still pained him, a pike thrust to his knee received boarding a French privateer off Alicante.

Coming from a naval family himself, and having married into another, the Captain was mired in the history of his profession. His hero was the late Admiral Hawke, though he was honest enough to admit to that man's trying temperament: Hawke had been foul-mouthed, bellicose and intolerant. To Locker that counted for nothing when compared with his exemplary behaviour in the face of an enemy, a policy the Captain had committed himself to follow. Over dinner in a shore tavern he regaled his officers with the mass of opportunities that might come their way: he had just heard that his ship had been ordered to service in the Caribbean.

'There are American privateers in those waters, as well as Frenchmen flying their colours. What we see, gentlemen, we will engage. And I give you this advice should we meet a Frenchie, which was the watchword of Lord Hawke himself: always lay a Frenchman close and you will beat him.'

His newly commissioned second lieutenant, who had been a glint in the parental eye when Locker had been wounded, could not hear enough about the heroic Hawke; Nelson encouraged the Captain in his historical ramblings, drinking in everything he had to say. There was no doubt that the older man was flattered by such unaffected attention. Waddle, of course, could not be brought to believe that such mutual esteem bore no relation to the position and influence of the young man's connections, which lowered Nelson even further in his estimation.

Nelson didn't boast of his relationship to the new Comptroller of the Navy Board, but it wasn't surprising, in a small world, that the first lieutenant soon found out. Waddle knew just how much power that office conferred on the holder. Though still only a captain, Maurice Suckling could look admirals square in the eye, since the power of his patronage was at least as great as theirs, and only marginally less than that of the First Lord himself. Such influence, dispensed wisely, would produce a positive response to any corresponding request.

It was two months before Nelson saw his uncle again. An enervating illness which had laid the Comptroller low precluded contact, even though *Lowestoffe* was being made ready for sea less than a mile from his office. Nelson joined him for dinner in his spacious accommodation, which alone gave ample evidence of both Maurice Suckling's elevation, his power and his connections. No cramped cabin here but a vast chamber in the former Royal Palace at Greenwich, with huge windows that overlooked the river Thames.

Everything had the feel of real luxury, from the polished mahogany and sparkling brass fittings on the doors, to a gleaming table that could host a conference or dinner for fifty. The walls were hung with portraits of his predecessors, as well as scenes of great naval victories. Yet there was intimacy too, as they sat in a pair of twin satin settles on either side of a blazing fire, a liveried attendant discreetly just outside the circle of candlelight ready to see to their every need.

'Sir James Douglas's nephew will never make a sailor. He's

green around the gills at the sight of a stagnant pond. But I have been able to provide for him a position as assistant to the master attendant at Chatham dockyard. In time, naturally, he will succeed to the senior appointment.'

Since the post he had been offered as second lieutenant on *Lowestoffe* had been granted by that same Admiral Douglas, his uncle had no need to spell out the connection. Reciprocal influence was at work, as was so often the case in the Navy. Maurice Suckling went on to talk about what opportunities might occur on this new commission.

The commanding officer in Jamaica, Admiral Gaynor, was due to be relieved. There was a queue a mile long of admirals wishing to take over, there being no better place to be in a war than the West Indies. A hundred thousand pounds in prize money was not unknown in those waters for an active admiral with enterprising officers.

Nelson listened attentively, yet could not avoid noting that the ravages of recent fever were still in his uncle's face, which had not filled out to the rounded healthy countenance that he remembered. Likewise his hair had lost its fine texture. But at least the eyes were still direct, piercing and without side.

'Whoever gets the post, Horace, I will be here acting on your behalf. A new admiral going to a new overseas commission will have requirements, some of which I flatter myself I will be able to meet. Your task is to achieve a degree of prominence so that whatever recommendations I suggest will be gladly undertaken. In short, you must excel yourself, boy.'

It took no great leap of Nelson's imagination to see himself fulfilling his uncle's wildest hopes: victorious, standing on an enemy deck accepting a captain's sword in surrender, a hero to the fleet. But when he spoke, he knew he had to sound modest and grateful. 'I will do my very best, sir.'

'I'm sure you will. But it's not as easy as it sounds. Your new commander is a fine sailor who loves a fight. But I've seen men as good and even better than William Locker who have spent their whole service life without so much as a sniff of powder. Just pray that *Lowestoffe* puts you the way of a trifle of glory. Then, when the new admiral arrives he will have no difficulty in showing you preferment. Never forget, Horace, that whatever he decides, even three thousand miles away, will have to be confirmed here in London.'

'I will pray to God for guidance on the voyage, Uncle.'

'Just don't get your head blown off,' said Suckling, his voice gruff. 'God knows, I'd miss you if you did.'

CHAPTER 18

Nelson never knew who informed the premier that the new Comptroller had chaired the body set to examine Midshipman Nelson, to ensure that he was competent to receive a lieutenant's commission. And, despite the evidence of his own eyes as Nelson carried out his duties, Waddle rarely lost an opportunity to diminish Nelson by alluding to that fact, the implication that he had only passed because of his uncle's presence.

And it was always allusion, never a direct insult. But, as the man who chaired every meal at the wardroom table, and who had the authority to control the subject of conversation if he so chose, Waddle never lacked opportunity. He took a savage pleasure in discussing it at their present mooring off Woolwich, so close to the office Captain Suckling occupied in the neighbouring parish of Greenwich.

'The service stands in peril from the misuse of influence, gentlemen, do you not agree?' Even if the sentiment was accurate the murmurs of assent were muted; too many people knew the target to be comfortable, but that was enough to encourage Waddle to continue. 'At peace, it might make little difference, but in a time of war it is perilous indeed to go placing people in positions of authority merely because of their connections.'

With his pallid complexion, and smooth, moon-like face, the premier could never smile without causing unease, since what should have been an amiable gesture too often hinted at conceit. He was a competent, if uninspiring seaman who held the loyalty of his juniors through his office, not through personal affection. But he was not actively disliked. He could appear interested in everyone, and it was only when each member of the wardroom was asked, for the third time, the same question regarding background or past experience that they realised he rarely listened to their answers.

'For it is in the heat of battle that the mettle of officers is tested,' the premier added, 'though you would scarce think so when you see the ease with which some of our number achieve their rank.'

'I'm sure, when the time comes, we need only follow your example, sir.'

Waddle's eyes narrowed a fraction, but he didn't look at Nelson. Instead, his gaze ranged around the others present: the master, Mr Bootle, the purser, Abel Corman, Pryce the schoolmaster and finally the marine officer, Lieutenant Livingston. Not one met his gaze, suddenly more interested in their food than conversation.

'What about that skirmish in the Indian Ocean, Nelson? That's one treat you've yet to regale us with.'

'It was a trifling affair, sir,' Nelson answered, suddenly wary. Under normal circumstances he would have obliged happily, but with Waddle looking at him in that jaundiced way he suspected he was being drawn into a snare.

'Come along, sir,' said Waddle, leaning forward with an insincere smile. 'No false modesty, if you please.'

All eyes were on Nelson now, eager to hear the details of any action, even if he had described it as trifling. Nothing excited a ship's wardroom more than tales of a fight that resulted in the taking of prizes. That meant a money reward, which, to a profession with few wealthy men, was the stuff of every dream, waking or nocturnal. There was no alternative but to comply, and it was a requirement that he set the scene, with the names of ships, number of guns, plus the course and weather. Questions were posed, especially by Mr Bootle who knew Surridge, though all fell silent when it came to the capture.

'So you didn't actually board yourself?' asked Waddle.

'No, sir.'

'I'm surprised, Mr Nelson, that you could resist it. Still, having been so newly appointed to your division you could hardly be expected to be sure of your duties.'

There was little he could say in response, having been put in his place by a man far more experienced at dinner table talk. The telling of such a tale required a degree of modesty anyway, if he wasn't to sound boastful. And he had been below decks at the point of boarding, which robbed the conclusion of much of its impact.

'A very creditable action, I'm sure,' said Waddle, with another smile. Then he turned to the purser, the thin, pinch-faced Abel Corman. 'You were a resident in Jamaica, Mr Corman, do tell us what we can expect when we arrive there.'

Nelson wanted to decline the command of a press gang, but the look in Waddle's eye left him in no doubt that such a request would be denied. The premier spotted his hesitation to proceed though, and commented on it. 'You find the idea uncongenial, I can see. The trouble is, Mr Nelson, if your uncle and the Navy Board cannot supply the fleet with enough men, we must go out and press them ourselves.'

'Estuary boats would be better than prowling the streets, sir.'

'They would not! Every ship-of-the-line will have their longboats off Margate and the Essex coast. Take the word of one who has real experience. I was active there during the Falklands quarrel. Blood was spilt then and there will be blood once more. And it won't be merchant seamen with dented skulls, it will be the crews of the men-o'-war doing battle with each other for some minor advantage, rather than searching for the few scarce hands they can take up.'

There was no denying the truth of that; two ship's crews in the same location, on land or at sea, seeking to recruit or press men for their own vessel, invariably ended in a brawl.

'Then let me go further out, sir, south of the Downs, if necessary.'

'A letter to your uncle would do more good,' Waddle snapped. 'We're still eighty men short on our complement, and that with the conflict barely begun.'

'Perhaps some of the men who would naturally volunteer dislike the idea of fighting the American colonists.'

'How about you? Are you one of those dissenting Fenland types?'

Nelson refused to be drawn on that, even if he did have some sympathy with the revolutionaries. The affair had been badly handled. And the good folk of Norfolk, many of whose Puritan ancestors had provided the first settlers, had been quick to say so. His own opinions didn't count. He was a serving officer holding a King's commission. If the sovereign decided that the Americans must be chastised rather than persuaded, he had little choice but to obey.

'We are unlikely to find eighty sailors wandering the streets.'

'Bodies will do, Nelson. We'll make sailors of them when we get to sea.'

'What's the tally, Mr Waddle?'

The premier raised his hat as Captain Locker approached, his limp exaggerating the rolling sailor's gait. The information that a hundred men had come forward was treated with a grunt. *Lowestoffe* was detailed to escort a convoy already assembling in the Downs.

'We need more'n that to do our duty!'

'I agree, sir. I was just about to detail Mr Nelson to press more hands, but he seems to harbour a degree of reluctance.'

Locker's eyes, lit by flaring torches, seemed to blaze with more ferocity than the flames. 'Does he, by damn?'

Waddle's explanation made much more of Nelson's disquiet than was strictly true, but he couldn't complain. Locker had set up a rendezvous near the Tower of London, and that had brought in volunteers, but they were a sorry bunch, with few real tars among them, dregs tempted by promises of regular food, clothing, West Indian sunshine. Poster parties were still out in strength, proclaiming Locker of the *Lowestoffe* to be a follower of the great Admiral Hawke and as like to achieve success as his mentor. They were also busy ripping down the proclamations of rival ships, replacing them with their own. That the other ships' companies were likewise engaged was held to be common practice, and as long as they were not caught in the act of destruction, nothing would be said or done.

'I agree with Waddle about the estuary, Nelson,' said Locker. His voice carried no trace of anger as he continued, 'And don't go thinkin' your reluctance is singular. Pressing men is a damned unpleasant business and not one that I ever took pleasure in.'

'But it is, sir,' insisted Waddle, 'very necessary.'

Locker nodded, eyes still on his second lieutenant. 'We have no other way of crewing the ship, Mr Nelson, and what cannot be gainsaid must be borne. Now, go about your duty, and do as well as you are able.'

'There's two ways of doin' this, your honour,' said Giddings, a short, burly bosun's mate, with a flat face made more so by an oft broken nose. Waddle had put Giddings at Nelson's disposal along with seven other crewmen, and Bromwich, a twelve-year-old midshipman, was bringing up the rear.

Nelson knew the latter better than Giddings since he had made a point of ensuring that the midshipmen's mess was being run in the proper manner. Thanks to his strictures, Bromwich, tall, gangling and a touch bovine, was in more danger of bumping his head than being bullied by his messmates. Giddings was a different case altogether. You could see from his face, squashed nose and a cauliflower ear, that he liked to scrap. As a man who would inflict punishment with the cat he had to be a hard case. Nelson always had to fight his own natural dislike of a breed like that, reminding himself that, from his privileged position, he was in no position to carp at how others made their way in the world.

'I've done this afore,' Giddings added, 'an' you either has to get them drunk, or find them that's had too much ale already. The former be the easier.'

'The first way wouldn't entail the crew enjoying a drink as well, would it, Giddings?'

The bosun's mate didn't see the faint grin on the officer's face as he grunted his reply. The street was too dark and Nelson was ahead of the lanterns. These men barely knew him and they would assume he was a soft touch until he proved otherwise. That was a notion of which they needed to be disabused.

'Else we find a rookery, surround the place,' Giddings added, 'an' take out every man who's able of body.'

'Ten men to surround a rookery that might contain several hundred souls?'

There were enough dwellings of that nature around the areas that abutted the London docks, rambling ramshackle affairs, one hutch tacked on to another in a dizzying configuration with no thought to order, home to people well versed in avoiding anything smacking of authority. The whole south bank of the Thames was lined with them, the homes of those attracted to the work the docks provided, a place where criminality flourished alongside poverty and disease. The locals knew their patch, alleys no bigger than an inadvertent gap between two shacks, trapdoors and roof spaces that provided ready exit in a way that no outsider could hope to unravel. There was only one way to take a rookery: seal the external exits with one large body, while another systematically searched the interior.

'It's not a lot I will grant, your honour, but it might serve to get us what we want.'

Why didn't Giddings share his own revulsion at what they were being asked to do? The man might be a volunteer himself, and as a bosun's mate he had achieved some status. But he had more in common with the men they were seeking to take up than he had with the officer leading him. The rest of his party were just as ardent, and he knew that one or two of them, peacetime sailors, had been initially pressed in wartime themselves. Surely, from what they knew about life before the mast in wartime aboard a man-o'-war, they would be more inclined to run than gather more victims. Nelson knew he couldn't ask, but his curiosity was so acute that a way of proceeding came to mind.

'I had a friend once, Giddings, a man called John Judd. I served with him on a merchant vessel.'

The bosun's mate was genuinely surprised. 'You did merchant service, your honour?'

'I did, and as a common seaman. A round voyage to the Caribbean in which I learnt a great deal not vouchsafed to many officers, most of it imparted by that same John Judd. He even spoke of the activity in which we are presently engaged.'

'So what did this friend of yours say?' Giddings asked, guardedly.

'I fear I must quote him at the peril of my soul. He said that pressing men was a job for a poxed son of a shit shoveller's bitch, but that there wasn't a King's hard bargain born that didn't fucking love it.'

Giddings hadn't gasped at the language, the like of which he had heard often enough on an officer's lips. But the man he was with now was reckoned to be pious, free from harsh judgement and disinclined to raise his voice or bark his orders. There was a different note in his own voice as he replied, 'I've never been one to deny another a favour, your honour.'

Nelson laughed. 'A favour?'

There was a note of emphatic sincerity in the man's voice as he responded. 'For certain, your honour. Don't forget that I've been ashore, man and boy, and I know how hard it is to make a crust. 'Tis no different for others that we take up, half starved, livin' by beggin' or riflin' the rich man's bins. Least we feed 'em 'board ship. And providin' they don't pine too much for home, and they attend to what they're shown, well, they come to love the life.'

'I imagine John Judd would say bollocks to that.'

'Just how long was you on this merchant barky, your honour?'

'Long enough, Giddings, to know when I'm being invited to piss into the wind.'

Giddings chuckled. 'How about the fact that if I ain't got a warm feather bed and a wide comfortable arse to snuggle to then I'm damned if anyone else will be free to enjoy the like?'

'Now that has the ring of truth.'

'Sir,' called Bromwich from the rear.

'A hush, sir, if you please.' Nelson heard the singing as soon as he stopped talking, drunken warbling that was plain at a distance.

'Sounds like trade to me, your honour,' hissed Giddings, shading his lantern.

'What's the best method?'

'Doorways, lads,' muttered the bosun's mate, ignoring his officer. 'Keep hidden and come out on my yell.'

Nelson found himself in a doorway too, his own lantern shaded, listening as the noise grew louder. The cold night air had already penetrated his boat cloak and now, standing still, it was chilling him to the marrow. He couldn't see their prey, but the shuffling, uneven feet told him they were very drunk indeed. He knew they wouldn't be sailors, even here, close to the docks. Seamen might not be noted for true wisdom, but any man who sailed a vessel into the Pool of London couldn't fail to see the ships fitting out for the Americas further downriver, and blue-water men, according to John Judd, knew how to keep away from the press.

Giddings didn't yell. Indeed, he hardly raised his voice as he said, 'Take them, lads.'

Ghost-like, in the dim light from the stars, the men emerged. The trio tried to resist, to insist that they were of gentle birth. Neither was much of a success. They were too drunk to stand upright and even in dim of a lantern Nelson could see they wore clothes that were close to being rags.

'Might I suggest, your honour, that we whip this lot off to the premier. The racket they're making will scare off any more prospects.'

'Make it so, Giddings,' Nelson replied, shivering slightly.

'Are you all right, sir?' Giddings asked, holding up his lantern, and peering into the officer's face.

'Fine!' Nelson insisted, though he felt anything but. The cold and damp seemed to have seeped right through his body, which shuddered uncontrollably every few seconds.

'You don't look it,' Giddings insisted, with real concern.

'Are you a surgeon, man?' Nelson snapped. 'Attend to your duty and let me do the same.'

'Aye, aye, sir,' Giddings replied, his voice, for the first time, stiff and formal now, thinking, Happen this officer weren't so soft after all.

He detailed two men to take the captures, now with their arms bound, to the Tower. Within the hour they would be entered on the *Lowestoffe*'s books. Then the party set off down more narrow, stinking alleyways. The ever-present smell of human waste and filth seemed to press in on him like the buildings above his head, adding to Nelson's discomfort. The streets, if such lanes could be flattered by such a description, cleared ahead of them. The locals knew who they were, and if some of the men were too drunk to flee, they had womenfolk or friends around who, when alerted, dragged them to a secure place. They tried one tavern, but it was full to bursting with scarred, tough looking individuals, too numerous for such a small party.

'If we mark the spot, your honour, we can come back with more men.'

'Yes,' Nelson responded weakly.

Giddings's lantern was lifted high, to show a pale sweating face, eyes that were without spark, and a mouth that was slack at the corners. 'You ain't on the up and up, sir, no matter what you say. Death's door be more like it.'

Nelson waved his hand to push Giddings and the lantern aside, but his gesture was too feeble to achieve anything, serving only to confirm that he was sick. He fell forward slightly, the bosun's mate grabbing his arm to steady him.

'Thank you, Giddings,' he whispered, pulling himself upright, willing himself to fight the desire to let go.

'Mainmast goin' by the board,' the sailor replied, as Nelson started to fall over. Giddings caught him, and with one easy arm hoisted him on to his shoulders. The protest died in Nelson's throat as the world around him, dark night pricked with lanterns, lost focus.

'Back to the Tower, lads. Mr Nelson has passed out.'

'Weak as piss, is he?'

'Don't know, matey,' Giddings replied, half turning with the comatose officer on his shoulder. 'He ain't half bad as commissioned sods go. But I'll wager this, if the little bugger fights like he swears, he'll be a rare plucked 'un.'

CHAPTER 19

Being seasick for the first time was an added burden for a man already weak from fever. Nelson was self-conscious about his condition, though none of his fellow officers referred to it, aware that they, too, might succumb to a different motion than the choppy seas they were now experiencing. At least he knew it would pass, which was more than could be said for the pressed men they had hauled aboard. Exposed to their first taste of the North Sea off Ramsgate, they were convinced they were about to die. Given they had lacked good health before going to sea, several looked as though they might be right.

Not knowing their duty they had to be driven to even the simplest task often with the end of a knotted rope, a starter that stung the back of the ribs as the petty officers applied it with relish. Grey skies, a heaving ocean and sporadic rain added to the discomfort of working on deck. Hands that had clenched on a rope became blistered and raw as they heaved on the braces, or hauled on lines to get sails and spars aloft.

Sentiment had to be put to one side. An inexperienced crew, indulged, might sink them, and Lieutenant Nelson was as harsh as his own condition would allow him to be. He yelled as loudly as Waddle, though he eschewed use of a starter, instead pushing men into place with his bare hands. On several occasions he knew how close he came to receiving a return blow for his efforts. But before they had put to sea, William Locker had read them the Articles of War, so each landsman knew that death was the penalty for striking an officer.

As second lieutenant, Nelson was in charge of half a watch, with only a quartet of proper seamen to help him control over fifty men, not one of whom seemed ever to have laboured in his life. A very few had some semblance of brain, but most were thicker than the wood on which they stood, gormless individuals who could not comprehend any request to haul on a rope, even if it was accompanied by careful, repeated explanation.

'Come along, Mr Nelson,' yelled Waddle, moving forward from the quarterdeck to where his second was supervising a party just in front of the gangways overlooking the waist. Free with his starter, the premier laid into every back that presented itself, leaving the unfortunates cowering in his wake. 'You must get your men on to the mainmast braces quick, or God knows what fate we'll endure.'

'They'll be slick enough when they know their duty, sir.'

Waddle swung at another head that was trying to retch into the sea, catching the man across the cheek. 'By damn, they'll know their duty or take a turn at the grating.'

That was Waddle's response to all transgressions – a good flogging. Nothing would persuade him that there was another way and Nelson was in no state even to try now; he was so weak he had to take hold of the hammock nettings to remain upright. Another sudden shower hit them as he opened his mouth to protest. 'They are my division, sir. Might I be allowed to discipline them?'

'They are my responsibility, sir!' Waddle yelled, swaying easily on his good sea legs as the water streamed off his oilskins. 'So is the whole ship. And take care that I do not see fit to discipline *you*.'

Waddle pushed the thick, knotted rope into his second lieutenant's hands. 'Take this, sir, and apply it heartily. And that, Nelson, is an order.'

The weather worsened as they rounded the South Foreland off Dover, to beat down the Channel into the teeth of a westerly rain-filled wind. The watch was changed, and a new set of sick, useless individuals came on deck, those going below staring at him in disbelief as he told them to piss on their hands so the blisters would heal. If anything, having been confined below, the new lot were in a worse state than their companions, the rags they wore soon drenched, their hair matted over low, confused foreheads.

Aware that Waddle was watching him, their officer swung the rope, adding the obligatory curses, although the starter landed with little venom. Yet such consideration was wasted. These men had so little experience of the sea that they considered themselves hard done by and they saw the man who commanded their division as a tyrant.

Life below was just as rough. Experienced hands were determined that these lubberly newcomers should defer to them. As cold air whistled around them, men soaked to the skin shivered in damp hammocks, occasionally retching over the side, though their stomachs contained nothing that would stain the red-painted deck. Two men died before their watch was turned out again, either from despair or fatigue, their emaciated frames testifying to the life of poverty they had abandoned in order to enlist in the King's service.

Facing a five-day blow with a brand new crew taxed all of Captain Locker's ability as a seaman. The master and he were rarely off the deck, as they shifted canvas and wood to haul round so that *Lowestoffe* could make some headway into the screaming westerly wind. There were ports off his lee that would harbour the entire convoy if conditions worsened, but Locker wanted no safe anchorage if it could be avoided. So Portsmouth, Lymington and Poole were ignored until, due south of Plymouth, he put his helm down and took the wind a few points off his stern. His bowsprit was now set on a course to weather what they must pass with plenty of sea room, the coast of Brittany off Ushant. The manoeuvre was copied at once by every one of the merchant captains for whom he was responsible, each one heaving over to show the copper that lined their bottoms as the wind drove into their side.

With the wind abaft their beam the pitch of the vessel eased. Men who had survived in the choppy waters of the Dover Straits and stayed upright in the English Channel were struck down by the change in motion. But it was an easier movement, which served Nelson well: he lost the yellow look of fast-approaching death, and got some colour back in his cheeks. Now that the sails were set true he could attend to the needs of his watch, most of whom now struggled to walk on a deck that was not only rising and falling but canted like a gentle slope.

'Giddings,' he ordered, 'get some food into any man who has not eaten.'

'That'll do the decks no good, your honour,' said Giddings, crossly. 'Let them lay till the weather clears. 'Sides, you could use some victuals yourself.'

What colour he had gained disappeared as he paled with anger. 'Two men have died already. If we leave them there'll be more. Do as I say, and any man who refuses food, force some well-watered rum and ship's biscuit down his throat.'

'Permission to set some of them upright to act as swabbers. There's shit all over the lower decks from them that know no better.'

'Make it so,' Nelson replied, heading for the wardroom. That matter would have to be sorted out before divisions on Sunday. He couldn't blame the lubbers who had had no chance to be educated, but they must be told to use the heads, on fear of some punishment, otherwise the ship would stink throughout the whole commission.

Little did he know that Giddings was below, telling his sickening charges just how lucky they were. ''Cos if it had been any other officer than Mr Nelson, you stupid cunts would be had up already. And I tell you, one more steaming turd found between the hammocks and it won't be the grating you'll get, it'll be my fist down your throat.'

As soon as he entered the wardroom Nelson accosted the purser, his pinched face pink from sitting near the stove. 'How soon can we issue the new hands with some proper clothing?'

Like all pursers, Abel Corman had a sleek appearance, although he was personally of slight build. Perhaps it was the quality of his clothes, and that he had been below all the time they had battled their way down the Channel. The bottle of claret, secure in the rack by his left elbow, might also have added to his overwhelming appearance of well being.

'Best left till the weather moderates a trifle, Nelson. We can't go laying out good canvas on a wet deck. And with all this heavin' and hoin' there'd be no end of waste in the cutting.'

'We've lost two men already.'

Corman sniffed, pulled out his bottle of wine and hinted, with a forward push, that Nelson might like some. 'Happens every commission, young fellow. They come aboard with every manner of disease in their frames. It's the hovels they live in, of course, and the salt water and air does for them. I remember when I was assistant in HMS *Ardent* we lost a round two dozen, most of them overboard, between Harwich and Leith.'

Even sick with fever Nelson had gone out with press gangs until the ship had its complement. The purser's air of complacency riled him, but he controlled it, albeit with difficulty. 'Would it surprise you, Mr Corman, that having gone to great trouble to acquire them, I'd be mighty loath to lose any more.'

Corman blinked then: the tone had been polite enough but the ice-cold blue eyes and the pale drawn face hinted at deep anger and frustration. 'And I think that men dying of wet and cold might be more wasteful than a few shreds of canvas.'

'Spoken like a fellow who has no need to account for it,' Corman said, sitting forward, skinny chest puffed out, his tone pompous. 'But I do, sir, and to men who can spot the waste of a farthing fraction.'

'Nevertheless,' Nelson hissed.

Corman held up his hand, aware that the youngster was close to losing his temper. 'It is the Captain's decision, Nelson, not mine. I suggest that you eat and drink something yourself, or perhaps you will be the one to expire.'

Waddle, in oilskins, entered behind them. 'Mr Nelson, we shall be returning to normal watch keeping, now conditions are somewhat eased.'

'Sir.'

'Which means that, if I were you, I should get some sleep. I've set Midshipman Latimer the first dog-watch. You are due to relieve him in less than two hours.'

'I asked Corman if we could issue some clothing to the landsmen.'

Waddle staggered as *Lowestoffe* pitched over in the wake of a large wave. 'In this? Are you mad?'

'No, sir, but I am concerned for the condition of the men.'

The round face, red from wind and rain, still seemed smooth, though the eyes, red-rimmed and tired, were less so. 'Take it as a blessing, Nelson. Weather like this weeds out the weaklings for you. Saves you the trouble of having to deal with them for the rest of the commission.'

'Quite,' put in Corman. 'The weeds usually end up at the grating, and if they expire from that it causes ill feeling in the crew. If it's not that, the sods tumble overboard for no reason.'

Nelson glared at him. 'I must ask again, sir.'

'And I must refuse.'

'Sir,' Nelson protested.

'You mistake your position, Mr Nelson, which I attribute to the influence of your connections. Let me remind you that we are at sea now.'

'Permission to see the Captain.'

'Denied!' barked Waddle. 'He is even more exhausted than you look. The men will be issued with their ducks when the sun is out and the deck even. Do I make myself clear?'

'Aye, aye, sir,' Nelson replied, pushing past the premier.

'Where the devil are you going man? I told you to get some sleep.'

He was sick of Waddle and his attitude that men were lower than the animals cosseted in the manger, and expendable. He was even more tired of deferring to his malice.

'I do believe, sir, that even in the bounds of naval discipline, that is beyond your remit.'

'Damn you, sir.'

'And damn you Mr Waddle.' Nelson's blue eyes were blazing with passion. 'We have the good fortune to live in a country where opinions may freely be stated, and these are mine. That your actions are a disgrace to human decency. Worse, they are more likely to sink us than save us. You, sir, are nothing short of a bully, and while you may instruct me in many respects I will never obey an order that forces me to emulate what I consider base behaviour. I will earn respect, not enforce it.'

'How dare you?' Waddle spat, his knotted starter raised to strike.

Nelson didn't flinch. 'Use it, Mr Waddle, and I'll call you out.'

There was a moment when it looked as if Waddle was going to succumb to temptation. He was bigger, stronger and healthier than the man challenging him. But he lacked the strength of will to impose himself on a personality that he must have known would never buckle. As soon as the moment of danger had passed, Nelson spun round and left the wardroom. He heard Waddle curse as he departed, then the words, faint but clear, addressed to the purser: 'There's a lily liver in that breast, Corman, mark my words. He thinks me blind, thinks I can't tell the odds between a proper blow with a starter and a dumb show. I've come across the type before, who're soft on the hands. It would not surprise me to learn that Mr Nelson would rather bed them than work them. No doubt he thinks to win their affection, but I know it to be as true as the nose on my face that when the time comes, and there's death flying about, they won't follow him.'

'He certainly has a great deal to learn,' Corman replied.

Waddle's reply had real venom in it. 'No, he doesn't. Not with his uncle so well placed that every senior officer will grovel to appease him.'

Was that true? Would he be favoured even if he was useless? The way Waddle continued certainly meant he thought so. 'That whey-faced pup will rise like well-mixed dough in warm air and, no doubt, have a ship of his own, while I am still some other captain's whipping boy.'

Eventually the weather did ease, though the sun didn't make an immediate appearance. Badgered on a daily basis by Nelson, Corman finally relented and hauled the necessary bolts of canvas from the sail locker. Each man was issued with enough to make a set of trousers and provided with cloth to knock up a shirt. Then, amid much grumbling, the better-qualified hands were set to teaching them how to sew their ducks, with Mr Nelson prowling on the main deck to ensure that none of the usual jokes were played. He wanted no three-legged men in his division.

Easier weather provided a chance to train the men rather than drive them. And once they had a uniform appearance, and had been fed for a week on plain but proper food that they could keep in their stomachs, they began to look like a reasonably healthy bunch of hands. Those with hair long enough had already begun to plait it, taking in good heart or ill the taunts of the long-serving, pigtailed topmen.

'Christ, your honour,' said Giddings, who had taken to

breaching the bounds of proper discipline by talking to an officer without permission, then doubling the offence by taking the Lord's name in vain, 'if I didn't know better, I'd say they almost looked like sailors.'

'They do that, Giddings,' Nelson replied.

The two men exchanged grins as the clouds parted at last, and the first burst of sunshine they had seen since leaving the Downs bathed *Lowestoffe*'s deck.

As they sailed south to the Azores, where they would put up their helm to head west on the trade winds, faces became names, and names became people, with homes, families and problems they could always raise, providing Giddings had laid the way, with the second lieutenant. There were those who would never make seamen as long as they lived, the mere act of hauling on a rope nearly beyond their mental powers, but in some sense every man took on a role aboard ship, even if it was only as the butt of endless ribbing.

Nelson was reminded of the voyage on *Swanborough* in the way that relationships changed between the experienced tars and the newcomers. Except here, if there were fights and other vices, he as an officer was kept unaware of them. And in a man-o'-war the hands were allowed no idleness to brood. There was too much to do: sail drill to perfect the frigate's ability to manoeuvre, gunnery practice to up the rate of fire – dumb show mostly, merely hauling the guns in and out so that the ten men per cannon could act as a team, powder being too expensive to waste.

There was practice in boarding with boats over the side, with one half of the crew trying to get back on the deck in the face of the others. Wounds were common, since no one wanted to play such games in a gentle fashion. Officers were not spared, and Horatio Nelson garnered as many bruises as the rest, but he handed out more, surprising and overcoming many a robust opponent with the sheer tenacity of his effort, his pike, marlinspike or sword wrapped in canvas doing sterling work.

The truth was he loved battle, even a mock one: it made his blood race in a way that he found exhilarating. Any feeling of weakness could be banished in an instant if he was offered the chance to lead a boarding party. That he sometimes ended up in the sea, thrown back by a strong defence, only occasioned laughter, both from the crew and the victim.

His problems were not on deck or with the crew, or in the sailing of the ship on watch. They were in the wardroom where the premier disparaged his actions as a futile attempt to gain popularity, a dangerous way to behave with men who, if you were an officer with a proper sense of discipline, you would have to send to the grating.

CHAPTER 20

Dinners with Captain Locker tended to be relaxed. He liked company, especially that of the younger members of the crew, and a ravenous midshipman was seen commonly on his left, usually taking little part in the conversation, but consuming as much as he could cram into his mouth.

'Tell me, Mr Bromwich,' Locker said, with a twinkle in his eye, to the youngster who, probably because of his height, tended to put his fellows in the shade in the article of greed. 'Does your coat have deep pockets?'

'Yesh shir,' the boy replied, his mouth full.

'Then we'd best eat up, gentlemen,' Locker whooped, aiming his knife at the great joint of roast beef in the middle of the table, 'or there will be scant fare for the adults.'

Bromwich blushed to his roots, even though his commander was grinning at him. 'Have you fed up the rats for consumption yet, young fellow?'

'No, sir.'

'You will in time, lad. A mid's hunger knows no bounds. I remember that well. Pounded ship's biscuit mixed with a drop of rum gives the beasts a very singular flavour.'

'I was taught to feed them the bargemen, sir,' said Nelson. 'We'd hover round the mess tables and scoop the creatures up as the hands banged them loose.'

'A bit of lobscouse does wonders for the texture,' added Pryce, the schoolmaster, who had served on a line of battle ship, which opened up a general discussion of the best way to catch, prepare and eat rats.

'Slow roasting over wood,' said Waddle, 'if you can persuade the cook to let you at his fire.'

Locker was of the opinion that they were best in a stew, as

fine, any day, as chicken if you added some dried peas and a pint of blackstrap wine to the mix. Bromwich took little part in the discussion, continuing to eat his fill rather than miss the opportunity. Who cared about rats in the presence of a baron of beef? He was still at it when the conversation moved on to the American rebellion and the conflict it had caused.

'The rebels have no navy, of course,' said Locker, 'and barring the intervention of the French, we won't see much in the way of proper action. But there might be the odd privateer preying on our merchant ships.'

'Yet our duties will be congenial, sir,' replied Waddle. 'The seditious swine are still trading into the sugar islands. Let us scoop them and turn their loss to our profit.'

Locker looked at his premier. 'The taking of prizes is all very well, Mr Waddle, and fine for the prosperity of our endeavours, but nothing elevates a man like a sea fight with a proper warship. Ain't that so, Nelson?'

Waddle's face clouded and he looked hard at Locker, as though he sensed a deliberate insult. He knew that the Captain was aware of Nelson's and his mutual antipathy, even though it wasn't allowed to surface in his presence. On a small ship like *Lowestoffe*, such things could not be kept hidden. Preference couldn't be kept secret either, and Locker clearly appreciated the company of his second lieutenant, a man keen to reprise at the table every battle the British Navy had ever fought. Waddle felt such games to be crass.

In Waddle's opinion, Locker could bore for the nation on the subject of naval history, especially regarding Hawke, his own personal hero. The actions off Quiberon Bay and Brest were a constant refrain and the captain always concluded with a statement so frequently expressed that, to his premier's way of thinking, repetition had rendered it fatuous: 'Always lay a Frenchman close,' he would exclaim, his hand invariably thumping the table top, 'and you will beat him!'

Nelson would always applaud the sentiment, which damned it as even more stupid in Waddle's eyes. But Locker's story-telling wasn't confined to his own years of service: he could recount the details of every sea battle since ancient times and, encouraged by Nelson, did so. Waddle put this down to the fact that Locker came from a long line of naval folk: grandfather, father and numerous sea-going uncles. He had even married the daughter of a naval officer, which hinted at a damaging degree of in-breeding. Nelson might not be cast from the same mould, but he behaved as if he was.

Waddle, with his more classical turn of mind, thought they exhibited a damning degree of simplicity rather than any deep knowledge. The Latin poets quite foxed them and any mention of Greek tragedies inevitably prompted a return to the naval battle of Salamis between the Athenians and the Persians. Waddle also saw Nelson's flattery of the Captain, his continual questions and enquiries regarding naval folklore, as nothing but the crawling of an officer determined upon advancement. What was even more galling to the bored observer was that it clearly paid dividends.

'It certainly did my uncle Maurice no harm, sir,' Nelson responded, when Locker reprised his mantra about beating the French. He had not looked at the premier as he spoke, so that he was unwittingly sailing into stormy waters.

'You cannot claim it is mere battle that has made him what he is,' Waddle growled. 'From what I know of your uncle, which I admit is only hearsay, he is a man of some culture, an avid reader and a presence at the cultural life of the nation. He has, of course, the advantage of being a bachelor without issue, which gives him time to indulge his wide variety of tastes.'

It was a finely balanced insult to Maurice Suckling, who lived alone, had never married and was known for a fussy attention to cleanliness and tidiness. Nelson had no knowledge of his sexual orientation, but he knew that to reply harshly to Waddle, to demand that he withdraw what was only an insinuation would reinforce rather than kill it.

'I think he applied the same abilities you mention to the proper running of a ship, sir.'

'What does this imply, Nelson? That the other officers who successfully fought the enemy during the Seven Years War did not?'

'That's certainly an accusation you could level at some of the admirals,' Locker joked, the only person at the table who could advance such a jest. He was trying to lighten the atmosphere, though one glance at Waddle was enough to tell him he had failed. 'They were not all like Hawke. At Quiberon Bay he risked his entire fleet to sail in after the French. If they'd guessed his purpose, and run their own ships into shoal water, the whole English fleet could have been lost.'

'If I may be permitted to continue, sir,' the first lieutenant said. 'Do you really see the skirmish your uncle took part in as in any way vital?'

Nelson replied coldly, 'I think it was something more than a skirmish.'

'Forgive me,' Waddle replied, pleased to have riled Nelson and making no attempt to hide his insincerity. 'I have no wish to diminish the action off Cape Francis Viego, but does that really explain your uncle's present position? I would wager that a busy application of flattery to superiors might achieve more in the way of advancement than a single sea battle.'

'I'm sure you mean no such thing, Mr Waddle,' said Locker. He then forgot his own remark about admirals. 'But you have just seen fit to disparage a senior officer. He also happens to be a close relative of one of your fellow guests.'

'I intend no disrespect, sir, the point is general, and—'

'Good.' Locker cut across him. 'So now we can return to the subject of American privateers.'

Waddle had been put in his place and had no option but to comply. But he engaged in the conversation in a sporadic moody manner that further diminished him in the opinion of his captain. Nelson was much more alert, eager when the master produced his charts to spread them on the table and point out the various routes through the islands that the Americans might use to evade British cruisers.

'Are we required to proceed directly to Jamaica, sir?' Nelson asked.

'Oh, yes, young fellow,' Locker replied, with a laugh. 'Admiral Gaynor will not thank us for deviating.'

'What if we were to turn up with a capture?'

'Then we'd be praised and damned at the same interview. But never fear, he won't keep us tied up at the quayside for long. It's no profit to him unless we are at sea.'

'Is he a friend to your uncle, Nelson?' asked Waddle.

'I have no idea, sir,' Nelson replied, 'but if he is, it's not something I can help.'

'Yet it is something you will most certainly profit by.'

Nelson jabbed the chart. 'I hope for us all to profit by taking the enemy ships that are smuggling contraband into the sugar islands.'

'All of us, Nelson?'

'Yes!'

'So now you add piety to all your other virtues.'

'Enough!' said Locker. Conveniently eight bells rang out to denote the change of the watch. 'I suggest that it is time you return to your duties.'

Locker proved to be absolutely right about Admiral Gaynor, who was full of impatience, harrying him to revictual and get *Lowestoffe* to sea. Gaynor knew he was due to be relieved and was all for 'making hay while the sun shines' and 'striking when the iron is hot'. Locker was ordered to take station covering the wide straits between Hispaniola and Haiti to intercept Americans trading into Jamaica itself. The three thousand-mile voyage, during which Locker had lost only a dozen hands to sickness and accident, had done more than turn the crew into a single unit: some of those snatched from a London street had shown enough aptitude to become topmen, the cream of the crew, who would even sit aloft talking when not required so that they could carry on yarning in peace.

But the same thing applied to all the divisions. It mattered little the watch they served with: they dressed the same and talked the same. Convention stilled the animosity between Waddle and Nelson. Mewed up as they were, in such close proximity to one another, their feud had to be tempered if it was not to burst into another open challenge. Locker helped by behaving as if the dispute didn't exist, and forcing his officers to do likewise. If the two men could not be brought to love each other, at least they wouldn't resort to the violence that would end in a court martial.

Matters eased when they took an American carrying a full cargo of rice, a commodity easy to dispose of, and the prospect of money, even if it was distant and at the whim of the prize courts and the depredations of individual prize agents, cheered the whole crew. That was what the volunteers had signed on for, a redemption of the promises made on Locker's posters. To those pressed, it was the final compensation for a forced life at sea. So when, in heavy seas, they spotted the armed American Letter of Marque, a two-masted barque, cruising between Cape Maize and Cape Nicola Mola, the whole crew cheered when they sought to engage.

What ensued was a long, exhausting chase, one that in such a sea, aided by a stiff quartering breeze, favoured the heavier ship. Now the months of blue-water sailing and steady training told as the master used all his skill to coax out of the frigate another ounce of speed. The American privateer was a good ship, well manned with a crew that had no desire to see the ship they had a share in fall into British hands. But the fates were against them, and the heavy press of sail they were forced to carry did nothing to aid their escape. In fact, it did the opposite, the wind forcing the ship head deep into the water so that a great quantity was shipped aboard, not all of which was discharged as the barque rose again.

As the afternoon wore on *Lowestoffe* steadily closed the gap. She had the weather gage and with land to leeward the lightly armed American, up against the superior firepower of a British man-o'-war, was soon in a hopeless situation, losing speed as the shipped water began to fill her 'tween decks and slow her even more. But the Captain had no intention of dipping his flag without showing his mettle and he let off his forward guns just as the frigate came within range. That and the reply from his own ship brought William Locker stamping unevenly on to the quarterdeck, to join Waddle and the ship's master who had the con.

'Gunnery, by damn,' Locker exclaimed. 'He's a plucky fellow and no error. Do we need to clear for action, Mr Waddle?'

'I cannot believe so, sir. Our friend yonder has a stark choice between surrender or destruction from Mr Nelson's maindeck cannon.'

'Then let us get that boat to him.'

Locker looked over the side to where a prize crew waited, with Giddings on the tiller, the longboat lashed fore and aft to the side of the frigate, bobbing up and down alarmingly and needing a great deal of fending off to keep it from crunching into the planking.

Waddle stiffened perceptibly. He had decided on a course of action and was less than happy to see it questioned. 'A chancy affair in this kind of sea, sir. I would rather lay him close and threaten him with our great guns.'

'Time might not favour that course, Mr Waddle.' His glance at the heavy clouds scudding above was eloquent enough not to require explanation. Night came quickly in the tropics, and with such a sky it would be pitch black within the hour. 'If we fail to board before dark he may be able to give us the slip. You have a boat in the water. I suggest it would be better used than just lying tied to our hull at risk of being swamped.'

'He will not prevail against the threat of guns, sir.'

'He might not have to without a prize master aboard. Lacking the benefit of moon or starlight our plucky fellow might choose to run.'

'In his present waterlogged state he would struggle to make enough headway to put the horizon between himself and us before dawn.'

The frustration was clear on Locker's face, and the cause was not hard to fathom. He couldn't order Waddle to take to the boat and secure the prize. That was beyond his power. He could suggest, but every officer had the right to decline a duty, and the Captain had to acknowledge that his own instincts, which were of the board them and be damned variety, might not always be correct. His premier knew this too, knew just what his rights were in relation to his responsibilities. To the first lieutenant's way of thinking the risk wasn't justified. In this sea a boat might easily capsize too far away from the frigate to effect a rescue. Waddle felt he could secure the initial surrender of the privateer without risk to the crew. And even if the prize did, by some fluke escape, he reckoned he'd be able to justify that decision.

Many a ship's captain, frustrated or not, would have left it at that, more concerned to maintain good relations with their second in command than risk a breach. Not William Locker! The look on his face had changed to one of anger and he spoke, as he later admitted, without giving much thought to Waddle's *amour propre.*

'Have I no officer in this ship who can board that prize?' he cried.

The premier opened his mouth to protest, but any words he was about to utter were forestalled by the master. He called to one of his mates to take the wheel, headed for the gangway. Nelson, who had commanded the guns that had so recently responded to the American salvo, abandoned his post at the same time, beating the master to the gap in the bulwarks by a hair's breath.

'I have the right, sir, as second,' he shouted, using what weight he had to block access to the gangway. 'It is my turn. And if I fail then the duty falls to you.'

The master, a big man, tried to squeeze past, but failed against the second lieutenant's tenacity. He was left on the deck, watching his chance of glory recede as Nelson dropped into the bobbing longboat. The boat was away from the side in a flash, Nelson in the thwarts urging the crew to row like the devil. That was easier said than done with half the oars out of the water at any given time. For the rest the bows were either aimed at the heavens as they crested a wave, or towards hell and damnation as they dropped sickeningly into the subsequent trough.

The prize was in a bad way, nearly waterlogged, proof that in his desire to evade capture the American Captain had risked a great deal. Indeed he was still trying, keeping his sails aloft and drawing when prudence surely demanded that they be let fly. The bulwarks amidships were under water every time a wave struck, and as much as he was able, Nelson ordered Giddings to set the tiller to aim at that point, ignoring the look of disbelief that engendered. But Giddings was a good sailor, a long-pigtailed hard case who had spent all his adult life at sea. He was yelling now, swearing imprecations at the oarsmen, ordering each blade to draw as it bit so that he could keep way on the longboat.

They dropped into a trough, the effect lessened by the bulk of the American ship, which steadied the boat so that all the oars could operate effectively. Still under orders to 'pull like

Old Harry', the sudden release of pressure, added to the combined pulling power, took the longboat right into the water above the American deck. Nelson could see the startled faces of the Captain and the crew on either side, watching, waiting for the ship to lift and tip these heathen interlopers into the heaving water where they would, no doubt, drown.

Aboard *Lowestoffe* every man, from quarterdeck to bowsprit, was holding his breath. Expressions varied from downright anxiety through silent encouragement to that of the premier, who could not keep from his face the look of justified satisfaction that came from being proved right. He heard Locker, by his side, emit a fear-filled hiss.

'Pull off, man.'

'Haul away!' Nelson yelled, at exactly the same moment, his voice drowning even that of the equally alarmed Giddings. Heads down and pulling oars the boat crew knew little of the danger they were in. But when the second lieutenant, normally a quietly spoken individual, yelled like that, they knew the situation was parlous. Doing as he bid them, they just managed to take the longboat out on the scud of discharged water, clearing the rising bulwarks that would have tipped them to a certain death by the width of a hair.

'God be praised,' whispered William Locker.

'They are still in danger, sir,' Waddle replied.

'I know that,' Locker snarled. 'But even a man who cannot summon the spirit to carry off such a feat must surely applaud it in another.'

'I—' Waddle spluttered, but in the face of what was almost an accusation of cowardice, he could not continue.

More commands hauled the longboat's head round and better timing on the approach put Nelson on board the prize, knee-deep in water. Giddings had lashed the boat to the side and the crew scrambled to follow their officer, running to obey his orders to reduce sail. Aware that further effort was futile the Captain had let the ship's head fall off, which eased the pressure on the hull and steadied the darkening deck. Across the water the huzzahs broke the tension, as the crew of the frigate cheered their mates to the grey forbidding skies.

Meanwhile Nelson had made his way aft to the wheel, now

barely visible in the fading light, and was accepting the surrender of the vessel from its master. The words, as he spoke them for the first time in his life, were sweet to the ear. 'Lieutenant Nelson, sir, of His Britannic Majesty's frigate *Lowestoffe*, at your service. I must, sadly, command your surrender.'

The American Captain, soaked like the man taking his ship, gave a courtly bow and replied in a thick rolling Devonshire accent that nailed his place of birth if not his port of residence. 'You have it, sir.'

'To whom am I obliged?'

'Jahleel Wilkins, of Boston, Massachusetts.'

'And your ship?'

'The *Torbay Lass*.'

'We must reduce sail even further, sir, and do something to get the pumps working in a more effective fashion.'

'It be yours to command, sir.'

'I would be obliged if you would alter course to ease the effect of the running sea.'

'You want me to con the ship?'

Nelson smiled, grabbing the rail to steady himself as a wave swept under the counter. Behind him he could hear Giddings yelling at the American crew. 'You know her ways better than I, sir, and even in the unhappy position you now find yourself I doubt that you have any notion to let us founder.'

'Everything I possess is in the ship, sir.'

'Everything except body and soul. I suggest a course that keeps us before the weather until such time that we can pump some of the seawater out and get a sight of the bilge.'

'You have not required my parole, Lieutenant,' said Wilkins.

'I'm sure you're a man of honour, sir. What other kind of person would let fly with his guns in the situation you so recently found yourself? And by your accent, even if you now hail from Boston, you were born an Englishman. I cannot believe that anyone of my race would so debase themselves as to withdraw their word of surrender.'

'I can barely see *Lowestoffe*, your honour,' Giddings shouted. 'Happen we should rig some lanterns.'

'If you can find dry flints make it so,' Nelson replied, taking off his hat and waving it at his mother ship, hoping that they could see it.

'We've lost him, Waddle,' said Locker, 'but he's got her head round on to a safe course.'

'Sir,' Waddle replied. His face was mask, but inwardly he was cursing both his superior officer and the man who served beneath him. Word of what had occurred would spread, that could not be avoided, and his decisions, which only an hour before had seemed rational and proper, would be made to look like cowardice. What interest he had was small and distant, a kindly disposed yellow admiral, one not trusted with a command, who hadn't been to sea in the decade following his promotion.

'Shape a course to match that of Mr Nelson,' Locker ordered, his voice hard and unfriendly. 'I want to see the topsails of that barque at dawn.'

'Aye, aye sir.'

Waddle wasn't sure he did. Apart from his long-term prospects, which, no doubt, had been irretrievably damaged by Nelson's behaviour, there was the immediate effect it would have on his life. Could he sit opposite that man in the wardroom knowing of what he was suspected? Even at this moment the effect of the day was apparent. Under normal circumstances Locker would have been cock-a-hoop enough to host a dinner to celebrate the capture. The invitation would have come to him before the Captain left the deck. Not today.

'Do me the honour, Nelson,' he murmured under his breath, 'of drowning.'

That was not an impossible prospect, as Nelson soon discovered. Even with the sails eased and on a new course, the pumps were struggling to cope with the water the barque had shipped. One of the reasons was that Wilkins was short-handed: a number of his crew had succumbed to a fever on the outward voyage. On top of that, he carried as cargo a mixture of molasses and rum, and some of his men had got to the latter when they saw that capture was inevitable. It had been lack of people sober enough to send up which had kept his sails aloft and drawing when common sense dictated they should have come down. It was the absence of any sense in their now addled brains that had the pumps working at only half their capacity.

'We'll have to put our own men to working the pumps, Giddings, and let the crew sleep it off.'

'That ain't right, your honour,' the bosun's mate protested. 'Let me get at their bastard backs with a starter and they'll pump us dry in a trice.'

'Whipping drunken men will not help.'

'They'll be sober in ten strokes.'

'No.'

Giddings looked into the officer's eyes, half intending to protest further, which he knew with a decent soul like Mr Nelson he was at liberty to do. But what he saw stopped him. The man before him seemed somehow different from the same officer on the deck of the frigate. He was more in the boarding mould, no longer the pale fellow who gave his orders in a quiet voice, but a harder creature altogether. It wasn't that there was any anger in the gaze – indeed the face had the customary half-smile. The cheeks were rosy, but that could be put down to the amount of seawater that had battered them on the way over. Locker's hard-case bosun's mate couldn't put a finger on what the difference was. But he knew one thing for certain: you just didn't argue with that look, not lest you wanted to waste your breath.

'Our men, of course, will benefit from a tot of that rum after the soaking we've endured.'

'Why that's right kind of you, your honour.'

'Just one tot, Giddings. Two sets of drunks will see us drown.'

'You'll join us?'

Nelson shivered in his wet clothes. He was cold too, but that was only skin deep. Inside he was elated, well disposed to the notion that a tot would be fitting to celebrate his first capture. Like any man he had doubted himself, unsure when it came to the test whether he might falter. That had gone. He closed his eyes, recalling the vision he had had on the way back from Calcutta. He was a long way from the goal he had set himself then, but the first rung of the ladder had been climbed.

'I shall, and fetch me a tot for Mr Wilkins,' he added, nodding to the American Captain, still on the wheel. 'Poor fellow, it may help to raise his mood.'

CHAPTER 21

From her position at the rear of the stage Emma couldn't see much and her frustration ate at her loyalty to her mother's wishes. The drapes hid the ceiling and the tops of the heads of the beauties in the alcoves, and all she ever saw was a back view of the nymphs that surrounded Dr Graham when he went on stage. She could hear enough though – the buzz of the crowd, the way it fell silent as Graham spoke, his opening words followed by oohs! and ahs! – reactions to the various demonstrations she ached to witness.

Her mother was behind her in the workroom, her task to ensure that everyone was correctly costumed now complete. It was then that Mary Cadogan would allow herself a little gin, a sip from the stone jar that she hid in her cupboard. There she would sit, staring into the middle distance, occupied with her thoughts and recollections, sipping until she dozed off. That was how Emma found her most nights, head dropped on to her bosom, eyes shut and a slight smile on her face, a woman seemingly contented, happy and mildly drunk.

Even now that they shared a room, Emma felt that they had never really talked, that they were not as close as mother and daughter should be. There was too much hidden in her mother's past. She had always been a distant presence, a provider of money, certainly, and orders as to Emma's path in life. But the love Emma craved seemed missing.

The distance between them might have been tolerable if Emma had been happy at the Adelphi, but that was far from the case. In front of her all was light and noise, which she craved; behind the stage it was messy and dark, barring the candle that lit her lectern. Invisible to the audience she was not afforded a proper costume, and felt drab in the presence of the nymphs and goddesses, who attracted so much attention from the male members of the audience. Hints that she might move from backstage to stand in front as part of the show were firmly sat on by her mother.

The evening ended in a walk back to their lodgings and a meal. A candle was sacrificed so that daughter could read to mother before they repaired to bed. Mary went to sleep, but Emma lay awake and thought of the pleasures she had had in the past compared with the tribulations she endured now. She planned ever more elaborate escapes that took her to the far corners of the globe on the arm of the man of her dreams.

Kathleen Kelly was no prince, and her charm was directed towards profit not kindness, but when occasion arose she could act the part of Lady Bountiful. So when Emma turned up again, bundle in hand, outside the basement kitchen door, Mrs Kelly left her clients to their amusements and came down to her. What she found was a drab creature, both in her dress and her manner, far from the ebullient girl she had been intent on grooming.

'Tut, tut, child,' she said, lifting Emma's chin. 'You look peaked.'

Forced to look at the Abbess, Emma tried to make out what she was thinking. The older woman's lips were pursed, her eyes narrowed, as though she couldn't quite believe what she had before her. Kathleen Kelly was thinking about Emma's eyes, seeing them with a just a little kohl top and bottom to frame them, thinking that they alone, regardless of the girl's fine figure, would seduce any man, regardless of what clothes she wore.

'I was not pleased to find you gone.'

The reply was bold and honest. 'I wasn't pleased to be away.'

'Your mother is still with Dr Graham?'

'You knew where we were?'

Mrs Kelly laughed. 'God in heaven, child, of course I did. If you're wondering why I didn't come to get you . . .'

Emma recalled her mother's warnings. 'My ma said you would.'

'Only to scare you child. Was I an ogre to you when you were under my roof?' Emma recalled only amiability and attention, of the kind she should have had from her mother. 'There you are. And I'm no different now. Have you eaten?'

'No.'

'Then set yourself down at that kitchen table and I'll see you fed. I must go back upstairs, but I'll be down presently to see how you're faring. We need to have a little talk, you and I, don't we?' That earned a nod, as well as a feeling of gratitude. Emma had feared to be turned away. 'You won't run away, now, will you?'

Emma thought of the streets she had existed on when she left the Linley house, and the cold charity of that life. She could no more go back to that than to her mother and Dr Graham's fanum.

'I have nowhere to run to,' she replied truthfully.

Mrs Kelly didn't return, but sent a servant to say she was too busy, and that a bed had been prepared for Emma in the attic. Even going up by the back stairs she could hear the gaiety of the ground- and first-floor rooms: laughter, singing male and female, the smell of food mingled with perfume and pipe tobacco, which suddenly made her feel at home. The attic was the same: familiar, a place of security. The other beds might or might not be occupied later by those working below, but right now she was on her own, and that was delicious in itself.

'Well gentlemen,' said Kathleen Kelly, when most of her clientele had departed and only those she called her stalwarts remained, 'I have some good news for you. A little flower you were keen to pluck, who chose to abscond, has returned to take her place under my roof. You will remember her, I'm sure, young Emma, with that flaming hair and those green eyes.'

'*Intacta*, still?' asked Jack Willet-Payne, a naval captain with a florid complexion and a loud, braying voice.

'I believe so, and will know for certain in the morning.'

'Then the bids will stand?'

The questioner, Capscombe, was a petty sessions judge, a grey wizened creature with rheumy blue eyes and purple-veined skin, really too old for the task of deflowering such a morsel. But he had bid the most, and wished to know how he stood. The rest of the dozen or so were men of property or business, all of whom had homes to go to, all of whom preferred to be here.

'They will,' Mrs Kelly replied, 'but the opportunity is still open.'

'Then you are undone, Capscombe,' hooted Jack Willet-Payne, 'for I have just had some of my affairs resolved in the article of prize money. My American captures have paid out.'

'You'll need deep pockets, Payne,' replied Capscombe, with little humour.

'I have those, man, and a breech deep enough to put your oversoaked prunes to shame.'

'Spurting salt water, I don't doubt.'

'Spurting none the less, Judge.'

'Gentlemen, I am put to the blush by such exchanges.'

No one was ungallant enough to say that she could blush all she liked, for under all that powder they would never observe it, and they knew she was no stranger to ribald conversation, so matters carried on in the same vein until it was time for each to go his separate way.

'I mean to have her, Kathleen Kelly,' whispered Jack Willet-Payne, as he made his final farewell.

'What, Jack?' Mrs Kelly replied, well aware that he was drunk. 'Would you make all my other nuns cry for the want of your attention?'

'Never in life. You can tell them all that after I aim my cannon at our nymph and board in the smoke, it will be back to a general fleet action damned smart.'

Her smile never wavered as she took his arm to see him down the steps to the street, but in her heart she hoped that some other suitor would come forward for Emma. She liked many of her clients for themselves, but Judge Capscombe and Willet-Payne were not among them. Not that they'd ever know – she was too much the professional for that. But the judge was a man of jaded tastes, like to indulge in sodomy when no virginity was on offer, while Willet-Payne was a braying oaf and, from what some of her nuns had told her, a log of sodden wood when it came to the point of congress: heaving, selfish and damned slow with it.

At least whatever Emma faced would be less of an ordeal

than Mrs Kelly's own, raped by her brothers and run from a sod hut where her father seemed set to follow. Now, one of her footmen was waiting to hand her a candle, to follow her up the stairs and extinguish those in the sconces behind. In the parlours the cleaning was finished, the white damask cloths drawn, bottle and glasses cleared away.

'Young Emma Lyon will need a dress for the morning. See that one is put out for her.'

Kathleen Kelly beamed at Emma, having made her twirl round in the dress she had been given. The girl stopped before the long mirror to inspect her own image, which pleased her mightily. She looked and felt wonderful.

'Well, young lady, I've always thought that a light cream colour was just right to set off your eyes.'

The dress was of silk overlaid with muslin, low cut at the front to show her *décolletage* to perfection, gathered at the waist by a silken burgundy cord. Mrs Kelly's own maid had dressed her hair high on her head, twisting plaits to support the mass of curls that accentuated her long neck, and showed clearly the full roundness of her unblemished jaw. How different from the plain flannel garment she had arrived in the night before.

'Now, disport yourself on that chaise and let's see how it appears.'

Emma complied, sinking on to the buttoned dark brown velvet that covered the seat, one arm raised to rest on the high back, her hand flopping at the wrist though the placing of the fingers was controlled. She leant into the back to appear relaxed, the picture of what she imagined to be elegance.

'God in heaven, girl, you're a natural.' Emma sat forward excitedly to offer her thanks, only to be ordered abruptly to resume her original pose. 'Never forget that you are on show at all times, Emma.'

'Am I to be on show?'

The well-powdered face creased into a frown, and the heavy silk dressing gown swished as Kathleen Kelly began to pace up and down. 'Sure, I doubt you're as innocent as you make yourself out to be.'

Emma couldn't help the way she used her long eyelashes

then, as if to denote innocent wonderment, but instead of being angered by it, Mrs Kelly let out a raucous laugh so coarse in both volume and tone as to leave no doubt that, dress and powder as she might, Kathleen Kelly was no lady. The laughter died to be replaced by a more serious look.

'You aware that I do what I do, girl, for profit?' A maidenly drop of the eyes and a bow of the head acknowledged that Emma did. 'And so will you! I know my trade, Emma, just as I know that there are a thousand ways for a woman to ensnare a man. I said a moment ago that you were a natural and you are. Sure, you have artifice by the cartload, and a beauty that leaves you free not to speak at all. But there are tricks. Shall I run through a few for you?'

To see this much older woman acting the coquette looked strange to Emma; the fingers snatched to pursed, virtuous lips, the arm thrown across eyes in a head bent ready to weep, the hurt look that proceeded a turning away so swift it was like the reaction to a slap, and finally the sinking to the knees in supplication. Then Mrs Kelly rose and looked hard at her newest nun, clearly pleased by the look of wonder on the young face. 'I know them all. Sure, I've seen them time and again, an' it never ceases to amaze me that the poor creatures fall for it.' She gave a satisfied sigh. 'But they do and I'm grateful, for it has seen me into a life of comfort. I may want for many things Emma, but money will never be one of them.'

Emma's eyes could not help but see that comfort around her; the room, the polished furniture, the sheer luxury. 'Then you are to be envied.'

'I think I am. And I think that you want what I have.'

Emma blushed, which produced another unladylike cackle. 'Sure, that's the prettiest yet, those rosy cheeks. If you can command that to order you'll have me paying for your company.'

Mrs Kelly replied to the knock at the door with a sharp command, and a slip of a girl, no more than twelve years of age, garbed in drab grey, entered with a tray. 'Tea!' she exclaimed, as the tray was put on a side table. 'Wait!'

The girl stood rigid, her eyes fixed above the heads of the two women in the room.

'That was you, Emma, not six months gone, though I grant you filled out the servant's dress a bit more.' Kathleen Kelly walked behind the child, who showed real fear in her face. 'Three days she's been here, this Hilda, not knowing what to make of the place, have you girl?'

A slight shake of her head was all the response Hilda could muster.

'A saint's name that, a good Catholic name. All her life she's been lectured about sin and here she finds herself surrounded by it. Lectured but not free of it, are you, Hilda?'

The serving girl's voice was almost a whisper. 'If you're hoping to persuade me—'

'Don't interrupt!, Mrs Kelly snapped, then resumed her normal tone, glancing at Emma. 'This child's father sold her to me, bonded her to my service. But he had to tell me, as he haggled for a price that she had known men. That she was no virgin. What men? Him? His friends? An uncle or the priest supposed to care for her soul? Him, I'll wager.'

The cruel tone was having the desired effect. The slim unformed body began to shake. 'Don't cry, Hilda. Don't you dare cry. Look hard, Emma, and when the time comes to choose the course of your life recall this moment. You may go, Hilda.'

The smile that lit the older woman's face as the girl left was like the sun coming out from behind a cloud. 'Now, Emma, I shall pour you some tea, and then we can discuss the arrangements I have made for you.'

Emma wasn't sure if going to the kitchen instead of her room was a way to avoid thinking about what Kathleen Kelly had said. Not that it had come as a shock. She had known before she rang the bell at that basement door what she was letting herself in for. After all, her mother had made it plain enough. But, still, the bald statement that she was to be auctioned like some prize bull at a county fair took away her breath.

'Hilda.'

The girl looked up from the mixing bowl, her eyes red with crying. Emma wanted to tell her that Kathleen Kelly had only been cruel to Hilda to increase the pressure on her. But she couldn't.

'When you are free of your chores, would you care to come up to the top floor and try on some of my dresses? We could talk if you like.'

Hilda looked at her in a way that made the words seem absurd, then went back to her mixing.

'You could choose to go from here if you wanted.'

'How can I,' Hilda spat, 'being indentured? I've been bought an' must stay.'

Emma turned away from the loathing in her eyes, the jutting jaw and disapproving mouth. She fingered her silk dress, wondering if she, too, was indentured.

'I often wondered, when I first enjoyed a tumble with your father, if there was any change in me afterwards that people could see.'

Emma hadn't noticed her in the doorway, and her heart jumped as her mother emerged and spoke. She seemed smaller somehow, her face more lined, her staid clothing adding to the impression of someone shrunk from former distinction. But her eyes were still as penetrating as ever. That, added to a determined stance, made her seem quite formidable. Emma fought to compose herself, to show that she was not afraid.

'And was there, Mother?'

'Should I call you Miss Hart? That is how you style yourself now, is it not?' Emma nodded, but declined to add that she had changed her name only because her parent had set the example. 'I will not enquire if your first experience of a man was pleasant.'

'You may, if you wish, and I will tell you that it was most pleasant.' The eyes were hard and unblinking to support the lie. 'Captain Jack is a gentleman.'

Mary Cadogan raised one eyebrow. 'He was never that when I knew him.'

'*You* knew him?'

'He's a rake, girl, and has been since he was a mere midshipman. Being a bosom friend to the Prince of Wales makes no odds. There'll not be one of Kathleen Kelly's nuns has not suffered his attentions, and they would tell you so if you asked them.'

Emma was damned if she was going to tell her mother just how unpleasant it had been, not just the searing physical pain at the loss of her virginity, but the boorish behaviour of the man who had won her in the auction. He had been drunk from his victory celebration, where he had crowed over the losers while filling the entire assembly, himself included, with claret. Then he had insisted on showing off his conquest in half the bagnios and coffee-houses in Westminster. In each one he consumed more claret, braying that he was about to pluck the sweetest flower, which left the object of his intention blushing and crushed. Everyone who knew Jack Willet-Payne bellowed crudities and traduced his prowess, offering her a better awakening to the joys of the bedchamber.

His gross consumption of drink had spared her on that first night, apart from ten minutes of painful fumblings, after which she lay sleepless due to the resounding snores of a companion who made her think of a beached whale. He lay, his great white belly free from its corset, rising and falling, arms akimbo, breeches half undone, as he sought by sound alone to dislodge the rafters from the ceiling above. He took his prize in the morning, his breath stinking fractionally more than his heaving body, the voice by her ear cursing his lack of spark one minute, the next mouthing filth to aid his purpose. Then it was her screams that sought to loosen what his snores had failed to fracture the night before.

'Then he has changed,' observed Emma's mother.

He had thrown the bloodstained sheep's intestine at Emma with a command of such insensitivity to see it washed that she had wondered about crowning him with the now redundant warming pan. She might have done it if the pain inside her had not rendered her almost immobile.

'The next thing you'll be telling me is that you've found true happiness.'

'I have found my place, Mother.'

'After a fortnight of Jack Willet-Payne I daresay you're glad to be back in it.'

Then it was hard to maintain her look of ease and

confidence. The fat slug had had the temerity to say that he was tired of her. Not that she was sorry. But it hadn't been all bad; he had sobered up eventually, and though he would never be a capable lover according to the little she had gleaned after that first night, he had more than once been less gross than on that first morning. And she had plucked up the nerve to reject him when he was drunk or hung over. When he had treated her as a normal mistress, those who had yelled bawdy abuse at her turned out quite pleasant companions, eager to compliment her and tell her that they were waiting in the wings.

The real joy came from being on the arm of a well-known and well-heeled man of parts. He knew his duty in the article of gifts, and Mrs Kelly's dressmaker was kept busy running up new gowns for the entertainments to which he took her. What a pleasure it was to sit in the stalls of Drury Lane, rather than be an underpaid runner engaged to deliver a costume. Though he rarely introduced her to anyone of importance at Ranelagh or Vauxhall she was at least free to enjoy the jugglers, the acrobats, the singing and dancing as though she was indeed a person of some standing. When she sat in the barge hired to take them to picnic at Hampton Court, she occupied the place reserved for someone of quality, and received as her due the love sonnets of the lute player that Jack the Whale had employed for the journey.

'How many times have I approached this doorway and wondered at the notion of turning away?' Mary Cadogan asked.

'That is not a notion I have ever had, Mother. You may enter now if you wish.'

'No, Emma. And not just 'cause Kathleen Kelly wouldn't make me welcome. Age has made me put behind what sense should have done long ago.'

'I'm never to be free of this, am I?'

'I won't disown you.'

'Will you cease to carp?'

Mary smiled gently, in a way that her daughter remembered so well. Emma wanted to tell her that she loved and esteemed her, but was afraid to do so lest the freedom she had gained be lost.

'I am finished at Graham's medical folly, and have taken

service in a house not three streets away in Jermyn Street. Number fifteen, if you ever need comfort or even just a sip of tea. I have the key to the caddy.'

The touch of the hand was soft but heartfelt, then Mary Cadogan was gone.

CHAPTER 22

1778

'That's Uppark Harry, my dear Emma. Called Fanshaw, though they choose to spell it Featherstonehaugh.'

Her companion, a marine captain named Lyttelton, spelt it for her, planting a kiss at the end of each finger to go with every letter. 'Eight thousand a year, a palace on the Downs and a mad passion for women, horses, shooting and the tables.'

'You don't like him?'

'Nonsense. Everybody likes Harry. He's so damned generous.'

'Why have we not entertained him before?'

'The Abbess has, before your time. He's been on the Grand Tour. Came back from Italy with all sorts of virtu, sculpture, paintings, pots and the like, as well as tall tales of escapades with the ladies. Probably not so tall tell the truth.'

He was singing lustily, a Purcell song called 'Come All You Spheres', and at the last word of the title he tried to kiss the breasts of the nuns who surrounded him. All were drinking champagne at his expense, and that included the half dozen male companions he had brought along.

'He has tremendous dos at Uppark,' Lyttelton added. 'Up to fifty guests at a time. Gaiety ain't the word.'

'He seems full of himself.'

'That will be because he is. Uppark Harry bends the knee to no one except his mother, and that is only because she holds the key to the last of his inheritance, the house itself.'

'It does no harm to disobey your mother,' said Emma, grinning. The song reached a crescendo, with a dozen voices singing at once. Emma looked over to where Kathleen Kelly stood. Normally such a racket would have had her intervening, but not tonight. She watched instead with a benign look on her face, of the kind a tender mother might bestow on a favoured child. Perhaps it was as her marine had said, that everybody loved Uppark Harry.

'I will require you to introduce me, Captain Lyttelton.'

'Even at the risk that I might no longer enjoy your company?'

Emma looked at him, to see that even if he was smiling he was far from joking.

'I'll wager that Harry has already clapped eyes on you, Emma, and has marked you down as a conquest to make.'

'This seems scarce to trouble you.'

'Why should it? I am an honourable man who has enjoyed your favour. Given that your vocation demands that you shower affection on more than one deserving case, it would be churlish to stand in his way.'

'You are a gentleman.'

'I have tried to be,' Lyttelton replied, again kissing the end of one of her fingers.

Emma wanted to tell him how different he had been after Jack the Whale: tender, a handsome man with a body to admire and a regard for hers that bordered on adulation.

'Let us do it now,' he said, standing, taking her hand and bringing her to her feet.

They moved across the crowded room, through tables where men of all ages, from mere boys to aged, creaking specimens sought to continue their exchange of endearments despite the din. Lyttelton had to shout to make himself heard, and push hard to get himself and Emma into the centre of the group surrounding his quarry. But he did so eventually, bellowing loud enough to make the introduction.

'Damn me, girl, you took your time.'

The babble of noise and chanting died away. Emma examined Uppark Harry intently, now that she was close enough to do so. The skin of his face was smooth and full, the eyes dark brown and dancing. The smile filled out his ruddy cheeks, and her impression was of a happy man under the influence of continuous debauchery.

'In what way?' asked Emma.

He shouted then, throwing up his arms. 'God's teeth, I've been here an hour and you've yet to kiss me.'

His arms enveloped her and his lips were full on hers before she could move. In that split second she smelt him, a mixture of tobacco, drink, a perfume and his own powerful odour. All she could hear were cheers and laughter as his coterie egged him on. His arms had slipped below her waist, and he pulled her forcibly into his grinding groin. Good sense told her to put her hands on his chest and push him away, but the taste of his tongue as it forced its way into her mouth stopped her. Somehow it felt right.

'There you are, girl,' he cried, as he released her. 'Your first taste of Uppark Harry, and I'll wager not the last. I eyed you the minute I entered, and I mean to leave in your company. Where's that damnable woman Kelly?'

That would have earned any other man a meeting between the outside pavement and his head, but not this one, loud, brash and seemingly unconcerned for whatever rules governed the running of the house. Kathleen Kelly came forward, to be embraced and kissed in a like manner. The way her lower body moulded with his gave ample proof that whatever her affectionate feelings towards him they were not motherly.

His face emerged from the embrace coated in powder. 'God Kathleen, there's a ride or two in you yet.'

Emma had never before seen Mrs Kelly simper, but she did now, in a face that was too much like floured tree bark to carry it off.

'I've a good mind to stick my hand on your muff and see you squirm.'

'Oh, get away with you now, Harry,' she trilled.

'I'm hung like a stallion, as you know, Kathleen, and ready to impale you here on the floor.'

Emma tried to conjure up an image of this young rake and the Abbess at it, and just could not. But clearly, from the look in Mrs Kelly's eye, it had occurred in the past.

'But I want Green Eyes.'

'Emma?'

'Is that her name?' he said, looking at her, taking in the

Titian hair, the eyes and the figure that was now fully developed. 'I'm not a man to share. How much?'

'She's a jewel, Harry, worth a mint of money to me.'

'You'll never see my cock again, Kathleen Kelly, if you price her too high.'

'This should be a private bargain,' she murmured.

'You're right.' He spun round and called to Emma, 'Drink champagne. Eat, if you want, on my tariff. I will be back shortly.'

With that he took Kathleen Kelly by the arm, and, with scant manners, hauled her from the room, accompanied by loud cheers.

Everything Harry did had a breathless quality, as though there were not enough hours in the day to encompass his requirements. How he struck his bargain with Kathleen Kelly was not discussed, but he had Emma and half a dozen of the other nuns – one for each of his companions – out of Arlington Street and into carriages within half an hour. In seconds Emma was on her back, a champagne bottle still in her hand, silk skirt and undergarments around her ears, with Uppark Harry heaving away before the closed carriage pulled out into Piccadilly.

What he had said about his endowment was no lie: it gave pain and pleasure in equal measure. Yet for all his behaviour it was impossible to be angry with him. His deep voice in her ear, mouthing endearments, was warm, the movements inside her exciting in a way that they had not been with Jack the Whale or gentle Lyttleton. In a house of whores, who were free in their private discussions, Emma knew what pleasure she should expect, just as she knew she had yet to experience it.

Was it his voice, the smell of his body, the girth and length of his cock, that wayward finger playing with her arse or just the sheer excitement of being ravished? It made no difference as she felt the waves of sensation ripple through her. The groans she fought to contain escaped anyway, low and pleading to begin with, high and demanding to follow, ending in a series of screams and frantic jerking, nails digging into her grunting lover's coat. Then she began to giggle.

'You're laughing, damn you,' he hissed, with difficulty, his chest heaving.

She was panting too, her body still racked by the slowly decreasing waves of pleasure. 'Is it not good to laugh when you are happy?'

There was just enough light from the interior lantern to see his twinkling eyes, as well as the sweat on his brow. Then he smiled and moved his body, inducing even greater sensations. 'By damn, Green Eyes, you'll do.'

She awoke in the morning, naked in the large dishevelled bed, wondering where she was. The call of the crowing cockerel had penetrated his brain too, but he only turned from one side to the other. The recollection of the wild night came back to Emma slowly. Of Harry and his companions drinking, each one attached to the lady of his choice, each couple eventually slipping away to a room of their own. Uppark Harry had been the last, drunk himself, with an equally inebriated Emma on his arm.

What had followed was wild, as Harry, who had whored his way around Europe, set out to teach her in one night everything he had learnt in several years. Drink seemed to affect him little, except in the article of emissions, and he had taken her in every way his imagination could recall. Parts of her body ached, but the overall feeling she had was of sated languor. The only question in her mind was whether he could have used her so freely had she not been drunk. It was with that thought, with a warm hand on her lower belly that she drifted back into sleep.

The curtains were open, and the sun was up, birds singing when she woke again. Harry was still asleep, his blond hair tousled and his full face bearing the expression of a petulant child, the lips thicker in repose than when awake. Pulling a sheet around her she examined him in the increasing light. He was handsome, even without the gaiety that animated his features. She touched his mouth with one finger seeking to lift the corner to produce half a smile. The hand that brushed hers away struck his face, causing him to wake with a start.

'Green Eyes,' he mumbled, producing the smile she wanted.

'Sir Harry,' she whispered, tracing the outline of his cheek.

'My mind is blank, yet I think we took great pleasure in one another last night.'

'I can speak only for myself.'

'Then speak.'

Instead she moved closer to him, first planting a kiss on his forehead, them snuggling down till her body was against his. 'I feel this is a better answer.'

The crack of a gunshot, distant but clear, made him jerk away from her, his eyes alert and fearful. 'In the name of Christ, what time is it?'

'I do not know.'

He was out of bed, dashing naked to where a dressing gown lay folded by a jug of water and a basin. The water went first down his throat then over his head. 'Get up, damn you. Get dressed.'

'Why, that's rich.' Emma was hurt.

'Do as I tell you,' he shouted. 'Now!'

He was struggling into his dressing gown, his eyes full of anger, and coming towards her. Emma was out of the opposite side of the bed in a flash, grabbing her clothes.

'Put your dress on,' he snarled, pulling furiously at a bell rope. 'Never mind the rest – you can carry those.'

Emma was confused, trying to equate this furious man with the fun-loving fellow she had met the night before.

'Just do as you're told.' The door opened to reveal a liveried manservant, who stood in the doorway and bowed. 'Damn you, Finch, why didn't you wake me?'

'Your own instructions last night forbade me, sir.'

'I was drunk, man,' Harry screamed, grabbing Emma by the wrist and dragging her towards the door. 'When have you ever had any reason to listen to a word I say when I'm drunk?'

'When you're drunk, sir,' Finch replied, not seeming in the least bit cowed.

'My friends from last night?'

'Are still abed, I believe,' Finch said.

'Then rouse them out, man. Get the coaches round to the north entrance.'

Suddenly he spun to face Emma, his face seeming confused as he looked into her eyes.

'Rosemary Cottage, Finch. Send someone down to get it ready for occupation.'

'Sir.'

'Quickly, man.'

The bow was low and courteous, the departure slow and measured. Whatever panicked his master clearly hadn't fazed the servant. Harry, still holding Emma by the wrist, rushed past him. He took her down the long corridor, their bare feet silent on the highly polished floors. He was out of the house by the first available set of windows, running across the still damp grass dragging Emma behind him, down the slope towards a line of trees that, when she got close enough, Emma could see hid a stream.

The cottage nestled under the branches of the biggest; small, grey-walled with a thatched roof and crabbed windows. Harry scrabbled at the door, cursing to find it locked, his temper not improved by the time it took a servant to arrive with the key. Behind him came a line of maids, bearing sheets and the means to clean the place. As soon as he had Emma inside, Harry made to leave. 'I must attend upon my mother before she completes her toilet.'

'But—'

'I will come back to see you this afternoon,' he called as he made his way out of the door, his last words barked at a servant. 'Get some food down here!'

Emma found it hard to maintain her dignity as the trio of maids dusted, made up the fire and lit it and laid sheets and blankets on the bed. She was still wearing only her dress: her shoes were in her hand, the rest of her garments still back in that bedroom in the main house. She felt close to tears. The maids didn't look at her, but went about their business as if she didn't exist, eloquent testimony to the way they thought of her. That invisibility brought forth anger, then the first smile. That was followed by a fit of giggles, which forced them to look at her, but as if she was mad, not bad.

Sir Harry Featherstonehaugh did not arrive until the evening, but food preceded him, delivered to a girl tucked up in bed and asleep. Really she should have gone back to Arlington Street,

269

but as she had little idea of where she was, and even less how to get home, no money and inappropriate clothes, staying in place seemed the best option.

His servants were efficient enough. A cold lunch followed the untouched breakfast, and a supply of candles arrived long before the light began to fade. When she awoke to attack the cold fowl, there were flowers in vases, a bowl of fruit, water to drink and wash in, and a clean chamber pot under the bed. A pair of footmen arrived with baskets brimming with bottles of claret. They greeted her question as to their master's whereabouts with the information that Sir Harry was waiting upon his mother's pleasure.

She said, 'Bugger his mother's pleasure,' to see how they would react. Two loud sniffs of disdain were pleasant indeed.

Harry arrived after dark, seen across the lawn and Deer Park by lantern light. As well as the young baronet, there came a posse of servants, all new faces, one to serve the dinner that the others carried. Food appeared from wicker baskets; a tureen of soup, a covered salver, which opened to reveal half a dozen cooked beefsteaks in an Italian sauce. There was a long bain-marie containing a whole cooked turbot, with just enough hot water in the base to keep the fish hot, and all the sauces and spices needed to make a memorable meal. Crockery and cutlery, fine bone china and heavy silver, knives, forks, spoons, all sparkling in the light shed by high six-branched twin candelabra. In the pool of light around the linen-covered table it was hard to recall that they were in a two-roomed cottage.

'I swear my mother fags me out more than any trollop,' Harry said, tucking into a thick slice of game pie, while the other dishes were prepared for serving.

He had offered neither explanation nor apology for his abandonment or the daylong absence, which Emma was determined to be cross about. She had even planned what to say to this wayward aristocrat, to the effect that good manners clearly had nothing to do with birth. But it died on her lips when he appeared, wearing that engaging grin.

And this was a different Uppark Harry, less raucous and boisterous, a quieter fellow, who seemed to lack the confidence that had marked him out at Arlington Street. There was something almost shy about the way he hogged the conversation, telling wild tales of schooldays and grand tours to impress her with past exploits rather than present behaviour. But the voice was still warm and deep, and his sensibility, when he chose to cease boasting, was almost feminine in its gentility.

Claret clearly affected him, and his conversation grew more bold with consumption, peppered with crude expressions that owed more to bravado than necessity, but Emma didn't flinch from rude words, since he failed to use one she had never heard before. As he talked Harry revealed his love of horses, food, wine, women and singing. But it soon became clear that most of all he loved Sir Harry Featherstonehaugh, Baronet.

Like most men he was the centre of his universe. Indulged since birth with every advantage, Harry saw himself in a flattering light, and never stopped to consider that his behaviour might be suspect. How could it be when he had so many friends prepared to share his company and to rock with laughter at his witticisms? He saw himself as loyal, brave and truthful, with no sense of his selfishness.

The meal finished, and another bottle uncorked, the servants were sent back to the main house with instructions to rouse their master, with breakfast, at seven of the clock. They had hardly got through the door before Harry was on her again, half carrying her through to a bed more cramped than the one they had occupied the night before. Their lovemaking was just that, far removed from the previous frenzied coupling, and Emma had no cause to be disappointed, pleased to discover that the magic sensation she had experienced in the back of that coach was no one-off pleasure.

'My mother would see me wed if she could, but that's a fate I'm determined to avoid as long as possible.' A dollop of coddled egg slipped off the spoon on to Harry's hairless chest. The 'Damn!' turned to a grin as Emma leant across him and licked it off.

'Mind you, Green Eyes, it would be worth it just to get her to cease her carping.'

'Is she aware with what you stuff your tied cottages?'

Emma only realised the *double entendre* when Harry raised a comic eyebrow, before his chest heaved with laughter. Emma joined in, which pleased him mightily, and it was a couple of minutes before he returned to the subject. 'Finch will tell her about you. The swine tells her everything, regardless of the silver with which I cross his palm. I daresay he duns my mother for the information he passes on.'

'Why pay him if he's not silent?'

Harry was slightly startled by that, until he recalled that Emma was unused to servants, therefore had no idea of what a duplicitous bunch they were. 'To prevent him from making things up. He's her man, and he'll go the minute she does. But now I have to suffer him. Damn all servants to hell, I say.'

'I must return to Mrs Kelly's.'

There was the faintest pause while he considered this. 'No,' he said finally. 'I struck a bargain with the Abbess.'

'Am I permitted to know how?'

For the first time Emma saw real anger in his face, a clouding over of his features that quite altered Harry's appearance. And the furious gesture that accompanied his ire sent the rest of his breakfast flying. 'You are permitted to know only what I tell you, and if you don't like it, you can damn well clear out now.'

Then he bellowed to his valet, who was waiting in the small parlour. 'Where, in the name of Christ risen, are my breeches?'

What followed was an exercise in calculated fury, as the valet, John, was treated to a stream of abuse for being cack-handed and for the state of his master's clothes. It was important to Harry that this girl knew her station, that he decided what happened and what did not. Emma, wrapped tightly in a sheet, had the good sense to stay silent, warned by a look from Harry's man, who was coolness itself under the onslaught. It was the only look John threw her way, but when his irate master had slammed out of the cottage door, he said, 'Best to let such gales pass, I say.'

'He is often in a temper?'

The valet glanced at her, with a look that told Emma he was wondering if he could trust her. Then he smiled. 'Sir Harry cannot abide things going against his wishes, and since his wishes are of the moment he is given to flying off the handle.'

'Am I the first to occupy this cottage?'

Another long pause. 'I doubt I'll break a confidence when I say no.'

'Should I stay or run?'

Emma delivered the question in the same flat tone, though she felt anything but calm. She had no idea what she was being offered and no idea what she might be sacrificing. But aristocrats were not always above marrying beneath their station, and whatever reputation she had acquired it was not enough to damn her if Uppark Harry wanted her. Mrs Kelly's nuns had mentioned predecessors who had gone on from Arlington Street to a life of grace and comfort.

Reality should have intruded to convince her that such a thing was impossible; the mother alone, close and concerned, would be an obstacle too great to surmount. The big house through the window, with its imposing façade and dozens of windows looking out over several thousand rolling acres, was unlikely to be the place for a girl raised in an earth-floored cottage. But she was barely fifteen, and tender enough in years to allow fancies to override indisputable barricades to dreams that might one day come true.

'You will have pleasure here, miss, that I can say without fear. What else you will have I cannot essay, or how long its duration. Who knows? It may last quite a while.'

John had turned away as he said that, busy with his master's discarded clothes. He didn't want to look into those green eyes when he suspected that he might be required to tell a lie.

CHAPTER 23

'You must command a horse,' said Harry. 'If you do not, it will command you.'

'Much like a woman, what?'

Charles Greville shook slightly as he laughed at his sally, although it had earned a ghost of a smile from his host and a nod of acknowledgement from Emma. She was just glad to be in the stable block out of the fierce heat of the summer sun. Harry had forbidden her a parasol on the grounds that it might scare the horses. 'They have all the instincts of an animal that, in its natural state, is prey to everything that lives off meat.'

One of the biggest animals, a gleaming black with wild eyes, snorted, as if to give the lie to that remark. Harry moved towards it, patted it carefully to avoid being bitten by the sudden display of large white teeth. 'Come Emma, say hello to Montenegro.' He clapped hold of the beast's ear, which stilled the constantly moving head. Emma walked towards it, eyes wary for the sudden thrust that presaged danger. She had been bitten by a horse before and harboured no desire to repeat the experience. But caution was not fear, so she proffered a flat hand, so that he could smell it and search for a morsel.

'Greville?' Harry asked.

'Never fear, Harry. I am all for a calm cuddy and a canter on a nice dry day, but you can keep your fiery thoroughbreds to yourself.'

'You don't know what you're missing. There can be no pleasure greater than flying across the Downs on the back of a stallion like this. It feels like the very edge of extinction.'

At that point Montenegro tried to bite Emma, but she moved back sharply.

'Do you ride, Green Eyes?'

'I have sat astride a horse many times, but never with a saddle.'

He grinned. 'Would you ride Montenegro here?'

'Not first off I wouldn't. Happen I would if I got to know him.'

'She's game, Greville.'

'Would that I was a hunter, then.'

If Harry noticed this foray, aimed at someone he claimed as his property, he didn't let on, leaving Emma at the mercy of a stare that was nothing short of hungry. Those soft grey eyes could look ravenous, Emma knew, since she had seen that look on Charles Greville's face before. It was a moot point as to whether it was fitting coming from such a close friend to the man who had, at present, exclusive rights to her bed.

Slim, with narrow shoulders and a pale complexion, Greville seemed fastidious in the face of Uppark Harry's healthy outdoor manner. He smiled a lot, but in a way that seemed to question the intelligence of his companions. And his constant sly barbs were evidently designed to establish that he was Harry's intellectual superior, and that he was not in the least cowed by his friend's wealth.

'I'll wager ten guineas, Green Eyes, that you'll never manage this beast,' said Harry.

He had no idea that one of the games she had played as a Cheshire child had been catching and mounting the horses of the local gentry. With nothing but a makeshift halter and bare legs she and her friends had dared each other to get astride and control some very unwilling beasts. They hadn't been thoroughbreds, of course, but to Emma one big strong horse seemed much like another.

Montenegro snorted again, this time seeming to agree with his owner that she was not fit to ride him. 'What can I possibly lay against your ten guineas?'

'That,' Greville said emphatically, 'is an unnecessary question.'

Harry's eyes were twinkling. 'Ten guineas to a kiss, Emma.'

'You can have a kiss any time.'

'You decline such a generous wager?'

'You must teach me to ride with a saddle and reins first.'

'Are we not too late for that, Harry? A bit of sporting carnality, what!'

Harry was finally riled enough to glare, receiving in response from Greville a shrug that almost implied that it was someone else who'd spoken.

'Groom!' Harry shouted. 'Get out Register and bring a saddle.'

Register was a mild mannered twelve-year-old gelding, not large. 'Now that,' Greville declared, as Harry pulled himself on to its back, 'is my kind of mount.'

'First, Emma, I will show you some very simple things, then you must try to ride Register yourself.'

'Not in that saddle, I presume, Harry. I know from just walking down Rotten Row that ladies do not sit astride a horse.'

'Do you think I would teach you to ride like that? Do you think you can mount Montenegro with a side-saddle? No, Green Eyes, you are going to have to learn to ride like a man.'

'In a dress?' she asked.

'No. I fancy you in a pair of breeches.'

Emma heard Greville draw in a deep breath.

'And not today. Now, you watch me in the paddock while I show you what you must do.'

Most of what he said she already knew: that you turned a horse with your knees as well as the reins; that if you sat back they walked and if you sat forward they would canter. It was the difference the saddle made that intrigued her, the way it altered the manner in which the rider sat, the support afforded by the stirrups and the gentle use of the reins.

'Tomorrow, Green Eyes,' he said finally, sliding off Register, 'I will bring you some breeches, so that I may try them on you.'

That made Greville grunt.

It was a strange life at Uppark, divorced in her little cottage from what happened at the great house. Harry's mother was a generous chatelaine, host to everyone in the neighbourhood with any kind of social pretensions, but also keen to receive her equals from the other great Sussex estates. Emma saw carriages arrive and depart; almost knew by the quality of each which visitors would detain Harry and which would not. She suppressed the desire that filled her to be part of the entertainments at the great house. This was the stuff of her dreams, gilded folk in gilded surroundings, yet here, though they were within sight, they were so far from touch that they might have been on the moon.

On many days she was left alone, save for those who delivered her meals or the maids who came to attend to her personal requirements. The latter, taking on the task in rotation, were like some silent order of nuns, carrying out their tasks without either a look or a word, clearly of the opinion that they were in the presence of sin and likely to be damned by association. They carried away the soiled bed sheets as if they were stained with the plague.

The footmen were the opposite, chatty, indiscreet, happy to while away time in the company of a pretty young girl, so she always knew what was going on up at the house: who had visited, how they stood in relation to the master and mistress, what their manifest faults were. Rank had no bearing on this; they castigated dukes and duchesses as much as the latest visiting curate. No one was fit to hold a candle to the owners of Uppark. And Emma could see in their eyes that they too dreamed of a life of ease, of having her in the same way as their master – which sometimes rendered her cruelly coquettish.

Her lover was with her as often as his social duties permitted, hours, day or night, when the drapes were pulled, all servants barred from entry and the two occupants naked and entwined on every available surface. Emma had no idea that Harry was insatiable, believing, partly due to the teasing of her old Arlington Street companions, that all men under a certain age were like this. And she was no victim. Having discovered the pleasure to be had from sex, she was as willing as he to experience it.

'God, if Montenegro was a man the beast would not disdain to have you on his back.'

Emma was dressed not only in a pair of Harry's breeches, but his shirt, coat and boots as well. She even had his riding crop and was standing, legs akimbo, before her baronet, a bottle of claret in her other hand. He was clad in one of her silk dresses, a compliant victim in the game they were playing, in which

Emma, with an occasional sharp flick of the crop, was about to ravish Harry's fair maiden. They had played this before, swapping roles with much laughter, especially on the first trial when Emma ripped her dress trying to get him out of it.

'I will ride him soon,' she said, taking a deep swig from a bottle already three-quarters empty. Then she dropped her voice to a rough approximation of a man's. 'But tonight I shall ride you like the beast you are.'

It was impossible not to laugh at Harry's simpering response, as he cowered on the floor, arms raised, pleading for mercy. Then Emma, struggling to contain herself, swung the crop too hard, missed her lover's hands and caught his cheek. Instantly she saw the expression in his eyes change from false fear to genuine anger. She tried to step back, to say she was sorry, only to be caught by the foot and tipped on to her back.

The curses flew from his mouth in an incoherent stream. There was spittle on his lips and he had bunched both his fists. She was stunned momentarily as one caught her on the side of the head. Only her thick hair protected her from real harm. Then he was astride her, fists flying until he grabbed the crop from her hand. The blows from that began before he was on his feet.

'Whore, bitch, strumpet, cunt, whore!'

He grabbed her hair, dragging her head up so that he could slap her hard, hauling at the collar of his coat, demanding she get the damned thing off. Her pleas for release and forgiveness were ignored. In his passion, his breath rasping, Harry lacked true focus, flaying her instead of administering the beating he intended. Emma curled into a ball to protect herself so he kicked her with his bare feet. Then suddenly he was gone, still in her dress, striding towards the Deer Park, nursing his badly wounded cheek.

It was Greville who came the following day, with the object of making the peace. He took hold of Emma's chin and turned her this way and that to examine the bruises on her forehead, as well as the black eye, which was already turning a horrible shade of yellow around the edge.

'You will be gratified to know that Harry bears a scar of his own, a thick red weal across his cheek.'

'Why are you here?'

'I am a friend.'

'He should be here.'

'No, Emma,' Greville replied emphatically, with rare certainty. 'Never expect that of Harry Featherstonehaugh.'

'So you came all the way from London to do his crawling for him.'

'I had arranged to come today anyway. And disabuse yourself of the notion that he will ever crawl. He is too secure in his station ever to do that.'

His voice wasn't envious exactly, or angry. Resentful, perhaps?

'If you are not here to say sorry, Greville, why have you come?'

'As a friend, Emma.'

'What kind of friend?'

Greville smiled, thinly. 'As much of one as you would let me be. But I am Harry's friend too, so I seek to repair a breach between two passionate creatures who are fond of each other.'

'Can it be repaired?' Emma asked, imbuing the words with as much drama as she could muster.

'It can, if you wish it to be. Do you wish it to be?' Emma nodded. 'Harry means a great deal to you?'

'Yes!'

Emma spoke with a passion she didn't feel. Harry's beating had knocked the gloss off infatuation. She was a kept woman, indulged with a degree of luxury, free from the commotion of Arlington Street, not sure if she was entirely happy, not sure what to do about it if she was not.

Greville sighed and dropped his eyes, then looked up again. 'Then let time heal things. Say nothing about the fact that you struck him.'

'Accidentally.'

'Say nothing,' he insisted, 'and seek nothing from him. Act as though naught has happened.'

'You have seen my face, Greville.'

'Call me Charles. The bruises will fade. Harry's mark will go too. And so that you are not reminded of it he has undertaken to go hunting in Kent.'

'I'm to be abandoned, then.'

'Never in life!' Greville exclaimed. 'I have undertaken to be your caretaker while he is away.'

Charles Greville was all attention to Emma for two weeks, in which her bruises faded. As soon as they could be covered with powder, her riding lessons recommenced under the tutelage of the Uppark grooms. Emma's caretaker watched with amusement as she wooed the men and boys of the stables with disingenuous ease. Ogling her in her breeches interfered with their duties, anyway, but all she had to do was smile at them and they dropped whatever they were engaged in to come and proffer advice. Since several of them had ridden Montenegro on his daily exercise, that help proved invaluable. Within ten days they were taking her along on her gelding, so she could see the thoroughbred outside his stall.

'I believe I'm ready now,' Emma said, as she dismounted, breathing heavily from a long gallop. Greville gave her a shawl to wrap round her legs, lest she be observed from the house, walking towards the cottage, attired like a man.

'Without Harry to witness it?'

'Let it be a surprise.'

'I would not want it to be a shock, Emma.'

The head groom was just as reluctant, knowing how much his master esteemed the animal. There was an Uppark race meeting due in a fortnight and if Montenegro wasn't fit to ride it would be his back that would feel the lash. But head groom or not, he was just as subject to flattery and female wiles as his younger assistants. And he had no real notion of how this young filly stood with his master. Happen he would cause himself as much trouble by saying no as yes. So he consented to Emma being led on the morning exercise, though he would not countenance any notion that she should be on the animal when it turned for home.

'For 'e'll have you off, sure as ever it was, what with his reckoning on a stall and a bag of oats. Folks often enquire if 'orses be stupid, an' I tell 'em, no error, that a horse is wise enough to know what it wants.'

There was mist on the Downs the day they set out. One of the grooms, named Caleb, had held Montenegro's head while she mounted, had seen her pale slightly as she observed how far she had to fall. She had a mounted groom on either side, Caleb with a lead rope that would hold the monster back should he be tempted to take off. But on this morning the normally fiery animal was as benign as a lamb.

'Reckon he's taken to you, miss,' said the head groom. 'Horses often like girls more'n men, I've found.'

'He may have a touch of the Minotaur in him,' said Greville, from his place behind the stall door. 'In which case he will eat out of your hand.'

The route was as familiar to the horses as it was to the grooms. Montenegro tugged at the bridle, but with no great passion since he knew that on the outward stretch of his exercise he would walk, then he would canter. Only when he turned for home, and was halfway back to his stall, would whichever groom rode him let have his head. Emma moved easily on his back, eyes watching the horse's ears for the first sign of those temper vanes flattening.

Her thoughts were not entirely equine. Uppark Harry loomed large. She missed his laughter, his gaiety and, it had to be admitted, his body. But she also wanted to tell him that she would not suffer to be beaten so, which Greville had insisted she avoid. Yet for her own self-respect Emma had to do something.

'I could do without the lead rope, with him being so docile.'

'Don't know 'bout that, miss,' said Caleb, shaking his tousled, blond hair.

'Give me your hand,' she said, transferring the reins, so they could hold them jointly. The lad obliged readily, it being something he had dreamed of, the chance to touch her, and the emotion that caused was transparent in his gaze. 'See how I hold him in. He is easy with me.'

Caleb was treated to a dazzling smile as well. He hesitated for a second, then kicked his mount forward, lent down and untied the lead rope from Montenegro's bridle. The horse didn't pull away at this, he just maintained his steady trot.

'Near to turning now, miss,' Caleb said, indicating the clearing ahead which was the furthest point of the daily ride.

'Let me take him to the end.'

The boy couldn't argue with the smile and the green eyes, nor could he fault the way that Emma, with a heavy haul on the reins, and a loud command, halted the animal. Caleb dismounted and held up his hands. 'You just slip down now, miss, and Caleb will catch you.'

Emma responded by kicking Montenegro into motion. The horse moved forward towards the line of trees and began to spin as she hauled hard on the right rein. His nostrils flared at the sight of the two grooms holding up their hands before him. They knew better than to shout. That would only spook the beast.

'Stand aside, stable lads,' she called, as she urged Montenegro forward.

The surge of energy as he took off was awesome, rendering futile Caleb's attempt to snatch his bridle. Emma raised her hips from the saddle, transferring all her weight to the stirrups, wrists and reins over the animal's neck. The path was clear and open, and hair and mane flying the pair raced across the Downs, cresting a hill that gave a view of the great house in the distance. The only sound she could hear, apart from the thud of the hooves was the wind whistling past her ears. Emma's heart was racing with the exhilaration of riding at such speed.

After two full miles Montenegro was tiring, the foam from his mouth flecking his rider. He was sweating too. Slowly Emma began to rein him in, pleased to feel him check slightly as she did so. It took time, he was not one to be easily commanded, but eventually Montenegro slowed to a canter, then to a walk. It was on the back of a heavy breathing and sweating thoroughbred that Emma entered the stable block. Greville and Harry were there, the sound of hoofs on cobbles making them turn round, both their eyes opening wide with wonder.

Harry was looking at the state of his horse, the cloud of steam that rose and seemed to envelop his Emma. She brought Montenegro to a halt and spun him with ease to face her lover. His face was clear of the weal, as fresh and ruddy as it had always been. He was smiling hugely as a groom took the horse's head and Emma slid into his arms.

'By damn, Green Eyes, you will do. You will most certainly do.'

'There, Harry,' said Greville, with an element of pique in his voice. 'I told you your damn beast was in safe hands.'

CHAPTER 24

1779

For a man like Frank Lepée, steward to the captain of HMS *Hinchingbrooke*, any change in his circumstances was unwelcome, none more so than the replacement of one master with another. He had watched his old commander over the side wondering if, when his replacement came aboard, he would be able to hold on to the best billet on the ship. The next captain might arrive with a servant in tow, which would mean a shift for Lepée to a hammock on the lower deck: back to poor food, no wine, hauling on a rope instead of the cork of a bottle.

It was an anxious steward who watched the barge pull out from the quayside of Port Royal harbour, oars steadily hitting the blue water as it wove its way through the anchored warships of the Jamaica squadron of the British West Indies fleet. *Hinchingbrooke* was berthed inside the great sweep of the bay, the bastion bristling with cannon off either beam, the white and red brick houses of Kingston dissected by the bowsprit, with the blue hills of Jamaica rising behind it.

The recently promoted Captain Horatio Nelson sat in the thwarts of the barge, though it was a while before Lepée caught sight of him, hidden behind the men rowing the boat. With the noonday sun high in the sky, the gold-edged tricorn uniform hat shaded his face, leaving only the impression of a slight individual, staring ahead, seemingly unconcerned.

Nothing was further from the truth. Nelson was in turmoil, half anxiety and half ecstasy. After only eighteen months on the station he was about to take command of a frigate, his first rated ship. Looking back his progress seemed seamless: the capture of the *Torbay Lass*, Waddle's decision to declare himself unwell and go ashore rather than face a daily accusation of cowardice, facilitating Nelson's elevation to first lieutenant. The joy of serving with Locker in that rank, harrying the enemy trade, taking capture after capture, had been huge. But even that paled when he was given command of a schooner, taking charge of a capture bought in to the service by the newly arrived admiral on the station, Sir Peter Parker.

Six months' independence ended abruptly when Sir Peter, a friend and admirer of his uncle Maurice, took him into his own flagship as third lieutenant. There was no better station than the West Indies for rapid promotion: the climate and disease saw off more senior officers than enemy action. And the ships that became available went to those closest to the admiral. Within four months he had progressed from third to first lieutenant, and two months later he was appointed as master and commander to the sloop HMS *Badger*.

He had enjoyed his six months in *Badger*, free at last to make his own decisions, to mould a crew in an image personal to him. While he could never be sure, Nelson hoped that the men had responded to his easy-going friendly manner, his way of treating them like human beings instead of cattle.

Opportunity was multiplied by the entry of the French into the American war, even more so when Spain was dragged in on Gallic coat tails. Together they had earned his ship and its commander an enviable reputation for activity and zeal that augured well for future promotion.

But the truth that nothing could be guaranteed came home to him the day he had learnt that his Uncle Maurice had died at Greenwich of a paralytic seizure. There was compensation in the will, from which he received a bequest of five hundred pounds, plus the assurance of the last words Maurice Suckling had said to his father, words that he had read several times:

Even in the crisis of his affliction his grip never faltered, and when he uttered these words he held my arm with the strength of a vice. 'Never fear, Rector,' he said, 'you will live to see your Horace an admiral.' Depend upon it, my son, those words have the ring of divine providence, coming as they do from a dying man. Take heart from that, and dedicate your prayers to his departed soul, and your mind and body to the memory of his reputation.

That stroke had taken from him his patron, and therefore the interest he relied on for advancement. Even with a good reputation he could not guarantee that he would be elevated any further than his present rank. No doubt Admiral Parker had given his word to Maurice Suckling that he would look after his nephew, but it was not a promise he was bound by. The question that nagged at Nelson, knowing that Sir Peter had other claimants to his good offices, was whether it still held.

The cry '*Hinchingbrooke!*' from Giddings, the coxswain of his barge, induced a glow of pride in Nelson. A captain arriving aboard was always referred to by the name of his ship, which made him wonder now at the trepidation of his last interview with the Admiral. There had been the worrying wait while Sir Peter offered his condolences, praising Maurice Suckling for both his sea and land service. There followed a period of anxiety while the operations he had undertaken in the previous six months were dissected and examined, looking less note-worthy under scrutiny than they had at the time.

But finally Parker came to the crux of the interview, to pronounce that Lieutenant Horatio Nelson had earned promotion to post rank on merit. Master and commander was nought but a courtesy title, to be given and taken away at a superior's whim. But to be made Post Captain was to have certainty in your life. Henceforth no junior officer could bypass him on the Captain's list. The date of his promotion would guarantee, should he be able to gain service, that he would rise from command of a Sixth Rate frigate, through all the rates to a majestic 100-gun ship-of-the-line. And in time, should he survive and the Grim Reaper remove those above him, would see him, as his uncle had predicted, promoted to admiral.

Giddings guided the barge to touch the side of *Hinchingbrooke* as gently as a feather and Nelson stood up, stepped neatly over the side of the barge on to the gangplank. On deck he raised his hat, acknowledging his officers' salutes as well as the line of marines behind them. To Frank Lepée he looked too young to be a post captain; slight of build, with blond hair and the soft features of a growing boy. Yet that he was, with eight years' near continuous sea service at his back.

'Good day to you, Mr Preece,' said Nelson, to the first lieutenant he had inherited, a dour-looking Welshman with a face like unrisen dough. 'Please muster the hands aft so that I may read myself in.'

The crew were not tardy in assembling, being as curious as Frank Lepée about their new captain. Horatio Nelson, his commission in his hand, gazed over the sea of faces that filled the space between the poop and the waist. His look commanded silence, and with a steady voice that hid his excitement, he began to read his orders.

'By the powers vested in me by the Lord Commissioners of the Admiralty, I am hereby instructed to take command of His Britannic Majesty's ship, *Hinchingbrooke*.' There was much more since those in power wished captain and crew to know their duties, including the reading of the Articles of War, which promised death by hanging the most common punishment, so these men before him breached such ordinances at their peril. But it ended eventually, and the hands were sent about their duties.

'Pray join me in my cabin, Mr Preece.'

Frank Lepée set the silver jug of coffee on the desk. His new captain, of whom he was still a trifle cautious, responded with a polite, 'Thank you,' though he didn't lift his head. The steward stepped back to examine him instead of leaving the cabin to return to his pantry. Nelson had only been aboard two days, yet already the ship had a different feel. His predecessor had been a distant figure to his men, sickly and a touch indolent, dependent on his steward, which had suited Lepée. This new fellow was too active, eager to meet the crew, to put names to faces and histories to those names; wives, children, the place they came from and how long they had served, even to talk to them about seamanship. Luckily, though, he had accepted Frank Lepée as his steward without a murmur.

The instructions to Lieutenant Preece on the running of the ship had been firm. Nelson disliked flogging as a punishment, the withdrawal of privileges was more to his taste. The men should be clean in their habits, which would be reflected in the state of the ship and their own health. The blind eye was to be employed, but anyone who stood out in terms of theft, gambling, violence or sodomy he wanted off the ship. Care was to be taken with the midshipmen: they were to be taught their trade assiduously and any form of bullying in the berth had to be stamped out forthwith.

Giddings had followed Nelson from *Lowestoffe* to *Badger*, likewise Bromwich, who was now in the mid's berth, and both were questioned for information on the new captain. Giddings couldn't praise him enough, especially for the way he had stood up to Waddle, who was cursed as a hard-case miserable sod and a bit shy when it came to action. He assured Lepée that Nelson was anything but shy, evidenced by the number of captures that had come in under either his own name or that of William Locker during the last eighteen months, every one of which Giddings listed.

'He'll line your pocket, mate,' Giddings confided, 'no error.'

While that appealed to Lepée, who loved money as much as he loved a drink, other habits and traits did not. Nelson was abstemious in the article of wine, not good news to a man who craved a regular tipple; it was easier to pilfer from an imbiber than a near teetotaller. The good news was that Nelson was the type to entertain his officers and midshipmen frequently.

Nelson scribbled away, writing letters home to his family; his father at Burnham Thorpe and his sister Susanna who had been in London working as a seamstress, but had decided to use her bequest from Maurice Suckling to buy out her bond and move back to Norfolk. His eldest brother Maurice was still at the Navy Office, though far from content, and Suckling had gone into trade in London using his own inheritance. They were both close to Anne, who was lace making in Ludgate Circus. Edmund was footloose and unsettled. Kitty, still at Burnham, he included in his letter to his father, with an addendum to be passed on to George at his school.

He was vaguely aware of his steward's scrutiny and not sure how to respond. Accustomed to messmates and shared servants, he was less familiar with the notion of solitude and a steward all to himself. What enquiries he had made of the man had established that Lepée was of Huguenot stock, from a family of French Protestants that had been booted out of Catholic France a hundred years before. The man looked French with his shiny black hair swept forward, flared nose, deep brown eyes and swarthy skin, but he was English through and through, and carried a dislike of the country of his ancestors even more rabid than that of his new master.

The Reverend Edmund Nelson had servants at home, Peter within and Peter without, as well as a parlourmaid, and since he had joined the Navy Horatio Nelson had been attended to by someone. But his relationship with Lepée would be different, more intimate, and that made him uncomfortable. He was aware that he was more likely to make some social gaffe than Lepée. Nelson did not know that his steward was working on this, making small alterations to his behaviour. Lepée had begun to remind him of lapses in his manners lest he embarrass himself, happy in the knowledge that he was getting on top of the man he would serve, which to his way of thinking was only right and proper.

The last thing Horatio Nelson wanted was to be stuck in harbour, and it wasn't long before his wish for action was indulged. Plans had been afoot ever since Spain entered the war to carry off a landing on the Mosquito Coast, its object to harry the Spanish and to secure a bridgehead from which Britannia could create a passage across the Panama isthmus. From there they could begin to wrest control of Central America from those who had held it since the arrival of Columbus. It wasn't just territory that London was after, but the wealth that flowed from the Spanish Main to the coffers of Madrid. Cut that off and Spain as an adversary would be crippled.

As a one-time merchant vessel, captured and converted to a Sixth Rate, the 28-gun frigate *Hinchingbrooke* was perfect for the task. With copious holds, there was ample space to bed troops. Nelson took aboard a hundred regulars from the 60th Foot. The accompanying transports carried volunteers from Jamaica, three hundred strong, a mixed bunch from Irish Volunteers to remittance men, some genuine in their desire to best the Dons, most more interested in carving out a life and land for themselves on enemy soil.

The primary task was to take possession of the fort that stood at the eastern end of Lake Nicaragua, at the head of the San Juan river. From there it would be possible to subdue the garrisons that protected the rich cities of Leon and Grenada. Everyone, governor, admiral and Major Polson, the man who commanded the expedition, was brimming with confidence. So too, it seemed, was the government in London. In his final letter to his father, Nelson had stated his true opinion of their plan, which was less sanguine: 'They will struggle to achieve their object before the rains, which will make military operations near impossible. We approach an inhospitable shore with barely enough men for such a task. How it will turn out, God knows.'

The estuary of the San Juan river was dotted with sandbanks dissected by sluggish streams. Behind the blinding white strip of narrow sand the jungle was deep green and impenetrable, the course of the river no more than a black break in that endless arc of vegetation.

To Nelson, it spoke of the voyage here, the creeping sense of gloom that had overtaken what residue of faith he had had in the operation. A landing at a logging settlement, supposed to produce another hundred regulars as well as the native levies necessary to get them up this river, had been nothing short of a disaster. The natives had run, fearing slavery as soon as they had seen the frigate's topsails. The regulars made their rendezvous, but in such a weak condition that Nelson wondered if they should be in hospital rather than assigned to this grand design – even their officers were sickly and weak – barely able to stand let alone march and dressed in uniforms that mould had turned to rags. The physician was obliged to begin dosing them against malaria at once, while Nelson assigned a midshipman to take the pinnace back to Port Royal with a request for reinforcements.

He had also sent the longboat ahead so that his sailors, bearing trinkets and gifts could gather the native assistance the expedition needed as the frigate made her way down the coast.

These natives possessed shallow draught boats, a most useful addition to the enterprise given that they were required to transport all their supplies and men up this watercourse.

'The Governor,' Major Polson insisted, 'was sure that the enemy is weak and under-prepared. A ripe fruit waiting to be plucked.'

Nelson looked at the man's heavily freckled face with ginger eyebrows, which seemed odd against the pure white of a fresh powdered wig. His pale green eyes were daring this naval officer to disagree.

'It is a bad idea, sir,' Nelson said, 'to ever imagine your enemy in such terms.'

Polson stiffened at what he clearly saw as a rebuke from someone who looked more boy than man. Yet he had to acknowledge that this slim, fair-haired fellow, who looked as though he had yet to shave, was a Post Captain in King George's Navy. He thus outranked him.

Nelson joined his premier, Preece, by the wheel. 'This is as inhospitable a shore as I've ever clapped eyes on. And the water level in that river is so low I'll wager they'll be able to wade the first mile.'

'We dare not wait for the rains, sir,' Preece insisted.

Nelson sighed. 'Signal the transports to begin lowering their boats.'

That presented the next problem. The soldiers had received no training in boat drill. The oarsmen couldn't row, and those on the tillers were unable to avoid anything, including their own comrades. The air was rent with cursing as, watched by stoical Amerindians and disbelieving tars, collision after collision occurred, with each boatload convinced that they were the party affronted. Never had 'bullock', the naval nickname for soldiers, seemed more apt. This was a force designed to operate on the great expanse of Lake Nicaragua, once the castle dominating it had been subdued. The dilemma, for Nelson, was clear.

'Mr Preece.'

'Sir?'

'You will take command here. I will undertake to get these bullocks to their destination. For that I will require my barge, plus a crew for each boat. You will strip down the transports to skeleton crews and send them back to Port Royal. You will remain on station here to defend the mouth of the river.'

Preece tried to hide his shock. 'And my instructions if an enemy appears, sir?'

Nelson was almost as shocked to have to tell him. 'You are to act as you see fit.'

Preece looked unhappy. 'Within what guidelines?'

That made Nelson testy. He was offering this man independence of action, yet obviously Preece, a man whom he had not chosen to serve with him, didn't relish it. He had noted the man's reluctance to act without clear orders on the voyage from Jamaica.

'The choice is simple, is it not? Depending on the force you face, you must stay and fight or run for Port Royal. Should you do the latter I'd be obliged if you'd send a boat upriver to keep us informed.'

'Sir,' Preece replied, touching his hat, his expression still full of doubt.

'You may have them in writing, Mr Preece.'

The relief on the man's face was almost palpable. 'Obliged, sir, most obliged.'

'You do not fear to stretch your orders, Captain?' asked Major Polson, when Nelson informed him of his intentions. It was a remark that caused Lepée to growl his assent, which Polson noticed but Nelson ignored.

'It is the nature of the service to which I have the honour to belong, sir, to allow for a degree of independence.'

His reply was the truth, but stretched to the limit. He would be grossly exceeding his instructions, relying on his own reputation for enterprise and his standing with the Admiral to protect him. Yet there was little alternative, apart from abandonment. Nelson couldn't face the idea of sailing back to Port Royal on his first command, to report abject failure.

'If you do not object, I will command matters till we reach the fort. Then, naturally, since we will be on *terra firma*, I shall defer to you.'

'You intend to fight alongside us?'

Nelson was genuinely surprised at that. What point would

there be in struggling all the way up the river just to turn round and return before a battle? 'Rest assured, Major Polson, when the lakeside fort is in our hands, the credit will go to you and your soldiers, not me and my tars.'

'Credit be damned, Captain Nelson,' Polson replied, eyes alight. 'You may have it, if you wish, just as long as we have the object we seek.'

CHAPTER 25

The light diminished as soon as they started up the watercourse under a thick jungle canopy, joined above their heads to create a fetid tunnel in which the miasma from the swamp-like mud rose to offend their nostrils. Everything about them reeked of corruption, death and rot, in a closed world where the humidity was such that sweat poured from every pore. With little water under the keels they were obliged to wade alongside their heavily laden craft.

Relief from this came at the odd clearing, but those had their own obstacles, the sandbars that had risen as the river dried out. When it came to unloading the boats and transporting their supplies to the next stretch of deep water the soldiers proved useless. Even in the intense heat of the glaring tropical sun they could not be persuaded to remove their kit: heavy coats, thick belts and pouches. The work was left to Nelson's tars and the Indian levies. Even the cannon had to be hauled by the gunnions across the blinding white sand, so soft and dry that a good footing was rare. And finally came the boats themselves, the most awkward of all, especially the flat-bottomed affairs specially constructed for the river journeys the troops would need to make in the interior.

Nelson ranged ahead in an Indian canoe, compass in hand, cursing the inadequate maps, peering up various creeks trying to find and mark the main channel that would take them to their destination. Lepée cursed too, an endless chant of misery drowned by the cacophony of forest noise: monkeys, birds, the occasional crashing as some larger creature burst through the undergrowth. Nelson was searching for a set of falls, above which he might find continuous deep water, aware that if he did not the expedition upriver would take four days, not the two he had envisaged.

He found the falls, then had the unpleasant task of getting the party and their supplies over them. It took an age, each individual piece, from water and beef to biscuit barrel, needing to be hauled up on a line rigged to a sheer block lashed to an overhanging branch. This proved invaluable when it came to the ordnance, but the time it took put them perilously close to darkness. Nelson and Giddings went ahead in search of a clearing, but had to admit after a while that the chance of finding one in this jungle was slim, and that a night in the boats, in what was now deeper water, was a better option.

As the light faded they lit torches steeped in pitch, a warning to the creatures of the jungle to stay away. And in the glow from those, men sat, or lay, and consumed hard ship's biscuit washed down with cold water. If anything, the noises around them increased, and since to conserve fuel only two torches were kept alight, most of the party was surrounded by Stygian darkness. Given the screeches and groans of unseen beasts no vivid imagination was required to anticipate a truly horrible fate at the hands of something real or mystical.

Bats swooped through the night air, missing hats and hair by a fraction of an inch. Insects abounded, never there when the hand slapped the skin, but biting for certain. Superstitious minds conjured up all sorts of demons and the night air was often rent with human cries as some poor soul convinced himself that he had seen some hellish vision.

In the grey light of morning, Nelson looked around a sea of tired faces. Lepée particularly looked like death warmed up, in no fit state to see to his own needs, let alone those of his master. The soldiers looked the worst, even though they had undertaken the least of the exertions. But all were afflicted, their faces swollen with insect bites, eyes red-rimmed after a miserable night of discomfort.

'Captain Nelson,' a voice called softly. He turned to see that the doctor accompanying the expedition had crossed two boats to speak with him. 'I fear I must insist on a rest for these men. That, and a chance to wash both themselves and some of their filthier kit. The boats also have served as latrines and must be doused. Clean water will do in the absence of vinegar.'

'Major Polson,' Nelson called, 'I suggest that we advance to a clearing before attempting to eat or drink. The good doctor also recommends that we look to matters that affect the men's health.'

The voice that replied was cracked with fatigue. 'I am in your hands, Captain Nelson.'

The lashings came off quickly and Giddings sorted the boats into two columns, taking advantage of what was now a wider stream. Rowing against the run of the river was hard work, but within an hour they had anchored around the hump of a mid-river sandbar, with every man in the boats grateful for solidity beneath his feet. Nelson ordered the soldiers to undress and bathe, assuring them that the water was too swift in its flow to present any danger from aggressive reptiles.

The Amerindians immediately produced spears and began to fish. Within minutes they had Nelson as a pupil, his inept attempt to spear the slithering silver objects beneath the water producing much hilarity. He earned a cheer when he finally had a success, and enjoyed gutting and eating his own catch, a pleasure he had not enjoyed since, as a boy, he had fished off the Norfolk coast.

He had to calm a worried Polson. They were safe to rest: nothing on water could pass them and they were protected by an impenetrable forest through which no enemy could approach. A respite of a couple of hours would restore the men's spirits. That was more true of his sailors than the soldiers, some of whom were sitting, muskets between their knees, shivering despite the increasing heat. Nelson moved them: once the sun rose high enough to crest the treetops, this pleasant glade would become like a furnace.

Staying with the shaded bank, they followed the river along a great arc called Monkey Bend, which took it almost back upon itself, so full of primates and their noise that even cannon fire would have been drowned. Approaching St Bartholomew's island, which they suspected might be fortified, they stopped by another sandbar to redistribute the troops. Two thirds of the party were left to guard the supplies while the rest, each boat rowed by tars, moved swiftly upriver, once more under an overbearing canopy. Using hand signals, Nelson, in the lead boat, indicated that the river was opening out, a sure indication that, if the maps were even remotely correct, they should be approaching the island.

Sure enough, through the increasing light, he saw the outline of a wooden palisade, with a decaying breastwork on the downriver point. Now they were travelling in almost total silence until a scream of alarm rent the air. In the widening stream, now no more than fifty feet from a landfall, two supporting boats had come alongside the leader, muskets pointed forward to deliver the first salvo.

The guns spewed forth on Nelson's command sending chips of wood flying and it was hard to know if the yells that followed were from wounds or mere alarm. No shot was returned towards them as the boats, with the muskets now reloaded, scrunched into the sand of the island. Nelson, Giddings beside him, had already leapt over the prow and charged the breastwork, with Polson yelling at his soldiers to come on, which they did at a shuffling gait. Nelson's tars managed a rush that put the bullocks to shame. The whole assault made for the low palisade wall, the sailors cupping hands to provide a leg up for their mates. Within two minutes of landing they were over the wall and inside the compound.

'Deserted,' gasped Polson to his naval companion's back. Nelson had carried on, sword up before him, until he could see the river again. What he saw didn't please him: a boatload of Spanish soldiers pulling furiously to get away.

'We won't surprise the Dons now, Major Polson,' he said, with clear frustration, when the soldier joined him.

'We had the right to anticipate that they would stay and fight.'

Nelson was angry with himself, at what he saw as a simple error. 'But they didn't and that ought to have been allowed for. I should have kept one of the boats manned to chase them. They would never have got clear of sailors.'

Polson patted his shoulder. 'Then we must move with even more speed, sir, and get to them before they can begin to put their defences in order.'

*

Surprise had indeed been lost: as soon as the party came into view several cannon balls blasted the beach on what was the most obvious landing site, three miles from the fort itself. Polson seemed to have recovered his composure, standing in his boat, telescope in hand, red-coated and obvious, almost inviting the enemy to take a shot at him.

'Would I be allowed to recommend a course of action, Major?' Nelson asked.

'I will welcome any advice, sir,' he replied, without conviction.

'At St Bartholomew the Dons ran without putting up any resistance.'

The telescope dropped, though the gaze remained fixed on the beach. 'Matters stand differently here, Captain Nelson. We face stone walls after a three-mile forced march, not a rotting wooden palisade.'

'What time have they had to improve the defence of the fort? One day at most, surely not enough to affect their sense of well-being. That island had a breastwork near falling down for want of repair. I would hazard that their main fort, stone notwithstanding, is in a similar condition.'

Polson's expression was cold. 'I fear you are going to suggest a *coup de main*.'

'It is a sailor's way, sir. When we encounter an enemy, we're not gifted the opportunity to employ siege. We must carry the day, if we are to do our duty, by main force swiftly applied. I suggest that the same tactic will work here. Let us land through their gunfire – which is useless as it is dropping into sand – cut our way up the paths to the fort and take it in a swift assault.'

'I cannot agree, Captain.' His telescope was fixed on the objective again.

Nelson contained his irritation. 'May I be allowed to enquire why?'

'Because if it failed we would suffer so much as to render the idea of another assault impossible.' Polson dropped the glass again and pointed to the fort on its elevated escarpment, the tops of its grimy grey walls just visible above the trees. 'No, sir, I envisage no assault at all. For I cannot stand the losses if I am to move on from this place. Instead I will institute a proper siege. We shall surround the citadel and cut them off from all succour. Then we can sap forward as the terrain permits, and achieve a position that renders our enemies' resistance impotent. Then I will invite their commander to surrender, affording him a proper exit with the honours he deserves.'

Nelson fought to keep his voice calm. 'Take this by main force and the other objects you seek will fall all the more swiftly.'

'I am mindful of your advice, Captain Nelson, but I seem to recall that this is the position in which I assume command.'

Nelson touched his hat, as much to hide his disappointment as to acknowledge the truth of the remark. 'You are correct in that, sir. And if you wish to afford me orders, my men will do all in their power to aid your plans.'

'Handsomely said, Captain,' exclaimed a relieved Polson, who had clearly been expecting the argument to continue. He raised his sword and pointed to the beach, still under desultory fire. 'We must secure that landing site, then we must force to retire the guns they have sited to play on it. Once that is achieved I will disembark the rest of our troops, taking care to let our enemy see the strength of our ordnance.'

Polson spoke on, ordering another officer further upriver to outflank the castle and cut it off from the lake. 'Destroy any and all boats that you see there. With the encirclement complete we can set about siting our batteries.'

'You do not fear they may essay out to attack us?' asked Nelson.

'No!' Polson exclaimed, as if the question bordered on the idiotic. Then he realised it was a genuine enquiry from a man who didn't know the answer. 'That's as foolish as us carrying out an immediate assault, merely depleting their ability to withstand us. In the open we outnumber them. If they had the strength to prevent us landing, it would be lined up on that beach denying us the opportunity to impose a siege.'

The Major was right, of course. He knew, as Nelson did not, that there was a method of siege that had about it all the elements of a formal dance. First, cut off your enemy from resupply, then search his defences for the weakest points.

Having identified those, all the artillery that can be mustered must be brought to bear on that at maximum range. Then move forward as the soldiers sap closer to the enemy, digging trenches across the slope and throwing up earthworks to protect themselves from enfilading fire. Once a new position had been established the guns could be brought forward, an emplacement constructed, and supplied through those same trenches with powder and shot, the cannon could play on the weak points at a shorter range.

That was the theory, and surely it would have been the practice too if it had not been for two factors. The tenacity of the Spanish commander was one. He made sapping difficult in what was shallow soil by the direction of his own defence, cleverly using the elevations afforded by his fort to delay those digging. But he had a greater ally in disease and natural hazards than he ever had in musket or cannon ball.

The soldier first bitten by a snake had suffered while standing upright carrying a barrel towards the forward camp. The creature, apparently hanging in a tree, had struck at him without warning, inflicting a bite on his upper cheek. His screams owed as much to internal demons as fear, not aided by the shaking heads of the natives who had killed it.

But Polson had no illusions as to how acute the supply problem was, how difficult the terrain made it to transport even the smallest item from the beach down below to supply the forward operations. Time did not allow him to put one man's well-being before that of the assault parties. The doctor made the soldier comfortable, while Polson tried to ignore the black swelling that already afflicted his face, ordering his men to move on.

What caused alarm among the other soldiers was not the fact that the man died, but that within two hours of being bitten his body had already begun to rot. Faced with death so swift and unpleasant, not one of the sappers could be brought to wield a spade until they were sure no reptile lurked in the undergrowth waiting the opportunity to do the same to them.

Matters moved slowly but inexorably. A small, tented encampment was set up, with latrines well away from the sleeping quarters and a tiny hospital to care for the increasing number of sick. As the first two weeks went by the forest echoed to the sound of cannons, spades in deep earth and the groans of the infirm.

Nelson and Giddings had set up a battery, moving it forward twice as the soldiers sapped to create new positions. Nelson knew it was a situation where rate of fire was less important than accuracy. The powder charges were carefully measured, the balls chipped with a sharp eye to ensure they were round and smooth. The battery commander, in this case the Captain of HMS *Hinchingbrooke*, stripped to the waist and wearing a bandanna to keep the sweat from his eyes, took personal charge of aiming the piece.

He saw both Polson and the doctor approach and wait in the stifling heat till Nelson had fired, eyes more concerned with the heavy banks of cloud in the sky than the fall of the shot.

'Six more men have fallen foul of the Yellow Jack in the last hour,' said the doctor, gloomily. 'That brings the total number to over two hundred. I have recommended to Major Polson that we must suspend operations for a period and construct some kind of shelter that will keep them clear of the elements. Otherwise we will require no more than an expanded burial plot.'

Nelson looked at Polson, seeing before him a recurrence of indecision rather than the spirit that would bring them success. He had to remind himself that command was not his, so carping was easy. But they all knew that the rains, which in being late had aided their cause, were now about to begin. One look at the leaden sky, an ear cocked for the rolls of thunder getting ever closer, was enough to establish that fact. They had to act.

The first spot of rain struck an outstretched leaf like a bullet, quickly followed by several others. Nelson was too preoccupied by the needs of his battery to respond. He began yelling at his men to cover the touchhole of the cannon, to get the slow-match under some protection, and to ensure that the tarpaulin he had rigged in anticipation was still in place to keep dry his powder barrels. By the time these had been instituted the rain had turned into a deluge so heavy they had to shout to each other to be heard.

'The sick will have to fend for themselves, Doctor,' Polson yelled, rain cascading off his face. 'I must get what troops there are digging out of harm's way. This downpour will wash away any earthworks they have constructed and leave them exposed to gunfire from the fortress.'

'Major,' Nelson yelled back, his face likewise running with rain, 'we must protect the battery positions or they will likewise suffer.'

'Make it so, Captain Nelson,' Polson roared, as he rushed away, his red coat turning to a deep soaked burgundy before he had gone ten yards. The sailors leapt out from the battery position and started to carve deep channels that would take any rainwater coursing down the hillside past their position. Eventually Nelson made his way back to the small hospital by the main command position, passing the cemetery that already contained, in two weeks, forty crosses of men who had died from fever.

Sapping in such wet conditions was impossible. Firing off cannon wasn't much better, only undertaken when the rains eased enough to observe the fall of shot. Different tactics had to be employed, which did not appeal to Polson, frontal attacks by small parties to disrupt whatever repairs the Dons tried to make to the breaches the gunners had made in the walls. Day by day this had to be undertaken with fewer and fewer men, as the continual damp, added to the other miseries of the jungle, decimated their strength.

Nelson felt the first signs of his own recurring affliction two days after that first noisy raindrop, a weakness in all his limbs, aching in his back and thighs, plus a general lassitude that made any activity a struggle. But struggle he did, helped along by Giddings and an amazingly tender Lepée. His servant clapped a stopper on his moaning while the coxswain took charge of the construction of new gun emplacements, using rocky outcrops with natural protection from cascading water, and revetted breastworks to protect them from enemy gunfire. When not engaged in that activity, with both Giddings and Lepée by his side, Nelson led forward groups of his sailors under the walls. Edging along they tried to catch the enemy by surprise, often succeeding, sometimes failing and suffering the casualties that such failure entailed.

The cemetery grew in direct correlation to the falling spirits of the attackers, not from death by action but from the effects of Yellow Jack. Funerals took place each evening, as the light faded in a sky the colour of filthy flannel. Those saying prayers for the departed could barely stand themselves and many knew that they were witnessing what might befall them in a matter of days.

After a day of loading and aiming ordnance Nelson often had to be supported by two of his own men, openly weeping as he counted the number of Hinchingbrookes that had been laid to rest. And then the reinforcements arrived, not many but enough to raise the spirits of those still upright. Brought from Port Royal by the sloop *Victor* they carried the news of Nelson's appointment to a new command.

'You are to be congratulated, sir,' said Midshipman Beevor, who had been detailed to deliver the news. 'You have been given a fine ship, a forty-four-gun frigate and near new.'

The man before him was too weak to respond with any enthusiasm, and Beevor thought him more scarecrow than Post Captain, a sallow-faced individual, all skin and bone, who would scarce make it back to the coast. The military commander Polson was not in a much better state, and the news he had received was bound to lower his spirits.

'I am superseded, Nelson,' Polson said, wearily, rubbing a hand over his lined forehead. 'I have Colonel Kemble coming to take over the siege.'

Nelson replied, with pursed lips, 'I am sorry to hear it, Polson, and I know you will not take credence to it but I will be sorry, too, to depart this place.'

Frank Lepée shook his head, the first sign of open dissent for weeks.

'You feel it too?' Polson asked, his now gaunt face eager.

'I do,' Nelson insisted, a smile on his wan face. 'Our Spanish friend yonder is closer to collapse than we. Were you not on the verge of a success I'd ignore my orders and stay.'

'In the name of Christ, Capt'n,' hissed Lepée, and for once Giddings supported him, though only with a look.

Nelson heard his servant's words, and wondered that Lepée didn't understand. This was his first independent command. He wanted to be there when success was achieved and Fort Nicaragua compelled to surrender. That would justify the faith that people like Locker, Admiral Parker and his uncle Maurice had shown in him, as well as his own certainty that he was destined for greatness. It would also elevate him in the firmament of his family. His exploits would be the stuff of dinner-table recollection, not those of the raft of ancestors who had preceded him.

'Which would force me to command you to depart,' Polson continued, ignoring the servant's intervention. 'Your health alone demands it. I have no desire to attend your funeral as well as all the others we have witnessed.'

Nelson hit Polson weakly on the shoulder. 'Finish it, man, before Kemble gets here.'

A hand came out, to be grasped firmly. 'God speed, Nelson.'

The trip downriver was very different from that experienced on the way up, taxing all Giddings's skill at boat handling. The San Juan was now close to a torrent. The sandbars they had rested on were submerged and hazardous rather than havens of calm. The banks no longer showed the mud that had sent up such foul air: that, too, was under water.

Action alone had kept the malaria from downing Nelson. That removed he lay in the thwarts like a man close to death, white of face, shivering uncontrollably, muttering to himself the names of the hundred of his men he had left in that waterlogged cemetery. Over and over again he recalled them, a toll of death to which Lepée, watching him, fully expected to add the name of Captain Horatio Nelson.

CHAPTER 26

1780

Race day at Uppark brought *tout le monde* to the Sussex countryside, some with horses they wished to run, others just to eat, drink and make merry. It was always held when Harry's mother was away for her annual summer sojourn in Bath, to give her son the run of the great house. It also gave his closest guests a guarantee that the revels wouldn't cease when the sun went down. Emma had received several hints, and knew Harry well enough to be sure that they were in for a wild night.

Kathleen Kelly must have closed Arlington Street for the day. The Abbess was present with all of her nuns, who greeted Emma like a long-lost sister, though a few could not hide their envy at her situation. Most of Mrs Kelly's customers seemed to be in attendance too, one or two of whom knew Emma sufficiently well from her past existence to essay the odd familiarity. These she took in good part, secure in her station for this day at least, as mistress of the house.

'Sure, it's always like that with men, my girl,' Kathleen Kelly said, when Emma alluded to such attentions being unwelcome. 'They can never let a girl forget that they've enjoyed her favours, nor pass up a chance to inform their companions. They'll even make it up to impress. They're sad creatures in the main, our menfolk, led by the breech into all sorts of foolishness.'

The Abbess had never treated Emma as an equal before, and it was a pleasant sensation. Letters passed back and forth to Arlington Street, as well as hints from Harry and his friends, told her that her tenure at Uppark had lasted a good deal longer than most. Her man was held to be notoriously fickle, a rake in every sense of the word. But since her arrival on the scene he had cut a more sober figure. If Kathleen Kelly behaved towards her as a person of some consequence that only coincided with Emma's view.

They were promenading under parasols across close-cut lawns towards the marquee Harry had set up to serve refreshments. The sun was shining, the sky was blue, and everyone, conscious of the gaiety of the occasion, had elected to wear as much colour as possible. Horses were being paraded and admired, wagers placed and odds discussed, in a babble of noise and laughter that caused a swelling of pride in Emma's breast. She felt this was as much her race day as it was that of the heir to Uppark.

'Harry tells me you're engaged to take part in the ladies' race.'

Lessons in riding side-saddle had followed her excursion on Montenegro, with a specially purchased and expensive habit to go with it, and she was accomplished now in both methods of riding. It had become her chief pleasure, since she had the run of the stables when Harry was absent from the estate.

'I am under instructions to win, on pain of a thorough lashing.'

Said humorously, it wasn't taken that way. 'He is known as a beater.'

'Kathleen,' Emma replied, 'he is an over-indulged child. But it is my fond wish that he can be tamed.'

Head bent, she didn't see the look on Kathleen Kelly's face, the mixed expression of doubt and surprise that a slip of a girl like Emma should be talking in such a vein. The beating Harry had given her was no secret, just as it was fully expected that at some time in the future it would recur. The Abbess had been a girl once. She could have recounted Emma's dreams of bliss with her lover, as easily as she could tell how misguided they were. They were a commonplace in immature minds, just as the dashing of them was a near certainty. True, she had seen one or two of her nuns catch a man well above their station, but it was rare, and she would bet a guinea to a clipped farthing that Harry Featherstonehaugh wouldn't be one of them.

'I must have a wager,' the Abbess said, to change the subject.

'Charles Greville has opened a book, I believe.'

'Then I shall keep an eye on him, Emma. If he's successful he can pay some of his outstanding debts to me. Not that I won't have to stand in line.'

'The queue, according to Harry, is a long one.'

Friends they might be, but Uppark Harry was as prone to pillow gossip as the next man, prepared to traduce the reputation and behaviour of his companions with the same passion he employed to castigate the actions of his perceived enemies. Few, regardless of how close they were as bosom friends, were spared a critique. Greville, he insisted, was a schemer, and generally an unsuccessful one. Emma, forewarned early of the trait, had observed the look that lay behind the eyes rather than in them, an impression of secret inner thoughts that gave the Honourable Charles the air of a conspirator.

But she had observed something else: a gentility of manner that contrasted sharply with that of her lover. It was hard to accept that Harry could be jealous of Greville, but he was and it emerged when he spoke of his friend. Not of his life or his conquests, but of his social standing as the second son of the Earl of Warwick, while on his mother's side he was allied to a raft of Hamiltons, a family awash with dukes, earls and influence. For all his wealth, Uppark Harry was perceived as frivolous. For all his endless speculations, debts, pursuit of rich heiresses and failures in business ventures, the Honourable Charles Greville was treated as serious.

He was a Member of Parliament, a passionate collector of virtu, mostly of the mineral variety, and a keen horticulturist, an expert on Italian art, paintings, sculpture and ancient artefacts, who acted as an agent for some of the wealthiest people in the country. But, more than that, he showed Emma a rare politeness, treating her as he would a lady. In the interregnum, while Harry had been absent, Greville had made no secret of his admiration for her, but had never so much as hinted at impropriety. And he had ceased his barbs. In sharp contrast to the absent host, Greville was wont to praise his friend and forgive his faults. The way he commended Harry, flying in the face of what Emma already knew, blunted her initial resentment. In fact, she had grown quite fond of him, a consequence of his almost permanent presence and exposure to his gentle demeanour.

'Mrs Kelly, Emma,' said Greville, bowing. He stood beside an easel, on which he had pinned a list of horses and riders, each with a set of odds against their name.

'I require your advice, sir,' said Kathleen Kelly, peering at the list. 'What should I back?'

'Nothing.'

'What? Are you not running a book?'

Greville threw her a sideways glance, in the way Emma had come to know so well, eyes hinting that the import of his thoughts was far removed from his words.

'My dear lady, you must differentiate between my advice and the occupation I have chosen for the day. In the latter guise I would point you towards the odds, but as a man who has attended many a race meeting I know that all the advantage lies with me. I am more likely to be left in possession of your coin rather than you in mine.'

'Then little could be said to have changed, Mr Greville,' Kathleen Kelly responded tartly. She had seen the look he had thrown Emma, understood the significance, and was still woman enough to be jealous, even if she cared little for him. 'I have often had cause to notice that you leave my house with a full belly while my purse is somewhat light.'

'True. And I cannot thank you enough for the way you indulge me.'

A hand was thrown out to the list of runners, but still accompanied by that slightly mocking grin. 'But fate has presented you with an opportunity to reverse that. Place a wager on any beast of your choice, Mrs Kelly, but gift me with no money. Should you win I will accept it.'

'And if I lose?'

'You may set that loss against my bill at Arlington Street.'

'You owe me in excess of fifty guineas, sir.'

'Fifty guineas it is, though if you are to profit from it you must be quick. The runners are coming under the orders of the starter. Which horse?'

People were drifting past, heading for the growing clamour at the start line. Horses were snorting and swinging their heads, voices were raised to encourage or denigrate, and grooms and riders struggled to calm their excited charges. Marquees had been erected around the start line with brightly coloured heraldic pennants fluttering in the light breeze, like some archaic jousting contest. The course itself ran circular on the rolling downland, marked by flags.

With the start of the first race fast approaching the noise had increased till it was a continuous roar, in which few individual calls could be heard. Kathleen Kelly, no doubt flustered into her selection, jabbed a finger at one runner, waited until Greville acknowledged it, then dashed off to witness the race. Greville offered Emma his arm, and followed.

'Was that wise, Charles?' she asked.

'Did you observe which horse she backed?'

'No.'

'You should have done, Emma. Never bet in haste, it is usually fatal. The nag our Arlington Street Abbess has chosen is a true donkey.'

'It may still win. Tortoises have been known to triumph over hares.'

He spun her slightly, to look straight into her eyes in a way that made her heart skip a beat, his words coinciding with the crack of the starter's pistol. 'That is a sustaining thought.'

She thought he was going to kiss her then, in public, and she was confused about the prospect. But he turned her just in time to see the runners go by, their great hoofs throwing up sods of soft turf.

'Look, Charles,' Emma cried, 'it's Harry out in front.'

'For now,' Greville replied, but in a voice so low she didn't hear it.

Emma was aware of being slightly drunk long before they sat down to dinner, though she was far from alone. Half a dozen races had been toasted by the guests, either in triumph or defeat, so that the forty people who had been invited to stay were all feeling the effects of day-long imbibing. That lent a raucous edge to the gathering, which obviously pleased the host who headed the table, a beaming, red-faced Sir Harry.

Emma sat near him, taking precedence over Kathleen Kelly

and her nuns, who made up a third of the number invited to join in the feast. At one end of the great dining room a group of musicians played, their efforts overlaid by the unrestrained talk. The liveried servants were so numerous that there seemed to be one for each guest, ensuring that the delivery of food was prompt. So was the pouring of claret and champagne.

No diner was allowed an empty glass, and consumption was encouraged with numerous toasts: praise to the King, the country and Harry's victorious horse, Montenegro, interspersed with more libations damning such creatures as the French, the watchmen, and pious, quiet souls everywhere for their hatred of riot. By the time they got to the syllabub, things were getting out of control, much to Harry's delight.

There was no conversation now, just shouted exchanges of half-intentional insults. Several of the Arlington Street nuns were already embracing their neighbours at the table, while one empty seat, added to the benign smile and slouched attitude on the face of the man next to it, testified to the fact that a pleasing service was being provided out of sight under the linen cover.

And still claret and champagne was being gorged by the pint. Emma lost track of the number of glasses she had emptied, and was so drunk that it was impossible to form an opinion on the state of everyone else. Things really degenerated after Harry, responding to a jest from one of his friends, aimed the remains of his pudding at the fellow's head. It missed by several feet, and hit the laughing creature next to him in the gap between her neck and the swell of her breasts. The chill made her scream, but not as much as the sudden planting of a tongue on her flesh, eager to lick off the cream.

Not to be outdone, another rake lifted his dish, pulled open the front of a dress, and emptied the contents down it, this accompanied by a loud cry to tell everyone present of his intention to eat it wherever he found it. Soon puddings where flying everywhere, the table abandoned by those either seeking to coat someone or to avoid the mess. Female squeals rent the air. Commanded by the host to play louder, the musicians launched into a sparkling reel that induced wild dancing.

The servants withdrew, taking with them most of the candles. The room now plunged in gloom, Emma no longer had any idea of the person she was reeling with, male or female, or who was planting kisses on her bosom or seeking to lift her dress.

She didn't want to look at the other occupants of the great bed, four in number, sprawled in varying directions, all still asleep. The quick glance she had allowed herself showed three naked men, none of them Harry, and one half-clothed female. For the first time in her life Emma couldn't clearly remember the night before, which had been a whirl of half-caught images, of dancing, laughing and lewd behaviour.

It took a hard tug to dislodge a sheet from under a couple of recumbent bodies, but since her clothes were nowhere to be seen she had little choice. Thus wrapped, she began to search the house, discovering that each bedroom was occupied by everything from couples to quartets. A pair of rakes had collapsed in the hallway, one, breeches round his ankles, sat in a pool of vomit and piss. The sound of argumentative voices coming from the dining room drew her.

They were sitting at the table, surrounded by bottles, in a room littered with discarded clothes and half eaten food. Harry was perched on a chair in just his shirt, which was open at the front to reveal his chest. Greville wasn't elegant, but at least he had on his coat and breeches, though his stock was loose and his wig was askew. Both were drunk, talking across each other with much finger-pointing. She watched them for several minutes, tightening the sheet around her body for comfort more than warmth. It was a glassy-eyed lover who, finally realising she was present, turned and peered at Emma as if he was attempting recognition.

'A ghost, Charlie,' he slurred. 'We have a ghost.'

Greville pointed towards the drapes on the long windows, one of which was open just enough to admit the light by which they could see each other. He spoke slowly, proof of inebriation. 'I am reliably informed, my friend, that spirits cannot abide the light. You will see, Harry, should you cast a glance behind you, that the sun is up.'

Harry had stood up, glass in hand, the long shirt covering him to mid thigh, and staggered forward. 'If I want a fucking ghost, Greville, a fucking ghost is what I will have.' He came close to Emma, the smell of stale drink strong on his breath. His eyes were bloodshot, the stubble on his chin picking up the glimmer of light. His voice dropped to a near whisper as he addressed her. 'Have you been fucking, my ghost?'

She couldn't answer. Nor could she hold his penetrating look.

'I hope you have, Green Eyes. I promised you to several of my friends. It would be a damned infernal nuisance if you'd let me down.'

'I . . .'

'I gave the Abbess a fair rogering,' he continued, in a louder voice, his hand going unsteadily to his crotch to rub it hard. 'She's an ancient baggage I'll grant you, but very obliging in the matter of portals. Old Harry can enter where he likes.'

'How do you tell the wrinkles from the portals?' asked Greville, collapsing in a fit of giggles on to the table. He was trying to say something about a slack arse but could not get it out.

Suffering from a headache, with a tongue that resembled leather and the fear that she had, indeed, obliged several of Harry's friends, Emma spun on her heel. She was aware of a feeling of disappointment. Not at Harry, he was as he had ever been – coarse and vulgar. It was Charles Greville's condition that affected her, as if in a way he had fallen from grace.

'Where you going?' Harry demanded.

'To the cottage.'

Greville had pushed himself up from the table, waving one hand to encompass the whole room. 'Then you will want your clothes, Emma. I assure you they are here somewhere.'

'I grant you it was a crass remark, Emma, but it was at least well intentioned. I was, as you have so rightly pointed out, as drunk as a baronet.'

Greville tried to look crestfallen and apologetic, but it didn't work. He felt quite plainly that Emma was in no position to chastise anyone. The conversation that had preceded the complaint had been like a game; she enquiring in an orotund way about the events of the previous night, and he, with the limited amount he could recall, attempting to spare her blushes.

He knew Emma to be relatively uninhibited when sober. Drink made her more so, but last night was the first time he had seen her truly intoxicated. She knew filthy songs as well as sweet ones, and delivered them with gusto, at one point baring her beautiful breasts to underline the lyrics. For all her present maidenly blushes, she had not objected to any of the advances made to her and had required no persuasion to enter into the orgiastic spirit of the previous night. Watching her now, sitting demurely before him, he felt he was looking at and lying to an altogether different creature. But for all that, it was impossible to avoid the fact that she had distributed her favours to those chosen by her lover.

'It seems I am a chattel, then,' she snapped.

How could he say it? That Harry would lend her to a friend with the same alacrity he would provide a horse for a canter over the Downs? That he had enjoyed her but, very likely, was tiring of her? He couldn't, because it would be too cruel, but he could move closer and hold her hand. And he could introduce a deeper note into his voice to establish his concern.

'My dear Emma, you must not dwell on that which you cannot recall. You will create fancies that are worse than truths.'

'*That* I cannot imagine.'

'Do you find it so strange that men desire you?' She stiffened slightly, so he carried on quickly. 'I cannot disguise the fact that I am smitten.'

The head went down. 'You should be more of a friend to Harry then, Charles.'

'Believe me, Emma,' he replied huskily, 'I am friend enough.'

That made her look into his pale grey eyes, her own gaze half shameful, half curious. His grip on her hand tightened, and he moved so his thigh was touching hers. 'I fear I am not rake enough in these matters. Do not accuse me of having higher standards for I assure you my thoughts are as base as those of the next man. Harry has invited me to approach you more than once. Were we not here two whole weeks without him being present?'

'He proposed—'

'Hinted, Emma. Yet I shied away, out of weakness, from such a gift, even if in my heart and soul I longed to possess it. The fool in me wants to know you intimately, but for you to give yourself willingly. Not as part of some Faustian bargain.'

'I do not know what that means.'

'It is a legend, recently penned in the modern idiom by a German fellow named Goethe. His man Faust sells his soul to the Devil so that his wishes may be gratified.' He sought to interpret the look in her eye, but that would have foxed Goethe's devil, Mephistopheles.

Part of her was thinking that Greville could not help showing away with his knowledge; the other half was grateful that he took the trouble to explain. Not many men she had known had tried to defeat her manifest ignorance outside the bedchamber.

'What I mean, Emma, is this. That I do not fear to be here in this cottage with Harry absent. Should he happen by, there would be, in my case, no brawl over the slight to his honour. Damn, I've made you cry.'

'Not you, Charles,' Emma replied, wiping the first tear from her cheek.

That made Greville move back, still holding her hand but breaking all other bodily contact. He was experienced enough to know that tears were a poor precursor to lovemaking; that to press his suit now was not only vulgar, but doomed. Yet a clever man, aroused, rarely falters when seeking a solution.

'Nothing would permit me to press my attention upon you under Harry's roof.'

'Did that apply last night?'

The question, he realised, was partly a fishing expedition. It was a pleasant coincidence to be able to nod, without saying that he had been unable to get close to Emma the night before, so eager and numerous were the suitors who had got there before him.

'What I would ask is this. That you come to visit me in London.'

'I do not go to London.'

That was said with a sense of regret and longing, but also with a degree of caution. Emma knew enough to be aware of what Greville was saying, and was, as yet, unsure of how she wanted to respond.

'You have but to ask. Harry will provide the means and the money. It will not surprise him to find that you wish for company, and entertainment.'

'Go when you please,' Harry shouted, 'you don't have to ask. Just tell the coachman and leave me a message. I will instruct Finch to provide you with something to spend.'

They were pounding across the Downs at a steady canter, the morning sun and their mounts' withers picking up the last of the dew from the tall stalks of grass.

'I thought tomorrow,' Emma called back.

As she did so she lifted her eyes, trusting her horse, looking hard to see if Harry could discern any hint of her intended destination. Greville's suggestion had alarmed her, but then, as the prospect of cuckolding a man who had treated her so shabbily took root, it excited her. A dry stick compared to Uppark Harry, Greville did not arouse the same feelings of excitement in her breast as her present lover. His suggestion that she ask Harry for the means to visit, where most men would have offered their own, was typical. But, for all that, he had qualities she liked, not least in the way he sought to please her as a person, not just as a lover. In a way, she had come to trust him.

Harry's next words seemed to confirm exactly where she stood in his affections. 'I am off coursing in Hampshire, so I'll be gone from here anyway.'

'You came,' said Greville, as he personally opened the door.

'I'm expected, am I not? I wrote.'

'Yes!' He smiled, and pulled her gently into the hallway, nodding to his servant to take her cloak, as he thought about that note, so badly spelt, so stunted for grammar, that had announced her acceptance of his invitation. Everything was prepared for her visit. Cold food and champagne, enough of the latter to break down the residue of her tenuous fidelity.

In the end, the seduction of Emma was easier than he had supposed. Having determined to indulge him, her mind had

315

been working on the prospect throughout the journey from Uppark to Westminster. By the time she made his front door, Emma was as eager to use his bed as he was himself, determined to demonstrate that this was a mutual bargain, not the seduction of a gormless young female booby. The cold collation and champagne provided an epilogue rather than a prologue to their first coupling.

'. . . and this is an emerald, Emma. Were it extracted from the surrounding rock and polished it would match your eyes perfectly, especially when held up to sunlight.'

'And that?' she demanded, pointing with a chicken leg to a dull black lump that stood erect on the glass shelf of the cabinet.

'Lava. The product of Mount Vesuvius, which as you will know spouts continually outside the city of Naples.'

'I don't know that.'

'You're a rare thing, Emma,' he replied, leaning forward to kiss her, catching the grease from her chicken on his own lips.

'Why?'

'You admit easily to ignorance, which is not a common trait in any class of society. Most people pretend to knowledge they do not possess.'

'Do you?'

Greville grinned, which completely changed his normally serious demeanour. 'I am a Member of Parliament, Emma. To feign knowledge one does not possess is a demand of the occupation.'

'When you know as little as I do, Charles,' she replied, her eyes running over the rows of books that stood above the display cabinet containing his mineral samples, 'it would be foolish to pretend.'

'Yet I sense you are eager to learn.' The smile, as well as the demure dropping eyelashes, encouraged him. 'I would happily be your tutor.'

'When I was taught the little gifted to me there was a fee.'

Greville pulled her close and slid his hand inside his dressing-gown, which looked better on her than it ever had looked on him.

'To be paid in kind.'

*

It was a game, entertaining and full of pleasures, two lovers instead of one, the contrast so great. Harry would call on her at Rosemary Cottage after shooting, hunting or arguing about matrimony with his mother, his method of lovemaking usually reflecting his passionate mood. He would be a physical, frequent and ardent lover, still the boastful, spoilt Harry she had first met, a man who saw his life in a roseate glow.

She would visit Greville for an altogether less frenetic afternoon of copulation, mixed with a tender care for her continued education. It seemed that Greville wanted her to change, to develop, to become a companion in conversation, to cease to be, in all respects bar one, the Emma that Harry had plucked from Arlington Street.

She loved the way that small things excited Greville. It seemed that a deft turn of her ankle could rouse him as much as her entire anatomy, a word he had taught her early, just as he told her which painting he had in mind as he ran his hand over her soft skin. He compared her raised foot to a Michelangelo drawing, her breasts and belly to a work by Giotti. And dressed again, Greville would read to her from books she could never have understood on her own, teaching her words in French and Italian, insisting that she broaden her mind, inordinately proud that she remembered a great deal of what he imparted.

His gentle attention stood in contrast to Harry's coarseness. Emma, curious to test the difference, attempted to apply some of Greville's tutoring to Harry, careful to disguise the source, pretending that it was her own knowledge she was disseminating. It didn't fall on deaf ears so much as a scowling indifference. Harry wasn't interested in art, books or foreign languages as much as he was in himself, hunting, fishing and shooting. He seemed to see her attempts to converse as a device to diminish him.

Yet Harry's enthusiasm, when he was allowed to gabble, as well as his rustic wit, with which she could naturally identify, could still bury Greville's tenderness. Alone, she would compare the two men, totting up their good and bad points. Harry's generosity set against Greville's careful way with money; the joy of riding flat out across the Downs with sessions listening to the writings of Greville's Dilettanti Society friends; riotous couplings that left the cottage a mess set against the fastidious neatness of Greville's bachelor lodgings after their lovemaking.

She would ponder the benefits of residence in this cottage, against the need to make her own way, since Charles Greville never mentioned taking over responsibility for her well-being. He was content to feed at the table of his wealthy friend rather than expend coin of his own. In the end, no balance could be concluded in favour of one or the other. Emma enjoyed them both when she was with them and had doubts when they were absent. And since no conclusion was possible without some declaration, Emma drifted along, enjoying what she had without worrying too much about the future.

Matters became more complex when the shooting season began. Now Greville was at Uppark, and that meant exciting trysts with him as he slipped away from the butts. Invited to take out a gun herself, it was agony mixed with ecstasy to have them stand either side of her, each admiring her in their own way. Then Greville went back to London, with the intention of going on to his family seat in Warwickshire. At the last parting he gave her some franked blank letters, a parliamentary privilege, so that she could write to him at no cost to herself. Now there was only Harry.

'I have arranged for you to take lodgings, a pleasant set of rooms according to Finch.'

Harry, with an air of forced unconcern, bent to his breakfast beefsteak, slicing through it and shipping it to his mouth in one movement. The next remark was delivered through the food. 'You will readily understand, Emma, that I must spend the next two months in London and I cannot accommodate you in Piccadilly.'

'Your mother,' she replied, without passion, picking at the food on her own plate.

'Not just her, Green Eyes. What will pass in the country will cause talk in town. Arlington Street will have given you an inkling of the cruelty attendant on London gossip. I will not have people exercising their wit at my expense.'

'So I am to be a secret?'

'You're far from that,' he said, trying to inject enthusiasm into his words. He pointed his knife at her plate. 'And eat up or you'll fade to nought.'

'My appetite is quite gone.'

'Mine ain't,' he cried, throwing down his napkin. 'What say you to a tumble before we take the horses out?'

Emma stood, wrapped in a sheet, watching as they closed the main house, a stream of carts at the entrance loading all the things that both mother and son would need for their sojourn in the capital: plate, silverware and linen, clothes and crystal, dogs and pet birds. The senior servants had already departed to prepare the Piccadilly house for the arrival of their master and mistress. And, like the possession she was, she would depart too.

CHAPTER 27

The state of Emma's finances, not least in regard to payment for rent and provender, was mirrored in Mrs Mulderry's face. That lady's disposition, when Emma had taken possession of these lodgings, had been established by her beaming countenance and the happy chatter at her guest's good fortune in 'being under the protection of such a "noble gent"'.

Obviously Finch had not been discreet. Hot water arrived promptly, and the fire in the grate was kept blazing with a seeming disregard for the expense of wood or coal. Clean linen graced the bed twice weekly and the plentiful food was served on the best plate the household could offer. From her top-floor window Emma looked down on a busy Whitechapel street, her residence close to the eastern edge of the City of London.

The room itself was pleasant: whitewashed walls and ceiling that made it light during the day, with heavy curtains and a good fire to blot out the cool night air. Her bed was in an alcove by the chimney-breast and on the other side of the fire she had a screened-off space to hang her clothes. Meals were taken at a table by the window; tea and comfort in the deep chairs that stood opposite the door, behind which stood a washstand, a good mirror and the chest that contained her possessions.

The constant congratulation had been the first of the Mulderry traits to evaporate, soon to be followed by the smile. One by one all those little habits that projected contentment followed, until, owed several weeks' monies, she went about her daily chores in silence. Sir Harry not only forgot to call on his young 'niece'. He also forgot to forward the requisite payment for her lodgings or any excursions. Letters to Charles Greville went unanswered, while the posting of them, to a man who was not the 'noble gent', only increased the depth of her landlady's suspicions.

The time duly arrived when Mrs Mulderry was scowling continuously, with scarce a civil word to spare for her lodger. There were mumblings about the appellation of 'niece' being misapplied, though the terms 'mistress' or 'bawd' had yet to be uttered. Emma knew that she would have to act if she was to avoid being cast out into the street or, even worse, had up for debt. Harry's injunction to send no letters to Piccadilly, two miles away on the other side of the city, had to be ignored: matters were approaching a crisis.

She did her best to ignore the change in her landlady's manner. In her first weeks in the house the older woman had been all agog to hear about Uppark: the dimensions of the house, the Deer Park, the rolling acres of grounds that ran across the Sussex Downs, carefully landscaped by the famous Capability Brown. The shooting parties and race meeting, which her young guest described so colourfully, interested her immensely, though the old lady was spared too clear a description of the revels which had followed. She alluded openly only to the consumption of claret and champagne, an excess that was greeted by a satisfied nod.

Like most people of her station, Mrs Mulderry loved a lord, prepared to forgive actions by those she considered her betters that she damned without hesitation in those less fortunate. That was the only weapon Emma had left to dent what was fast becoming open hostility. She employed it relentlessly, her face and eyes alight with seeming happiness. But as she spoke now, she knew in her heart that the owner of the house was not going to be fobbed off for much longer with tales of grand living. That threw her back on to her last defence. Her lover's station in life.

'You cannot fathom the cares that a man like Sir Harry has to shoulder. His dear mother is not in the best of health, and he so dotes on her that his concerns give him great burden. He must see to his estates all the while or they'll go to rack, with all his improvements yielding no gain. Then there's his house in London, peopled, he tells me, with servants who would rob him blind if he didn't keep a sharp eye on their doings.'

The scowl deepened, till the landlady's eyes seemed to sink into her round, puffy face. 'I has cares, Miss Hart, like paying for victuals and heat.'

'That I know, dear lady. And I have penned a note to my uncle castigating him for his oversight in the matter of your payments.'

'A week forgetful is oversight, a fortnight in any man I calls a disgrace. But three weeks and then a month without so much as a farthing! That, Miss Hart, makes me wonder if your uncle remembers your needs at all!' The word 'uncle' was accompanied by a look that told Emma that Mrs Mulderry knew her to be no better than she ought. 'I have no choice but to inform you that should his memory fail till Sabbath next, I'll be required to take what I can from you to cover the loss.'

Emma knew that that would amount to very little, something of which Mrs Mulderry must have been aware since she had observed the quantity of luggage, a single light chest, with which her guest had arrived. When Emma had been ensconced at Rosemary Cottage, Sir Harry had been spared the expense of fitting her out in the kind of clothes she would have needed to cut a dash in town. He had been content to let her wear what garments she had brought from Mrs Kelly's – that is, when she wore anything at all.

Nor had he seen fit to supply her with any jewellery that she could pawn. Anything she had been given to wear had been borrowed from his mother's box, to be replaced on the following day. Certainly there was insufficient in her chest to pay off the outstanding rent. There was the riding habit he had given her. That was worth something. Her mind went back to those days on the Downs, racing through the tall meadows with wild abandon, jumping hedgerows that even some of Harry's cronies had shied away from. It was less than six weeks ago, yet it seemed like an age.

And she had no chance to ride now. If she didn't return to Uppark the garments were useless. She opened her mouth to offer them to Mrs Mulderry, only to be interrupted by a loud and sustained banging, as someone beat heavily, with what sounded like a club, on the downstairs door.

'The devil damn that noise,' cried Mrs Mulderry, and rushed out the door.

Emma suspected it was Harry, though her first fleeting thought was that Mrs Mulderry had sent for the tipstaff. But not even a bailiff arresting her for debt would set up such a racket. Uppark Harry would, especially if he was taken with drink. His voice, floating up the stairs, confirmed her suspicions. Lately Mrs Mulderry had experienced no difficulty in showing condescension to Emma. Now, by the sound of her whining voice, she was grovelling before the noble gent she had been traducing a mere minute ago.

'Surely you cannot be concerned about such a trifle, madam.'

'Saving your honour's presence, it never crossed my mind that you wouldn't take proper care of your pretty niece. It's only . . .'

'A few guineas, madam.'

'Naught to you, sir, an' who's to say that a man of your parts don't deserve it? But to a poor woman like me a-struggling to make ends meet, with the price of all and sundry differin' from one day to the next?'

The chink of coins followed the voices. 'I will require some wine.'

'At once, sir,' Mrs Mulderry replied, in a satisfied tone.

'Not your normal cellar-made strap. Send out for something that a decent man can drink.'

Emma couldn't help herself. She had sworn that if Harry answered her call for help she would be cold, this so that he should know what trouble he had caused. But his voice, loud and demanding, sent the blood racing through her veins, and induced in her a longing that had been barely submerged since he had left her six weeks previously. She rushed to a small mirror glass that stood above the jug and washbasin, biting her lips and pinching her cheeks to induce some colour.

As she brushed her hair she had to fight not to laugh. She would keep him here all night, and with a damn to what her landlady thought of their relationship. Not that she imagined Mrs Mulderry would be shocked. As long as the old woman was paid promptly, she would rest content, and sleep even if the whole house shook.

Her mind was full of images of the time they had spent together. Surely he had not forgotten the pleasure he had taken in her company. Emma certainly hadn't. No other lover had induced in her such sensations. Greville, though accomplished, was different, a man who would devote a whole afternoon to observation and touch before consummation. Harry was her bull, man enough, drunk or sober, to perform prodigiously, with a devil-take-the-hindmost attitude that made their couplings as full of humour as they were of lust. She had learnt early how to tease him, how much he liked to see her demure and virginal; then overwhelm her supposed innocence and debauch it, playing the lord and master having his way with his inferiors. Luckily, she was dressed in a simple white garment that showed her figure clearly when she moved. It would offer no bar to speedy gratification.

She had to get back into his close favour. It would be a torment to be stuck here, in these lodgings, waiting for such occasional calls; much better to return to her little cottage. The thud of his boots announced that Harry had reached the small landing. Emma grabbed her embroidery, threw herself into her chair by the fire, and sought hard to give the appearance of a truly innocent girl, pressing the edge of the sewing ring into her lap in a futile attempt to suppress her desire.

'Damn that woman,' he said, from the open doorway. 'D'ye know she had the gall to dun me for a month's rent?'

Emma spoke without thinking, or raising her eyes to look at him. 'Consider yourself fortunate, sir. My ears have been dunned these last fourteen days. Assaulted till they are sick of it, and not a word of comfort from you to set against it.'

Harry grinned. 'A small price to pay, Emma, is it not, to have a connection to a fine fellow like me?'

There was nothing emollient in that slurred reply, only arrogance. That, coupled with her state of libidinous anticipation, made Emma snap at him, something she had rarely dared before. When she looked up her deep green eyes blazed with anger, and the colour in her cheeks owed nothing to being pinched. 'I scarce call it attention, sir, to be left to shift for weeks without even any knowledge of you or your whereabouts.'

His lack of sobriety was obvious: his face was flushed and the thick fair hair a mess. Emma felt as though she was looking at him for the first time, since his puffy appearance robbed him of that which she had previously considered handsome. Even his brown eyes had lost their lively, mischievous look, seeming glazed and dull. He blew out his cheeks angrily, which did nothing to decrease her impression that she was looking at a rake going to seed. Harry didn't raise his voice to counter her accusation, replying in a tone that was as flat as his general demeanour. 'What I'm about, girl, is none of your concern. Nor am I obliged to inform you of my doings. You'd best recall that you're merely here to serve any purpose I command.'

Part of Emma's brain was willing her to stop, to rise from the chair and throw herself at his feet, there to beg for his mercy. She ached to hold him close, to subdue the unbearable tingling that filled her body. But another part of her was too incensed to let matters drop. Furious at being ignored, even angrier at his indifference, she threw her sewing on the floor and stood up.

'A plague on your purpose, Harry. It's no service to be left here to beg for my supper. To have to write you—'

'Which I expressly forbade you to do,' he shouted. 'I do not want letters from the likes of you on my salver. Especially when my mother is present to enquire as to where the damn missive is come from, an infernal scrawl with a House of Commons frank that I suspect you extracted from Greville.'

'Forbade? I am to starve rather than risk upsetting your precious mother! Are you afraid that she might discover that her dear sweet son is nowt but a whore-chasing coxcomb?'

Harry emitted a barking laugh. 'I have scant need to chase the likes of you. King Street doxies queue up for my company, and the door of Arlington Street is never closed.'

'The wine, your honour.' He spun round to see Mrs Mulderry standing in the doorway. She was holding two dust-covered bottles. 'A fine claret of the Brion variety, so the vintner tells me. Says it's a rare 'un.'

'Leave them!' he snapped.

Her servile manner had gone now that she had been paid. Clearly, with guineas in her possession, she had less of a mind to be talked down to. 'I hates to see a family quarrel, your honour. Breaks my heart, it does.'

Harry's stick was in the air, and Mrs Mulderry was gone before he issued his threat to break her head. He swung it round towards Emma, only to see that her anger had evaporated and that her chest was heaving with laughter. Emma saw his eyes drop to her breasts, clearly visible in their shape through the thin white dress.

'Oh, Harry, I've missed you so.'

'Take it off.'

'With the door open?' she asked.

He turned swiftly and slammed it. By the time he spun back to look at her Emma was naked, the dress crumpled in a heap on top of the sewing ring. The stick was flung into the corner as he charged towards her, pressing her back against the sharp edge of the wooden mantel. His head dipped immediately to suck one erect nipple, while his hand rammed up between her legs, his grunt of pleasure matched by hers. Harry dropped to his knees and his tongue ferreted around, poking forward, seeking entry. That pushed her even further to the fire, which threatened to scorch her backside.

'Oh, Harry,' she gasped, 'my arse is near burning.'

He jumped to his feet and let out one of those whooping hunting calls she remembered so well. Spinning her round, he threw her back on to the bed, wrestling with his coat and breeches. 'It will be so, Emma, my girl. I'll burn your arse, and no mistake.'

'But I don't want to stay here, Harry,' she said. 'There's nothing to do except sit and embroider, or listen to Mrs Mulderry moan about her rent. I don't even have the money to cross the street.'

His voice had the sated quality of a man who had drunk too much. Certainly his promise had remained unfulfilled. Given her knowledge of his prowess, plus his allusion to Arlington Street, Emma had the feeling that he had probably stopped at some point on the way here. He lifted the goblet of claret to his lips, taking so a deep a gulp that some spilled over and ran down his hairless chest. Emma licked it eagerly. The smell of cheap scent on his body confirmed her suspicions. Even so, she employed her hand to try and revive his ardour. The continued flatness of his tone was evidence that she was wasting her time.

'I shan't be back at Uppark for two months, and I can't keep you anywhere near Piccadilly. Quite apart from my mother, there's the expense.'

'Am I not worth an extra shilling?'

'Don't carp at me, Emma. Be grateful for what you have.'

Her fingernails dug painfully into his groin. 'Grateful? I can smell the whores on you, even through your sweat and drink.'

'Damn you!' he cried in agony, arching forward and sending the contents of his goblet flying.

'And damn you, sir,' snapped Emma, rolling out of bed. 'I don't see you for near a month and you can't cross the distance without paying for something I give you free.'

'Free! You're as much of a whore as the pair I bedded earlier.'

She seemed to lose some of her strength as she bent to lift the dress off the floor. The sewing ring was entangled with it, and Emma answered with resignation as she tried to separate them. 'I am to you.'

'Not just to me, girl. Don't you think I know how many of my friends you've serviced?'

'At your discretion, sir.'

When he replied his expression was close to a sneer. 'A fine thing, Emma, when you term your natural inclination a command from me.'

'You wretch!'

The sewing ring, flung with all her strength, took him on the ear. Sideways on it would have split the skin, even flat it caused pain. Harry leapt from the bed, one hand on his head, the other balled into a fist. Emma ran to the corner and picked up his silver-topped cane, holding it out like a club. 'Lay a hand on me again, Harry, and I'll dash out what passes for your brains.'

It wasn't fear that stopped him from hitting her. Emma knew, as he pulled himself upright and reached for his breeches, that his movements were composed of indifference.

'Never fear, Emma, I shan't lay a hand on you, ever again.'

'Harry?'

'Desist. I am tired – just as much of your company as I am fatigued.'

'I'm sorry.'

He laughed, buttoning his shirt. 'Are you, Emma? I'm damned if I am.'

'You can forgive me, surely. Had you the means earlier then I would have less passion now.'

The anger returned, but not in a loud way. He spoke with more of a growl, as if he was intent on ensuring his own superiority. 'It is even more galling to be rebuked on that score by a woman who has forfeited any ability to ply her true occupation. I have paid your bill, but I'll not give you another penny. From now on you must fend for yourself. Do not, under any circumstances, write to me again.'

He picked up his jacket and went out of the door, leaving her naked, silhouetted against the glowing embers of the fire, and still holding his silver-topped cane like a club.

'The offer is no more than temporary, Emma, as one of the good doctor's goddesses has a fever. But an empty alcove is no good to man nor beast, and I daresay you can fill it better than most.'

The lady who had taken over her mother's position at Dr Graham's spectacle was like him, Scottish, with a slow, deliberate way of speech that made her employer, by comparison, sound like a gabbler. She had turned down flat the request that Emma be allowed to take back her singing duties, since that position was now ably filled.

'Should I not see the doctor?'

'Not unless you have an ailment, girl.'

Having turned away, the Scotswoman didn't see Emma's face drain of blood, and by the time she looked again the rosy countenance was quite restored. As if fortune had deserted her completely, the morning sickness had come to Emma the day after her row with Harry. Fortunately she had always emptied her own chamber pot, so as long as Mrs Mulderry didn't hear the retching, she would remain in ignorance. The problem was the continued payment of rent.

'Dr Graham leaves matters of this nature to me. All that is required is that we alter the Hygenia costume to fit you.'

'I am forced to enquire about the payment.'

'Two guineas a week is what you will receive. But that can be multiplied by what is on offer from the male custom.'

That was something Emma knew already. In her previous spell here she had seen the passage of notes from the back entrance to the dressing rooms, invitations to supper or a rout, routinely delivered to one or other of the statuesque beauties her mother had costumed.

'Indeed, if the Hygenia you are to replace took more care of the chill night airs, when she was bestowing her favours, she would not be confined to her bed now.'

It wasn't what she wanted, little better than a return to Arlington Street, which Emma was determined to avoid. There were sound reasons for that, quite outside the loss of face, the almost certain feeling that she was with child being the greatest. Her mother would help but she couldn't face her either, having refused her advice so comprehensively. What Emma needed was a breathing space, with enough coming in to pay her rent until such time as matters resolved themselves. A week or two with Dr Graham would provide part of that, and if some fellow wanted to take her to supper and pay for her food she would agree.

'Get out of that dress,' the Scotswoman barked. 'We have but an hour till the doors open.'

CHAPTER 28

'Dr Graham's fanum is the most amazing thing, Nelson. You simply must let me take you there. Quite apart from anything else it might lift your spirits and aid you in your recovery.'

Lieutenant Tom Foley's face was alight with enthusiasm. With his dark curly hair, hazel eyes and the lilt of a Welsh accent it seemed for him a natural condition. They had been friends and correspondents ever since they had been midshipmen together in the *Raisonable* all those years before, Tom the bravest of his companions in the fight to contain the tyranny of Rivers and Makepeace. Nelson had been called to London by the prospect of a ship. Tom, in town while his own vessel refitted for service in America, had immediately offered him a share of a set of rooms he had taken.

Right now Nelson was in limbo, with letters flying back and forth between himself and the Admiralty, aided by dozens of missives from friends and relations. The American war presented opportunity to a serving officer, though there were, as always, more applicants than ships. A queue of unemployed post captains filled the First Lord's anteroom hoping for employment.

In his case he had the patronage of Sir Peter Parker, the backing of William Locker, who was trusted for his honesty, and a residue of goodwill left over from his uncle's tenure at the Navy Board. There was a brief note on the First Lord's desk from his second cousin the Earl of Orford to the effect that the Walpole family deserved recognition for services to the realm; since Captain Nelson was the only candidate available to receive it, he should have it as his due.

The Admiralty secretaries would weigh all this and when recommending appointments to Lord Sandwich they would seek to offend as few people as was humanly possible. The First Lord, adding politics to the brew, would consider the needs of the administration, already under serious strain from the lack of military success in the American colonies. No one too closely identified with its critics could hope for preferment, which bothered Nelson, who had been sometimes a touch too free with his views.

His health would give them cause for concern, and all the gossip of the Pump Room at Bath, where he had convalesced on his return from the West Indies, would be pored over to see if his infirmity could save the Admiralty making a decision. Nelson didn't like Bath any more than he liked being ill: it was a place that sustained itself on a diet of gossip and a most exacting social grading that afforded scant attention to a mere naval captain. But his father had insisted he come to where the best doctors practised, rather than return to Norfolk where medical help was less accomplished and the county, at this time of year, was in the grip of a harsh winter. That it coincided with the Rector's annual visit to Bath, made every January, was never mentioned.

Then there was the expedition that had brought on the illness. Success would have brought him great credit. As it was, he now had to worry about being associated with failure. The Lake Nicaragua fortress was captured not long after his departure, but it lacked the supplies to sustain further operations. Worse, of the two hundred men from his ship eventually committed to the operation, only ten had survived to see Jamaica again, and that included himself, Giddings and Frank Lepée. The price for the soldiers had been even higher, to the point where, with three times as many in the cemetery as still effective, all discipline had vanished. The final result had been an ignominious retreat.

That weighed on him the closer he came to success. It was unofficial, but Locker had hinted at a frigate bound for Baltic service. Yet nothing had come yet and the ugly face of Lord Sandwich gave little in the way of hope.

'I've had enough of physick, Tom. The doctors in Bath pored over every inch of me. I have been bled, blistered and every motion I've passed for three months has been examined.'

There had been his father too. Whatever good Lepée and his ministrations had done for him during the journey home, it was still a weak, skeletal individual who had been hoisted ashore at Portsmouth. He could not but admire the way his father had cared for him, carrying him to and from his bed, seeming to suffer as much pain from the excruciating torture of movement as his son. Weeks had gone by before he could fend for himself, weeks when his father had never flinched from his duty, regardless of the unpleasant tasks he had been obliged to carry out.

'And as to recovery,' Nelson added, 'I feel I am a new man.'

'Yet you're still troubled by that arm?'

'Intermittently, Tom,' Nelson replied, failing to add that the affliction in his left arm, which felt stiff and painful, now extended to his left thigh and leg.

'Twice last week you complained of it,' Foley insisted, his open face a mixture of worry and excitement. 'How can you contemplate taking up your duties until you have tried every method to effect a cure?'

'I'm not yet convinced I have a duty.'

'You're better placed than I, Nelson. I've yet to be made Post.'

'Electricity is so much stuff.'

'How do you know that?'

'The doctors in Bath told me. Not one of them had a good word to say in its favour.'

'Hardly surprising, Nelson,' Tom said, 'since they don't make use of it themselves. But opinion here in town has Graham as a sort of genius. Stories abound of cures he has engineered with his delivery of shocks.'

'And just as many speak of tomfoolery.'

'I hazard only from bodies that, like those corpses in Bath, have not paid a visit.'

Tom was not to be gainsaid and eventually time and his eloquence wore Nelson down, until he agreed that a visit to the Adelphi was essential to his well-being.

The sight of the two giants at the door, in their gaudy uniforms under the flaming flambeaux, nearly put the putative patient into reverse. But Tom grabbed his arm, which was enough to remind him of why he had come. It had been white and dead that morning but now it was swollen, red and painful to the touch, so he allowed himself to be led through the narrow entrance, in the midst of the shuffling crowd of well-heeled patrons. The pile of discarded crutches and peg legs caused him to raise an eyebrow. But he parted with his guinea, the fee that allowed him to reach the inner sanctum, which smelt of eastern perfumes, the soft singing of high-pitched voices like that of the cathedral cloister.

Inside, the walls were lined with flaring flambeaux, which gave the room an ethereal look as the flickering flames played on the silks and curtains that covered both walls and ceilings.

'Look at that, Nelson,' Tom whispered, pointing to one of the young ladies in the alcoves. 'If that ain't enough to cure your arm, nothing is.'

'The ability to be crude comes easy to you, Tom.'

'Don't you go getting pious, Nelson. Remember you was a midshipman once. I have shared a mess with you and heard you at your nocturnals. One hand clapping is never as silent as the perpetrator supposes.'

That made Nelson blush and look away, to be immediately confronted by a scantily clad young woman draped in muslin and silks that did little to hide her charms. Most striking was her auburn hair, which fell in wavy tresses from under her tawdry Greek helmet. The spear she held was set like that of some archaic sentry and her gaze was so direct and level as to make her look like a character in a tableau. Yet she was no figure of *papier mâché*. The shape of her thigh was as unmistakable as the rise and fall of her breasts.

'Ain't she just the thing, Nelson?' whispered Tom. 'And there's five more like her. Graham is not one to stint his clients when it comes to shocks, natural or otherwise.'

Nelson had to drag away his eyes so as not to be caught in the act of staring. But even if he sought to disguise it from his friend he felt a surge of energy through his limbs. The creature was striking in her beauty. And even as he looked at the occupants of the other alcoves the image of that full-lipped face stayed in his mind. He knew, without looking again, that her eyes were green and felt, without knowing why, that her disposition was kindly. Then he had to remind himself of past experience, of the times he had been fooled by other impressions, seeing a kind heart only to discover at the end of the carnal transaction that it was in reality made of silver fed stone.

Yet he kept glancing back as Tom prattled on about the other models, the machines and contraptions that Dr Graham employed in his treatments.

'Now there's a bed fit for a king,' he enthused, dragging Nelson's eyes to the great round couch, padded with satin, decorated by near lewd furbelows that, in his present state, brought about a degree of tumescence. A mighty clap came forth next, and the stage behind the bed was suddenly occupied by even more scantily clad beauties, with that sweet female voice rising to a warbling crescendo. One man stood in the middle, in powdered wig and sober black, his eyes lively and his expression animated as he accepted the applause of his audience.

'Ladies, gentlemen and sufferers, welcome,' he intoned, his voice heavy with a Scottish brogue, arms outstretched like a Christ receptive. 'I come among you as a healer, a humble servant of God, who has put me on this earth to advance the cause of a troubled humanity.'

Some of the flambeaux had been extinguished, and the room had darkened. Nelson half listened as the good doctor began his lecture, talking of the connection between the soul and the body, and his claim to have found in electricity the umbilical cord that connected them. References to the act of procreation he handled with a skill that could scandalise no one, as he wandered from afflictions in general to his particular subject, the begetting of children and the problems associated with any man's inability to sire an heir.

'For it is with we, the heirs to Adam, that such responsibility lies. You would shudder to see the brave men I have had weep upon my shoulder when forced to admit that they are unable to provide the seed of life. And all, my friends, is not dissipation. Our God, in one guise, may be our saviour, but in another he is tormentor enough to leave innocent souls bereft of the process of the mind that turns a limp sliver of useless flesh into the spear of creation.'

Nelson turned to look back to that alcove. The girl had relaxed now, almost a shadow in the dim prevailing light, leaning against the side of her perch. Her spear was at rest and he observed that her eyes were closed as if she was asleep. Eyes that could see a distant ship under a gloomy sky had little difficulty in assessing those features in repose. Like those of a child, they bespoke of an innocence that was at odds with her occupation. Behind him Graham spoke on, his voice sinking to a deep, soporific drone, as he sucked in his audience. Vaguely he observed some attendants approaching the snuffed flambeaux, in preparation for lighting them again, which acted as a cue to the alcove attractions to re-adopt their poses.

'Now, friends,' Graham barked, his voice returning to normal at the same time as the lighting, 'is there anyone here with an affliction that requires attention?'

Nelson heard Tom's voice. 'My friend, doctor.'

'Tom!'

'He is newly returned from Bath, Dr Graham, where he has been recovering from a malarial fever.'

Graham stepped down from the stage and came up to Nelson, to stand so close to him that the herbal odour on his breath was easily discernible.

'Not wholly recovered, I fancy,' Graham said softly, 'judging by the peak of the skin. Your name, sir?'

'Nelson.'

'*Captain* Nelson,' added Tom, with just a hint of envy.

'Your coat tells me that, sir. What it does not tell me is how and when you came by your fever, and how often it recurs.'

'It is not something that falls within your province, sir.'

'Captain, how would you react if I told you how to sail a ship?' Nelson didn't answer. 'I fancy you'd tell me that you knew your business. Please allow that I know mine.'

Graham put a thumb below his eye and pulled the skin down to expose more of the pupil as Nelson talked. He told him briefly of the first fever in the East, the number of times it had recurred, and of the state in which he had been obliged to quit the attack on the San Juan Fort. At the same time Graham's other hand went to Nelson's wrist, two fingers on the flat, the thumb pressing at the back.

'Your tongue, sir, if you please?' He had to comply, given that he was now the centre of attention. 'It is not a healthy specimen, I see, and there is a fetid odour on your breath.'

'His arm pains him,' said Tom.

'In what way?'

Nelson had no choice but to answer, nor, when Graham insisted he remove his coat, could he demur. The doctor prodded and poked, sensing the pain he was causing to a man who had no desire to show it publicly. A call over his shoulder produced a contraption that consisted of a handled wheel inside a wooden frame, with bright metal connected, plus two flexible metal strips with amulets attached.

Graham first had his man wind the wheel, then held the two amulets close to each other until a series of sparks flew across the gap. That was accompanied by cries from his audience that ranged from fear to wonder. Graham insisted that Nelson remove his shirt from one arm and shoulder, then place one amulet on the wrist and the other high on the upper arm.

'You have a blockage, sir, which does not permit the message of your vital spirit to transmit itself to the extremities of this limb. It is my aim, using the latest discoveries of the sciences, to undo this. You, sir, when I wind my wheel and generate the force that will course through you, will think you are partaking of a miracle. You are not, sir. You are merely in receipt of God's good grace. What we have has been on this earth since Creation. Only now has God seen fit to enlighten us as to its use.'

The first tingling sensation was pleasant, of the kind he had experienced when in anticipation of some great treat. But that didn't last as the wheel was spun faster.

'Stand back there,' Graham barked, mostly to Tom Foley, but also to the curious crowd. 'You will transfer the cure, and perhaps even the affliction if you touch the patient.'

The tingling grew in effect, no longer a tickle, though not quite a pain. 'The power courses through you, sir. The pain you suffer will begin to increase.'

Nelson had to nod to Graham, because the man was right.

His arm was hurting like the very devil, but it was tolerable. That lasted only a few seconds, until it increased in intensity causing him to gasp. He could feel the sweat on his brow, smell his own armpit, and he was conscious of the sea of faces that seemed to press in on him from the crowd. The effect now began to extend from his arm to his whole body. The limb to which amulets were attached began to jerk in involuntary spasm, and Graham's face, leaning forward, had taken on a demonic cast. Nelson knew his lips were open, pulled back over his teeth, and he was just on the verge of screaming enough when the wheel stopped. The sensation ceased immediately, but left him feeling so weak that Tom had to support him.

'Do you feel any pain now?' asked Graham. His arm felt numb, but not sore so he shook his head. The doctor turned to the room and said, 'There! I credit that as a success.'

The applause was spontaneous, and others pressed forward to request the doctor's services. They were directed to a clerk with a book, whose job it was to register them for appointments.

'I cannot treat the entire populace of London in public. Besides that, some of the patients I administer to have things it would be unbecoming to reveal to an audience. See my good man here, he will appraise you of times and charges.' He spoke softly then to Nelson, who was putting his uniform coat back on. 'You, sir, presented a most enlightening case. You therefore owe me nothing.'

'Sir, I insist.'

'Pray, Captain Nelson, allow me to follow what I consider my professional duty. Your illness, sir, came upon you through service to your King and country. Believe me, I love both too much to be able to receive anything by way of payment.'

They eased out of the crowd, Tom gabbling away enthusiastically, Nelson ignoring him as he concentrated on two things: the numbing of his arm and that Greek goddess with the spear and the flowing auburn hair. She was looking at him now – the eyes, indeed, were green – almost staring in fact.

CHAPTER 29

Charles Greville entered Emma's Whitechapel room with the caution of a man expecting to be robbed. He cast about him with that same air and finally looked at her so directly that she smoothed the folds of her dark, satin dress involuntarily, and wondered what was the matter with him. He was behaving as if he hardly knew her.

'You look exceedingly respectable, Emma,' he said, making no attempt to disguise the irony in his tone.

Damn him, she thought, as she favoured him with a smile as demure as her clothing. For him to see through her so quickly boded ill for the forthcoming interview. She shouldn't have dressed like this, in a solemn, plain garment. He knew her too well to fall for such a subterfuge.

'Why did you not reply to my letters?' she asked.

'Have I not done so by coming here in person?'

'Then you have responded to the last. There was more than one.'

'I sit for a Warwickshire seat, Emma. If you knew anything about the life of a Member of Parliament you would have some notion of how it can occupy every waking hour.' Greville looked hard at her, forcing her to accept the lie. 'And then I return to find you the talk of the clubs, my dear. Every loose fellow who's been to a pleasure garden these last few weeks claims to have secured you as a prize.'

There was little doubt that Greville disapproved, just as there was no doubt that he would fail to understand how she had been driven to accepting invitations that, under better circumstances, she would have refused. Her employment at Graham's spectacle had lasted no more than two weeks, barely long enough to keep her head above water.

Emma had often been told that the road to hell was paved with good intentions, and she had intended to remain chaste – but how could she laugh, accept food and drink, dance and sing in the company of an amusing companion, then turn them away from intimacy, especially when he offered her some badly needed money? The only defence she could offer was that she had accepted no more than was necessary for survival.

'I am pleased that seems to give you cause for disquiet,' she said.

His smile didn't disappear, but the slight lines that marked his high forehead indicated the degree of his resentment. 'I think you're aware of my feelings in the matter, Emma. I seem to recall that while you were still at Uppark you came to understand that such behaviour carries risk. I certainly thought that when you visited me you paid attention to my advice on the best way to disport yourself.'

'What risk is there in dancing, sir?'

'When it is accompanied by drinking to excess and the loud rendition of bawdy songs . . .' He left the rest in the air, merely adding a shrug.

Emma was curious to know if Greville had learnt this by his own application, or if the gossip was so prevalent that picking it up had been a commonplace. The former would help her case, the latter probably destroy it. And, annoyingly, a direct question was impossible. She decided on a brave face as the best defence. 'Am I to avoid pleasure altogether, Charles? Are not drinking and dancing the very stuff to which Vauxhall and the Ranelagh are dedicated?'

'I daresay, Emma,' he replied, his face stern, 'just as I daresay that's why I so heartily dislike them when the hour has come for respectability to exit, allowing vice to enter. I take leave to doubt that you were an early-evening visitor.'

If that was close to an insult it was also true. She had never gone to either pleasure garden before the firework display, which was usually the signal for the innocents to depart and for the revels, for which such places were notorious, to become more free. She had to bite back any response, since she was in no position to challenge him.

He picked up a high-backed chair and moved it to the other

side of the fire. Once seated, he examined her closely. For all the displeasure he had espoused regarding her recent behaviour, there was admiration in his eyes.

'Not that your carrying on seems to have blighted you. If anything, you're more beautiful than ever.'

'Then, clearly, a life of unremitting pleasure suits me.'

'Are you sure it's not your condition, Emma?' He held up his hand as she opened her mouth to protest. 'Your landlady, Mrs Mulderry, has a sense of discretion that does not extend to the refusal of a shilling. She informed me, with some relish, that you wake the whole house of a morning with your retching.'

Emma looked straight at him, hoping that he would see in her eyes that she was speaking the truth. 'I had intended to tell you, Charles.'

'Am I the father?'

'It's more likely Harry is.'

'Are there any other candidates excepting Harry and myself?'

'That's a damned unkind thing to say.'

'Remember, I was at Uppark on more than one riotous occasion. I have already alluded to your being the talk of the town. I won't do so again. I will merely ask you this: under those circumstances, why did you leave a letter requesting that I call?'

'I had every reason to believe that you still think of me kindly.'

'I do, Emma. And I will add that I think of you often. It gives me no pleasure to return from Warwickshire and hear you discussed openly by people I regard as rakes and fools.'

Finding she was the subject of common gossip nearly broke Emma's resolve. It brought home to her how far she had fallen. It took great effort to keep her composure, and to demand defensively, 'Who are these people?'

The slight smile returned. 'I daresay you know that better than I, having spent so much time with them.'

Remaining calm might be a necessary requirement, yet in the face of such an accusation it was near impossible. Emma fought to keep any hint of pique from her voice. 'You imply a want of discretion, Charles, but I have not once set foot outside the circle of Harry's acquaintances. These are all people whose company you seemed to enjoy.'

'I rest my case,' he replied, with a wide grin.

'That included you, Charles. How can you forget the attentions you paid me? And that while I was still under Harry's roof, let alone his protection.'

'I had hoped that you'd see me differently, you know that. But my humble means cannot compete with your keeper's.'

'I've seen precious little of his money.'

'Indeed!'

'Do you think I would run around with such people if I had Harry's attention? I've been forced to fend for myself.'

'I heard he had cooled.'

'Froze, Charles, not cooled. I haven't seen him for near three whole months. And these lodgings, in which he undertook to support me, are my own to maintain.'

'Given your evident charms, my dear, that should present little difficulty.'

'I am not a whore, Charles,' she snapped, goaded by his studied air of serenity.

'I have what I hear.'

'And I require a roof over my head, as well as food in my belly.'

'Since you owe rent, I must assume you have not pursued a new career with gusto.'

'Is there anything Mrs Mulderry didn't tell you?'

The smile returned. 'That was the first thing she said, no doubt hoping that I would satisfy the debt.'

She dropped her head, unable to look him in the eye. He stood up and leant over to squeeze her shoulders. 'I'm not a fool, Emma. You're sure you suspect Harry to be the father?'

'It is the most likely,' she replied softly, making no attempt to keep the hurt out of her voice.

'Then you must go to him and tell him that it is so.'

That produced a humourless laugh. 'He forbade me to call at Piccadilly, or to write to him there.'

'He's not even in London, Emma. At this very moment he is in Leicestershire.'

'That might be the moon for all the difference it makes to me. I lack the means to stay or go.'

He traced the outline of her cheek with one extended finger. 'Come along, Emma. Do you think that I would leave you in such a bind? I've already promised to pay your arrears to Mrs Mulderry.' Emma looked into his eyes and took his hand, trying to convey in her tight grip that she was fond of him. 'As to your travelling expenses, I will cover those as well.'

'How can I ever repay you?'

'If Harry acknowledges parenthood, then you can reimburse me from what he will, as his honour demands, settle on you. Now cheer up, and behave to me like the Emma of old.'

'I think I've quite forgotten how to do that, Charles.'

'Nonsense. My first suggestion is that you change that dress. It makes you look like a mourner at a particularly dull funeral.'

She brightened at that, and smiled properly for the first time since he had arrived. 'What should I put on in its place?'

He bent forward to kiss her, but before their lips touched he halted, then smiled again. 'I think that is a matter to be set aside for the moment, don't you? Just let it fall so that I may inspect what is, in my opinion, the living Venus.'

The hoofs of the shay that was to carry Emma to meet the Leicester coach at the Strand still echoed in the street, as Greville returned to face Mrs Mulderry.

'Now, madam, I require from you a final account of the amount Miss Hart owes.'

'I have it writ here, your honour,' she replied, proffering a small piece of paper, 'so's there can be no a-arguing. An' might I be allowed to say that I've rare met such a good soul. That young lady needs proper lookin' after.'

As he counted out the coins into her hand, he couldn't help noticing the change in her manner. Finally satisfied, she clasped the money in one fist, then put her other hand on top of it, the two being clutched to her belly. Her round face was no longer supplicant and the way her shoulders lifted around her thick neck displayed the level of her disapproval.

'Not that such beauty will want for long, I daresay. But bloom won't last. It never does with that sort.'

Greville was tempted to tell her just what an unpleasant creature she was. But his mind was more with Emma and how much he had missed her. He knew Uppark Harry well enough to be sure that he would deny paternity, quite possibly shifting responsibility to him, a notion that was quite conceivably true. Whatever, that would leave Emma unsupported. His mind was reeling with the notion that he had won out over his rich friend; that he could finally offer his protection, the search for ways in which it could be managed financially began at once. Calling her a beauty did her scant justice, and having her all to himself was something to look forward to with keen anticipation.

Not that it could happen immediately, of course. There was the final despatch of Harry to resolve. Regardless of the outcome of that, which, if he knew his friend, would do nothing for Emma, she was with child. There was little point in him maintaining her in that state, when for several months she would be unable to fulfil the purpose of her presence. But once the child was born, then Emma Hart would be grateful for his continued concern. And with his superior intellect, and her manifest needs he was sure he could lure her into another experiment as a kept woman.

The Strand was crammed with coaches, so deep in horse dung that the sweepers struggled to keep it clear for the passengers, some alighting after their arrival in London, most waiting to depart. The noise, to Nelson's mind, sounded like the Tower of Babel, with drivers yelling at each other and flicking whips for right of way, the owners and ticketing vendors of the routes jostling and hustling their customers to their conveyances, servants near to brawling so that luggage could be loaded, all that mingled with the cries and sometimes tears of welcome and farewell.

'Worse'ner than a maindeck first day in port,' snarled Frank Lepée, simultaneously elbowing a hired porter who tried to cross his route. 'Mind how you go, mate, or I'll fetch you a clout with that there valise you're hoickin'.'

'Go fuck yourself, mate,' the porter replied, with little rancour.

343

The string of invective with which Lepée answered that was brought to an abrupt halt by a command to belay from his master, who turned quickly and raised his hat to the porter's client, a well-dressed lady with a hooded cloak and a veil covering her face, the scent of which, necessary to keep out the malodours of the street, wafted over him. Her face was hidden by the cowl of her cloak and she didn't respond, but she was no more than twenty feet away when she removed it and clambered aboard her coach, showing thick auburn hair and a classically beautiful profile.

Nelson recognised her immediately as the semi-clad nymph from the Adelphi, and tried to move forward to make her acquaintance. But too many other passengers blocked his progress and she was aboard before he had managed a yard. That halted him. The prospect that he would have to open the door to address her in front of other passengers was too much for him and the courage he relied on at sea was not up to facing such a potentially embarrassing encounter. He watched as the coach driver, whip flicking, drove his horses' heads out into the Strand.

The image of that auburn-haired goddess recurred in Nelson's daydreams as he took his own coach north, with no firm news of a ship, acceding to his father's request to visit Norfolk. The landscape was flat under the grey skies, as the coach rattled along at a good pace on new roads built by turnpike trusts. A change of conveyance at Norwich took him through the towns on the Pilgrim's Way that ran north to the coastal towns of the Wash. The sights and sounds of his own county, now bathed in a summer sun, evoked a degree of introspection.

From Burnham Market he took a hack to his home, through rolling hills that cut off the nearby sea from the flat plain to the south. He had run around here as a child, coursing hares, raiding birds' nests, stealing fruit, trapping rabbits and hunting foxes. He heard the cry of the gulls a mile and a half inland, at the same time observing from the coach window the swallow-tailed butterflies and hawker dragonflies that buzzed across the hay meadows. The faint smell of the North Sea brought back memories of fishing, of gadding about in small boats when he'd been entranced to see on the horizon the occasional sail of a great ship. The light of the sun, as it sank below the cloud in the West, had a quality that existed nowhere else he had ever been; a streak of low gold that cast shadows that seemed to run to the edge of the world.

How would he be received here in the Burnhams now that he was a Post Captain? Even unemployed and far from complete health, that made him somebody, perhaps enough of a person in the county not to fear too much from his present situation. Against that his elder brother Maurice, now toiling in the same Navy Office his uncle Suckling had run, warned him of the poor prospects facing idle captains forced to exist on half pay.

Rattling along past sights so familiar they tugged at his emotions, it was easy to conjure up the image of a rural idyll: a place of content, where the well respected Captain Horatio Nelson would be of some standing in the community, a man to elicit a raised hat from the gentry, and a doffed cap from labourers and tenant farmers.

Yet it was foolish to compare his standing here with the respect he was shown aboard ship. What could he hope for here except obscurity? The notion of being indistinguishable from the herd had never appealed to Nelson. Though he knew that his desire for recognition carried within it the sin of vanity he could not help but crave it. It had been with him all his life – even as a child he had sought to outdo his siblings.

His father would be there to greet him, the same man who had looked after him so assiduously in Bath. Illness had not spared the Rector's son oft-repeated homilies regarding his manners, the forthrightness of his opinions, or how those impacted on his prospects for advancement. That his father insisted he recuperate in Bath had made sense, but the fact that he actually liked the place amazed Horatio Nelson. Why leave his parishes in Norfolk, where he was a highly regarded individual, to travel to a West Country town where he melded seamlessly into a flock of nonentities taking the waters, bowing and scraping to those they considered their social superiors?

With an uncomfortable vision that his own life might take a similar course, he mouthed a silent prayer that their lordships at the Admiralty would give him a ship.

CHAPTER 30

Albemarle shuddered, her head falling off in customary fashion. Though Nelson could never be brought to say so, this ex-merchantman turned frigate was the most crank ship he had ever set sail in. It was a true example of the parsimony of a government that failed to build men-o'-war when they should, then could not provide them to defend Britain's interests when required.

Of shallow draught, broad beamed and unstable in any kind of sea, she was even worse on a breeze, a ship that had her crew toiling aloft endlessly even on a calm day. Useless on a bowline, sailing into the wind was a struggle, and that had applied on the Baltic convoy as much as it did here, off Boston and Cape Cod. Her head would keep falling off, obliging Nelson to tack constantly, struggling to keep up with his better-sailing charges.

Locker had advised him to decline the command, and that had been when the captured French ship was still in the dockyard being converted. Nelson was never sure if it was pride or fear for future employment that had made him ignore such sound advice. Whatever, he had had ample cause to curse ever since, in which he was outshone by a cantankerous Frank Lepée, who had assumed certain rights and privileges – not least that of hinting to his master that he was frequently in the wrong, and that their presence aboard this barky proved it. That this, said openly, embarrassed his officers seemed to bother Nelson not one jot, just as the fact that Lepée was frequently drunk when serving table seemed to escape his notice.

The first cruise had seen Nelson trying and failing to keep a swift-sailing French privateer from snapping up some of the merchantmen, loaded with naval stores, he had escorted from the mouth of the Elbe. A month spent dragging her anchors in the Downs had worn him to a frazzle, that culminating, after a particularly nasty five-day gale, in a heavy collision with another warship. Any hope that the damage was permanent had been cruelly dashed by the dockyard superintendent: with a war on anything that could float had to be pressed into service. He announced the ship repairable and had her back at sea in a month.

The second convoy, from Cork to St John's, Newfoundland, had been even worse. *Albemarle* had become separated not only from the cargo vessels, but from the second escorting frigate, *Daedalus*, and had behaved so badly in the Atlantic swell that her arrival at the destination port was a whole two weeks behind the vessels she had been detailed to escort. He touched with the fleet at the Isle of Bec in the St Lawrence river, but was ordered back to sea within two days. This afforded him scant opportunity to replenish his stores, or to observe the town of Québec and visit the spot on the Plains of Abraham where his hero General Wolfe had fallen.

At least here, astride the main supply routes to the Continental insurgents, they took some prizes, mainly deep-water fishing vessels with cargo and ships that were easy to sell in the St Lawrence and Newfoundland settlements. He had sent in four prizes already, calculating to within a golden guinea how much they were worth, while gnawing at the knowledge that, with the provision of prize crews, he had left himself perilously short of both officers and men. And by staying at sea for the maximum time possible he was also short of victuals. His water was good, having been replenished at Québec, but his fresh greens were quite used up, the crew diet reduced to barrels of beef, pork and dried beans that did nothing for their health.

Those left aboard had a lacklustre appearance, and were slower in going about their duties. Their skin had a grey tinge and the breath of most was fetid on the nose of anyone they talked to. Staying at sea was partly orders, but it was also the inclination of a captain determined to prove that his ship, the butt of many a joke in harbour, was a match for any frigate on the station.

Lepée, had Nelson enquired, would have told him of the brawls the crew had engaged in to protect the honour of their ship when they were berthed at Portsmouth and the Downs. He would not have mentioned, even if pressed, that some of the fights had been about Nelson himself, who was mocked by other crews for his height, his appearance, his gentle manner and the continuous presence of one of his midshipmen with him wherever he went.

'Fog bank ahead, your honour,' said the man on the wheel.

'Thank you, Nichols,' Nelson replied, stretching himself.

That shortage of officers meant Nelson standing a watch himself, so that Midshipman Bromwich, the last young gentleman he had aboard, could get some rest. George Bromwich, coming up sixteen, was the son of a blacksmith, a youth without any influence whatsoever. Tall and golden-haired he now had a ruddy complexion much marked by the scars of the skin eruptions that had accompanied the change from boy to man. He had written to Nelson for a place as soon as he heard that the man who had left him at the mouth of the San Juan river had a ship. Nelson, knowing him to have the makings of a competent seaman, had been happy to reply in the affirmative.

Now he wondered how Bromwich felt. Was he glad he had joined Nelson, or silently cursing the luck that had put him with such an unfortunate ship and commander? Loyalty, that necessary commodity, only stretched so far. A year on *Albemarle* for a man in his position, even with the courtesy rank of acting lieutenant, could feel like a decade.

'Deck there,' the voice called from above, just loud enough to be heard, obeying the standard order not to use more voice than was necessary. 'Ship!'

'Where away?' Nelson demanded, lifting a telescope from the rack.

'Dead ahead, your honour,' the lookout replied. 'Just got a sight of some upper poles before they were swallowed agin by the fog.'

Nelson turned to Nichols. 'Please, send someone to rouse out Mr Bromwich. I want you to hold the ship steady on this course.'

He climbed the shrouds quickly, telescope tucked into his breeches, joining the lookout in the crosstrees. Thorpe had a good pair of eyes, better than those of his captain, and even if they could see nothing now, Nelson was sure that the man was right. But he could add little to what he had already imparted. The swirling bank of fog ahead, a commonplace in these waters at this time of year, could have hidden a fleet.

'If he saw us he will have changed course.'

'Stayed on the same heading for the little time I saw him. His fore and main never wavered.'

Nelson had to ignore the foulness of Thorpe's breath, assuming as he did that his was just the same. He rated the able seaman highly as a willing hand, a man who could hand, reef and steer, who was content to sit aloft for the whole of his watch if asked, keeping a lookout with one of the best pair of eyes on the ship. Apart from that he was a Norfolk man, and that pleased a captain who liked nothing more than to crew his ship from the men of his own county.

'Two masts?'

'Aye. And no pennant.'

'On course for Boston, then, Mr Thorpe, and damn nearly home.'

That made the able seaman smile, it being one of his commander's little habits to address the commonality as gents, in his customary unaffected manner. On his Sunday inspections, Nelson trod the decks avoiding what he knew would be accusing eyes, a crew that cursed him as much as they did the ship, never realising that his men esteemed him very highly indeed. They knew he had served before the mast and were given ample evidence that he had never forgotten it.

Notions that they might guy him or fail to carry out their duties properly fell at that hurdle. Nelson knew what to look for and where to look, and could put an expression on his face when dissatisfied that made the perpetrator feel like a scrub. There was no pomposity and neither could they complain for the fair way in which he behaved. There had been no more than two floggings in the six months since they'd weighed from Cork, and both, by common consent, had been well deserved.

'Happen he's laden right enough, your honour.'

'Then, with your permission, Mr Thorpe, I may increase sail.'

That brought forth yet another wide grin. But Nelson didn't see it. They were approaching the edge of the bank, and looking down he could see that Bromwich had taken up his station on the quarterdeck. Soon the whole ship would be swallowed up and those below would be lost to sight. If he wanted to con the ship that was where he should be.

'I'll send aloft a youngster. No shouting, Thorpe! If you sight anything send him down.'

'Aye, aye, sir.'

'And, Thorpe, if you need to be relieved, send that message down too.'

'I'll be fine, your honour, never you fret.'

'I never do when you're aloft,' Nelson replied, his hand on the backstay.

They were into the bank of fog by the time he reached the deck, orders given quietly to increase sail added to a small change in course to close one side of what he hoped would be a triangle. Two pairs of the maindeck guns, on either side, were manned, loaded and run out. Bromwich, his huge frame tense, was dying to ask, but convention denied him the right. Nelson was quick to put him out of his misery. 'Thorpe has her as two-masted, another fishing schooner most likely. Reckons we weren't spotted.'

'He's a good man, sir.'

'That I grant you.'

Just then a cry drifted through the air, a call amplified by the mists that had every ear cocked to trace the sound. Nelson put out a hand and pulled the wheel two points to starboard, nodding to one of the crew to mark the course alteration on the binnacle slate. Silence descended then, the only sounds, apart from the odd cry of a seagull, the creaking of their own ship's timbers, ropes stretching and easing.

An hour passed in that state, the ship seemingly alone and abandoned on the great ocean, held in place by the damp, cloying fog. His course, he suspected, was taking him into the Boston Bay, so he put a man in the chains with a lead, plus messengers to warn of shoal water. It was a dangerous place to be, but he calculated that at such a slow rate of sailing if he did run aground, provided he avoided rocks, he would have little trouble in hauling off.

Eventually the light increased as the fog thinned, first just a play upon the eye, then the hint of a watery centre to the radiance. Within a minute they could see the outline of the sun, no more than a yellow-tinged rim. That was when Thorpe, in defiance of his instructions, shouted down to the deck in a voice that would have woken the dead. 'Ship two points free on the larboard bow, not more'n half a cable's length.'

Nelson was halfway along the gangway before he had finished, rushing for the bows. The fog had turned hazy, and in the sunlight the wisps of mist could be seen moving. And as he leapt on to the tight ropes gammoning the bowsprit, hanging on to a stay to lean out over the bows, he saw the outline of their quarry. 'Hard a-starboard, helmsman,' he yelled. 'Larboard cannon fire before you bear.'

The head came round agonisingly slowly, the *Albemarle* behaving in its usual crank fashion. The gunners didn't wait as long as they might, but fired off two balls low, which landed well in the wake of the target. By the time they had reloaded the warship was beam on to the American ship, with Nelson calling through a speaking trumpet for the master to heave to. Unarmed, the schooner had little choice when faced with heavy cannon, and it was with lifting hearts that the Albemarles saw the sails loosened to spill the wind.

Bromwich hadn't been idle: the boats, towed astern, had been hauled up to the rope ladder that hung below the open gangway. Nelson was over the side on the heels of his barge crew, and with a swiftness that belied their aching limbs the men pulled for the capture, hauling alongside so that their captain and half of the crew could go aboard. The mist had cleared now, and the spires and roofs of Boston were plain to the naked eye, proof of just how close their quarry was to home. As if to underline his capture, the wind suddenly grew in intensity, blowing away what haze remained, ruffling the waters and showing the first signs of white caps.

'Good day to you, sir,' he said, as a tall, imposing man, clearly the master, stepped forward. 'Captain Nelson, of His

Britannic Majesty's frigate *Albemarle*. Whom do I have the honour of addressing?'

The voice that replied was deep and rather attractive. 'Nathaniel Carver, sir, native of Plymouth, Massachusetts, owner and master of the schooner *Harmony*.'

'Your cargo, sir?'

'Reckon you can smell that, Mr Nelson.'

The odour of fresh fish was strong and, judging by the overflowing baskets that lined the deck, the vessel was full.

'Do you have a licence from the authorities to fish these waters?'

'Not any authority you will recognise.'

'Then unfortunately, Mr Carver, I must confiscate both ship and cargo, as being the property of a rebellious subject of my sovereign.'

Nelson was pleased that Carver seemed an honest fellow, not one to try to pass off a forged certificate marking him out as an American Loyalist. Such documents were never good enough to deceive him and made what was an unpleasant duty that much worse, especially since there could be no doubt of where he intended to make his landfall.

'You have your duty to do, sir.'

Nelson was only half listening, his eye caught by a degree of activity in the harbour. The gunfire would have set off every bell in every spire. Boats, no doubt, were being manned to come out and retake the vessel. And the wind had increased even more, making the two stationary vessels pitch. For a ship like his this was not promising. He had to go, and quickly, but so close to the shore he knew he was among the shoals, banks and reefs that, with any kind of sea running, made the approach to Boston treacherous.

'Mr Carver, I find myself at a stand. I have too few officers to man your ship, and I find myself close to a hostile shore that must, in all conscience, be more familiar to you than to me.'

'That I would not disagree with, sir.'

'You will also observe yonder that attempts are being made to launch boats to effect a rescue. In shoal water an armed cutter can be deadly even to a frigate. That means that I must depart this place in some haste, not a course I would normally adopt where I run the risk of grounding my ship.'

'Grounding be damned, sir. You can founder in this bay, sir, if you do not know where the rocks lie.'

'Quite,' Nelson replied. 'I would therefore be obliged if you would come aboard my vessel and con her out of these waters. In fact, I require you to be my pilot. *Harmony* will follow in our wake until we are clear of danger.'

'You ask a great deal, sir,' said Carver.

'I am aware of that, sir, but I fear I must insist. My only other choice is to sink you, and as a sailor I find that notion repugnant.'

'Then, Captain Nelson, I am at your service,' Carver replied, showing both his palms. 'I had a hand in the building of this ship, and I would be loath to see all that labour go to naught. I would have her still float, even under another's hand.'

'May I request your parole?' Carver nodded, so Nelson added, 'A word to your crew, if you please?'

Carver obliged, telling his men to stay in *Albemarle*'s wake, to attempt nothing in the way of recapture, for there would be stern chasers trained on their ship. 'Any promise I give, boys, not to attempt recapture is yours too. Mark it.'

On coming aboard *Albemarle*, Lieutenant Lenham, the marine officer, once appraised of the American's role, assigned two marines to guard him, an order his captain overrode with a rare show of asperity. Carver nodded at this and thanked him. But he spoke little after that, except to order a change of sails, his face wearing a heavy frown when the crank ship failed to answer to her helm as any decent vessel should. If he noticed that the crew were a touch sluggish he said nothing and the way he manoeuvred showed how at home he was in these waters, with their shifting, treacherous currents and flukes of local wind.

He had the parochial knowledge to take them close to hazards, evidenced by the breaking waters that marked them, without ever putting either vessel in danger – so much so that Nelson left the deck for a while, trusting Carver enough to leave him unobserved. He came back to find his faith well placed, since finally, after two hours in which the crew had worked to

Carver's orders, they were safe in deep water, and the forced pilot handed the ship back to his captor.

'That was most handsomely done, Captain Carver. You have the thanks of both my men and myself. Would you join me in my cabin, where I will offer you some refreshment?'

'Obliged.'

He followed Nelson into the great cabin, spacious as befitted a converted merchantman, though rather bare since the furniture had been displaced by the need to use the rear pointing cannon that sat, squat, black and still run out, a menacing reminder of what damage *Albemarle* could inflict. Lepée glared at Carver as he poured the wine, and stood swaying while the two men shared a toast to all sailors in all seas. Nelson was then obliged to rather force the conversation on a taciturn guest, relating to him their Atlantic voyage and all that had flowed from it.

'We have barely touched shore since April, and that at Portsmouth. I must tell you that we dine on naught but salt beef and pork.'

'Well you have fresh fish in abundance now,' Carver replied sadly.

'Would it was green stuff. Tell me about yourself, Mr Carver?'

'Not much to tell, Captain Nelson. I was born on yonder shore, and that don't leave much choice when it comes to occupation.'

'Damned rebels,' growled Lepée, in a voice he obviously thought couldn't be heard.

Carver expected the man to be put in his place, and was as nonplussed as everyone else who had ever witnessed such behaviour when Nelson ignored it.

'Your vessel *Harmony*, is she part of a fleet?'

Carver emitted a deep, humourless chuckle. 'I was spawned without much, Captain, and have worked my way up to that ship. Everything I have in the world is tied up in her.'

'Your antecedents are English?'

'Welsh.'

That brought another growl of dissent from Lepée, who considered anyone not pure English to be of mongrel blood.

355

This time Nelson threw him a look designed to silence him. 'Would that you were loyal to King George, sir.'

Carver squared his shoulders. 'Would that King George could put aside tyranny, and accept that we have a right to determine our own future.'

Nelson smiled. 'It is as a serving officer of my sovereign that I am here, sir. And I know Mr Carver that such a sentiment applies to many of my fellow officers. Yet that is sorely tested when the French fight alongside you. Can you not see a way to make an accommodation?'

'I'm a fisherman, Captain, not a politician.'

'You are also a gentleman, sir.'

'I hardly qualify for such a title.'

Nelson felt weary, the wine acting on an already debilitated constitution to bring his tiredness into the open. He had to lean forward and rub his eyes before continuing. Carver had the good manners to look away so that his host would not be embarrassed.

'Many think it is an estate conferred by blood or money. But I know better, Captain Carver. It is a cast of mind and you have it.'

'Why, thank you, Captain.'

Nelson stood up, picked up a piece of paper and led Carver out on to the deck. There, watched by every unemployed member of the crew, he handed it to the American.

'You shall also have this.' Carver took it, nonplussed. 'It is not in the nature of British sailors to be ungrateful, sir.'

Then Nelson raised his voice loud enough to carry to the whole busy deck. 'You have behaved in a most exemplary manner, carrying us out of danger without a thought to your own loss. I therefore return to you your ship and cargo. That paper you hold attests to your good character, and it is my fond wish that should any of my fellow officers apprehend you in the future, they will respect the sentiment it expresses and leave you free to go on your way.'

'Captain Nelson, I don't know how to thank you.' Confusion mingled with hope and gratitude chased each other across Carver's features. Observing it increased Nelson's feeling of self-satisfaction, and the knowledge that what he had done was right and proper. 'That is simple, sir. Boston is under our lee. Make a happy return to that harbour and my crew and I will be content.'

They cheered Carver over the side, which confused the crew of his own ship. That is, until Carver told them what the piece of paper said. Nelson had the satisfaction of looking along his own deck, and observing that his action had caused just as much joy aboard the *Albemarle*.

CHAPTER 31

Another dawn, and another coastal fog, but Nelson reckoned that this one, too, would burn off with the morning sun. He also knew that he was in a safer part of the bay that marked the approach to Boston, with plenty of water under his keel. That was very necessary, given the reduced state of his crew. They had been at sea too long, and the effects were now increasingly obvious. To slack behaviour and smelly breath had been added a miserable cast to the eye, spongy gums and constant aches from deprived muscles. He and Bromwich suffered more than anyone, forced by the lack of officers to stand watch on watch.

Bromwich longed particularly for the return of his superiors, the ship's lieutenants who had been sent off with the captures, tasked to take Nelson's prizes into Québec where both the hulls and the cargoes could be sold at auction. In his present state moving his large frame around had become a real test of character. His captain worried for a different reason: if the prize crews had not returned to the ship, there was a strong possibility that they had never reached Québec, either falling to American privateers or, even worse, recaptured by the French ships known to be active in these waters. All the money Nelson had imagined would accrue from his captures might have evaporated. Worse, his sailors, officers and men might be prisoners.

'Holy Christ almighty,' called the lookout. The blasphemy would have annoyed Nelson if it had not been immediately followed by words that portended enough danger to warrant them. 'Four – belay that, five sail off our larboard quarter.'

The mist was lifting like a stage curtain, and within half a minute that warning, alerting him to such a danger, seemed inadequate. What he saw, too close for any sense of comfort, was a strong squadron of warships: four line-of-battle ships, a 60-gunner and three 74s with a frigate in company.

'Part of Monsieur Vaudreuil's squadron, I presume,' Nelson said calmly, as a signal went off in the flagship and all four battle ships obeyed the instruction to tack in succession. A different set of orders had obviously gone to the fifth enemy vessel, the accompanying frigate, which was piling on sail and coming round to close with *Albemarle*. 'Mr Bromwich, an appreciation if you please?'

Bromwich swallowed hard and his normally ruddy face, now pale, looked so weary in his musings that his captain nearly answered for him. But he managed the words before aid was provided. 'The frigate will seek to close with us and engage, sir, allowing the line of battleships time to come up and force us to strike.'

'Correct. I will note the accuracy of that assessment in the log.'

'Thank you, sir.'

That reply was more animated, as befitted a midshipman who would dearly love to be a real lieutenant. Which he would be, if ever he could sit the examination. His captain never ceased to test him, preparing him for his interrogators. There was nothing he didn't know about single ship actions, lee shores and fires on board line of battleships.

'The next question, Mr Bromwich is, what do we do?'

'We must run sir. We can't face one ship of the line, let alone four.'

'I remind you of the sailing qualities of *Albemarle*.'

Bromwich shook his head then, loath to speak the word 'strike'. In his opinion his captain should not be calmly standing here discussing tactics, he should be getting everything aloft he could and running for safety.

'Forget the capital ships. We would never get away from that frigate in open water, Bromwich. She is, I think, the *Iris* of thirty-six guns and from what we know a fine sailer. She would close on us and force an engagement that could only end in one result, especially with us carrying a crew that is well below its best.'

'I cannot believe you contemplate surrender without a fight, sir.'

'Surrender, Mr Bromwich!' his captain snapped. 'Never in life!'

Nelson felt animated now, his love of action stimulating him, and if his eyes were not exactly alight, they had a flicker of excitement in them that had been absent recently.

'You will oblige me by letting fall the fore and main course so I can get some way on the ship. We will require the topsails to be loosed and drawing in the light airs as well, but with the shortage of hands and the condition they are in we must show care. Only when the sail plan is complete can we ask them to clear for action.'

Scanning round the bay Nelson's glass swept across the roofs and spires of Boston. There would be a crowd gathering already, appraised of the possibility of a sea battle on their very doorstep, a mob aware of the odds and keen to see perfidious Albion trounced and taken prisoner. What flags flew were blowing towards the north on the light southerly wind. Nelson had to find a way to confound them and the only one that presented itself was a reduction of the odds. To stay in deep water was to invite the line of battle ships to partake in his inevitable surrender. He must change the nature of the engagement, find water shallow enough to make pursuit by such deep-keeled vessels impossible.

He forced himself to appear calm, to reassure his troubled crew. It was agony to observe the way they moved, lassitude more obvious than effort. The time it took to loose the sails seemed like an eternity. In truth, there was no point in fretting. The *Iris* was closing fast, everything aloft that she could safely bear. Anxiety, however, would aid neither him nor his intentions.

That steadiness was maintained as he gave the orders to the helmsman to come round, personally calling for the yards to be braced then sheeted home. His ship was moving, slowly but perceptibly, but never fast enough to outrun the enemy. He set her bowsprit for the shore to the north of the town, heading for the shoal waters of St George's Bay. Then he retired to the master's day cabin, right by the ship's wheel, using the charts and tables to calculate the tidal times and the possible depth of water he would encounter.

'Stern chasers first, Mr Bromwich,' he ordered, as he rejoined the small knot of people on the quarterdeck. He was assuming that Lepée was sober enough and had had enough time to clear his possessions below. Those guns were in his cabin. 'You will aim them yourself and only fire if the chance of striking the target is high.'

'Aye, aye, sir.'

'If you can wound her masts I'll see you get a gazette.' He gave orders to his warrant officers to clear for action. 'But with care, gentlemen. I would not want to see any of our men suffer injury through unnecessary haste.'

They were looking over his shoulder at the French frigate, clearly less certain than their captain that time was available. The next task was to get the best eyes on the ship in the right places: two on either side of the foremast and one right out on the bowsprit, men who could not only see but shout loud and soon enough to let him change his course.

'Thorpe, I want you as far out on that pole as you can go. And I want to hear you shout as loud as you did when we spotted that fishing boat.'

That made the sailor hang his head. He had disobeyed a standing order by not sending the boy down as he had been instructed, and had been expecting to be chastised immediately after. But with time elapsed and nothing said, he had thought himself safe. He should have known that Nelson, with his sharp eye and memory, would forget nothing.

''Bout that, your honour.'

'Hold, Thorpe,' Nelson said, his eyes wide with shock and a friendly arm on the able seaman's shoulder. 'I recall, to my shame, that I forgot to thank you for that. Forgive me.'

'Thank me, your honour?'

'Of course. It's a bold man that has the sense to know when to disobey his captain. Had you delayed we might have run foul of our quarry and that would have ruined me. Now, get out on that bowsprit and save me from my follies again.'

Back on the quarterdeck, he addressed Nichols, the quartermaster's mate, who had taken his station on the wheel. 'I may have to attend to other matters when our lookouts call. Obey them, and use your own instincts, d'ye hear?'

'Aye, aye, sir.'

Looking over the side, he saw pea-green choppy water, reasonably calm; he hoped that on any shoal or bank the difference would show, either through sudden calm patches where it eddied or in increasing white caps where it broke over rocks. One thing he was sure of: if capture threatened he would run her hard on to something. She might be useless as a ship but *Albemarle* was important as a trophy, so he would wreck her rather than strike. But before that happened he would fight.

'Ship cleared for action, your honour,' the master at arms called.

'Note the time,' he said, before he realised that he was the only person present to do that. Just then Bromwich fired his first salvo, two shots from the stern chasers that fell well short of the target, sending up twin plumes of water that spread out and stayed in the air long enough for the *Iris* to sail through them.

'Roberts,' he called to a ship's boy, 'my compliments to Mr Bromwich and tell him his range finding was excellent.'

The boy rushed off, and Nelson smiled to himself. Bromwich would accept the compliment but he would also get the message.

'Water breaking two points to starboard.'

Nelson looked over the side, using his telescope to see what the man aloft had identified with the naked eye. He caught sight of the white water quick enough, caps breaking over what should be rocks. His instructions to the helmsman were to ease towards it not away. He wanted his pursuer to see it close, and perhaps to include an extra degree of caution into the chase. Behind the French frigate, two of the 74s had come round to pursue. Those rocks alone would take care of them. Monsieur Vaudreuil would not risk a capital ship to catch a sprat like him.

It was a tricky manoeuvre in a crank vessel, to ease it close enough to imply another hazard to starboard. But he had the wind and the leeway to aid him and to carry him away if it all became too critical. *Iris* tried the range with her bow chasers, likewise falling short, the disturbed plume of water thrown forward on the breeze.

The next hour was a constant triangular perambulation between the wheel, the master's cabin for another look at the charts, then forward to check on his lookouts. In between, Bromwich blasted away, with the enemy now in range, no doubt wondering why his French counterpart didn't reply. His captain knew: they were far from their home shore these Frenchmen, in a land that had only the capacity to build small ships for fishing and whaling. A frigate, even a converted merchantman, was a prize worth having intact.

Of a dozen salvos, only one ball had struck home, catching the Frenchman on the waterline and extracting a weary cheer from the Albemarles. And up ahead, his lookout continually warned him of hazards under the surface, sandbanks and reefs that forced him to alter his course, and to ease his sails to take the way off the ship so that the manoeuvre could be successfully completed. The French captain would have his own lookouts. But he would also be taking a close observation of his quarry's course, knowing that he had only to follow it to maintain safety.

Eventually they were crawling along, under reefed topsails, hardly making any way at all. The obstacles to a smooth passage had increased substantially, and the lookouts were hoarse from shouting as each new risk was identified.

'Roberts, my compliments to Mr Bromwich again, requesting him to desist and secure the stern chasers.'

By the time the tall midshipman had reached the deck, still wearing a bandanna round his ears, black from head to foot with the powder that had blown back through the portholes, his captain had slowed the ship to a mere crawl. Deafened by cannon fire, Nelson had to shout to make himself comprehensible to his junior. 'Mr Bromwich, you will oblige me by breaking out our stern anchor. I will also require a spring on that hawser so that we can haul our head round. Once that is completed you may display to our friend yonder the muzzles of our maindeck cannon.'

The Frenchman had matched his pace to that of *Albemarle*, not coming on any faster than his enemy, which to Nelson was a failing. The gap that existed between them was so great that it would take an hour to close at the present rate of sailing. That would be an hour when the *Iris* would be exposed to a great deal of fire from the British ship.

'You see, Bromwich, we have turned the tables on them. The deep-keeled ships, for all their power, dare not approach us for fear of running aground. Now, imagine yourself on that French deck. Our friend will see us work our spring to come round beam on to his bowsprit. Then he will observe us drop a bow anchor to hold us in position. He will see our cannon run out, a dozen guns of which he must run the gauntlet for some time before he too can anchor and turn to oppose us on equal terms.'

'Is that what you think he will do, sir?'

'No, Bromwich, I don't. If he were a British naval officer, I would not only anticipate such behaviour I would expect it. But observe his admiral, standing well off, and imagine his thinking. To capture a frigate is all very well, but not at the risk of so damaging one of your own, so far from home waters and a decent dockyard that your strength will not be augmented but weakened.'

'Yet he comes on.'

'He does so when the risk is slight, but in a few minutes' time that will cease to be the case. The fellow will be within range.'

Nelson looked along his deck to where his gun crews waited, kneeling by their cannon, some so fatigued that they were resting their heads on the cold metal. He was almost loath to make them stand, but it had to be done. He called the orders softly, allowing them time to obey, then waited a whole minute before giving the order to fire.

The waters around the bows of the *Iris* boiled as the shot struck. A few balls hit wood, sending the audible crunch of cracking timbers across the calm intervening waters. The reloading was slow and laboured, but before the guns could be run out again a single, distant shot punctured the silence. A stream of pennants streamed aloft on the flagship, and it was not long before the order they relayed became obvious. The yards on the Frenchman suddenly went limp and his head began to haul round.

'We must gift him something to see him on his way, lads,' Nelson shouted. As soon as *Iris* was beam on, the Albemarles let fly with a second salvo. Given a bigger target, they enjoyed a degree of success, removed several stretches of the bulwarks, which flew up in the air to cheer the crew. Another salvo or two would have been possible, but Nelson decided against it. His crew was too tired and ill to be so employed. Besides, at this range the damage they could inflict was not sufficient to disable the enemy.

'Secure the guns, Mr Bromwich, then get the ship back to rights.'

'Ahoy, *Albemarle*.'

The shout, two hours after the action had ceased, with *Albemarle* still anchored in the shoal water of Boston Bay, caused some panic. It was evidence of their state that, in the failing light, a ship had got close enough to hail them without being seen. The voice was American too, which had the more alert crew members rushing to cast off the guns. Others stood open-mouthed and shocked at the thought that they might be taken.

'Who are you?' demanded Bromwich, who had the watch.

'*Harmony*. Captain Nathaniel Carver requesting permission to come aboard.'

Nelson came on deck then, slowly, more weary now than he had been the whole voyage, but able to answer. 'Permission granted.'

He heard Carver order the fenders over the rail, and waited until the schooner bumped into the side of his ship. The American crew lashed her to the frigate's side, and by the time it was secure the whole ship's company had made it to the deck, most to stand slack-jawed, glassy-eyed and confused, observing their recent captives come aboard.

'Captain Nelson.'

'Welcome aboard, Mr Carver,' he said softly. 'I will not ask the purpose of your visit for fear you'll tell you want to be taken to Québec.'

'Never that, sir. But I do have a kindness to repay.'

'Indeed?'

'I take it I have the right of it that you have not returned to revictual since we last met?'

Nelson had to drag out his response he was so tired. 'That is so.'

'I observed some sickness in your crew two weeks ago, and even in this fading light I can see matters have not improved.'

'No.'

'Then I have a gift for you, of some fresh meat, a supply of green vegetables and some fruit. I have been at sea on a whaling ship when this has happened to me, sir, and observed that an injection of fresh victuals works wonders.' Carver half turned and hailed his own deck. 'Bear a hand there and get that stuff aboard.'

'Mr Carver, this is most generous. But I must also say that it is not yet completely dark and what you are doing will not go unobserved.'

'I know that, sir.'

'Are you then not in danger of sanction from your own fellow countrymen?'

'If I am, Captain Nelson, I care not for it. There cannot be a soul in Boston who has not heard of your treatment of me. If they are such as to think that what I do now is any more than just, then I am sorry for them.'

Nelson was shocked. 'You made public what happened?'

'More than that, sir, I boasted of it. Rest assured, your country may be damned in Boston but the name of Nelson is not.'

The first batch of cabbages hit the deck, sending out an odour that the crew of *Albemarle* had not sniffed since the tip of southern Ireland. Pile after pile followed: cauliflower, kale and sweet potatoes, as well as a batch of fresh fruit – apples, lemons and limes. Last aboard were four live sheep, bleating mightily as they were lifted into the air.

'I cannot thank you enough, sir,' said Nelson, turning away slightly so that Carver would not see the tear in his eye. 'Now, as to payment, if you will render me a bill I have in my cabin the means to satisfy it.'

Carver's voice dropped a whole octave, which, given its

standard depth was remarkable. 'It grieves me, sir, that you seek to insult me.'

'I do no such thing, sir.'

'You offer payment, Captain.'

'I offer you just reward, sir.'

'It ill becomes you to do such a thing in the face of what is plainly a gift.'

It took Nelson half a minute to digest that, half a minute in which the stony look on Carver's face made the American's sincerity obvious.

'A gift?' Nelson asked, his shoulders sagging.

'Indeed it is, and one that stands as less than a small percentage of what my last catch fetched in the Boston fish market.'

'That is a kind statement, sir,' Nelson replied softly, 'but you know I cannot in all conscience accept.'

'Then we are at a stand, sir, because I cannot agree to any form of payment. Nor will I lift a finger to get what provender has come aboard off your deck and back on to my own.'

'A gift?' Nelson repeated the words to give himself time. He also needed to press his fingertips to his eyes to hold back the sharp sensation that affected the corners of his eyes. He was weary from bad food and a long day's fighting, but he was also deeply affected by Carver's generosity.

'None more deserved, sir,' Carver said, raising his voice. 'I recall that the sentiment leading to my release was cheered by your crew, not one man dissenting even if it meant a loss of money to him. With such fine fellows in danger from scurvy, a disease which if not attended can kill, I could not stand by.'

Not letting show the wetness in his eyes became progressively harder, and Nelson would not give way at once, continuing to insist on payment. But Carver, who accepted that a drink of wine was in order, was adamant, and wore down a man who was willing to be overborne. Even when the food was below, and the smell of its preparation drifted out through the cook's chimney, he continued feebly to offer payment.

'I have done what I came to do, sir,' Carver said finally, drawing himself up to his full height and towering over Nelson. 'But before I depart I would like to opine that this stupid conflict will one day be over. I will also predict that two groups of proud and independent souls, bred from the same stock, cannot long be enemies, and that I look forward to the day, not too far in the distance, when our mutual esteem will resurface.'

'Allow me with all my heart to share the sentiment, sir,' said Nelson, holding out his hand.

CHAPTER 32

There was little pleasure back at the Steps, no warmth or family affection to speak of. Grandma Kidd, though still active, was near bent double now with age while her grandpa had lost the ability even to recall his own name, and his eyes were vacant and confused when she first faced him on her return. Uncle Willy, grey now, still occupied his place by the fire, never having laboured one day to provide wood to sustain it.

Emma now styled herself Mrs Hart. No one in the family commented on this, even though they knew there was no husband. Appearances, for shame's sake had to be maintained: she could hardly come home so obviously with child and admit to no legal father.

Harry had proved impermeable to any sense of either responsibility or charity, quite certain that, despite any evidence to the contrary, the child was the offspring of another man. Not that she had seen him; her first note, sent from a nearby post-house, had brought a reply in which he had forbidden her to call on him in person. Several more missives had been exchanged, each one less polite than the last, until he had finally written insisting that the connection be broken. Greville wrote too, responding to Emma's reports on her progress, advising and commiserating from the sidelines.

It was he who had provided her with the funds to take the coach to Cheshire, as well as the means to keep her and pay for the attentions of the midwife. Once she had arrived, his letters, carefully addressed to Mrs Emma Hart, grew longer, as he laid out conditions for her return to London. Emma was wise enough now to know that Greville was motivated by something other than kindness. She had known from their first assignation that he had always hoped to elbow Harry aside in favour of his own suit. Yet, despite the certainty in her heart that he had a deep affection for her, she was confused: clearly he wanted her to be his mistress, providing that the long list of conditions which filled his letters were met, but the negotiations were so dispassionate.

There was no mention in writing of anything deeper than a respectful affinity, no hint of a magnetism that drew him towards her, the kind of mood that would make a man occasionally act foolishly. It was as if he was drawing up a business contract, demanding she respond in full to any points he raised. In her more emotional moments Emma, used to open affection, damned him and resolved to have nothing more to do with him. Yet a swelling belly always stopped her penning her frustrations, the knowledge that her options and those of the child she was carrying were few. And despite her misgivings, she was extremely fond of him and grateful for his offer. She convinced herself he must love her, otherwise he would hardly go to so much trouble.

Greville would pay to have the child looked after: first by a wet-nurse, then by a decent family to care for the upbringing. Schooling would be a charge upon his purse as long as he and Emma had a connection, almost as if he was the legal father. Once the child was born she must return to London and occupy a house he would provide. A woman of a sober disposition would be employed to do the chores, while she would be obligated to remember to whom she owed her good fortune, and to behave appropriately.

Greville wanted none of the riotous behaviour in which she had indulged at Uppark. He was a man taken seriously by his contemporaries, which did not debar him from keeping a mistress; it did necessitate, though, that he acquire the services of a woman who gave no cause for scandal. Where Harry merely disliked being the subject of risible gossip, Greville, desirous of making his way in the world, could not countenance talk of any nature. The other manifestation that stopped Emma responding with a passionate refusal was the arrival of her mother.

As usual, little explanation was provided for the maternal presence. Vague mention was made of a housekeeping job that was in temporary limbo because her employer was travelling. But that person had no name, no address, and was the cause of no description, leading Emma to suspect that Mary Cadogan, which she insisted she be called even in her family home, had returned because she had heard of her daughter's condition. She accepted without demur that Emma had changed her own status, and became outside the Steps party to the fiction that a Mr Hart was awaiting eagerly the news of the birth of his child.

Her own lack of openness was no bar to a demand to know every detail of Emma's recent past. Never able to stand against her, Emma had produced the letters for her to peruse. 'Read them for me, child, so that I can form an opinion on this fellow.'

'You said you knew him.'

'Knew *of* him, Emma, a mere slip when he first came to Mrs Kelly's, as like to take his pleasures on another's bill than dip into his own pouch. I daresay I exchanged the odd word with him, and shared a song or two after supper, but as to knowing him, that I cannot claim.'

It took some time to read the dozen or so of Greville's letters, each one interrupted by Emma's reprise of what she had sent in reply. Mary Cadogan sat silently, eyes half closed, nodding, saying nothing, imagining, toying with and discarding various possibilities, until her daughter had finished, sure in the end that she had arrived at a conclusion that would offer them both advantage.

'Safe to say he is not a wild man, which at least I did discern on earlier acquaintance. But such caution I have rarely heard of. Yet what he offers is not to be lightly dismissed. A home, raising and education for the child, the job as a housekeeper, which your mother could fill as best as the next.'

'You?'

'Why not? You need someone to care for you, girl.' She saw Emma about to object and cut her off sharply, voice hard and eyes angry. 'Your condition swears testimony to that better than any words I could conjure.'

Emma dropped her eyes, sat down and let her shoulders slump, the epitome of shame in her pose. Her mother knew her well enough to wonder if the emotion was real, or a contrivance. Annoyed already, the thought that she was being guyed made Mary Cadogan seethe. She had done everything possible to keep Emma from this, only to be thwarted at every turn. Time to tell her daughter a few home truths.

'The fellow, it is clear, fears your wild inclinations, and to tell you plain, Emma, so do I. Twice, good positions have gone because of it. How many times did I try to warn you of the fate that awaits girls too willing? But do you listen? No! Mrs Kelly's was bad enough, but to allow yourself to be taken up by a drunken, horse-mad rake, with not a word said or witnessed as to how he was to treat you, was more than folly. And what's the result? You end up with child on the wing of another man's charity.'

'Don't call it that!' Emma cried, looking up, green eyes full of pain.

'Penniless, I say,' Mary Cadogan insisted, 'when you can bet Kathleen Kelly made a coin or two out of the exchange. I don't suppose it occurred to you to call on her and ask for a share of Uppark Harry's payment, did it?'

Emma looked shocked. 'I didn't know there was one.'

'Which damns you even more as a fool.'

Mary Cadogan saw her daughter's shoulders shake and her anger evaporated. She also felt the sting of tears in her eyes, part sympathy, part self-pity. Too many times in her life she had been party to such an exchange, too foolish to see herself as a victim. She couldn't crow at Emma, given the number of her own mistakes. She had come back to the Steps with the express purpose of sorting out her daughter's life once and for all; Emma couldn't be trusted to look after herself. What was proposed from this Greville had its drawbacks but, given Emma's situation, it offered the best way to gain a reasonably secure future. She went over to stand by Emma, a light hand touching her shoulder.

'I am as much of a fool as you, girl. Have I not fallen for the promises of men to end up a housekeeper? When I was your age I dreamt of luxury for all, of a free hearth and no toil for my ma and pa. Uncle Willy would sit beside a blazing fire by invitation, and such would be the connection that your aunts, instead of being damned to the spinster estate, would have been sought after by men of parts. It fell away, Emma, as dreams do when you find how cold the world really is.'

With some difficulty she crouched down and lifted Emma's chin, looking into the tear-filled eyes. 'I have one more dream that still has life, and that is to see you better placed than I. Your Charles Greville is no flash catch, I'll grant you. But a man who goes to such lengths to make his contract is more like to keep it than your baronet.'

'Why?'

''Cause your gaiety-loving Harry cares not a jot what people say of him. He expects to garner admiration, not to be cursed for his treatment of you. Daresay he'll be wont to boast about it in years to come. But Greville, he is opposite in tone. He's a man who wants to be seen as fair. I do not say that whatever connection you agree will be lifelong, that might be casting a bit high. What I do say is this: he has an affection for you. And should the connection be broken, it is like to be on terms that will not leave you in the gutter. That is something to think on. Now can I get up from this bending? My knees are not the springs they once were.'

Emma had to help her to stand upright, and saw the pain in her mother's face as her legs straightened. The lines had thickened round the now baggy eyes too, and her nose had broadened from its previous elegant shape to render her somehow common. There were few areas of likeness between them, the receding chin being the most prominent, but Emma could see her future in that weary face, and it was not one that entranced her.

'Old bones, Emma. You never think they'll come. But here I am, not yet reached my fortieth year, and I can scarce bring myself to get in and out of a church pew. Am I to end up like your Grandma, I wonder, bent so you can sup your dinner off my back?'

It was no great flaring insight that Emma had then, just the cold, slow realisation that as well as the baby she was carrying, she was now responsible for the future comfort of her mother and all those who would stay behind in the Steps. Only she could ensure a supply of money that, though it would not provide luxury, would keep them off poor relief.

'But you must ask yourself one more thing, child. It is easy for me to say what you should do, but as you're the one who has to do it, it falls to you to decide whether it is a burden that can be borne. You might find life with your cold fish too chill for comfort.'

Emma brightened then, in a way her mother knew well – she had never known anyone who could go from deep despair to elation so quickly. It was a fault, but a hard one to resist. 'You're judging Charles by his letters, Ma. Let me tell you, he is not like that in the flesh.'

Mary Cadogan sniffed loudly and held up a restraining hand. 'Spare me the flesh, Emma. I've had a surfeit of male flesh.'

But Emma was not to be overborne. Her face alight again, she said, 'Mr Greville is sweet and kind. He teaches me things, never treating my ignorance as stupidity. I will grant you that my baronet was more of a force of nature, but none can fault Greville for the attentions he pays me.'

The maternal eyes narrowed, as Mary Cadogan looked closely at her child, particularly taken by the light of passion in her large green eyes. 'Do I detect an affection in you as well, Emma?'

The reply came without hesitation. 'Yes, Ma, you do. And when you meet him, and see him in his own circumstances, instead of those imposed by the written word, you will come to esteem him as much as I do.'

'Mrs Cadogan,' said Charles Greville, with as much enthusiasm as he could muster, 'I am pleased to make your acquaintance.'

The curtsy, given the state of her knees, was not as deep as she would have liked, but the smile on Mary's Cadogan's face was full of gratitude. It was brought on by the realisation that if Greville remembered that they had met in different circumstances, he was determined to preserve, like her, the fiction that it had never happened.

'You do me honour, sir, in agreeing to my taking service with you.'

The gruff cough behind her forced her to move, to allow the coachman and his boy to carry the chest in through the narrow doorway. With a practised eye, Emma's mother used the moment to assess their benefactor, all of the details she needed being in plain view in this simple house.

Not grand but comfortable, set back from the road with a small garden, a new structure of a mere three storeys, it was part of a ribbon of expansion on the road to Edgware village, houses built not for proper gentlemen but for men of business of the superior sort. The ambience reeked of discretion, sobriety and frugality. Mary Cadogan knew, before Greville told her, that the allowance for household necessities, food, heat and light, would not allow for either peculation or excess.

She would have two of the attic rooms to herself, one for use as a private sitting room. The two maids would share the third, the cook and the skivvy bedding down in the room next to the kitchen. There was a bedroom, dressing room and parlour for Emma, as well as a spare that would act as a study and bedroom should Greville wish to work or sleep alone. He would employ no valet, since he would rarely spend the entire night under this roof.

He seemed to reflect the nature of the place, caution in his stance, leaning slightly forward, hands held behind his back, as if he feared to display them less they detracted from the sober character he was determined to project. His dress was plain but of good quality, even to the dull, light brown watered silk of his waistcoat. Mary Cadogan didn't rate him handsome, though apart from the obvious nose his features were even enough and the skin unblemished. It was the eyes and brow that detracted, with an air of permanent concern that hinted at a suspicious mind. In her experience such people who worried so much about being dunned by others were usually more culprit than victim.

'A perfect establishment, sir, if I may be permitted to say so.'

It was far from that and Greville knew it. It was a hideaway, but he smiled, which removed that set of lines from his forehead. 'The child is healthy?'

'Ever so, sir, and content with a good Cheshire wet nurse.'

'The lying-in?'

Those forehead lines were back, proof that he was worried about complications. 'Went as smooth as silk, Mr Greville, as I believe my Emma imparted in her letters. She delivered in the hour after her waters broke, and was back on her feet in a day or two.'

'And how does she appear?'

'In full bloom, sir. You know a child brings colour to a woman's cheeks. If anything, though I claim a leaning, Emma is more beautiful than ever.'

She hid her amusement, seeing the hope and doubt that she was telling the truth cross his face. But Mary Cadogan had to pinch herself mentally; she must stop thinking of this man as the callow youth she recalled from Arlington Street. He was to be her benefactor too. The obvious affection in which her daughter held him was welcome, but for her irrelevant. She had her duties as part of the compact. He would need to be made as happy in the parlour as he would in the bedchamber. That was her task.

'I take it, sir, I am free to engage the rest of the servants?'

'You are, Mrs Cadogan, within the proviso of my approval.'

'Why of course, your honour.'

'No one loud or indecorous, is my main concern.'

'Quiet souls, sir, that is what I will seek, who can hold their tongues as well as they can hold their places.'

'We must to work then, madam. Your daughter will be here within the week. I would want all found and in harmony when dear Emma arrives.'

He called regularly over the next few days, eager to check on things and near to dying for the presence of his mistress. For a dispassionate creature, which by his written words he most certainly was, Greville had trouble in containing himself. Try as he might he couldn't keep his excitement from the surface, which pleased his new housekeeper since it hinted at a long-term occupation of Edgware Road. He was present when Emma arrived. She had taken her mother's advice and stopped at the last post-house on the journey, so the woman who emerged from the chaise sent to fetch her had spent only a short time in travel, and a long time at that morning's toilette.

Under a muslin shawl Emma's hair, brushed a thousand times before a mirror glass, shone in all its auburn glory. Her mother had the right of it about her features: having a child had enhanced the colouring of her cheeks while an added year had helped to remove the excess flesh of the young girl from her chin. But her body had blossomed and she was now a full woman, beautiful and glorious enough to make staid Greville catch his breath and dash to hand her down.

'Welcome, Emma, to your new home. Allow me to present you to those who will care for you.'

Being introduced to the servants was odd, especially since the premier servitor was her own mother. That occasioned a spontaneity typical of Emma, as she leant forward to kiss the cheek of her 'dear Mama'. It helped, too, in easing her own awkwardness at having presented to her people of a station that she had occupied herself not too many years ago.

'Pray come indoors, Emma. The parlour awaits you, with a splendid feast prepared by these good people. I admit to being made near ravenous by the mere sight of it.'

'I will see to the dunnage, your honour.'

'Thank you, Mrs Cadogan,' he replied, a hoarse note in his voice.

She did too, harrying the men to get Emma's chest into the bedroom and depart, leaving it in a corner. Then she shooed the rest of the servants back to their places of rest, with a repeat of her instructions to stay out of sight. She guessed that food would not occupy Greville for long, that the bedchamber would be his priority, not his stomach. Mary Cadogan was determined to do as much as she could to ensure that engagement went smoothly. So much depended on it.

CHAPTER 33

Since reaching post rank Horatio Nelson had had gifted ample time to reflect on the constraints placed on him by a captain's role. As a midshipman he had had his ups and downs in the berth, yet set against that was a degree of comradeship and devilment as compensation. The wardroom was a more formal, less boisterous place – lieutenants seemed to shed their sense of frolic as soon as they were commissioned. But promotion brought a welcome private space, screened off by canvas, servants and civilised eating. To be promoted from there altered everything.

A captain occupied an area equal to that of every other officer on the ship, and he occupied it alone. He had a day cabin opening on to a dining cabin, the pair easily combined for formal entertaining. His sleeping cabin, with his cot slung above a stern chaser cannon, lay to starboard while on the opposite side he had an equal sized coach available for any use he chose. In front, between him and the ship's company, lived Lepée, his pantry to one side of the passage, sleeping quarters to the other. At the end of that passage stood at all times a marine sentry. Nelson had craved the rank and space only to find that his elevation imposed distinct disadvantages.

The bulkheads that stood between him and the rest of the ship sometimes seemed like prison bars, so much did he miss the easy comradeship he had enjoyed before promotion. Strive as he might, he could not break down the invisible barrier that existed between himself and his officers, which was multiplied a hundredfold when it came to the crew. On Sundays he often felt like an impostor when, before divine service, he would tour the ship, unable to put out of his mind the artifice he had employed in the past to fool those who been in command.

He knew the formality of the officers was essential, but it seemed to him too unbending, and the looks on the faces of the men in each division left him convinced, after every inspection, that they saw him as a gullible fool. Certainly the man closest to him, his servant, saw him like that; at least Frank Lepée had no desire to disguise it, especially when, as seemed to happen more and more frequently, he over-indulged in drink.

The vision he had had of a great and glorious destiny, as *Albemarle* ploughed through the icy waters off New England, seemed to mock him. He was immodest enough to think himself a good seaman, but honest enough to wonder if his dislike of flogging did him any good either with those he led or with his naval superiors. Certainly he had few warm relations on the St Lawrence station. The Commodore was cold towards him, and it seemed his fellow captains took their cue from that source. There were invitations to other ships to dine, hospitality that he returned in full measure, but he couldn't recall one single occasion when he had felt either wholly happy or relaxed.

In entertaining his own officers, despite every attempt made to put them at their ease, he had hardly dented the rigid naval convention that no inferior should speak until spoken to. The only time he succeeded was with his midshipmen, whose natural lack of restraint led them occasionally to treat him as a human being instead of some kind of god. The crew either declined to look in his direction or favoured him with a disquieting grin and a touch of the forelock, and when he spoke to them he was sure he could see in their eyes a mixture of amusement mixed with sympathy.

Only ashore had he felt fully the advantages of his position. A naval captain was a person of some worth in the world, more so in a place like Québec, cut off by three thousand miles of ocean from Europe, the seat of everything fashionable. Among the people he had met and become friendly with, Alexander Davidson stood out. A Northumbrian, Davidson was a merchant adventurer who had taken advantage of the American war to amass a sizeable fortune. He had a comfortable house, and when in harbour Nelson, tired of on-board isolation, had accepted his invitation to share it.

It was a busy household and Nelson had enjoyed meeting

many of the leading men of Québec, all of whom were, at the very least, frank in their acknowledgement of his place in the order of things. That despite his youthful appearance the rank he held, allied to skills he possessed, made him a man of parts. When he spoke, they listened, but as equals not subordinates; Army officers, fellow traders like Davidson or civilian officials, they liked to drink, eat and talk, as well as put to rights what they saw as an imperfect world.

Nelson had visited the Plains of Abraham often in this last year. Overlooking Québec City, this was where his hero, General James Wolfe, had fallen in the battle that had secured Canada for the British Crown. The emotions he felt there varied from envy to wonder; a tinge of jealousy at the almost mystical power of Wolfe's fame, the same feeling he had experienced before the memorial in Westminster Abbey; awe at his achievement mixed with doubt as to his own ability to accomplish anything of a similar stature.

Now he stood below the cliffs Wolfe had scaled to outflank the French. It had been the Anse de Foulon then, now it was Wolfe's Cove. In the background lay the mighty St Lawrence, a mass of moving water a mile wide, dark grey and brooding even on this clear frosty morning. Looking up at those sheer cliffs between the river and the battlefield he wondered at the strength of leadership that had taken ill-equipped British soldiers from one level to the other, then inspired them to mount a stout defence, that was followed by an attack that had overwhelmed their enemies.

Alexander Davidson stood a few feet away, his hat in his hand, his dark reddish hair exposed. Slim, tall and handsome, with graceful manners, Davidson knew that the friend who had shared his house was troubled, and his own concern that this should be so showed in the worried creases round his narrowed eyes.

'Wolfe humbugged the French here, Davidson. Is that what I have been reduced to, a humbug?'

'Foolish, Nelson, perhaps,' Davidson said, with a sad smile, a dismissive wave of his hand and an arching of his prominent eyebrows. His voice, light and slightly affected took the sting out of the accusation. 'But your over-zealous spirit will surely guarantee that if you persist, that will be your fate.'

'How can you be so sure?' Nelson demanded.

'I know this place better than you.'

'And the lady in question?'

'Is part of a society that is strange to an occasional visitor.'

Davidson paused, searching his mind for the right words, those that would impart an unpalatable truth without inflicting too deep a wound. In the short period that they had known each other he had come to love Nelson for himself, and to esteem him highly for his professional ability. Then there was his manner; nonjudgemental, always willing to see the best in people, never wishing to enquire beyond what he needed to know for friendship. If he had a fault it was an endearing one; that once he had set his mind on a project, however inappropriate, he went at it with every fibre of his being. Davidson was convinced it was that which had led to this present situation, and not, as some might suspect, an almost blind naivety.

He was wrong in that assumption, but Horatio Nelson would never tell him so. He would never mention the night at sea, months before, when Frank Lepée had been so drunk that he had let his tongue run away with him, and bandied about his erroneous accusations about Davidson, not forgetting to include his captain, in his slurred and incoherent speech. Nor on how such an association reflected on Lepée himself and the whole ship.

Not only was Nelson 'mewed up with a Jenny Jessamy and his sodomical ilk, setting every tongue ashore wagging, but he would never be off taking one of the ship's youngsters with him wherever he went, an' though that was his way and had ever been thus it looked odd nonetheless'.

What had followed was a poor imitation, albeit recognisable, of Davidson's singular manner of speech. Horatio Nelson had sat in shocked silence, listening to Lepée clattering about in his pantry, knocking things about, berating the bulkheads. He was accustomed to his servant's drinking and his way of carping loudly and inappropriately, even when he had guests, but nothing like this had ever assailed his ears. It was equally shocking to hear Lepée traduce him by saying that as a commander he was 'too soft by half'. His fellow captains, according to his servant's ramblings, laughed up their sleeves at his lenient ways and his kindness to 'cheeky able seamen, upstart enough to talk to him unbidden, and jumped up mids who he was forever touching, which just goes to show there might be something in this Davidson lark after all'.

Nelson rarely raised his voice, but he did so that night, commanding his servant to 'Stop your gob and get to your hammock'. Lepée, bleary eyed and swaying, obeyed, staggering to his berth, still mumbling imprecations against 'sodomites, pansies, goat-shaggers and the like'.

They were the ramblings of a drunk for certain, and a man who cared more for being damned by association than he cared for much else. Certainly Davidson had an effeminacy of manner and quick mobile hands, allied to a high tone of voice. But Nelson, though he had no clear idea of his friend's sexual orientation, knew him to be kind and considerate, too generous by nature certainly, and as honest and upright a fellow as he had ever met.

It was a poor specimen who served Captain Nelson his breakfast the following morning, a man whose hand shook so badly he had trouble placing the plates and pouring the coffee. A pointed enquiry established that Lepée couldn't remember a single thing about the previous night. Not the dinner for his officers that his captain had hosted, nor the uncut rum he had consumed, nor the stolen wine that had followed it, nor his tirade in the pantry, once everyone had departed.

Lepée stood, head bowed, as Nelson told him, in his customary gentle voice, how intolerable his behaviour had been. He listened, without looking his master in the eye, to the threat that one more occasion like that would see him dismissed. It wasn't the first time he had heard it and Lepée reckoned it wouldn't be the last, but there was little fear that the threat would be carried out. He might not be the best servant in the world but he tended to a captain who was too soft a soul ever to send a man like him back to serve before the mast.

What Lepée couldn't know was the effect that his words had

on his master. If, over the next two months, the Captain seemed to brood, when not doing the hundred and one things that fell on his shoulders, that wasn't unusual. The log was still written daily, the sheaves of papers regarding the state of the ship, from the sail maker, the carpenters, the gunner, as well as all the other warrant officers, arrived and were despatched speedily. Every few days there was a ritual argument with the purser, regarding what was due to the men in terms of rations. He still invited his mids and officers to dine with him and if he was a trifle more taciturn on this voyage than previously that was his right.

But at the back of Nelson's mind, gnawing at him, was the notion that there might be some germ of truth in Lepée's opinions. In the years since his experience in Calcutta there had been no women in his life apart from a Caribbean servant and the wives of fellow officers who had nursed him as he lay under the blight of his fever. Certainly there had been no romantic attachments. As for the use of the brothel, his own early experiences with Amos Cavell and John Judd, plus the evidence of his own eyes in observing his less virtuous fellow officers, had convinced him that he had been lucky in the Orient. Only disease and eternal damnation would follow from indulgence in that quarter.

Recollection went back to his schooldays, that foolishness aboard *Raisonable* and a dozen other events or relationships that dredged themselves up for examination. Certainty of intention tended to become blurred when sleep became impossible, imbuing innocent acts and gestures with a more sinister overtone. He had worked alongside men he knew to be attracted to their own sex, had laughed with them, joked, drunk and danced hornpipes with them, shared endless banter and thought nothing of it.

He knew himself to be tolerant of what many of his peers saw as a mortal sin, his blind eye turned through benevolence rather than the necessities imposed by the running of the ship. Called upon to comment on the love of one man for another, he would damn as sin the physical expression of such regard, but he was inclined to accept that it was capable of being based on nobility, the same as any other, more natural relationship.

He would not tolerate that such things should be too overt, or that any unwelcome attentions be paid, just as he came down hard on bullying.

As for himself, a life constrained by his rank would have been wholly intolerable if he could not take pleasure in what companionship was available. At sea that was wholly male. Even ashore the preponderance of males to females, in a colonial outpost like Québec, ensured that most social gatherings were single sex. There were balls and parties, of course, but opportunities for dalliance were rare, men being protective of their wives, fathers of their sought-after daughters. As for Davidson, he had never, by deed or gesture, given indication that their relationship was based on anything other than mutual esteem, which allowed him to banish Lepée's ramblings.

But what really troubled Nelson, alone, lacking anyone to converse with, was the notion that if Lepée had thoughts of that nature, so might others. Was that the reason for his cool relations with the Commodore and his fellow captains? Did the society of Québec look at the domestic arrangements he had with Davidson, wonder at their relationship, and put on it a damning interpretation?

Before they berthed again, Nelson had made a decision. Marriage had always been something to which he had aspired, and only a lack of the means to support a wife had constrained him. Gradually he deduced that he must find a wife, so by the time he came ashore again he was afire with passion. Money be damned! Marriage was an estate he should join sooner rather than later. The trouble was that in embarking on this course, he had made, according to Davidson, a complete mess of things.

'You must understand, Nelson,' Davidson added, his face still serious 'that any visitor to this outpost—'

'How can you call Québec an outpost?'

'It is that, man,' Davidson insisted, his high voice exaggerating his Northumberland accent, 'even from the French who still reside here. This is not London or even Paris. True, we have fine buildings and a vibrant society, and a collective attitude to outsiders that insists on a hearty welcome over all other

considerations. That receptive nature is apt to be misunder-
stood, to impart a gloss it does not truly have. Your Miss
Simpson has that same trait in abundance.'

'Have you ever been in love, Davidson?'

The way Nelson asked that had an odd ring to it, as did the
direct gaze that accompanied the question, but Davidson put
that down to his anxieties and answered it honestly. 'Perhaps
I've been too busy in trade for that, my friend. I love ships,
cargoes, bills of lading, profit over loss . . .'

It was the wrong word to use, and Davidson knew it as soon
as he had uttered it. Nelson responded bitterly. 'Then if you've
never been smitten you cannot even begin to contemplate the
depths of my attraction.'

Davidson closed his eyes and spoke in sorrow, not anger.
'She is sixteen, and I grant you that she's a beauty.'

'A veritable Diana,' Nelson exclaimed. 'I quote there the very
words of the *Québec Gazette*.'

Nelson had chosen to set his cap at the one girl who dazzled
everyone who came into her orbit. Mary Simpson, with a father
who was Provost Marshal to the garrison, was at the very peak
of Québec society. She was dazzlingly beautiful and vivacious
and to be attached to her was to enter in upon that provenance,
a heady prospect for a naval captain of slender means, far from
home. All Nelson had succeeded in doing was making a fool of
himself.

'How much do you value your naval career, Nelson?' asked
Davidson, suddenly inspired with an argument that might have
some effect.

Nelson tried to wave that aside. His barge was waiting at the
river edge to take him aboard. *Albemarle* had orders to join the
New York squadron under Admiral Digby. His premier was, at
this moment, making preparations to weigh.

'You propose to stay,' Davidson insisted, 'abandoning both
your ship and the orders to sail for New York. For what? In
order to throw yourself at the feet of a child who even if she did
know her own mind, may not have the same *tendresse* for you
that you claim to carry for her?' He was tempted to say that the
girl flirted with everyone, and the only person who hadn't seen
it for what it was stood before him, but that would be too cruel.

'I do not just claim it,' Nelson replied wistfully. 'It would be true to say, Davidson, that I live it.'

'So you will retire from the Navy?'

Intended to shock, it had the desired effect. 'That isn't necessary!'

The reply was sharp, querulous and proof to Davidson that what he suspected was true. His friend, in his impulsive way, had simply not thought matters through. He had watched him carefully since that first meeting, noticing that, as a creature suffused with natural spontaneity, he could charm people with ease. It was amusing to witness him engage in conversation, to see that a person only had to propound an idea he half agreed with to face the full force of Nelsonian verve.

Having been a guest aboard *Albemarle* several times, Davidson knew how much his officers admired their captain, just as well as he knew how little the object noticed. It was in their eyes when, his attention elsewhere, they gazed upon him with something approaching awe. In conversation, when he wasn't present, they would never fail to tell the visitor of his competence as a seaman and his care as a commander.

As an experienced trader, he had great knowledge of ships and the men that manned them. Never had he seen such regard as Nelson received from his crew, such ease of communication between the two constituents, the best part of this the captain's ignorance, as with his officers, of the depth of the common seaman's esteem.

'Not necessary?' Davidson insisted. 'You do not think her father, a man of some means and position, might not object to your suit? What are you, my friend, but a post captain with few prospects?'

Davidson saw the hurt, and hurried to ease it. 'I do not say these things to diminish you, Nelson. I count you a friend and believe that one day what you vouchsafed to me as a friend will come true, that you will astound all who know you. But I doubt that Colonel Simpson could be brought to that view. I do not say he lacks soul, but talk of visions of greatness and a destiny foretold by the Almighty would harm rather than aid any suit. I also doubt, given his obvious regard for his daughter, that he would agree to a marriage that saw you leave here with no known idea of when you might return.'

The shoulders had slumped, the head was bowed. 'In short, my suit is pointless.'

'I truly believe that it would not succeed. And if, perchance, I was wrong, I do not think it would bring you happiness. You would be forced to resign from your command and take up residence here. Do not be deceived by the vivacity you witness. That is the desperation of those cut off from the real world. Right now the frost and ice are fresh and pleasant. But be here when the weather truly turns, with a winter six months upon us and you will see a depression of spirit that would make you weep.'

'Yet you stay here.'

'I make my way here,' Davidson replied. 'And I do not intend to stay for more than another winter. The best advice I can give you is to go about your duties. If your heart is so smitten that you cannot stay away I'm sure you'll contrive a way to return. Then, if you still wish it and I can be of any help, I will aid you to press your suit.'

Davidson hooked Nelson's arm and led him back towards the steps where his barge lay. Nelson looked down at the faces of his crew, red and healthy now. The hesitation was minimal, and once he moved one foot the other was easy. But it was a crestfallen creature who stood in the thwarts as the oars bit the water, a man too sad to return Davidson's encouraging wave.

CHAPTER 34

It was a doleful commander who had sailed his ship from Québec, a fact noticed by every member of his crew. It was in the nature of sailors to watch carefully the behaviour of a ship's captain, the man who, without recourse to higher authority, controlled their lives. It was generally held that a man could go mad with solitude or repressed passion and turn from kindness to tyranny in the blink of an eye, and, in the superstitious world of tars, women and their wiles lay at the root of many a puzzle. Horatio Nelson thought that his crew knew nothing of his loss. In this, as in so many other things, he was wrong.

They observed that his spirits began to lift once they had passed Cape Cod, and the prospect of action lay over the horizon. By the time they had entered the Long Island Sound the regular life of a ship at sea, bells, watches, punctual dinners, gunnery and fencing practice and midshipmen's lessons had salved his wounded soul and returned their captain to the human race. He smiled again, talked to them in that easy manner they had come to expect. Entertaining was possible once more and Nelson was invited to the wardroom, which was preferable to all of his officers than dinner in the great cabin, where Lepée seemed to rule, not the Captain.

Then they opened the mouth of the Hudson river, crossing that to their berth at Sandy Hook off the New Jersey shore, and saw there not only the ships of the New York squadron, but elements of the Caribbean fleet. Nelson rattled off the names of both ships and officers, what action they had seen and how they had fared. He seemed to know every fact of every ship in the entire fleet, and it was clear that the sight of these vessels had excited something in him. *Albemarle* had barely dropped anchor before Bromwich was despatched with a letter to the commander of the Caribbean fleet, Admiral Lord Hood.

'Lord Hood will see you now, Captain Nelson.'

Nelson followed the secretary into the great cabin of HMS *Barfleur*, leaving behind the midshipman who had attended upon him when he came aboard. Hood, too, raised an eyebrow at Nelson's appearance, which made the visitor look like a vision from another age. Laced uniform coat, a long waistcoat with flaps, undressed fair hair with a pigtail exceedingly long and old-fashioned, more fitting to a topman than a commissioned officer. The effect, to Hood's mind, was showy.

In his turn Hood was under scrutiny, though he took his visitor's look as a bid to establish some kind of parity. It wasn't, Nelson being frank and open in his admiration. Here before him was the junior admiral who had been under a cloud for failure to prevent the surrender at Yorktown the previous year. Within twelve months of that disaster he had redeemed himself by helping to beat the French fleet in the Caribbean. The battle of the Saintes had been a great victory, but Hood, not content, with ships still battle damaged, had pursued all the way north those Frenchmen who had escaped, scattering them, finally forced to anchor his twelve sail-of-the-line off Sandy Hook. To Nelson, Hood was his kind of admiral.

'Be seated, Captain Nelson. Can I offer you some refreshment?'

'A small glass of wine, sir,' Nelson replied.

'Then I shall join you, and toast the memory of your late uncle.'

'You knew Captain Suckling, sir?'

'Not only knew him, young man, but esteemed him as the kind of officer that this service often lacks, a man of application and proven bravery. And he was as fine an asset to the Navy ashore as he was at sea. My wife's father was mayor of Portsmouth when your uncle had the seat, and never have I heard anything but positive words attached to his name.'

Nelson's heart lifted at that, the association and the advantages that might accrue from it raising the hopes with which he had come aboard.

'That is most kindly put, sir.'

Hood raised his glass, followed by his visitor. 'Let us hope that blood ties mean the same qualities reside in you.'

Nelson found it easy to conjure up a vision of his late uncle then, the kindly face, its similarity to his mother's, but more than that his ability, application and reputation. That was what he craved more than anything, to be seen as other officers had regarded Maurice Suckling: brave, resourceful and, most of all, successful in battle, just like the man opposite, whom he was so desirous of impressing.

'Rest assured, sir,' he replied, blue eyes fixed on Hood's, 'that I can open my character to all scrutiny with confidence. I also will say that my late uncle saw me destined on his deathbed as fitted for the highest attainment.'

'Quite,' replied Hood, taken aback by the way Nelson had reacted to a very ordinary compliment.

Hood picked up Nelson's letter, leaning forward to reread it by candlelight: the grey winter skies allowed little light to filter through the long row of casement windows. That allowed the visitor to examine his host: a large man, but not gross, with a kindly countenance. Hood had blue-grey eyes under heavy brows of a whiteness that matched his powdered wig, and a nose, forehead and cheekbones that indicated a strong spirit.

He had made enquiries about Nelson before granting an interview. Admiral Digby had been less than flattering, which was hardly surprising since upon his arrival at Sandy Hook, Nelson had taken the occasion of his first interview with his new commander to ask for a move to the Caribbean. He had also learnt that among most of his peers Nelson was highly esteemed, though held to be a trifle odd. There were those who spoke ill of him, and more who were indifferent, but the most active officers were keen to praise his zeal, expressed envy of his seamanship, and pointed up the fact that, though it had no effect on the recipient, his crew adored him.

'This is a somewhat unusual request, Captain Nelson.'

'That you should say so surprises me, sir.'

'I have officers in abundance asking for a move to New York, but only you seem willing to travel in the opposite direction.'

Hood was looking at him keenly now, trying to discern if

there was some motive that made sense. Right now, money was to be made on the North American Station. With a blockade on the harbours north and south of Chesapeake Bay, the pickings in the Caribbean islands were slim indeed.

'I cannot believe that Admiral Digby will engage the enemy in a fleet action, sir. Money is his object. That may be enough to satisfy his duty to his King and country, but it will not suffice for me. I see my duty – and my destiny – as being to engage the enemy in battle.' Nelson paused, suddenly aware of his own bombast, and the effect it was having on his host, who had looked away. But he had to finish, even if it sounded in his own head like outrageous flattery. 'I cannot doubt that you, at the very first opportunity, will do just that, sir.'

Hood coughed to cover an extra degree of embarrassment. The loss of eye contact with Nelson had nothing to do with the young man's sermonising: Hood had just heard one of his fellow admirals traduced, which he should have checked, and it caused him acute discomfort to let it pass.

But Nelson was right. Digby had been shy when it came to searching out the enemy. All his captains were too busy lining their pockets with prize money to care about defeating the French. The indolent Admiral Digby was in the enviable position of being in receipt of an eighth of their profits.

'All I ask, sir, is a better ship than my present command, and the opportunity to confound my country's enemies in a fashion that will bring about a satisfactory conclusion to this conflict.'

Listening, the Admiral was still searching for the pretence that would normally be part of such sentiments. He had heard it often enough in his service life, men claiming one thing while meaning another. But it was absent now. Nelson was sincere, which was of itself somewhat singular.

'I feel I am ready for a line-of-battle ship, sir, for preference a seventy-four. And should we meet with our enemies I do not fear that either I or those under my command would shrink from any engagement, however hot.'

'I don't doubt it, Nelson,' said Hood, standing up. 'You must leave this matter with me and allow me to see what I can do. Meanwhile, I feel I have a duty to introduce you to someone.'

Hood marched out of the great cabin, forcing Nelson to

follow in his wake. The midshipman who had shown him to this place was there, waiting to escort him back to the entry-port. He stood ramrod stiff when Hood appeared. 'Captain Nelson, allow me to name to you His Highness Prince William Henry.'

Nelson tried to prevent his eyes opening wide. Could this slim, unprepossessing youth really be the son of his sovereign? He was unaware that the youngster was wondering if the man before him, who looked as if he carried fewer years than himself, could really be a post captain.

'Captain Nelson has requested to be allowed to join our fleet, Your Royal Highness, preferring the prospect of honour in battle to that of wealth through taking prizes. He stands as an example to us all, wouldn't you say?'

'Why, sir, I'm amazed. When I next correspond with my father I will not hesitate to tell him of Captain Nelson's sacrifice.'

Nelson was slightly confused, since to him what he was proposing was only right and proper. 'How can it be a sacrifice when I am merely showing a desire to serve my King?'

'He will be most grateful, Captain, I'm sure,' the Prince stammered.

Nelson was wondering if his blood was blue instead of red, this pink-faced youth with the faraway look to his eye. Never having been in the presence of royalty he was at a stand as to how to behave. This boy was by several fathoms his social superior, but by the same degree he was his service inferior. And then there were Nelson's political inclinations, which were more to the Whig tendency than that of the Tories: he supported monarchical limitation rather than any increase in the royal powers. But there was also the fact that the King was his ultimate superior, the person to whom, on taking up any commission, he swore an oath of allegiance.

'If you are writing to your father, sir,' Nelson said, 'it would be a kindness of you to include the regard in which all we naval officers hold him. And I know that I speak for my men when I say they see in him the father he must be to you.'

Hood coughed, wondering at which poor school Nelson had learnt his social conventions. The only thing that saved his words from sounding like complete tripe was the sincerity with which they were expressed.

'You might want to pen that very soon, Your Royal Highness, lest you forget the depth of the sentiment.'

'Sir,' the Prince replied. The Admiral nodded and Nelson left the pair with a lift of his hat, admiral and prince of the blood staring after him as he walked across the main deck of Hood's flagship. The Prince could not quite believe what he had just seen and heard, and took advantage, as he was wont to do, of his position as the son of the King. 'Would I be permitted to opine, sir, that Captain Nelson seems an odd fish?'

Hood was tempted to say, 'You're a royal prince, jacko, you can say what you like,' but instead he sought refuge in a change of tack. 'Perhaps a little oddity would not go amiss in others. He is very much a complete officer, steeped in the history of the service and wholly committed to it. If you wish to know aught about naval tactics, that fellow has a mind to plunder. I heard of him before he ever wrote to me, and from people whose opinions I esteem most highly.'

'Does he really not want prize money, sir? I intend no insult when I say that by the manner of his dress he looks in some need of it.'

'Pen your letter now, then return to me,' Hood growled. 'I have a request to deliver to Admiral Digby.'

When Hood's fleet weighed from Sandy Hook, their course set south, Hood wasn't the only one who wondered, as he watched *Albemarle* in its futile attempt to stay on station, if he had made the right decision. The man conning the ship had no doubt.

Nelson never saw his longed-for fleet action, nor did he get another, more seaworthy ship. Instead he spent months cruising around the Caribbean, with a few runs ashore, pursing an enemy determined to avoid engagement. He watched, with increasing frustration, as other frigates, swift vessels built for the task, were despatched on independent missions. No such opportunity fell to slab-sided, slow-sailing *Albemarle*, stuck to the coat-tails of the flagship.

One thing he had managed, though, was to keep his crew

intact, tenaciously fighting off any attempt to pluck men from his ship to man other vessels that were short-handed. Nor would he allow overbearing senior officers to land him with the dregs of their men in exchange for his own, trained by him to be good hands. He even fought off the attempted depredations of Lord Hood, courting unpopularity in an area where it was dangerous to do so.

Then, in the spring of 1783 came news of the peace. The Americans had won their land for themselves, and both France and Spain were exhausted. Nelson's orders were to return to Portsmouth and decommission the ship, which made him wonder if he had been right to act in such a fashion regarding his crew. Some of the captains to whom he had denied hands had earned prize money. He hadn't put a penny piece in the pockets of those who followed him, nor had he garnered them anything in the way of glory.

When they sailed in to anchor at Spithead, Portsmouth was a town in a state of riot. The end of the war occasioned the rundown of the whole fleet. Dozens of ships were being paid off in theory, the only problem being that all they were being given was freedom. Pay, even in the simplest case, was a mere warrant to be redeemed at a future date, there being no coin in the coffers to meet the obligations. On top of that, any man who had served in more than one vessel found himself chasing payment for several warrants, forced to sell them at a discount to sharps who lived off the trade.

Standing in the Port Admiral's office, in a first-floor room that overlooked a courtyard full of noisy sailors, Nelson was obliged to listen to a whole spate of excuses from the incumbent, Admiral Sir Ralph Burnaby. All were based on official humbug, with never even a mention of the truth: that the pay for the men, given by the government to their own Paymaster to the Forces, had been lent by that official at a favourable rate of interest as though it were his own money. Since he refused to call in the capital of those loans there was no coin for the men who had served the nation, because those who ran it had no conception of the meaning of the word corruption.

There were dozens of officers present, a few who had come

to seek redress for their men. The majority were there to demand that the atmosphere of riot, which had seen many of them jostled and insulted both aboard ship and in the street by common seamen, be put down, if necessary by armed marines and cannon in the streets. Nelson knew that some of those most vociferous in the cause of violence had made a great deal of money in the recent war. Quiet-spoken he might be, but he could hail the masthead in a howling gale and be heard if need be. So when he raised his voice to defend the sailors every head turned to hear his words, many having to search for his slighter figure among men both taller and more rotund than himself.

'I cannot believe my ears, gentlemen. I cannot credit that you, as commissioned officers, are proposing to turn guns, cannon even, on men who have a legitimate cause for grievance. It makes me ashamed of the service. We, as captains, would be better pledging our own credit so that the men and their wives get the full value of their warrants, rather than leaving them to sell them at a discount to the same calibre of thieves who robbed them in the first place.'

Everyone in the room replied in some way, a cacophony of noise in which few voices supported his plea. Admiral Burnaby was glaring at him. 'You would have your commission insulted, sir?'

Clearly Burnaby didn't know him. 'Captain Horatio Nelson, sir, HMS *Albemarle*. As for insults, my opinion would be that they stem from an empty chest. I dislike being jostled any more than the next man, especially in place of the swindlers who hide behind their office.'

It was clear that Burnaby took this as a personal insult, even though he was merely the purveyor of the bad news, not the architect. His red face went purple and his bulging eyes protruded even further out of their sockets.

'Then I suggest, sir, that you act as your conscience dictates, though judging by the state of your dress you would be hard found to get credit from a trader in used rags.'

Nelson blushed as those who disagreed with him laughed, poking each other and repeating, 'Used rags'. Two years away, sea air and salt had rendered the deep hue of his best uniform coat a sky-blue colour. What gold lace still decorated his hat had fared little better, his breeches and waistcoat were grey and his stockings so often darned that they looked like patchwork. Set against the dress of an officer like the Admiral, he looked like a naval vagabond.

There should have been words to say, a witticism clever enough to put this pompous red-faced oaf in his place, but Nelson was not gifted in that way. He raised his scruffy hat, spun on his heel and elbowed his way out through those officers who stood between him and the door, his mind trying and failing to produce a simile based on silk purses and sows' ears.

Outside the entrance there was indeed a marine guard, there to keep back a mob of protesting sailors. Nelson marched towards those red-coated backs with a purpose that made the officer in command order them to open ranks and let him through. His mind was in turmoil, the personal insult to which he had just been subjected mingling with a feeling of inadequacy in the face of official obfuscation. He felt utterly useless. Once among the unhappy tars, he barely noticed the pushing and shoving that made his path difficult, and the roar of insults heaped on him and his kind were just an unintelligible clamour. Then a sailor plucked off his hat, forcing Nelson to stop and seek the culprit.

He saw it raised and the face of the man who had taken it just before Thorpe, he of the lookout's eyes, felled the thief with a punch to the jaw, his other hand reclaiming the hat as the man went down. Suddenly Nelson was surrounded by Albemarles, who formed a cordon around him and berated those who would insult their captain. The scorn with which they were rebuked was mingled with words he could hardly credit: that he was the best captain any man could serve with, no flogging hard-horse bastard but one who saw his men fed fair and clothed proper, and a damn to the purser's accounts.

More followed, all flattering, until his crewmen grabbed him and raised him to their shoulders, still declaiming to those outside their circle that they would be lucky sods if they ever got to sail with Nelson. He sat atop, swaying left and right, back and forth, looking at the sea of faces that surrounded the Albemarles, wondering what his men were about. He had gone to the Port Admiral's office to get their due and emerged empty-handed, but still they cheered. The mob had begun to cheer too, most on the fringe not sure why, but happy, like any mob, to be part of the general mood.

He tried to look round, to see if those first-floor windows in the Port Admiral's office were a sea of commissioned faces, but he couldn't crane round enough. Pleased as he was to be rescued in such a way he could not help but feel that the impression he had created back there would not be elevated by this. Then he thought, Damn them. Many of them were little better than rogues. What they thought of him counted for nothing. What his men thought of him counted for everything.

The day came when the crew were finally paid off, with the ship going to a berth where her masts would be removed, her stores unloaded, her sail-locker emptied and all the sailors and commissioned officers would depart, leaving to look to her welfare only the officers warranted by the Navy Board, the purser, the carpenter, the boatswain, the cook and the gunner, men who belonged to the ship throughout its service. Nelson's barge lay alongside, sea chest loaded, Lepée and the boat crew led by Giddings ready to take him ashore. It was time to say goodbye.

The gathering of the hands on the quarterdeck replicated the day he had commissioned her for service, and a hundred Sunday divisions, in which the men had gathered before him for divine service and a reading of the Articles of War. There was a catch in his voice as he thanked them for their loyalty and abilities, then offered his deeply held hope that they would find prosperity ashore or at sea, should they choose to go back to it. When he finished, Thorpe, certainly one of the best hands on his ship, stepped forward, pulling his woollen hat from his head.

'I speaks for all, your honour, afore the mast, elected to do so by the whole crew.' Nelson nodded for him to carry on. The seaman scrunched his hat nervously between his hands. 'What I's been asked to say is this, that never have we here served with a better captain, such a good seaman and a fair-minded man.'

That occasioned a murmur of assent. Nelson stared up over their heads unable to look them in the eye.

'I have been asked to say an' all that there is not a man aboard this barky who wouldn't willingly serve under you again, so should you get another ship, which you so richly deserve, then just put the word out an' we'll all hot-foot to join it.' There was a slight pause before he shouted, 'Three on three for Captain Nelson, lads.'

Nelson left the poop to the sounds of that cheering. They were still at it as he stepped through the entry port to make his way to his barge. Then they manned the yards, and as he looked back, hat raised in salute, he saw that the whole ship's crew, including his officers, had taken station either aloft or at the bulwarks to cheer him across the Spithead anchorage.

BOOK THREE

CHAPTER 35

1784

This morning, Emma felt she was at loggerheads with everyone, not least George Romney, who was sketching her for yet another portrait, this time in the pose of wild-eyed Medea, classical slayer of children. The clothes she wore were tattered and revealing, her hair teased out wildly with twigs, face streaked with dark lines of heavy make-up. It was her eyes he needed most, that look of near madness he had struggled hard to create, which Emma kept discarding.

Old Romney, with his lined, walnut-coloured face and unruly grey hair looked up from the pad on his lap and glared. They had already had words about her inability to sit still, Romney pretending he had no idea of what triggered her fidgety behaviour. Yet he had seen Greville's face that morning, when he had delivered her to the studio; the black looks and stiff bearing that had characterised their exchanges, he all formality, Emma all meekness, until Greville departed.

Emma had spent the last half-hour locked in an internal argument in which she naturally cast herself as the aggrieved party. Playing both roles, her face was animated by point and counterpoint. She was winning of course, an imagined Charles Greville being easier to deal with than the real person, especially as she was of the opinion that the previous night's behaviour had been due to nothing more than high spirits. How dare Greville insist that if she couldn't learn to contain herself he would never take her out again!

As ever, when he was working, Romney's grey hair stood on his head, giving him the appearance of an elderly monkey, the impression heightened by his large, dark brown eyes. The old man was kindness itself, and Greville's black mood of this morning was no fault of his, so Emma worked to put the mad stare back in place. Romney nodded and went back to his frenzied sketching.

She should be angry with her lover about this too, being sold like a carcass. Greville had an arrangement with the artist: he provided the model, Romney provided the oils and the talent; the money from the sale of the resulting portrait was split between them, Greville's portion to set off the cost of keeping her. Romney had painted her a dozen times now; every picture had found an eager buyer.

Romney's eyes darted back and forth, boring into her. Did he, with his artist's insight, see how she felt? She loved Charles with a passion that had grown deeper through three years of attachment, and enjoyed their domestic harmony. Yet certain losses rankled, like the social life she had enjoyed on first arriving at Edgware Road, which had been slowly choked off. Her life now seemed sober and confined. After a year, Greville had moved into Edgware Road permanently, imposing his fussy bachelor habits on what had been an easy-going household; he had let the townhouse he had built in Portman Square to ease his debts. However, it had obviously not eased them enough: only the week before he had scolded her for giving a halfpenny to a beggar.

Excursions from the house had been rare of late. She could never be brought to the notion that her own natural vivacity was in part responsible for this. Was it her fault that when they went to a ball or a rout nearly every man in the room sought to engage her attention? Was she to blame if powerful and well-connected men cared not a whit if their outrageous gallantries offended her lover? It was not her fault that Greville was so jealous and insecure, unable to accept her repeated assurances that he had no cause for concern.

He had insisted that she had made an exhibition of herself the previous night. To Emma, singing and dancing were the stuff of life, and a glass or two of champagne encouraged her. She knew that Greville had cause to celebrate. As a collector he acquired only to sell, and was careful in the way he built up collections to make sure that the whole was always vastly superior to the sum of its parts. Many a time quick disposal had saved him from ruin. He had been corresponding with his uncle in Naples, using his good offices to amass a set of Roman and Etruscan artefacts that he had already sold on at a substantial profit. The news that his virtu, in the company of his uncle, had arrived in England had sent him into raptures of delight, and loosened his normally tight purse strings to such a degree that he had insisted on taking Emma to the Ranelagh Pleasure Gardens.

Could Greville not see the joy she felt in wearing a fine dress, having her hair tended for a night of entertainment, and crossing the portal for pleasure not duty? This was the first time in an age that Greville had offered to take her out to somewhere fashionable.

'Rumour has it,' Romney said, 'that you were the *belle amusement* at last night's rout.'

'I greatly enjoyed myself, I admit,' she replied defiantly, wondering how he knew.

'More than you have on previous visits?'

'Who said I have visited the Ranelagh before?' Emma demanded.

Her mother had told her she had a duty to deny her previous existence, even to those who must know it well. She was the semi-respectable Mrs Hart now, not the wild, promiscuous person of her former incarnation.

The old man grinned, laid aside his pad and ran a hand though his spiky grey hair. 'The two different faces of the gardens have always fascinated me, Emma – the decorum of the early evening contrasted with the riot of the later night. It seems that two different worlds occupy the same space. Reynolds captures the first, Hogarth the second.'

'With some men in both,' Emma replied firmly. Having been lectured by Greville she was in no mood to take the same from Romney.

But it was true what he said, just as it was true that she had misread the place, never having been there at what Romney called the Reynolds time. Then the prostitutes who plied for trade were still outside the gates. The gardens in the early evening were patronised by respectable London, who admired the carefully arranged plants, listened to good music and short, amusing dramas. They were not a scene of riot, with couples cavorting in the bushes, lewd songs and risqué plays, all aided by the consumption of vast amounts of wine.

'All I did was stand to sing,' she insisted.

'With a much admired voice, I'm sure.' Emma blushed and dropped her head. 'Take the compliment, my dear. You do have a sweet voice and the lessons Greville arranged for you have made it sweeter yet.'

'If I'd seen his face I would have stopped.'

He might have been scandalised, but others weren't. Compliments and drinks arrived before her in equal measure and she knew she had become drunk on both, the depth of her inebriation only serving to deepen her lover's disgust. She had seen that go skywards when she had got up, acceding to a request to dance. He demanded that they leave and the atmosphere on the way home had been icy. Once inside his own house Greville blew up like the volcanoes he was fond of describing.

Her mother, roused by the clamour, had advised Emma to apologise, grovel a bit if necessary to appease the man who kept them. Emma had taken a great deal of persuading, especially when Mary Cadogan had insisted she change into a drab grey dress to indicate penitence. It had been in vain. Her lover had even refused to share her bed, retiring to his study for the night, and in the morning, still under the burden of his anger, he had delivered her to this studio.

'I begged him to forgive me, even changed out of my finery to do so. You should have seen me, Romney, in that drab outfit, on my knees weeping in despair.'

'Show me the pose you adopted.'

Emma sank to her knees, her hands joined in supplication. The old man gazed on her shaking his head. 'Too biblical for my taste. I prefer the Greeks, though it would be a charming notion to paint you in a more modern pose.'

'But would that sell?' she asked sarcastically.

'An artist does not always toil for money.'

Their shared look was proof enough that such a sentiment did not apply to Greville. 'The mood you saw him in this morning was evidence that I am still not forgiven,' she said.

'You shall be, Emma, never fear.'

'How can you be so certain?'

The large brown eyes, normally so expressive, took on a certain blandness. The truth was that she was a beautiful bargain, a woman who might have commanded a much more puissant lover if she had so decided, might have moved in the grandest circles with a little education. There was a touch of love in Romney, old as he was, for the best model he had ever had. Greville kept her out of sight as much for fear of loss as he did to save coin. He had seethed with anger when the Prince of Wales had waxed lyrical on Emma's beauty, since his admiration was bound to be followed by an attempt at seduction. What Greville could never accept was that while male attention flattered her, and she responded, Emma wasn't interested.

'Greville will forgive you because he is so very fond of you, Emma.'

'Is he, Romney?' she whispered.

'Most decidedly so. He values you so very highly.'

Visitors to Romney's studio were frequent, and people who might become clients took a chair to watch the artist at work. His ever-attentive son, who was also the person charged with encouraging commissions, served refreshments. Emma had witnessed much of this, and was normally unconcerned by others' presence. But this day she was less than happy, given the pose she had been asked to adopt. It wasn't Greville who bothered her, it was the person she suspected to be his uncle William, as she reprised her wide-eyed and unattractive pose.

Greville had seen her in such a state of *déshabillé*, wrapped in their shared bed sheets, but for a total stranger to see her so was a different matter, especially one whom he esteemed so much. As soon as Romney declared the session closed Emma dashed to a private room to repair her appearance, then emerged with her hair brushed, face clean and properly dressed.

'Allow me, Emma, to name my uncle William,' Greville said. 'He is, as you know, His Majesty King George's ambassador and minister plenipotentiary at the court of Naples.'

'How you load me with honours, Charles.'

'They are yours by right, sir. Or should I say Chevalier?'

'But they are also much less impressive than they sound. Mere trifles, I would say, of some use in the Two Sicilies but of small account in a London full of grand titles.'

Charles had been talking about his uncle for days, with an increasing excitement that was hard to fathom in one so naturally reserved, yet nothing in either voice now suggested the kind of blood tie that would hint at an emotional attachment. Certainly the uncle was a kindly looking soul, soft voiced with an ease of manner that came from having mixed from birth with the cream of society. Greville had told her more than once of his connections, of the fact that, as a child, he had been a playmate of King George.

'I confess, my dear, to being quite startled when I entered. The face you presented to the world then was frightening in the extreme. Now I find myself gazing at untrammelled beauty.'

Emma smiled sweetly but without sincerity, recognising in the voice the muted tone of dalliance with which, in the past, she had been so familiar. Compliments would come easily to Sir William Hamilton, as would the desire to seduce her should the chance present itself. His manner stayed in that vein on their return to Edgware Road, to a supper prepared for them by Emma's mother, who was introduced and treated to as fine a piece of noblesse as Emma could remember. While they ate, Sir William and his nephew talked of family, politics, land, inheritances and the older man's recent widowhood.

It was in the latter that he showed real emotion, his sadness at the loss of his late wife, who had been for many years an invalid. But, for all that, the conversation carried little resonance for Emma.

Greville's hint that she should retire and leave them to talk was made abruptly enough to stir her rebellious spirit, but only in her breast: she had enough sense with Uncle William in attendance to suppress comment. To answer back would have made her Ranelagh misdemeanours look tame. But at least the Ambassador knew his manners. When she rose he leapt to his feet and came to hold her hand.

'Mrs Hart, I cannot say how much I have enjoyed the pleasure of your company.' The eyes that held hers were blue, steady, slightly watery and benign. 'I intend to presume upon my nephew's good graces to see you again – that is, if the prospect of such does not repel you.'

'How could it, sir?' Emma replied, in a lilting voice of which her singing teacher would have approved heartily. 'I revel in good company.'

'Revel?'

Sir William rolled the word around in his mouth, as if it was a sweetmeat he had never tasted. Out of the corner of her eye she could see Greville watching this exchange, a slight smile playing on his lips. When other men had tried the same, he had been furious.

'My nephew tells me you like to sing.'

'I do.'

'Then may I be permitted to visit when you are in a mood to do so?'

'Of course, Uncle,' Greville barked. 'You must come and see Emma at any time of your choosing. I'm sure she will enrapture you.'

'My dear Charles, she has done that already.'

'Good night, sir,' Emma said, curtsying.

Sir William kissed her hand and then she left. Greville's words followed her, and as she closed the door, she pressed her ear to the panel.

'I see that you approve of her.'

'That is understatement, Charles. Were she not in your care I swear that, old as I am, I would set my cap in her direction. She is a rare creature, and her manners are of the highest.'

'She's decorous now, I grant you, sir. But you have no idea how many rough elements had to be polished to produce the diamond you now observe.'

'Emerald, Charles! With such eyes she can be nothing less than that.'

'Then it is, no doubt, with some reluctance, Uncle, that you must once more turn your mind to Wales.'

After that first visit Sir William came often, accepting with pleasure the way that Emma called him uncle. He called her 'the fair tea-maker of Edgware Row', alluding without the least trace of restraint to his appreciation of her beauty. She returned his affection in full measure, happy to spend time with a man so congenial, who was not just urbane but could take and give a quip in equal measure. In that he showed up his nephew, who was wont to examine raillery aimed at him for an insult, and to include in his own attempted witticisms a degree of cruelty that robbed them of their humour.

Uncle William was an easy man to be with, and the occasional gallantry did not seem amiss from a man who still had his good looks. It was rare for Greville to leave Emma alone with any man, but he seemed to have no fear of his relative. Though in his mid-fifties, the Ambassador looked younger, which, when she remarked upon it, he ascribed to his love of walking.

'And you shall walk with me, Emma, should you and Charles come to Naples. I'll take you to Pompeii and Herculaneum, and show you what beauty lies under the mountain of ash that Vesuvius spewed forth to cover them.'

Seeing her confusion, he smiled. 'These names mean nothing to you?'

'No, Uncle William, they do not.'

His patient explanation was similar to that undertaken by Greville when he had first made her acquaintance. He described the volcano and the destruction it had caused, spoke of how he and others initiated digs to extract objects of great beauty and antiquity that had been wholly preserved by the ash.

'There's a fine collection of such virtu, many of the pieces acquired by me, in the house of a friend. Should you desire it, I will take you to his gallery for a private viewing.'

'I'd like that very much, Uncle, though if this volcano is still a danger, a visit to Naples is something I might not greet with the same joy.'

'I would never say not to fear it, but it can be approached as easily as I approach you, my dear. And the effect is somewhat similar. I got so close to the summit one day that I singed the soles of my boots.'

'Then for all you're a clever fellow, Uncle William, you have a streak of foolishness.'

Sir William was as good as his word: he took her not only to his friend's gallery but to any place she chose to visit. He escorted her to the Pantheon in Oxford Street, where society gathered in the daylight hours to gossip, exchange pleasantries and indulge in attempts at seduction. Sir William Hamilton commanded attention in his own right, but he clearly enjoyed the extra consideration he received with a beautiful woman on his arm. And Emma responded by behaving with becoming grace, commanded by Greville to be on her best behaviour, determined not to let down either him or the uncle they both admired.

There was a changed feeling in the household with Hamilton a frequent visitor. He came for tea most days and supper many nights, either at Edgware Road or at the house of a friend, singing round the harpsichord, games of Blind Man's Buff and the like. Life was once more the charmed existence Emma had enjoyed on first arrival. The Chevalier, as Greville called him, made no secret of his admiration for Emma, but never once did he overstep the bounds of good taste.

Occasionally, Greville would look at her with that hunger she knew so well, which never failed to produce a corresponding response in her breast. In the bedroom, he seemed restored, more relaxed, the Charles Greville she had known from her days at Uppark. He laughed more, his sallies lost their cruelty and Emma's love for him deepened accordingly, while gratitude was boundless to Sir William, who had brought this transformation.

There were worries, she knew, to do with Sir William's estates and what would happen to them after his death, undercurrents of anxiety that still troubled Greville. He greeted his uncle's suggestion that he and Emma visit Naples enthusiastically one day, with a frown the next. And Emma nursed her own hope to use this new household mood: she wished to advance the notion that her child, now three years old, should be brought to London. Greville wouldn't hear of it, but Sir William, when she mentioned it privately, saw no objection, and undertook to broach the subject with his nephew at an appropriate moment.

'Perhaps he will be more amenable when we are on our travels.'

'Travels?' Emma asked.

'You go to Chester, I believe?'

Sir William saw the confusion on Emma's face, and had the good grace to show embarrassment. 'Charles has not told you?'

'He hinted,' she lied, to recover her poise.

'We go to Wales on Friday, my dear, to look over my estates, while you journey to see your relations in Chester, including your child. You will travel with us as far as Cheltenham. I suggest the timing for what you desire could not be more appropriate, you with the child, me nudging Charles to agree.'

Emma was still confused, and her response showed it clearly. 'How long are we to be away?'

'A month.'

CHAPTER 36

'Look lively, lads,' said Giddings, at the sight of the hatless midshipman who was desperate to reach the quayside before Captain Nelson's carriage appeared.

All but two of the barge crew slipped down the slimy wooden stairway, taking their allotted places in the boat, clasping and raising their oars till they stood, regulation fashion, pointing towards the grey sky. The rattle of iron-hooped wheels set up a steady tattoo as the coach bounced on to the cobbled hard of Sheerness dockyard. Midshipman George Andrews skidded to a halt and jammed his hat back on his head. He had just enough time to raise it again as the door opened. His hair was whipped to one side by the steady wind, which also carried his high-pitched voice to the waiting sailors' ears.

'Mr Andrews, sir, at your service.'

Nelson returned the salute with a smile that carried more than his normal ration of paternalistic good humour. He had met the Andrews family in St Omer, in what now seemed like a futile attempt to better his French. The clerical father had been happy to entertain a naval officer bent on improving himself. Once he met the parson's daughters his studies had lost their lustre. Kate Andrews, at eighteen the elder of the pair, had occupied his waking thoughts, filling his mind with imaginings of the blessings of matrimony, even if, as an officer on half pay, he couldn't afford it.

Letters to relatives had not produced the desired financial assistance, probably due to Nelson's inability to guarantee that the object of his affections held him in the same regard. It was the kind of bind from which it seemed impossible to escape: he couldn't propose marriage because he lacked the means, but couldn't acquire the means without some indication of commitment from the object of his affections.

That short exchange with young George brought the memories flooding back: sweet Kate, who sang like an angel and played the piano with grace; the secret glances they had exchanged to fool those present. Jealousy surfaced in Nelson when any other seemed to occupy Kate's attentions and he recalled the way her lips pursed with annoyance at the sharper tone his voice took on in such circumstances. It was love of the truest and purest kind, painful in an almost physical way.

And here before him stood Kate's sibling brother, who had been at school in England while the rest of his family had been in France. He had the same corn-coloured hair, blue eyes and fair complexion, features that produced a physical reaction that ran through his entire frame. Nelson had a ship on foreign service, with every hope that his fortune might improve; at the end of this commission he might well find himself in a position to call on Kate with the means to make a proposal. Having returned the salute, he stuck out his hand. 'Why, Mr Andrews. I am happy to make your acquaintance. Might I be permitted to enquire after your family?'

'My father asked particularly to be remembered to you, sir. Both he and I are conscious of the honour you do us by taking me on board.'

'How could I refuse?' he replied. 'Was it not Kate who requested it?'

The boy's eyes opened wide in surprise. 'Why, no, sir. If anything she's dead set against it.'

That made his new commander frown; it indicated that his pursuit of Kate Andrews was stalled. 'Did she say why?'

'My sister thinks me too young, sir.'

'Did your father not inform you that is exactly the same age at which I came to sea?'

'Why, sir, that is amazing.'

The wonder on George Andrews's face, the startled look in his cornflower-blue eyes, restored Nelson's dented spirits. He, too, could recall the impossibility of the thought that his seniors had once been just like him: young, gauche and inexperienced. He looked up to see Giddings approaching, reminding him that the midshipman, in his enthusiasm, had forgotten to attend to his duties. And Frank Lepée, never one to shirk in articulating his displeasure, was frowning, though whether at the boy for his failure or the master for his indulgence was impossible to say. Giddings saw the look, observed that the servant was about to speak out, and solved the problem by acting as though the order had just been given.

'Aye, aye, sir,' he barked, turning back towards the hands who had yet to take their place in the barge. 'Sharp now, an' see to the Captain's dunnage.'

Andrews's whole frame shook, in a manner that reminded Nelson of the charlatan Graham's electric therapy. He sought words to cover his lapse.

'Holy Christ in heaven,' growled Lepée, which earned him a stern look of reproach from his captain.

'You must ask me to step into the barge, young man,' Nelson whispered. 'That is, once the sea chests are loaded.'

'Aye, aye, sir.' The boy gulped.

His voice was restored by the time they came alongside. The way he yelled '*Boreas*', to inform the crew that their captain was coming aboard, would have been heard halfway across the Medway. It was also quite unnecessary, since the first lieutenant had given the lookout orders to keep his telescope trained on the shore.

The barge crew hooked on to the chains and Nelson leapt for the rope ladder that rose towards the gangway. As his head appeared above the level of the deck, the pipes blew and the marines crashed their boots on to the planking, producing a resounding salute. Ralph Millar was the premier. A florid-faced American Loyalist, he had served as a midshipman aboard Sir Richard Parker's flagship, HMS *Bristol*, when Nelson was first made Post Captain and had never ceased to correspond with a man he openly admired. The last time he had seen Nelson was as an invalid being shipped home after the San Juan river fiasco. Millar stepped forward as Nelson's foot made contact with the deck, hat raised, his round face showing with subdued pleasure. 'Welcome aboard, sir. It does my heart good to see you fit and well.'

Nelson raised his own hat in return, both to his first

lieutenant and, facing the quarterdeck, to his new command. 'Assemble the men aft, Mr Millar, so that I may read myself in.'

As he glanced up from a document he knew by heart the eager faces cheered him mightily. Giddings had volunteered; Thorpe was there, as well as Nichols, and Bromwich, standing head and shoulders above the rest – still not promoted, despite Nelson's best efforts – had agreed to serve him as a master's mate. There were numerous others, who had formerly served on *Albemarle* and had now volunteered for his new 36-gun frigate and a return to the Caribbean. Nothing made coming back aboard a ship as pleasant as this.

Nelson glared at the stack of papers on his dining table. It served as a desk as well, a piece of fine mahogany on bare planking in a wooden-walled space painted pale green. There wasn't much else: a wine cooler, the gleaming brass instruments he used for navigation, two Harrison chronometers, which would give him his latitude, and enough chairs to host a decent dinner.

'A summary, Millar, if you please.' Millar rattled off the facts, in his twangy Yankee accent, which covered myriad items: sails, spars, rope, tar, nails, turpentine, even bales of tow. 'Combustibles?'

'Fully loaded, sir. Deficient only in wood and water.'

'Powder and shot?'

'Your predecessor was all husbandry in that department, sir. The hinges on the shot store hatches are rusty.'

'And likely to remain so, Millar.' The premier's thick black eyes betrayed just a hint of what must have been deep surprise. Nelson pulled a second oilskin pouch from his pocket. 'We have become a mere postal packet. If you peruse that you will see that we are to be burdened with passengers.' Millar reached forward to take it, as Nelson continued. 'Twenty-five midshipmen, enough to man every vessel on the whole Leeward Island station, with a few to spare for Jamaica. Added to that we shall be carrying the wife and daughter, no less, of our future commander, Admiral Sir Richard Hughes. I doubt they'll take kindly to their repose being shattered by daily gunfire.'

'The lady is a sailor's wife, sir.'

'Wrong!' said Nelson, with a grin. 'She's an admiral's wife.'

'Should I be a-continuing, your honour?' Lepée, busy unpacking, had a face to match his grumbling voice. 'If we has an admiral's wife aboard, she'll have the use of most of the cabin.'

'As like as not I shall have to shift my cot into the privy.'

'So, no gunnery, sir?' asked Millar.

Nelson grinned even wider. 'Let us see how she shapes up. Maybe she will love the smell of powder as much as we do.'

The sound of the marine sentry, coming noisily to attention, made both look to the door, which opened abruptly at Nelson's command to reveal the swarthy, handsome face of the second lieutenant, Edward Berry.

'Pilot coming aboard, sir.'

'Good. Mr Millar, stand by to weigh at first light tomorrow morning.'

Spithead, 18th April
To Mr Stephens,
Secretary to the Admiralty,
Dear Sir,
I have the honour to acquaint you that His Majesty's ship, under my command, arrived at this place yesterday, and enclosed is her state and condition.
Yours,
Captain H. Nelson.

'And damned lucky we are, Millar,' he added, putting down his quill. He sanded, folded and sealed his letter to the Port Admiral at Portsmouth.

'The man was clearly drunk, sir,' Millar replied. He referred to the Nore pilot who had run them fast aground in water so shallow when the tide went out that an audience had gathered to walk round the ship. He got her off at the next high water, only to be bound to the shore by a gale and a blinding snowstorm. In the Downs, still suffering from seasickness, he had got into a quarrel with a Dutch captain, who laid a complaint at the Admiralty about his behaviour. Unusually to Nelson's way of thinking, they had backed him up.

A knock and the sudden appearance of Andrews disturbed his thoughts. 'We've been hailed by a whole fleet of bum-boats, sir. They're full of women and servants who claim that one is the wife to Admiral Hughes.'

'The lady is sharp, sir,' said Millar. 'We've barely made our number.'

'Perhaps she fears I'll sail without her,' replied Nelson.

'You are most gracious, Captain,' said Lady Hughes, for the tenth time.

'The offer of my table is trifling enough, madam,' Nelson replied. 'The food, as well as the plate, is all yours.'

Aboard three days now, she had dressed for the occasion, head turbaned in silk, jewels flashing each time she moved her head and neck. From the little he knew, she had been a beauty when young, and some of that had stayed with her into middle age. But the line of her jaw had hardened, spoiling what might otherwise have been an elegant, if matronly, countenance.

'I do so think there is nothing like an occasion for making proper acquaintance. Especially, sir, with members of the gentler sex.'

The great cabin was full to overflowing. Practically every officer and midshipman aboard *Boreas*, including Lady Hughes's own son, was present to consume the ample dinner. Naturally she had yielded the head of the table to the commanding officer, but she had taken station to his immediate right and showed equal care in the way she placed her daughter, Rosy. The girl, plain, plump and pitifully shy, had been sat within full view of the Captain, her position close enough to the lieutenants to ensure that, should Lady Hughes's premier stratagem fail, these junior officers were there to fall back on.

Almost her first words on coming aboard had been a polite enquiry after Mrs Nelson. The predatory gleam in her eye as he replied that he had no wife had troubled Nelson. Trapped at table, with George Andrews a visible reminder of his hopes, he was brusque with both. This wounded the girl and bounced harmlessly off the mother. Her 'butterfly', as she so inappropriately called Rosy, was off to the West Indies unattached. Clearly, Lady Hughes had no intention that she should return to England in that same estate.

'You're sure the hour of dinner is not too early for you, madam?' he asked, seeking to shift the conversation towards alimentary rather than matrimonial pursuits.

For once his passenger replied precisely to the point. 'A trifle. I reckon my disposition, after long abuse, will bear it. Your three of the clock dinner is a naval habit that the Admiral insists on when he's ashore. My butterfly greets his determination to dine early with much grief, claiming it plays havoc with her digestion, which is, I may say, as delicate as her manners.'

'Then she must take care to avoid sailors, madam,' snapped Nelson. 'We engage in a rough trade and perforce make poor husbands.'

It had been too good an opportunity to miss, but he had spoken with more force than necessary. Lady Hughes might be single-minded, but she was far from stupid. More than that, she was not one to suffer so without retaliating. Her glance strayed down the table to where Midshipman Andrews sat opposite her own son, Edward. She had noticed that among the ship's youngsters the Captain had afforded this blond child extra attention.

'You do not hold with officers marrying, sir? Perhaps you find it unnatural.'

The inference was evident. He had to fight the temptation to administer a public rebuke at such a charge. Only her position as the Admiral's wife saved her. But his reaction clearly alarmed the lady since she sat back abruptly – anyone who had seen his face at that point would have recoiled: his eyes were as hard as gemstones, the skin round his jaw was fully stretched and his reply was delivered in a subdued hiss so at odds with his normal manner. 'You will oblige me, madam, by leaving off with your matchmaking. I expect you to apply this injunction to both myself and my officers. Your position affords you many advantages, but trapping your husband's inferiors is not one of them.'

'I dislike your tone, sir!'

Nelson deliberately looked at Andrews. 'And I, Lady Hughes, dislike your insinuations. I will have you know that I have an arrangement with that young man's sister.'

She didn't flinch, being of the type who didn't require her husband's position to provide a defence. Lady Hughes was formidable in her own right, quite strong enough to examine Nelson with open curiosity, as if seeking to determine whether his words were true. He, on the other hand, could not respond in kind: he was well aware of the flaws in his forthright rejoinder and he was obliged to concentrate on his plate to hide his thoughts. He was contemplating putting the Admiral's family ashore, with a 'goddamn' to the professional consequences.

When he looked up again Lady Hughes had turned away. Her eyes were roaming the table and when she spoke Nelson knew that, despite his clear injunction against it, her attention had shifted to a new target.

'Lieutenant Millar, I've scarce been afforded a chance to make a proper acquaintance.' Nelson's premier bowed his head in acknowledgement. 'I am sure your duties have precluded it. You're from the Americas, I'm informed, that melancholy country. My boy tells me you keep them to their tasks. Rest assured that my husband will be made aware of your zealous endeavour.'

'You are most gracious, milady.'

'Did you know that my husband once had this ship?'

His reply, when he took in the look on his captain's face, was nervous: 'No, madam, I did not.'

'And very fond of her we were. To me she will always be dear *Boreas*. Why, I felt as though I was stepping aboard a private yacht when I came on to the deck.' The hiss beside her, from the present commander, did nothing to deflect her. 'Perhaps, Mr Millar, with your captain's permission, you will escort me in a turn around the deck after dinner.'

Millar could not refuse: to a man of his rank the lady's expressed wish was as good as a command. And his captain could not intercede for the sake of good manners. But it was gratifying to him, at least, to see Rosy Hughes drop her head into her napkin in a vain attempt to hide the embarrassment.

At that moment Lepée, leaning close to whisper in his ear, distracted him.

'Mr Berry's compliments, your honour. The Port Admiral has made our number and sent us a signal to weigh.'

'Mr Millar will be relieved when he hears that,' replied Nelson softly.

The forward half of Nelson's cabin was partitioned so that he occupied his own sleeping and working quarters. The Hughes family had the day cabin as theirs, though they were obliged to shift to the coach during daylight hours. Despite his respect for Lady Hughes's position, Nelson did not set aside the midshipmen's lessons to accommodate her presence. A class of twenty-five, of whom all but five would shift to different ships when they raised Barbados, required space to learn their lessons. In truth, when it came to the majority their education was none of his concern, but if anything cheered him it was imparting knowledge to youngsters. To him, Edward Hughes was no different from the rest, and suffered not one jot from his mother's poor relations with the Captain.

Nelson was also on deck at midday to oversee the noon observation, where the young men would learn to use their quadrants. They studied mathematics, trigonometry and navigation with the master. At night they were lectured on the stars, so that they could read their way around the world by merely looking aloft. Then there were their duties as young gentlemen.

Though not commissioned, they were officers as far as the ship was concerned. Fencing lessons would be given daily. There was gunnery and sail drill; how to recognise which knot to use and when, then instructions in the actual tying. In calm weather, each mid in turn would be given command of a ship's boat, with Giddings and an experienced master's mate on board for company, their primary task to sail in strict station on the mother ship.

This manoeuvre called for seamanship. The run of the sea and the play of the wind on the frigate's larger area of sail ensured different rates of progress. In time they would be ordered away to identify some imaginary sail on the horizon, with a rendezvous provided for the following day. These orders would be delivered by an officer standing on the poop, speaking trumpet in hand, yelling a stream of instructions, none repeated, which the candidate had to memorise without benefit of pen or paper.

Nelson's greatest concern was for the youngest of his charges, an eleven-year-old child whose small build exaggerated his lack of years. Called Henry Blackwood, he was under four foot tall and so scrawny he looked like an eight-year-old. Nelson had paid particular attention to him from the first day, knowing that his appearance would leave him open to abuse from his fellows. Words with the gunner's wife had him removed from the mid's berth after dark, to be accommodated in the gunner's own quarters, as Nelson had once been.

But that only protected the lad at night. During the day he was exposed to all the perils of his peers. The Navy required each young gentleman to progress at the same pace, and being the runt of the litter afforded the boy no special privilege. The first time he was ordered to go to the masthead nearly proved his undoing. *Boreas* was making around six knots, pitching and rolling evenly on what, for the coast of Brittany, was a calm sea. Nelson, pacing the windward side of the quarterdeck, well away from Lady Hughes taking the air on the poop, was watching the noisy group of mids out of the corner of his eye.

Each in turn was required to climb to the tops. He observed the way little Blackwood eased himself back into the crowd, hoping that Berry would fail to notice him. But the second lieutenant knew his duty. He had twenty-five mids to send aloft, and only twenty-four had performed the task. When he enquired as to who had ducked their duty, every eye turned to the stripling boy, and a path was cleared between him and Berry, leaving the miscreant nowhere to hide.

'Mr Blackwood, you are required to proceed in a like manner to your fellows, that is, to the masthead.' The boy, who had never been further than the main cap, began to shake from head to foot, the image of terrified reluctance, which made Berry snarl, 'It is your duty, young man!'

'Aye, aye, sir,' he piped, though his feet remained rooted to the spot.

'Then proceed.'

'With respect, sir, I can't.'

Berry's already swarthy face went two shades darker as he shouted his response, a bark that stopped Lady Hughes in her tracks. 'Can't, sir? You are in receipt of a direct order. You must and will obey.'

One foot moved but not the other. Blackwood, looking aloft to a point one hundred and twenty feet in the air, tried to suppress a sob, but it came out nevertheless. Nelson stepped forward on to the gangway, which immediately brought the entire party to attention. Berry whipped off his hat in a respectful salute, but his expression showed his true feelings: this was a situation in which his captain had no right to interfere.

Nelson couldn't fault him: he had every right to require obedience to his orders. But this child was so small, and clearly so frightened, that he was in mortal danger. He would go aloft eventually. Berry, and the fear of derision from his peers, would ensure that. But would he reach his destination? In his terror he might slip. Luck, if it could be termed that, would take him overboard, to the chancy hazard of a difficult rescue from the cold sea, but if he mistimed his fall, he would land on the deck. That would see him entered in the ship's log as 'discharged, dead in the execution of his duties'.

'Mr Blackwood,' Nelson said, moving forward.

'Sir,' the boy squeaked, spinning to look at the Captain.

'I am about to go aloft myself. I'd be obliged if you would join me.'

With that Nelson stepped on to a barrel to aid his ascent to the bulwarks. He turned and smiled at Blackwood. 'As you will observe, I am not as nimble as you. Why, I daresay you could leap to my side without the aid of that cask.'

The eye-contact produced the desired result. Blackwood's expression changed from fear to something akin to trust. He did as he was bidden, and jumped up on to the bulwark, grabbing at the shrouds to steady himself.

'I see I shall need to be quick, Mr Blackwood. You're even more lively than I supposed.'

He started to climb, slowly at first, but with increasing speed as he sensed the boy following. The shrouds stretched like a long rope-ladder all the way to a point just below the mainmast cap, every movement of both ship and climber combining to alter the shape. After some forty feet the shrouds presented two avenues. One took the climber on, through the lubbers' hole, on to the spacious platform of the mainmast cap. The others rose vertically, skirting the rim to rise even higher. Nelson had no need to hesitate. He increased his pace, arching backwards as he gripped the ropes. He slipped past the edge with ease, leaning forward again to ascend this narrower set of shrouds.

Up he went, fifty, sixty, seventy feet from the deck. Out again, this time as *Boreas* dipped into a trough, which left his back in line with the sea below. The slim strip of ropes led on past the tops. He knew Blackwood was with him; not close but there, his eyes fixed on the Captain before him, rather than the frightening panorama below. Once at the crosstrees, Nelson threw his leg over on to the yard, easing his back till it rested against the upper mast.

'Come along, Mr Blackwood,' he called. 'There's no need for you to favour an old man in this fashion.' As the boy's head came level he held out his hand to help him up. 'Mind, respect to the Captain is a very necessary notion, I suppose. It would never do to show me up. Bad for discipline, eh! Now, young sir, clap on hard to this rope and sit yourself down. Then we will have the leisure to look about us, and the chance to talk for a while.'

'Aye, aye, sir,' gasped Blackwood.

'Is it not a fine place to be?' Nelson saw the boy's face pale as he looked down towards the deck, where the assembled mids now looked like a colony of ants. 'I remember when I was a shaver, just like you, an old tar, who had sailed with Anson, brought me up here. I remember him saying that once you was above ten feet, it don't signify. As long as you clapped on in a like manner.'

'Aye, aye, sir.'

'Now, Mr Blackwood, being a captain has its advantages. But one of the drawbacks is this, sir. You rarely get a chance to be alone with anyone. Now that we're up here, just the two of us, it will give you a chance to tell me all about yourself.'

The boy's mouth opened and closed, but no sound came.

Nelson had to prompt him with a direct question. The tale the boy told was a depressingly familiar one. As the younger son to a middling family there had been little prospect that he would receive a decent education. Nor did the Army, with its bought commissions, present a realistic prospect of advancement. The family had few connections and, lacking interest as well as money, could not place their son in any milieu other than the King's Navy. But as the story emerged, Nelson couldn't help but wonder, for the hundredth time, whether some sort of age limit should not be placed on entry, so that boys like Blackwood were not exposed too early to the rigours of life afloat.

Nelson felt like a youngster again as he grabbed for the backstay and slid down to the deck, wondering halfway if his dignity as a captain would be impaired by such behaviour. But it had the desired effect, Blackwood following him down in a heartening sailorly fashion, to be greeted by a grinning Nelson.

The arch look Nelson received from Lady Hughes, still on the poop as he turned to return to the quarterdeck, made his blood boil: it was nothing less than a repetition of her insinuation that his interest in youngsters was at best misplaced, at worst impure.

CHAPTER 37

The last time Emma had seen her daughter she had been in swaddling clothes. To gaze on her now, a child of three years, induced the most unwelcome sensations. The large eyes held her smile in place for a lot longer than she had intended, but there was no change in the little one's expression when Emma spoke her name, nor when she held out her arms to enfold her.

'Say a welcome to your mother, Little Emma,' encouraged Grandma Kidd. The old lady was now so bent that her head was almost at the same level as that of the suspicious child. But there was no doubting the deep affection in the look, even if it was from a face lined like tree bark. Her smile exposed that what few teeth she had had left were now gone. 'She's come all the way from London Town just to see you.'

It required a gentle push to get Little Emma any closer and a tug from her mother to make enough contact to complete the hug. But the ice of greeting had been broken and the little girl, a lively child, soon began to chatter, first to her great grandmother, then slowly including this stranger called mother. Emma found the transition harder than her daughter, and constantly referred to her grandmother for clarification of the child's unformed speech.

'You'll get used to it, girl. She's a rare one when it comes to tattle, bit like you was when you were a bairn.'

That induced a rare silence in Emma. Grandma Kidd was one of the few people who could mention her past and evoke unpleasant thoughts. Her life had not turned out in a way that anyone in the family wanted. Her grandmother was an upright, honest woman, though not a hypocrite when it came to accepting money help from whichever source provided it.

Yet the old lady must have been saddened to see the way her

brood had gone, first her daughter, Mary, then her grand-daughter, not settled but living off the good grace of men who thought them too lowly to marry. The way she was looking at the child now, as she played with and talked to her doll, carried with it some of that sadness, as though she was seeing Little Emma grown and in the same predicament.

'How do you cope with the burden?'

'Bairns ain't no burden, Emma. They is a joy, least at that age.'

'It may be that the child can come and reside with me.'

'In London?'

'Yes. With my mother as well, a proper family.'

'That would be good,' Grandma Kidd said, without conviction.

Emma imbued her voice with as much enthusiasm as she could muster. 'I have engaged in this the good offices of Mr Greville's uncle, the one I wrote to you about.'

'Old Tom Fort reads for me. He says it be called Napoli where this uncle comes from, not Naples as you wrote, and with him being an old sailor, well, happen he knows.'

The way it was said implied some lack of honesty in the man who had lived there, though Emma struggled to find what difference it made.

'Old Tom Fort is just showing away 'cause he's been there. I've yet to meet a sailor who don't boast. Stands to reason the locals term it different to we English.' That earned a loud sniff, as if the matter was to be considered but not too readily accepted. 'Tom would have doffed his hat soon enough to our uncle William.'

'He ain't your blood.'

'It is a liberty he allows, in fact positively encourages. He is, Grandma, the most gracious of men, with a smile that would have you over in no time.'

'Wed? Only you didn't mention.'

'Widowed, with a heart still bruised from the loss. Not that it depresses his spirits. He loves to be gay and has a ready wit as well as stories you would scarce believe about the scrapes some of our English folk get up to abroad.'

'There's not a lot he could tell me about folks, and that's without ever leaving my own parish.'

Grandma Kidd was disposed not to like Sir William Hamilton, that was clear, but then she had not much good to say for Charles Greville either, even if he did foot the bills for Little Emma. To the old woman they were cut from the same cloth: the kind that had exploited the girls she had raised.

'Uncle Hamilton has undertaken to seek permission for Little Emma to move to Edgware.' Hearing her name, the child stopped talking to her doll, and raised a pair of large green eyes to stare at her mother. Emma addressed her directly. 'You would like it there I am sure, for Mr Greville is a kinder person than he will at times let show. I'm sure a few of your smiles would melt his heart just as quick as they have mine.'

'Whatever's best for the child,' said Grandma Kidd. 'That's all I care for. That's all I ever cared for.'

Charles Greville was reading, silently, Emma's first letter since their parting, as usual half amused, half despairing of the breathless way in which it had been composed. But the 'Damn!' he hissed was loud enough to make Sir William Hamilton look up from his labours.

'She has given that old woman, her grandmother, near a full fifth of the money I allowed her for the month.'

'That is bad?' Sir William's reply was halfway between a statement and a question. Greville was clearly displeased, but that didn't signify since his nephew was prone to disapproval of many things, something he found trying at times.

'Apparently Mrs Kidd bought the child a coat she couldn't afford.' He spoke brightly now, because he had read the words that followed. 'Emma promises to make good the loss. She tells me she has taken cheaper seaside lodgings and is eating frugally.'

'Does she mention her health?' asked Sir William.

'Blooming, Uncle, as is that of the child.'

'Then that at least is good news.'

'Sea bathing, both of them,' Greville added, tossing the letter aside. He went back to his own set of books, the accounts for the present year that would have to be checked before being passed to his uncle. Greville was the man responsible for the stewardship of these Welsh estates, an obligation to which he devoted considerable time. 'Do you really believe such immersion can be efficacious?'

'Not in these northern waters. But I have a small villa at Posillipo in the Bay of Naples. In summer, when the sea is warm and the body is robust enough to withstand the power of the waves, it does wonders for the ague.'

The voice drifted into silence, and the older man had a wistful look in his eyes. It was hard to compare in any favourable way this house, this dark, oak-panelled room and its musty, unoccupied smell with either Posillipo or his apartments in the Palazzo Sessa and the freshness of the Mediterranean sea breeze that wafted through them. Nor could he conjure up much affection for the green Pembrokeshire countryside that rolled away from the windows. He yearned for the warmth of the sun, and the smell of lemons and abundant flora that filled his rooms, for the sight of his collections and the excitement of a dig when the first sign of some artefact emerged from the ash.

Absence kept him from recalling the smell of the city when the wind blew from the east, the beggars and the light-fingered, noisy inhabitants – the court, too, which was full of intrigues that seemed so petty they might be amusing, had they not been so deadly. Neapolitans loved to sing and dance the *saltarella*. They loved food, wine and blatant carnality. But, most of all, they loved to hate. There were family feuds, political enmity, and a visceral hatred of all other nationalities; Spanish the most, Austrians the next. His duty was to ensure that Britannia retained if not affection at least no increase in animosity.

He had a duty here too: to pass the accounts with which Greville had presented him, books that covered the years he had been away. These showed he had well-managed assets that yielded him an income, without any effort on his part, of some five thousand pounds per annum. Not that he was unaware of the profit: spending it wisely was a major concern.

'I cannot bring myself to decide whether to be pleased or angry with Emma.' Sir William looked at the bent head, knowing that the face he could not see wore a frown. 'I suppose

'I should be sanguine about the way she has behaved. I have to tell you, Uncle, there was a time, and not so very long ago, when she would not have shown the sense necessary to make good the loss.'

'Hardly a loss, Charles. It went to the child.'

'I make provision enough for the child. Little Emma wants for nothing.'

Sir William forbore to say that his nephew was clearly wrong, since the purchase of a coat, in a Cheshire winter, would be a necessity. 'There is the matter of parental affection.'

That made Greville look up. 'I didn't have you as a lover of Rousseau.'

'The fact that I do not have children of my own . . .' His uncle had to pause and look away to avoid the avarice in Charles Greville's eyes. 'It does not mean that I do not ponder on the proper course of raising and educating them.'

'And?'

'I look to my own past. I was put out to a wet-nurse on the very day of my birth.'

'With a king for a companion on the other teat.'

'A prince then. But that is to digress. What I mean is that Rousseau has identified this as an unsatisfactory way of rearing infants. And it is not just he. The Duchess of Leinster I consider a friend, and she in her letters cannot be brought to think of child rearing in any other way than by the natural mother.'

Greville favoured him with a thin smile. 'I sense a reason for the route of this conversation, Uncle William.'

'I doubt it is a secret to you that Emma herself inclines that way.'

'The books bore you, I fear.'

'They do, nephew, they do. You have carried out your stewardship in a splendid fashion. Were it not that you insist, I could scarce be brought to check the figures you produce.'

'A turn round the garden?'

There had been a shower earlier, so although the grass was damp, the air had a clear odour to it that was pleasing. Less engaging was the turn the conversation had taken, with Greville's point blank refusal to consider that Little Emma should live with her mother. His reasons, though they sounded practical, were based on selfish motives. He was a fastidious man, a lover of order who would find the accommodation of a child's needs, the sheer disruption, impossible to cope with.

'You only see Emma, Uncle, as she is now. You do not see the wild, untamed creature she once was. Keeping that which has been achieved intact is paramount.'

'If what you say is true, that is so.'

'Yet you admire her.'

'It would be hard not to, Charles. She is, even you admit, a rare creature. Were she not under your protection I doubt I could be saved from a foolish attempt at dalliance.'

'Hardly foolish, sir, and do not fear that any attentions you paid to Emma would evoke a jealous reaction in me.'

Sir William looked sideways at his nephew's profile, the set of the jaw, the look into the far distance meant to convey sincerity. Perhaps he did mean what he said, but his uncle had seen him react to the presence of other men around Emma Hart, and nothing he had observed had led him to believe that he took kindly any form of attention to her.

'The foolishness would stem from my age. Besides, it would scarce be fitting. Suffice to say, Charles, that I consider the obligation of family.'

Greville tried to suppress the combination of anxiety and excitement in his voice. 'Do you truly think of me as family, Uncle?'

'How can you doubt it, since you're my blood nephew and I consider you my heir?'

That was an amusing moment for Sir William, who was too wise and urbane ever to be fooled by his nephew. He didn't dislike Charles, quite the reverse, but there were traits in his character, the most notable his endless calculation, which he found reprehensible. As a younger son himself he knew what it was to lack an inheritance. And there was the clear memory of his own marriage which, while founded on a degree of regard, had had as much, if not more, to do with the stipend produced by the very estates they were now inspecting, property that had come to him through his late wife.

Charles worried that he would not succeed to the income.

He knew that his mother had been Sir William's favourite sister, and that once she had realised her brother was childless, she had pleaded eloquently on behalf of her younger son. Sir William had been happy to oblige, with the caveat that should he predecease his wife the estates would not be in his gift. He considered it a point of honour that, having made that promise and having survived Lady Catherine Hamilton, he could not go back on it.

Yet he couldn't help teasing his too-serious nephew with hints that he might remarry. Such talk, though Greville tried to disguise it, threw the young man into a frenzy of doubt. With a shaky concept of honour himself, he could not ascribe unselfish motives to others, and constantly saw barriers to his inheritance where none existed.

'There is some pity in the fact of our blood ties,' said Greville, holding up his hand to feel for the first spots of rain.

'In what way?' Sir William had already turned towards the house, thinking that the rain, a cause for some celebration in Naples because of its rarity, was all too commonplace here.

'I speak of Emma, of course. She is, I must tell you, the sweetest bedfellow a man could crave, as capable of gentility as she is of abandon. Had you been afforded a chance to discover her charms, I assure you, no barrier of age would have ruined your pleasure.'

Hurrying for shelter now, Sir William noted the words but not the expression that accompanied them.

However, over the next week, as the subject of Emma and her obliging nature came up again and again, it was not difficult to see which way his nephew's mind was moving. Sir William was unsure whether to be offended or pleased, to anticipate delight or ridicule, to agree to what was being hinted at or scoff at it: the proposition that a man of his age should investigate the possibility of housing, and quite possibly bedding, a lively creature considerably less than half his age.

Trained as he was in diplomacy, Sir William did nothing to commit himself to any course of action. But he was not immune to imagination, and he had to admit that though the thought didn't entirely please him, it didn't appal him either.

*

A month with Little Emma had not only affected the child, it had had a deep impact on her mother as well. There were tantrums, of course, times when Emma's patience was sorely tested, such as when she encountered her daughter's reluctance to put more than one foot out of the bathing machine and into the sea, or to go to bed when the appropriate hour had struck. Hunger made the child fractious, as did tiredness, and it was plain that Grandma Kidd had over-indulged her. But on the whole she was a joy to be with, a source of endless wonder with her chatter and her childish view of events and objects.

There were moments that would live with Emma for ever: the first voluntary taking of her hand, the morning when a sunny smile greeted her, the look in those green eyes, so like her own, when she read her daughter a story, the peals of laughter that accompanied a session on a swing. But, most of all, she loved that moment when Little Emma, tired after a day on the beach collecting shells or searching for crabs, fell sound asleep on her mother's breast, the gentle pounding of her own heartbeat timed exactly to coincide with that of the child.

In Southport Emma was anonymous, just a mother with her child, a Mrs Hart whom everyone assumed had a Mr Hart in the background. Hints of a man serving at sea were accepted without question by the lady owners of the lodging house, who were too polite to enquire after an excess of detail. She was nodded to by strangers as a decent woman, and eventually engaged in conversation about matters domestic that had her falling back on her years in service. It was so long since Emma had experienced respectability that she was disinclined to give it up.

Against that she missed Greville, even his moods. She had sense to see that this seaside interlude was just that: a short break from the life she had chosen; a chance to play the part that might have been hers, had she not allowed her life to take the course it had. Having corresponded with her lover before, she knew better than to look for affection from his pen, but the coldness of his writing, especially on the subject of her daughter and Edgware, still wounded.

That absence of emotion served to rekindle her natural spirit, the need to challenge, rather than just accede to the wishes of others. Her growing attachment to Little Emma made the thought of giving up her daughter more and more difficult to bear. Emma swung between confidence in her own ideas and a fear of the reaction they would provoke, but finally, with no one present to check her, she determined to act as her conscience dictated. The first thing to do was to get both of them to London and installed before Greville returned.

'If she is already here, then it would be a stone heart that had the inclination to turn her out.'

Mary Cadogan watched her granddaughter playing on the floor with the same affection Emma had experienced at the Steps. It wasn't just the blood tie either: the child had a winning way as well as an open, trusting gaze and ready smile that was heart melting. The surprise of the child's arrival had faded in her, but not the notion that Greville would ever stand for it. He was a man who liked the house tidy. You only had to look at his choice of furnishings, which inclined towards the dainty rather than the robust, and to observe how he checked them continually for position and cleanliness to understand how finicky he was.

Greville liked things just so, and however sweet Little Emma was, she was still a child, prone to speak when not asked, cry when hurt, demand attention when inappropriate and leave her playthings wherever they fell when she tired of them. Though Mary suppressed these thoughts in order not to spoil a happy interlude, she had good reason to feel vindicated when the master returned.

'If anything, Emma, I am more vexed now than I was when I read your letter.'

Greville was pacing back and forth, hands behind his back, in the master-of-the-house pose that had become an increasing feature of his behaviour since he had moved in. Emma sat, head down, careful to avoid adding an eye challenge to a domestic one.

'Did you tell your uncle?'

'How could I not when you'd engaged him as advocate on your behalf?'

'I believe he shared my view that it would do no harm.'

'A stand of which I would take more cognisance if he would be obliged to suffer the consequences of such an arrangement.'

'Suffer, Charles? She's only a child.'

'The only is singular, Emma, given that her being an infant is the whole point of my objections. The household is simply not suitable . . .'

'She has her own room, and both my mother's and mine when matters permit. She need never come downstairs at all when you are about. You won't even know she's with us.'

'Nonsense,' he replied, impatiently, his voice rising as he spoke. 'And what I do and do not know is hardly the point. Do not tell me that in some crisis you will not put her needs as paramount. Do not tell me that when I have friends in my own house some act of the child will not be noticed.'

'Who can object to the sound of a child?'

'I can!'

Mary Cadogan was listening behind the door, and when she heard Emma reply to that, she noted there was real steel in her daughter's voice. It wasn't anger but determination, and for once her mother, who feared to be cast out on the street more than any other fate, was with her.

'I require you to indulge me in this, Charles.'

'Require? Am I to be required of?'

The answer to that was no. Pleading, tears, tentative intercessions from an uncle who knew the bounds placed on interference had had no effect. Charles Greville ordered his life just so, and would not stand to see it altered.

Returning Little Emma to Grandma Kidd was heart-wrenching for Emma and ultimately sad, too, for the old lady, given that Greville had decided that the child must be placed with some respectable family to secure her future. That his notion had wisdom attached did not detract from the melancholy such a suggestion provoked. If the child stayed at the Steps, she would grow up in the same manner as her mother and grandmother before her. Who was to say that she would not turn out to follow the same occupation? It was a notion that Greville, for very good reasons, could not countenance.

'The choice will be yours, Grandma,' said Emma, the

offending letter in her hand, her eyes, like those of her grandmother, red with tears, 'though Mr Greville's approval will be most essential.'

'It should fall to you, Emma, not me,' croaked Grandma Kidd.

'I would not pick someone close by. You will, so that at least you can see her when you want. It sounds cruel I know, but I cannot abide the way I feel. I would send her to a family so far away that even should I come to visit you I would not have the chance to see Little Emma.'

'I never thought you'd turn your back on your own child.'

'I do it for her,' Emma sobbed, her eyes turning to the curtain behind which her daughter slept, 'so that she will not see tears every time she beholds her mother's face. Let her grow up thinking someone else her true parent.'

Grandma Kidd stood up, if her bent frame could qualify for such a description, and both her face and the tone of her voice showed her anger. 'I was never one for falsehood, Emma, and I reckoned you the same. But all this "doing it for the little 'un" is stuff and nonsense. You'se doing it like this for your own ends. It's your heart that is uppermost, not the bairn's.'

'I—'

'Say no more, Emma. Go to the Post House, where you took care to leave your possessions, and wait for your coach to London.'

'You speak as though I have a choice.'

'You do, child,' Grandma Kidd replied wearily. 'You could stay put and raise your own. But you're too like your own mother, always looking for others to fend for you.'

Emma tried to embrace her grandmother, but was foiled as she moved away. 'I'd like to part in harmony.'

'You could stay in that, Emma, but as to parting I can't see how. Tell your man to write his conditions for the child. Rest easy that I will place her where she will be happy.'

CHAPTER 38

1785

A lively sixteen-year old, Miss Parry Herbert, daughter of the Governor of Barbados, was enthralled by the approach to the island of Nevis, St Kitts just visible beyond it, beautiful Montserrat over the stern. Conical in the clear blue sky and water, with the tip of the old volcano topped by a ring of mist, the high cirrus clouds of a Caribbean dawn formed a perfect backdrop. Whatever doubts she had had about taking passage from Antigua on HMS *Boreas* had long since evaporated. She had discovered very quickly that the supposed ogre, Captain Horatio Nelson, who was standing with her now, was nothing of the sort. He was a kind, considerate man who ran a ship that defied everything she had ever heard about naval service: it was clean, free of fear and crewed by men who treated her as if she were a princess.

It was hard to credit that this man who never raised his voice was, according to his servant a real Tartar when it came to a scrap; that he was so in love with trouble that if it didn't present itself he went out of his way to find it. Frank Lepée was often a trifle inebriated when imparting this information, indiscreet in the way he talked about his master and the troubles he brought on his own head, both with the ladies and authority.

Not long after arriving on the station Captain Nelson had fallen out with his commanding officer, Admiral Hughes, though some put that down to his relationship with Lady Hughes. Then there had been his unfortunate association with the wife of a fellow naval officer, which had set tongues wagging all over the region. Captain Moutray, retired from the active list and in some ill health, was married to a woman twenty years his junior. Mother of two children, she was reputed to be a beauty, though of a rather faded kind.

Gossip had it that Mary Moutray was a flirt, always keen to ensnare any passing young officer in the web of her vanity, managing to keep several gullible swains on tenterhooks at any one time. At worst, Nelson had been a fool among many, perhaps a greater one for the depth of his attraction and the directness of his method. He had made matters worse by entering into a dispute with the lady's husband to do with the prerogatives of serving officers as compared to those afforded to a man who'd retired, some nonsense about a commodore's pennant, which many ascribed to jealousy more than professional pride.

It was all stuff to a girl of her age, and that included the most boring subject of all: Navigation Acts. Nelson had set the sugar islands on their ears by insisting that an adherence to the laws, which obliged British subjects to buy British goods solely from goods shipped in British-owned bottoms. Anything brought in by foreign ships, especially Americans, might be cheaper but, in the eyes of the law he represented, it was contraband and would be seized as such.

Nelson watched her face, noting the excitement, responding as she pointed out some feature of the island that had caught her attention. Miss Parry Herbert was an engaging creature, full of the enthusiasm of youth that Nelson so admired yet could not but feel had long departed from him. For Nelson the Caribbean was a sea of troubles. Mary Moutray had gone home to England a few months before, leaving an aching void. With her corn-coloured hair, flawless skin, deep blue eyes and winsome manner, she had led him to believe that all was possible, then broken his heart.

Frank Lepée reckoned he had been a fool, and in his drunken ramblings told him unwelcome truths: that the barbed remarks from his commanding officer about Nelson's responsibilities, the gentle nudges of friends and the warnings to desist, had sprung from genuine concern, and not, as he had supposed, from envy. Now, in his prayers, he begged forgiveness for having conjured up a base vision of Mary Moutray as a widow, her sick husband dead, and himself inheriting both her and the couple's two young children.

Heartbreak was not his only trouble: having risen to become second in command on the station, he was at loggerheads with his admiral, one-eyed Sir Richard Hughes, who would not support him in obliging the island traders to abide by the law. He claimed that if Nelson persisted, he would ruin the economy of the islands. Nelson had been forced to go over his head and appeal for support from the Admiralty, which had soured relations even more and did nothing to ease his present difficulties: they could not respond from London in less than three months. Nearly everyone in the islands cursed him as an infernal nuisance, and that included many of his fellow officers. But he had right on his side, and he was determined to prevail.

A puff of white smoke emerged from the bastion covering the anchorage, followed by the first of several booms from *Boreas*'s signal cannon. Nelson insisted to Miss Herbert that the courtesies exchanged between the shore batteries and his frigate were a salute to her, not him. That had pleased her mightily, and underlined to her how wrong she had been to listen to those who had advised her against requesting this passage. How could this gentle fellow, with his shy manner, threaten the very fabric of society?

She did not know that she herself had been a boon to the ship's captain: her lively nature and genuine interest in all things nautical served to keep his mind off the worries that assailed him.

'Mr Berry, my barge,' he said, 'and Mr Hardy to join me ashore when he has completed his lessons.'

Martha Herbert, daughter of the household and a year older than her cousin, was on the porch to greet them. There was a moment of appraisal between the two girls, who were strangers to each other: Miss Parry was fair-haired, bright-eyed and pretty, while Martha, no beauty with her pinched face, had hair that was near black and contrasting almost translucent pale skin. Nelson observed them, and could see that while Miss Parry was happy to be visiting, her cousin was not so outgoing. Beside Martha stood the youngest member of the household,

Josiah Nisbet, and Nelson's glance in his direction broke the contact between the cousins.

'This, Miss Herbert,' said Martha, stepping to one side, 'is Master Josiah Nisbet, son of Mrs Fanny Nisbet, your cousin, whom I'm sure you know is held in high esteem by my father.'

The boy didn't move, but concentrated on not meeting her eye. Miss Parry Herbert moved forward and held out her hand. 'Captain Nelson has mentioned your mother many times since we left Barbados.'

'Have I?' asked Nelson. He was as surprised by this as Martha Herbert, who raised a quizzical eyebrow.

Miss Parry continued, 'All praise, sir, I do assure you. I believe you even went so far as to advise me to model myself on the lady in my relations with my uncle.'

'Wise advice, cousin,' said Martha, rather formally. 'Mrs Nisbet runs Montpelier on my father's behalf, removing the care of domesticity from his shoulders, allowing him ample freedom to attend to his more pressing affairs. Is that not correct, Josiah?'

The reply was halfway between a grunt and a hiss. Josiah was clearly determined to give away nothing in front of this strange girl. Nelson, though smiling at the boy, was thinking about those 'pressing affairs'. John Richardson Herbert, president of the Island Council, was the wealthiest man on the island, so rich that half of the other planters annually mortgaged their property to him. Certainly he behaved with great generosity, scattering gifts with little regard to depth of acquaintance or cost. He carried himself well, as befitted the grandson of the Earl of Pembroke, and this house, Montpelier, white and imposing, stood as testimony to his taste.

The floor of fine English oak was highly polished and all about them in the hallway was evidence of a high appreciation of fine objects and furniture. At night, when the chandeliers were ablaze, they combined with the decoration to create an almost magical effect, which was enhanced by a steady stream of visitors whom Herbert seated, dined and entertained, his only complaint being that the business of playing host fatigued him.

Martha, having informed the visitors that her father was still at his toilet, offered to take her cousin to her room. As they disappeared up the grand open staircase, Nelson turned to the boy, whose mood had changed abruptly: with the females gone he was looking at Nelson with open affection, which was not reciprocated.

'I have to say to you, Josh, that you did not acquit yourself well with your cousin.' The boy's eyes dropped, and Nelson felt a bit of a scrub, especially since the child was not his to chastise. 'But she is near enough in age to you to understand, so no harm will be done.'

'Thank you, sir,' Josiah said, abashed.

Nelson could never be stern with a youngster for more than a few seconds, so he adopted a pleasanter tone. 'You look a bit peaked. How have you occupied yourself since I was last here?'

The boy gave an exaggerated sigh. 'At my books, sir, which is tedious, though Uncle Herbert has promised me that I shall have a pony if I do well.'

'You must do well, Josh,' Nelson insisted, 'otherwise I will not be able to ride out with you when I next sail this way.'

'*Will* you ride out with me?' Josiah Nisbet asked eagerly, taking Nelson's hand.

'Most assuredly, young sir. It will be a pleasure.'

The tug to demand attention was unnecessary, since Nelson was looking right into the boy's eyes, and smiling. 'Can I come aboard your ship again?'

'If time and your mother permit. Indeed, when you are a little older, perhaps you may spend a spell with us, take a trip around the islands as my guest, as your cousin Miss Parry has done.'

'Why sir, that would be splendid.'

'Where is your mother?'

'Off the island, sir, at present, visiting on Montserrat.'

'That is a great pity,' Nelson replied, his smile evaporating.

'She will be back before nightfall, Captain Nelson. It will please her that you have called. I know for certain that she esteems you.'

That made Nelson smile again. 'Does she, Josh?'

'Highly, sir.'

'Then that is gratifying to know.'

'Will you play with me?' the boy asked, tugging again.

'How can I refuse, when there is nothing to distract me?'

'If you run down the stairs, sir, the floor here provides the most satisfying slide.' Seeing the raised eyebrows, Josiah added, 'That is, if you can be brought to remove your footwear.'

'It's a good notion, but I fear for my stockings.'

'Tear them, if you must, sir. Uncle Herbert has pairs by the hundred.'

They were under one of the hall tables, quite oblivious to his presence when John Herbert appeared. He was a small round man, balding, with tidy features who cultivated his movements in the same way that he carefully modulated his voice. Fastidious of dress and behaviour, he had been caught out by the sudden arrival of his niece, forced to make a hastier than usual toilet. What he saw before him did little to restore his equanimity.

Josiah Nisbet was squealing mightily, emitting almost endlessly a high-pitched, childish yell. Nelson manoeuvred through the table legs, growling like some great jungle beast, grabbing him and snarling then letting the boy's foot slip through his fingers. The queue that tied back the Captain's hair had come loose, and so had his stock. But that was not what alarmed John Herbert most.

'Captain Nelson, sir. Do I find you my guest and in disarray?'

Their sudden awareness of the owner of the house had a great effect on both man and child. Josiah Nisbet scurried away, looking for a place to hide, while Nelson, caught only half dressed, sought to rise and fetched his head up hard against the top of the table with an audible thud.

'Mr Herbert,' he said. He crawled out, pulled himself to his feet and straightened his coat, stock and hair. 'Forgive my appearance. I could not refuse a request to play from a youngster. He is a sprightly fellow, as I'm sure you know.'

Herbert was looking at his feet, at the stockings that now had holes at the toes. He could scarcely credit the dishevelled apparition before him: this man sent shafts of fear running through all of the islands, with his accursed enforcement of the Navigation Acts threatening ruin to many. Herbert's fat face was a mask of controlled anger. 'The boy can be a damned nuisance, sir. I have often had occasion to remind my niece that, if she is absent, there is no one here at Montpelier to hold him in check.'

'He is no pest to me sir,' Nelson responded. 'Indeed, being a hearty young fellow I enjoy his company. He reminds me of my midshipmen.'

That brought a frown to Herbert's face, as though what Nelson had said edged the bounds of good manners. 'You enjoy the company of the young, I perceive.'

Nelson looked hard at Herbert, before deciding to treat his remark as an innocent one. 'Of course.'

'That, sir, is singular. I find children a bore. Those misguided modern nostrums as to their care are all stuff and nonsense. I was wet nursed, fostered and left to the care of my father's black servants and it has done me naught but good.' He continued to look at Nelson as, voice raised, he said, 'Josiah, if you have not breakfasted, do so. If you have, go to the schoolroom and await your tutor there. And do so in silence.'

He looked Nelson up and down once more. 'As for you, Captain, I think you need some privacy to compose yourself. That, and a new pair of stockings.'

'They have suffered, sir, but in a good cause.'

'The room you occupied on your last visit is empty. Might I recommend that? I will send someone to you with the means to effect a toilet.'

'Thank you, sir.'

He was moving away before another thought struck him. 'How did you find Miss Parry? Her parents tell me she is a joy, which I hope to establish as being true. I am, as you know, Nelson, plagued by female relations as it is. It would grieve me if she were to prove tiresome.'

'My acquaintance is of short duration, but I certainly found her an entertaining companion.'

The look on his host's face told Nelson that someone he found good company would not necessarily find the same favour with Herbert.

'You must join me at the breakfast table, and acquaint me with her nature,' said Herbert, in his troubled, fussy way. 'I am so often at a loss with the younger family members, fearing to open my mouth lest I offend some unknown sensibility.'

Nelson knew that to be the opposite of the truth and was confirmed in this opinion that evening just before dinner when, rum punch in hand, he sat in silence, while Herbert monopolised the conversation. It was the typical planter statement: about sugar, its price and position in the creation of a strong British nation; the way West Indian traders were ignored in the councils of government. He made the obligatory slash at the fools who would abolish slavery, with an aside to the effect that if they knew the black man better, they would be less forceful about freedoms.

Midshipman Hardy, lessons and duties completed, had arrived in the early afternoon, it being Nelson's policy to introduce his youngsters to polite society as often as possible. Thus he rarely went ashore without one in tow, or ordered them to join him when he was being entertained, in the hope that by example and exposure to non-naval company they would improve their manners, as well as the quality of their conversation.

Hardy now sat rigidly on a hard chair as Herbert droned on, bored by all of this, his stomach rumbling for the food he could smell already, his eye fixed on a glass he had long emptied and hoped to see refilled. But Herbert rarely even flicked an eye towards the youngster. To him the lad was just one of Nelson's foibles, one of that group of spotty midshipmen he always seemed to have in tow.

For all that conversational dominance, and his host's utter determination not to acknowledge Hardy, Nelson had to admit that John Herbert had a kindly streak. Most planters did, with their easy come, easy go attitude to money, which would have been seen as reckless in colder climes. They gave gifts with a freedom that staggered new arrivals, and expected nothing in return. Herbert was exceptional only in that the base of his wealth was so secure that he did not, unlike most sugar planters, run into debt on an annual basis.

'Ah! Fanny,' Herbert exclaimed, caught in mid-flow as his niece entered. Nelson had no idea that she had returned, but he was aware that he was happy to see her. 'You have come most carefully upon your hour, as the bard said. I must visit your aunt Sarah in her sick bed, so for the next quarter of an hour I would ask you to entertain Captain Nelson.'

Just then Josiah Nisbet appeared from behind his mother, which made his great uncle frown. He then glanced at the rigid midshipman. 'Josiah. You are much of an age with Mr . . .'

'Hardy, sir,' the midshipman replied, in his Devon lilt, his voice betraying the cracks, wheezes and strains of puberty. Spotty-faced, with thick lips that were designed never to smile, he was a big youth, broad, heavy jowled, and slow thinking.

'Quite. Take him out into the garden to work up an appetite.'

Thomas Masterman Hardy's face was a picture of self-control that amused his captain. Was that ire due to being thrown into the company of a five-year-old, or the host's failure to recognise his near starvation? Nelson reckoned on a combination of both.

'I will send a servant to sit with you and Captain Nelson, Fanny,' Herbert stated. He never forgot the need for propriety.

'Run along, Josh,' said Fanny. 'That is, if Mr Hardy does not mind?'

'Ma'am,' Hardy replied, in a strangled tone.

Her voice was soft and melodious, reminding Nelson instantly of Mary Moutray, an impression that was strengthened by the elegant way in which she moved towards the fireplace to pull a bell rope.

'I shall summon a servant myself, since I suspect that between the door of this room and another my dear uncle will have quite forgotten. Believe me his many cares make him unmindful. You only see the obliging host, never the much put upon plantation owner. Might I request for you another rum punch, Captain?'

'Thank you, no, Mrs Nisbet. I fear my head is swimming enough with what I have taken in.'

He was only aware then that he had been staring hard at her, giving a *double entendre* to his words that was unintentional. She blushed and dropped her eyes. He took the opportunity to admire the slim figure beneath the light muslin dress she wore.

'I must say I like your boy,' Nelson stammered.

She gave an engaging and musical laugh. 'Not half as much, sir, as he esteems you. I cannot thank you enough for the kindness you have shown him. He insists that you are the only person to whom he would issue an invitation if the right lay with him.'

'Then perhaps a turn in the garden, Mrs Nisbet, to see how he and Mr Hardy are faring.'

He held out an arm, which she accepted and they made their way out into the warm evening air.

CHAPTER 39

The garden was like the house, exquisite in the way each of the plants, shrubs and trees had been placed to provide gentle promenades. They soon came upon Josiah, who had persuaded Hardy to push him on the swing, the cry of 'Higher!' repeated several times. Nelson felt her tense beside him as Hardy responded positively to the request, sending her son so far in the air that the tension broke on the ropes.

'Have no fear for him, Mrs Nisbet,' he said reassuringly. 'Observe the grip of his hands. Josiah has clapped on like a true topman and nothing will dislodge him.'

'I cannot pretend to share your faith,' she replied with a slight gasp.

Nelson inclined his head towards hers, enjoying the gentle aroma of her lemon verbena scent. 'That is, dear lady, because you have never yourself been aloft in a gale of wind. I do assure you he is in no danger.'

The tiniest squeeze she administered to his forearm as she replied to that was as pleasing as the sentiment she expressed. 'I must accept your word, Captain. Josh wouldn't thank me for interfering in a situation that his father would have let stand. I cannot tell you how the boy needs a man to help raise him.'

'Mr Hardy,' he called, aware that the authority he was about to show was designed to impress.

'Sir,' the midshipman replied, standing to attention then skipping smartly sideways to avoid a blow from the returning swing.

'I would request that you ease up on young Master Josiah. Not that I believe him at any risk, but it does no good to worry his mother.'

'Mamma,' Josiah wailed.

'It is my injunction, young man,' Nelson said, coming closer. 'Though I expect your mother to be worried she has made no move to interfere.'

'Thank you, Captain,' said Fanny Nisbet, softly.

'I fancy you for a future sailor, sir,' Nelson continued, 'like Mr Hardy here. Should you be lucky enough to be accepted into a King's ship, I hope the first thing you would learn is that good manners towards the gentler sex are of primary importance. Is that not so, Mr Hardy?'

'Aye, aye, sir.'

A gong rang out from the hallway to announce dinner. Nelson escorted Josiah's mother back into the house, bowed to both Miss Martha and Miss Parry, then took up his place at Herbert's right hand, several places up the table from Fanny. But as he ate and listened to Herbert, he watched her carefully. Fanny Nisbet was younger than Mary Moutray and pale of complexion, a tribute to the care she took to stay out of the fierce Caribbean sun. She had fine, if quiet manners and a cultivated mode of speech, peppered with enough French to let any listener know of her fluency in the tongue. The linen napkins they were using had fine embroidery at the edges, all Fanny's handiwork, according to her uncle.

'I can't think how I would manage without her, Nelson,' he insisted, after both ladies and youngsters had withdrawn, and his guest had alluded to her capabilities. 'Montpelier is never run half as well in her absence, which I cannot help but notice as I am dragged away from some task to deal with domestic disputes. I swear she's dearer to me than my own daughter.'

'I believe I have already said I can see ample cause for your esteem.'

'Then, sir, we shall drink to the lady, you and I.'

'Most heartily, sir,' Nelson replied, his mind suddenly a turmoil of future possibilities. Fanny Nisbet was not only attractive as a person, she was in all respects sensible. And as a favoured niece of a rich man, the lack of funds that had restrained him from proposals of matrimony in the past might be removed.

Young, vibrant creatures were all very well, but a sober spouse might serve him better. He could see her as an admiral's

446

wife, able to entertain the very best of society with an ease born of long experience. And she had shown her fecundity in the production of a son already, so that his potent desire to be a father would be likely to be satisfied.

'You would not, however, stand in the way of Fanny's happiness, sir?'

'Of course not, Nelson,' Herbert replied, seeking to relight his pipe.

'Damn the man to perdition,' said Nelson, having read the latest letter from Admiral Sir Richard Hughes.

He was looking through the casement windows of his cabin to the packed anchorage of St John's harbour, Antigua, the busiest port in the Caribbean, scene of his own first landfall in these waters as a mere child. If he recalled it as welcoming then, it was less so now.

He threw the letter aside. It was a reminder from on high that regardless of Nelson's view on illicit trading into the islands, his commanding officer was not minded to act by ordering every ship in his squadron to intercept foreign vessels and seize their goods, nor to impound whatever they landed. The trouble was that Nelson had with him on his quarterdeck a whole posse of representatives from half a dozen islands, who wished to ensure that he followed the same course.

'Our visitors, sir?' asked Lieutenant Millar, anxiously.

In the silence that followed Millar reflected on the relations he had with Nelson, an intimacy he had never enjoyed with any other captain. No one had ever taken him into their confidence in a like manner, not just in a professional way but almost as a friend. Yet, while harbouring nothing but admiration for Nelson as a seaman, Millar often wondered if he knew what a fool of himself he made when he stepped ashore. This desire to take on the established order and turn it on its head was just one example. Right was only one of Nelson's motivations, the other being an almost visceral need for conflict, a trait often to be found in men of small physical stature. Sir Richard Hughes disgusted Nelson, with his fiddle-playing indolence and his fear of confrontation, a man who would agree with the last person he spoke to, who was very often his wife. Yet he had the prestige of his office, powerful friends and supporters at home, and was a person it was unwise to cross.

But that was as nothing to the Captain's romantic attachments, Millar mused. Nelson had offered him many confidences for he saw the premier as a good and compliant friend. And Millar knew he would back him, even if it blighted his own career. He spoke to remind him of the need to act. 'Sir!'

'Hold them for just another minute.'

'They have all said most forcefully that they have business to attend to, that they are civilians, and are not subject to the arbitrary power of the service.'

Nelson didn't reply. He wanted his minute to make up his mind as to what to do. His inclinations were to ignore the Admiral and continue. But for once he heeded the advice of others and, instead of charging like a bull at a gate, stopped to consider the consequences. Taking on Sir Richard meant taking on the entire West Indian establishment: planters, traders, corrupt officials and even a number of his fellow naval officers, happy to accept gifts in lieu of action. The only help he could muster was an authority three thousand miles away, which was scant comfort, especially since Admiralty support was not guaranteed. Against that, though, he was faced with withdrawal from a position that was, without doubt, right. No matter what opposition he could imagine, nothing was worth that. He looked into his premier's florid face, a man who had stood by King George when his countrymen wouldn't, and had lost everything because of it. How could he relent before such a man?

'Send them in, Millar.' He turned to Lepée, who was already glassy-eyed and it was only ten of the clock. 'Start pouring, man. When they hear what I have to say to them they'll need strong liquor to stay upright.'

It was a noisy, quarrelsome group who entered the great cabin of *Boreas*, yet they were overly polite in the way they gave precedence to each other, as if to underline to this upstart naval fellow that they were all men of position. Nelson looked hard for his host from Nevis, and was relieved to see that Herbert wasn't present. He stood to greet them, indicating that Lepée was standing by with refreshments, and waited until they all had a glass in their hands before raising his own. 'Gentlemen, the King!'

'The King,' they replied in unison, drinking and talking noisily to each other. To their rear Lepée joined in the toast and downed another glass.

'Who is our anointed Sovereign, gentleman,' Nelson continued. 'He has, through his ministers, instituted a series of laws known as the Navigation Acts.' That rendered the group silent and wary. 'You know what these are so I won't bore you with repetition. What I will say is this. That a *laissez faire* attitude to the landing of illicit cargoes falls without those laws. I will therefore see it as my duty to clap a stopper on such activity. From now on any foreign vessel claiming the need to land a cargo, may do so.'

That made a few, the more foolish ones, nod. Other wiser minds were staring at him as though he was some kind of animal to hunt. 'That cargo will be seized by His Majesty's customs officials and destroyed. It will *not* be sold through the back door. Any customs officer colluding in such an act will end up in my cable tier, there to repent his sins.'

The cabin erupted, each man shouting in an attempt to overcome his neighbour. Hughes was mentioned somewhere in that cacophony, as were justice, poverty, local rights and the inadvisability of such high-handed tactics. Nelson stood in the face of this barrage, thinking it worse than cannon fire, until it began to subside.

'The law rules in these islands, as elsewhere. If you wish it changed I suggest that my cabin is not the place to make your representations.'

'You will regret this, Captain!' shouted one voice, exciting a general murmur of agreement.

'How can I, sir, regret doing what is right?'

'I cannot do other than agree with you, Captain Nelson,' said John Herbert, appraised of what had happened, though surprised to receive another visit so soon from Nelson, 'though it is like to cost me dear.'

They were walking in his gardens again, with Fanny Nisbet and Midshipman Andrews several paces to the rear, Josiah

449

between them holding a hand of each. A sudden laugh from George Andrews caused the face of the boy's sister to come to Nelson's mind, which he suppressed quickly and guiltily. How long ago that seemed, St Omer and the beautiful Kate, yet it was only eighteen months.

'I am grateful for that, sir,' Nelson said, aware that Herbert was expecting a reply.

Herbert stopped, frowning, closing the gap between themselves and those bringing up the rear. 'But you will struggle, Nelson, to persuade others of the rightness of what you do. You fail to understand the nature of the beast you attempt to control. As men they suffer from all the follies and vanities that are prevalent. They make vast sums after the harvest, yet spend even more to display the extent of their wealth. Every year most are obliged to mortgage their land to find the money to carry out planting, which they pay back from their crop before frittering the residue on outdoing each other once more. They drink heavily, gamble to excess and purchase luxuries with an abandon that would shame a sultan.'

'You do not fall into that trap, sir,' Nelson replied, with some feeling.

'I have better land and I have husbanded my resources when times are lean. I must say, most of my fellow sugar planters do the opposite.'

'I cannot lay aside the law to oblige the profligate.'

'No. But do not think for one moment that reason will affect their opinions.'

The group behind had caught up and, to Herbert's annoyance, Nelson offered his hand in place of Andrews's to swing young Josiah. He hadn't finished lecturing his guest about the ways of the plantation fraternity.

'I fear you have vexed my uncle, sir,' said Fanny. Andrews had moved on, as politeness demanded, to walk beside Herbert. 'You leave him in the company of enthusiastic youth, in which he finds scant comfort.'

'I would not upset him for the world, Mrs Nisbet, only for you.'

That reply lost some of its gallantry through Josiah's insistence on continued swinging. But the look in the grey eyes told Nelson he had struck home, that if he chose to pay attention to her it wouldn't be unwelcome. They chatted happily, assessing each other's antecedents in a way that caused no offence. He mentioned his Walpole relations and his father's clerical lineage, while she alluded to her connection to the Scottish Earldom of Moray. Her late husband, from a good Ayrshire family, had qualified as a doctor, though he found practice in Nevis hard due to his propensity to suffer from sunstroke.

Their sparring reassured her suitor. Nelson knew that she would not have volunteered such information without at least a passing interest in some future connection between them.

Lieutenant Ralph Millar put as much emphasis as he could into his latest set of objections, though it signified little to the recipient, his captain, lost as he was in the throes of yet another romantic attachment.

'Sir, how can you even consider such matters when you are confined to your ship and in danger of being clapped in gaol should you step ashore?'

To Millar's mind, Nelson replied like a spoilt child. 'There is a lady on Nevis to whom I can only communicate by letter, while I have to stay here in St John's harbour to ensure that these damned planters do not humbug me with the first enterprising American trader.'

His premier wanted to mention Mary Moutray, not six months gone from the islands, who had so affected his captain that he had claimed to be unable to breathe. But then he recalled the way Nelson had talked about Kate Andrews, when they had first become close enough to share intimacies. And he had heard from others, mutual acquaintances, of his attachment to the Saunders girl in Québec. He just had to conclude that his commanding officer was an incurable romantic, a slave to his passions, inclined to fall in love at the drop of a hat, never having succeeded enough in any of his suits to be exposed to the unhappy consequences of his actions.

The troubles he had now outweighed anything he had faced before, with the entire Leeward Islands establishment combining to sue him in their own courts for the cost incurred in his enforcement of the Navigation Acts. They claimed the loss of £100,000, and demanded that Nelson make redress. Millar had offered to take on some of the responsibility, even though he was as poor as his captain, only to be rebuffed with a reminder that Nelson's rank demanded that it was he who had to face them down.

How he was going to do that, with few means, wasn't clear. He couldn't afford the lawyers necessary to defend himself and was at present confined to *Boreas* for fear of arrest if he stepped ashore. Yet with all that hanging over his head it was hard enough to get him even to consider the subject, so taken was he with the idea of matrimony and the occupants of Montpelier.

'Herbert is a man after my own heart, Millar, able to go against the herd. He offered to post bail for me to the value of ten thousand pounds. Ain't that the finest thing?'

'Of course, sir,' said Millar, who had met Herbert and found him a fussy old goat. 'But does that mean he sees you as a future relative by marriage?'

Nelson frowned. 'I cannot read him. One minute he is all encouragement, the next as cool as a glacier. I have no real certainty that he is not toying with me.'

Millar had another vision of the wistful Mary Moutray. 'As long as the lady is not toying with you.'

Nelson put his head in his hands. 'I cannot believe she is, though I admit that my letters have yet to receive a reply.'

'Have you asked for one?'

Nelson fixed Millar with a petulant stare. 'I don't see the need.'

Millar might be half the sailor Nelson was, but when it came to the fair sex he had a better idea of procedure. He tried to keep his exasperation out of his voice. 'She is a widow, sir, dependent on her uncle, who is stiff when it comes to doing what he perceives to be right, and mindful of the opinion of others. She cannot volunteer herself to you without you requesting it.'

Nelson's blue eyes opened wide with revelation, though inwardly he felt foolish. 'I never saw that, Millar. How could I be so blind?'

His premier denied himself the pleasure of telling him that in matters of the heart his blindness was as complete as it was when it came to his servant. Millar had often hinted that Nelson should remove Lepée, who grew more drunk and less respectful in equal measure. Nelson couldn't see that the man who had nursed him down the San Juan river was not the same person now. He was a thieving rogue and rude with it. But this was no time to ruminate on that: there were more pressing matters to attend to.

'That, at least, you can repair, sir, but I beg you to allow yourself time. The most pressing thing is to see off this suit from the planters.'

'The most pressing thing is for you to take over here, Millar, while I have Giddings get the cutter rigged and head for Nevis.'

'Nevis?'

Again Nelson showed the petulance of a man who hated to be thwarted. 'How can I be idle in such a matter?'

'You'll end up in a debtor's cell.'

Nelson brightened then, looking for all the world like a mischievous boy. 'Only if they know I am ashore. But since I shall depart and return in the dark, I shall confound them.'

John Herbert loved to worry and he did not confine his anxieties to his own cares. With Captain Horatio Nelson a frequent visitor in the last two months he had taken on the burden of his concerns too, though it didn't take precedence over the care of his garden, which they were, at that moment, walking through. 'It must be another several weeks yet, Nelson, before you can hope for any reply from London.'

Nelson nodded agreement, though the subject bored him and he did not want to talk about it. He half suspected that Herbert had deliberately brought it up to avoid engaging in the one his visitor desired. It had been a strange interlude, these last few months, with the planters huffing and puffing yet fearful to go too far until Nelson heard from the Admiralty, a message they feared might praise his high-handed actions.

Even more odd was the way he had to skulk about in his cutter, leaving ship and returning in the dark, sneaking ashore on Nevis and making his way to Montpelier in secret. But if things had gone badly on water, they could be said to have progressed on dry land. He was far from having an arrangement with Fanny Nisbet, but enough had been imparted in a dozen meetings and over fifty letters to convince him that a formal request for her hand in marriage would not founder on an objection from that quarter. He was desperate to pin down Herbert, who was eel-like in his determination to avoid being ensnared.

Now good manners overrode Nelson's impatience and forced him to reply. He acknowledged the truth of what Herbert had said. They talked of Admiral Hughes, due to be relieved, too taken with imminent departure to bother with his second-in-command.

'He is determined to get away before the hurricane season makes it too dangerous. I think he's only awaiting the arrival of Prince William.'

At that name Herbert lifted his head. 'You know the King's son, do you not?'

This was a question he had asked before. The prospect of royalty being present in the islands excited him. But that was not what animated Nelson, and his exasperation was evident in his voice. 'You may recall me saying I served with him in Lord Hood's fleet during the American War. I—'

'He will come here, won't he, Nelson?

Nelson looked away for a second so that his sigh would not be obvious. 'Nevis is high on the list of places His Royal Highness must visit. Naturally, as president of the council, the task of greeting him will fall to you.'

An already puffed chest swelled even more. 'Most satisfactory.'

'I have,' Nelson said nervously, 'come here upon another matter. That which I wrote to you about.'

'Quite,' Herbert replied, noncommittally, pausing to examine a brightly coloured flower.

Exasperation finally broke the bonds of politeness, and Nelson spoke quite sharply. 'Do my attentions to your niece offend you?'

'Never, Captain Nelson,' Herbert said calmly, still fingering his flower. 'As a man I esteem you, though I would never allow personal taste to interfere with my duties as the head of the family. Your own family connections raise you to the rank of suitor, regardless of my opinions.'

'I must advise you, sir, that I am poor as a church mouse.'

Herbert laughed. 'Never fear, sir. I have seen many an officer arrive out here penniless, only to return home as rich as Croesus.'

'That would apply only in wartime. I am obliged, before pressing forward in any way, to ask of Mrs Nisbet's circumstances.'

Herbert's small eyes were on him. 'She hasn't a penny to her name, sir.'

Nelson felt his chest constrict and he struggled to hide the shock. This news flew in the face of all that he had observed of her here at Montpelier. Frances Nisbet played the hostess to such perfection, in this grand mansion on an island crowned with wealth, that the idea that she had no money of her own was ridiculous.

'And her expectations?' he asked, breath held.

Herbert waved an airy hand. 'Without my good offices she has none.'

For the first time they locked eyes. 'Then I must ask you, sir, if you intend to endow her?'

Herbert held the stare. 'And I must ask if you are intent on pressing your suit.'

Nelson had to hesitate then, faced by a Rubicon that, once crossed, would provide no retreat. 'I have expressed certain sentiments to the lady by letter, Mr Herbert, that make the subject of income delicate.'

The words were burning in his brain: that he would as happily occupy with her a cottage as a palace; that esteem founded on sound reasons was more to him than money. He was forced by these surprising revelations to ask if such statements were true. But as he conjured up a vision of wedded bliss, of young Josiah running riot in some well tended cottage garden, he was happy to acknowledge the warmth of his feelings.

Besides, he was convinced that Herbert was just being coy, a wise move for a man who, for all his display of generosity, had had the sense to be careful of his money. He esteemed his niece,

455

that was certain, rarely missing an opportunity to praise her. When the time came to show how much he cared, Nelson was sure that his bounteous purse would be loosened.

'I have set my heart on a course of action, sir, from which I would be desperately disappointed to be deflected.'

Herbert nodded sagely, forcing his chin back into his chest. 'You propose to take on a heavy burden. And I propose to think on the matter if that answer satisfies you.'

'Only a wedding will satisfy me, sir.'

'So ardent, Nelson, so damned ardent.'

Herbert nearly blurted out his concern then; that this suitor was a man who made trouble wherever he went, and none of Herbert's fellow planters would take kindly to him being welcomed into the Montpelier household. Yet clearly Fanny was smitten. He had heard that Nelson was as mercurial in a fight as he was as a suitor, as determined to succeed professionally as he was to dun him out of a dowry. And what then? He had just as likely get his head blown off in some action and leave him, John Herbert, to take on the burden of a niece who had been widowed twice.

'I have told you, sir,' he said, 'these are matters to be thought on.'

In the face of that Nelson had to be content.

CHAPTER 40

1786

Mary Cadogan's relations with Charles Greville were based on one principle: he was the master and she, though of the superior sort, was his servant. It was an arrangement she worked hard to keep in place, never assuming as Emma's mother any prerogative that didn't come naturally to her through her position. Never once did she presume to comment on their relationship, content to accept that, despite occasional disputes, it satisfied something for both parties. In so much as he was capable of affection Greville cherished her daughter. Emma, emotional always, veered between submissive love and occasional bouts of intense fury, but on the whole seemed content with her lot.

That Emma loved him mystified her mother, but she had seen too many unlikely couplings in her varied life to indulge in any deep reasoning. When he was absent Emma praised Greville to the skies, quite forgetting that her mother saw nearly as much of the man. Even the pain of Little Emma's removal, which had come closest to breaking their connection, faded within weeks of the child's departure, leaving an atmosphere once more calm, as though she had never been a resident.

Mary Cadogan was too wise to try to comprehend the ways of love. The most inappropriate pairing often lasted longest and perhaps this was one of them. Her interest was to keep them in the house, in relative comfort, to satisfy the fussy Greville and smooth the odd bouts of rebellion in her daughter. She and Greville talked often, of course, since the maintenance of the house required it. There were menus to discuss, guests to accommodate as well as the mundane costs and quality of the keeping of the house.

No meeting was an occasion for comfort. Greville lacked that ease of manner with servants that made for a simple exchange. He tended to bark his enquiries rather than speak them. He worried over the smallest amounts of money but insisted that when he entertained nothing should be left aside that his guests had a right to expect from a host.

He was constantly on the cusp of ruin, speculating here and dealing there to keep himself and his way of living afloat. The building of a collection for future sale and keeping Emma Hart ate up money that had to come from somewhere. The annual five hundred pounds allowance from his father didn't go far, so he tried to make up the shortfall by dealing in pictures, acting as his uncle's agent, and accepting commissions to act for others. The rental of his house in Portman Square failed to produce the required income, leading to a sale, which resulted in losses once he had paid the builders.

His endless search for a rich wife was no secret, though it was never openly discussed. Nor was it a cause for much anxiety. If Greville did land an heiress the match would be for money, not love. It was tacitly accepted that success was not intended to affect the arrangements at Edgware Road. They would continue, albeit without the permanent presence of the master.

So Charles Greville existed in a financial and social circle whose ends couldn't meet. But his housekeeper, a clever woman, manipulated his moods and her expenses in an attempt to satisfy both his purse and his aspirations. The knowledge that this was so did little to temper his moods at their weekly meetings.

Mary Cadogan sensed that this interview was to be different when Greville invited her to sit. It was not the normal day for their perusal of the accounts and the commitments for the coming week; that had already taken place. And he was nervous rather than cranky, fiddling with papers or moving the candles, occasionally jumping up to poke the fire before throwing himself back on to his chair. The opening remarks had the general quality of gossip, as if he was in some doubt as to how to proceed.

'Tell me, Mrs Cadogan, what did you think of my uncle William?'

'A fine gentleman, sir.'

She meant it, but considered it a daft question. How could she say any different? Uncle William, as both Greville and Emma called him, had been a breath of fresh air in the house, with his worldly manners, ready wit and lack of side. He was a man who found the lower orders easy company, was of the type to make them feel comfortable attending on him – that evidenced by the genuine tears that had accompanied his departure. Yet she had heard his name damned only two days previously on receipt of his latest letter by the very nephew who claimed to esteem him most.

'It seemed to me that Emma was exceedingly fond of him.'

'She was and still is, sir.'

'Has she spoken to you of this?'

He had turned away to poke the fire again, but his voice gave a lie to the impression he was trying to create, that the question was of little import.

'Emma talks of him often, sir, to you as well as me, I'll wager. He was kindness itself and not above an excess of flattery to please her. It wouldn't be going too far to say she misses him. We all do in the house, from scullery to attic.'

'What you term flattery was nothing more than the plain truth, Mrs Cadogan. My uncle regarded your daughter in the highest possible light, not only for her beauty but for her manner and her accomplishments.'

Mary Cadogan wanted to say that that was obvious, as obvious as the attentions paid to Emma by everyone Greville introduced her to. How many times had he come back from some event railing against some poltroon for his forwardness? Mary Cadogan reckoned that through usage, Greville had lost sight of what a prize he had captured.

'It is pleasing as her mother to hear that, sir.'

'I have arranged for Emma to visit him in Naples,' Greville said abruptly, sending up a shower of bright orange sparks as he poked at the coals. 'Naturally I would like you to accompany her.'

The obvious question to follow that was a request to know

what he was going to do, since there was no 'we' in the proposal. But that was one she felt it would be unwise to ask. Mary Cadogan knew, or at least formed judgements on, more than Charles Greville imagined. It was one of the advantages of being a servant that you were free to observe what others involved in such exchanges failed to see: the pitch of a voice, the undertones of a statement, the look the listener couldn't see were all objects of acute interest to a person rarely included in the conversation.

Little could be hidden from someone who occupied and supervised the house. It was her task to take in and pay for the post, so even if the contents of any letter were unknown to her, the name and location of the correspondent were not. If a verbal message came when the master was absent it fell to her to take it. With her daughter the mistress of the house, Mary Cadogan had more than a passing interest in the relationship between her and Greville. Having suffered so many changes in her life she was attuned to the atmosphere that preceded a shift. And right now that extra sense was at full stretch.

'I must go to Edinburgh for six months,' Greville said finally, a slight growl in his tone, evidence to Mary Cadogan that he had been waiting for her to ask. He threw the poker at the fire and himself into his chair. 'I had considered taking Emma with me, but it won't answer. Nor, as I'm sure you will agree, would leaving her here.'

Again Mary Cadogan didn't respond. There was a sniff of finality in the way he was speaking. Was Greville the type to cast Emma out like Uppark Harry before him? A vision of her and her daughter on the street again was hard to keep out of her mind.

'Sir William has written to say he is happy to accept you both into his household until I can join you.' There was a vague wave of the hand. 'Some time in September or October, I would say.'

It wasn't that which had caused the shouted goddamns she heard from the outside of the parlour door. The invitation from Sir William that the trio of nephew, mistress and mother should visit Naples had been made often in this very room.

'You have told Emma this?'

'No,' he said slowly. 'I fear that after our last parting, as well as the loss of Little Emma, she will take it badly.'

With another man it might have been easy to accept his every word at face value, but not with Greville. He surely didn't want her to tell her daughter of his plans. That was a task he could not pass to another. So why tell her first? There would be scenes for sure, tantrums from Emma, the kind of tears and wailing that wouldn't go amiss in a stage tragedy.

'I want her to be happy, Mrs Cadogan. I hope you know that.'

'I do, sir,' she replied. Once more, what else could she say?

'If I do anything, I do it for her own sake.'

The word 'liar' was in her mind but not on her lips as he continued, forced jollity evident in his voice, his words jumbled. 'My uncle has painted such an enchanting picture of Naples, I am afire to see the place. Emma will share a similar excitement, I'm sure, and he is so fond of her and she of him, they are so very easy in each other's company, that the visit is bound to be a success. I must in truth tell you I am already suffering pangs of both loss and jealousy.'

'For six months?'

'Quite,' he replied, avoiding her eye. Then, warming to his theme, he spoke with calculated enthusiasm. 'Think of it. He will be able to take her to dig for his treasures. She has often said she would enjoy that. And Naples is not London. My uncle remarked on the ease of manners. I daresay Emma will meet the very cream of Neapolitan society.'

'That will be very nice,' Mary Cadogan replied, in a voice that earned her a sharp look.

'You do not agree?'

'Why, sir,' conjuring up an expression of false innocence, 'whatever gave you that idea?'

'I have arranged for a fellow to accompany you, David Gifford, a pupil of Romney, who is charged to visit Rome to improve his skills. He has French and Italian, so will be useful.'

So Romney knows, Mary Cadogan thought, and this pupil knows. It must be that uncle William knows. How come Emma don't know?

There was something afoot that she couldn't fathom right off. But it was there and a clear mind was needed to discern it.

She was tempted to challenge him, to demand outright what he was up to. But there was no point. He wouldn't oblige her with the truth.

'When do you intend to tell Emma, sir?'

That made him look exceedingly uncomfortable, causing him suddenly to shift his body in the chair as though he itched all over. 'As soon as she returns from her singing lesson.'

'Would I be permitted to enquire how far your plans are advanced, sir?'

That made him shoot out of the chair again, so that he could turn his back and avoid her eye. 'The decision is made.'

'And when would you be expecting us to travel?'

Another vague wave, as though that part of what must occur was a fresh thought. 'The middle of the month.'

'No more'n a week away.'

'Matters have come to a head in less time than I allowed.'

'Best prepare for a squall then, sir, for my Emma will not take kindly to your notion.'

'I cannot see why,' he insisted, more to convince himself than her. 'Naples, in the company of a man she is fond of. It's an exotic place, you know, very exotic. Emma has been entranced to hear my uncle describe it. I've seen the look in her eye when he tells his tales. I cannot see how it can fail to appeal to her sense of adventure.'

'Change is never as welcome to those doing it as it is to them that proposes.'

In the end, Mary Cadogan was surprised by the meek way in which Emma reacted to news of the arrangements. Perhaps Greville had persuaded her that there was some advantage in his proposals, benefits he had not vouchsafed to herself. Also, she knew that Greville had cowed Emma's spirit somewhat, but only realised now how much. An earlier Emma would have raised Cain at his plans and rightly so. Mary Cadogan, for all the strictures she herself had employed with her daughter, wasn't sure that she was as fond of this humble apparition as she was of the old contrary one.

Since a storm-tossed crossing and that first night in the inn at Montreuil, the journey had represented six weeks of sights, sounds and smells larded with discomfort and misery. The latter, in Emma's case, stemmed from the need for a six-month parting between her and the man she loved. For her mother it was the need to listen to the endless expectations her daughter espoused that Greville would fly to her side long before the due period was complete.

That served to keep David Gifford at bay. He was a handsome young man, with an enthusiasm for art so profound it could be wearing. And charged with looking after Emma, he didn't see his responsibility as any bar to an attempt at seduction. Neither did the object of his desire entirely accept the need to discourage him. But however far he proceeded Gifford ran into the wall of affection Emma carried for the man who had paid his passage.

Off the subject of art Emma did find Gifford attractive. He had an open, honest face, made engaging conversation, and had a pealing, infectious laugh. To flirt with him would have been easy, yet the determination to be good overrode that; Emma needed to prove to her absent lover that her attachment to him was total, that she knew what Greville required and was determined to abide by the principles he had laid down. She must avoid becoming the object of gossip or speculation both on the journey and in Naples.

She was convinced that Greville was putting her through some form of test, an extended parting in what would be seductive society. The cost of failure was one she dreaded so much that it was pushed to the back of her mind. The lack of someone to confide in was a burden: she needed a person in whom she could trust and to whom she might relate the happy memories that raised her spirits. Her mother was no good in that respect: she didn't like Greville, much as she tried to disguise it. All she saw was his public face, serious and a bit self-righteous, which exasperated Emma as much as anyone.

Mary never saw the private Charles, the person on the other side of that bedchamber door, who was capable of being boyish, light-hearted and wickedly funny, a gentle but potent lover still intent on improving Emma's mind as well as enjoying her body. Alone, provided she had not upset him in some way, his demeanour changed, and he became the man that Emma so much wanted to please. The thought that she would, by some inadvertent act, cause Greville to break from her filled her with apprehension.

Besides memory and inner fears, there was the futile attempt to avoid discomfort on the coach, which bucked and rattled across roads too rough for its springs. Stops were frequent, the cacophony of languages barely comprehensible even to Gifford, who spoke them. This left Emma and her mother adrift and helpless when he was absent, seemingly intent on searching every church, monastic building or nearby chateau for a work of art. The simplest request without him, the water to wash, a pan to warm a bed, drink, food, gave cause for an elaborate mime. Emma, never having feared the need to perform, overcame this, and by the time they reached the Italian border she excelled in her ability to garner proper attention without a word being exchanged.

The smells were not all foreign: the odour of an open sewer, a French barnyard or cow stall was the same as it was in England, likewise rain on grass, though the further south they travelled the more that turned to the unfamiliar smell of baked earth. Mary Cadogan, not deeply religious, maintained that the locals, all the way from Picardy to Calabria, gave off the stench of Papist heathens. Every inn they stopped at on the well-travelled route saw a battle over price and what was provided for coin expended, clean linen, always at a premium – especially in the Italian inns – and some way of dealing with the fleas that infested the horsehair mattresses.

Emma found the sights astounding: Paris, with its teeming narrow streets and rookeries cheek by jowl with the great aristocratic hotels, the vast expanse of Versailles, teeming with those dependent on the King's favour; great cathedrals in towns that seemed too small for their towering campaniles. The vineyards of Burgundy, stretching away on red-soiled hillsides, became real villages with real people instead of half-remembered names from some dusty bottle on Greville's table. In this part of the world towns, even a city like Lyon, were built on the tops of hills, what buildings stood now, Gifford explained, resting on what had once been the great hill forts of a Celtic

France subdued by Julius Caesar. They rose to the Alpine pass at Mont Cenis in tolerable heat, alongside a rushing torrent of icy water that could be gathered to cool the brow and spent nights in inns where the air was crisp and clear. There was ample snow still left at the peak of the route, which had the whole coach party engaged in a snowball fight.

Little pleasure was afforded in the steep drop down to the Lombardy plain, a cauldron even in the late spring that left the party near ill with heat exhaustion. Turin heralded a two-day delay while Gifford, with Emma on his arm, scoured the ducal palaces, likewise in Genoa, Lucca, Parma and the Medici fortresses in Florence, she turning heads with the radiance of her beauty and her smile.

Gifford left them in Rome, and Emma and her mother, now seasoned travellers, continued south on their own, staying in inns on the Via Latina where the level of filth increased as the latitude fell. A full month of travel in a coach gives such an existence an air of permanence: it comes to seem like a natural state instead of an uncommon one. Beside that was the notion that it was here in Naples that Emma risked the kind of gaffe that, reported to Greville, might alter their relationship. Was Sir William Hamilton her friend, as he had appeared in London, or an uncle so conscious of his nephew's wishes that he would act for him, not her? As a consequence of these thoughts Emma had mixed feelings when the end of the journey arrived.

Sir William was there with his servants to greet them as the coach, having struggled up the steep hill, turned into the open gates of the Palazzo Sessa, his handsome face and kind smile helping to wash away some of the recent, less pleasant memories. The sunlight, till then a glare to be avoided, mellowed to a welcome choice between heat and shadow.

'My dear Emma,' he said, in his familiar baritone, as he bent to kiss her hand, 'welcome to my meagre lodgings.'

Mary Cadogan was forced to mind her manners when he turned to greet her, realising that the look on her face was less than friendly – a fact attested to by the alteration in Sir William's own expression. After near six weeks of speculation she found herself looking at their host as if the answer to all her disquiet lay in his face. A curtsy took that out of view, and it was a countenance of due deference that appeared as he raised her up. 'Mrs Cadogan, how good of you to accompany your daughter. I know only too well the discomforts of the journey. Allow me to commend you for being so intrepid as to undertake it.'

Greeted with such easy familiarity Emma felt herself relax. How could good, kind Sir William ever be a threat to her position with Greville? He took her hand and escorted her up the broad staircase to his first-floor apartments, a spacious residence full of light and shade, littered with vases, ampoules and archaic statues set off by motes of dust hanging in the sunbeams. The floors shone with the beeswax, and the view from the windows, across the Bay of Naples to the distant offshore islands, took Emma's breath away.

'This,' Sir William said, 'will be your private drawing room. There is a comfortable apartment for you, Mrs Cadogan, which adjoins the music room. The bedchamber I have made ready for Emma is across from that, likewise overlooking the bay.'

If he knew how closely Mary Cadogan was examining him, he gave no sign, and it was a moot point as to whether the thoughts she harboured would have pleased or disturbed him. Now there was a solicitous air about the Chevalier quite at odds with his previous persona. He seemed too much the supplicant. Perhaps it was the charge of being host instead of guest, or even Emma's mood. She had mentioned Greville when they came through the gates and her mother wondered, for all her daughter's smiles and gracious acceptance, if that thought was still with her.

'You will find much to occupy you, my dear,' Sir William continued, addressing Emma. 'I have engaged both a music and a singing teacher to continue the lessons you had in London. Since you are to be here for some time I have also taken the liberty of asking a few of my friends to converse with you in the language. That, I find, is the best way to learn.'

'I must write to Charles, to tell him of our arrival,' said Emma, brightly.

Sir William seemed rather crestfallen as he pointed to a set of double doors and said, 'The materials you require are on the escritoire in the music room.'

'Thank you.'

Emma headed for the doors, which were opened and closed behind her by one of the servants. Only then did Sir William give Mary Cadogan any real attention. And when he spoke to her, the tenderness he had shown Emma slipped somewhat, to be replaced by a hurt tone. 'A letter to Charles could surely wait awhile.'

'Not for a second, Sir William. Scarce an hour has passed since we departed London that he was not mentioned.'

He waved a hand towards the large windows, and the Bay of Naples beyond, gleaming in the sunlight. 'This generally gives people pause. Their arrival in Naples and first sight of the view is held to be an occasion to remember.'

'There's little doubt she would rather spend any occasion with your nephew than here, pretty aspects notwithstanding.'

The expression on the Chevalier's face was a mixture of perplexity and disappointment. Quite clearly he had built up to the moment of arrival, only to find his hopes dashed by Emma's behaviour. But that only lasted a second or two, his cheery air returning, although it was probably a mask. His hands waved elegantly once more towards the blue bay. 'She will come to love those pretty aspects, Mrs Cadogan, as much as I do, I am sure of it.'

The temptation to issue a challenge, a demand to be let into whatever was going on, was as strong as it had been when she had talked to Greville. But Mary Cadogan resisted it. Happen it would emerge naturally. If not, she would ask in time, once Emma had settled in and she had her own feet well under the table. She had noticed that the Chevalier's servants spoke good English. Quizzing them might produce something. Servants always knew what was going on.

Sir William Hamilton was an easy man to admire. He knew that Emma thrived in company, and made every effort to ensure that she was never without it. Into the apartments came an endless stream of visitors to add to the teachers. Count This and Baron That, visitors from home as well as half the countries of Europe, courtiers, doctors, writers, scientific thinkers and artists, who begged to be allowed to paint her. All, whatever their speciality, paid court to her, which was hardly surprising since her radiant beauty was enhanced by the sunlight and warmth of the city, yet never did anyone go beyond the bounds of proper behaviour, for which Emma was grateful.

Then there was the Chevalier himself, dancing on her as much attendance as his duties would allow. The residence of the King was close to the Palazzo Sessa; a short walk away the Palazzo Reale hugged the shoreline. The journey there and back was one he made several times a day, so ensuring that his beautiful guest was rarely, if ever, alone.

Being an ambassador required frequent attendance on the King, even more upon his wife, Queen Maria Carolina. She was the daughter of the formidable Maria Theresa of Austria, sister to the French Queen Marie Antoinette. Ferdinand, her husband, was a simple oaf, though in truth his lack of dignity was not entirely his fault. When his eldest brother had gone mad it was decided that education of any sort might have a deleterious effect on the unformed mind of this future sovereign. So, instead of being taught those things necessary to run a kingdom, martial skills, financial acumen, shrewd evaluation of advice given and a degree of manners, he had been left to his own devices and passions. The centre of these was hunting, both wild animals and ladies of the court, closely followed by an appetite that bordered on gluttony.

Tall and imposing, with a direct demeanour, he looked at a distance every inch the King. Close to, the corpulence was less impressive, the vacuous look in the eye and the lack of intellect obvious. He was a buffoon, but an amiable one, a combination that had great appeal to his fickle subjects. They saw a man who looked like a monarch and behaved like a peasant, a fellow who was not above relieving himself over the walls of his various palaces, spraying his subjects with a generous dose of royal piss.

Emma was fascinated by the regal goings-on. The Queen was as much an object of interest as her husband: mother of a dozen children, the voice of power on the Royal Council, the real ruler of the Kingdom of the Two Sicilies. When he spoke of her Sir William praised her sharp mind and deep intellect, her sense of duty and purpose, as well as her devotion to her husband. This not only saw her forever brought to the delivery couch, but extended to ensuring that when he strayed, which he did often, the women she chose for him were either poor and clean, or well born and already married, so of no risk to her position.

Emma's mother watched all of this with an acute eye and, when she was reasonably certain of her suspicions, on a day when Emma was out of the Palazzo Sessa visiting a dressmaker, asked the Chevalier if she could have words with him.

CHAPTER 41

The meeting took place in Sir William's apartments, which were crammed with the results of his digging and his purchases. It was difficult to move without knocking over some valuable object or bumping into a case full of antique coinage. Seated, Sir William enquired as to what she required.

'Little, sir, 'cept enlightenment. I would like to know, Sir William, why there's not a soul in the town who does not, by look and deed, think my Emma your mistress.' Mary Cadogan received a dismissive wave. The air of the professional diplomat was more obvious in this setting: the bland face and slight smile meant to convey friendship without commitment, the slow use of the hands to ward off anything unpleasant. 'And I has the further impression that such an opinion has been held since we arrived here three months past.'

'Idle tongues, madam. Neapolitans love to gossip.'

'They were not the source, sir, since I've yet to comprehend the *lingua*.'

Sir William responded, in a bluff manner, 'Our English visitors are equally afflicted with that particular disease, Mrs Cadogan. They chatter and they write letters home, few of which contain a single grain of truth. It is the bane of my existence mollifying both a court and a ministry that choose to give their ravings credence.'

'I asked for this interview, sir, with the intention of speaking plain. Not gossip or ravings but open, and I wish to know if in doing so I will be indulged with the true state of things.'

He didn't reply immediately. Instead, he held her gaze for several seconds, wondering whether to allow her to proceed or to point out politely that she did not have the right to challenge him. To open himself to her scrutiny would lead to certain admissions; one being that things were not proceeding as had been hoped. Could he face that?

Sir William thought Mary Cadogan a good woman, a beauty herself once, though not in comparison with Emma. In any exchanges they had had he had been happy to acknowledge her good sense, as well as the wry wit that never exceeded the bounds of her position. She had even managed to impress his irascible nephew. Here, in his establishment, she had fitted seamlessly into the domestic arrangements, undertaking tasks his own servants were happy to surrender, never interfering in duties that didn't concern her.

'It would grieve me to be treated as just a stupid woman.'

'And I, madam, would be a fool to do that, for you are very far from it.'

'Then I'd be obliged if you would tell me what is going on, sir, not that I ain't formed a notion of my own.'

'I'd be interested to hear it.'

'Folk hereabouts have Emma as your mistress. That you make no attempt to deny them leads me to believe that you would wish that was true.'

'She is attached to my nephew.'

'Would that he was attached to her,' she replied briskly. 'You don't see it, 'cause my Emma hides it from you. She writes sometimes more than one letter in a day. In three months not one reply has come from Mr Greville.'

'He is a poor correspondent.'

'He has found time to pen several letters to you.'

A flash of annoyance crossed the Chevalier's face. The quizzical expression on that of Mary Cadogan was evidence that she had noticed it.

'You get a lot of letters from Greville,' she continued. 'Your man was happy to save his legs and let me bring them up.'

'A glass of wine?' said Sir William, standing up quickly. He manoeuvred his slim frame between the statue of a bearded ancient and a large decorated pot, poured from the decanter and returned to present her with the glass. 'What is it you want?'

'The truth, sir. I expect you have an arrangement with Mr

Greville. What I see is my own girl near to despair sometimes, she loves him so.'

'I doubt you approve.'

She took a deep drink of wine before replying. 'I learnt long ago, sir, an' in a hard school, that the heart don't often adjoin to the head. Whether I approve of your nephew is neither here nor there. What my Emma suffers because of it is. If she is to be cast out I need to know of it.'

Sir William helped himself to a glass of wine and sat down again. 'There is no intention to cast her out, I do assure you. She'll always have my protection, should she want it.'

'The question is sir, does she need it?'

Again, he had the temptation to dismiss her, to say that what she was asking might be her business but she was being above herself in demanding to know. But he had a nagging thought that would not go away: matters were stalled with no sign of a way to break the deadlock. Was the key to that sitting before him? The natural diplomat in him rebelled at revelation; the frustrated suitor in him demanded that something happen.

'Would I be allowed to tell you a story, Mrs Cadogan?'

'I judge it to be a long one, so I'd be obliged to see my glass recharged.'

That made him laugh and he rose to accommodate the request. There was a moment when their hands touched, as he took her glass, a moment when he thought he saw the woman she had once been, the lively eyes that could hold humour so easily, the notion that in her mind there was judgement, but rarely condemnation.

'Your Emma is quite remarkable, but so are you. You'll be aware of my nephew's prospects, but I doubt you've any inkling of his inability to indulge in decisions that would materially advance them.'

'He always seems in a stew about money, that I do know.'

'The solution lies within him. There are people who esteem his gifts, not least those who'd help him to achieve office within the ministry. Opposition can lead to advancement too, yet Charles dithers, says that he cannot support either Fox and the Prince of Wales or Pitt and the King.'

'I thought he had it in mind to marry well.'

'In his mind, yes, Mrs Cadogan,' Sir William growled. 'But his aim is so inept that if he were a hunter needing to live off his kill he'd starve. But you must let me tell you what happened in England or, to be more precise, in Wales.'

He paused for a moment to gather his thoughts. 'It's no secret that I had tender feelings for my late wife, attachments based on those most solid foundations, trust and esteem. In short, Mrs Cadogan, though not accomplished in any startling way, my late wife was a good woman.'

'Everyone below stairs says so, sir.'

'They talk too much below stairs,' he snapped.

'Funny that, Sir William,' Mary Cadogan replied, dipping her head to her glass. 'That's what folk attending usually say about those they serve.'

'Something tells me that I have just been humbugged,' Sir William admitted, before continuing. 'My late wife's estates, bequeathed to my nephew, will ease his burdens. But, being Charles Greville, he will not come out and say so. He's a schemer even when such behaviour is unnecessary. He seeks to tie me to what my inclinations direct me towards, notwithstanding the fact that I may, at some future date, decide to marry again.'

Mary Cadogan smiled. 'It would be a lucky woman who got you, sir.'

'Thank you for that,' he replied, genuinely touched. 'I have named Charles as my heir and that makes him happy, though the notion that I might take another wife renders him anxious. Matters came to a head on my return to Naples. I travelled part of the way with the widowed Lady Clarges. In a moment of madness, in Rome, after a good supper and much wine, I let my tongue slip enough to emit what might have been construed as a proposal of marriage.'

The Chevalier told a good story, describing both the supper and the conversation, his face animated enough to convey the depth of the shock at his own stupidity, plus the nature of the farce that had followed.

'Luckily the lady either missed the nature of the allusion or chose to ignore it. I wrote to Charles recounting this vignette in the most light-hearted vein, presenting myself as a buffoon who had, by sheer serendipity, managed a narrow escape. I need hardly tell you of the effect on him.'

'He offered you Emma?'

'Quite,' he responded, uncomfortable again at being so rudely reminded of the point. 'I doubt to a woman of your sagacity that much more explanation is required. The regard I have for your daughter's beauty must be plain to the dimmest eye. I made no secret of it in London, though she, besotted with my nephew, chose to see it as mere gallantry.'

'Understand, sir, she receives that kind of attention all the time.'

'Don't I know it!' Sir William replied. He stood up suddenly and fingered the motif around the rim of a tall Roman vase. It was sad to see his shoulders sag a little and his voice, though not weak, was melancholy. 'You forget, Mrs Cadogan, that I have been out on the town with her. It has been my duty to confound the attentions of those who know both my nephew and Emma, even the Prince of Wales himself. I also confess myself flattered that those who did not know her thought her attached to me. And I can assure you that delivering her back to Charles Greville was often the occasion for a sad reflection on the burden of age.'

'You was telling me about Wales.'

'It was there, while we were touring my estates, that Charles first mooted that I might take on responsibility for your daughter.' He ignored Mary's loud sniff of satisfaction, the certain knowledge that she had been right, and carried on, gently turning the tall vase to admire the artwork. 'I believe I had said to him many times that her beauty was so classical. Do you know how often I have seen her face on objects such as this?'

That made Mary Cadogan look more closely at the decorative friezes that adorned the vase he was fingering, at the reclining beauties holding lyres or grapes. In profile they were, indeed, like Emma.

'From my point of observation,' Sir William continued, 'the idea has obvious attractions, as well as uncertainties. To Charles it is all advantage. Don't think he doesn't esteem Emma, he does. But love is not an emotion to which his heart is open. My nephew is a man so practical that it is sometimes necessary to wonder if he is actually flesh and blood.'

The look he gave her then, as he turned to face her, was unblinking. 'The rest you can guess. If I take on responsibility for Emma, Charles has less to fear in the article of my marrying again. He also offloads the cost of keeping a household for her and, as a *quid pro quo*, he has a lever on which he can work to get me, publicly and legally, to name him my heir.'

'You have not done so?'

'No, Mrs Cadogan, I have not!' he replied, the snap back in his voice. 'I will not see everything I own entailed by some extravagance, for he would be bound to borrow on his expectations. He plagues me in the letters you deliver to stand surety for a bond, which I will refuse to do. Should he inherit, which is my intention barring the caveats I have already stated, then I want that bequest to be that which was left to me, not the residue of his speculations.'

'One of which is Emma.'

'I'm very fond of her, I hope you acknowledge that.'

'It's our lot to be used, sir. I had decades of it, and had hoped for better for my only child.'

'That was wounding, madam.'

'Then forgive me for my honesty. And forgive me for observing that I had your nephew as less the rogue than you.'

'I think it a bit high to term him a rogue.'

Mary Cadogan lost some of her reserve then. Her voice was emphatic. 'He has sought to profit from Emma since the day he moved her to London. How many times has Romney painted her and how many pictures do you see? Sold, near every one, not kept to gaze on in admiration. And now that he tires of her he barters her off in order to maintain a grip on your good intentions.'

'It is not as mean-spirited as you make it sound. He observed my attraction to Emma and thought he saw that it was mutual in its potency. And I do not think that he has the capacity to return the level of affection she demonstrates for him.'

'So he'll break her heart?'

'I seek to mend it.'

'Without success.' That sharp rejoinder caused Sir William to respond with a curt, unhappy nod. 'It was the attentions you paid her that caused me to ask for this chance to talk.'

'I am more concerned with what your daughter thinks, Mrs Cadogan.'

'Why, sir, if she notices at all, she ascribes it to kindness, not desire. My Emma does not think of you as a gallant.'

'That is the unkindest cut of all,' he replied, crestfallen. 'It is true to say that I am aware of being well past the first flush of youth, but the prospect of never being anything other than an uncle is not one to savour.'

'What would happen if Emma and I were to return to London?'

'The true answer madam is that I have no idea.'

Mary Cadogan suspected that he was lying. If they had discussed Emma coming to Naples, they must also have talked about what would happen if the hoped-for result didn't materialise. Set against that would be Sir William's reluctance, having invested so much, to admit to failure. No man would embark on such a deep-laid plan of seduction contemplating outright defeat.

Sir William Hamilton, harbouring that very thought, had been made uncomfortable by Mary Cadogan's question, the assumption that failure would see Emma and her mother back in Edgware Road. Every time he had mentioned it to his nephew the idea had been swept aside as absurd. He realised just how much Charles had flattered him, playing on his vanity to achieve an object that, in truth, held more advantage for the proposer than it did for the supposed beneficiary. Had he been alone he might have voiced the thought that there was no fool like an old one.

'The question, sir, is where we go on from here?'

'I confess myself at a stand. I am unable to offer any solid opinion.'

'What would you offer Emma?'

That made him look at her sharply. She dropped her head to examine the back of one of her hands.

'I cannot be certain I know what you are saying, madam.'

She looked at him, her eyes hard. 'Then you are not the clever man I think you are, sir. It be simple enough, Sir

William. Does my Emma have a better prospect of happiness here than elsewhere?'

'And if she does?'

'Then I'd see it as my duty to help persuade her of it. And I might add that, given your nephew has gone to such lengths to create such a situation, no doubt he will take a mighty unkind view of a contrary outcome.'

'He will meet his obligations, madam, I will insist on it.'

'I know you will forgive me the liberty I take when I say that don't reassure me.' She ignored his flash of irritation and carried on talking. 'You know something of my life, sir, and can guess what you don't, just as you know all about Emma's. I want for her now what I have wanted from the day she was born. That she should not have to bend to the will of any man who—'

'I have no desire to bend her to my will,' he interrupted. 'What I desire I would want to be surrendered willingly.'

'And having won that, what then?'

'Security and the knowledge that as long as I live Emma will be a charge upon my honour. And I would add this, I am not like my nephew.'

Mary Cadogan stood up. There was little more to say, except, 'I will not assure you that all will work out as required, but if Emma is to be persuaded to see where her advantage lies, then I am the one she will listen to.'

Months of carefully dropped hints and allusions to betrayal did not dent Emma's attachment to Greville. Throughout the summer and early autumn she still spoke of him as if he was just about to walk through the door, and in such an obsessive way that her mother sometimes wondered if the oppressive heat had addled her brain.

Mary Cadogan had experienced love in her own life, as well as infatuation and all the shades of regard in between. She had also been part of a society of women where the ability to hold on to a fantasy, despite ample contrary evidence, was endemic. But never had she come across something of the depth of Emma's enthusiasm. It took the transfer from comfortable, warm Naples to cold, lonely Caserta, to bring matters to a head.

Sir William attended the King's annual hunting expedition, for which he had been allotted what he liked to call his cottage near the Winter Palace, a stab at humour that had some merit since it could accommodate over forty souls. Occupied for two months of the year, it lacked any sense of permanence, but what was worse for those not engaged in blasting every living thing that crossed the landscape, was the lack of company.

Sir William would set off every morning clad in ample clothes to ward off the chill, weapons cleaned and gleaming with fresh oil, several flasks of ardent spirits in his servant's saddlebags. The hunt would last all day, Ferdinand leading furious charges over his land in pursuit of wolves, foxes, bears, stags, and, when none of those larger creatures would oblige, any small bird demented enough to fly within the range of his weaponry.

At night they consumed the day's bag, long feasts well oiled with drink, all-male affairs at which the hunters would eat to excess, drink bumper after bumper in endless toasts, sing vulgar songs, exchange lewd anecdotes, and end up in furious arguments regarding the claims of rival noble families. At some point several of Ferdinand's courtiers, having watched him eat for four men, would be required to accompany him to the privy, there to wait patiently while he burbled on in his nonsensical way and eased the pressure on his bowels.

Back at the cottage, Emma and her mother were left with a few servants, to sit in a draughty house in which every doorway required a bolster, every room and passageway a blazing fire. During the day, if the sky was clear, the aspect of distant snow capped Apennine peaks was pleasant, but there were rain-filled days, when the landscape seemed to close in on the royal enclosures, making the place feel like a prison.

There were few visitors for Emma, no teachers or aristocrats to sit at her feet and admire her beauty. Outdoors it was nothing like teeming Naples, where the *lazzaroni*, the peasant class of the city, on seeing her face would seek to touch her hem and hail her as the living embodiment of the Madonna. Good rider though she was, Emma was forbidden to join in the Royal Hunt, her status forbidding attendance at an event often observed by the Queen. With no recognisable social standing, she couldn't be presented to royalty. Indeed, if she was out riding and saw the hunt heading in her direction, she had to turn and flee lest she cause a scandal. Accustomed to better treatment, this led to many a tantrum, stormy sessions during which Italy was cursed, the weather likewise, and Sir William castigated for his ill-treatment of a guest he often admitted as his favourite person.

'I shall tell him as soon as he walks through that door, Mother. I have had enough of his damned Italy.'

'And what d'you reckon his response will be, Emma?'

The surprise was genuine, the way she treated the answer seen as obvious. 'Why, he will arrange for us to return to London, of course.'

In all the three months since that talk with Sir William, Mary Cadogan had tired of the game she had been playing with Emma. She was also irritated by the ague, brought on by the draughty residence she was forced to occupy. Her joints were stiff, and the morning and evening chill had her sniffing and wiping an almost constant drip from her nose. It was no preparation for a game requiring patience, and neither Sir William nor any of the endless stream of guests who attended her daughter in Naples was here to restrain her.

'So you've finally given up on your Greville ever coming here to you?'

'No!'

'Then you're a fool, girl. If you still hold a candle for Charles Greville you're worse than that.'

'How can you say such a thing?'

'Cos it be right. How many letters have you penned these last months?' Eliciting no reply Mary Cadogan continued, in a harsh voice that had as much to do with her condition as it had with her daughter's stupidity. 'Dozens, and not so much as one word to say he's even read them.'

'It's his way. It was the same when he was with his uncle in Wales.'

'His way is to ignore you, then, lest you be right by his side.'

Emma threw herself into a chair, hand over her brow like a lovelorn stage heroine. 'You cannot fathom how much I miss him.'

'Ain't hard, girl,' Mary Cadogan replied, with scant concern to be polite, 'since you never leave off telling me.'

'You must want to go home as well, Mother. This house, and this particular climate, little suits you.'

'Cold air suits better than cold charity,' Mary Cadogan snapped.

'What does that mean?'

That was the moment at which maternal patience fractured, for reasons numerous and manifest: but especially Emma's blindness to the fact that Sir William was, and had been since their arrival, paying court to her. How could she not see his endless attention to her and her education, his occasional salacious sallies, for what they were?

Personal discomfort also played a part to shorten Mary's temper, the aches and pains that racked her body, but most of all it was the weight of keeping a secret from someone who had every right to her support. It was as if a dam had been breached, and a torrent of words told Emma just what arrangements had been made for her, and just how she stood in regard to the man she professed to love.

'She fled the room in tears.'

'I wish she had been made aware more gently,' Sir William replied. His voice was slightly slurred from the drink he had consumed in the King's company and his face was flushed, but what was most striking was his air of depression.

'You're more'n fond of her, aren't you, sir?' asked Mary Cadogan gently.

'I won't deny it,' he said sadly. 'I made no secret to you or my nephew how attracted I was to Emma. But it was an appreciation of her beauty you saw in London. My doubts as to the wisdom of her coming to Italy you must be able to guess at, leaving the bed of a young and virile fellow to go to that of an old and somewhat diminished man.'

'That, I sense, has changed.'

'Do you look at her, Mrs Cadogan, and see what I see?'

'I see my girl, your honour. I see beauty and her lively nature. I see her make you and other men laugh. I see the look of lust that your friends take care you should not notice.'

'I notice, madam,' he replied, staring at the burning logs, adding a small, humourless laugh. 'You have no idea how it pleases me to do so. I am flattered by it, especially since Emma seems so ingenuous as to positively encourage the notion that I am her lover.'

'She wants to touch often those she is fond of.'

'If I didn't know better I would think she was teasing me, flattering my vanity as Charles did my mind, leading me towards an indiscretion so that she could play the shocked innocent and embarrass me.'

'My bones ache for the chill, Sir William. I am about to help myself to that ardent spirit you recommended. Might I be so bold as to suggest that you would benefit from the same?'

'Let it be so.'

Half of the bottle of grappa disappeared while they talked of the spectre in the background, a distraught young woman, who might at this very moment be sobbing herself to sleep. Mary Cadogan wiped a maudlin tear from her eye, then took another stiff drink to kill the temptation to weep.

'It just came out, what with her on yet again about going home.'

Sir William had a lump in his throat. The open admission that Emma had captured his heart had escaped suddenly.

'It is, you must understand, an expression of feeling I thought to leave behind in callow youth. To be moonstruck at my age is to be made ridiculous.'

'Only if it is not requited, your honour,' sniffed Mary Cadogan.

'What chance is there that it might be?'

'You must own that I know my Emma better than you, sir. She might seem to you just a flighty creature whose heart has been won by an undeserving knave. But she is far from that, albeit in her mind's eye she has a vision of a future that cannot be.'

'What are you telling me, madam?' Sir William demanded.

Mary Cadogan drained her glass, as if by doing so she would fortify her train of thought. 'You must offer her better, sir.'

'I cannot compete with Charles Greville.'

'I don't mean in the bedchamber,' Mary Cadogan replied

testily. 'I will not say it is a place where Emma cares naught for who she's with, but you must know that your nephew was not the first man to bed her.'

'I cannot hold that against her.'

'Nor should you, sir, never having had to make your way in our world. It's not the same as yours.'

'It is not so very different, Mrs Cadogan.'

'Two things must be done, sir and the first is to persuade her that there is no future for her with your nephew.'

'That is not something of which I am certain.'

'But I am, sir,' Mary Cadogan protested. 'The next thing to do is to present her with a picture more rosy than the one she harbours now.'

'I have no assurance I can do that.'

'Then send us home.'

'What cruel alternatives.'

'Which be the lesser of twin evils?'

CHAPTER 42

Sir William was out hunting again the following day, so was spared Emma's ranting and the need to listen to the words used about him and his nephew, language so coarse that even her mother pretended to be shocked. It wasn't the cursing that upset Mary Cadogan, so much as the effect of her daughter's shouting on a head suffering from the previous night's excess.

Greville was a lecherous, penny-pinching arse, his uncle a spavined old goat, her mother a snake in the grass. Rogue, scoundrel, villain, cheat were spattered about among swearwords that would have shamed a sailor, the whole tirade liberally sprinkled with bouts of weeping and demands to be taken back to the arms of the man she loved. There were endless dashes to the escritoire to start angry letters that ended up as balls of parchment on the floor. Mary Cadogan held her tongue, waiting for the storm to pass. But, with less of a sore head as the day progressed she offered some wise words regarding the good of flogging a dead horse, which reduced Emma to another bout of weeping.

Mary Cadogan was glad now that she had spoken out. The matter was in the open, there to be discussed when Emma calmed down. And she flattered herself that she understood her daughter, passionate and less versed in the application of wisdom to any predicament. When the time came to make a decision, she could rely on Emma's good sense. In that she was too sanguine by half.

Even back in Naples, a less glamorous location in midwinter, Emma refused to give up on Greville, and brooding on that made her a less engaging companion for those who called at the Palazzo Sessa. Sir William was the first to drop away, happier at the gimcrack Neapolitan court – anything to be spared the accusatory looks of his beautiful young guest. Others who had that summer sat at Emma's feet found her sudden recourse to tears, without any indication as to what had triggered them, tiresome, especially since she made no move to enlighten them.

Matters were scarcely improved by the arrival of letters and gifts from Greville, finally stung into a response by Emma's anguished pleas. The blue hat and a pair of gloves were well received. The enclosed cold missive, which advised Emma to 'Oblige my uncle', was enough to near break her heart.

It took the festivities of the Nativity, a week-long orgy of celebration of the Birth of Christ, before even the glimmer of a chink showed in her longing. It was a time to be out in the streets, to see the endless processions with hand-carried tableaux – three wise men, the shepherds in the stable, the Virgin holding her child under a glowing star, made by rich clans determined to display their wealth. The singing of Christmas hymns in the crowded squares of Naples was uplifting to Emma, but not to Mary Cadogan, who dismissed it as Papist nonsense.

The effect on Emma was marked. She was much taken by the natural theatricality of the people, which lifted her mood. Perhaps it was the commemoration of that birth, when she had been denied a life with her own child, that finally made Emma realise the connection was broken: that a man who could sever so cruelly his relationship with a child who might be his daughter could steel himself to deny anyone.

Drink helped, and her mother encouraged her, knowing that wine-induced moods, though tending towards the maudlin, at least contained an acknowledgement of the facts. When she felt it would serve, Mary Cadogan encouraged Sir William to resume his courtship, glad to see that although Emma struggled she did so to accommodate not discourage him. Another man might have stumbled, but Sir William had the bedrock skills of his diplomacy. Emma gave silent acknowledgement, in mood not words, which indicated to Sir William that she was prepared to go further than mere gallantry.

All that was needed now was the moment.

*

'It is a rare thing, Mrs Cadogan, yet pleasant all the same.'

Mary Cadogan nodded to accept the compliment. It had been her idea that, after all the mad revelry of the last three weeks, masques, balls and open-air festivities, a private supper would be a blessing. Thus, instead of the usual nightly throng that graced the Ambassador's table, or a coach trip through the crowded streets to dine at another board, they were having a quiet, intimate meal, just the three of them, in his private apartments.

Soft candlelight played over the stone statuary and white porcelain vases, blue glass and red, the table a brighter pool in the centre. Servants came and went as silently as ghosts, as if they, too, knew what was afoot and were determined to ensure success. The paintings on the walls, each with a candle to illuminate them, seemed to aid the intention, being composed of cupids and nymphs, or lovers separated by a fate they longed to overcome. Even if she thought herself detached from what was happening, Mary Cadogan knew that she was part of the performance. Her role had been in organising this, her presence adding a veneer of innocence. It was pleasing to see the pretence played to perfection by the two other participants.

Emma was all gaiety, dressed in a gown of light muslin that betrayed the full flower of the figure underneath, drinking a little more quickly than she should, making occasional conversational gaffes that caused her to giggle and Sir William smile. It was the way she had worked for Kathleen Kelly. There was no intimacy of the kind that would occur between friends. It was as though Sir William and Emma had only just met. An unkind observer would say it was a tart's performance but Mary Cadogan didn't care, because it was a damned fine one, so fine that withdrawing, which she had to do, was painful. She longed to be a fly on the wall, to see how Sir William Hamilton would manage the final step from surrogate uncle and detached benefactor to lover.

He used his latest purchase, a large urn dug up by another collector from the ashen mud of Pompeii, to set the mood. It was a vase that carried classicism to a point well beyond the borders of good taste, depicting an orgy of sexual couplings. Men and women were entwined, of course, but there were other images of guests consorting with a variety of animals or with their own sex. Standing behind her, Sir William slowly turned the vase to point out each detail of the frieze.

He was taller than Emma, and the scent of her body, rising on the heat from her skin, was overwhelming. The sight of her exposed shoulders, catching the candlelight, made breathing an effort. With his head by hers, as he leant forward to indicate another point of interest, he brushed her auburn hair. Emma leant back slightly, affording him an alluring view of her voluptuous breasts.

'I fear we are a sorry crew compared to the ancients, but they had their pagan gods as examples.' He pointed to a reclining female figure, naked, head back. Even with primitive art it was obvious that she was enjoying the attentions of her lover, on his knees, head between her legs. His voice was soft and hoarse, low enough to vibrate though her head and neck. 'And this, Emma, this creature in profile, is so like you. All that is different is the adornment of the hair. I have often wished you would dress your hair like a Roman courtesan.'

Emma experienced none of the sensations she had enjoyed with Uppark Harry or Greville at his best, that racing of the blood that made every nerve end tingle. But she did feel flushed, and the languor induced by good food and wine made leaning into Sir William seem natural. Nine months of being denied the company of her lover also had an effect on her, since she enjoyed physical love as much as she longed for emotional security.

And though it was something of which she was unaware of, Emma Hart was honest. The road to this moment had been long and painful, streaked with nocturnal tears. Even though tonight had been a performance, she lacked the duplicity necessary to be a whore with an eye for a prize. The part of her being that longed for gaiety – singing, dancing and drinking – was balanced against a need to feel secure, to be loved for herself, not just for her accomplishments in the bedchamber. So, having finally acceded to the inevitable, she would not tease the man who offered her that.

There was no resistance as Sir William placed his hand flat on her belly, pulling her backwards so that she could feel him through her thin garment. She closed her eyes for pleasure's sake, not disgust, as he leant to kiss her shoulder. This he did several times, each touch of the lips and gentle movement of his hand interspersed with paeans to her looks, her hair, her body, her accomplishments and his deep regard for her. He pointed to the reclining courtesan again. 'I would give much to see you thus.'

To oblige him, and slip out of a thin dress lacking undergarments, was easy. She didn't turn right away, aware that he had stepped away and was silently admiring her back. After several seconds he moved forward, a hand on her elbow to spin her round. She stood, one foot slightly raised while his eyes ranged over her body. He cupped his hand under one breast, lifting it slightly so that the erect nipple pointed straight towards him.

'Truly, Emma, you are fit for an emperor.'

The touch had made her shudder, sending a clear signal to her putative lover that she could match his passion. He bent and kissed that same nipple, at the same time taking her hand, so that when he raised his head again he could lead her to his bedchamber. Accustomed to a man who was young and passionate, Emma was surprised and pleased by Sir William's gentility. What he lacked in ardour he more than compensated for in patience and experience. He was adept with hand, tongue and voice, mixing flattery and touch to achieve his purpose, which was to raise Emma Hart to a pitch of sexual expectation so high that the pleasure she craved must follow. In doing so he worked the same effect upon himself, leaving his new lover with the impression of a man not far from the full flush of youth.

Emma returned to her own apartments halfway through the night, wrapped in Sir William's dressing gown, leaving him to his slumbers. Her mother was asleep too, in a chair, head lolling forward, probably too anxious or curious to go to bed and intent on waiting up for her daughter to return.

Looking at her, mouth open, jaw slack, Emma went through a gamut of emotions: anger at her mother's machinations, gratitude for the concern that had prompted them, a renewed stab of passion for Greville, swiftly followed by a feeling bordering on hate. What had happened tonight she knew was not enough. She could take pleasure from Sir William's company both in bed and out, but one coupling did not make for a commitment. That expression nearly made her laugh out loud. She thought she had that very thing with Uppark Harry and Greville, only to see it snuffed out by indifference.

The balance of what was on offer had been spelt out, albeit with much circumlocution, by her mother. Fine bones and youthful mettle were all very well in a lover, but they did not keep you fed and clothed. Beauty, her only asset in the eyes of most men, was not going to last for ever. If she craved comfort, and she did, then any arrangement that provided it was better than one that promised only passion.

'I must be more like you, Ma,' she said, 'and look out for what suits me in advance.'

Mary Cadogan opened her eyes and, seeing what Emma was wearing, Sir William's patterned dressing gown, she smiled and nodded.

'Did I do right, Ma?'

Her mother's voice had the croaky quality of one who had drunk too much wine and slept badly. 'How's to know, child. Only time will tell us that.' She heaved herself stiffly out of the chair, a hand going to ease her aching back. 'But I will say that what went afore is dead and buried now, even if you find that hard to accept. Take it from one who knows, that pain don't last for ever. A mind on what's to come is worth a ton weight of memory. I take it the Chevalier didn't disappoint?' she added, with arched eyebrows.

'No,' Emma replied softly.

She was unable to give the true answer; that however accomplished Sir William seemed, however kind and wise, she was not in love with him. For five years she had shared her bed with a man she loved, and nothing merely physical could compare. She felt empty.

'You do like him?'

'Yes.'

Mary Cadogan hooked her daughter's arm to lead her to her own bedchamber. 'Then that is where the likes of us start from, Emma. We can ask no more'n a chance, and if what we are faced with ain't too low to contemplate, then we can bear with it.'

'I want Greville to pay for this.'

'His type don't suffer. Take what you can get and leave the rest to God.'

'There should be more.'

'Happen there is, girl. And happen you will find it.'

CHAPTER 43

1787

Though the dispute over enforcement of the Navigation Acts had been resolved in Nelson's favour, the Admiralty backing him to the hilt, several obstacles still hampered his pursuit of Fanny Nisbet. With Sir Richard Hughes now departed there were his duties, as the commander on station between admirals. Second, there was her uncle, who still seemed to blow hot and cold, sometimes a touch of both on the same day. Would he give her a dowry? He declined to be drawn. Did she have expectations for his estate? Perhaps! How went Nelson's own requests to his family for financial assistance? How could he answer when a reply might be six months in coming?

Then there was the difficulty of explaining his feelings when he was mostly confined to letters, his fulsome and excitable, hers sweet and full of gossip. A dashed visit to Nevis, with a brusque demand for clarification, extracted from Mr Herbert permission that they might become engaged, provided his niece had no objection. That was a difficult moment, one which Nelson dreaded. But Fanny assented to his suit, and even allowed him a gentle kiss to seal their bargain.

But if any cause could be laid at the root of his difficulties it was His Royal Highness, Captain Prince William Henry of Hanover. The slender youth of previous acquaintance, full of respect and wonder for a senior naval officer, had quite gone. Instead, Nelson had to contend with a porcine, gluttonous creature, who could never be brought to admit he was in the wrong profession, a potentially fatal trait in one who, though he commanded a frigate, should never have been entrusted with a coracle; a man who had achieved his rank because of his blood, not his ability. Whoever had chosen his officers had done so on the grounds that seamanship was necessary, and a Germanic background was an asset. Where they had failed was in the notion that in dealing with someone like Prince William, tact was also required.

On arrival at Antigua, Prince William delivered a brusque and rude demand for a court-martial. He wanted his first lieutenant, Schomberg, removed for failure to show due respect to a superior officer. Horatio Nelson wanted to remind the Prince that he was signally failing in that respect himself. Barking at the senior captain on the station was not a right even gifted to a king's blood relative. But the need for tact applied to him as well. It was nothing new for a first lieutenant to fall out with his captain – it happened all the time, the confines of a ship almost inviting conflict between the two senior officers if there was any grit in the oyster of their relationship. Those faced with solving such a confrontation knew that a court was a poor solution, since neither party would emerge unscathed.

Prince William didn't know that Nelson had on his desk a letter from Schomberg detailing his own accusations against his captain: failure to keep proper logs; arbitrary misuse of his power to release rations and accusations of collusion with the purser to deny the rights of his crew; drunkenness; a wanton disregard for the safety of the ship; and a failure to heed the advice of his officers, as well as the ship's master.

The list was endless and, if Nelson recalled his visitor properly from their time spent together in the Caribbean, probably true. When serving under Lord Hood Nelson had tried to bring on the Prince's nautical education, with little success. The boy was dogged but useless at mathematics, slipshod in his attentions to the needs of his division, an embarrassment at sword practice and something of a boor at the dining board. In the circle of those who could speak openly to each other, it was agreed that such things mattered little. No royal prince would forsake home for life aboard a man-o'-war. This one had confounded them by pursuing a naval career, though whether the notion had been his or his father's was not known.

'Now, Nelson—'

'Captain Nelson, Your Royal Highness. Or sir, if you prefer.'

Unaccustomed to being checked, Prince William managed a stuttering reply. If he blushed, which he should have done, it was not obvious on such a rotund, high-coloured face. 'Yes . . . Yes. I wanted to ask you about the tour of the islands.'

'Which part in particular?'

'Your suggestion that we use your ship. I'd much rather captain my own. Let my father's subjects see a prince who is not some stuffed affair, but a real man with a job to do.'

That was the last thing Nelson wanted. He knew Schomberg and esteemed him as a very competent sailor, honest though somewhat dour of temperament. Added to what he had experienced of the Prince, the accusations he had made were likely to be more truthful than spiteful. Not that it mattered much; no one, least of all Captain Horatio Nelson, was going to bring charges against a member of the royal family. That would be professional suicide even for an Admiral of the Fleet. But he knew if he agreed to sail in Prince William's own ship, he might find himself in the same bind as Schomberg, forced to interfere in the running of the frigate, especially in entering and leaving the difficult West Indian harbours. That was where the Prince's lack of even the rudiments of seamanship would be most exposed.

'I fear you will find the journey exhausting enough, sir, without the need to captain a vessel as well.'

'Nonsense, Nelson,' Prince William replied, angering his host again with his lack of respect. Yet that turned to amusement as he wondered whether the son of His Majesty could be guilty of lèse-majesté. This clearly showed on his face, since his guest enquired with furrowed bow, 'Something amuses you, sir?'

'I was anticipating the pleasure you'll bring to your father's subjects.'

'Especially in my own ship!'

What followed was pure inspiration. 'Even with Lieutenant Schomberg on board?'

'He must be removed, naturally.'

'That, as you know, Prince William, is beyond my power to do. Schomberg was appointed by the First Lord. Only he can remove him.'

In the weeks that followed, Nelson had constantly to remind himself that he was Christian, and that since he had claimed a kind of friendship with the Prince, it was his duty to forgive his royal passenger a great deal. His misfortune was that William of Hanover would have tested the patience of a whole bevy of saints. Inclined to boorishness when sober, he became a positive menace when inebriated, which was frequent.

On deck when Nelson wasn't present, he interfered in the way the ship was run, which cut down what little time the Captain of the *Boreas* had to himself. He was exhausting, not least in the endless gaffes he committed socially by seeking to seduce every attractive woman he met. Few were unmarried; all the unattached had fathers; princes did not apologise, so it fell to Nelson to mollify the locals this sprig of Hanover offended. He undertook his duty with a sore head, since his guest was addicted to the tavern and the whorehouse. Nelson tried to be abstemious, but that was a hard task in the company of a man determined to prove he had hollow legs, to prove that the Navy could not be bested in the article of consumption by 'these damned planters'.

Worse, Nelson's duty to visiting royalty threatened to keep him away from Nevis. There was a pecking order in the West Indian islands, though to persuade the inhabitants to agree to a listing would have been impossible. Jamaica was the largest British possession, the jewel of the Caribbean, which must be visited first. But what came next was at Nelson's discretion and, still unpopular over his enforcement of the Navigation Acts, he took advantage of that to push Nevis well up in the itinerary.

John Herbert was thrilled to receive a royal prince in his capacity as president of the council, and by the time they landed Prince William was aware of Nelson's attachment to his niece, which added a *frisson* of deeper excitement to the visit. And the way the Prince flattered Fanny held none of the innuendo for which Nelson had been forced to apologise on other islands. For once acting like a gentleman, Prince William absented himself so that Nelson and Fanny could spend some time together. The gardens at Montpelier were big enough to find a secluded spot where they could sit and talk, though not so cut off from view as to offend propriety.

'He seems to think highly of you, your prince.'

'I flatter myself that he thinks me a friend. Indeed he has shown me the content of the letters he sends home to his father, which say so.'

'Who could have a better friend than you, Captain Nelson?'

'Fanny,' he replied earnestly, 'you know my feelings for you.'

She dropped her head slightly, in a way that he found enchanting. 'I blush to recall some of the things you have written.'

'All true, I do assure you. It is my heart that pens my letters.'

'Who can doubt that? I fear my replies must seem dull.'

Just like his reply regarding the Prince, Nelson had to sacrifice truth to the greater goal. Fanny's letters indeed lacked the depth of passion he had hoped for. In his own daily missives no image of bliss had been excluded: rose bedecked cottages and ebullient children; her on his arm as he accepted the greetings of neighbours that went with his status as a senior naval captain; the fact that he would astound the world with his exploits and that she would find herself betrothed to an admiral and a hero. Even the bliss of conjugality had been gently alluded to, in an attempt to draw her out into admitting that she too craved the physical side of marriage.

Yet for all his passion Nelson admired the sense of proper behaviour that debarred the woman he sought to marry from responding in a like manner. The desire for respectability was strong and what could do more to grant to him that status than a woman of such accomplishments as Fanny, with her French, her music, her embroidery and her kind, gentle manners?

'Your letters, Fanny, are meat and drink to an aching heart. I own up to my emotional nature, of which you are tolerant. I confess that when we are apart I am afire with curiosity. Where are you? What are you doing? Is some other creature paying court to you in my absence? When you write, and when I receive what you have written, it calms me. I swear it is no secret to my officers and my men, all of whom wish nothing but happiness for you and me and young Josiah. They know that I am a different man after a packet of letters from Nevis.

Only the reservation of your uncle stands between me, even us, and bliss.'

'You must forgive him, Captain Nelson. It is not that he does not consider you worthy, it is more his concern for my happiness, for which I cannot do other than respect him.'

But Nelson harboured the suspicion that Herbert thought him not good enough for his niece. As a direct descendant of an earl of Pembroke perhaps he felt the Nelson bloodline less blue. Or was it just parsimony, the knowledge that by giving permission he would have to open his purse to an unrestricted commitment?

'You do wish for us to be married?' he asked, deliberately sounding doubtful.

'With all my heart.'

'Then if you can forgive your uncle, Fanny,' he lied, 'so can I.'

Herbert, happy to receive Prince William, was less than enamoured of the abrupt way in which he departed. Nelson heard all the reasons as they weighed, none of which sounded even remotely like the truth, which was that Nevis did not enjoy much in the way of entertainment. The inhabitants were sober and industrious, and because the island was not a port for ocean-going vessels it lacked the kind of palaces of entertainment so beloved by sailors. In short, there were no whores, no riotous establishments and few women to whom His Highness could pay court.

So, as they continued their tour, touching at the other Caribbean possessions of the King, it was back to letters to Fanny and attempts to pin down her uncle on the matter of a dowry or some future allowance. Herbert's replies deftly turned that responsibility back on Nelson, reinforcing the feeling that though Herbert had agreed to a match he was not settled as to its entire suitability. Worn down by that and his attendance on his charge, liverish in the extreme from over consumption, Nelson became so melancholy that others saw his distress.

Even the Prince noticed, and quizzed him on the state of his suit. 'You are sure that this lady is the one you wish to wed?'

Nelson was thinking two things: first that it was really none of his business, and second, how like a parent Prince William sounded. He might have been the Reverend Edmund Nelson, except that he was round and red, instead of tall and saturnine.

'Because if you are, Nelson,' the Prince continued, 'I may have the means to effect a conclusion to this affair.'

'In what way?'

There was a long pause, and much pacing to and fro designed to convey that Prince William was giving his reply careful thought. 'Have you engaged anyone to stand as your best man?'

'I would have hoped for a fellow captain but, failing that, I intended to approach Ralph Millar.'

'In listening to you explain the situation and, if you will forgive me from what I have gleaned in conversation with your officers, it seems to me that you require some lever to force Herbert's hand.'

'He will consent to it in time.'

'I am surprised, Nelson, that you did not see fit to approach me.'

'You?'

'Does the thought of a prince of the blood as your guarantor depress you so?'

'I could not have presumed to make such a request.'

'I can see how my position might debar you,' the Prince replied portentously, 'but what if I offer my services, man?'

'It's not an offer any loyal subject of the King could refuse.'

That threw the King's son, who had clearly been expecting a more fulsome response. He cleared his throat. 'Well the offer is there, Nelson. Take it, if you will, and convey to Mr Herbert that my duties do not allow me much time to act in that capacity. That if he wants to see you wed with me alongside he must make some haste.'

When such an offer was put to him Herbert's response was swift. Fanny Nisbet and Captain Horatio Nelson could be married at the Prince's convenience. The financial matters, however, were not dealt with, so Nelson was left with the prospect of the nuptials yet no idea if he would have the means to sustain the married estate. But there was no going back. In his hearty manner Prince William had taken to the notion of a wedding so it was not only his intended bride's feelings he had to consider.

'Come along, sir,' cried Prince William, as they landed on the fateful morning. He had hosted a breakfast for the ship's officers and young gentlemen, consuming a couple of bottles of claret with his beefsteak, his high colour, as well as his jolly manner, attesting to that. 'I find it hard to believe you are shy, Nelson. I know you to be a warrior, sir, and there is a wench up that hill waiting to be conquered.'

Horatio Nelson had never felt less the warrior, never so unsure of his aim, and the sip of wine he had taken at the Prince's bidding had not been enough to grant him any courage. It was the press of his officers, midshipmen and friends landing behind him that pushed them forward, and once his feet were moving some of his confidence returned. The carriage ride up the hill to Montpelier, through what seemed to be the entire island population, exhilarated Nelson. They were there for the Prince, of course, not him, though they wished the bridegroom well. But it was pleasant indeed to bask in that kind of attention, to be allowed to return the cheers of the crowd with a wave that signified he was the man of the hour.

Naturally John Herbert was fussing before they arrived, darting about, pushing his plantation slaves into something resembling a line, checking that his daughter especially and the rest of the household were in place to receive royalty for an occasion of such magnitude. The clatter of the iron hoops on the roadway sent him into a near faint, the handkerchief he held wiping copious amounts of sweat off his face and absorbing that which ran from his hands.

Nelson had never known the Prince so regal. He handed the bridegroom ahead of him, ceding pride of place, a signal honour that earned a flutter of applause from those who had followed the carriage up the hill. Nelson addressed those assembled in a state that belied his inner nervousness, only relieved when he came to young Josiah. 'It will be a grand day, young Josh,' Nelson said. 'And think on this. Standing as parent to you, I can see to it that you join me aboard ship. How does that sound, sir, a career as a sailor in the King's Navy?'

Prince William Henry, behind him, heard the last sentence, and added, 'If your stepfather cannot oblige you, Master Josiah, then rest assured I shall.'

There were cooling drinks and a brief sojourn in a shaded part of the garden for the Nelson party as Herbert saw to the final preparations. Nelson noted that his officers and midshipmen had raided Montpelier's flower-beds for a variety of exotic buttonholes. Hardy and Andrews had gone further, and festooned themselves so comprehensively with orchids that their captain had to order them to return to a state of respectability. They were drunk, of course, having started on the claret at the Prince's breakfast and not having stopped till they landed on Nevis, only to resume consumption as soon as they reached this shaded arbour.

Eventually all was ready, a table acting as an altar with a lectern to the side so that the clergyman could read the service. They stood facing a set of high French windows, Nelson and the Prince hemmed in by the crowd, leaving only an avenue to their rear through which the bride and her uncle could enter. The scents of hibiscus, the perfumes of the assembled crowd and the smell of their massed bodies suddenly assailed Nelson. His eyesight and perception seemed very acute, allowing him to see that much of the silk on both men and woman had suffered from being in the Caribbean, a repair here, moth-attacked lace there. Along the base of the veranda a line of ants was at work, carrying off the detritus of the bed of roses that already looked limp, so hot was the air.

As Fanny appeared he was more conscious of the trickle of sweat down the centre of his back than of her appearance, and he had to force himself to concentrate. She was veiled, in a dress of old-fashioned cut that he knew to be an heirloom, the garment in which the late Mrs Herbert had married the uncle who was giving Fanny away. Somehow the veil, which he had expected, annoyed him. He wanted to look at his bride throughout the ceremony. Prey to commonplace doubts himself, he wanted to see if she was likewise, wanted to witness her overcome them as he did.

Beside him, he picked up the faint lemon smell he recalled from their early meetings. It was strong and clean. Fanny wouldn't sweat, she was too good and refined. His doubts were replaced by the heart-warming image of presenting his bride to his king, he having astounded all of England with a great victory, Fanny already well known as a hostess whose good opinion society considered essential.

'We are gathered here today, in the sight of God . . .'

Nelson was aware that he had dreamed throughout the whole ceremony: visions of battles, cannon blazing, sails and masts torn asunder; of the return of the hero, cheers from the rigging of every ship anchored at Spithead. Or of a glorious death, with Fanny and Josiah black clad and weeping before his memorial in Westminster Abbey, placed next to that of James Wolfe. At times he was bleeding on shattered quarterdecks, at others advising a roomful of gold-braided admirals, all of whom nodded with sagacious agreement at his tactical and strategic proposals.

'Captain Nelson.'

The ring seemed to make its own way to Fanny's finger, and as the clergyman pronounced them man and wife she lifted her veil to reveal damp eyes but dry cheeks, one of which he kissed, before bestowing another on her lips, and one for good measure on the back of each hand. In his ears, as though from far away, he heard the locals clap and his officers and midshipmen cheer.

CHAPTER 44

1790

It was Emma's habit to recall every date of significance in her life: her birthday; her first employment; the date on which Samuel Linley had died having held her hand throughout the hours in which he wasted away. There was the night she met Uppark Harry, the day she first gave way to the importunities of Charles Greville. The anniversary of her arrival in Naples, on a sunlit April day, was a time for reflection, a time to put together the advantages and drawbacks of her life. Four years on, she relived the moment of stepping into these apartments for the first time, thinking how much she and her circumstances had changed since then.

Slowly her longing for Greville had evolved into something near hatred. The letters they had exchanged grew ever more bitter, sometimes descending into bathos as Emma threatened to kill herself, to return to London and take to the streets, selling herself for a pittance, expiring in the gutter, which would tarnish him with shame for ever. When that failed to move him, she even threatened to marry his uncle and bear a child, though Greville saw through that. Even Emma had to acknowledge that he was *Sir* William Hamilton, with dukes and the like coming out through his ears when it came to relations. Quite apart from that he was the King's Ambassador.

'I sometimes wonder if I'm happy,' she said to her mother.

'What brought that on?'

'Thinking of Greville, and of the changes in my life since we came here.'

Mary Cadogan was sorting dresses and costumes for the forthcoming performance of Emma's *Attitudes*, the occasion to be celebrated on the date of her arrival in Naples, a day Sir William Hamilton insisted had been one of the most significant in his life. Not that the Chevalier needed much excuse: he would throw a dozen such balls in a year, inviting several hundred people, more if the calendar of social obligation permitted it. He loved to entertain.

'What looks bleak turns out to be for the best,' said Mary.

Her daughter was applying powder to her face, prior to making up her eyes, lips and rouging her cheeks. 'I wish I had a gold sovereign for every time you've given me that answer. I swear you'd say it on a sinking ship.'

'Said often don't make it wrong. If this ain't clover I can't tell what is.'

'I got my feather bed, right enough,' said Emma, more to herself than her mother, to whom she had never mentioned her visit to Lady Glynne's bedroom.

'What are you on about, girl?'

Emma just shook her head. Being mistress to Sir William Hamilton now had all the familiarity of habit. It was hard to remember a time when it hadn't been so. Only at such moments could Emma be brought to a position of deep introspection. The benefits she enjoyed far outweighed the sorrows. Half of Naples thought them husband and wife, joined in secret ceremony, though her letters from home told her that others were not fooled. In every respect, she was the lady of the house, acknowledged to be so by everyone who lived within or visited. The list of guests who'd enjoyed her company included the cream of society, aristocrats, painters, writers, thinkers; English, Scottish, Welsh and Irish fought with French, Germans, Austrians and the ubiquitous Italians for a moment of her attention.

She had achieved a social pinnacle that would have been denied her anywhere in England. But it wasn't the men who mattered when granting her that – they would have paid court to her for her looks alone. It was their wives. Quite apart from those she counted as close friends, the drawers of her escritoire were filled with letters from women whose station was of the highest, each one committing to paper kind sentiments and flattering references to some or several of what they considered her attributes.

Nor was she merely decorative. Her lover was besotted with her, and included her as much as he could in what he called his 'toils'. Every discussion with the court was reprised inside the Palazzo Sessa. Emma knew as much about affairs of state as Sir William, and was invited to comment and proffer advice, the sole caveat being that the Ambassador was allowed to ignore it if he chose. In the process she learnt a great deal about politics, not only in Naples, and her conversation, if she chose, rose well above the level of mere chat or gossip. She could now converse in French and Italian as well as in her native tongue. Gone were the days when every meeting had been a trial, where one or two words missed ruined a whole raft of talk. Now Emma could engage in an exchange of ideas, hunt down an allusion and exercise her wit with whoever came to visit.

When Emma sighed that she was, truly, far from content, her mother said, 'Strikes me you've got more'n enough to be going on with. Where does the Chevalier go that he don't take you along?'

'Court,' snapped Emma.

That was a constant bone of contention. She had met both the King and the Queen informally, the latter on dozens of occasions. On their first meeting Maria Carolina had been stiff, which befitted their respective stations, but the Austrian-born queen, who surrounded herself in her private life with forty servants from Vienna, was delighted to find that Emma spoke enough German to converse with her haltingly.

Two things grew from that: Emma applied herself to learning the Teutonic tongue and the Queen relaxed the rules of protocol that debarred her from receiving Mrs Hart on unofficial occasions. Lacking colourful people in her life, as well as those who had no thought for personal advantage, the Queen warmed to Emma and the two women became companions. As their friendship deepened, a daily visit to the Palazzo Reale when in Naples, or the Royal Palace when they were in Caserta, formed part of Emma's day. There she would sit with Maria Carolina and engage in gossip, or play with and assist in the English lessons of the numerous brood of royal children.

Sir William, taking both note and advantage of this, began by entrusting messages for Maria Carolina to his young mistress, then sought her help in nudging and persuading the Queen to adopt some particular policy. Because Emma was careful never to carry to her anything too radical, or to protest too loudly in support of any plan hatched in the Palazzo Sessa or the small seaside villa at Posillipo, the attachment had grown to a point where Maria Carolina acknowledged Emma as a confidante.

That made it doubly galling not to be officially received. Every formal court function, from the daily levee to the endless state balls, masques and entertainments, was barred to her. Emma could engage in games with royal children, sing to them, dance with them and squeal with them. She could have them as guests at the Palazzo Sessa. But she could not be seen on the arm of Sir William on any official occasion.

'If you're still fretting on that, girl, you're soft in the head. What will be will be, the locals say, and they have the right of it. And it won't do to be miserable, especially not this night.'

An anniversary party at the Palazzo Sessa, the cream of Naples in attendance; music, dancing and an opportunity for her to do what she loved most, to perform. Yet Emma wanted more. Did she really want to be Sir William's wife? It would damn Greville, impress her mother and she would have official recognition in society. But though she was fond of him, and much as she appreciated the attentions he paid her, it would not be something she would undertake for love.

Her elderly paramour had taught her patience. As a diplomat, especially in such a febrile posting as Naples, he insisted it was a trait required by the ton. Many times Emma had seen him receive what appeared to be terrible news and admired the way he never allowed it to prey on his mind. Equally, when requested by the court to pass on to his own government some stinging rebuke, he would pocket the missive for several days, then quietly dispose of it when the Neapolitan government, alarmed that it might have gone too far, added a conciliatory codicil.

But her patience was on the way to becoming frustration. All that held her back from the inevitable explosion was the simple truth: there were no more options to pursue and no Greville waiting in the wings to carry her back – the only thing that would bring her to break her commitment to Sir William. Was it just as her mother said, 'That she always wanted to be on a coach to someplace else'? Was it fear that her lover, now approaching the age of sixty, might die and leave her in limbo? Certainly he was less sprightly, but not much so. He still walked, still climbed Vesuvius, still scrabbled away at his excavations. But there were her looks, which would fade as she aged.

'Aged?' Mary Cadogan said, her voice full of reassurance. 'Name of God, child, you're not yet thirty.'

'I don't know why I tell you what I'm thinking. All you ever do is tell me to rest content.'

'There'll be no rest now,' Mary Cadogan replied, ignoring the true import of what her daughter was saying. 'There be near two hundred folk out there, as grand as you like, all waiting for you, Emma Hart.'

The shouts from the assembled guests were enough to banish Emma's earlier melancholy. Using no more than a pair of shawls and a Greek shield, the pose she struck was immediately recognisable, to an audience with a classical turn of mind, as Andromache mourning the death of Hector. Candles combined with cleverly placed mirrors ensured that light and shade added to the effect. Her mother used a thick black curtain at each change of scene, servants moving lights and mirrors, this accompanied by a clash of cymbals as the curtain was pulled back. Emma had rearranged her clothes to appear in another guise, that of the bronze statue of a dancer, recently excavated from the ruins of Herculaneum. The transformation was so swift and accurate that it drew forth gasps of amazement and a round of applause.

Behind her lay the Bay of Naples, moonlight playing on the water, with the occasional scudding cloud adding a dramatic backdrop to her pose. A trio of musicians played suitable airs, a dirge for Aphrodite, a minuet for the bronze dancer, something light-hearted and gay when she became the Comic Muse.

Abandoning her shawls, and with the use of a staff, Emma changed her attitude to that of the Goddess Circe, daughter of the Sun. A sorceress, she was leaning forward, arm out-stretched, her garment low cut and tantalising to lure Odysseus, sailing home from the sack of Troy, on to the rocks of her island.

Emma loved to perform, to enthrall her audience with these *Attitudes*, and in fact this was an extension of her personality: every move she made in company had a tinge of theatricality. She had rehearsed every gesture, every facial expression, many times in her mirror glass. She had an interior and an exterior disposition, the latter a critical eye that judged each act, each phrase and each movement against the aspirations she worked so hard to perfect. That watchful spirit was most active in performance. She could pose in any one of fifty guises, sing in four languages and loved to dance: sometimes stately gavottes, at other times, in the right company, the wild peasant *saltarella* of southern Italy.

She performed other *Attitudes* and executed dances more pagan in origin, embodying notions that Sir William had brought back from his excavations. Since these included the exposure of a great degree of flesh they were reserved for his eyes only. Much of his virtu – lewd vases, cups and statuary – carried graphic images. In addition Sir William had copies of frescos and drawings from the walls of the ruined houses of Pompeii, all of which Emma was invited to emulate.

Some of that art could not be reproduced, not even by her talent, so scandalous was the nature of the images portrayed. Humans in every kind of sexual congress; women with one man or several; old men with young boys; representations of Sapphic poses, painted lovingly before being sealed by disaster, to survive the passage of near eighteen hundred years thanks to the harsh hot ash of Vesuvius.

Sir William enjoyed these as much as he delighted in Emma's private performances. Early on in their relationship he had openly confessed to being a lover of licentiousness, even to being a great masturbator. He had not only his art, but books as well. Without Latin, Emma could not read them but she barely needed to given that he was only too eager to act as her muse, sure she gained as much gratification as he did from the retelling of these obscene stories.

Sir William Hamilton had grown up in a world in which the acquisition of sexual accomplishments was as much a requirement of his position in society as his undoubtedly polished manners. He had had a dozen mistresses before his marriage, and several after, and when young had been no stranger to the better class of bagnio. Courteous, kind, sometimes fatherly, behind his bedroom door he revelled in vulgarity. The carefully modulated manner, the pose of the diplomat deserted him, to be replaced by a mode of speech that owed much to the whorehouse. A loud fart would reduce him to uncontrollable giggles, and he was even more amused if he was not the perpetrator. Everything he had learnt from experience and his reading he passed on to Emma, happy to find himself attached to a companion who loved ribaldry and physicality as much as he did.

Quite prepared to acknowledge his age and the constraints it placed on his abilities, Sir William more than made up for his waning sexual powers with the sheer variety of his endeavours. He saw innovation as a challenge, and the presence of an uninhibited creature like Emma Hart as a licence to push back the boundaries of his own skills, and to lift to increasing heights the pleasures she should enjoy in his company.

And he continued to fill the house with visitors, determined that either during the daylight hours, or when the sun had faded, Emma should never feel any hankering to return to London.

Mary Cadogan observed them with a judicious eye, keeping her place, never presuming, notching up each point at which the relationship progressed, where it stumbled. She was always there to reassure Emma that what she had now was better than what she had left behind. She had a clear idea of what went on behind the closed door of the bedchamber. No man can keep a secret from his servants, least of all his valet, so Sir William's tastes were well known below stairs.

Only Emma knew the depth of her frustration, only her mother knew it existed. If Sir William guessed she was not unreservedly happy, then he had the good sense to keep it to himself.

CHAPTER 45

A dozen characters later Emma rejoined the party to partake of supper, more music and cards, accepting the compliments thrown in her direction. General Acton was there, the elderly Englishman who was minister to King Ferdinand, but was even closer to the Queen. She engaged pleasantries with the German poet and diplomat Goethe, who would amuse Emma by rustling up a flattering couplet in four languages with consummate ease. The Duchess of Argyll, her good friend, had her usual place by the door. Angelica Kaufmann, the most celebrated artist in Naples, had painted her several times already, yet was still sketching in the background.

There were half a dozen wealthy rakes on the last part of their Grand Tour, all of whom, during the evening, would seek to seduce Emma away from her older lover. They would not succeed, however handsome or well connected. This pleased Sir William mightily: although rumours abounded about his Emma, she showed him nothing but fidelity.

Sir William swore that this endless caravanserai fatigued him and kept him away from his five true loves: Emma Hart, the sea bathing villa at Posillipo, the hot lava flows of Vesuvius, his archaeological digging and the English garden he had crafted for King Ferdinand and Queen Maria Carolina at Caserta.

While Emma flatly refused to go near it in winter, Sir William's hunting 'cottage' provided an oasis of peace in the summer. The air there was clear and cool compared to that of the city, the smell of flowers and cut grass so much more pleasant than the rank odour of the open sewers that ran through the alleyways of Naples into the bay. The draughts that came through the gaps in the doors and windows were welcome, and with the mountains so close, and a great cascade coming straight off the glaciers, chilled water was always available to drink, or to dab on a heated brow.

Even if he wasn't much given to lifting spade or hoe, Sir William sweated as he ordered his gardeners about. They weeded and clipped, trying to keep alive plants accustomed to cooler climes and to check those that would run riot in the sunshine. Even though he spoke the language his minions took pleasure in misunderstanding every word he said to them and it was the frustration of that which brought on the perspiration. Disinclined to interfere, Emma wandered off to find a shady spot where she could sit with sketchbook and charcoal and entertain herself by drawing Vesuvius, smoking away in the distance. A liveried attendant fell in behind her, so that should she require anything, he would be on hand to fetch it.

Sir William had worked hard for over twenty years on his garden and much of it was now mature, small copses and flower-beds, bushes and hedgerows, cut by winding paths. It was a place of peace, a gift to the court of Ferdinand and Maria Carolina, a sanctuary to ease the burdens of statehood. It was pleasant to proceed slowly, to gaze upon the carefully arranged beds, then kneel to sniff the pungent scents that rose from a disturbed flower.

'*Buon giorno, Signorina.*'

The voice made her stand up abruptly. It came from within the small grove of trees, was a deep *basso profundo*, suited to the man who emerged, blinking like some wild animal suddenly exposed to the light. The King of Naples was tall, dark-skinned and a trifle unkempt, with food stains on his black coat. The hair, jet black and unbrushed, was sticking out in a dozen different directions from under his hat and in his blood-streaked hand he carried two dead rabbits.

Emma was unsure how to react. Incognito, Ferdinand had attended many a ball at the Palazzo Sessa, had watched her perform her *Attitudes* with alarming concentration. In complimenting her on her singing, he had even gone so far as to say that she sang like a king. This, she found out later, was a reference to his known love of his own voice, and in his mind was the highest compliment he could pay her.

The disguise was slight, but respected as far as possible by all those present. Even as a known glutton he never stayed to consume any food or drink, which underlined the fact that he had come to see her. Should she recognise him now, a man who plainly sought to avoid that at other times?

'Signore.' That made him grin, and Emma had the relief of knowing she'd chosen the right course. 'Do I perceive that you have been hunting?' she asked in Italian.

'I'm still hunting,' he replied.

'Is the garden not too cultivated for hunting?'

'There is sport all round for he who's determined enough to pursue it.'

It wasn't hard to get the drift of these exchanges. The King was known to lack education, but Emma knew from Sir William that when it came to pursuit of the ladies he was as direct as any hot-blood in Naples. A man who grew tongue tied and bored over affairs of state had great clarity of speech, and no subtlety whatsoever, when it came to fornication. Judging by the bulge in his breeches, which he was making no attempt to hide, that was his aim now. But knowing what he was after did not supply the answer as to how she should react. How do you say no to a king?

'I have admired you often, Signorina Hart,' he said.

A maidenly hand went to her mouth, to indicate surprise as well as to cover the incipient smile that threatened to break on her lips. 'You know my name?'

'Everybody in my kingdom does,' he replied gruffly, completely demolishing the pretence, that followed with a look of confusion. Emma curtsied, not the full depth due to a monarch, but certainly enough for a gallant prepared to flatter her.

'I've seen you make magic with just a shawl. There's not a man in the room does not yearn to see what is under so flimsy a garment. I want to see.'

'It would scarce do for me to reveal what it is in public, Signore.'

'Then let's go somewhere private.' He jerked his thumb over his head. 'These bushes will do.'

'I was in search of some shade, sir,' Emma said, thinking, but that bush is not what I had in mind.

'Shade?' he demanded.

'I was heading for the bower at the end of the lane.'

'Then I shall join you.'

Emma advanced down the path, hearing behind her a whispered exchange, which obliged her to stop and peer. She saw the servant palm a coin, which denoted a bargain struck. But she was on her way again before Ferdinand looked round, forcing His Neapolitan Majesty to scurry so that he could catch up. The bower was close, and within a minute they were under an overgrowing wisteria. Emma sat down without asking, which caused the King a split second of annoyance. Then he joined her, occupying the other end of a rough-hewn bench, his eyes boring into hers. Unable to return that look, Emma laid her parasol across the bench as a not very effective defensive barrier.

She might be sitting opposite a well-known ignoramus who loved to play the buffoon, but he was also a ruler of the most absolute kind and accustomed to getting his own way. Emma sought to find a method by which she could deflect his attentions, without insulting his person.

'Since you know who I am, Signore, you must also know that I have a present attachment.'

'I know the gentleman well,' he replied, edging closer, his hand on the parasol. 'We are good friends, close enough that he would gift me anything I asked for.'

'You may say that, Signore. I cannot be sure it is true.'

'You are a woman so that makes little difference.'

'To you.' Emma laid a firm hand on her parasol, to keep it in place. 'That gentleman is my protector, on whom I depend for everything.'

'What is wrong with me?' he demanded.

'Nothing, Signore,' she lied.

'I disgust you, perhaps?'

The truth, that she did not find him attractive, would not serve. But Emma was convinced that, whatever his rank, she was not about to succumb to such a clumsy attempt at seduction. To call it uncouth was by a long mile an understatement. It was positively insulting. The King was treating like a street whore the mistress of the British Ambassador.

'You say that the gentleman who is my protector would agree?'

'He will.'

Like a conjuror performing a trick, the sketchpad was open and the thin stick of charcoal offered. 'Then write to him. If he is such a friend and he agrees, then I do not risk my position.'

Ferdinand looked confused, so Emma continued. 'I cannot chance my present comfort, and that of my aged mother, on a whim of desire, Signore. The prospect of what you propose is not unpleasant, but sense informs me I must have permission to accept.'

'When?'

'I walk in this garden often and so I think do you.'

Ferdinand grabbed the pad and wrote quickly in large, untidy, childish letters. His scrawl, when she looked at it, was hard but not impossible to read. He had written to Sir William without the use of either name, identifying himself as a hunting partner who had, on more than one occasion, given him the kill of a stag. By the time she finished reading the King was gone. All she saw was his broad, retreating back, and two dead rabbits.

The question is this. What do I say to Sir William? Do I mention it at all? And what will he say if I do? Surely he would never suggest that I submit!

The questions multiplied the more Emma gnawed on the problem. A dinner with forty guests, and the social obligations that entailed, did little to ease her disquiet. At worst her keeper would accede to the King's request. At best that equable temper of his would explode. Rare as it was, she had seen it happen, usually when some visitor from home rudely demanded of him a service he was not obliged to provide.

Should she let her mother see it first? She was far more experienced, after all. But Emma was reluctant to do that, wishing for once to act on her own behalf. There was difficulty here but also, perhaps, advantage. This train of thought was interrupted continually by her requirement as the hostess of the evening, and it was the respect shown to her in that role which gave her an indication as to how to proceed.

'You cannot deny that my position is irregular?'

Sir William was reading one of his favourite authors, the Marquis de Sade. He didn't want to look up from the story of innocence corrupted to where Emma was sitting, poking at her teeth with a sharpened piece of hazelwood. There was a slight flash of annoyance as well, because his mistress clearly didn't quite comprehend that at his age he required a degree of stimulation prior to their love-making. He would have been doubly annoyed if he had known that Emma was deliberately interrupting him when she knew he needed to concentrate.

'I am at mercy of any number of male vanities.'

Justine was at the mercy of two callous monks, which to Sir William was much more important.

'Because I am attached to you in such an irregular fashion every lecher feels he has the right to try his luck.'

'I have always thought you liked the attention,' Sir William replied, his train of thought broken.

'I sometimes wonder, Sir William, if it is you who derives pleasure from that – the knowledge that while many may make the attempt, none succeed. Perhaps I am the victim of your vanity.'

'You are fractious tonight, my dear.'

Emma turned round to look into his bright eyes, at the lined face, the nose and the jawbones made more prominent by the passage of time. She composed her own features to convey a dissatisfaction to which he was unaccustomed. In three years Sir William could count on one hand the number of times that his mistress had argued with him. Greville's prediction that she was a sweet and willing bedfellow had been more than borne out. His further observation that Emma had a temper, which would break out occasionally, had not. More importantly, having acceded to the present situation, he had never once heard her complain vocally of her lot. She was too beautiful ever to look shrewish, but those green eyes could convey hurt with little effort.

'Something has happened to bring on this mood.'

'Yes.'

'Am I to be told what it is, or am I merely to be a gull to the consequences?'

'What is your true opinion of those men who leer over me?'

Sir William smiled. 'I admire their taste, my dear, while at the same time pitying their prospects.'

'What if I found such approaches offensive?'

'Then, my dear, I would be obliged to demand that those making them desist. But never having observed that and, I may say, trusting your own wit to take what care is required, I have never felt the slightest inclination towards even an ounce of jealousy.'

For the second time that day the sketchbook was conjured up. 'Then I beg you to look at this.'

It was with some reluctance that Sir William put aside de Sade to reach for Emma's sketchbook. Slowly he read the scrawl that requested of him, as a hunting friend, that he surrender his mistress.

'Ferdinand?'

'No less.'

'He pressed his attentions upon you?' Emma nodded, and Sir William smiled. 'It is not unusual for the King to behave so. Every woman in the court, from noblewoman to skivvy, has had his hand on her arse. You will have observed, if you did not know already, that his behaviour is that of a child.'

'If you had seen the stretch on his breeches you wouldn't say that,' Emma protested. ''Tis a wonder they didn't rip.'

'He is near permanently erect,' Sir William replied wistfully. 'The only thing that quietens his ardour is hunting, though a kill can often bring forth an unbidden emission.'

'Am I to be a kill?'

'From your tone, my dear, I observe the prospect does not entice you.'

'He smells to high heaven, and though I may not know I can guess that his attentions would be swift and selfish.'

'In that you are likely correct.'

'And am I allowed to observe that you are not taking the matter seriously? He will chance upon me again. What am I to do?'

'You must leave it to me, my dear, for it is a matter with which I know how to deal. And you must disrobe so that I gaze upon that which the King will see only in his imaginings.'

Emma obliged, as Sir William reached for his book, still open at the page. Then, intermittently raising his eyes to look at her naked body, he began to read aloud the de Sade story of the debauching of the young Justine.

CHAPTER 46

Sir William Hamilton was no booby, even if that was a face he often sought to present to the world. He knew that Emma and his nephew still exchanged letters, suspected that, vitriolic to begin with, they had probably settled down to mere correspondence. While he had never known the depth of Emma's written spat with his nephew, he could certainly guess at some of the contents: if Greville kept insisting that matrimony with Emma would be a disaster, then that had been a subject raised in their letters. That she never mentioned such a desire did not in any way diminish the notion that it was an estate she sought, either for the sake of permanence or to spite her ex-lover.

He had pondered on it often, weighing the pros and cons, aware that he would need royal assent from his own sovereign, let alone the nod from the Court of the Two Sicilies. Resignation would remove that requirement, but that was something he was loath to contemplate, even if his duties fatigued him. He loved Naples, the foothills of Vesuvius and the diggings that such a natural monster had provided.

There was also his desire to do the right thing. Though he felt fit and well, he could not ignore the difference in their age. Unless Providence dealt Emma a cruel blow, she would outlive him by many years, and without the protection of his name might descend into the hellish pit of poverty. Having already assigned his estates to Charles Greville he had little else to bequeath her. Yet much as he pondered on this, he always shied away from conclusion, reasoning that another day, another week, or another month would make little difference. Ferdinand's behaviour altered that, forced him to concentrate, and also presented a solution to a man who had a brain.

'The matter is delicate, Your Majesty, since it concerns your husband, the King.'

If ever any person lacked a majestic quality in the physical dimension, it was Queen Maria Carolina. She was a small, plump woman, inclined to wear drab costumes. Her face was plain and her eyes dull. She seemed permanently weary, hardly surprising since she had been brought to bed with child seventeen times since her marriage to Ferdinand. Other cares assailed her, as the true ruler of the kingdom, the day-to-day running of which would tax ten men. Events in France bore down on her, as they did on her brother, the Austrian Emperor.

'It is 'ard, Chevalier 'Amilton, to put together those two words, "husband" and "delicate".'

'I think you know how much I esteem His Majesty.'

She nodded at the diplomatic remark, aware that the Chevalier liked her husband, going well beyond that required of him in the matter of time spent in the King's company. He was unfailingly polite to her, as well, though she wished she could see the true face he must present when out hunting, for rumour had it that Sir William was a committed killer of game.

'I must pass this to you.'

Maria Carolina took Emma's sketchpad, already open, and read it, not once, but twice. Sir William Hamilton watched her face, noting the slight movements: a diminution of the cheeks, the thinning of the lips, the way the heavy eyebrows stretched a fraction. He knew she wouldn't be shocked: Maria Carolina and her husband were a tolerant pair. It was rumoured she had an attachment to General John Acton, though since he was said to be a pederast too that was open to question.

'This was written about Miss 'Art?'

'It was.'

'You do not approve?'

Sir William executed the tiniest of bows. 'It hardly falls to me, when dealing with a king, to entertain such a notion as approval.'

The Queen smiled: Sir William had found a neat way of deflecting her question while providing an answer. 'Poor Emma.'

'Indeed. It gives me no pleasure to admit that it is not an attachment she favours.'

'It is not one I favour, Chevalier 'Amilton. I allow his bestial attentions because it is my duty to do so.'

Sir William wisely chose to ignore that outburst, uncharacteristic in a woman who normally kept the unpleasant side of her marriage to herself.

'I have the problem of her very public attachment to me. I love His Majesty, and would under most circumstances seek to oblige him. But no gentleman could consent to another cuckolding him with his mistress. Aside from that, I'm aware of the passions to which His Majesty is prone, therefore I've come to the only person who could intercede without causing offence.'

'The best method I 'ave found is to distract him.'

Sir William Hamilton had encountered some such distractions and been subject to the odd pang of jealousy. Maria Carolina, or the agent she employed on her behalf, had an unsurpassed eye for beauty, of which there was no shortage in the area of Naples. Young peasant girls, with clear olive skin and figures just on the wrong side of being wholly formed, were the Queen's only method of contraception, the only way she could get enough peace to recover from her endless *accouchements*. Ferdinand was happy with a young and luscious bedmate while the girl chosen was happy with a financial reward that gave her the price of a good husband.

It is often the case, in conversation, that the import of a remark only dawns on the recipient after several more exchanges have passed. As Sir William and the Queen discussed how to deflect her husband, he could almost see on that square, unattractive face the notion, the seed of which he had planted, form in her mind.

'You said, Chevalier 'Amilton, that no man could consent to 'anding over possession of his mistress.'

'I would find that impossible.'

'We both know other men who would not.'

'With respect, Your Majesty, I am not other men.'

Maria Carolina gave a wry smile. 'It would be curious to

know how you would react if my dear companion Emma was your wife.'

'A man and his wife are different, Your Majesty. Having formed a bond and had it sanctified by holy matrimony, each party enjoys the right to seek pleasure, within the bounds of discretion, where they may.'

She was nodding slowly, since her visitor was only stating the obvious. Marriages in the upper layers of society were rarely made for love, but for financial or dynastic reasons. It was not unknown for a woman to leave the bed of her lover, attend church for her nuptials, see out the celebrations and return to her lover, presuming that her new spouse was doing the same.

There was genuine admiration for Maria Carolina, and not only from Sir William Hamilton. The diplomatic community praised her for her sagacity, were at one in naming her the true daughter of the formidable Empress Maria Theresa of Austria. Unlike her sister the Queen of France, Marie Antoinette, who was held to be frivolous, Maria Carolina had a brain, good deductive powers and the ability to take advice. It was such a pity, the same diplomats concluded, that she had to exercise her gifts on such a poor patrimony, and on such a husband.

'You are saying that, were Miss 'Art your wife, His Majesty's attentions would not offend you?'

'Let us say that I would leave it to my wedded wife to make up her own mind as to whether they offended her.'

'But you take leave to doubt such a suit would be pressed to the wife of the British Ambassador?'

'Knowing the King as I do, and cognisant of the source from which he receives his advice, I am sure he would see that if such attentions were unwelcome, the interest of the State would ensure that they be discontinued.'

She put her fingers to her lips, hands almost in an attitude of prayer, a slight smile hidden, just as were her thoughts. But it took no great powers of deduction to guess at their train.

'Would you wish to marry Miss 'Art?'

'The notion would not displease, Your Majesty, given the pleasure it would afford her. I believe you are aware of how attached I am to the lady.'

'I, too, am attached to 'er, Chevalier 'Amilton. She is a

presence that brightens my day and my younger children adore 'er.'

'Might I say, Your Majesty, that she has, in private, nothing but praise for you, both as a companion and as a monarch.'

'It had always caused me much pain not to be able to receive 'er. It is bad that at a time when one often needs a friend to add colour to a dull occasion, a person like Miss 'Art is debarred from attendance.'

'Again I would tell you that it grieves her also, though she would bear that and much more to maintain her attachment to you.'

'Then marry 'er, Chevalier 'Amilton, and make two women happy.'

'Alas,' Sir William replied, throwing up his hands, 'my position forbids it.'

'You require the consent of your king?'

'I do,' Sir William replied, his face bland at what was the crux of the problem.

Maria Carolina nodded slowly, engaging in a long pause, as if seeking a way out of an intractable problem – instead of immediately suggesting the solution that had occurred to her when she had sent the conversation in this direction.

'What would His Majesty King George say if you were able to tell him that a refusal to you would offend the Two Sicilies?' That got a raised eyebrow. 'What if you were to say to your sovereign that Miss 'Art is a friend to the Queen, a confidante she seeks to 'ave by 'er side as and when she chooses? What would the King of England say when 'e is told that my little princes cry to be told that the Emma they love cannot be with them?'

It took some effort to quell the beating of his heart. 'I cannot answer for my master. But I know in my dealing with both kings and queens, that they can rarely be brought to refuse a request from a person of equal rank.'

'Chevalier 'Amilton,' she said, in grave voice, quite at odds with the beaming face, 'I require you, for the sake of the peace of mind of the Queen of Naples, and for the cementing of good relations between the Court of St James and the Court of the Two Sicilies, to marry Miss 'Art.'

It took all Sir William Hamilton's skill as a diplomat to keep the triumphant note out of his voice. 'And the request to my sovereign?'

'The request to King George, Chevalier 'Amilton, that this should be so, will come from me. Might I suggest that it is one that you, in all duty, should deliver.'

The faint tinkling of the harpsichord, and Emma's sweet voice coming through an open window, greeted Sir William on his return. He made for his own apartments first. There, with great care and the assistance of his valet, he repaired his toilet and changed his clothes. He donned a cerise watered-silk coat that he knew Emma was very fond of, ordered that some flowers be formed into a bunch and, once that was in his hand, made for Emma's part of the palazzo.

Below stairs they were abuzz with curiosity at this unusual behaviour, and sensed that something was in the air. Mary Cadogan, with a firmness they had come to expect, made sure that not one of them tried to sneak upstairs. Whatever Sir William had in mind was to be carried out without disturbance.

Emma didn't hear him enter, concentrating on playing the harpsichord part of a Haydn concerto. That allowed Sir William to examine her, which he had done a thousand times these last few years. Dressed for the climate in garments of light material, he could see her breasts moving as she swayed across the keyboard. Her hair moved too, its ends close enough to the sunlight coming through the window to flash red at one second, then burnished gold the next.

Carefully, his silver-buckled shoes making no sound, he approached her back, admiring the way the tendons and bones flexed and moved as she played. Emma must have turned because she sensed him; he was sure she hadn't heard. But turn she did, swiftly, gracefully, her green eyes lighting up with pleasure as she saw him.

'Sir William?'

'My dear Emma.'

'Flowers. Is there some occasion that I have missed?'

'No, my dear. But there is, I am happy to say, one that you may anticipate.'

The frown of curiosity on such a flawless complexion was delicious, creasing her forehead slightly, moving those full red lips together without ruining their shape. The frown deepened as Sir William went down on one knee and placed the posy he was carrying in her open hand. Then he took the other and lifted it to his lips, holding on to it when he had kissed her hand.

'My dear Emma. You have been companion to me now for near five years, and I am certain my life has been improved by the association. It is my fond hope that the same truth holds for you. With that in mind, and knowing that it is something you desire to come to pass, I have come here, and gone on to one knee in time-honoured fashion, in order to ask you to be my wife.'

The green eyes opened wide with shock. 'Wife?'

'You would make me the happiest man on earth if you merely said yes.'

'Wife?'

CHAPTER 47

1791

'Charles, I swear to you, Emma couldn't say anything but "wife" for several minutes. She kept repeating that one word.'

'How amusing,' said Charles Greville, though both his tone and the sour look on his pale serious face belied his words.

They were in a coach, heading back from Windsor. Sir William had used his right as a returning ambassador not only to report to his sovereign regarding his Neapolitan mission but to pass over the request from Maria Carolina that King George's Minister Plenipotentiary regularise his position *vis à vis* her good friend and *confidante*, Emma Hart. Greville, returning from his family home in Warwickshire, had met him at the royal castle.

'She agreed to a wedding in the end?'

'Most assuredly.' Sir William could recall the scene now. Emma had flown around the room in a torrent of excitement, before acceding to his request that she help him back to his feet. Emma had obliged, showered him with kisses, rushed to tell her mother, embraced all the servants, who seemed just as ecstatic, then rushed back up the stairs to embrace him again.

There was pleasure here, too, in almost guying his nephew. Charles Greville should know he had nothing to fear in the matter of his inheritance, yet he was piqued by his uncle's intentions. It was as though he still considered Emma his own; was annoyed that the man he had put in as a surrogate had usurped his prerogative. Now, for the first time in five years, he was on his way to meet her.

'The King was gracious?' Greville asked.

'My old foster-brother George has no knowledge of grace. He

sees directness as a quality. It is a good thing that I represent him abroad and not the other way round. We'd be forever at war.'

'Any hint of madness?'

'None, unless you count that damned habit he has of saying "what, what" all the time. He was always a bit of an odd fish, even as a child.'

He had been a damned unhappy fish earlier, King George, searching for a way to refuse his ambassador permission to marry. Throughout a deeply uncomfortable interview Sir William had searched in vain for a sign of the child and young man he had known. Whatever his oddities, George had possessed a degree of humorous vulgarity. In the rollicking life they had led as young men he had always been to the fore when it came to causing mayhem. George loved women, married, single, betrothed; high-born, low-born and anywhere in between. He drank like a fish, sang loudly, badly and frequently, teased any watchman whose path he crossed and flew in the face of authority. He had also, as a prince, set up house and fathered a bastard by a commoner.

Now he was Farmer George, father of the nation, model husband with a dog of a wife who had raised dullness to a performing art. He preached marital fidelity as if he had never bedded the wife of another man, bore down on his sons in the article of low-born mistresses for behaving exactly as he had himself, and had hummed and hawed to his old friend like the worst kind of pious hypocrite. Sir William, angry at the hypocrisy, had enjoyed his discomfort: the letter from Maria Carolina had made it impossible for him to refuse. He hadn't quite squirmed, but it was a close run thing.

'Brown's Hotel,' said Greville, indicating that they had arrived at the place where Sir William and his intended bride had taken rooms.

It was with an attitude of studied calm that Greville ascended the stairs to their suite. It would be a curious reunion, which Emma had known she would have to face, and which she had signally failed to mention on the journey from Naples. Opening the door, Sir William was surprised to see Mrs Cadogan. But that made sense: Emma must be nervous that by some inadvertent act she would destroy a prospect of the happiness she had come to London to set in stone.

With that air of theatricality that never deserted her, she had taken station by the bow window. The light was nothing like as flattering as that of Naples: indeed, there was scarce any sun to speak of, even on this, a late-spring day. But what there was played across and flattered her features. Emma had dressed carefully too, in a dark blue dress that hinted at sobriety. Yet she had also taken care that it did not hide her magnificent figure, so that Charles Greville should be sure that the creature he had abandoned was even lovelier now.

Sir William had to admire her poise. The slow turn, the look towards him to receive a nod that told her of the King's consent. Then an even slower smile, followed by an advance across the room, both hands outstretched. Emma was every inch the lady.

'Charles.'

'Emma,' he replied, bending to kiss one of those hands.

This was a moment of truth for Emma, the point at which she would know her feelings. Would there be that *frisson* running through her hand and her arm? She knew she was being watched by her future husband, knew that Charles, if only for the sake of his pride, would be looking for a response. She felt nothing, just the touch of dry flesh on her moist skin. The breath that she had held, in fear of finding the love she had once harboured for Greville still there, was released. Greville saw it and the disappointment was plain in his eyes.

'I arranged to meet Charles at Windsor, my dear,' said Sir William, 'so that I could fetch him back to see you.'

A slight untruth. Greville had suggested meeting at Windsor, taking advantage of the interview to bring himself before royalty. His excuse was that gossip of the worst kind regarding Emma had flowed to the King's ears from every malicious voice in London. If necessary he wanted to be on hand to refute it.

'Then I thank you for that, Sir William,' said Emma, voice slightly over-modulated to show Greville she was truly now a lady. 'Your nephew and I have much to catch up on. Letters can never do as much justice to events as conversation. Mother, would you oblige me by ordering for us some tea?'

Sir William was content. The prospect of this meeting had caused him some concern. He disliked the notion of committing himself to Emma without being sure that her previous regard for his nephew had cooled. His concentration, at that moment of contact, had been total: he had seen her response and it had pleased him. But more than that he had observed how stiff Greville had become, like a man rebuffed. He could now leave them alone with an easy mind. And the way she had said 'your nephew' was like a deliberate blow aimed to wound Charles's pride.

To take Emma out into society carried many risks, but they had to be borne. Some people, Sir William knew, would slight her without ever allowing themselves the chance to test defamation against experience. Others, ogres to his mind, would come to peer, but with a set view that would not alter whatever Emma did. Yet, even in stuffy London, so different from pleasure-loving Naples, there were those who would receive both the Chevalier and his intended bride and make them welcome.

Sir William Beckford, author of *Vathek* and a famous pederast with a reputation to put Emma's to shame, accommodated them at Fonthill, eagerly discussing the plans for his new house to be built as a seal at the end of his ten-year self-imposed exile. Bath, home to the fashionable world in August, was split. Sir William's old friend the Dowager Countess Spencer fled to Longleat to avoid a meeting; her daughter, Georgiana, Duchess of Devonshire, welcomed the pair with open arms.

Emma sat once more for old Romney, feeling different from the chattel who had been painted so many times before. Now she was there in her own right, as a future ambassadorial bride, posing for pictures that would not be sold off for her keep. It seemed that every artist in London wished to capture her likeness, though time allowed her to accede only to a youngster called Thomas Lawrence. This came at the behest of his patron Lord Abercorn, Sir William's cousin, who had agreed to stand witness for her, this in a family that was scandalised in the main by the match.

There were parties at the Richmond home of the Marquis of

Queensberry, where Emma performed *opera buffa* songs that enchanted all present, one fellow so much that he offered her two thousand pounds to appear in a pair of concerts. That was something to make an old friend laugh when they went to Drury Lane. Jane Powell, Emma's fellow housemaid, was now a famous actress, ever grateful to that rat Gil Tooley, who had engineered her and Emma's dismissal from the Budd household, for forcing her into the profession.

Mary Cadogan went north, first to Hawarden to see her mother and settle some money on the family, then to see Little Emma. She was able to report on her return that the child, now supported by Sir William, was well, that her education progressed at a goodly pace, and that she had no idea that the lady she was talking to was a relation. 'Better to let her grow up in ignorance,' was the grandmotherly conclusion.

The temptation to send a note to Arlington Street, to Kathleen Kelly, was to be avoided. Besides, she was a woman with her ear to the ground. She would know that Emma Hart was back in London on the arm of a Knight of the Bath. Perhaps, on the day of the wedding at St Marylebone Church, she would be outside.

The sun shone as if by command, giving a golden tinge to the stone of the church. Crowds had gathered to watch the nuptials, the usual mob drawn to any hint of scandal, but leavened with more than just the curious. Some members of society might not be able to bring themselves to attend, but they were determined to see a woman famous now, all over Europe, as a beauty.

There was gentle applause mixed with ribald good wishes for Sir William, dressed in cream silk, the sash and brilliant star of his knightly order very prominent. Strangers watched for infirmity, but saw only the sprightly gait of a fit and healthy man, and a face that could only be described as patrician. A hush fell as Emma's carriage approached, open-topped, with the bride in a pale green dress of fine silk, set off by a dark green sash around her waist, both designed to show her fair unblemished skin and highlight her huge green eyes. On her head she wore a high hat of the same colour as the sash, held in place by a silk scarf and topped by a huge curled feather, both of a hue to match the dress. Her rich auburn hair, so beloved of every man she had known, she wore loose and long, the whole ensemble bringing forth from the crowd a spontaneous ripple of acclaim.

From inside the small church they could hear the music and the singing, not a choir, nor a doleful church melody, but musicians hired by Sir William to lend an air of gaiety to the proceedings with light, quick airs from Austrian and Italian composers. She stepped down from the carriage on the arm of Lord Abercorn, and went into the dim interior of the porch.

Few had attended the ceremony, at Sir William's request, and he stood at the end of the short aisle facing Emma, erect, looking proud as she walked slowly towards him, nodding to those present. Greville was facing her, his eyes searching her face, perhaps in the hope of seeing doubt. After a brief glance at him, Emma looked away and produced a dazzling smile aimed at his uncle.

Would Greville see it for what it was – performance? From her earliest days Emma had dreamed of marrying a prince. Sir William wasn't that, but he had a palazzo, he lived in the grand manner and she rode in carriages as fine as any nobleman could muster, and all worshipped at her feet. But she had also dreamed of an all-encompassing love, a depth of passion so profound that her heart would burst at the thought of union. But as she reflected on the life she had led so far, which was different from those childhood dreams, Emma knew that she was lucky. To ask for perfection at a moment like this seemed the height of selfishness.

Sir William bowed to her before turning to face the cleric, who stood ready to carry out the ceremony. As he spoke the words of the service she could hear the soft crying of her mother in the front pew. As a woman who had done much to engineer this moment tears seemed an odd response. Did she wish for better too?

Her future husband's skin felt as dry as parchment as he took her hand to put on the ring. She noticed a slight tremble as he aimed it at her outstretched finger and wondered what doubts he too harboured at this, the final moment, as he bent to kiss her hand.

'I now pronounce you man and wife.'

'Lady Hamilton,' said Sir William softly.

The musicians, silent throughout the ceremony, burst into a joyous *rondo* of harpsichord, violas and French horns, and all present applauded as the couple turned to them. At Sir William's bidding, he bowed and she curtsied, before they turned to enter the vestry, there to sign and solemnise their marriage. What doubts Emma had were now gone. Those words Sir William had used chased her demons away. She was now the lawful wedded wife of the Ambassador and Minister Plenipotentiary to the Court of the Two Sicilies.

She was Lady Hamilton.

Sir William, preparing to return to Naples, sent to tell King George of his intentions. That was, by custom, another occasion on which an ambassador was obliged to meet the monarch, also an occasion, if he was married, to present his wife at court. The reply came back from Windsor, couched in terms of no politeness whatsoever, that neither the King nor the Queen recognised Emma as his wife; that while he was welcome to attend and receive his instructions, on no account was he to be accompanied by her. Sir William had no choice but to go, but he used the occasion to tell the man with whom he had shared a nursery what he thought of such behaviour. Their meeting wasn't private, as it should have been, but held publicly at the normal weekly levee.

'I depart at the end of the week, Your Majesty.'

'Time to be gone, what, what?' King George replied, with a knowing look aimed at those courtiers close enough to observe and hear the exchange. 'I daresay you yearn for the warmer climate of Naples. They allow for things there that would not pass elsewhere.'

'We shall stop in Paris, Sire.'

Farmer George shook his head. It wasn't a happy prospect for a reigning monarch to look on, the events taking place in the French capital: King Louis and Queen Marie Antoinette had been dragged from Versailles to be kept in the Palace of the Tuileries and denied the freedom to move. Mobs gathered in the *faubourgs* and orators on street corners incited the mob to violence. Would the contagion spread to Farmer George's own realm? 'Bad business there, Sir William, what, what?'

That raised a murmur of assent from the eavesdroppers.

'But interesting, Sire.'

The bulging Hanoverian eyes bulged a little more. 'Interesting?'

'Of course, Sire. It will be instructive to observe how a king goes about his duties when his subjects are in a position to command his behaviour.'

Sir William bowed, turned on his heel, and left the audience chamber, which was buzzing with his carefully honed insult.

Emma thought they looked a sad pair, King Louis and Queen Marie Antoinette, as they made their way through the gardens of the Tuileries to attend mass, an absolute precursor of their holding court, a sign of their continued belief that the office they occupied came from God, not man. The nation, or at least the National Assembly, didn't agree, and was just days away from the ceremony that would inaugurate a new constitution.

Louis seemed vague, bereft of that regal air so necessary to command a nation like France. Dress like monarchs they might, but for both himself and his Austrian wife the appearance of their office had deserted them along with their power. After the mass, King Louis's conversation with Sir William and Lady Hamilton was perfunctory. His wife, however, knowing that Emma was a confidante of her sister, was eager for their company.

Observing Marie Antoinette as she talked, Emma could see a family likeness to Maria Carolina in her face, but that was where it ended. The French Queen was taller than her sister, a more willowy creature, had clearly been a beauty, and those physical traits seemed replicated in her behaviour. The eyes betrayed a weak, distracted personality, her conversation was floating and inconsequential, odd given her circumstances. The assurance that the prayers of Naples were with her and her family lifted her spirits somewhat, and she pressed on Emma a letter for delivery to Maria Carolina. The Hamiltons were also presented to her children, who showed punctilious behaviour in the way they greeted these visitors from England. Emma remarked after they left that the Dauphin was 'quite the little man'.

'More so than his father, I hazard,' said Sir William. 'If ever I saw a fellow defeated, then it is Louis.'

Two days later, Emma and Sir William made their way to the Champs Élysées on foot, all carriages having been banned from the city, to witness the celebrations of the new, constitutional France. A balloon, in the red, white and blue of the new tricolour, was sent up to a huge clamour of emotion; strangers kissed and embraced as they toasted each other and freedom.

But it was not all bliss. Making their way back to their residence, after a wearying day, the Hamiltons came across a mob surging through the streets, grubby individuals, shoeless, trouserless, wild-eyed creatures egged on by fiery demagogues. When the rabble stopped to listen to the orators, Emma heard threats of death uttered that chilled her blood, threats not just against royalty and aristocrats, but against all men of property, including the most rapacious landowner of them all, the Church.

The scenes of riot continued into the night and Emma watched from the safety of her window. Clutching in her hand the letter from Marie Antoinette to her sister in Naples, she felt more sympathy for King Louis than that evinced by her husband: she had seen in the faces below her and in those they had observed on the way home that he truly had something to fear.

Taking possession of the letter turned out to have been easier than delivering it. The King and Queen of Naples were at Caserta when the Hamiltons returned to the Palazzo Sessa, which occasioned a short stay, a hasty repacking, before they were once more in the coach on the way to the royal country palace. Sir William, as a returning ambassador, had a duty to present his credential, and the more pleasant task of finally presenting Emma at court. Powdered and dressed for the occasion, it was a blow to arrive at the palace only to be informed by the Court Chamberlain that, while Sir William Hamilton was welcome, he had no instructions regarding his wife.

Left outside while others passed through to be presented, for he had refused to enter without Emma, Sir William exploded. His voice, in a mixture of Italian and undiplomatic French, echoed off the high ceiling of the anteroom leading to the audience chamber. That was as nothing to the tirade he produced as, with the levee over, the Neapolitan courtiers departed while he and Emma still waited.

Emma tried to keep a brave face. She had been traduced many times and, even after a wedding that had been the stuff of fairy-tales, still had enough sense to know that her titular elevation left her exposed. She had kept from Sir William her hurt at not being presented at Windsor, laughing it off as the behaviour of people too stuffy to engage her interest anyway. Diminished as the French royal family were, presentation at their court had salved the wound. But she had expected that here, of all places, she would be fully welcome, and that, hard as she tried not to mind, engendered some tears.

Enraged, Sir William insisted he would leave the country, not just Caserta, and court officials were sent scurrying to seek a solution. In an establishment that moved slower than a wounded snail, a hurried compromise was arranged. The King was already gone, gun in hand to shoot any poor bird that flew over his head, but Maria Carolina agreed to return to the audience chamber and take her seat on the throne.

Sir William was tranquillity itself as he entered, Emma in court dress on his hand. He could feel her slight trembling as they made their way up the carpet, which was decorated with the royal coat of arms. She had practised for this a hundred times, dreamt of it a thousand. And here she was at last.

'Your Majesty, I bring you greetings from my Sovereign Lord, George, by the Grace of God King of England, Ireland, Wales and Scotland, Lord of the Isles, Duke of Hanover.' In a calm voice Sir William Hamilton reeled off the endless titles of his king. But the note changed to one of pride as he continued, 'And may I, Your Majesty, present to you Lady Emma Hamilton, my wife.'

Maria Carolina stood up, came down from the dais, and kissed Emma on both cheeks. 'We welcome you, Lady 'Amilton, and pray that you will grace our court often.'

Emma responded with a deep curtsy, her heart pounding with an excitement that far outweighed what she had felt at her wedding. Part of her dreams at least had come true.

BOOK FOUR

CHAPTER 48

1793

Scraping the ice off the inside of the window-pane did little to increase the light. The sky was slate grey. Only by peering through the glass could Nelson see the stark outlines of the bare trees in the Parsonage garden, a line of gaunt sentinels that, in fanciful moments, stood like gravestones for his naval career. Halfway up the hill, All Saints Church, grey moss covered stone, stood barely defined against frosty fields. The sneeze, loud enough to penetrate the closed parlour door, reminded him that he was not alone, though it seemed like it at times.

In the grip of a Norfolk winter, it was hard to recall the sublime moment of his wedding: the hot sun, the gardens of Montpelier in the same full bloom as his bride-to-be, the grin on young Josiah's face at the melting of his worries. Prince William Henry, now created Duke of Clarence, had behaved like a *grand seigneur*, and John Herbert fussing as he deferred to a man whose social position dazzled him. Nelson frowned. Herbert would have been less enamoured if he had known the Prince's true character, had had any inkling of the merry dance he had led the bridegroom on their travels round the Caribbean both before the ceremony and afterwards.

That association had done Nelson nothing but harm, which had been made plain to him since paying off *Boreas*. In four annual visits to Windsor to attend a levee, the King hadn't chosen once to engage him in conversation. He was more inclined to scowl at the man who, according to the reports he had received from outraged husbands and dunned tavern keepers, had allowed his son to make an ass of himself and the institution he represented.

It seemed that nothing he had tried to do in the Caribbean had worked in his favour. Admiral Hughes had enough friends on the Board of Admiralty to place a check on any career and he had not forgiven him, blackening his name at every opportunity, telling all that Nelson was a damned nuisance; that to employ him was to employ trouble. Instead of being grateful, the officials in the departments to which he had reported on the way the planters were bent on cheating the Exchequer were inclined to back up Hughes's opinion, on the grounds that Nelson had done nothing but aggravate their workload and disturb their measured, peaceful existence.

Many spoke for him, William Locker foremost among them, but Nelson knew from his own experience that one negative voice in a situation where employment was scarce could outweigh ten in favour. For some reason, Hood, the senior sea lord, who should have aided him, had turned his face away. The years had gone by: five years on half-pay when his only accomplishment had been to turn the gardens around the Parsonage from his father's untidy desert into something respectable. Five years of annual visits to his noble relation, Lord Walpole, where his wife could see in the broad acres and landscaped lakes what might have been hers had she married better.

Josiah, on his visits home from school, grew more morose and less joyful, the carefree infant rapidly turning into an adolescent irritant. Locally he had seen gawky girls turn from geese into swans, spotty boys grow to be men and stalwart farmers and their wives shrink into their dotage. His calendar revolved around local feasts and markets, coursing for hares with his dogs and shooting in the autumn. That was until he learnt that he was a deplorable shot; that his fellow hunters wished to steer clear of him from his habit of walking with his weapon cocked. Firing on sight, without proper aim, was no way to fill the larder.

Alarms and excursions abounded. Spanish bellicosity, re-volution in France, even fleets gathered and sent to sea so that Britannia's enemies should know that she was prepared for war. Hopes had been raised that he might stand for Parliament but they, too, had faded away. The list of correspondents to whom he sent pleading letters had grown longer as time passed, but not one had been able to alter his prospects.

He breathed on the window, then traced an outline on the steamed up glass with his finger, a rough drawing of a frigate under bare poles, half a dozen strokes, one from bowsprit to sternpost, the second the deck and the poop. Three masts were added and stroke six was a wave-filled sea. He imagined her as *Boreas* with everything aloft, royals, studdingsails and kites, to see that line of waves below the hull as the deep blue they had been when he had sailed from Barbados for home. He couldn't draw the vision of happiness that had filled his mind then any more than he could understand where it had disappeared.

Those unemployed years had felt like five decades, spent in the company of a wife who had good reason to be more miserable than he. Fanny hadn't taken to England, let alone isolated and windswept Burnham Thorpe, shuddering even when the sun shone and the garden on which he had toiled so assiduously was in bloom. She hated it when it rained, which was frequent, or when the east wind froze her to the marrow even on a day when the sky was blue. Grey skies and icicles reduced her even more, so that she could barely be brought to exchange a civil word with anyone, his father when he called, her husband or the servants, especially Frank Lepée, who was often drunk and always boastful. Her blood was accustomed to the heat of the West Indies while her domestic appetites hankered for the ease and luxury of Montpelier. Often these complaints were vocal and general, but it was with her silences and her personal frigidity that she punished him.

Leaving the window and his drawing, Nelson went through to the parlour, a hurried opening and closing of the door earning him a glare from the figure hunched inside a shawl by the fire. He replaced the bolster laid to keep out the draughts, jamming it hard against the gap at the bottom of the door, then walked past his wife to poke the logs, causing them to flare up and light what he could see of the pallid face.

'I shall need to get Lepée to fetch more wood.'

'Is there enough wood to fend off this chill?'

'This weather will pass, my dear.'

'To what?' she snapped. 'To rain, sleet, to a hint of warmth in the sun blasted to petrifaction by a North Sea gale, with you telling me of storms at sea and how you love a good blow.'

The words he wanted to say died on his lips, merely because he had used them before and failed to lift her spirits. For all his desire to secure employment, Nelson could extract some pleasure even from this ice-bound existence. It certainly suited his health. The fevers and agues, which had plagued him in warmer climes, were absent here in this bracing English air. Winter was a time to hunt for game and fowl, to skate upon frozen ponds with young Josiah when he was home from school. This part of Norfolk was blessed with hills, and snow allowed for the manufacture of ice slides, as well as providing the ammunition necessary to indulge in a snowball fight. The fantastic landscape afforded by a sudden thick frost, which covered the branches of the trees and made them into hanging sculptures, delighted him.

Society came from visiting neighbours, relatives or friends, and a day spent in Burnham Market, where he could share the newspaper in a snug coffee-house. There was a degree of frustration in reading in the *Register* of events outside the borders of the Burnham parishes; of who was received at court, who led fashion and how his nation stood in the councils of the greater world. Commenting on the news gave him a reason to correspond with people, allowing him a justification for putting his name before them.

He often accompanied his father as he visited his parishioners, all of whom never forgot to include Captain Nelson in their prayers. He would listen as the Rector ministered to their souls, seeing the other side of his parent's doleful nature, the part that could encourage and uplift. Edmund Nelson's sermons, delivered from his trio of pulpits, were stolid rather than inspiring, but they were designed to ease troubled souls, and to remind his flock of the dangers inherent in a lack of scrupulous observance to the teaching of their God. It was pleasant to stop outside the church and talk to these people; to remember that, but for fate, he might have ended up a farmer himself, obsessed with flukes of wind that presaged a storm, watchful of birds as they migrated and returned, caring for livestock that suffered danger from pestilence, weather and hunting animals.

And he studied and wrote about the lives of the lowest in the land, the farm labourers. It was no secret that the King was interested in the state in which they, his least blessed subjects, existed. Nelson could report that their lives were close to miserable, that what they ate would not and could not sustain them, and that recourse to the alehouse, their only relief, did naught but beggar them further. These reports were not sent directly to the King, but to Prince William, Duke of Clarence, for onward transmission to his father, as a way of alerting both to his continued existence. He longed to say more since the lives of these wretches depressed him. But tact was required, so the unpleasant truth had to be made palatable. At least he could openly tell their sovereign that they were loyal, that the sedition spreading from France had little influence in the hovels or alehouses of Norfolk.

He relished the feeling of frozen cheeks warmed by a welcoming interior and a blazing fire. The taste of spiced wine, mulled with a red-hot poker, was twice as pleasant outdoors than in. The sight of robins pecking the berries, hard because of deep frosts, could keep him still till his marrow froze. The moment when the weather broke, and the first green shoots of spring emerged through the morning mists, was a perfect joy, making him feel close to his Maker. Activity kept Nelson warm by day, and should have by night, but the lady he had married, in concealing certain things, had hidden most her fear of ardent desire.

Consummation, his wedding night, even after five years, was fresh in the memory, being so swift and dull, almost an agony to Fanny who had made it plain that, while her husband was entitled to his due, it was not to be freely and frequently offered. Nelson lacked the heart to press, to insist, nor was he good at signalling desire, either merely corporeal or his wish to father children, to which out of duty Fanny might have responded. The merest hint of disinclination drove him away. He wanted warmth offered freely, not cold charity, so that aspect of his marriage had now faded to nothing.

'Post on the way,' shouted Lepée, who managed to make the passing on of such mundane information seem like an imposition.

'Post my dear,' said Nelson, searching his pockets for the means to pay, glad to suppress the disloyal thoughts he had been harbouring.

'Another letter of regret, no doubt, husband.' Her voice took on an arch, shrewish tone, meant to convey the heartless tone of officialdom. ' "Their Lordships regret to inform Captain Nelson that they cannot oblige him in the matter of a ship. We are sure Captain Nelson will appreciate that there are many deserving officers and a want of opportunities, with the country at peace, to employ them".'

'We mustn't lose hope, Fanny.'

Her voice was weary, her head sinking even deeper into the shawl than hitherto. 'Your anticipation fatigues me so, husband. How many letters must you have before you see the truth? How many wasted trips to London and fruitless interviews can that sanguine nature of yours contend with?'

'I can't lose expectation, Fanny. It is all I have to sustain me.'

'Half pay is what sustains us both, and in a degree of cold and misery I never thought to experience.'

'These are the worst months, January and February. It will soon be spring.'

'With you throwing open windows as if what comes through passes for warmth.'

'The postman,' Nelson said, to avoid having to answer.

Muffled against the wind, the post messenger slithered up the slippery path, between the empty flower-beds, past the white frosted lawn and the frozen pond. His hardest task seemed to consist of keeping his feet on the uneven paving, reminding his recipient that repairing it had been a task he had promised for last summer, but had failed to fulfil.

'Post for thee, your honour,' the voice said from under layers of scarves.

Nelson took it, examining the seal, his hope evaporating as he saw that it was not from any official source. There was no crown impressed into the red wax, nor anchors to denote the Admiralty. He paid the fellow his sixpence, bade him God speed, and hurried back indoors. He had to heat his hands by the fire before he could begin to open the letter.

'It's from Davidson, my dear.'

'If he offers you a merchant vessel, you must take it.'

Nelson declined to reply to that. It was a long-running marital sore, the notion that he should take employment in a merchant ship and at least afford himself the chance of earning a decent stipend. Behind the insistence was the notion that Fanny would benefit too, perhaps to sail in his ship to some warmer shore or, failing that, being able to move to a less isolated spot, perhaps even to a house that might be said to be comfortable. He knew he could not oblige. It was one of the catch-all tenets of naval service: if you wanted advancement you must be available, even if there was scant employment. Taking service on a merchant deck meant no longer being on the active list. His naval career would be as good as over.

'Matters with France do not improve. Davidson maintains that despite the best efforts of the opposition war cannot long be avoided.'

'I recall he said the same last year and the year before that, when those *canailles* carried their king to Paris. Now they try him like a common criminal and what do we do? It was ever thus. Those cowards and placemen in Whitehall will do nothing.'

'How can you say that after last year's alarm?'

'You would do yourself a kindness not to mention that!'

He might not mention the Spanish Armament, but he thought often of that brief period when his hopes soared with the news of two English ships seized by the Spaniards off Vancouver Island, the crews confined in Mexico. The revolutionary government in France made ready fourteen sail-of-the-line, war was in the air and employment with it. High hopes had been raised, only to be dashed when the Spanish, once the proudest nation on earth, meekly caved in to all Britannia's demands.

'Things have moved on, Fanny. This time it is France. Their king I feel sorry for. But what is more important is that the revolutionaries have gone to war with their neighbours and they are beating them soundly. Britain cannot stand aside and see Europe engulfed.'

'Why do you talk to me so, Nelson?' she whined. 'Like some Westminster candidate trawling for votes. I cannot abide it.'

His reply was designed to mollify her. 'I merely seek to advise you, my dear, that matters move our way. War will see the fleet expanded, and I flatter myself that my character is such that they will never refuse me employment.'

'They have managed to do so for five years.'

'Davidson suggests it would be wise to be in London, that a call on Lord Chatham might serve best.'

'Then I hope he has enclosed the coach fare, for if he has not you must needs spend a week out in that wilderness shooting enough food to fill the larder.'

He smiled. 'I am reliably informed that I'd more likely shoot myself.'

Nelson bent down, pulling at the shawl enough to reveal the red end of Fanny's nose. He recalled those pale cheeks in sunshine, where they had been fetching. Now they were pinched and chapped, the lips that had smiled so sweetly likewise. 'Are there no words I can say that will bring you cheer?'

A mittened hand emerged to take hold of his. The voice ceased to whine, and instead seemed crestfallen. 'Forgive me, husband. The cold shrivels regard as quickly as it does the skin.'

'Not in my breast, Fanny.'

'Do I deserve such a sentiment?'

'You always will, my dear.'

'Little enough have I done to earn it.'

Nelson put a hand to her cheek, his fingertips welcome, being warm from the fire. 'If I repeat myself, forgive me, but I see all this as a trial from God, a test of my regard for my country. Can I let them treat me so ill and still retain the golden glow of my patriotism?'

'Can you, Nelson?'

'With you by my side, yes.'

'All I do is fail you.'

'I will not let you think that,' he insisted. 'You were raised to better things. I met you in sunshine and plenty, and have brought you to this. It is I who have failed you. But believe in my destiny as I do, Fanny. And know that there is a future day when this will be a humorous memory, a tale to tell your grandchildren that they will never understand, being surrounded as they are by everything material a man, a woman or a child could desire.'

She dropped her head to kiss his fingers. 'If God rewards a forgiving nature he will surely reward you.'

'He has done that already, Fanny, by bringing you to my side.'

'Go to London, Horatio. See Chatham, if you can, though don't ask me to hold out much hope, given the way he has abused your requests these last five years. I have seen his letters, don't forget, and read the sentiments that can only be described as cold rejection.'

Chatham had never mentioned the King, and neither had he to his wife. He was in bad odour at court, and while the Sovereign had no veto over naval appointments it would be a brave First Lord of the Admiralty who would gainsay his wishes. Lord Chatham seemed far from that. The trouble was that such an attitude denied him the chance to redress the low opinion in which he was held. An annual levee, which was his right as a post captain to attend, did nothing to thaw relations. No chattering king now, instead a mumbled 'How d'ye do?' from a cold and distant monarch.

'And,' she continued, 'I cannot fathom how you can even begin to tolerate the name of Admiral Hood, who does not even deign to reply when you write to him.'

Hood had wounded Nelson by his indifference, but he had his own problems with royalty. 'Do not castigate a good man damned by politics,' he said.

'Is there anyone you will not absolve?'

'My God would scarcely forgive me if I did not. And I know how deeply my father would chastise me for that sin. I think now, if we pray hard enough, God may answer our submissions.'

'The Rector's on his way,' shouted Lepée, 'looking as cold as charity too.'

Nelson stuck the poker in the fire, trying not to think of Frank Lepée, who could scarce be brought to lift a finger to undertake duties he saw as domestic. Five years on the beach had not tamed the sailor in him, just as it hadn't tamed his love of drink, his ability to relate a tall tale or his less than respectful relations with his master.

'I will fetch my father a posset to heat his bones, and add some brandy to it.'

Fanny smiled, though not much, since to do so fully hurt her lips. 'You'd best not tell him, husband.'

'No. He would see it as a waste of a gift from God.'

She clasped his hand. 'I'm sorry, husband. I promise, when the sun comes out from behind those infernal clouds, to be a better wife to you.'

'I cannot, my dear, see how that is possible.' He stood up as the Rector entered, his tall frame shivering with cold. 'Good news, Papa. Davidson has written to me to tell me there must be a war.'

'With France?'

'Who else?'

'Then God be praised,' said Edmund Nelson, raising the Bible in his gloved hand to point at heaven. 'The Antichrist will at last be slain.'

The sentiment and the way it was expressed made his son shiver.

He had no sooner arrived at Davidson's lodging than he was whipped off to a grand dinner at Hanover Square, home of the Duke of Grafton. Davidson had sent them a note to say he was bringing Nelson along. The welcome he was afforded did not extend to seating him close to his friend. Indeed, he was so far below the salt that he could barely see the carroty top of Davidson's head. The huge room was noisy with the buzz of a hundred conversations, and introductions were so garbled that he was unsure of the identity of his dining companions.

Nelson was seated between two women, both in their middle years. A fat fellow called Padborne, to whom Davidson had introduced him, sat opposite, so enamoured of gluttony that, once the soup was served, his head hardly lifted from the plate laid before him. When he did look up, his eyes, set deep in folds of flesh, cast a jaundiced eye at other portions, as if he were intent on consuming those too.

'Please, sir,' Nelson said, having taken just a few sips, 'my appetite is small. If you feel that you can manage it, have what I cannot eat.'

That earned him a loud sniff of disapproval from his left. The suggestion had come from five years in Norfolk, five years of care in the avoidance of waste. Nelson had forgotten where he was. Wearing his most pleasant smile, he turned to mollify the offended lady with an appropriate excuse. 'Short commons are such a regular feature of naval life, madam, that waste in any form is anathema. Why, if I had any midshipmen here they'd sweep the board like a biblical plague.'

'Who would invite a midshipman to an occasion like this, sir?'

'You would be surprised,' he replied, still smiling, though curious as to where he had seen her before. 'Some of the mites are well connected.'

'Obliged, sir,' said his fat dining companion, who clearly had no more manners than Nelson. He looked at his naval dining companion quizzically.

Nelson reminded him of his name, and added, 'Davidson introduced us.'

'Nelson?' said the same lady. 'Are you any relation to the Reverend Edmund?'

'Yes, madam. He's my father.'

'Then we have met before, sir,' she trilled, 'in the Pump Room at Bath. I scarce recognise you, sir. You were a skeleton when I last clapped eyes on you, with your dear father, who was quite fatigued by the care he administered. Did I not tell you, Padborne, about that naval officer at death's door after that foolish expedition on the San Juan river?'

The fat head lifted from Nelson's plate for a second. 'I cannot recall it, Mrs Padborne.'

'His mind extends no further than his last meal, sir,' she confided, in a voice that could be heard ten feet away. 'Your recovery is remarkable, sir. I take it the Bath waters provided an efficacious contribution.'

'That and Norfolk, where I now reside with my wife.'

'You were not married on our first meeting. You made a good match, I trust?'

547

He bridled at the question, but fought to keep his temper at this woman's impertinence. 'An excellent one.'

He had to look her right in the eye then, because in the sense that Mrs Padborne meant it his marriage had been far from a good one. Herbert had been parsimonious indeed when it came to granting any money to the newlyweds. Talk of a substantial legacy had been just that. Herbert had passed away and only a small bequest had materialised from his estate.

'A woman of means, then?' Nelson was just about to slap her down, to tell her that Fanny had few means, yet was blessed with a good heart, but he didn't get the chance. 'The Rector is still with us, I trust?'

'In such rude good health that it puts mine to shame.'

'Would I know the lady who is now your wife?'

'Do you have connections in the sugar islands?'

'Never in life, sir.' She waved a fan at her fat-faced husband, head still in his soup plate. 'Padborne there would speculate in that pit of thieves if I was not there to stop him, sir. But, by God's good grace, I am.'

'I was about to add that my wife is the niece of the late president of Nevis, who was himself grandson to the Duke of Pembroke.'

'An excellent connection, sir,' she replied with insufferable arrogance. 'I'm sure you have made a proper match.'

There was a snap in his voice when he responded: 'I did not wed the lady for either her dowry or her bloodline. I married her for herself.'

That earned him another sharp wave of the fan. 'How singular, sir.'

'I married her,' Nelson insisted, 'because I esteem both her person and her accomplishments. I must tell you that there is no finer companion for a man's heart than my dear wife. I cannot praise her enough. She is kind, good-natured in the matter of my manifest faults, a rock upon which my house can withstand whichever storm fate throws to test us.'

He carried on, all the time knowing in his own mind he was lying because, in truth, Fanny had been a sad disappointment to him. He tried to suppress his train of thought, but it would not go away. Where was the warm anticipation he had anticipated at Montpelier; where were the children he had written of in his Caribbean letters? His longing for physical contact had been broken on the granite of her coldness. What satisfaction was there in sex without even a pretence at emotion; what point if the prospect of procreation was greeted with horror?

'It was a great shock to me, Davidson,' he confided later, when they were back in front of his friend's hearth, 'as deep as any I have ever experienced. The sudden knowledge of my own unhappiness.'

Davidson leant forward to tap him on the thigh. 'You will have a ship soon. That will lift your spirits.'

'I don't love her, Davidson,' he said, pulling himself from his chair to lean on the mantel, his voice choked with emotion. 'And when I look backwards I cannot be sure I ever did.'

Davidson put his arm around Nelson's shoulders. 'You need sleep, my dear friend.'

'I feel I've been asleep for five years.'

He was just that when Davidson entered his bedroom, to stand and look over a man he admired more than anyone in the world. Certainly Nelson could be trying when he spoke of the follies of other naval officers or the certainty of his own destiny, but though he was full of confidence, he was a mass of inner tribulations – in his relations with his officers and men, his standing *vis à vis* his superiors, and most of all in anything to do with the heart.

In repose, his hair tousled, his face relaxed, those full lips slightly open, Nelson looked so young, still like a boy at thirty-five. He would find out tomorrow what Davidson already knew but was sworn not to reveal. That Nelson would have his ship and the gloom under which he laboured now would be lifted.

CHAPTER 49

The next morning Nelson arrived at the Admiralty still a half-pay captain. He departed after an interview with Lord Chatham as the commander of HMS *Agamemnon*, a 64-gun ship-of-the-line. Had the First Lord discerned his reasons for turning down a larger ship? Nelson knew that *Agamemnon* was faster than most 74s by several knots, the kind of vessel likely to be sent on detached service rather than tied to purely fleet duties, a ship in which he could individually distinguish himself. She was berthed at the Nore, but there was much to do before he could journey to Sheerness to join her. The next two weeks were all activity as he fired off and replied to endless letters.

Lepée was detached from his celebratory bottle and sent back to Burnham Thorpe, Fanny requested to keep him sober and oversee the way that his servant packed Nelson's sea chest. He added a detailed list of what it should contain. Josiah had to be alerted to join his stepfather as a midshipman aboard his new command. Another letter went off to his brother-in-law, George Bolton, to tell him that if he still wanted his boy, George junior, to be a sailor, then the time had arrived for him to take up his duties.

Using Davidson's credit he could gather the personal stores necessary to stock his own larder with the wines and combustibles he would need to maintain his station among his peers. He had officers to alert, to take up their duties, from Edward Berry, who would be his premier, to his fourth lieutenant, the faithful Bromwich, made up at last and sent to Norfolk to recruit men around his own locality, using the Nelson name. The parents and relatives of a stream of midshipmen were another group with whom he had to correspond, some to accept, many more to turn away. William

Hoste, the son of the Reverend Mr Hoste of Inglethorpe, in Norfolk, he would gladly accept since he knew the boy, and thought his shyness and reserve would disappear once he was serving in a mess. But Mrs Darby's son Henry, despite a connection to his Walpole relations at Wolterton, was, he regretted to say, too young.

There was a stream of missives to the warrant officers, boatswain, gunner, carpenter, armourer and purser, to report to the premier the state of the ship and stores. When it came to crew, sailors had a communication system that seemed to defy time and distance. They knew before the King's ministers that war was certain, knew before the Admiralty secretaries which captain had been appointed to which vessel. Anyone who had served on a man-o'-war wanted the familiar face at the helm, the face of a man they knew they could trust. Nelson hoped he could look forward to seeing a host of old acquaintances.

He would still be short-handed, even with his strong Norfolk contingent, but at the start of a war that would be made up easily from volunteers. On arrival at Sheerness he put up at the Three Tuns, known to all serving officers as the worst inn in the world. William Locker, who commanded at the Nore, joined him for dinner, as hearty as ever and remarkably well informed, eager to advise Nelson to plump for the Mediterranean fleet, since Hood would command there and not the Channel.

'Forget his cold behaviour, Nelson. Hood was frightened to upset the King, who blames you for his son's failures in the West Indies. He might be devious but Hood esteems you as an enterprising officer. The Channel goes to Admiral Lord Howe. He has his own list of deserving captains whom he will favour, and you ain't among them. And there's more chance of independent action away from the home shore for a ship-of-the-line, a chance perhaps to distinguish yourself.'

Locker didn't know he was preaching to the converted. Nelson wanted nothing more than to get away from the shores of England. He was still confused about many things, especially his relationship with Fanny. He felt he needed to be at sea, surrounded by familiar sights, sounds and faces, to put the last five years of inactivity into some kind of perspective. He couldn't wait to get away to sort out his life.

When the time came to go aboard George Andrews was at the quayside, just as he had been when Nelson took command of *Boreas*. There was no hesitation in Andrews now, a young man of nearly twenty years and *Agamemnon*'s third lieutenant. His orders were crisp and loud, and Giddings, who had arrived to take up his previous station without any form of communication from his captain, carried them out in his usual competent fashion.

'How fare you, Mr Andrews?' asked Nelson, looking up at the young man whose fair hair and blue eyes could still conjure up a disturbing image of the sister who had once been the single object of his captain's affections.

'Very well, sir, very well indeed. All the better for being in your ship.'

The sight of his first ship-of-the-line lying at anchor, rising and falling on the slight swell, lifted his heart. *Agamemnon* displaced 1300 tons, carried a crew of 520 men and sixty-four main- and lower-deck cannon. Built at Buckler's Hard in 1781, she was as handsome a vessel as he had ever clapped eyes on. The deck was certainly prepared, with every sign of the mess created by a vessel taking on stores hidden for the new commander's eye. Berry knew just what to clear away and what could be let pass. Captain Nelson was not the man to go prying for faults below decks or on the companionways as soon as he came aboard. He would settle for what he could see between the entry port and his cabin door, between the great cabin and the poop where he would read out his commission. And what he saw pleased him.

Then he set to work, to get ready for sea and, Nelson hoped, glory.

HMS Victory, off Toulon, 1st September 1793.
To Captain Horatio Nelson, HMS Agamemnon.
  Sir,
    You are required with the vessel under your command to proceed with all despatch to Naples, there through the good offices of the British Minister Plenipotentiary to press upon the Court of the Two Sicilies the need for troops to hold and protect that which we have gained on the French mainland.

Enclosed is a letter from myself to King Ferdinand, which I require you to deliver personally into his hand.

I am yours,
Admiral Lord Hood

'Are you familiar with the expression "See Naples and die", Josh?'

'I believe you did say it to me the other day, sir,' his stepson replied, without much spirit. 'When we first got our orders.'

Midshipman Josiah Nisbet was in titular charge of the Captain's barge, though he would in all respects defer to Giddings as coxswain. Such a duty was part of his training, which after four months at sea was moving along tolerably well. He had been seasick in the Thames estuary, for which Nelson, who was prone himself, could not fault him. He attended to both his duties and his lessons, and had progressed well in all departments. Yet Nelson was concerned for the boy, who did not share with the other mids a seeming delight in their station. It was as though he had come to sea to please his stepfather, not because he himself desired it. Even the sweep of the Bay of Naples, as noble an aspect as nature had ever created, failed to move him.

The six-week voyage to the Mediterranean had done Nelson a power of good. He had spent the time in working up both crew and ship so that whenever the Admiral called for any manoeuvre it was carried out swiftly and with grace. With Berry he tinkered with each watch to balance them out in efficiency. His cannon, eighteen and twenty-four pounders, had been run in and out so frequently that Nelson knew in a fight he would get at least two broadsides a minute from his gunners, a rate of fire that no Frenchman could match. Activity, distance and the companionship of sailors had eased his troubled mind, and allowed him to conclude that his difficulties with Fanny were more his fault than hers. A sailor, who by his very nature must hanker after the sea, must be a hard companion with whom to spend your life; a poor and frustrated one denied a ship so much worse.

Looking at Josiah, the thought did occur to Nelson that he was in such a buoyant mood that anyone else might appear glum. Since joining up with Lord Hood off Cadiz he had enjoyed an excellent rapport with the Admiral. Hood liked enterprising officers, and being back at sea had cleansed him of politicking. The kindred spirit who was prepared to stretch rules to gain a positive conclusion, the officer who talked about destroying the enemy not merely engaging them, was one that the admiral valued highly.

Hence this vital mission to Naples. The great French naval port of Toulon had surrendered to the British fleet, but Hood lacked the means to hold it against the revolutionary armies marching from Marseilles to recapture it. Nelson's mission, to him, implied that he had his admiral's trust, and it had also given *Agamemnon* the chance to snap up a prize on the way, a fully laden Levant merchant vessel, which Nelson had valued provisionally as worth at least ten thousand pounds. Three-eighths would be his share, less commission to Davidson, who was acting as his prize agent. Letters had already gone off to him and to Fanny, to tell her of the increase in their wealth.

And here in Naples he was going ashore as a man of substance, Hood's representative, to treat with a king and his ministers on behalf of his own sovereign. With his signal gun he had saluted the kingdom, and Naples had replied most handsomely. His launch was surrounded by boats of all shapes and sizes, some with fishermen, others carrying people of obvious quality come to greet a British man-o'-war.

They were not the only eyes on the barge. From one of the higher chambers of the Castel Nuovo, Maria Carolina, using a telescope on a tripod, had both launch and occupants in view. Emma Hamilton was trying to focus on the same with the naked eye, but the distance was too great. The Queen was calmer now than she had been at first light, when she had been alerted to strange topsails on the horizon. Like most of her wealthy subjects, she stood in terror of the arrival of the French who, having chopped off the head of King Louis, would bring with them the seeds of revolution and murder.

That had occasioned panic in her husband and most of her courtiers, to the point where many had a coach and four laden with their possessions ready to flee. The Queen's nerve had held firm enough to stop Ferdinand from leading a Gadarene rush to safety, which was singular given that her own sister Marie Antoinette was in grave danger of following her husband to the guillotine. There were enough elements in Naples, vocal ones these last months, who would gladly deliver her to the same fate.

As a witness to the earlier reaction of the nobility, Emma was somewhat amused at everyone's behaviour since the vessel had been positively identified as British. Inclined to boast without cause anyway, the Neapolitans she met now swaggered in a parody of bravery, and told her how they had spent the time since dawn loading guns, sharpening swords, preparing to repulse the French invader.

'Your British captain is not very imposing, Emma.'

'Might I be allowed a look, Your Majesty?'

Maria Carolina stood back from the spyglass and Emma peered through, adjusting the lens to get a clearer view. She homed in on the dark blue naval coat, but could see little of the face, obscured as it was by the crowd in front. The man was not tall, but that was commonplace. Few naval officers were, it being so uncomfortable to have too much height in a ship. Emma swung instead to look at the warship in the bay, twin rows of ports open to let in air, though with no guns run out. The sails were furled now, tight against the yards, but the vessel was still a hive of activity, ant-like creatures running through the rigging and traversing the decks. The tide had turned her near bow on to the shore, showing her as broad at the base and much narrower at the level of the deck, the figurehead a proud bust, coloured gold and carmine, with the royal arms at the base. Her pennants fluttered in the breeze and the boats that had gone out to her, to sell their wares and women, stood a way off, awaiting permission to come close enough to trade.

'It is the ship that matters, Your Majesty,' Emma said, as she swung the glass to the quay, fixing her gaze on her husband's back. 'That, I swear, is imposing enough.'

The reception committee on the public quay was numerous, led by the man Nelson must see first, the Ambassador, Sir William Hamilton, whose bearing identified him easily as an English *grand seigneur*. Nelson examined him carefully: tall, once handsome, now showing the lined face and prominent bones of his age. Nelson knew that Hamilton had been in his post for thirty years, and had become famous not only for his length of service but as a collector. There was also the matter of his marriage, which had occasioned a minor scandal, the ripples of which had reached Norfolk. The bride was thirty years his junior and a lady with a colourful past.

After weeks or months at sea, great self-control is required by a sailor to maintain his dignity when stepping ashore. Motionless dry land can easily make a man whose legs are in tune with the waves appear an idiot. Was Hamilton aware of this? Nelson didn't know, but the Ambassador aided him by grasping his hand so firmly that his natural inclination to sway was choked off. Indeed, Hamilton held him in such a strong grip that Nelson felt he was keeping him upright while they exchanged names and courtesies.

'Captain Nelson, you have no notion what it does to my spirits in these troubled times to see a British man-o'-war anchored off Naples.'

Though not yet steady, Nelson had achieved some sense of balance, enough at least to carry off the rest of the introductions without support. In between the exchange of names, speaking rapidly, he brought Hamilton up to date with events: what had happened in Marseilles, which had tried to surrender to Hood only to face the Red Terror. Men, women and children, whose only crime was gentility, had been murdered in cold blood on a guillotine set up in the main square. The citizens of Toulon, frightened by this, had surrendered their town to the British, along with the best part of the French Mediterranean fleet.

'A great coup, Captain,' Sir William cried, just before he introduced the Duke of Amalfi.

'A great burden, sir,' Nelson said, acknowledging the greeting of some count whose name he missed. 'The Admiral lacks the means to hold Toulon. The Revolution was already on the march to retake the town when I left. We had soldiers aboard in lieu of marines, but no more than two thousand in all. Even with the loyal French and half the sailors from the fleet we cannot hold out against a determined enemy. We must have more men, and Lord Hood has sent me here to request that the Two Sicilies provide them. What prospect have I of an immediate audience with the King?'

'Every likelihood, Captain Nelson. I sent my wife to see the Queen with that request in mind. Since Her Majesty holds her in the highest esteem I'll take the liberty of assuming acceptance and coach you directly to the palace.'

Nelson was surprised, but also pleased. He had little knowledge of British plenipotentiaries abroad, but he had them tagged as a slothful crew. Sir William Hamilton was clearly cut from a different batch of cloth, able to act with despatch even before he was asked, to the point of dragging him away from a crowd eager to press his hand. He got Nelson into his carriage, at the same time issuing instructions that would see the Captain's stepson and the crew of the launch catered for in the article of food and shelter.

'I have sick men aboard, Sir William, who would benefit from being ashore. I require fresh victuals, greens, beef and citrus fruits. My water is so brackish as to be undrinkable and I have little time for delay.'

'Use the credit of my office, sir, to purchase anything you need.'

'The expense will be great.'

'My credit hereabouts is greater, Captain,' said Sir William, without pomposity. 'Longevity and a consistency of policy have seen to that.'

'I thank you, sir.'

'It is I who must thank you and Admiral Hood. My task in Naples is never easy, but these last months since the outbreak of war have been strewn with difficulty. I must confess that, at times, my own conviction that we would see something of a British fleet in these waters has been sorely tried.'

They had to talk over the noise of cheering and the endless stream of flowers flung at them by an emotional Neapolitan mob, each man sizing up the other as an aid to those first impressions. Sir William, urbane and dignified, was struck by the seeming youth of this fellow, obviously a senior captain, as well as his application. He was in control of both his subject and his mission. While careful to be polite, Nelson nevertheless had a grasp of what he needed and how he intended to go about getting it. He spoke quickly and succinctly, describing the situation of Hood and his fleet clearly and graphically, explaining the terrain at Toulon and how he, if he were in command, would go about securing it.

'I fear you're wasted at sea, sir, given your grasp of the finer points of land warfare. For my sins I am an old soldier, so I know of what I speak.'

'Never fear, Sir William, I have chosen my career well. My name was unknown to you not half an hour ago. That will not long remain the case for our fellow countrymen. Soon they all will know the name of Nelson!'

Such self-assurance would normally have made Sir William uncomfortable, but somehow the way Nelson said it, the lack of artifice and the look of conviction on his face when he did so, rendered it truthful rather than conceited. Then Nelson demonstrated that he also had good sense, in the way he listened intently to his host as Sir William gave him a brief account of Naples, its court, its politics and the personalities who mattered.

'The Marquis de Gallo, who heads the government, is a man who feels his country is best served by doing nothing. He is the type who would neither support a friend nor oppose an enemy. He has one abiding wish, and that is to stay in his post and increase his already considerable fortune.'

'Does the King trust him?'

'It matters not one jot if he does. Flatter the King but place no store by his promises. The Queen matters most but avoid any attempt at flattery with her. She responds to clear ideas simply expressed, and whatever she decides will be in consultation with her favourite minister, General Acton.'

'Is he party to our cause?'

'He is an Englishman, Captain Nelson. He cannot help but be so. And it stands you in good stead that he is also an ex-naval officer. The "general" is an honorific from Ferdinand. Acton knows that he who controls the Straits of Messina controls the fate of the Kingdom of Naples.'

Hamilton, too, was under scrutiny, and Nelson liked what he saw. His manner was open and friendly, and he had about him an air of sound common sense. Accustomed still to the social mores of home, he was taken by Hamilton's total lack of condescension, his readiness to treat him as an equal and to defer to him in any area of his own expertise. At the same time he had a certain steadiness about him, and gave the impression that ample time was available even if there was, in truth, precious little. Nelson judged that if he had still been a soldier, Hamilton would be a cool fellow in battle, which was the highest praise he could bestow.

The crowds thickened as the carriage approached the gates to the Palazzo Reale. People were there, Hamilton explained, because they were unsure of what was taking place. 'They sway greatly, Nelson, from bellicosity to abject fear in seconds.' He indicated the floor of the carriage. 'Do not be fooled by these flowers. They're as fickle as they are emotional. Ferdinand fears his own people as much as he fears the arrival of the French – with good cause.'

'Then he must be eager for a military victory.'

'I daresay, such are his dreams, that he wins one every time he sleeps.'

Ferdinand, dressed in black and grubby in appearance, towered over his visitor. He greeted Nelson fulsomely, naming him as the saviour of his nation, and enveloping him in an embrace both crushing and malodorous. That remark raised a round of applause from the assembled courtiers to which King Ferdinand responded with a joyous shout. Then he introduced his chief minister, the Marquis de Gallo.

He looked as slippery as Hamilton had described: bland of feature, with blank black eyes and dry skin, vain in the way he spoke and moved, as if Nelson's presence had interrupted far more important business. It was the royal consort who cut across him. The Queen had a presence her husband lacked, and the wit to discuss with her Minister of Marine and the Army what response Naples should make to the request, which had been communicated to her a mere ten minutes before the audience had been granted. It was Acton who spoke; short, deeply tanned, with sharp bird-like features and a look in the eye that denoted deep intelligence.

'Their Sicilian Majesties are cognisant of the joint responsibility of both their nation and yours, Captain. The plague from France must be halted and thrown back into the gutters of Paris from where it emanated. Both my sovereign lord and his queen have had to bear the tragedy of personal loss as well as witness the turmoil released on Europe by these demons. But they are also responsible to the nation God has given them the power to rule.'

'That nation is safe,' Nelson replied, speaking somewhat before he should. 'The French have no fleet and what few capital ships they have at sea are poorly manned, ill prepared and blockaded in Hyerés Bay.'

'We have a land border as well, Captain.'

'You have even less to fear from that source, Sir John. There is no army closer than Toulon to threaten you.'

'It could be said, Your Majesty,' interposed Sir William, addressing the vacant-looking King, 'that the Neapolitan border stands at that very spot. Hold Toulon and France can never menace Naples.'

Sir William had warned Nelson not to expect any decisions, cautioned him that the court of the Two Sicilies moved at a snail's pace when it moved at all. Acton replied on the King's behalf. 'His Majesty King Ferdinand has already arrived at that very conclusion, and is prepared to put at the immediate disposal of Lord Hood a force of six thousand men, plus the vessels to carry them, which are at this very moment being made ready to sail.'

The slight nod between Acton and the Queen, allied to the faraway look in the eyes of King Ferdinand, was enough to tell all present who had really made that decision. The frown on the face of the Marquis de Gallo showed that not everyone agreed.

'I've never known the like, Nelson,' exclaimed Sir William, 'in thirty years of being here. Somnolence, not zeal, is the common currency around these parts, hunting and whoring excluded, of course.'

'I would have wished to decline this feast tonight. Apart from being knocked up from months at sea there are matters aboard my ship to see to.'

'It is one of the burdens of my office, Captain Nelson. A royal wish is not that at all. It is a command. And I fear that this means your ship will have to wait. Besides, I would be most upset if you declined to be my guest.'

'Perhaps for tonight. But I must get back aboard tomorrow.'

'Possibly,' replied Sir William, with an enigmatic smile.

Their progress to the Palazzo Sessa was just as noisy and flower-bedecked as their previous journey, it seemed, with every citizen of Naples eager to show their relief at Nelson's appearance. The noise died as the gates shut behind them, and Nelson picked blooms out of the brim of his hat. The cool of the entrance hall was pleasant after the heat of the open carriage, and Sir William was flattered by the attention of his visitor to the classical statuary that decorated the vestibule.

The rest of the palazzo was like that, an Aladdin's cave that he was encouraged to wander, cooling drink in hand, while Sir William went to find his wife, to tell her of their guest, and to forewarn her of the ball at the Palazzo Reale that night. Emma was in her music room, playing an early harpsichord piece by the recently deceased Mozart, from which she broke off as soon as he entered. She stood up, the loose gown dropping to cling to her figure, in a way that still took away her husband's breath.

'How fared our naval officer?'

'Captain Nelson fared amazingly, Emma. He has quite enchanted the King, and Acton has pre-empted the request he was about to make for military help. Six thousand troops promised in the blink of an eye!'

'He must be a magician. I was with the Queen when you came ashore. I'm not sure she had quite recovered from her fear that his ship was French.'

'He's a remarkable fellow, my dear, quite remarkable.'

That gained him raised eyebrows, for Emma knew her husband to be the least impressionable of men. New acquaintances, if they rated a mention at all from Sir William, rarely benefited from a favourable one.

'You will see in him what I did, I am sure.'

'Which is?'

'You know how rare it is, my dear, to meet someone to whom you take an instant liking.'

'I have no experience of you ever succumbing to that.'

Sir William smiled. 'I did with you.'

Emma brushed a hand across his cheek, her voice soft and ironic. 'It was your breeches not your heart that was smitten.'

'I protest,' he responded, without rancour, his hand reaching out to grab her.

Emma slipped into the seat at the harpsichord again and pressed a sharp key. 'So, tell me about your naval officer, and why you're so taken with him.'

'It's the oddest feeling. I have not, as you know, been a soldier for many a long year.'

'With not a good word to say of the breed in the meantime. Nor do I recall much praise of sailors. I've heard you trounce them as an uncouth menace.'

'This fellow is different. He has little height but a commanding presence.' Sir William stood with his head bowed in deep thought. 'Is it that he looks you in the eye? That there's no feeling of any thoughts harboured other than the ones of which he is speaking?' He looked up again. 'I don't know. But I would hazard that he will go far in the service. He certainly thinks so.'

Emma pursed her lips, looking doubtful. 'How do you know that?'

'He told me.'

'What?' she cried, hitting another sharp key. 'How vain!'

Sir William smiled, but there was still a look of wonder in his eyes. 'Perhaps you'll see what I see, perhaps not. He is to be our house guest. The King is throwing a feast in his honour at the Palazzo Reale tonight.'

She stood up. 'Then I must shift since I shall require the dressmaker. Shall I ask my mother to have a room prepared?'

'The apartments we had decorated for the Prince will serve splendidly.'

Emma could not hide her surprise. Sir William had lavished much money and time on decorating special rooms to accommodate the Queen's sixth son, who even at the tender age of seven was much attached to Emma.

'For a mere naval officer?'

'No, Emma,' Sir William replied. 'More than that. I think they are fitting for a man who one day may be vastly more important to both us and our mission here than Frederick Augustus, even if he is a prince.'

Passing, Emma pecked his cheek. 'I fear, husband, that you have been too much in the sun without a hat.'

CHAPTER 50

Instant attraction is such a rare thing that those exposed to it must distrust the immediate onset of the feeling. In seeing Horatio Nelson Emma felt as if some chord had been struck in her breast. He wore the blue naval coat and white waistcoat and breeches that had always given her cause to recall her first, heartbreaking, romantic attachment, when she had been no more than a housemaid, to sixteen-year-old Samuel Linley. Emma had never been able to see a sailor in uniform without being reminded of the Linley House: of Samuel's life, their stolen moments, but most of all of his lingering and tragic death.

But it was not just this visitor's attire and a tweaked memory that engaged her. The near-white hair might be less glossy but it was there in all its abundance. The skin was as clear as alabaster, the odd slight scar an enhancement not a blemish. But it was the eyes that struck her: light, blue and direct in the way they looked at her.

Nelson saw a woman of great beauty, flowing auburn tresses, startlingly green eyes, allied to a vague notion of recognition. The smile she gave him was all-enveloping, her hand held out to kiss far enough away to demand that he move forward to take it. As he bent over he could barely hear Sir William's introduction.

'My dear Emma, Captain Horatio Nelson of His Britannic Majesty's ship *Agamemnon*. Captain Nelson, my wife, Lady Hamilton.'

His fingers were under hers, lifting her hand to his lips, Nelson aware that each tip seemed filled with a tingling sensation. Emma was suffused with a rush of memory – youth, purity and breathless stolen moments in a corridor. There was a slight constriction in her chest, and her heart missed a beat as Captain Nelson's lips pressed themselves to her flesh with more pressure, and for a longer time than was either polite or necessary.

Nelson kept hold of her hand as he straightened up, looking at her unblinkingly, a stare returned in full measure. 'Lady Hamilton, it is a great pleasure to meet you.'

'And you, sir,' Emma replied, aware that her voice held a trace of huskiness. 'I cannot say how relieved my husband and I were to see your sails on the horizon.'

He let go of her hand at the mention of the word 'husband', turning in some embarrassment to look at Sir William, who had an odd smile on his face, knowing and amused, which led Nelson to suspect that his wife had the same impact on everyone she met. Then Sir William's eyes flicked slightly to his left, which reminded Nelson that he had another duty to perform.

'Lady Hamilton, allow me to name my stepson, Midshipman Josiah Nisbet. Josiah, Lady Hamilton.'

Josiah, brushed and powdered for the royal feast, stepped forward smartly, hat under his arm, his heels tapping on the parquet floor. He stopped and bent forward as if someone had slapped him on the back of the head, and missed with his lips Lady Hamilton's hand by the merest fraction.

'Milady.'

'Why Mr Nisbet,' she responded, gaily, 'what a smart fellow you are, a credit to your stepfather and your ship.' Accustomed to abuse rather than flattery, the youngster blushed to the roots of his hair as Emma took his arm and headed for the open double doors. 'And handsome to boot, in your naval blues. I shall have to guard you well, young sir, for I tell you no secret when I say that the Neapolitan ladies are all rapacity when it comes to fresh game.'

William Hamilton laughed, indicating that he and Nelson should follow, his voice near a whisper as he confided, 'Damn me, Nelson, she can spot shyness at a mile off. She has every young man in Naples, including the King's own son, in thrall to her.'

'Given her beauty, sir, I would hazard it's not only the young men. Your wife could rejuvenate the ancient statuary.' Nelson, who knew himself to be the least accomplished of men when it came to repartee, was quite astounded at his own ability to get that sentence out without a stammer.

'Handsomely said, sir,' Sir William responded, 'and very true. Emma does attract the eye. I allow my wife the degree of liberty her station commands, yet she has never once given me cause for misgivings.'

Nelson could not be sure that the older man told the entire truth, given the attention to which his wife was exposed both before they took their places and afterwards. His eye was drawn to Lady Hamilton in a way that he felt sure must be noticed, given that he had been allotted the place of honour at the King's right hand, an exposed position even in such a huge gathering. Ferdinand helped him, not being the type to engage in quiet conversation with a neighbour, more inclined to shout to someone a dozen places distant, with all his courtiers and their ladies hanging on to his every blaring word. He spoke in Italian, which Nelson couldn't understand, and the rare asides Ferdinand made to his premier guest had to be translated, which clearly bored the King.

General Acton was close enough to converse with, as was Sir William Hamilton, and much was exchanged about the need for Great Britain to protect such a stalwart ally as the Two Sicilies. Nelson agreed, with genuine feeling, being of the opinion that holding the Mediterranean without good bases was militarily impossible. He was less sanguine about a quick peace, convinced that, without a major rising of monarchical forces all over France, such a hope was wishful thinking.

'Even if Provence rises in its entirety, General Acton, it will not answer. It is an under-populated part of the French nation, and far from the seat of real power. Lyon, I am told, has suffered the same butchery as Marseilles. A coup in Paris might give grounds for hope.'

'I wouldn't hold out for that, Captain Nelson,' said Sir William. 'My wife and I came through the city on the way back from London, in the time of the Convention, before Robespierre and his regicides took over. Nothing depressed us more than the sheer stupidity of the mob. Parisians are drunk with power, so drunk that every man must fear even to be their leader.'

He could not avoid looking at her again. The object of his surreptitious attention was seated near the Queen, able to engage in pleasant conversation with her and her offspring, which made Nelson jealous. He also observed that Josiah, some distance away with the rest of the *Agamemnon*'s officers and midshipmen, couldn't take his eyes off her. But that bothered Nelson not one jot: young swains were supposed to be bowled over by such beauty and charm.

'Then we must fear for Italy, gentlemen,' said Acton, dragging his attention back to the conversation. 'Lombardy provides a route to Vienna. Let the Revolution defeat Austria, and the wolves will be at our throats next.'

Nelson thought Acton unduly pessimistic, but diplomacy forbade him to say so. For an ex-naval officer he showed a scant grasp of reality. France, having murdered its king, was isolated, with even their common ally Spain ranged against them. Their enemies included Austria, Prussia, the Russians, the United Provinces to the north, as well as a substantial number of French émigrés encamped on the Rhine. In turmoil, she could feed neither herself nor her armies. British naval power would choke off a goodly portion of what could be imported, taking ships and cargoes to deny French armies the means to sustain themselves. Defeating France was far from certain, but containing the Revolution within her borders seemed eminently possible.

He stole another glance as he raised his wine glass to propose a toast: 'Then let us hope that they murder each other until not a Frenchman is left alive to keep their damned Revolution going.'

He felt a delicious thrill as Lady Hamilton, mistaking the purpose of the raised glasses, nodded to accept what she took to be a compliment to her. Rejoining a conversation about fleets, bases, victualling and the progress of armies seemed to act like a strain on the muscles of his neck.

What Nelson failed to see was that Lady Hamilton was throwing as many glances in his direction as he was in hers, which was why she had mistaken the toast. Too experienced to suffer turmoil, Emma was drawn none the less towards Captain Nelson, without being sure why. His smile, which looked slightly melancholy as he listened to the King's translator, entranced her, as did the way he moved his hands as he ate or responded to a question: slowly, as if each gesture required deep calculation. The slight air of loss when the King made an obscene gesture to one of his subjects contrasted to the certainty that animated him when he made a point to her husband or Acton.

When not talking, listening, or thinking about Lady Hamilton, Nelson was wondering how this monarch had stayed out of confinement. He had heard that Ferdinand was uneducated, his ignorance a source of humour all over Europe. But the King was more than a buffoon, he was deranged, and would most certainly have been removed as the nation's ruler if he had resided in England, as King George had so nearly been when he had gone temporarily mad.

'He is a child, Captain,' said Sir William, once they were back in the coach. 'No more and no less, with a child's passion for that which pleases him. Hunting and procreation seem to be his abiding traits. The poor Queen is rarely out of the delivery couch, so ardent is he in the bedchamber.'

'She confides in me that conception is as painful a chore as birth,' said Emma.

Sir William responded with a weary air – but he was checking his wife none the less. 'I think that is one confidence that Her Majesty would not wish to be disseminated.'

Emma laughed, in a way that showed she was slightly intoxicated. 'You cannot chide me, sir, for there is no greater gossip in Naples than yourself. Believe me, Captain Nelson, you must beware in my husband's company for no gaffe will go unrecorded. Few English visitors to Naples leave without adding to his store of anecdotes.'

The light of the carriage lamp was just enough to let Nelson see that the rejoinder had been well received. Sir William wore a self-satisfied smile.

'I confess that is true. But I also sense Captain Nelson to be an upright man, my dear, so he has nothing to fear.'

'I daresay I shall find out if he has,' said Emma, nudging

Josiah, who was sitting beside her. 'Young Master Nisbet here will tell me all.'

'You're in for a dull exchange, milady,' said Nelson, without much thought. 'Josiah's mother and I hold each other in the highest regard, is that not so, boy?'

'It is, sir,' Josiah replied, with such conviction that he made his stepfather, who had had time to consider the statement that prompted the response, feel like a scrub.

'They say she was a whore, sir,' Josiah exclaimed, as soon as the servant closed the door to their rooms, 'and that she tricked Sir William into matrimony.'

'Enough of this!' Nelson was rarely sharp with any of his youngsters and that applied most to Josiah. The evidence of this was plain in the crestfallen expression on the boy's face. 'Is that the first thing you can say of someone who has treated you with kindness? Lady Hamilton is our hostess, so you will oblige me by containing the kind of talk that passes for conversation in the mid's berth.'

'Aye, aye, sir,' replied Josiah, stiffly.

'I suggest that you retire. We have a busy day tomorrow, that is, unless you'd rather not accompany me.'

Nelson knew that he was being cruel because his stepson was merely repeating things he too had heard, and which he had believed before making Lady Hamilton's acquaintance. Yet, having met her, how could he give credence to them now? His expectation of some coarse creature had been quite swept away on that first encounter.

The introduction, in her music room, had underlined what Sir William had told him: that she played more than one instrument and sang like an angel. No one had cut her at the Palazzo Reale, quite the reverse: people of both sexes and obvious merit had lined up to greet her. He had heard her speak French to one of the King's guests, German to another, and her Italian appeared close to fluent, accomplishments to make the most aristocratic woman proud. In translating the conversation between him and the Queen she had demonstrated the regard in which she was held in that quarter. No

London trollop could attain such a position – surely her reputation was the result of malicious and jealous tongues.

'Well Josh, do you wish to go to Portico tomorrow?'

'I do, sir,' Josiah replied softly.

'The company of kings clearly suits you.' Nelson put a hand on his stepson's shoulder and smiled. 'Well, I can say that your desire outweighs mine. Another royal feast will be the death of me, I'm sure. And I fear we will have to depart at such an early hour that it will afford me little time to visit those of our seamen who have been brought ashore.'

'Sir William assured me they were being well looked after, sir.'

'It is my duty to ascertain that for myself. The men expect and deserve it. Remember that when you command your own ship. Put the well-being of your crew above all other considerations. Then when they are required to fight, they will do so willingly.'

'Yes, sir.'

'I will require you to deliver some orders for me while I am thus engaged, so I suggest it is time we both retired.' He paused, looked around the well-appointed rooms, his mind full of the image of the lady of the house. 'This will be something to tell your mother, will it not?'

Sleep was hard, partly because of the amount he had been obliged to eat, all of which seemed stuck somewhere between his throat and his ribcage. But he was equally troubled by his thoughts. His relationship with Fanny, easy to suppress while afloat and occupied, was now thrown into such sharp relief by the vision of Lady Hamilton that he could not erase it.

There was guilt too, the memory of the relief he had felt when they had finally weighed, the cutting of the umbilical cord to wife and home, a feeling of being released from a prison of his own making. Home was never ashore, it was on a ship in the company of like-minded men: officers commissioned, warrant and appointed; topmen and upper yardsmen, able seamen and even landsmen fit only to haul on a rope. Lepée, for all his drinking and his foul moods, took on the attributes of a saint when compared to the dull, insular servants at Burnham Thorpe.

Nelson nearly groaned when he recalled the first dinner he had thrown for his admiral and fellow captains. He knew he was no drinker, yet he had allowed his normal abstemiousness a night off due to the joy of being at sea and the pleasure he took in the company of men who matched his rank. Naturally at an all-male table, with ample drink, an element of ribaldry had entered the conversation. Instead of diverting it, his responsibility as host, he had actively encouraged his guests.

Admiral Hotham had served with Captain the Honourable Augustus Hervey, famous throughout the fleet for his amatory adventures, twenty years before, in the Mediterranean. It was claimed he had seduced more than two hundred women, English, Italian, Austrian and French, in a two-year commission, fathering enough bastards to man a frigate. Those who approved of Hervey's record were matched by the number who thought it a disgrace to the service. Nelson had embarrassed several of his guests, including his good friend Troubridge, by the crass remark, 'Every man is a bachelor east of Gibraltar.'

'Am I that?' he asked himself aloud, before thumping his pillow and throwing himself on to his other side, determined to get to sleep.

Emma left Sir William with a light kiss of his forehead, his eyes closed and face relaxed. Drink affected him badly and tonight's coupling had taken time and effort, with her in the role of a supplicant wife seeking clemency for a condemned husband, Sir William fully committed to his performance as the tyrant who would accede only if granted certain favours.

Her husband made no secret of his need to conjure up images in his lovemaking, yet for all his knowledge and lack of hypocrisy it never seemed to occur to him that Emma might require the same. Every movement she had made tonight, every seemingly enforced submission had been carried out with eyes closed, the vision in her mind a jumble of places: Harry and the cottage, Greville at Uppark and Edgware Road, Nelson and the great cabin of a ship, all three faces blending into each other.

As usual, her mother was waiting for her, dozing in a chair, head lolling forward, jaw slack. When she awoke and helped her daughter to prepare for sleep, Emma was required to recount the events of the night's entertainment.

'So what's he like, this Captain Nelson?' Mary Cadogan asked, removing the ties with which earlier she'd dressed Emma's hair.

'A nice man, but too gentle for the task, I shouldn't wonder. He has none of the brash quality we associate with seafarers.'

'The Chevalier seems to rate him high enough. He dislikes seafolk as a breed, I know, for he has told me so more'n once. I could scarce credit it when I was told to prepare the royal apartments for this one.'

'Sir William has taken a liking to him,' Emma replied, yawning. She was tempted to say that she had, too, but with a mother as nosy as hers it was best to stay silent. 'He advises me that Captain Nelson is a fellow to watch, though how he can know this on one day's acquaintance escapes me.'

'Happen his servant, Lepée, has been a-tattling to him. God knows, I had my fill of the fellow, as much as he had fill of the Chevalier's claret. When it comes to his charge paragon ain't in it. There's not a virtue going that Captain Nelson don't have in spades from care of his men, the way he sails his ship, to being a terror in a scrap. It's a wonder he ain't the Lord High Admiral of England.'

Emma yawned again as her mother began to count off the brushstrokes on her hair. 'I can't imagine him fighting anyone. He looks too gentle by far.'

CHAPTER 51

'An awning will be essential, Mr Berry, for us, if not for our guests.'

'Aye, aye, sir,' Berry replied, wearily. If his captain had been busy, the premier had outdone him, not only obliged to attend the social events ashore but also to oversee the revictualling of the ship: wood, water, flour, fresh biscuit, greens, anti-scorbutics and meat, both butchered and on the hoof.

'The hen coop will have to be struck into the boats,' Nelson continued. 'Clear the manger of animals and douse the deck with vinegar.'

'Are we clearing for action, sir?'

Nelson smiled. 'Worse than that. We're receiving royalty, Berry. I want a special effort below deck, everything shipshape, with every man in his Sunday best, shot chipped and blacked, every rope from the sheets to the gun carriage tackle flemished and snow white.'

'Vittels is arrived from the Palazzo,' growled Lepée, interrupting without even a pretence at a cough. 'Who's to detail hands to get them aboard?'

Nelson looked up at him, the bloodshot eyes and grey face of a man who had spent the last three days drinking and boasting, taking full advantage of his stay at the Palazzo Sessa, a place with ample servants to do what he knew to be his duty and a cellar that was full to bursting with the means to get drunk. Lady Hamilton's mother had mentioned it when they had met, making no secret of the fact that she thought Lepée a poor servant, more concerned for his own comfort than that of his master. The good lady, who had struck Nelson as eminently sensible, didn't know the half of it. Liverish himself from three huge feasts in three days, he wondered how Lepée managed it.

'Should you not see to that, Lepée?'

His servant held out a hand, as proof of how unsteady it was. 'Got the marthrambles, don't know how, your honour. Like to drop most of it.'

'I hazard that wine and rum might have something to answer for.'

Lepée closed one eye, as if to confide in his captain. 'I reckon it be the stinking air and the heat. They be a filthy crew these 'politans. Shit where they like and don't wipe their arse, papist heathens that they are.'

'Ask Mr Andrews to detail some hands,' his master replied, wearily.

'I'll oversee to it, of course, your honour,' Lepée insisted. 'Sir William's steward promised to send us the finest from his larders and his cellars.'

'It will all make it to the storeroom, I trust?'

'What a thing to say, your honour,' Lepée replied, his protest so forceful he sent a blast of bad breath in Nelson's direction before staggering away.

'We may have to strike that one into the bilges, Mr Berry,' Nelson said as Lepée reached the doorway. 'His breath is enough to clear out the rats.'

'Be better off there than here,' Lepée growled, overhearing the remark. 'Slaving like a Barbary capture when it's not appreciated.'

Berry was looking at him and Nelson knew why, since there was hardly a member of the ship's crew who could understand why he put up with Frank Lepée. 'He can be a sore trial, Mr Berry, I know, but my needs in the servant line are modest.'

'With respect, sir, we have the King and Queen of Naples, their family and most of the local nobility coming aboard in two hours' time, not to mention Sir William and Lady Hamilton and every important visitor who happens to be here from England. And your servant, one of those charged with attending to them, is drunk. I suggest that the wardroom servants be left alone to look to our guests.'

'Lepée would be most offended.'

'You don't fear to offend a king?'

'You do not know this king as I do,' Nelson replied, with a wicked grin. 'He and Lepée will probably get on famously.'

Berry knew he would have to resolve that problem himself, since his captain, a man universally held to be one of the most competent officers in the service, could not bring himself to chastise the man. The premier was no martinet; he could not serve with Captain Horatio Nelson and be that kind of officer. He shared his commander's notions of training and responsibility, openly admired a quality of seamanship that he could never match.

He hoped and prayed that when he had his own ship the ease of manner Nelson had with everyone aboard would be gifted to him. The Captain knew the name of every man on the muster roll, where they came from, if they had a wife and children, which ships they had served in and what ailments they were prone to. He liked to talk with them, more to listen to them, his feel for the mood so acute that he could smell a reason for discontent before it had time to manifest itself.

Berry knew how the need to maintain a captain's dignity constrained Nelson. He had seen him itching to go aloft and show the upper-yardsmen, nimble boys all, that he could still set topgallants. When he talked to the gunner about his flintlocks, powder and guns, the conversation was one of knowledge on both sides, weight of shot, quality of powder, which gun fired best in length and power.

He and the boatswain spent hours discussing the crew, seeking to extract the best from them, to gain them skills that might see them raised to a better station on another ship. Likewise, Nelson spent extra time with the sailmaker, the carpenter, the master at arms and the ship's corporal. His coxswain, Giddings, as familiar as he'd been from their first meeting, acted as an extra conduit of information to a Captain always prepared to listen and learn. After five months at sea, *Agamemnon* was a crack ship, better than most frigates when it came to tacking, wearing or coming about. Clearing for action, practised every day, was down from twenty-five to seven minutes.

Even the purser, usually the most hated man on any ship, was popular aboard this vessel. Hand-picked by his captain he was allowed to make his profits, but only if it was fair. The provision of double hammocks had done for half a year of potential gain. Once past Gibraltar, Nelson insisted that, in the Mediterranean heat, a single hammock and fourteen inches per man to sleep in was a recipe for sickness. Each man must have two hammocks, one to be used, one to be washed clean each make and mend day. It was a fine notion, much appreciated by the crew, and the cause of mixed mirth and fury when, in a sudden squall, all the drying hammocks festooned around the rigging had suddenly been blown into the sea.

Gazing at them floating away, many already sinking below the waves, with no boats in the water to go after them, Nelson had remarked, 'The fish will sleep better than us this night, lads, and we'll rest better than the purser.'

They had laughed and cheered him for that calm response, their affection open, their faith in Horatio Nelson as their commander, judge and jury for offences, and in some cases father figure of the ship, quite obvious. And yet this man feared to tell his servant that he was a useless drunk.

'The King will want to see the great guns fired, so detail four of our best gun crews to oblige him,' Nelson said. 'I shall have to turn my cabin into a refuge for those ladies who will be affrighted by that.'

'Might I suggest, sir, that since it's royalty, your cabin should be set aside for the Queen's retinue, while the wardroom is cleared for the rest.'

'A capital notion, Mr Berry. Make it so.'

As the boats set out from the shore, the royal barge commanded the most attention. But Nelson found himself searching the flotilla for the craft bearing Sir William and Lady Hamilton. He had had only limited contact in the previous three days, his duties precluding any form of relaxation: attendance on a monarch who wanted to hog his presence; meetings with General Acton, the Queen and her council regarding the despatch of troops to Toulon. At the same time he had to look to the welfare of seamen, both sick and well, make sure his ship was victualled, write letters both official and personal, and issue orders to send out to sea a pair of boats. They were to take station in the approaches north and south of the Bay of Naples to ensure that *Agamemnon* would not be caught unprepared should an enemy appear on the horizon.

Fleeting glimpses, a hasty exchange of pleasantries, a view across a dinner table or an audience chamber was all he had been gifted. Josiah had enjoyed the bulk of Lady Hamilton's attention, a match that had benefited his stepson no end. She had brought the boy out of his morose shell and captivated him. No strictures were needed now to stop him traducing her reputation. Josiah was all praise and was given to extolling her numerous accomplishments in a way that made Nelson jealous.

He had spent almost all of the three days with Sir William, who had roused himself in the most admirable way to ensure that what could be done to aid Nelson was carried out with despatch. For a man who termed himself a lazy dog Sir William had great energy. He also had a deep and impressive sagacity, outstanding patience and a huge knowledge of who was for the British alliance in Naples, and who, fearing French reprisals, was against.

Nelson's initial approval had turned into a deep regard for the Ambassador. He had eased Nelson's burdens not only with his presence and his courteous way of deflecting the King's wilder flights of fancy, but also with his wit and conversation, his consideration and his open way of letting the naval officer know that he esteemed him personally as well as professionally. It was therefore uncomfortable to be with Sir William, enjoying his company, asking his advice, sharing plans and proposals while simultaneously being unable to get out of his mind the man's stunningly beautiful wife.

He spotted them under an awning, in a decorated *felucca* that was being propelled by a gaily dressed crew. Lady Hamilton, her mother and her maid all seated, Sir William, with his valet in attendance, standing behind them, hands clasped on the awning poles. Joy and anxiety were mixed in Nelson's breast: the pleasure to be had from seeing her again and in circumstances where, as the host, he could command some of her time, but against that was his desire to impress, and he feared he had failed in that. It might be his ship they were visiting, but it was Sir William's provender they would eat, his wine they would consume, the impression created that the

Captain of the *Agamemnon* could not afford to provide such a feast himself.

'The salute, Mr Berry, if you please.'

The guns, armed with powder only, blasted out twenty-one times, wreathing the ship in white smoke, leaving in the air that delicious odour of saltpetre. Eleven guns, the salute due to the ship, blasted out immediately afterwards from the battlements of the Fort St Elmo, which stood on the highest peak overlooking the city. And, in the background, Vesuvius billowed forth an extra puff of sulphurous smoke, as if determined not be left out of this occasion of mutual appreciation.

'Man the yards,' was Nelson's second command.

Berry bellowed the order and two hundred men raced for the shrouds, fore, main and mizzen, going aloft in controlled fashion, the less able at the rear. The older topmen fanned out on the main yards, the more nimble occupying the space between the caps and the tip of the upper yards, while the youngsters, small of build and feet, raced to the upper yards, some to stand in a death defying pose on the twelve-inch circumference of the topgallant poles.

'Three cheers, lads,' yelled Nelson, his voice loud enough to carry all the way to the tip of the topmast, where one sailor, with only a finger and toe-hold, had taken his place at the highest point on the ship. The huzzahs roared out, three on three, with every man on the deck, including the Captain, raising their hats as they cheered.

Nelson and his officers left the upper deck and made their way to the maindeck to take station by the entry port. The marines, red coats brushed, belts pipeclayed a startling white and boots polished, came to attention as the royal barge slid alongside the gangway, the bosun's pipe timed to begin the ceremony of welcome as soon as the first royal foot touched the platform. Two of the most reliable members of the afterguard, the oldest and most experienced seamen, hooked on to the barge, hauling it in tight to steady it. Another pair were on hand to assist the King.

Ferdinand had dressed for the occasion in a Neapolitan naval uniform. Out of his customary black food-stained garments and properly clad like an officer, he was an imposing figure, a man with whom it was a pleasure to exchange salutes. He also had the courtesy to tip his hat in the direction of the quarterdeck, a signal mark of honour from royalty.

It took nearly half an hour to get the entire visiting party on to the upper deck, to where wine and food were laid out under the awning on the wardroom tables: smoked hams, fowls by the dozen, oysters, crustaceans, pastries and fruits. The wardroom stewards, in brand new duck trousers and wearing their best kerseymere striped jerseys and stockings, moved smoothly through the throng serving wine to nobles English and Italian, women who looked more like courtesans than wives.

'Milady,' said Nelson, taking Lady Hamilton's hand to kiss. 'You do me great honour by consenting to be my guest.'

He had observed her taking the breeze on the windward bulwark, close to the master's day cabin. They were just far enough away from others to have a private conversation.

'I would look a fool, Captain, to ignore an invitation accepted by *tout* Naples.'

He looked at her then: his unblinking eyes, which could so unsettle the insincere, fixed on hers. Having rehearsed this meeting he had a whole string of polite conversation all ready to employ, every word sifted through his imagination a hundred times. It all deserted him now, to be replaced by that fearlessness of manner that had caused him so much trouble in the matters of the heart.

'Is that why you came, just because everyone else did?'

Allied to his stare, as well as the expression on his face, it was a bold remark, and she knew it. Her face reddened and she spoke as if she was short of breath. 'Why else, Captain Nelson?'

'As the Ambassador's wife,' he replied smoothly.

That flustered response, from such an accomplished person, had cheered him. His question and the way he had delivered it had bordered on the outrageous. Nelson knew that, but he simply had to know, too, if there was any feeling in her like the one he had experienced before, and was suffering from now. His chest was tight and his muscles, lower back and legs had a sensation in them somewhere between an itch and an ache.

'You have made a conquest there, Captain Nelson.'

'Have I?' he enquired.

His eyes bored into hers so that she was forced to look away. That took great effort, given that his nerves were jumping and his conscience was heavily pricked by images of both Fanny and Lady Hamilton's husband. He knew he was not good in situations like these, that he lacked the easy wit and charm necessary for seduction; that his habit of speaking direct truth, an asset sometimes, could damn him just as easily.

A part of Emma wanted to put this fellow down, to puncture the air of assurance in those startling blue eyes. Yet she was aware of her own physical reaction to his proximity, for she was trembling and confused. There was anger at her inability to master the conversation as well. In six years in Naples, with a string of male admirers, Emma had become adept at deflection. Why could she not do so now?

The door to the master's tiny cabin was open. Nelson wanted desperately to lead her into that confined space, to close the door behind them, to . . .

'I meant that you'd made a conquest in my husband, sir.'

Crashing from such a high-pitch emotion to quotidian reality was like an imagined fall from the rigging, half a second of suspension before his sense of his responsibilities as a ship's captain and a representative of his own king reconnected with the ground. Even so, his breathing wasn't right.

'Then, milady, I can only say that feeling is returned. Your husband is a man after my own heart.'

'He predicts that you will achieve great things.'

'I flatter myself that I shall, milady, should Our Lord spare me time to do so.'

'Your stepson is waiting to speak with you.'

That brought Nelson right down to earth and broke the train of conversation, which seemed to imbue every word said with two meanings. Realising he was standing too close to Emma Hamilton he stepped back a fraction then turned to face Josiah, noticing that his stepson was not the only one watching their exchange with interest. Lady Hamilton's mother was looking at him, a quite singular expression on her face.

'Mr Berry's compliments, sir, he asks me to inform you the

cutter is approaching at speed, flying a signal to say that the enemy is in sight.'

Everyone who had ever served with Horatio Nelson was aware of his absolute decisiveness, a speed of reaction to an event that could sometimes be said to border on the irrational. Most praised it and few damned it. Right now both would have been nonplussed at his reaction. Nelson was looking at his deck, covered in food, wine and guests of the highest station possible. The threat, whatever it was, lay outside any immediate assessment. The pace at which the cutter was approaching probably had more to do with the commanding midshipman's desire to impress his captain than anything requiring panicked response; an enemy close enough to be a threat would be visible from his own tops.

'Tell Mr Berry we will be putting to sea at once. A party to clear the deck while he assembles the men to weigh.' He spun round to Lady Hamilton. 'Forgive me, milady, but I must request that everyone goes ashore.'

'You speak of the King and Queen of Naples, Captain.'

'I have a duty to them, I acknowledge. But that includes defending their kingdom as well as my responsibilities as a serving officer of my own sovereign. I fear I must insist.'

'Then I suggest you inform the King of this.'

'I shall, if you will oblige me by passing on what I say to Sir William.'

Emma was forced to observe, as she watched the decks clear into the waiting boats, that if there was one thing the Neapolitans were good at it was panic. King Ferdinand, appraised of what might be in the offing, showed no pique at being unceremoniously ejected from the ship. Indeed, he led the charge, getting away just before the cutter hooked on and a message was passed to the quarterdeck that a French man-o'-war convoying three merchant ships had been sighted to the west of Capri.

No reassurance that the threat wasn't imminent had any bearing on that hysteria, and the sailors who had so courteously helped them aboard now found themselves required to be quite firm about the way the guests departed. The other visitors, English, émigré French, Germans and Austrians, were more stoical, moving to the poop as they were directed by members of the crew, busy striking everything off the deck. There was a degree of admiration for the sheer efficiency of a ship's company who could steal the food on the table while carrying it below at speed. What could not be transported was tossed into the Bay of Naples.

Eventually the noisy locals were gone, and the remaining guests were led down to the maindeck, Sir William and his wife bringing up the rear, Horatio Nelson stopping them to allow the gangway to clear. Mary Cadogan took the maid by the arm and moved her away from the conversation.

'Sir William, I apologise to you and your wife. I ask you to convey my proper regrets to His Majesty. My cutter, which was placed out as a screen to the west, has been told there is a French ship-of-the-line in the offing.'

'A threat to Naples?'

'A threat to shipping, our own and those of the Two Sicilies. My duty demands that I seek to engage and destroy her and that must take precedence over all other considerations.'

Emma wondered where that softness had gone. However, what had replaced it was just as telling, an air of command, the impression of a mind in control of what it observed. Captain Horatio Nelson was the only person, apart from themselves and a midshipman by his side, who was standing still. Everywhere else was movement as men rushed to obey a stream of commands from the Captain's inferior officers. Yet for all the seeming disorder it was far from that, this evidenced by the quiet way in which Nelson himself imposed his presence.

'I would ask you to care for those men I have left ashore, Sir William.'

'Leaving them behind will render you desperately short-handed.'

'I have enough to tackle a single Frenchman, Sir William, even if he outguns me. Look about you, sir, at these fellows I have the good fortune to command.' Nelson smiled then, which to Emma made his face look radiant. 'Why, if this Frenchman could just gaze upon them he would strike before I opened my gunports.'

'They are a fine set of men, I agree,' Emma said.

'Lady Hamilton, when we beat our enemies it is not men in blue coats who win the battle, it is these fellows you see now going about their tasks. All their officers do is get them to the right place.'

'Goodbye, Captain Nelson,' said Sir William. 'I wish you a speedy return to us, and good fortune attend you until then.'

Nelson raised his hat to salute the Ambassador and his wife, who curtsied in response, saying, 'A happy return.'

Agamemnon was hauled over her anchor and plucking it out of the sea before the ambassadorial *felucca* had got more than half a cable's length away from the warship's side. Aloft, the rigging was full of men loosing sails and the Hamiltons could just see Horatio Nelson, who had come to the leeward side of the quarterdeck.

'What a strange man, husband,' said Emma.

'An admirable one, my dear, who does not, it seems, worry about offending kings.' The ship heeled slightly as the wind took the now tautened sails. The great rudder was hard round to sweep it on a course that would take it out to sea. 'Something worthy of praise, I think.'

Emma was looking at the single figure on the quarterdeck, diminishing by the second, when she replied, 'I certainly have nothing but admiration for Captain Nelson.'

The object of her observation was looking at the gaily decorated *felucca*, wondering if his desire to get so hurriedly to sea was the prospect of a battle. Or was it to save him from making a complete fool of himself?

HMS Agamemnon, 18th September, at sea
   My dear Sir William,
   You will, I'm sure, already have heard that I missed my Frenchman, which makes the nature of my departure from the Bay of Naples all the more indefensible. I plead duty, which I am sure you will understand, and that you will convey to Their Sicilian Majesties the assurance that Nelson stands ready to defend their country to the dying breath.

   My compliments and deepest thanks to your dear lady wife, who has entranced every man aboard my ship, not least my

stepson, Josiah. We all look forward to a happy return to the
warmth of your hospitality.

I am yours,
Horatio Nelson (Capt)

CHAPTER 52

1797

Horatio Nelson couldn't stay in his cabin even if his dignity as a commodore demanded that he do so: he needed to be on deck, even if in the thick haze there was little to see but half the ships of his own squadron. HMS *Captain* ploughed through the grey Atlantic waters. His heart was pounding in his breast, blood racing, none of which altered the tactical situation in the slightest. Somewhere out ahead was HMS *Victory*, flagship of Admiral Sir John Jervis. Beyond *Victory*, between him and the southern tip of Portugal, also hidden from view, lay the combined fleets of Spain, so recently an ally against France, now as much of an enemy.

'Mr Hoste, be so good as to join me.'

The midshipman hurried over to join him on the windward side of the quarterdeck as he paced up and down, his heels beating a heavy tattoo on the planking. The prospect of action always excited Nelson. Prone to recurring bouts of malaria, nothing banished ill-health like the sound and fury of battle. In the four years since he had sailed to war he could think of no officer who had been as active as himself; single-ship actions, cutting-out expeditions: the siege of Bastia, and then Calvi, which had cost him clear sight in one eye but had secured Corsica for the natives. To that he could add diplomatic missions, sea chases and storms that had seen good old *Agamemnon* so reduced that she had had to be sent home for a refit.

Yet for all the success of the Royal Navy, France had been triumphant everywhere on land. Bonaparte, unheard of before Toulon, was now a national hero, his armies carrying all before them in Savoy and Italy until the states who had actively opposed the Revolution sued for peace. But the seas were British, Nelson able to sail where he wished, to support and harry the enemy, to hold Corsica and Elba and keep a promise to protect Naples.

He was hardly aware that he was talking, using Hoste, whom he counted as his favourite among the mids, as a sounding board to relieve his inner tensions. 'The defection of Spain altered everything. Combine the French and Spanish fleets, then place them in the English Channel, and the whole fate of Britain hangs in the balance. It would be the Armada all over again, with no guarantee of the result. That, Mr Hoste, is why the Mediterranean had to be abandoned, even Naples, to counter such a threat.'

'Aye, aye, sir.'

'You do understand all this, don't you?'

The boy's 'yes sir' carried a fair measure of doubt, as did his large dark brown eyes. He gazed at Nelson as if he was of another species, evidence that such patient explanation had only gone so far in clarification. Hoste, like many others, was in awe of him, and while that often had a pleasant feel, it also served to underline for Nelson the increased distance that now lay between him and his shipmates.

That lack of contact he had disliked, as a captain, was even greater now. Ralph Millar had been made post, but was serving with him as the Captain of his flagship, seeing to the day-to-day running of the ship, leaving Nelson free to oversee the rear section of the fleet, an admiral's command entrusted to him. Ralph Millar undertook the midshipmen's lessons now; it was he who took divine service and the divisional inspection. Commodore Nelson attended, of course, but the service over he retired to his cabin. If he wanted company he had to do what he had just done with Hoste and ask for it.

'This could be the most important day of both our lives, young fellow.'

Nelson could see the boy didn't comprehend that; didn't know that for all the success his commodore had enjoyed nothing could compare with what was possible now. All his naval life he had yearned to take part in a successful fleet action, the naval might of one nation pitted against another. It was why he had gone to the Caribbean in *Albemarle*, hopes dashed when the French declined to oblige a nation that had already beaten them in those very waters. He nearly had one with Admiral Hotham, the fool who had succeeded Hood, only to find the enemy taking action to avoid an engagement.

Single-ship combats were all very well, and good for a long report in the *Naval Chronicle*, but to take part in a successful fleet action elevated a naval officer to the pinnacle of his profession. Distinguish himself, and that plaque he so craved in Westminster Abbey, next to James Wolfe, his hero, would be possible. Lose? To Nelson the possibility did not exist. The possibility of death however, reminded him that he had yet to write a final letter to his wife, Fanny, and compose a will.

Back in his cabin he picked at his solitary dinner, served by Tom Allan, the servant who had taken over from Lepée. Allan was silent where Lepée had been vocal, sober where he had been drunk, Norfolk bovine instead of London sharp. But he missed Lepée, and would have kept him on if he had not become intolerable. It wasn't so much inebriation that had done for him but his increasingly loose tongue.

Servants were supposed to keep their master's secrets not trumpet them. Lepée, in his cups, had started referring publicly to a dalliance Nelson had enjoyed with Carlotta d'Ambrosio, a Genoese opera singer, not just to his fellow crew members but even at dinners thrown for important guests. Drunk, his voice would rumble on, and what should have been thoughts instead turned to ranting monologue. The time had come for him to depart, not to the lower deck, as feared, but with a discharge from the Navy. He granted Frank Lepée a stipend that would keep him from the gutter and, more importantly, since its continuance was based on silence, keep his mouth shut.

Nelson was back on deck as soon as a sharp ear heard the first faint echo of a signal gun. The haze had cleared enough to allow his one good eye to range over the whole fleet, sailing in line ahead. It looked imposing, fourteen line-of-battleships, but he knew just how long these ships had been at sea; how much wear and tear was hidden by endlessly applied paint. More guns sounded below the horizon that could only come from a

Spanish fleet on a working-up exercise that saw no reason to hide itself from an inferior enemy.

Nelson knew from conferences held aboard *Victory* that the plan was to close with the Dons and take them on where they found them and in whatever strength, notwithstanding that they would certainly outnumber the British fleet. The Spanish flagship alone, *Santissima Trinidad*, with four decks, mounted 136 cannon and Don José de Córdoba, the Spanish Admiral, had half a dozen ships carrying 112 guns plus a potential fleet strength of over thirty capital ships. To set against that Admiral Sir John Jervis had fourteen: two 100 gunners, two 98s and two 80s, plus eight 74s.

The afternoon wore on, signal guns booming out to the south, with the wind shifting to blow in from the open sea to westward. Frigates shadowing the Dons informed Jervis that they'd turned for home, on course for Cadiz, their premier Atlantic naval port, halfway between Portugal and Gibraltar. The flags ran up *Victory*'s yards to order the fleet to increase sail. Sir John wanted to be in a position at dawn to bear down on them should the wind favour him.

Aboard every ship they dined that night in full anticipation of a battle on the morrow, 14 February. Wills and last testaments were updated. Final letters to loved ones composed, promises extracted and exchanged so that whatever fate befell the individual someone would see to his effects and his responsibilities. Nelson had written to his wife and his family, father, brothers, sisters and uncles.

He also penned a letter to Naples, to Sir William and Lady Hamilton, with whom he had enjoyed a lively correspondence these last four years. He assured them that battle was imminent, of his fidelity to their mutual friendship and reiterated the Navy's determination to return to the Mediterranean as soon as the business was done. As he did so, the image of Lady Hamilton filled his mind: those auburn tresses, green eyes and lively animated face faded through a pang of guilt into that of his wife.

Had Fanny, in the way her husband had praised Sir William's wife in his letters, discerned the attraction he had felt? He had wrapped his own fascination in kind words regarding her treatment of Josiah. Would that make the mother in her jealous? It was a truism that praising people was as dangerous a game as damning them. Had Josiah seen the attraction? Though he had never mentioned that Genoese opera singer, his stepson must have known about her. Could he be trusted to remain silent? For that matter could Lepée? He went to his cot still gnawing on such concerns, lying in it, swinging softly, well aware that the following night it might not be his bed but his coffin. His favourite expressions, repeated over and over again, served to still the anxiety in his breast.

'Death, damnation or Westminster Abbey.'

'Twenty-seven of the line, sir,' called the lookout, who was above the mist and could see the enemy sailing on a parallel course, 'and ten frigates.'

'Nearly double our number,' said Ralph Millar, the twang of his Yankee accent evident.

'I'm sure our admiral will not shy away from that,' Nelson insisted.

In every meeting he had had with Sir John Jervis, Nelson had found him full of fight, dancing around in a way that belied his sixty-two years. Sir John was a scrapper by nature, an energetic little man with the face of a pug terrier and no tolerance whatsoever for slacking, inefficiency or the complaints of sailors about their lot. Unmarried, he was a martinet in the article of discipline, irascible, poor company at a dinner table, and inclined to rudeness if given an opportunity to rebut an ill-placed remark.

Nelson, when he first met him, had expected to have to defend himself. The opposite was the case. Though Sir John's reputation was proven with other officers, the Admiral was the soul of kindness to his boyish-looking commodore. They thought alike in the article of fighting and, it transpired, shared between them a perfectly attuned blind eye regarding the behaviour of men in their private life, as long as they properly performed their duties.

The Spaniard Grand Fleet had sailed on the wind overnight, a westerly breeze that was waning by the hour. When they spotted the British fleet bearing down on them they were some twenty-five miles west of the Portuguese headland at Cape St Vincent, and it was obvious by the untidy nature of their reaction that they had been taken by surprise. But they were clearly inclined to offer battle, holding on a course south of the British fleet, their bowsprits facing east and home, seeking no increase in speed, inviting Sir John to make the next move.

But that was based on the assumption that Sir John would attempt to get alongside his enemy on a parallel course, matching them in speed and course to engage in a gunnery duel. Given that Sir John would have to sail south-west in line, then bear up to the east on a converging course that would overhaul them, the Spanish Admiral felt he had ample time to prepare his fleet to receive the outnumbered and outgunned British.

Two things spoiled Don Córdoba's confident assumption. The first was the inability of the Spanish captains to form proper line. Their ships were bunched into two untidy squadrons; the leading group of nine vessels had got well ahead, leaving a gap astern of them of several miles. The main section of the fleet was also bunched in such a way that many of its guns would struggle to bear on an enemy in proper formation. Attempts by the Spanish captains to form a line were not going well.

The second wrong assumption was a belief that no British admiral would disobey the Fighting Instructions, which dictated the tactics the Spaniards anticipated. But Sir John Jervis did, on a course due south that didn't deviate. He held back, timing his approach to let the lead Spanish division cross his bows. As soon as that happened Sir John reacted.

'Flag signalling, sir.'

Nelson watched, full of admiration, as his admiral ordered a press of sail, and aimed his van like an arrow at the gap between the Spanish contingents. This action flew in the face of every tenet of British naval warfare. It was a crime by admiralty statute. Jervis, if he lost, would face at least disgrace and quite possibly a firing squad on his own quarterdeck.

Here seamanship told, as each line-of-battle ship in turn, in what seemed to be no more than minutes, got aloft a full suit of sails. The water began to cream down the side of each vessel, as she heeled over to take the west wind on her beam, yards braced right round to catch it. His old shipmate from the voyage to India, Thomas Troubridge, was leading the fleet in HMS *Culloden*, HMS *Orion* in support. Another friend, Cuthbert Collingwood, brought up the rear of the fleet in *Excellent*, just ahead of *Diadem*, which was behind Nelson in HMS *Captain*.

The plan was straightforward: to get between the two parts of the enemy fleet, isolate the greater part to westward then tack into the wind to take them on. Nelson, watching Troubridge, was full of envy, since he would be the first to engage. That feeling deepened as the Spaniards opened fire, which Troubridge chose to ignore, holding his response until it mattered, the point at which he turned to do battle. Troubridge was holding his course to cross the bows of Don Córdoba's flagship, *Santissima Trinidad*, the biggest fighting vessel in the world, leaving the Spaniard with the option to luff up or risk a collision.

'The Spanish van have begun to tack,' said Lieutenant Berry.

Nelson looked to the east, following Berry's gaze, to observe the front section of the Spanish fleet coming round to rejoin the rest of their consorts. Into the wind such a manoeuvre would take time. Don José Córdoba suddenly turned to sail north-east, angling his ships towards the rear of the British fleet, calculating that though they'd face fire from the likes of Troubridge, they would avoid the rest and would be able to slip past *Excellent*, last ship in the British line. Sir John, obliged to hold his ships together, would be forced to come round in succession, which would take an age to complete.

Time and the wind would be against the British, creating a chance by which the Spaniards, passing round his rear, could rejoin into a formidable whole. With both wings of the Grand Fleet reunited, Don José could then choose to retire, making for his intended landfall, or come round again to oppose the enemy as a vastly superior force. If he chose to run, Sir John's only option would be to pursue at a distinct disadvantage.

'They're going to get away,' said Nelson suddenly. He could see the course they were steering, and could calculate the triangulation and tell where each ship would be in an hour's time. Only Troubridge, and perhaps *Orion*, would fetch even the Spanish back markers. They would never head off the enemy flagship.

'Don José may choose to fight, sir.'

'No,' replied Nelson, who was wondering if it was already too late to change things. 'The Dons are not like us, Ralph. Even with greater numbers they'll run.'

Nelson had a sinking feeling in his breast. Ever since he had listened to his uncle Maurice recount his tale of the fight at Cape Francis Viego, he had yearned for a day like this. Whether it was to match his uncle or outshine him, he didn't know, but he did feel that his whole life had been a preparation for this moment: his visions of a brilliant destiny could be fulfilled or destroyed here. There was a solution, but it was so dangerous to his name and reputation that it took several moments of contemplation before he could bring himself to articulate it. Someone had to check the flight of the Spaniards; someone would have to supply a base and create a triangle, to cut them off and make them do battle. Succeed, and he would have fulfilled that vision he had had on the way back from India. Fail and he would be derided for a fool and very likely never command a squadron again. He would be like those sad cases he had seen in Bath, the so-called 'yellow admirals', incompetents who had risen to the rank by mere survival, but who would never be trusted with a command. What decided Nelson was the knowledge that, after this day, he would have to look at himself in the mirror. There was no way he could face looking at the reflection of a man he thought of as a moral coward. He spoke very slowly. 'Captain Millar, I require you to wear out of the line.'

'Sir?' said Millar, eyebrows shooting up, since that was to turn away from the enemy.

'We will come round full circle and slip between *Diadem* and *Excellent*. Once through and in open water, I wish you to put me across the bows of those Spaniards.'

Millar realised what Nelson was about in putting his ship in front of the fleeing Dons. He also knew, as much as his commodore, what failure would mean. To pull out of the line to disobey orders, not only those of his commanding admiral but those of the Fighting Instructions. Nelson was putting his whole career on the line, possibly along with that of every officer aboard the ship.

'I feel it is my duty to point out the consequences, sir.'

'Do you wish those orders in writing, sir?' he asked Millar, softly, so his voice did not carry to the other officers on the quarterdeck, Lieutenants Hardy and Berry.

'No, sir. I merely wish to make sure you know the hazards.'

'I know what I hazard if I *don't* act so, Millar, and so do you. The Dons will get away. You do agree, don't you?' Millar nodded. Nelson put as much into his voice as he could, seeking to persuade a man he esteemed as a friend and admired as a sailor. 'Then take it in writing. At least you will have the protection of that if we fail. The blame will fall on me.'

'Fail, sir!' exclaimed Millar, in a voice that could be heard all over the quarterdeck. 'I never thought to hear that word on your lips. Mr Hardy, hands to man the braces.'

Hardy possessed a voice to go with his stocky build. The order roared out and men moved. On the command the ropes holding the yards were hauled round, at the same time as the great wheel swung, the rudder biting so that *Captain* came up to take the wind and clear the line. The sails were then backed to bring her head round, then sheeted home and lashed off to take the wind on her larboard side, pushing the ship forward beam on to the wind.

Nelson raised his hat as HMS *Diadem* sailed past them, then heard Millar order the yards hauled round once more as the quartermaster put down his helm. Now *Captain* was sailing into the wind at an angle that had Nelson looking left into the stern casements of *Diadem* with the bowsprit and figurehead of Collingwood in *Excellent* to his right. Within minutes Millar was through, sailing away from his consorts, Nelson's hat off to exchange a salute, his ears full of the cheers that Collingwood must have encouraged. He could see Troubridge had tacked at the head of the Spanish line, and was coming up hand over fist to join him.

'Flag signalling,' cried Berry.

All the officers watched as various ships' numbers were hauled aloft to break out at the *Victory*'s masthead. Orders were sent to *Excellent, Blenheim, Orion* and *Prince George*. That was followed by the message instructing them to support HMS *Captain*. Nelson felt a release of tension, of which he had been unaware in the excitement and trepidation of his actions. The responsibility was no longer his: Admiral Jervis had approved.

Nelson allowed himself one more look around at the ships holding their course to follow Troubridge and those moving directly to his support. He felt his heart swell with the certainty that the fleet would be victorious. That he might not survive didn't matter. If he expired in the moment of triumph he would have achieved the single most important aim of his life, making it worthwhile.

'Lay me alongside the enemy, Captain Millar,' he cried, in a voice that travelled the whole length of the ship.

CHAPTER 53

Before those words had died away the closest Spanish ship, *San Salvador*, opened up, her guns aimed forward to take *Captain*, her whole side wreathed in smoke. Nelson was elated, even though some of the balls struck home, making the frame of the 74 shudder. He was in action.

'Note the time,' said Millar to Hoste, acting as his signal midshipman, looking at his commodore to see if he should reply.

Nelson shook his head, seeing that *San Salvador* had held her course, more intent on evasion than fighting. 'I believe we may lay that ship ahead by the board.' He pointed at the towering four-decker that would be unable to avoid them. 'If my memory serves me well, she is the *Santissima Trinidad.*'

'Allus the same with little fellers,' said one of the quarterdeck gunners, to his gun captain. 'They allus want to pick a fight with the biggest bastard in the room.'

'An' how many times have you see the big one taken down?' the gun captain replied. 'Old Nellie will have her over, you mark my words, mate.'

The approach was close to silent, though ropes creaked, timbers groaned and some warriors whispered prayers. Aloft, men were taking in sail, leaving only the high topsails to give steerage way. Nets were being rigged in their place to catch anything falling from above. Extra chains had been fitted to the masts to stop them going completely by the board, and Pierson, the marine officer, had his men in place, up in the caps, main fore and mizzen masts, with muskets ready to play across the enemy deck.

The Spanish ship, knowing that a fight was unavoidable, had replicated everything that had happened in the British 74, albeit without the same efficiency or speed, the loss of sail slowing her progress. She loomed up, two decks higher than *Captain*, the great gilded poop so tall that the men who stood on it were invisible. It was always like this before the guns spoke, that terrible period of waiting as two vessels designed for destruction approached each other.

Don José de Córdoba could not have ordered the first salvo, a ragged affair that came from the forward lower deck cannon, the only ones that would bear, 36 pounders, the largest calibre on the ship. The side of the *Santissima Trinidad* vanished as the smoke billowed skywards to hide the upper works. Several spouts of water shot up yards from the British hull to blow away on the breeze. Two balls struck home, making *Captain* stagger, but it was a wooden hull, built to take heavy shot, so they did little harm. The four-decker began to turn away, so that her course would run parallel to Nelson's, inviting a gun-for-gun duel that *Captain* would struggle to win.

'*Culloden* has a press of sail on, sir,' cried Berry, pointing south to where Thomas Troubridge, ignoring easier targets, was coming up hand over fist to the aid of Nelson.

'Then we shall be more than evenly matched when he is with us, Captain Millar, two seventy-fours to a one-hundred-and-thirty-six.'

'Permission to open fire, sir. I'd like to get the first true salvo in to disrupt the aim of their gunners.'

'Make it so, Captain Millar.'

Every gun was loaded and already run out, the crews with bandannas round their ears kneeling ready to reload, and the gun captain stood poised over his flintlock, ready to trigger a spark that would ignite the powder in the touch hole. It was the same on the lower decks, in the glimmer of light emitted by a string of fighting lanterns plus a small amount that came through the portholes. It was just enough to show the eyes of the men and pick up the rouge of the planking, which would show no blood.

Marine sentries stood at the companionways so that no one, panicked by noise or the proximity of death, could run. *Captain*, cleared for action, showed a clean sweep fore and aft, right from the peak of the bow to the stern where the cabins had stood, walls, stoves and furniture, all now struck below. The animals had been heaved over the side into the ship's boats, and were now well away from the noise and fury of the coming contest.

Behind each group of guns stood a blue-coated officer, in command of his division. He had the task of controlling the gunnery, trying to ensure that weapons didn't fire simultaneously. Better rolling fire than a single blast. Underneath their hats they, too, wore bandannas, an attempt to protect their eardrums from the stupefying sound of the blast.

'Fire!' yelled Millar.

They didn't all go off at once, the timbers wouldn't stand it. Instead the fire rolled down the side, each gun firing within two seconds as the one before it recoiled. The ship shook from stern post to figurehead and the smoke blew back over the deck, the acrid smell of powder and saltpetre catching in the throat. But that slowed nothing. The crew was as well drilled as any in the fleet. On the recoil two bars were shoved under the carriage to hold it steady against the roll of the ship. The first thing down the muzzle was the swab necessary to clear the residue of used powder. That was followed by the charge, already pricked by the gun captain so that a small quantity covered and penetrated the touchhole. It was rammed down the muzzle, next the ball chipped and rounded before the battle so its flight would be true. Last to go in was the wad, tamped down to provide a seal that the blasting charge could act against.

The crew hauled on the tackles as one, pulling the cannon into its firing position, black menacing muzzle out of the porthole, carriage hauled right up to the rings fixed to the ship's side. Timing his action to the gun preceding his, the gun captain would lean forward again to trigger his flintlock. If that failed there was slowmatch to ignite the powder, to make it hiss and flame, the fire igniting the charge behind the ball. Within half a second the gun would spew forth destruction, sending out a heavy ball and a streak of orange fire mixed with black smoke, the trail of the exploding powder. The ball, well aimed and properly fired, with the right charge of powder, arced across the gap between the ships, glanced off an open port lid. Unseen by those who had fired it, the ball ricocheted through, taking an enemy gun on the muzzle, dismounting the metal, smashing the wood of the carriage, trapping and maiming half the crew and killing two on another gun crew with wood splinters gouged out from the deck.

The noise was tremendous, a continuous barrage of sound and fury that made verbal orders impossible. On both vessels the officers walked slowly down the line of their cannons, touching each gun captain's shoulder to control the rate of fire, trying to ignore the effect of enemy shot on their own vessel, the way the timbers of the side suddenly cracked open, parts of the wood detaching to fly like spears across the deck. Men screamed and men died, with extra hands ready to take their places at the guns or to drag them away to the less than tender ministrations of the surgeon.

And all the while the ship's boys raced back and forth to the gunner, carrying powder charges. Others, not powder monkeys, were given the task of replenishing shot from the locker, a chain of small hands that kept the racks full by each gun. Some had buckets of water, and ladles with which to try to quench the thirst of the gunners, who, after just a few salvoes, were black from head to foot, their skin and hair singed by hot flashing powder.

Aim as they might on the first salvo, it was rate of fire that counted, the sheer volume of shot coming in from the British ship enough to suppress the Spaniard's reply. *Captain* was making little headway, wallowing on an Atlantic swell. Fire on the down roll and the balls hit the enemy hull. Fire on the up roll and the shot could go anywhere from the bulwarks to the rigging. The Dons laboured under the same conditions, and though they could not manage the same rate of fire, they had more guns and the damage they did was telling.

Blocks and pulleys cascaded down and whole yards were blown out of their chains, falling to rip through the netting and slamming into the deck, careering on to damage flesh and blood as well as wood. Backstay hawsers snapped, ropes parted and shrouds were shredded, with the foremast the first to go. It snapped above the cap like a matchstick, falling sideways, a creaking, groaning lament that could be heard above the pounding of the cannon, taking with it several men, some to die smashed on the deck, others tipped overboard into a sea from which there was little prospect of rescue.

On the quarterdeck Nelson stood rock still. Having brought HMS *Captain* into action, he was now no more than a figurehead. Others carried the fight to the enemy, but few were as exposed as he. There were several ways to die, and each man aboard knew them well. On deck a musket ball might fell you, or a stray roundshot cut you in half. Every cannon on the deck was a lethal weapon to those who fired it as well as to the enemy. Free of its breaching it would pulverise flesh, blasted from its carriage it could maim and kill. But of all the deadly things to face, splinters were the most lethal, malignant shards of wood, some bigger than the men they struck, some so small they were barely visible, capable of lopping off a limb or inflicting wounds that were nearly always fatal.

Through the smoke it was hard to see, but Nelson knew from what he could hear that *Captain*, with *Culloden* having come up in support, was inflicting as much damage as she was taking, and that was considerable. But the price was high. The mainmast followed the foremast, so fouling the way on the ship that a party with axes had to be formed to cut it away. The wheel was gone, shot away, taking the quartermaster and two of his assistants with it. In the lull that followed the *Santissima Trinidad* hauled clear, this before the next Spanish ship came up to engage. Millar ordered Lieutenant Josiah Nisbet away from his quarterdeck cannon to take an instruction below, to alert the men on the relieving tackles, heavy hawsers that worked the rudder, that the steering of the ship was now their responsibility.

Josiah shot down the companionway, immediately struck by the way the sound was muted. Looking along the open lower decks it seemed as if he was gazing into hell. Smoke hung in the air, illuminated by the orange flashes of firing cannon. There were dead men, and wounded, screaming for mercy, bleeding copiously, unceremoniously hauled away either to die or be tended in the cockpit. There, with only lantern light to work by, the surgeon used his probes, knives and saws, up to his arms in blood, lopping off limbs, rough sewing gashes, with only a swift slop of rum to ease any pain, that and a leather strap between the teeth of his patient. Hardly surprising that the lad took a little longer to return to the deck.

He emerged to find his ship fully engaged against another enemy, trading shot with a crew fresh and prepared. The air was full of missiles, chain and bar shot intended for the rigging but just as effective in slicing through men. And there, in the middle of the quarterdeck, stood his stepfather, in his uniform coat, one epaulette hanging off and half the rim of his hat blown clean away.

'Hot work, Josiah,' he said, clearly happy.

Another almighty crack, another wrenching lament, before the mizzen mast began to fall. It didn't come all the way, but held by the mass of torn rigging that had once held up the other masts, it settled at a crazy angle, the gaff boom jamming into the poop to form a triangle of useless wood. Men rushed to secure it, lashing it to any solid object to stop it doing more damage.

Looking back at *Culloden*, when the wind gusted enough to clear the smoke, Nelson could envisage what his ship must look like. Wallowing and useless, *Culloden* had fallen out of the battle, rudder shot away and not more than a stump of any mast standing. It was easy to imagine blood flowing out through the scantlings by the gallon, but whatever the cost, Troubridge could be proud. He had done his job.

'Enemy approaching on our larboard quarter,' shouted Millar. 'All hands stand by to engage.'

'*Excellent* is coming up to help us, sir,' cried Josiah.

She was, too, with enough aloft still to overhaul the enemy. By the time *Captain* opened fire with a ship they knew to be *San Nicolas*, Collingwood had put up his helm to place himself no more than twenty feet from her beam, opening up with a salvo of gunnery that tore the Spaniard apart. Great chunks flew from her side into the air; the rigging was shredded on the second salvo, and on the third the lower ports were smashed in, the clang of metal on metal so loud it was audible across the intervening water.

To the rear of that *Prince George* had engaged the three-decker *San Josef*. One Spanish ship sought to edge away from Collingwood, with what few tattered bits of canvas she still had aloft. The *San Josef* was seeking to get across the bows of *Prince George*, to a point where she could pour fire into an enemy who would struggle to respond. Instead she ran foul of her own consort, checking her way so comprehensively that *Excellent* shot past to cheers from *Captain*.

'Captain Millar,' called Nelson.

'Sir?'

'We are useless in the line,' he shouted, pointing to the nearest enemy. 'Please be so good as to put us at a point where we can board that ship.'

'Mr Nisbet, pray return below again and ask Mr Hooper to put the rudder hard a-larboard.'

It was agonisingly slow, the way that *Captain* inched towards the *San Nicolas*, both ships firing ragged salvoes. But Millar had done just the right thing, using the run of the sea to put his prow right in line with the poop of the enemy vessel. Men gathered around their leaders, with knives, clubs, muskets and pikes. Pierson, leading the marine detachment, had his men lined up as if on parade, ready to put their first fusillade into whatever resistance formed itself on the Spaniard's deck.

Berry was already out on the bowsprit, edging on to the spirit sail yard as the two ships collided, sword in hand, yelling like a banshee, preparing to jump. Around him Nelson could see other old Agamemnons, Thorpe, Warren, Sykes and Thompson, both Johns and Francis Cook. Beside him, swearing loudly, stood William Fearny, one of his bargemen, normally the quietest soul in creation, now raring to get into the fight.

'Permission to lead the boarding party, sir?'

Nelson turned to answer Millar, his look almost pleading. 'We cannot both leave the deck, Ralph, and I cannot stay while there is a fight. My nature couldn't bear it.'

The silent exchange lasted only a few seconds, enough for Ralph Millar to impart his opinion that commodores had no right to lead boarding parties. But then neither, really, had captains. Behind them Berry was swinging his sword, driving down the heads of those who would stop him, allowing those behind him to drop on to the poop and take them on. Marine muskets were fired and reloaded to clear the enemy deck of opposition. And the ship was spinning slowly, now locked into the *San Nicolas*, hanging on to the enemy stern. Millar smiled, touched his hat, and went back to his station.

'To me,' Nelson called, leading a group of men forward to the quarter-gallery windows, now nestled up against a point where the bulwarks were smashed open. A marine stepped forward and smashed the glass, Nelson immediately leading his party, seamen, marines and three midshipmen, through. They found themselves in a small cabin with a locked door. That, too, fell to the butt of a musket, allowing his party into the fore part of the great cabin, led by a wild-eyed commodore, repeatedly shouting, 'Death or Westminster Abbey!'

'Heads!' Nelson yelled, pushing one midshipman one way, a second the other, then diving himself for one of the bulkheads as a fusillade of musket balls, mixed with the sound of shattering glass, came through the skylight above their heads.

'Marines, clear them!'

That order was aimed at the rest of the party, still exiting from the quarter gallery. The muskets were up and fired almost before the words were out of his mouth, a salvo that killed several men and aided Berry, still fighting desperately on the poop. Nelson was already out of the cabin on to the open deck, heading for a companionway full of Spanish sailors. He discharged his own pistol, before turning it to use as a club, felling a man who had been stabbing his pike towards one of his mids.

He had to step back to get his sword free, then lunged immediately, missing his main target in his haste but taking another enemy sailor in the thigh, enough of a wound to make the fellow collapse in a heap. In a fight that is a mêlée, all the swordsmanship practised on deck counts for nothing. This was hacking, jabbing work, with the hilt just as vital as the blade, close-quarters fighting in which instinct, or a flash of something in the corner of an eye, counted for as much as skill.

It was that which alerted him to the swinging club. Even though his sword sliced into it, the jarring up his arm was painful. Keeping his embedded sword aloft exposed his assailant's lower body and a swift kick in the groin doubled him over. It was his own club that finished him, retrieved and swung by Nelson so hard he could hear the fellow's skull crack open. A pike, pointed and serrated, shot past his nose, missing him by a fraction as he fought to dislodge his sword. Thorpe, who had jammed a hand on to the shaft just in time, unbalancing the pikeman, had disrupted the enemy aim. The blade of Nelson's sword sliced up under the pikeman's throat, cutting through his neck so hard that his head nearly came off.

Fighting their way up the companionway was hard, a compact mass of British facing an even more dense crowd of Spaniards. Willpower won out over numbers, aided by the first sight of sunlight at the enemy back. Jab – cut – jab – cut, slice – parry – jam the hilt into a face, kick, bite, scratch, anything to keep the forward momentum. Nelson was soaked with sweat, his mouth dry and his arms aching. But he was leading his men to a point where the enemy must break, which they did with a suddenness that nearly had him falling on to his knees.

He emerged on to the deck to find Berry in occupation of the poop, in the act of hauling down the Spanish flag. Odd that the lower deck guns were still firing, unaware of what was happening above their heads, still trying to fight *Prince George*, probably convinced that she had stopped firing through their efforts rather than the dropping of the Spanish ensign, unaware that the British ship was now concentrating its fire on the *San Josef*; this while their officers, on the deck, were in the act of surrendering their swords; this while all fighting had ceased on the upper and maindecks.

'God bless you, Berry,' Nelson croaked. 'She is ours.'

'A party below, sir, to still those guns.'

'Make it so, Mr Berry.'

Berry hadn't made it to the companionway when the fusillade of musket fire swept across the deck, fired from the cabins of the *San Josef*, still stuck fast to *San Nicolas*, scything through a party of sailors and marines celebrating their victory. Several fell in such a way as to make Nelson think them dead. But that was not foremost in his mind.

'To me, lads,' he shouted, waving his sword, which gathered every available man. 'Marines form up and give them a volley. Mr Hardy, a party at the hatches to keep those below in check.'

Pierson had his red-coated bullocks in line and ready within half a minute, their fusillade poured into the area from which the gunfire had come. Nelson followed the musket balls at a rush, jumping from the bulwarks of one Spanish ship, a Second Rate, on to the main chains of another, to grapple his way on to a First Rate three-deck 112-gun ship.

Berry was with him, using main force to push his commodore up high enough to get over the bulwark of the bigger vessel. Nelson was shouting, his cracked voice sounding mad. He emerged on to the deck prepared to kill everyone in sight, only to find a line of Spanish officers, swords extended, waiting to surrender to him. One, on his knees, informed him in stilted English that his admiral was dying. Nelson took his hand to lift him to his feet, and requested of him in even worse Spanish that all the ship's officers should be informed of the surrender.

A salvo from *Prince George* slammed into the side of the *San Josef*, to remind Nelson that a battle was still in progress.

'Berry, the flag, cut it down.'

Berry rushed to obey as Nelson took the swords, handing them to Giddings, who, with an air about him of studied calm, tucked them under his arm.

'They've struck already, sir,' Berry shouted, from the poop.

'Then show yourself to *Prince George*, but don't get your head blown off doing it.'

Thorpe grabbed his hand and shook it, gazing into Nelson's astounded face. 'You don't know it, do you, yer honour, what you've done? I'm shaking your hand now while I has the chance. When this gets out they'll be queuing up.'

'*Victory*, sir,' cried Berry, bloodstained but unbowed, pointing to the approaching flagship, fast coming down on the three closely entwined warships, *Captain*, *San Josef* and *San Nicolas*. The rigging was full of sailors. On the quarterdeck Nelson could see Admiral Jervis, Captain Calder and all the flag officers. As they came abreast Sir John raised his hat, and led, in the most flattering fashion, the cheers of every man aboard his ship.

CHAPTER 54

Emma Hamilton read Nelson's letter for the third time that morning, trying to imagine the battle that had taken place a month before, not helped by the way her correspondent played down what must have been a bloody affair. The Spaniards had been soundly trounced, those not taken forced to run for the shelter of Cadiz.

Both she and Sir William had had other letters, from London, that told of how the news of the victory had been greeted. The bells had rung, gold medals had been struck and every civic body in the land vied to give one of the heroes the freedom of their city. Sir John Jervis had been raised to the peerage, and was now Earl St Vincent. Nelson had become both a rear admiral and a Knight of the Bath. And those letters also told of that new raree-show that was enacted in all the pleasure gardens and playhouses: Nelson's Patent Bridge for the Taking of First Rates, in which the feat of crossing one ship to take another, never before achieved, was played endlessly to an adoring, patriotic audience.

Sir William had been right all those years ago, when he had introduced Horatio Nelson as a man of exceptional ability. Emma began a reply couched in warm terms that would, of course, include a fond wish that a British fleet should once more come to Naples, and that Admiral Sir Horatio Nelson would lead it.

Fanny Nelson, staying in Bath with her husband's father, couldn't deal with the letters she received. They were too numerous. Everyone who knew Admiral Nelson wanted to write with praise of his actions. But so did many who had never made an acquaintance: people from all over the country who had read of his exploits in the newspapers, eager to tell her that her husband, by his actions and his application, had saved the nation.

She had letters from him, too, in which she knew he had played down the blood and danger, more eager to tell her that her son had behaved well, that money would flow from the battle: head money for the enemy sailors captured, gun money for the guns, as well as prize money for the ships themselves.

With *Captain* a near wreck he had shifted his flag to HMS *Theseus* and hoisted his blue pennant at the mizzen, the flag of his new rank. It worried her that the acclaim he had garnered didn't seem to satisfy him, and that he was already talking of a new adventure which, if it succeeded, would eclipse the fame he had already acquired. Together with the Reverend Edmund Nelson she pored over maps to locate an island somewhere off the coast of Africa she had never heard of: Tenerife.

There is always a moment before going into action when a sailor faces the prospect of death, convinced that this is his day to succumb. Pessimism abounds at the moment of composition, when it is easy to conjure up images of those you love and cherish: family, friends, fellow officers and seamen in a world in which you no longer exist. Nelson had written just such a letter off Portugal in February, and he was writing another off Tenerife in July. That pessimism, in Nelson's experience, usually evaporated as soon as he turned his mind to more practical things. But not on this occasion! Not for the recently promoted and knighted Rear Admiral Sir Horatio Nelson KB!

First mooted after the victory at Cape St Vincent by a junior admiral keen to enhance his already glowing reputation, the operation to take the island had been viewed with confidence. Tenerife lacked a full garrison; what forts it had were weak and under-gunned. Land a substantial force, take those forts and invest the main port of Santa Cruz, and it would only be a matter of time before the island fell, there being no hope of relief from Spain who had seen its Grand Fleet soundly beaten six months previously.

Surprise, a vital element of the plan, was lost when the weather turned against him: a strong gale allied to a foul current meant his frigate commanders couldn't land their troops in the dark. The next attempt involved landing forces in broad daylight while the line-of-battle ships pounded Santa Cruz. This was frustrated by a flat calm that had him wearing to and fro off the bay called the Lion's Mouth, unable to aid the progress of Troubridge, who battered uselessly against the hillside forts until he was forced to withdraw, re-embarking his landing parties, weary and unsuccessful.

When proposed, Nelson's latest plan, a direct attack on the town via the mole that protected the harbour, caused even his bravest subordinate to pale, making him wonder if it was a product of his vanity rather than sound tactical sense. With the success against the Grand Fleet he was loath to return to Admiral Jervis, now Earl St Vincent, without a triumph under his belt. The last time he had seen him his irascible commander in chief had been up to his ears in the suppression of mutiny, the tidewash of the insurrections at Spithead and the Nore, which had led to the unpleasantness of two hangings.

Nelson was glad to be away from that, an impossible conundrum. He sympathised with the sailors' demands while at the same time deploring the methods chosen to effect change. And in a fleet at sea, which might face battle at any time, sentiment had to take second place to the maintenance of efficiency. He hoped another resounding success would do more to stifle discontent in the fleet than any number of yardarm ropes.

'Gentlemen, I shall lead this attack. Please be assured that my desire to do so has no bearing on the conduct of any officer in this room. I think you know my character, and will readily understand that I find it ten times closer to hell to be a mere observer, rather than a participant.'

The numerous nodding heads reassured him. There would be no jealousies, but he would have been cheered by more smiles. 'I intend to anchor off the town and give every indication of my intention to bombard. Conscious of the difficulties, and not wishing to keep his troops under heavy cannon fire, the Spanish commander must assume another landing and I hope will reinforce his forts, thus denuding the town. In darkness complete, which at this time of year will be close to midnight, we will take to the boats and secure the mole. From there we will attack and take Santa Cruz, manning the walls on the landward side to repel any attempt at a counter attack.'

Plans for timing, numbers to be employed, which boats to take which parties, marines or sailors, signals, both to advance and retire, used up most of the afternoon, so that when the captains left to return to their own ships it was time to stand into the bay. Now it was dark in his great cabin and, with all his affairs in order, Nelson took his sword and pistols from Tom Allen and went on deck. His sight, once it was accustomed to darkness illuminated by stars, alighted on an officer preparing to board one of the boats.

'Lieutenant Nisbet, a word, if you please?'

'Sir?'

'Do I observe by your dress that you are about to embark?'

'I am, sir.'

'You know that I lead the attack?'

'I look forward to the honour of accompanying you, sir.'

'Josh, what if we were both to fall? What would become of your poor mother? The care of this ship is yours. Stay, therefore, and take charge of her.'

'*Theseus* must take care of itself. I'll go with you tonight if never again.'

'I cannot insist,' Nelson responded softly, but sadly, hiding his foreboding. 'Not for an answer I myself would have given.'

He could feel the wind on his face, and the swell lifting and dropping the ship under his feet, neither a good omen for what would be a difficult task even on a calm windless night. At least the Spanish governor had fallen for his ploy. They had observed a great number of men departing Santa Cruz for the forts, lessening the numbers he and his men would have to face.

Troubridge and Waller would be embarking the left flank party from *Culloden*. Captains Freemantle, Thompson and Bowen would join him in the central division once he was in the boats from *Theseus*, and young Sam Hood and his own flag captain, Ralph Millar, would take the right. Movement was always preferable to being stationary: better to worry about keeping your footing when getting into a boat than standing on the deck thinking of the ball from musket or cannon that might kill you.

The slight swell on the 74-gun *Theseus* was more telling once he had lowered himself in to the ship's cutter. That and the tide had the boat crews hauling like madmen just to get them inshore, their efforts not aided by the way the boats were lashed together to ensure they maintained cohesion. Off to the left firing broke out where he perceived the head of the mole to be, though he could not be certain of his own heading, a sharp fight with muskets, the yells of hand combat floating on the wind. Suddenly rockets shot up from behind the arc of the mole, illuminating the stone structure, showing in the harbour behind it several vessels warped right into the beach, as far away as possible from any impending harm.

'Señor Guiterrez is expecting us,' Nelson called, naming the Spanish governor. 'Let us hope he has laid out a decent table for our breakfast.'

It was a feeble joke, but enough to make his men laugh, even those who, by the light of the rockets, could see that they were now within gunshot range.

'Cast off,' he shouted, adding, as soon as the cutter was free of its rope, 'pull like the devil, give a hurrah to let them know we're coming, and when you get ashore remember your orders. All parties to make for the main square and wait.'

The water before them was suddenly full of canister and grapeshot, each small ball tearing up its own patch of seawater, so heavy that it looked as though nothing could live through it. Off to his right the boats led by Captain Freemantle had already made the mole and were clambering on to the stonework, engaging defenders. Nelson's blood was racing, as it always did when he was going into action. The thoughts he had harboured in his cabin, that this was an action from which he would probably not return, were suppressed by the sheer excitement that animated him.

Crunching on to the soft ground that lay at the foot of the harbour mole, he was first out of the boat, the sword that had served his ancestor, Captain Gadifrus Walpole, held out to lead the charge. And charge they did, his men, screaming obscenities, firing pistols and muskets, clubbing, stabbing, jabbing with pikes, driving back the strong defence. Nelson, seeking to get everyone on to dry land, was waving his sword, yelling to cheer on his fighters, one eye noting that Josiah was fighting like a demon.

Then he felt himself spun round so hard he nearly fell to the ground, the sword knocked from his hand by the blow. His reaction, to pick it up with his left hand, was automatic, taken before he realised that his elbow was smashed and that his right arm was hanging at an odd angle. He felt no pain, just the shock of recognising the wound and watching his own blood pump from his arm to stain the stonework, and glisten in the light from the rockets fired by the defenders. Then he fell to his knees, aware that he was going to die.

'Father,' said Josiah, taking his upper arm in a tight grip.

That word opened his eyes, the silhouette of his stepson outlined against the rocket lit sky. Nelson wanted to say to him, 'You have never called me that until now and I had wanted so much to hear it these last twelve years.' But he couldn't. Instead he asked, 'How goes the fight?'

'Well . . .' Josiah said evasively, knowing that all along the mole, even though they had carried it, the British assault was on the defensive from a strong counter-attack launched from the town. Cannons were firing from the streets that led down to the port, while at both ends guns were still in Spanish hands, playing on the flanks of the assault. 'We must get you to a surgeon.'

'Take the town, forget me.'

'To me, Theseus,' Josiah shouted, a call that was immediately acknowledged by half a dozen voices. 'The Admiral is shot in the arm. Get him down to a boat.'

The pain came as they raised him, so acute that he nearly passed out, but they lowered him on to the thin strand of beach, Josiah holding his arm to slow the blood flow. Then they lifted and laid him in the bottom of the boat. A rocket obliged with a strong light overhead, and that showed how much blood he was losing.

'A tourniquet,' Josiah demanded.

One of the men pulled off his shirt and, completely ignoring the balls whizzing past his ears, tore it and wrapped one sleeve round Nelson's arm as a tourniquet, the remainder being fashioned into a sling.

'I thank you, Lovell,' Nelson hissed, recognising a man who had served him on three ships. 'Should I expire take a shirt from my cabin, the best you can find.'

'You'se going to be all right, your honour, don't you fret.'

'Mr Nisbet, now that Lovell has given up his shirt, do not let the purser dock his pay warrant.'

Nelson heard those words, but no one else did. They were too busy heaving the boat off the sand so that it would float, grunting and cursing as they rocked and pushed.

'Man the oars,' Josiah said, as they got it into the sea. 'Set me a course to go under those guns. We must make dark water.'

Nelson was in a state of suspended animation. Yet he was *compos mentis* enough to admire Josiah's thinking. To row straight out to sea, with the sky still illuminated, was to invite every cannon left on the mole to take a shot at them. Josiah had them row under those very guns, so close they could not depress enough to reach, aware that their attention would be concentrated on what they could see far off, not at the water twenty feet below them. Once out of the arc of light, he put down the tiller and headed out to sea, before handing it over to another so that he could attend to his stepfather.

'How fare you?'

It was a weak left hand that lifted his great uncle's sword. 'I still have my weapon.'

'Your arm is shattered, sir.'

'I saw, Josiah.' He let go of the sword to clutch his stepson's hand. 'I thank you. You have shown great ability tonight. Your mother would be proud of you. I know I am.'

'It would be better to rest, sir,' said Josiah, taking off Nelson's hat to put it behind his head. 'You will need all your strength for what is to come.'

'An amputation, at the very least.'

'The surgeon may be able to save it.'

The shake of the head was firm. 'I have witnessed more of wounds than you, and I have looked at this one. Can you raise me a bit, so that I can see?'

Hands got him to an upright position, so that he could look

back to the shore, a place of flame and fire, sound and fury. He had only been upright a minute when a great flash lit the sky to the right of the boat. Nelson saw the silhouette of the decked cutter *Fox*, heard the flimsy timbers tear under the sudden weight of the salvo that struck her hull. Her masts, lit by the flares from the shore, immediately tilted over towards the sea.

'*Fox* going down, your honour,' called one of the men. 'Her larboard bulwark is shipping water already.'

The shouts floated across the water, the cries of men, ghostlike apparitions in the blue lights, screaming for salvation as they jumped into the sea.

'Survivors!' cried Nelson. 'Steer for survivors!'

'Your—'

Josiah never got a chance to finish his plea. Nelson might be gasping, but there was no doubting what he said. 'That, sir, is an order.'

Josiah changed course to set the boat in among the flailing figures in the water, his men shipping oars each time they got a chance to haul some poor near drowning soul inboard. The need to save seamen seemed to revive Nelson, so that he could sit up without assistance to ensure that the search was thorough. He took no account of his wound. There were other boats, which depressed him, since they could only be returning from the shore, where the firing was dying away. Men were calling out for those still in the water to alert the rescuers to their presence, but all response had ceased so they began to row again for the fleet.

'Ship ahead, your honour,' said the shirtless Lovell, after about forty minutes. 'I think it be the *Seahorse*.'

'Steer for her and call for a seat from the yard,' said Josiah.

The left-hand grip became like a vice, the voice like a whip. 'No!'

There was no sound of firing now from the shore, and no *feu de joie* to indicate a British triumph.

'You must have the attentions of a surgeon,' Josiah insisted.

'Not the *Seahorse*. The man is a butcher and a drunk. Besides, Freemantle's wife is aboard, barely wed six months and too young to witness this. I could not face her without news of her husband. Get me to *Theseus*.'

'Time is not on your side, sir.'

'Do as I say, Josiah,' Nelson said softly. 'Let me be the judge, and if I do expire, take no blame upon yourself.'

Midshipman Hoste heard the shout, the hail *Theseus* a strong one, and he recognised the voice as that of his mentor and admiral. Within two minutes he saw Nelson, arm still in a sling, jump for the side, haul himself aboard with one hand to stand on the deck, his eyes bright.

'Tell the surgeon to get his instruments ready, Mr Hoste, for I know I must lose my arm, and the sooner it is whipped off the better.'

'Bowen's dead, sir,' said Ralph Millar, reading from the list he had in his hand. Nelson was sitting in a chair, one sleeve empty and pinned to his coat, his eyes showing the grief he felt for a lost friend, as well as the pain from his wound. *Theseus* was engaged in a bombardment, beating to and fro in front of the town. 'Captain Freemantle is under the care of his surgeon with a wound that may well carry him off.'

'Not that, Millar, not with Betsy so newly wed to him.'

'She is tending to him as well, sir. If anyone can provoke his vital spirit to pull him back to health, it is she.'

'Boat coming off, sir,' said Hoste, popping his head round the door. 'Captain Troubridge in the thwarts.'

When he stood up, Nelson felt weak, grateful that he was in Millar's cabin, which led straight on to the quarterdeck, rather than his own, one deck below. Tom Allen tried to assist him, and was shooed away like a foolish cat. As he emerged, he was aware of the eyes of the crew upon him. Giddings, his coxswain, was close, his gaze full of concern.

'I'm no use for fishing now, Giddings,' he said. 'I fear if I am shipwrecked like Crusoe you will have to come with me or I shall starve.'

'Twould be an honour to serve you wherever, sir.'

Nelson had to turn away then, and it was not the pain he felt that nearly made him cry.

'Captain Troubridge had no choice but to surrender, sir. He was outnumbered a hundred to one.'

The Earl of St Vincent managed a grim smile on that pug-like face of his. 'No blame attaches to any one of your officers, and I have nothing but praise for your actions.'

'The losses, sir.'

'We cannot make war without them, Admiral Nelson.'

Nelson knew his commander to be a more callous man than he. St Vincent never showed much in the way of emotion, gruff kindness being the best Nelson could expect.

'I have written out orders for *Seahorse* to take both you and Captain Freemantle home.'

'Thank you, sir, but I would say to you that, my affliction notwithstanding, I am fit for duty.'

'I hope you are, Admiral Nelson. I want you back under my command as soon as you feel up to a return. And I would suggest that the sooner you are gone, the sooner that will be.'

CHAPTER 55

1798

Return Nelson did, to the blockade off Cadiz six months later, with his rear admiral's flag flying above HMS *Vanguard*. St Vincent was delighted to see him, matters in the Mediterranean having gone from bad to worse. News had come of a fleet of twelve French ships-of-the-line ready to depart from Toulon; infantry and cavalry being loaded into four hundred transports that this fleet would escort. Bonaparte, who had done so much to save the Revolution from collapse, was on the move, destination unknown. Nelson's task was to take a detached squadron back into the Mediterranean, find Bonaparte, his warships and transports, and sink them, an assignment that had caused a furore at home, where several senior admirals were incandescent with rage that such a task should be given to so junior an officer. St Vincent was happy. He wanted ability, not seniority.

'I am obliged to ask if you are fully recovered, Admiral Nelson.'

Nelson could never get over the way he was treated by his beagle-eyed commander-in-chief. It was common knowledge that St Vincent was at the mercy of constant headaches, which partly explained his normal behaviour: orders barked, insults heaped, and professional reputations traduced in this very cabin. Suggested courses of action from his junior admirals or captains were generally met with withering sarcasm, any failure of his exacting standards brutally excoriated.

There were things this sixty-three-year-old bachelor believed with all his heart: that the best way to clap a stopper on mutiny was a swift hanging; that any officer who showed slackness in the way he handled his ship should be sent home; that a man once married was lost to the service and near to useless as a commander; that one Englishman in a ship was worth ten of any enemy. Yet Nelson was shown nothing but kindness, which had preceded the loss of his arm, and he had even heard Josiah, who stayed on the station and now had his own ship, praised for the way he emulated his illustrious stepfather. As a member of the inshore squadron blockading Cadiz he had distinguished himself in three separate small-arms actions.

St Vincent showed a hard carapace to the world, but was more emotional than his visitor knew. He loved Nelson for his zeal, for his determination to fight whenever the opportunity to strike presented itself, for his ship handling which was of the highest, and not least for his own earldom, which would have gone begging had not Nelson risked all at the battle from which St Vincent's title came.

'I am, sir, in better health now than when I left for Tenerife.'

'Then the bosom of your family has done you the power of good.'

'It has, sir.'

'You may have *Alexander* and *Orion*, Captains Ball and Saumarez,' St Vincent continued breezily. 'They and a squadron of frigates will see you into the Mediterranean, and I will reinforce you as my situation permits.'

Nelson pondered those names. Saumarez he knew of old, a good-looking Guernseyman, a fine seaman whose main problem was his own awareness of his appearance. He was always immaculately attired and had a reputation as a man who could paint the whole ship without a speck of it marring his dress uniform. Ball, he was disposed to dislike. He had met him in St Omer all those years before, and bridled for the man's unwarranted attentions to the lovely object of Nelson's affections, Kate Andrews.

'Send me fighters, sir,' insisted Nelson, 'for I intend to find the enemy and send both Bonaparte and his Italian army to the bottom of the sea.'

'Do that, Nelson, and we'll take our seats in the Lords together.'

They discussed plans to co-ordinate if it turned out that

Bonaparte was heading for the West Indies. With cavalry aboard that was unlikely. But, then, he was unpredictable by reputation, and successful to an astonishing degree. Never one to waste time, Nelson's squadron fired their salutes, formed line and set their course for the Straits of Gibraltar. With a fine topgallant breeze they entered Rosas Bay under the towering rock, to anchor, replenish their stores before proceeding into the Mediterranean.

In Nelson's heightened imagination, exiting one sea to enter another was like cutting a chord. He was leaving behind one set of doubts to be replaced by another. He knew – despite all the efforts he made to convince himself that it was otherwise, despite all his protestations to anyone close enough to hear him that she was the object of his deepest regard – his relations with Fanny had not been resolved.

The homecoming, or rather his journey to Bath to meet wife and family, had been muted. Nothing Nelson had written to tell Fanny of his wound would have had the same effect as the writing itself, a left-handed indecipherable scrawl that Fanny openly admitted had reduced her to tears. Her husband could not confess that the loss bothered him too, or that the wound hadn't healed properly. He still, mentally, reached for the quill with the missing right arm, was surprised to look and see that, although his brain had issued the command, and he could feel his right arm moving, nothing was there. That and his constant pain had to be hidden from Fanny to avoid another bout of weeping.

Right handed or left, in four years away, none of his letters home ever intimated that his regard for Fanny had wavered, neither from Naples, in that silly infatuation with Lady Hamilton, nor even from Genoa when he had gone further and transgressed his marriage vows. He had always written to her as his loyal wife, bosom companion and lifelong partner. The simple truth was that he didn't know his own mind, and since he was disinclined to discuss it with anyone he was unaware of how common such a notion could be. He wasn't even sure if the doubts still existed, the mere act of homecoming lending deep sentiments to his feelings. The dread he had had at seeing her again when he had set out four years ago had faded.

Their meeting had been marked by a gentle touch of lips on cheek. Yet that had satisfied him in a way he found hard to define, making him realise that there was more than one strand to his personality. The part that craved action and excitement found Fanny trying: the part that loved domesticity, a blazing hearth, gun dogs and the idea of rubicund children conjured up an image of her as the perfect companion.

Davidson had done a sterling job as his prize agent, and while he wasn't rich he certainly had enough money to live in comfort. His old friend had also done a sterling job for himself, marrying a very pretty and vivacious lady, who had promptly presented him with golden-haired twins, something to make the father *manqué* in Nelson truly envious.

One worry had been laid to rest: the failure at Tenerife was seen as folly, except by those who actively disliked him. Most people he had met, and all of the press, while they had harped on about the loss of the *Fox* and some hundred members of the crew, had concluded that it stood as a heroic failure, a defeat caused more by poor intelligence on enemy strength and the Admiral in command having been asked to do too much with too little.

He was Nelson of the patent bridge, the man who had captured the public imagination. So his credit stood high, and his fellow countrymen demanded the right to place his image upon their walls. This he knew from Locker, to whom he had given, some fifteen years previously, a portrait of himself by John Rigaud. His old mentor had been approached with a request to make prints from it, for sale to the public. How good it was to be praised instead of damned, to have his knighthood conferred by the King in person, and not just sent to him on some foreign station.

King George, no longer irascible in the face of a man now a hero, had asked for a written history of his Mediterranean service, and Nelson knew that that which he had returned was impressive: four single-ship actions, six engagements on land commanding batteries, the cutting-out expeditions numbered ten and he had captured a couple of towns. That, and his wounds, won him a welcome annual pension of a thousand pounds.

The best day had been when his doctors, reaching for the string that held the ligature inside his wounded stump, had pulled, and instead of acute pain, the whole affair had come away, taking with it all the poisons that had kept it from healing. That was the day he went to the Admiralty to say he was again ready for service.

So he had said goodbye to Fanny in the same gentle way he had greeted her, a dry peck on a dry cheek, still uncertain of his feelings. But for all that, when he thought of her as he penned his near daily letter, it was with kindness and warmth.

A red-coated band played them away from Gibraltar, the God-speed of an Army garrison who had entertained them royally, soldiers who never felt quite safe unless a British fleet was in the Mediterranean. Having raised his hat to the island, and waited till *Orion* and *Alexander*, with four frigates and a sloop in attendance, had cleared the bay, Nelson turned to his new flag captain, Edward Berry.

'My lucky sea, Captain Berry. Set us a course for Toulon. Let's find this Corsican menace and destroy him.'

Berry grinned. 'What a contest, you and Bonaparte.'

'I long to try him on a wind, Berry, for landsman or no, I wager that the Corsican will ignore his admirals and try to control the battle.'

'I take leave, sir, to differ,' Berry replied. 'I would wager that whatever battle we have will be controlled by you.'

Nelson was not one to be haunted by words, but that expression of confidence made by Berry and wholly endorsed by him produced a sickening sensation when he recalled them. His return to the Mediterranean had not been the success he had craved, quite the opposite. Between Toulon and Corsica *Vanguard*, caught in a violent storm, had lost every one of her masts, and had been left to roll so heavily on a menacing swell that Berry had been forced to flood the lower decks just to gain some stability. Lacking steerage way the heavy seas of a week-long storm had nearly driven her on to the rocks of several dangerous shores, only saved by the application of Captain

Alexander Ball, who used his vessel to tow the flagship out of danger.

At the subsequent interview, which took place in a placid bay resounding to the clatter of shipwright's hammers, Nelson faced Ball with some trepidation. Having been brusque with the man on the few meetings he had attended, he now had to thank him for his ship and probably his life. If Ball knew that his admiral disliked him, it didn't show, and as they talked Nelson felt his aversion evaporate in the face of the man's modesty. He refused to acknowledge that his exceptional behaviour and courage had been anything but the action any other captain would have taken.

What was intended to be brief extended itself to an invitation to dine, and as the meal progressed Nelson found his feelings growing warmer by the course. Ball was a man after his own heart, a fighter, a sailor, and modest with it. Nelson couldn't understand his previous animosity. How could he have so misjudged Ball? It was an indication to him to be more cautious in future, never to let his heart rule over every emotion. When they parted, he was sure that he was saying goodbye to a friend.

They got *Vanguard* back to sea in an astonishing four days, and resumed the hunt for Bonaparte. Nelson's hopes were lifted off Cape Corse by the sight of Thomas Troubridge in HMS *Culloden*, sailing to join him at the head of ten sail-of-the-line. Now a battle fleet, they sailed north to close Cape Sicié, only to discover from a Marseilles merchantman that the Corsican's armada had already departed Toulon. But there was no information as to where he was headed. At least he could call his captains to meet him, so that they could have no doubt about their commander's intentions.

It was a gathering of old friends as well as new faces: Ralph Millar, Troubridge, of course, dark of countenance and doleful by nature. Tom Foley was there, his friend from his first ever ship, now in command of HMS *Goliath*, tall Sam Hood, the son and nephew of admirals, who had been with him at Tenerife. There was also the round-faced and cheerful Louis, his second-in-command, and Galwey, who was mad, Irish and looked it, with his protruding eyes and unkempt ginger hair, and Darby, another Irishman of a more sober disposition. These were good men, the best St Vincent could send him, fighters all.

'Gentlemen,' he had begun, 'we will, as a fleet, pay not one jot of attention to the Fighting Instructions.'

The faces of his captains betrayed no hint of the import of those words. The Fighting Instructions, as rules of engagement, were not designed to confer outright success on a battle fleet: they were designed to avoid complete failure. A maritime nation like Britain couldn't afford to entrust its fleet to the mere whim of an admiral, especially since the appointment of a commander-in-chief might often have more to do with politics than ability.

It was the bane of the service that a captain became an admiral by mere seniority, filling a dead man's shoes. A promising midshipman did not always pass for lieutenant; a good premier did not always rise to be a competent captain. Nor did a man who could command and manoeuvre one ship necessarily have the ability to manage a fleet. To take a fleet into battle, risking death and destruction and win, required skills granted to few.

So the Admiralty had evolved a set of rules tying the hands of individual commanders. A battle was considered a victory if the enemy withdrew. A stalemate, in which no side could claim an advantage, was seen as a positive result; defeat was unthinkable. Failure had dire consequences. Admiral Byng, after a farce of a trial, had been shot on his quarterdeck for failure at Minorca thirty years previously, as Voltaire, the French sage, had put it, '*pour encourager les autres*'.

'Gentlemen,' Nelson continued, referring to that disgraceful episode, 'is there one of us present who has not wondered if we'd share Admiral Byng's fate at some time in our career? I am the Admiral. That risk is mine. I would ask you to obey the orders I give you in writing and put aside all thoughts of what consequences might attend upon failure.'

Nelson rarely raised his voice in company, his even temper being one of his great qualities, but he did know how to be emphatic. 'Why? Because we cannot fail. We have ships and men that have been at sea for years. Our gun-crews achieve a rate of fire that will be double that of our enemies. Not a day goes by that does not include practice in boarding. In short, gentlemen, we are professional naval officers. Our opponents have been decimated by the guillotine and politics, and are led by a bullock, a blue-coated one, I grant you, but a soldier nevertheless, and like to be a buffoon on water.'

Some applauded, others grinned. Fat-faced Louis cried, 'Hear him.'

'Our fleet will be split into three divisions. The pair closest to the enemy battleships, wherever we find them, will engage them immediately, the third will seek to destroy the transports. Since the object of the French plan is to carry troops to whatever destination they have in mind, defending those will become a priority. The first two divisions must and will interpose themselves between the transports and the enemy flag. We will make them fight their way through to provide succour.

'My signals lieutenant will give you the outline of a set of flags each, relevant to your own ship. But we all know that flags can be obscured. I therefore expect you to act according to your outline instructions without recourse to a command from me. These, too, will be in writing.'

There was more to discuss, a dozen different outlines. Where would the enemy be? Would it be day or night? The sea-state would have a bearing, as would wind direction. Would the French have an anchorage under their lee to which they could run for safety? What if they split their forces? Nelson had to make sure that every one of his inferior officers understood that their ships were instruments of war; that an individual loss was acceptable, given a positive result to the battle. The conference broke up in a happy mood.

What followed was the worst sixty days of Nelson's life, a seemingly fruitless voyage around the Mediterranean. His instructions from St Vincent, to find and destroy the enemy, fell on the hurdle of his lack of frigates. They were the eyes of the fleet, able swiftly to seek likely rendezvous, the bays and harbours where the French might congregate, then report back to an admiral who could mount an attack. He had too few for an expanse of water that stretched from Gibraltar to the Black Sea.

Bonaparte threatened Malta, Tuscany, Naples, the Adriatic, Tunis, Algiers, Egypt and the rest of the Ottoman Empire. If there was a grand design, it was secret. Nelson sailed to Alexandria, only to find the anchorage devoid of French shipping. On his return to the Straits of Messina he heard that Malta had fallen to the French, but that Bonaparte was no longer there. He had disappeared again! Faced with a frightened King Ferdinand, still at peace with France, he had to use subterfuge to keep his ships victualled, using what frigates and sloops he had to scour the seas while he remained inactive at Syracuse.

Reports came in of sightings at every corner of the Inland Sea. Thomas Hardy, now master and commander of the brig *Mutine*, spoke with a Ragusan trader in the Adriatic who had sighted a fleet heading east. Was this Bonaparte? Had Nelson guessed right about Alexandria, only arriving too soon to catch a slow-sailing convoy of four hundred transports?

Off they sailed again, Nelson sick, so great was his anxiety. Hailed as a hero in England for his exploits at St Vincent, forgiven for heroic failure at Tenerife, he knew that whatever reputation he enjoyed would disappear like a puff of smoke from a chimney if he failed to find Bonaparte. How confident he had been at those early conferences, how foolish his plans seemed now.

And this voyage to Egypt seemed just as fruitless as the first. Two ships had looked into Alexandria only to find its harbours empty, a fact signalled to Nelson as soon as the fleet came in sight. It was with a heavy heart that the Admiral ordered a signal to turn eastwards for what he suspected to be a futile search of the coastline.

'Frigates,' he said to Tom Allen, as his bovine servant served him a solitary dinner. 'When they cut me open, Tom, they will find that word engraved on my heart. If I had half a dozen, I'd have Bonaparte.'

Allen regarded the man he served with an experienced eye, wondering if he should say something. Nelson was so jumpy he daren't knock one salver into another. The slightest unusual noise made him jerk round to look, evidence of the tension he was harbouring in what he thought was a calm demeanour. He had heard that Frank Lepée had never feared to advise Nelson or to tell him he was wrong. But Lepée had been shown the cabin door, which was the last thing Tom Allen wanted. Serving the Admiral was a soft billet, which he was not about to sacrifice. Let the Admiral tie himself in knots, it was no job of a servant to act the doctor.

The food lay uneaten on the plate, to get cold and congeal. Nelson, looking at it, was inclined to see his career in a similar light. He knew from the faces of the ship's officers that they felt the same. They had started out with high hopes under a commander who never missed a chance for action. This was the place to be; he was the man to be with, yet it had all fallen flat. Berry, he knew, would be above him with his officers, eating a silent repast, thinking the same as his admiral, that they had missed the boat.

All those admirals at home, above him on the list, would be crowing now, telling all who would listen what folly it had been to appoint such a junior and vainglorious character to command. People who had treated him as a hero six months before would shun him now, the man who couldn't find an armada of over four hundred ships. And just where was Bonaparte, a man who had taken on the features of a demon in Nelson's mind? He was attacking something somewhere, and the man ordered to stop him was in the wrong place.

Nelson started to shake. Was it a recurrence of the malaria, a disease which always came to attack him when his spirits were low? Or was it just the lack of sleep, endless nights spent lying in his cot gnawing at the problems he faced both professionally and personally? Tom Allen, had he dared, would have told him to eat, which he had scarce done for a week.

The scraping of a dozen chairs, followed by the sound of running feet, distracted Nelson but did nothing to dent a miserable, sickly mood that had him close to seeking rest. Even the peremptory knock on his cabin door failed to rouse him and he left Allen to respond. But the flushed, excited face of Midshipman Hoste, sent to give him a message, set his heart racing.

'*Zealous* signalling, sir. The enemy is in Aboukir Bay, fifteen sail moored in line of battle.'

CHAPTER 56

At those words the enervating malaise fell away. The whole ship was alive with cheering by the time he made the deck. From his position in the line Nelson could see little of his leading vessels, but he trusted to the ships in the van to take the appropriate action, Foley in *Goliath* and Sam Hood in *Zealous*. It was after one-thirty, and raking the high masts that lay in Aboukir Bay with a telescope, their hulls cut off by a headland, he began to make his calculations. He had already sent a frigate ahead to lay off and repeat signals to his leading vessels, which would attack unless he issued orders to desist. Was that wise?

Hood and Foley would barely make the bay before sunset, and the rest of his ships would engage in the increasing gloom, the last ships in the line going into battle in darkness. That particularly applied to *Alexander* and *Swiftsure*, straining to catch up, having been detached to look into Alexandria. A night battle was always a chancy affair, with the exercise of command impossible. And the French were anchored in a strong defensive position. But Horatio Nelson had laid out his principles, which were based on an abiding trust in his captains and a deep faith in the men they commanded.

'Captain Berry, be so good as to signal to the squadron, prepare for action.'

'Sir,' Berry replied, beaming.

'My dinner is on the board, and I intend that this day it should be eaten. If you wish you may join me.'

Information came in piecemeal over the next five hours: signals from the frigate standing off to pass orders, through speaking trumpets over the taffrail of HMS *Minotaur* sailing ahead of *Vanguard*, through excited midshipmen sent by their captains in boats, and all that was allied to what his own lookouts could see. Nelson perceived that the French Admiral, de Brueys, had anchored with his strongest vessels to the rear of his flagship, the 120-gun *L'Orient*. The vessels closest to the approaching British squadron were the weakest in his fleet.

By the amount of activity on the beach there appeared to be numerous shore parties, some of whom would struggle to get back to their ships before battle commenced. There were also gaps between the anchored ships large enough for a 74 to sail through, so orders went out to all ships to prepare sheet anchors that would hold the warships by the stern and keep steady and true whatever fire they poured on the enemy.

'Monsieur de Brueys is not anticipating a fight today, Mr Hoste.'

The youngster fixed Nelson with his huge soft brown eyes. With his now spotty skin, no one could look less the warrior and, indeed, so small had Hoste been that Nelson had worried for him when he first came to sea. He had grown now, and was nearing an age to sit for lieutenant. As for fighting, he was apparently a right Tartar when it came to fisticuffs.

'He will get one, sir, won't he?'

'It would be interesting to know what would prevent such a thing.'

Hoste knew he was being tested, just as he knew that there were no traps in the examination. 'We lack charts, sir, so there may be shoal water that would run us aground.'

Nelson smiled. 'There's enough for the French.'

'There might also be shore batteries, given all the men that have vacated the ships.'

'Well spotted, Mr Hoste.' The youngster talked on, mentioning the lack of light, the possibility of the unexpected, as Nelson listened. 'And given all this, and assuming you were Monsieur de Brueys, what would you have done?'

'I'd want to fight in open water, sir. I'd have put to sea as soon as I spotted our topsails.'

Nelson lifted his telescope then, and fixed it on the Admiral's pennant flying at the masthead of *L'Orient*. 'So would I, Mr Hoste, so would I.'

Goliath was just edging *Zealous* to be first into the bay, both ships with leadsmen casting for sandbars. Captain Tom Foley could hear Sam Hood over the gunfire exhorting his men to greater efforts as they rounded the headland protecting the anchorage. The cannon fire came from a French sloop inshore, trying by its pinpricks to persuade either of the captains to pursue it into water shallow enough to run them aground. Foley had made his way to the forepeak, to raise his glass and look at the enemy, the sides of the vessels aglow and orange in the light of a sinking sun. In twenty-seven years, much had changed about the midshipman who had challenged his admiral to a pissing contest, but he still had sharp, bird-like eyes and tidy features, even if they were lined with age.

Foley could see men hurrying about the deck of the lead French ship, *Le Guerrier*. He could also see that, with the tide running east, she was straining on her single forward anchor cable. There wasn't much tidal movement in the Mediterranean, a rise of two feet or so, but there was enough. That meant his enemy, when the tide turned, would swing through an arc of 180 degrees. The deduction that followed was simple. *Le Guerrier* had to have enough water under her keel to do that, which meant that ahead of that anchor cable was a whole ship's length of water deep enough for *Goliath* to sail through.

'Quartermaster,' he yelled, 'bring her head round and point me to the shore. I want to shave that anchor cable.' More softly, he added to the midshipman at his side, 'Get off a signal to the flag and tell him of my intentions, and ask the premier to take us down to topsails.'

The whole bay was bathed in orange light, the tops of the wavelets pink instead of white. Nelson's lookouts had told him of *Goliath*'s change of course. Silently he blessed his luck in having such men along with him, men who understood not only his orders but also his philosophy: that it was necessary to look for all advantage and take it without recourse to a higher authority. Foley was going to sail inside the French line, and take his opponent on a side that was likely undefended.

The first boom of cannon fire rippled through the twilight air, and Nelson heard Berry order that the time, 6.28 p.m., be noted. His nerves were jumping again, worried that Foley might ground his ship and leave himself at the mercy of shore batteries. Hands clenched, he willed his lookouts to yell that he was through, but whole minutes went by without a sound. Looking round, Nelson realised that the whole ship was holding its breath.

'*Goliath*'s through,' came the yell, 'with *Zealous* in her wake.'

'Signal to all captains, Mr Berry, to hoist out distinguishing lights.'

Within minutes men on every ship had raced aloft to lash lanterns to the upper masts, combinations and colours that could be noted. Now Nelson knew that neither he nor those to his rear, in the pitch black of a moonless night, would fire into their own. Over the next hour, as darkness fell, he watched the lanterns of *Orion*, *Audacious* and *Theseus* follow Foley's lead and take the French on the inshore side of the bay, pouring into them a pounding rate of gunfire that sent visible parts of the ships flying into the air.

Sixth in line, Nelson ordered Berry to stay on the open flank, sailing straight ahead to take station of the third ship in the French line, *Le Spartiate*, reducing to topsails just before commencing to fight. High flaring lanterns, clear against a black sky, told Nelson that *Theseus* was bombarding the other flank.

Berry dropped the sheet anchor to hold his stern, *Vanguard* within pistol shot of the enemy, then gave the order to open fire. The Frenchman, with guns that could be put to good effect, had already raked him twice with two quick salvoes but that rate of fire did not survive the first British broadside. It was only by the flash of cannon fire that Nelson saw what damage his flagship did; that and the sound of screaming men.

He saw in one flash that the mainmast was going, taking with it rigging, spars, chains and men. Parts of the bulwarks of the French ship flew off, exposing those on deck to the withering fire of the next salvo. He could imagine the hell between decks on both sides, so much worse for the enemy than for his gunners toiling below. There would be men here dead and dying, but not as many as on *Spartiate* and that was what counted. Eight ships now battered five Frenchmen. In the flashes of gunfire they could see that *Spartiate* was completely dismasted, its bulwarks in shreds, the deck covered in men whole or in bits, glistening blood running out of the scuppers. Wisely, those to his rear had passed him to seaward to take on unengaged enemies further up the line.

That was where he should be, opposite the largest ship in the battle, and the enemy Admiral. Nelson was just about to request Berry to haul up the stern anchor and move on to face *L'Orient* when he was felled by a tremendous blow to the head that sent him flying backwards into his flag captain's arms. The pain was instant, as was the certain knowledge that he was going to die. As if from a mile away he could hear voices around him, commands to get him below to the surgeon.

'I am killed,' he croaked, as Berry lowered him to the deck. 'Remember me to my wife.'

How stupid those words sounded once he had uttered them, how pointless and futile. But for all that, if he was going to die he had God to thank that it was at this hour. Battle would still rage, but he knew de Brueys would not beat him, that what had happened already presaged a great victory. He could pass on in the heat of battle like James Wolfe, and there was nothing he would have wished for more if he could not have life. And perhaps, if God were kinder still, he too would, like his hero, expire at a moment of triumph.

He did know that he was blind; the eye that had survived the shattering of stones at Calvi, and which had been milky ever since, gave him only a dim view of what was happening around him. The other was just blackness, with warm blood running down to give a salty taste to his parched mouth.

Arms lifted him and he recognised the voice of Giddings in his ear. 'You'll be all right, your honour, when we get you below.'

Berry reached forward to lift a long patch of skin off Nelson's face, pinning it back to the forehead from which it had been sliced. Other arms took him and, jerking, eyes closed, Nelson was carried below to the cockpit, lit by shuddering lanterns and full of the dull boom of cannon fire and the screams and moans of wounded sailors. Above their heads gun carriages rumbled out, blasted forth, then groaned as they were flung back by the recoil.

'Mr Jefferson, the Admiral,' Giddings yelled, lowering Nelson so that he could stand supported on his own two feet.

'No,' said Nelson, opening his eyes and realising that he could still see. Jefferson was up to his armpits in blood and gore, the area around his feet awash and shiny red, sprinkled with limbs that the surgeon had already sawn off. 'Let me wait my turn.'

'Your honour,' insisted Giddings.

'There's near a hundred men in here, I fancy, Giddings, all as good as their admiral.'

Giddings didn't argue, but by supporting Nelson more fully he allowed the other sailor to detach himself and go to the surgeon. Nelson was laid on some sacks by the time Jefferson came and probed the huge gash. He announced that the wound was deceptive, not as bad as it looked, and that Nelson was in no immediate peril. Unconvinced, his admiral sent for the parson, Mr Comyn, so that messages could be written now, to be sent to his wife and his second-in-command.

Lying on his sacks, with the bleeding ceased but the pain increasing, Nelson listened to a stream of messages, slowly but surely coming round to the view that he was indeed going to live. *Spartiate* struck at eight-thirty, and here before him, as Jefferson stitched his wound, stood Berry with the French Captain's sword, plus the news that two other Frenchmen had been struck, while three more, including *L'Orient*, would shortly be overcome.

To get him away from the noise of men wounded and dying and the rumbling of cannon overhead they shifted Nelson to the bread room, and there, deep in the bowels of the ship, in a room lined with tin to keep out rats, he heard the depth of his victory increase at what seemed no more than ten-minute intervals. Demanding pen and paper, Nelson began to write his despatch to the First Lord.

Admiral Sir Horatio Nelson KB.
Aboukir Bay off the coast of Egypt
  My Lord,
Almighty God has blessed His Majesty's arms in battle . . .

The door opened and Berry was there once more, to tell him that *L'Orient* appeared to be on fire. 'Her cabin is ablaze, sir, and I can't see they have left the means to check it while they remain under bombardment.'

Nelson struggled to get up, but failed. He felt weak, but his voice was strong. 'Help me, Berry. We must see if we can save her.'

'The doctor, sir—'

'Is not your superior, Captain Berry.' Nelson grinned to take the sting out of the words. 'I must see for myself.'

He arrived on deck to be told that three more Frenchmen had been struck, an almost unbelievable result. Berry took him to the side and pointed out the flames leaping about the stern of the French flagship, a conflagration that illuminated it all the way to the bowsprit and bathed the whole bay in an ethereal light. In the water hundreds of heads bobbed, some clinging to wreckage, others swimming or floundering.

'Captain Berry, get boats out to rescue survivors!'

It was light enough to see *Swiftsure* and *Alexander*, late arrivals at the battle, pouring a merciless barrage into the stern of the French flagship. If they had the means to stop the blaze the pounding of British cannon prevented them from doing so. The poop was a mass of flames but brave men on the lower deck were still working her guns, replying to the two British 74s. Nelson pointed this out to the crowd of officers and mids surrounding him. 'Look hard, gentlemen. We do not have an exclusive call on bravery and honour.'

The flames hit what rigging was still left standing, shooting up to the tops like a racing squirrel. They could see ships close by, faced with the sailors' greatest dread, a spreading conflagration, cutting cables and sheet anchors to get clear. Only Ball stayed in position, his pumps working flat out to drench his decks and upperworks with water, this so he could keep his guns firing in the increasing, metal-melting heat. But when the decks were alight even Ball knew that the enemy was doomed and hauled himself clear of danger.

Nelson saw the flames suddenly balloon out, mixed with a mass of timber. A wall of air hit his face followed by an ear-shattering boom that pressed in on his flesh. Looking up he saw

L'Orient disintegrate, even her guns tossed skywards by the force of the blast that ripped out of her magazine, the hull driven down into the encroaching waters so that the flames, which had illuminated the whole battle scene, were suddenly extinguished, plunging everyone into stygian darkness.

It was minutes later that bits of *L'Orient* came back to earth, wood, metal, tattered fragments of sail and the limbs of men blown to small pieces by the force of the explosion. By then, aboard the ships of Nelson's fleet, the cheering had already begun.

CHAPTER 57

The sight of a British frigate, beating up into the Bay of Naples, flags streaming from the masts, was enough to cause panic in some breasts, anxiety in others and hope in a few. Sir William, trusting the eyes of others, received the news at his dressing table and immediately ordered that a boat should be sent out to greet the new arrivals, with instructions to carry to him at speed whatever message they bore.

Standing by the windows of Emma's private apartments, her new friend Cornelia Knight observed the way the frigate anchored, saw the speed with which two young officers alighted into Sir William's boat, and felt a frisson of fear as she contemplated what news they might carry. France had been triumphant everywhere these last five years. The Revolution had humbled all of northern Italy, overrun the Papal States and Rome itself, taken and held the Low Countries and Flanders. Bonaparte, their famous Corsican general, was abroad in the Mediterranean, seeking God only knew what lands to conquer.

The whole world knew he was at sea with a strong fleet and transports carrying the army with which he had humbled Austria. The destination of that fleet had been the only subject of conversation for a month, since the news had arrived that Bonaparte had captured Malta. Had he gone east to threaten the Adriatic or Egypt? Had he gone west to threaten Gibraltar? Or was he coming here, to burn, destroy and loot Naples?

'They are close enough to see their faces, Emma.'

Emma left the writing table to take the telescope from her friend. The first image to fill the glass when she had adjusted it was that of William Hoste, whom she named to Cornelia. The other officer, a lieutenant, was a stranger to her. Then she lifted the instrument to look over the ship, sitting on the still waters of the bay, sails now neatly furled, an image of peaceful intent.

Mary Cadogan entered, wearing her customary apron, tied at the waist by the chain that held the heavy keys to the palazzo. 'Sir William asks that you join him in his library.'

'He will insist on greeting them formally,' Emma said, for the benefit of Cornelia Knight.

'Will my presence affect that?'

'No Cornelia, it will not.'

The trio stood to greet the two officers as soon as they heard their footsteps echo on the marble staircase. Sir William was wondering, as he had since they'd been spotted, whether what they said would be a prelude to flight or celebration. If the former, what should he take with him and what should he leave? If the latter, what was the state of his larders and cellars? Years of waiting for news had inured him to over-reaction in either direction. How many times had he anticipated a momentous despatch only to be handed a packet of social letters?

The double doors swung open to admit the pair. Naval officers they might be but they looked absurdly young, no more than boys, two faces that were struggling to appear controlled.

'Sir William,' said the one who could barely be said to be the eldest, 'I am Lieutenant Capel, and this is Mr Hoste. We bring despatches from Admiral Sir Horatio Nelson.'

A second's pause followed, in which both young faces contorted with effort, before breaking into full grins, their voices rising to near shouts as they imparted the news. 'A great victory! The French fleet is utterly destroyed! Admiral de Brueys was brought to battle in Aboukir Bay and . . .'

Sir William saw Emma begin to go, but could not react quickly enough to catch her. Neither could his two visitors, though they moved with speed in an attempt to break her fall. She hit the stone floor with an audible thump partly covered by cries from her husband and her friend to fetch the smelling salts. Capel and Hoste lifted her inert body on to a divan, then stepped back to stand like mourners at a wake.

'Months of worry have caused this.'

'You may worry no more, sir.'

'Admiral Nelson?'

'Bears a wound, sir,' replied Hoste, 'but though he suffers from the effects of it the surgeon assured us they would pass.'

'Tell me what happened,' demanded Sir William, standing to allow a servant to administer the salts. 'Briefly.'

'We caught them at anchor, sir,' Capel replied, his near black eyes flashing with the memory, 'though they were ranged in line of battle. It has been proposed that de Brueys did not consider the possibility of an immediate attack, so had made no preparation.'

'The result?'

'Five ships-of-the-line taken as prizes, two burnt and Admiral de Brueys' flagship, *L'Orient*, blown to bits. Two 74s, we believe under Rear Admiral Villeneuve, escaped, *Guillaume Tell* and *Généraux*. They had with them a trio of frigates, but that is all. To all extents the French menace in the Mediterranean is gone.'

'We must tell the King,' said Sir William.

The carriage that had brought them from the mole was still harnessed and it was but a short journey to the Palazzo Reale. Admittance to the royal chamber was immediate, and there sat King Ferdinand and his queen, with all of their children, apparently breakfasting quietly as if all was well with the world, as if no frigate had entered the bay that morning. But Sir William knew that this was window dressing, an act designed to demonstrate that they were brave enough to face news good or bad. In truth Their Sicilian Majesties would be in turmoil. Somewhere close by, loaded and ready to flee, would be a line of carriages.

'Your Majesty, I bring you good tidings. Admiral Nelson, on the afternoon of August first, found and engaged the French fleet in Egyptian waters. I am happy to say that he has achieved the most astounding of victories, and that the French menace to your kingdom is no more.'

The Queen had a hand to her throat, as though the guillotine blade that had beheaded her sister was on her flesh. Sir William could see that Ferdinand was trying to be regal, trying to play the role his titles and birthright demanded of him. But the natural child in him could not contain his joy.

Suddenly he rushed to embrace the British Ambassador, yelling, 'You have saved my kingdom! You have saved my family!'

The elder children were weeping, the younger ones confused. Their mother was on her feet now, moving around the chamber, swaying as if to swoon and looking to various statues for support. Ferdinand was babbling away to Sir William while the two messengers stood confused, not understanding a word. It was ten minutes before the wailing ceased, during which Maria Carolina had sunk to the floor to pray. Evidence that the news was abroad came from the sudden cacophony of church bells that pealed out over the city. Within the hour all of Naples was celebrating its deliverance, an hour during which, with Sir William translating, the two young naval officers described the battle in detail.

'You know, sir,' said Capel, 'of the chase we had. I have never seen my admiral so vexed and anxious as the thought plagued him that he had missed Bonaparte.'

'He so much wanted to encounter him at sea,' added Hoste, 'to prove that Bonaparte's success on land counted for nothing.'

'Nelson said so in his letters,' Sir William replied, this while Ferdinand was asking him a question. 'His Majesty counts himself a sea officer, gentlemen. Please explain the disposition of the fleet.'

Neither Hoste nor Capel was fazed by that request. In the week it had taken them to make Naples they had had precious little else to talk about. They knew that they were privileged to have been present at the greatest feat of naval arms since the destruction of the Spanish Armada. In the week following the action, before they received their duplicate despatches to carry to Naples, every story of every officer, French as well as British, had been condensed into a narrative account of the battle.

They spoke in turns, using maps when Ferdinand produced them, tracing the route Nelson had taken in his pursuit of Bonaparte. East, west and east again, the information that he had missed them by a whisker twice. They described the

636

disposition of the fleet, the King nodding sagely at each piece of information as though these were decisions he himself would have made, had he been in command.

'We have it from the French prisoners that, seeing the time of day, de Brueys though it unlikely we would attack.'

'He should have studied Nelson,' said Hoste, eyes alight with hero-worship. 'When he did clear for action, he did so only on the seaward side.'

When this was translated, Ferdinand looked confused. Capel was busy arranging model ships, ten or so in line with another eight bearing down on them, a cloth rolled up to represent the arc of Aboukir Bay. With his finger he showed Foley's route, looking at the King to ensure he understood.

'They fought well, the Frenchmen,' said Hoste. 'There was no thought of surrender, and every one of our ships suffered great damage, *Bellerophon* particularly, she losing a full third of her complement as casualties. But they were out-gunned, out-manned and out-fought. *Le Peuple Souverain* cut her cable and ran aground, *L'Orient*, it appeared, had been painting and some of the residue of that caught fire. The rest, barring *Guillaume Tell* and *Le Généraux*, struck.'

The destruction of Admiral de Brueys' flagship had been heard ten miles away. Troubridge, so eager to enter the battle, had run his ship aground at the head of the bay. Later he said he thought that he had suffered some form of explosion below, so great was the force of the blast transmitted through the water. It transpired that the treasure of the Knights of St John, looted from Malta, with sixty ingots of gold to the value of £600,000, had gone to the bottom with her.

'The cost?' asked Sir William. He did not mean in terms of money.

'Some two hundred dead on our side, sir,' Capel replied, 'with seven hundred wounded. The enemy losses were of the order of two thousand dead or missing.'

'This will mean a peerage,' said Sir William. A servant entered to give the Ambassador a message. He smiled, looked at the two young officers, and said, 'My wife seems quite recovered. She is in an open carriage at the gates and desires, if you have finished your report, that you join her.'

Half in love with her already, both young men rushed to comply. They found her as Sir William had described, wearing on her head an embroidered turban that read 'Nelson and Victory'. Emma Hamilton took them through the streets, singing patriotic songs, shouting that Britannia had triumphed and generally whipping up an already excited populace to a frenzy of celebration. She was aided by two young men who thought her a most remarkable creature, young men who spent as much time admiring her and thinking about bedding her as they did about the victory at the Nile.

The arrival of the Vanguard in the Bay of Naples, under tow, part of the trickle of ships that made up Nelson's victorious fleet, came as no surprise. Fishing boats, trading-vessels, lookouts on high points of the southern Italian coast had been searching for her topsails for weeks. The journey from the Straits of Messina to the Bay of Naples had been regal progress as ships altered course to hold some tenuous link to an English sailor who had saved Europe and had placed the most telling check for five years on that monster, the French Revolution.

Hardy had been made post after the battle and had taken over as flag captain, while Berry had been sent home with the despatches announcing the victory, which would surely get him a knighthood. Despite his best endeavours, Thomas Hardy, big, bluff, red-faced and a bit of a quarterdeck tyrant, couldn't get his admiral to rest. Bandage over his bad eye, in constant pain from the wound it covered, letter after letter poured from Nelson's pen, as he sent what frigates he could muster flying in all directions, promising, pleading, flattering or chastising, depending on who was the recipient. When not writing he was pacing the deck, thinking and planning, as if there were still a French menace afloat to chase, his good eye searching the horizon for the return of his messengers.

Contact with ships from home brought out-of-date news, the despatch of the victory at the Nile yet to reach London. Fanny was pleased with a portrait by Lemuel Abbot, now finished, that he had sat for on his last leave; her son Josiah, previously praised, was for some reason in bad odour with St Vincent, and was to be sent to serve with his stepfather. That troubled him little, since hardly an officer breathing was not in trouble with the acerbic St Vincent. Davidson wrote, creating the usual pangs of jealousy when he mentioned his offspring. He had answers from friends and the Admiralty to the requests he had made for this person or that to be advanced; bills, pleas for intercession, enough to keep him occupied for a week, all of which would have to be replied to. And having discovered his secretary was useless – the man had fainted at the Nile – Nelson had dismissed him and undertaken the correspondence with the help of the parson, Mr Comyn.

Nelson came on deck without his bandage as they opened the bay, hair swept forward to cover the angry scar. He began pointing out the landmarks to a pair of the younger midshipmen, part of a group who never ceased to trail him, as if by touching his hem they could pick up an ounce of glory. He named the two great castles, Dell'ovo and Nuovo, that dominated the approaches, detailing the armament that made it a dangerous place to attempt to take from the sea. There were bastions, too, covering the arms of the bay, full of great guns that could send a ball though a wooden ship's hull. The battery of St Elmo was right above the Palazzo Sessa, and that got a special mention.

'Take note, young Pasco, of the dangers of sailing into such a place. See how, at a mile distant, they will make it warm for any vessel caught in a crossfire. They are cunningly placed so that an assaulting fleet must wonder at which fort to return fire, and the wind in these parts is fickle enough to see you becalmed under the guns.'

'You could take it, sir,' protested Quilliam, the other young mid, his freckled face alight with faith.

'Not I, Mr Quilliam, but I do reckon that if any men could confound those defences it would be British tars.'

'How would you assault Naples, sir? asked Pasco.

Nelson was tired, Hardy could see that, and he moved to send these pests about their occasions. For a moment the expression on Nelson's face lightened, as if the pain and all his cares had dissolved. 'Why, I should use charm, young sir, which is what you must do when you go ashore.'

'They say the ladies are very fine in Naples, sir.'

'They are to heroes, which is what you are. Every man in this fleet is a hero.'

'We are about to anchor, sir. Permission to signal our tow.'

'Make it so, Captain Hardy.'

'Mr Pasco, Mr Quilliam, you must have duties to attend to when anchoring. I suggest that is where you belong.'

Anchoring in a bay full of boats come to greet them was a tricky matter, especially since *Vanguard*, having lost her foremast and four seamen with it, required to be towed by a frigate. There were barges with bands playing 'Rule Britannia', 'Britons Strike Home' and 'See the Conquering Hero Come'. Everybody of quality in Naples was there to greet the victor of the Nile, and they had banners to prove it, some woven with images that were far from true representations of the man they admired. Behind him, the quays were lined with a mass of people, all cheering.

'Sir William Hamilton,' said Hardy, pointing to a barge pushing through the throng to head for the side of his ship.

Nelson leant over the bulwark and saw Sir William, but searched for his wife. Lady Hamilton was sitting down, but her head was up, looking towards him.

'Five years,' he murmured to himself, his eyes fixed on the woman who had so made his blood race. As the barge got ever closer so did her face, under a broad brimmed hat and muslin scarf. The pain in his head grew worse as he stared, but it was not the cut that caused it so much as the way his heart was thumping in his chest. He didn't want to go down to the entry port to greet her, that being dark and shaded. He wanted to see her here on his quarterdeck, in the sunshine, perhaps with her hat off, to find out if he felt now as he had the last time they met.

'Hardy, my apologies to the Ambassador. If he has no objection I will receive him here.'

Hardy smiled and tossed his square head, as if to say, 'He'll damn well see you where you please.'

It was a tense five minutes, from the point at which the barge disappeared from his eyeline, to hooking on and the passengers coming aboard. For some reason he found himself thinking of his wife again: the image of Fanny gazing admiringly at that

Lemuel Abbot portrait she'd written of induced feelings of deep guilt. He knew that his God could see into his soul, was aware of every thought and every action. How could he forgive him for what he was thinking now?

The guilt evaporated at the moment he saw her. Emma Hamilton emerged from the companionway, smiling, her cheeks red with excitement, followed by a bright-eyed Sir William, who was much aged and thinner than the man Nelson remembered. Suddenly he realised that he, too, must present a very different apparition to his guests.

'My dear Admiral Nelson, you have joined the immortals.'

Nelson locked eyes with Sir William's wife, who stood examining him, taking in the empty sleeve and the mist-covered iris of his damaged eye. 'I fear I am a much-reduced creature, milady.'

'You are very much more substantial to me, sir,' she replied.

He almost didn't hear the words, so taken was he with the look in those huge green eyes. They were like a mirror to her soul and carried in them something deeper than mere admiration. Suddenly she flew at him and, in a very unladylike fashion, threw her arms around his neck and kissed his cheeks.

CHAPTER 58

The Palazzo Sessa was illuminated by three thousand candles, liveried servants lining the entrance to greet the stream of guests. The King and Queen attended, though not in a fully royal capacity, because Naples was supposed to be at peace with France, even had plenipotentiaries in Paris discussing an alliance. Yet the battle of the Nile had changed everything; France was not to be quite so feared, with no ships and no army, and ambassadors, princes, the cream of the Neapolitan aristocracy mingled with streams of naval officers from the victorious fleet.

Emma Hamilton's entrance was the kind of staged affair she loved. Her dress had been specially made, very low cut, blue and gold with an edging embroidered with the intertwined names of Nelson and the Nile. The transparent shawl with which she preserved some modesty was white, liberally sprinkled with gold anchors, while on her head she wore a cap of victory, which kept her hair high. On the arm of her elderly husband, she entered the room that had once held the bulk of Sir William's excavated treasures. These had been packed ready for shipment to England, there to be sold, allowing the room to be turned into a space that could accommodate the three hundred guests.

Now Nelson toyed with the thought he had entertained when the couple had come aboard *Vanguard*: that Sir William had aged much more than he. Wounds, battle, constantly being at sea and the strain of command had done for Nelson, implanting lines on his skin and greying his once blond hair, while at sixty-eight, age alone seemed to have altered the Chevalier. He was thinner all over, but particularly so in the legs, which looked spindly in his tight white breeches. The nose, which had always been prominent, now stood out starkly, this in a face that showed an excess of definition due to taut skin.

Nelson was seated in the place of honour, with the King and Queen on his left, while Emma and Sir William sat to his right. A slightly unusual arrangement, in terms of rank, had him between the two ladies, both husbands outside them, for which Nelson was grateful. Sir William he could abide, but he had eaten enough meals beside the gluttonous Ferdinand to want ever to do so again.

If the food and the setting were magnificent, the proximity of Lady Hamilton was agony. The Queen had no English and his foreign language skills extended no further than the need to ask for an enemy to surrender, so any conversation with Maria Carolina had to be translated by her good friend Emma and, in a room full of noise, she found it necessary to lean across the guest of honour to undertake that task.

Physical contact was constant, on one occasion her hand actually rested on his knee, squeezing it as she made some pertinent point to the Queen. Asked for his impressions of the battle, Nelson obliged, while claiming that his position in the line, followed by his wound, precluded him from being the best-placed observer. But he was observing Lady Hamilton with a proximity that both excited and appalled him. Her head was often no more than an inch from his, a beautifully formed ear enticingly erotic. Nelson had always been attracted to voices, and hers, low, varied and always with that hint of amusement, entranced him. He could smell her perfume and her hair, and sense the heat of her body, so had to fight to avoid looking down the front of her dress to her alluring bosom. An occasional squirm was required to ease the pressure on his groin, his napkin pressed into service to cover an embarrassment he could do nothing to control.

Such a situation drove Nelson to drink more than was usual, a greater quantity than the Queen, though less than Lady Hamilton, who grew bolder the more she consumed. Any attempt at modesty by her guest was overborne in a flurry of arms and loud laughter, with many a plea to Sir William to intercede and tell Nelson he was a hero, and should behave as such; that he was their shield and must make Naples his Mediterranean base.

'I had intended to use Syracuse, milady.'

'Sicily!' cried Emma. 'We will not hear of you departing, Admiral Nelson, will we, Sir William?'

The Chevalier nodded gravely. 'It would certainly grieve us, sir.'

'I won't be off just yet, Sir William. You will have noticed, even with an unpractised eye, that my ship lacks masts. I doubt the dockyard can repair her in less than a week.'

'But we wish you here for more than that, Admiral,' Emma pealed. 'A month, a year, for ever. If you do not promise me, I shall request a royal command.'

That had her leaning across to the Queen again, babbling in German, and what ease Nelson had managed was ruined. Emma Hamilton had put one hand behind his back, better to reach over. The absence of his right arm brought her closer to him than would otherwise have been the case. He could see her lips moving even if he couldn't understand what she was saying. He wanted to grab her there and then with his one good hand, but he sat back instead, forcing himself to look right past her to Sir William, smiling at the Ambassador, an expression that was returned in full measure.

He can't see it, thank God, Nelson thought.

Sir William Hamilton, with his acute sense of observation, was thinking that his wife had gone slightly overboard with regard to Nelson. The nautical simile made him grin just as the man in question looked at him. Certainly the Admiral was a hero, who deserved the thanks of half a dozen nations. He deserved this celebration, too, and all those that were bound to follow. Every city in Britain would want to toast him, and since he was such a hero, women by the yard would fawn over him. The fact that this was true did not alter the fact that his wife was one of them.

Emma's husband put it down to the heightened sense of theatricality that was one of her abiding traits; that and her need to be at the centre of things. Nelson might be the nation's hero, but Lady Hamilton wanted him to be her hero as well, somehow to give the impression that she had had a part in the Nile victory.

'Have you thought, sir,' asked Sir William, 'about your title?'

'I wouldn't wish to tempt Providence.'

'It would be improvident of His Majesty King George, if not downright imprudent, to hesitate in granting you a peerage. I daresay the thanks of the nation, in financial terms, would not be too much to ask.'

Of course Nelson had mulled over these things since the morning of victory. He would have been stupid not to. A title was a near certainty, indeed there were those who had insisted he deserved one after St Vincent. He had scotched that suggestion. A peerage required deep pockets to support it. A knighthood cost nothing. But if they voted him a pension as well . . .

'Nelson of the Nile,' cried Emma, pulling herself back far enough to look into his eyes. 'That should be your title.'

'I had thought of honouring my birthplace.'

'Which was?'

'Burnham Thorpe, in Norfolk.'

'Then, sir, that is the whole of it.' She rose to her feet, which alerted all the diners, who, seeing her standing, glass raised, followed suit. The toast she gave was in French. '*J'offre à vous, Monsieur le Duc de Burnham Thorpe et le Nile.*'

The roar that filled the room made Nelson blush, which endeared him to the lady looking down at him with unabashed admiration. Even Maria Carolina had raised her glass, though her dignity as a queen forbade her to stand. Ferdinand looked bemused, as if the idea that anyone else could be toasted in his presence, that cheers could ring out for another, was impossible.

Emma's chest was heaving, as if she had taken part in some taxing physical activity, her face flushed with pride and happiness. She did feel that she had a right to some reflected glory. Had it not been she, with her husband's blessing, who had gone to the Queen when Nelson was stuck in Syracuse needing supplies? It had been Emma, Lady Hamilton who had used every ounce of her credit to persuade Maria Carolina that

Neapolitan neutrality, which forbade giving assistance to Great Britain, should be breached.

Had that not happened, Nelson could not have continued his pursuit of Bonaparte. Without that, no battle of the Nile could have taken place. So, the very fact that this man was sitting here blushing at the praise being heaped on him was, in a large part, due to her intervention. Emma believed that when they toasted Nelson, they inadvertently also toasted her. As she sat down, the cheers still ringing, she saw that Nelson now looked uncomfortable.

'There's something amiss?'

'I wish I had the French for another toast, milady, which would be to my captains, my officers and my seamen, for in truth they are the people who won at the Nile.'

'I would not waste your modesty on this crew, Admiral Nelson. They wouldn't understand it.'

'Do you understand it?'

'I applaud it, sir, here,' she replied, putting one hand on her heart.

Eyes locked for just two seconds, both Nelson and Emma Hamilton were aware only of their own thoughts; that emotion was taking control of them. The noise of the packed room had faded so that they seemed to share a cocoon. Emma suffered a moment of confusion, under the strain of a raft of feelings she had not allowed for years, the kind of sensuous passion she had felt in the company of Uppark Harry and Charles Greville. Her whole life seemed to be encompassed in a thought that lasted no more than a split second before, for the sake of propriety, that mutual stare had to be broken.

She couldn't read Nelson's mind. Looking into his one good eye gave her no clue as to what he was experiencing. He felt the same set of sensations that came upon him as he went into battle, familiar from so many engagements: racing blood, acute awareness, the ability to see things in a detail denied to him normally, access to those juices that made a fighting man aware of a threat, and gave him the speed with which to counter it and stay alive. What seemed odd to Nelson, when he realised his state, was that for the first time in his life, he should feel all this in the company of a woman.

However, concentration on each other was impossible in a banqueting hall containing three hundred people. And when the meal finished and they repaired to the ballroom to dance, Emma was engaged by a variety of partners. Never much given to formal dancing, more at home with a hornpipe, Nelson had the excuse of only one arm, as well as a degree of exhaustion, to avoid participation.

It was unlikely that what happened that night would have occurred if he hadn't been quite so fatigued. An added complication was that Nelson wasn't alone in feeling so. When it came to saying good night, Sir William made it plain that he was worn out by the events that had preceded the ball, never mind the assembly itself. Emma wasn't put out by this nor was she surprised: her husband's desires had diminished steadily since he had turned sixty-five. In the last year that had accelerated, since Sir William refused to abandon his other pursuits. He still coached out to Pompeii for his excavations, still climbed Vesuvius, albeit slowly, and he continued to oversee the care of his English garden. He claimed he had scant energy left for copulation. Tonight was one of many in which he made it plain to Emma that her presence in his apartments was not obligatory.

The absence of servants was also due to the night's entertainment: clearing up after so many guests saw everyone busy, with few to spare for lighting candles, warming beds, or seeing to a most important guest. Under the supervision of Mary Cadogan, the entire staff, including those brought in especially for the occasion, was busy washing, drying and packing crockery or filling hessian bags with linen and breaking down the dozens of assembled tables. Aware of this, Emma Hamilton saw it as her duty to ensure that the hero of the Nile was comfortable.

Illuminated only by the pair of candles he had used to guide himself to his accommodation, the suite of rooms Nelson occupied was in near darkness. A portrait of George III above the mantel of the fireplace in the drawing room rendered a glowering rather than an inspiring image, which reminded him that royalty were a fickle crew. There was no sign of Tom Allen, who'd last been seen heading for the kitchens, which were full to overflowing with local women.

The act of undressing was difficult without assistance, barring his dress coat, with the embroidered star of the Order of the Bath, which slipped off easily. When it came to the heavy brass waistcoat buttons it was a struggle, and he cursed his servant for deserting him. That was until he recalled that Tom had been at sea as long as he had himself and was, like him, a man. The sight of all those olive skinned jades would have been enough to inflame any red-blooded fellow. That brought back to him the way he himself had behaved, and he recalled the thoughts he had toyed with earlier, which caused him to smile, then frown, then mentally beg forgiveness from his all-seeing God.

When a knock came he assumed it was from a household servant and called that he or she should enter. The breath stopped in his chest as Emma Hamilton came through the door.

She was still dressed in the costume that had been created to flatter him. What light there was, was playing across her face and hair, as well as the gold embroidery of her clothing.

'I came to see if all your needs have been met.'

Was the *double entendre* deliberate? Nelson didn't know, and his reply, which was automatic, only added to the confusion. 'Without aid and only one arm, I find it difficult to undress.'

'Your servant?'

'I fear after months at sea some Neapolitan lady has claimed him, leaving me to struggle with these waistcoat buttons.'

Emma was halfway across the room by the time Nelson had said that, close enough for their eyes to lock. 'Allow me to aid you,' she said.

'That would be very kind,' Nelson replied huskily, his mouth as dry as it had ever been in battle.

She stepped up close, so that the faint light from the candles on the mantel shone over his shoulder into her eyes. The green orbs seemed huge, steady and direct. He knew that any woman with a modest desire just to undo his waistcoat buttons would not look at him like that. She knew that no man making an innocent request would jerk as he did when her hand moved down to the lowest button on the long garment.

Several spasms ran through Nelson's body as each button came loose. He was achingly aware of her long fingers, her smell, a mixture of bodily musk and perfume, the way that her shawl was less than modest and that the breasts it was designed to cover were rising and falling too fast for a woman hardly engaged in anything like exertion. He wanted to touch her but was frightened to move, fearful that even now he was mistaking kindness for passion and that any act on his part would break the spell.

Emma, with much more experience, supposed Nelson was suffering from a mixture of shyness and fear. Ever since her first days at Mrs Kelly's she had known there was a breed of men frightened of their own passions, so unsure of themselves as to freeze when they should act. That this man, a garlanded hero who could board an enemy deck without fear, should show such an emotion when faced with Emma Hamilton, made her hand tremble slightly.

She was also aware that, in coming here, all her excuses of seeing to Nelson's comfort were just that, pretexts to cover an irresistible desire to be close to him. His mere presence set off something she found hard to control, which had existed since their first meeting five years before. Absence made such a thing seem foolish, but proximity made it so forceful it could not be gainsaid.

She knew because of what had happened on first acquaintance that it was the man, not just his fame. Besides that, Emma wasn't the type to dwell too long on wondering. At dinner, all that contact had been no accident. She had known what she was about as she pushed herself close to him, eager to feel the tingling sensation his close presence brought her. She had it now and, in the glow of the candlelight, looking at his hooded eyes, feeling the trembling of his body through the slightest of contact, she knew he had it too.

Taking hold of his stock to untie it, she exerted a degree of pressure. Instead of holding his body tense against it, Nelson allowed his head to be brought to within an inch of Emma's. To kiss seemed natural, a gentle meeting of lips stretching little to touch each other, the increase of pressure as Nelson slipped his good arm round her waist to pull her body into contact with his. At the back of his mind he knew that what he was doing was wrong, sinful, but elemental.

The lips parted and Emma put a good foot of distance between them and Nelson felt disappointment overwhelm him. Then her hands came up, and slowly, her eyes still fixed on his, she began once more to undo the stock, slipping it off slowly and sensually. At the same time his fingers found the edge of her shawl, which slid from her shoulders to the floor.

Emma continued to take the lead, knowing that this man would hesitate at every stage of what was now inevitable. Her body was on fire, she wanted to rip off his shirt, with its one pinned-up sleeve, and her dress with it. Yet there was great pleasure in denial, gratification in lack of haste, in putting her hand behind Nelson's head and pulling it to her bosom. The throaty chuckle that emerged when his lips brushed the top of her breasts was caused by a thought, not the touch; that a man who couldn't undo his waistcoat would probably have trouble with the button on his breeches too.

'How odd,' Nelson murmured. 'I feel as though both my hands are upon you, even my right. I swear I can feel your skin through my missing fingertips.'

His left hand was pulling her hard, and through the thin material of her dress she could feel his cock pressing against her belly. Nelson's head came up and the kiss he gave her this time was crushing and passionate. Suddenly Emma put two hands on his chest and pushed him away. Nelson tried to resist, but with only one hand she spun out of his embrace.

Seeing his crestfallen expression Emma put a finger to his lips, then slipped across the room to the double doors, turning the key smartly, before spinning round to lean against the wood. Her dress, new and for the occasion, hooked at the back where she couldn't reach, gave way at one of the seams as she tugged hard to pull it down. Everything underneath seemed to go in that one swift movement till she stood naked, one foot raised, the flat of her hands on the lower door panels, inviting him to gaze on her.

Nelson's groin was aching. He felt as if he wanted to do ten things at once: rip off his own shirt and the buttons on his breeches, kiss her, fuck her, caress her, worship her, yet he did nothing. He just stood, feeling a little foolish, until Emma, laughing, came back to him, to help her one-armed hero. His shirt was pulled over his head, Emma's hand, then her lips, caressing his chest before wandering to the stump that hung off his right shoulder, to kiss the point where the healing skin had puckered at the base. Her other hand was at his breech buttons. Nelson nearly ejaculated as her fingers took hold of his prick to ease it out of the restraining clothes.

She had to hold up his falling breeches to get him to the bed, making Nelson feel slightly ridiculous, and propriety resurfaced. But contact with cool sheets as Emma pushed him back, the sight of her kneeling to take off his shoes, her head, still in her cap of victory with his name sewn into the band, bobbing at either side of his erection, produced the first feeling of humour he felt he had had for months, a deep chest-heaving laugh. There was a feeling of evaporation as he lay there, as though every thought that bothered him, every difficulty that assailed him, marital and professional, was being chased away by the action of this stunningly beautiful woman.

Emma wasn't at his feet for long. She knelt on the bed beside him, her hand once more caressing that stump. Her lips were parted showing the tip of an enticing tongue, her eyes full of amusement, her beautiful breasts rising and falling evenly in a way that made him want to raise himself up to suckle the nipples. Then she spoke.

'I fear, hero that you are, that I must take command here.'

Nelson laughed again. Then, using his good arm, he raised himself up with every ounce of force he could muster, the weight of his body throwing hers backwards. Emma let out a peal of laughter as he rolled her on to her back, his knee immediately jabbing between hers to open them, not difficult since she was a willing victim. Looking up she saw in Nelson's eye a look that only men who had gone into battle with him had seen. It told her without words that no one commanded Horatio Nelson.

His stump was jabbed into the bed to hold his right side, both his legs now between hers, his hips jabbing forward to get inside her, a manoeuvre that had to be repeated several times before she reached down to help him. Nelson had to struggle to contain himself under the coercion of that cool hand. His lips were buried in her neck and in his head it was as though that orb of the vision he had had when he was sick on his return from India came back again to tell him that what he was doing was right.

He tried hard to be the practised lover, to hold himself, but the passion was too great, uncontainable. The groan as he came was a mixture of deep relief, overwhelming gratitude and the boyish shame that always afflicts a man who feels that he has failed. Emma, one hand behind him pulling his buttocks in tighter, legs lifted from the bed, pelvis writhing and lifting and falling, was laughing, a deep gurgle that Nelson thought was ridicule and she knew was gratification.

He collapsed on her body, his head sinking into her breasts, feeling the chest below them heave as he continued to jerk inside her, small, delicious spasms that slowly but steadily diminished. Her hands were stroking his back, both of them, palms pressed into his shoulder blades and spine as if that alone would convey to him the feelings that racked her body.

As he rolled sideways Emma followed him, so that it was now Nelson who was thrown on his back. She lay over him, to gaze down at him with a mixture of gratitude and wonder. 'Have I just been conquered, Nelson?'

'No, madam,' Nelson said, softly, 'you have just been victorious.'

Sir William, on his way to give a message to Emma, had gone to check on his guest for the same reason as his wife. He was just in time to see the door to Nelson's apartments close on that well-lit and unmistakable dress, blue and gold, decorated with entwined embroidery of Nelson and Nile. He stood for several moments, his mind going back to the dinner, to the way that Emma had fawned over her hero. Recollecting what he had observed, he saw her behaviour as different from those times when she had allowed other men to raise in themselves expectations that would not be met. Her reaction to Nelson had been different, more tactile and very effusive.

There was a sobering moment when he remembered the dozens of letters they had exchanged over the last five years, since Nelson's visit to ask for aid at Toulon. Every one had contained a request to pass on kind sentiments and flattering comments to Lady Hamilton, even though she, too, was his correspondent. He had only been in Naples four days, and had left in a rush that seemed, in retrospect, over-dramatic. Had there been another reason, outside the need to engage an enemy warship?

Close to the door, Sir William had heard the muted voices of a conversational exchange. But that was followed by silence, which lasted a long time. Then he heard the faint sound of pressure on the door, followed by the grate of a turning key. A man of the world, Sir William Hamilton could easily deduce what that meant.

They lay together, Emma face down while he lay on his back, talking intermittently, she fondling his limp cock until the blood began to flow again. As soon as he was erect she threw one leg over his body and raised herself up to look down at him. The previous tussling had thrown back his hair, exposing the scar where a piece of langridge from *Spartiate*'s cannon had sliced into his forehead. She bent to kiss it and his lips found a nipple as her breasts sank to his face.

They made love slowly, Emma in charge of both pace and passion. Her own hair, now loose from that cap of victory, would occasionally brush his chest as she bent closer, while her inert lover gazed up in wonder, sure he must be dreaming that this perfect creature was intent only on his pleasure. Sometimes she would sink low to kiss him, pressing her breasts into his, her whole upper body in contact.

Then he was lost again in that mental wilderness of conflicting images; thoughts of what they were doing and might yet do, the feeling of her belly, warm against his, the way her thighs pressed into his side, the texture of one buttock as he held it and squeezed with his one good hand. The groans that seemed to come from the very base of Emma's spine as she quickened her pace, the rising feeling in his own groin.

When Emma Hamilton left, Nelson lay on his back, his mind racing over what had just happened, the pleasure of which made him writhe with recollected memory. The murmured name of his wife turned that to a guilty squirm. Then he thought of his host, a man who had shown him nothing but kindness and consideration, such nobility repaid by a scrub who had just made love to his consort. It made no difference that she had been willing, had in some senses taken the initiative. But that still made him an ungrateful louse when it came to Sir William, a man who had boasted to him of his wife's fidelity.

Regardless of how much he chastised himself he knew in his heart that he wanted what had occurred tonight to happen again. He felt as if he had been struck by lightning, a *coup de foudre* that no amount of self-control could overcome. The word love barely registered, but lust did, of the most unbridled kind. He could try to put his love of God and his regard for Fanny as a shield between himself and Emma Hamilton, but he knew in his heart it would never answer.

Nelson resolved to move out of the palazzo and go back to the cabin on his ship; to put seawater between himself and temptation. The excuses he would use began to form in his mind, based on the knowledge that in such a large establishment, the chances of Sir William being aware of what had taken place were slim. Lady Hamilton would never have allowed it to happen if there was a risk. He would say that he needed to harry the dockyard or *Vanguard* would never be ready. That even if he had defeated the French fleet in Aboukir Bay there were still two capital enemy ships at sea threatening trade. Sir William would understand, and Nelson could get away from Naples, as he had before, without any damage to either his reputation or that of Sir William's wife.

As he knelt to pray for forgiveness and help, he was conscious of his nakedness, of the stickiness of his body as well as the smell, a combination of her perfume, their sweat, and the odour of stale carnality.

Mary Cadogan was waiting when Emma came back to her own suite of rooms, sitting in the chair she often occupied, but awake. She looked her daughter up and down, noting that her dress was not as well fitted as it had been earlier, her hair not as neat, the cap of victory nowhere in sight. And Emma had her slippers in one hand, almost a badge to tell anyone who saw her in the passageways what she had been doing.

'Sir William seems to have recovered some of his ardour,' Emma said.

'Has he?'

'I think Admiral Nelson's victory must have inspired him,' Emma added, throwing herself into another chair. 'He was quite the bull and I am quite exhausted.'

'You're a fool, Emma, and what is worse for me is that you think I am too.'

Emma leant back and yawned, slightly more elaborately than was necessary to express her tiredness. 'What do you mean?'

'I mean, girl, where you have just spent the last two hours.'

'With Sir William.'

'Your husband called for his carriage about an hour and a half ago. He left a message to say that he had gone to spend the night at Posillipo.'

Emma was upright now. 'In the name of heaven, why?'

'I daresay it's because he has a fair idea of where you were, Emma.' Mary Cadogan's face softened in the face of her daughter's confusion. 'Do you realise what you have done, girl? You have gone and thrown away whatever chance we had of peace and happiness in the future. And for what? For a couple of hours with a passing sailor, and not even a whole one at that.'

To be continued

AUTHOR'S NOTE

This book is fiction based on the facts surrounding two remarkable people. While it is historical it is not meant to be a history. There are hundreds, if not thousands, of books on Horatio Nelson and Emma Hamilton in libraries and bookshops everywhere. Nothing would please me more than that the reader should become so enamoured of the subject as to take a deep interest in the mass of biographical information available.

Allied to the reading of original sources, I too have consumed numerous books. The best biography of Horatio Nelson, to my mind, is still *Nelson* by Carola Oman, first published in 1947. Someone should reissue that for the 200th anniversary of Trafalgar in 2005. Likewise *Beloved Emma*, by Flora Fraser, which ranks equally when it comes to the life, loves and tribulations of Emma Hamilton.

There is some confusion about Emma's birth date. Some writers give it as the year of her baptism 1765, others go as far back as 1761. For the sake of my story, I am assuming 1762, which puts her birth before the marriage of her parents. Given the times in which they lived, and her mother's subsequent career, it is entirely possible that Emma was born out of wedlock and only baptised after they had regularised their relationship.

As regards Nelson's officers, I have played ducks and drakes with them, putting men such as Millar, Berry and Hardy in situations *vis à vis* our hero earlier in their lives than actually occurred. There are also invented lower ranks, who stay with him throughout this book. My reason for this is simple. In his time at sea Horatio Nelson must have served with hundreds of officers and thousands of men; to use the muster rolls of his ship to name them all accurately would have created deep confusion.

My justification is also simple: it is no desire to denigrate anyone, merely the fact that most would have remained obscure footnotes in history if they had not served with Nelson. Likewise the title: Emma Hamilton was a fascinating character; clever, beguiling, mercurial, theatrical and beautiful, who would have achieved some recognition as an artist's model.

But fame? No, that came from being the lover of the greatest fighting sailor this country has ever known.

David Donachie
Deal, Kent, 2000